THE TALISMAN OF FAERIE

To Jeremy —
a kick-ass singer
and kind of a cool guy.
Hope you enjoy the book

Jason R Beil

THE TALISMAN OF FAERIE

Jason N. Beil

iUniverse, Inc.
New York Lincoln Shanghai

The Talisman of Faerie

iUniverse, Inc.

For information address:
iUniverse, Inc.
2021 Pine Lake Road, Suite 100
Lincoln, NE 68512
www.iuniverse.com

ISBN: 0-595-32320-0 (pbk)
ISBN: 0-595-66525-X (cloth)

Printed in the United States of America

Contents

Prologue: The Bargain

Black clouds hung heavily over the immense tower which thrust its way out of the dry, desolate land. A low wind moaned quietly, kicking dark sand into the air and into the eyes of the horseman who approached the tower's gate. He sighed and stopped to adjust his scarf to better protect his face from the storm. He and his black horse were the only living things within miles of the tower; for nothing could exist long in the ravaged land of Mul Kytuer. Nothing, save the one who sat waiting in the tower.

The horseman appeared to be a very old man. His skin was deeply creased, his eyes sunken and dull. His hair was thin and gray, his flesh spotted with age. He was wrapped in a dirty gray cloak, a dark hood pulled over his head. At his side was a glimmering sword with strange markings running along its length and large gems set in the hilt.

Eventually the rider reached the massive tower, which rose into the gray sky almost higher than he could see. A wide, long row of gray stairs led to the black tower's gate, which opened with a great grinding as the rider neared. The rider urged his mount up the stairs and rode into the tower.

The near half of the tower's first level was a great open area with a dirt floor. The far half held hundreds of empty stalls where horses, presumably, were kept at one time. One stall was prepared with feed and water, and it was here the old horseman left his mount. Then, slowly, the old man climbed a staircase upwards.

The old one climbed for more than an hour, stopping to rest only once. He rose level by level through the great tower, hardly bothering to ponder the significance of each floor. Here, perhaps, was a sleeping quarter for soldiers; here, a dining hall. Perhaps this level, divided into smaller rooms, was for officers or important visitors. The next, perhaps an armory. Each tier grew increasingly smaller as the tower narrowed.

At last he reached the top story of the tower, a full one hundred levels above the ground. This uppermost floor was by far the smallest in area, but it was still as large as the halls of the great kings of old. It was decorated in silver and gold and fine works of art. In the center of the room was a large, black throne, and upon it sat a thin figure in black robes. The figure was skeletal and hideous, its gray flesh stretched tightly over its frame of brittle bone. Its sunken eyes sat so far back in its skull they were hardly visible. Its hands were thin and gnarled and its bony fingers ended in long, yellow talons. The creature pointed at the old man as he entered the room, sending a shiver down his spine. The horseman was a dark and mighty sorcerer, but the creature on the throne was darker and mightier still.

"Salin Urdrokk, you have braved the lands of Mul Kytuer and come to the tower of Vorik Seth. What is it you seek and what have you brought with which to bargain?"

"Great Vorik Seth, I seek information and wish to bargain with the same. It is only as your humble servant I stand here before you."

Salin knelt before the great Vorik Seth, who spoke again with a voice as dark as night and as quiet as death.

"Rise, Salin. You have served me well for many an age of this world. Yet you have not sought me out, nor have I had need of you, for centuries. I have watched you, however, since last we met, and I have seen you destroy kings and build empires in my name. Things go well for our side, as they have for the last thousand years. What is it you seek?"

"Great Lord Vorik, the world is large and much of it is uncharted and unknown. We have conquered the realms of Margon and Northern Eglak. Our servants hold the lands from Middle Estron to Riglak Nord. Yet beyond are realms of strong men, and further still live the Fair Folk in lands of peace and beauty. They have never submitted to your will and they grow stronger by the year. Soon they will dare to march westward into our lands. Because they refuse to recognize you as their Lord and Master, they will challenge all we have built. They still believe the One, the bringer of Light and giver of Life, will ultimately destroy you."

The Seth smiled, showing a row of decayed teeth. "They are fools to think it so. The eternal battle between light and darkness rages on, as it has since the world was new. The balance of power is forever shifting, but this is foreordained: In the end, Darkness will swallow Light, and Death will come to all things. And you are mistaken when you say the Fair Folk have never submitted to me; for once, long before your time, I ruled over them in their green forests. Oh, yes, I was younger then and fair to behold. Terror was not my only weapon in those days. I was beautiful, and all who looked upon me were charmed and swore to do my bidding. What I could not take by force I took by lies, deceit, promises of greatness and power. I gave them many gifts and taught them the ways of Shaping. And so it was I gave them the very tools with which they eventually defeated me and cast me out. Still, the Fair Folk's victory is only temporary. I will reign again."

"It is as you say, my Lord. Still, there is reason to worry. We are losing ground to the men of the east. The Fair Folk themselves are amassing armies which may one day rival our own. And there is another reason to be concerned. You have not forgotten *the Three*, have you?"

"I forget nothing, young Salin. The Three have certainly been a hindrance to my plan over the years, but their time is ending. Already the First of the Three has succumbed to my will, and the Second has lost interest in his sacred mission. The Third still may pose a threat, but it is a small one. Only together could they hope to stand against me. I assure you, our empire will not fall. Under my shadow it grows stronger each day. When the entire world falls to me, then I can, at last, fulfill my true Destiny. Now, Salin, enough banter. What is it you wish to know?"

Salin drew in a deep breath. It was not lightly he sought advice from his dark master. Always it was better to serve at a distance, for to look into the Seth's gray, decayed face was to remember the truth: Salin was just another slave to the greatest dark power in the world.

"My lord, I was studying a long forgotten text of high sorcery which I discovered within a buried vault in the archives of Old Syngara, in the west of Riglak Nord. It told of the Talisman of Unity, which binds together the minds of the Fair Folk and allows them to act and think as one. It is the crux of their power. He who holds the Talisman wields great influence over the minds of the Fair Folk. Great Vorik, if one of your servants were to find and wield the Talisman of Unity, we could at last bend the Fair Folk to your will. Then, truly, you will be close to achieving your Destiny."

The Seth laughed. "And you would be the one to wield this power? Salin, do you think I cannot see through your schemes? It is plain you wish to advance your own position. I know you care not if I achieve my Destiny. You *fear* the day, as well you should! My true purpose is known to no one save me and the gods, as was ordained when I first entered into this mortal realm. Yes, I can help you locate the Talisman. After all, I helped the fools create the cursed thing. Long has it been lost, but even buried and forgotten it still continues to function. It still gives the King of the Fairies insight into and influence over the minds and hearts of his people. But if it were in our hands, warped to our purpose...it could be a valuable tool indeed. I wonder, though...why should I help *you* acquire it? Why entrust the greatest of all Faerie artifacts to one such as yourself? After all, I have already granted you a Sorcerer's Chain. Is this not enough to satisfy your lust for power?"

Silently, Salin cursed his master. The Sorcerer's Chain was a rare and immensely powerful tool, but over time the use of it bound its wielder ever tighter to Vorik Seth's will. Salin needed something else, something safer. Putting the Chain out of his mind, he forced himself to smile. He knew his dark master would not be able to resist the bargaining chip he had brought with him. "In the ancient text were written other great secrets. It spoke of the Three. The First, you say, is already in your power. The Second has lost interest in his former cause. But the Third. Ah, the Third. He still seeks to thwart you, to end your reign once and for all. It is the Third I wish to speak of. In the text I discovered his Name. His Secret Name."

For the first time in hundreds of years, Vorik Seth's sunken eyes grew wide in excitement. His lips curled in an evil but sincere smile. He rubbed his hands together and rose from his throne, laughing a coarse, raspy laugh.

"Salin, you have done well! Try as I might, in all my long years I have never managed to uncover the Secret Names of the Three." He began to pace excitedly, and Salin could almost sense evil plots hatching in his master's skull. "With the name of the Third I can summon him to my lair, bind him with great sorcery, and destroy or enslave him as I fancy. O joyous day! Tell me the Name."

"I will, Great One. And yet, I have come to bargain. Will you trade information on the Talisman of Unity for the name of the Third of the Three?"

Vorik Seth's face grew grim. His eyes flared with anger. Then, almost instantly, he was again as calm and unreadable as a corpse. "I would not have to bargain. I could dig my fingers into your skull and suck the information from your little mind. I could bind you here and peel your flesh layer by layer until you told me what I want to know."

Salin licked his lips nervously. He could barely control his shaking hands. He was afraid of no mortal man, but Vorik Seth was no mere mortal. Salin began to wonder if he would escape the Seth's tower with his life.

Vorik looked Salin up and down, as if judging his worth. "Hmmm…I suppose, all things considered, you are still valuable enough to keep alive." Salin's relief was almost tangible. "*For now*," added Vorik. "Since you have proven your usefulness throughout the centuries, I will tell you what you wish to know." Salin's heart leapt. He could barely suppress a smile, for this was his chance to gain power beyond imagining! "The Talisman of Unity," continued Vorik, "was lost three centuries ago in a battle in Tyridan. Go to the small farming village of Barton Hills, in the far north of Tyridan. The folk there are a simple, silly folk who you will find easy to manipulate. Seek out one Alec Mason. He is the key."

"Alec Mason in Barton Hills, Tyridan. What will he know of the Talisman?"

The Seth grinned darkly. "I will say no more. From here, you're on your own. Now, uphold your end of the bargain. What is the Name?"

Salin Urdrokk looked into his master's eyes and spoke the Secret Name. Vorik smiled widely and hideously and rubbed his gnarled hands together. Suddenly Salin knew his master had gotten the better end of the deal. Still, if Salin could indeed find this Talisman and gain control of the Fair Folk, his power would grow tenfold. He would rise even higher in Vorik Seth's councils, and when Vorik at long last ascended to his Destiny, he might take Salin with him.

As Salin Urdrokk rode away from the tower, he thought on this and decided it was unlikely. He was damned. When the Seth was through with him, he would be discarded like the rest, his immortal soul destroyed.

Ah well, he thought. *In the meantime, I will hold power the likes of which mortals only dream. In the meantime, I will be a god.*

CHAPTER 1

Bard's Day

The heat of the summer sun beat down on Alec Mason as he thrust his shovel into the ground. The hole was getting larger, but there was a long way to go before he would strike water. Alec paused a moment to mop the sweat from his forehead, and then, sighing deeply, he continued to dig.

A young woman stopped along the road to watch Alec work. He did not notice her at first and kept to his task. He was not really cut out for such toil, as the observer might have noted. He was rather small in frame, save for a roll around his midsection which jiggled as he worked. His arms were thin and his hands small. His face was fair and handsome and his curly hair was sandy blond. He was still a very young man, perhaps only twenty or twenty-one. Each time he heaved a shovel full of dirt over his shoulder he grunted with the effort.

"What I want to know," said the girl, giggling, "is who had the bright idea to assign the task of digging a new well to the baker's apprentice? Why not someone with some muscles, like the blacksmith, or maybe the tavern's peacekeeper, Kraig?"

Alec looked up at her and frowned. "Laugh all you like, Sarah. All the men have to take their turn at digging."

"And all the boys, too, it seems," she laughed.

Alec tried to be mad, but her laughter was contagious. He dropped his shovel and started laughing along with her, holding his shaking belly.

"Sarah, you are a piece of work. Shouldn't you be helping your mother in her shop instead of harassing men trying to do an honest day's work?"

He looked at the girl as she laughed again. She was short and slim with long blond hair and delicate features. She had just celebrated her seventeenth birthday, but looking at her, Alec still saw a child. He loved her like a sister, and like all sisters, she got on his nerves.

"The shop is closed today, Alec. It's Bard's Day, or have you forgotten?"

Alec's smile widened at the mention of the holiday. He folded his arms and, shaking his head, said, "Grok's beard, girl, of *course* I haven't forgotten! Who do you think you're talking to? There'll be a grand celebration tonight at the Silver Shield, with singing, dancing, plenty of drinking; I've been looking forward to it for weeks! Oh, I hope old Jordi Luppis is going to play his lute and spin a tune or two."

Bard's Day was Alec's favorite holiday. It came in midsummer, when holidays were few and far between. It was always the most festive of times, save Yule. The holiday was held to commemorate the great bard Ottis Brachnitter, who composed some of the greatest ballads and tales ever to be sung or told in Tyridan. On this day all the local singers and storytellers would gather and entertain the townsfolk until late into the night. Alec's favorite bard was Jordi Luppis, who always told the famous tale *The Battle of the Hill*, which Alec had loved since he was a small child.

"Jordi'll be there," said Sarah. "He's already at the tavern getting ready. By sunset there won't be a seat in the place, and folks will be gathered outside, as well. Mother closed the shop early to prepare a song of her own."

"Your mother's going to sing? Well, this certainly will be a day to remember."

"I guess it will. Well, have fun digging. I'll see you tonight."

With a smile and a wave, she continued down the road. Alec watched her for a moment, smiling. He noticed some curves in her body which were not there a year ago, and he decided that perhaps she wasn't a child after all. Then he continued his work, looking forward to the night of revelry ahead.

The village of Barton Hills was established two hundred seasons ago as a farming community to help feed the people of northern Tyridan. As the country of Tyridan grew, great cities and mighty castles were built, and many people migrated there from neighboring realms. Soon, there was a need for more farmland and people to manage it, so scouts were sent northward into the unexplored territories to find fertile ground. What they found was a godsend: miles upon miles of gently rolling hills with some of the most fertile soil in the eastern lands. Soon, over one hundred families moved to Barton Hills and began farming the rich land. It wasn't long before the village became an important addition to Tyridan.

The folk of Barton Hills and the nearby villages led simple lives. They were happy to till the earth, leaving larger concerns to the people of the cities. Except for the few merchants who came to trade, there was little contact with the world outside the village. Once a month wagons came from other parts of Tyridan to cart off food grown by the farmers of Barton Hills. The farmers were paid mostly with other goods, for they had little use for silver. The little coin circulating in the farming town was spent on new farm equipment, drinks at the Silver Shield, and trinkets and curiosities from the Dragon's Den; the antique store owned by Ara Mills, Sarah's mother. Ara made her humble living by selling strange antique items for a few silver coins. Most of the trinkets were in fact handed down from her grandfather, who once ventured across the known world seeking wealth and fame. He found neither, but he did collect a myriad of curious but virtually worthless items.

Alec Mason was born in Barton Hills, the son of a hunched farmer named Brok and his young wife Karlyn. Karlyn took ill and died when Alec was only six, and old Brok was so heartbroken he wandered off one night and never returned. Alec was taken in by the baker and his wife and eventually learned the baking trade. Alec never had much of an adventurous spirit, so he never ventured far from home. He had never been to a large city, never seen a grand castle. He had heard tales of wars and of magic, of ogres and Fairies, but to him they were just stories to pass the time around the fire at night. Even so, there were some stories he enjoyed hearing again and again. He was fascinated with local history, for he loved hearing about the early days of his village and the part his ancestors had in founding it. This is why he loved Bard's Day, for on this day the tales of the village were told by the best story tellers in Northern Tyridan.

As evening approached, Alec finished his work for the day and returned his shovel and pick to the village storage house. Tomorrow it would be back to the bakery for Alec, and someone else would continue digging. This suited Alec just fine, for he enjoyed baking, working along side Stan Kulnip, the master baker. Still, he knew he would be sore in the morning. Digging a hole all day was a lot more strenuous than baking bread, muffins, and cakes. He already felt the strain across his back and in his arms and chest.

Alec went to his home, a small hut beside Stan's larger one, to prepare for the celebration ahead. The hut was modestly furnished with a small straw mattress and warm wool blankets, a three-legged wooden table for eating and writing, and two wooden chairs. Across from the table was a small wood stove to warm the hut in the winter, and beside the bed sat a simple wooden chest in which Alec kept his few possessions. Alec opened the chest and began to rummage through it, picking out his newest brown tunic and pants, some fresh towels, and a clump of white soap.

Before he closed the chest, he paused for a moment over a painting of his parents he kept inside. He looked at it every now and then so he wouldn't forget them, for he had been very young when his mother passed away and his father vanished. He remembered the day when the picture was made: an artist was passing through Barton Hills, painting simple portraits for silver. Brok and Karlyn had taken Alec for a walk in the garden of the Temple of Grok when the artist approached them, and they agreed to pose for him.

Those were happy days and Alec smiled remembering them. The likeness of his parents was quite detailed. Karlyn had flowing long hair and wide, gentle eyes. Brok was not a handsome man, but he had a kindly tan face and a compact but strong body. They looked genuinely happy, as did the five-year old Alec standing between them.

But Alec had not come here to muse over the past. He gathered his things, shut the chest, and left his tiny house. He wandered to a little stream on the west side of town, where he sometimes came to bathe. He found his favorite spot, a small area secluded by willow trees and green bushes where clear, crisp water poured over white rocks. Making sure there was no one else about, he stripped off his dirty work clothes and waded out into the stream. The water chilled him, but he dived under it gladly, happy to wipe the day's filth from his body.

When he felt clean and refreshed, he left the water and toweled himself dry. He dressed quickly, anxious to make it to the tavern before nightfall. He took his soiled clothing back to his home and set out at once for the Silver Shield Tavern.

When Alec arrived ten minutes later, there was already a large crowd gathered outside. Townsfolk stood among the trees or sat on the grassy hills behind the Tavern. A platform was set up in the yard on which singers would later perform. The really good bards would be performing inside, and Alec was a little disappointed he might not be able to get in. Once the seats inside were filled, the rest of the villagers had to be content with the outdoor show.

No sooner was Alec about to take a seat on a green hill when a head poked out a tavern window and called his name. It was Sarah and she was smiling.

"Alec Mason, you fool! I told you not to be late!"

"Don't rub it in, Sarah," he called. "I'll have to enjoy the celebration from here."

"No you won't, silly. I saved a seat at my mother's table for you. It's my privilege since she's a performer tonight. Just tell Kraig you're with me and he'll let you in. And hurry! It's about to start!"

Alec didn't waste any time. The townsfolk on the hill looked at him as he passed, some calling out jests like "Hey, there goes his highness Prince Alec; he gets a reserved seat every Bard's Day!" and "Who do you have to know to get a seat in the tavern?" He turned toward them and made a rather obscene gesture, which set them all into fits of laughter. Alec laughed right along with them, for it was all in fun. Soon he came to the door, which was guarded by Kraig, a huge man who worked for the tavern's owner as a peacekeeper. Kraig's dark hair was short in back and long in front, and he wore his long bangs swept off to one side and hanging down over half his forehead. He had a very short beard, little more than dark, course whiskers, which added to his air of rugged strength.

"Hold on there, Alec," said Kraig, putting a big hand on the smaller man's chest. "Tavern's full."

"It's all right, Kraig. I'm with Ara and Sarah."

"Oh, that's right. Sarah told me she was waiting for you. Go ahead in."

Alec entered the tavern, which was already filled with drunken, jovial people. The large common room had a wooden floor and a roof of wooden rafters. There was a bend in the room at the far end, an alcove where people who desired more privacy could sit. Alec stood in the doorway and listened to the townsfolk shouting and laughing, gossiping and singing. He breathed deeply, smelling sweat and ale and cooking food. Although the night was still young, the celebration was well underway. Alec had some catching up to do.

Alec cast his eyes to the bar, which was situated along the right wall. The barkeeper, Derik, was busy filling glass after glass of ale. For him, it was the busiest night of the year. Alec laughed, seeing sweat dripping from the brow of the fat, bald man.

Alec scanned the many tables searching for Sarah. He saw many people he knew, including Stan and his wife Matilda, whom he greeted as he passed. Finally he came to a table near the back and saw Sarah, waving her arms wildly to attract his attention. He went over and took a seat.

"Hi. Sorry it took me so long. This place is crowded!"

"It sure is. You should have gotten here sooner."

"I had to work until sundown. It's the rules."

"Rules? Rules are made to be broken, especially on Bard's Day, Alec. Hey, here comes my mother."

Ara sat down, placing three large mugs on the table. "I thought you might be here by now, so I got you a drink, Alec. It's good to see you. You don't come by the shop much anymore."

"Hello, Ara. It's good to see you, too. It's hard to get away from the bakery these days. I'm working to master the craft so I can take over when Stan retires. That's only three years away, and I'll have to be at least a journeyman by then."

"Knowing you, Alec, you'll be a master in half that time. Still, I'd like it if you stopped by more often. So would Sarah."

Sarah glared at her mother. "I couldn't care less!" she protested.

Ara looked at her daughter and raised an eyebrow; then she looked at the silent Alec. "At any rate, I could use your help in the shop. I need some things brought out of the basement to put on display. You've always helped me out and I'm willing to pay twenty silvers."

"Twenty!" cried Alec. "That's a month's wages!"

"You're worth it. Two women can't carry some of the heavier things I've got down there, trunks of gems and whatnot."

Alec rubbed his chin. "I'll do it this Sunday. I'm off at the bakery. I could use a day to rest, especially after a day of digging, but I'd love to help you. You know I'd do it for free."

"I know, but there's no need. Business has been good. Some of the merchants who come through town are often intrigued by my more unusual pieces. Sometimes they're intrigued enough to pay in gold coin. I don't know why. My grandfather collected junk all his life. I opened the shop just to get rid of some if it; I never thought people would actually want it."

Suddenly the room became quiet. A slim, bearded man in a cape and fine clothes had jumped up on a table and raised his hand. Everyone's attention focused on him, for they knew it meant the evening festivities were about to begin.

"Greetings, my friends. I am Landyn, son of Gordon, minstrel of the city of Freehold. I will be your host for the evening. As you know, Bard's Day is celebrated all throughout the north of Tyridan to commemorate Ottis Brachnitter, the Great Bard. I will be singing one of his greatest ballads at evening's end. Until then, enjoy the songs and stories of your friends and neighbors and the bards who travel this great country of Tyridan."

Alec leaned over to Sarah and chuckled. "He's awfully long winded. Let's stop talking about singing and just have a song!"

"Shhh! We're lucky to have him here. He's one of the best."

"He's no Jordi Luppis."

"Jordi Luppis!" she spat in mock disdain.

And so the celebration began. According to custom, the first performer of the night was the town mayor, who in Barton Hills was Brian O'Lynnen. The fat old mayor climbed onto a chair and began to belt out a familiar drinking song. He was loud and off key, but everyone laughed and cheered as the normally stoic O'Lynnen drunkenly sang his bawdy tune.

> *There was a girl from Guildenheim*
> *I used to see her all the time*
> *With golden hair and bright green eyes*
> *Bosoms large and gen'rous thighs*
>
> *A dancer she was, it was her trade*
> *She jiggled with each move she made*
> *The way she'd dance was so sublime*
> *All loved the girl from Guildenheim*

Alec downed his drink as quickly as he could to overcome his embarrassment. The mayor would never live down his ribald performance! The song grew more and more lewd as it went on. The drunken revelers cheered at each verse, raising their mugs and singing along.

"This song is terrible!" exclaimed the baker.

"Lighten up," said Sarah, jabbing his side with her elbow. "Have another drink."

Alec took her advice, and by the time he finished his second ale he was enjoying himself a bit more. The next singer, old Doc Hamlick, was somewhat better than the mayor, although his song was equally silly. Doc danced and kicked his legs out as he sang, and he even juggled some mugs he grabbed off a nearby table. Derik watched with a horrified expression, fretting over the safety of his mugs. Alec didn't know what was funnier: Derik's worried face or Doc's mad performance.

Hey dilly dilly
You dance worse than Millie
The maid with the king-sized feet

"Grok's beard!" cried Alec. "Now he's singing *The Maid with the King-sized Feet!* Doesn't anyone here have any taste?"

Despite his comment, Alec was feeling quite happy now, his head light from the drink. He laughed right along with the others when Doc came to the part of the song which compared Millie's feet to squash and other large vegetables.

As the night wore on and ale was consumed in vast quantities, there were cheers and jeers and shouts from all corners of the room. Some of the singers were much better than O'Lynnen and Doc Hamlick, especially Jon Dugan, a young minstrel from Riverton. The crowd roared approval as he sang the classic *Tale of Preston the Ogre.*

Said the knight to the ogre "I've been thinking it over
And I don't think I can agree.
A man's heart is pink, not green as you think
It's a simple fact, you see."

Said Preston to knight, "Let's settle this right,
The facts we must make clear."
So without too much art he tore out Knight's heart
"By gum, you're right, I fear!"

No less than five people slid out of their chairs, laughing furiously as they rolled on the floor. When Jon finished the song, thunderous applause filled the room. He bowed, smiled, and rejoined the crowd.

Not all the singers were met with such a warm reception. Brik Masterson, the Blacksmith's son, drunkenly climbed on the table and began to mutilate *It's Time for Figgy Pudding,* a favorite song normally sung at Yule. Halfway through the song, a mob of revelers grabbed him from the table and threw him out the nearest window. The crowd laughed uproariously at this, and Brik, unfazed, joined the celebration outside. Several more performers throughout the night met with a similar fate, but it was all in fun and no one was seriously hurt. If things got out of hand, the massive and always serious Kraig was there to keep the peace.

Alec had drunk six huge mugs of ale and was feeling happy when he saw the man in the corner looking at him. The man sat quietly in his chair, nursing a single mug of ale, seemingly oblivious to the drunken revelry around him. His eyes were gray and sunken, his spotted flesh was deeply creased, and his hair was thin and gray. He wore fine leather garb and a heavy black cloak. When he saw that Alec had spotted him, he simply smiled and sipped his drink.

"Weird guy," said Alec. Sarah followed Alec's gaze and nodded in agreement.

"At least he knows how to dress. Why's he looking at me?"

"He's looking at *me*, Sarah. He smiled when I met his gaze a moment ago."

Ara looked over. "I never saw him before. Ignore him. He looks harmless enough. I need another drink, and then I have to sing. Excuse me." With that she got up and drifted somewhat drunkenly in the general direction of the bar.

Soon Alec had forgotten the mysterious stranger in the secluded alcove and was raising his glass in song, singing along as Jordi Luppis retold the famous *Battle of the Hill.*

In tears of drunken joy, Alec cried, "Grok's Beard, I love this song! I love this man!" He began to wave his arms around and sway in his chair to the beat of Jordi's song.

"Oh, please," muttered Sarah, finishing her second ale.

> *All harken now to this, my tale true*
> *And hear ye of the knights so bold and brave*
> *Who died upon the hill beneath skies blue*
> *And carried honor even to the grave*
>
> *It came to pass two hundred years ago*
> *That out of darkness came an ogre raid*
> *To stamp out light and life and grief to sow*
> *To kill and maim and cut with ogre blade*
>
> *The town militia met them on the Hill*
> *With bow and blade and axe they bravely fought*
> *But never could they match the ogres' skill*
> *And so the day was lost: or so they thought*
>
> *But hope rode in on noble horses white*
> *For Eglak sent her Bladeknights to the fight*

The old, wrinkled minstrel continued his song, which stretched on for nearly twenty minutes. By the end Alec was crying unabashedly, moved by the story of the knights who gave their lives to save Barton Hills and the surrounding villages. Finally Jordi Lupus finished his song and left the center table. The celebrants cheered him and chanted his name. No one loved him quite as much as Alec did, but his stirring performance left an impression on all of them.

After a few moments, the handsome minstrel Landyn helped Ara up onto the table. A joyous uproar filled the room as the townspeople saw the popular Ara take the stage. She waited until the cheers died down and then introduced her song.

"This is the story of a man and a woman in love. It's also the story of the war which came between them. It's called "Lydia's Lament.""

Unaccompanied, Ara's beautiful voice filled the room. The revelers, captivated by her, forgot their drinks for a moment and sat in silence, mesmerized by the tale and the woman who spun it. Alec shook his head in wonder.

"I'm impressed, Sarah. I never knew your mother was so talented."

Sarah just sat there, smiling. "Neither did I, Alec. She's wonderful. She's in her glory."

Sitting back, Alec listened.

> *Fires die and winds are still and oceans cease to churn*
> *The skies grow black and music dies and grieving hearts do yearn*
> *For sadness fills the souls of those who hear the tale spun*
> *Of the war where dreams and lives at once became undone*

The song went on for several minutes, telling the story of the War of Madagon, which, according to legend, began when an evil spirit from the unexplored plains to the North corrupted men and spurred them to attack their neighbors. The King of Pren Dalah, the land to the south of Madagon, ordered his army to battle this ravaging spirit and its followers. Lydia was the wife of a Captain in the King's army, and she begged him not to go. She was a wise woman, and she sensed the spirit's power and knew a mere mortal army would never prevail. She knew as he left that her husband would die.

> *Her sorrow wrapped her like a shroud as he marched off to war*
> *She watched him cross the field green toward lands of death and gore*

Her poor heart broke as she went to beg the King to call them back
He ignored her plea for he was blind to the spirit's powers black

The tale went on, alternating between a grieving Lydia and the futile battle against the spirit. It wasn't until the army was destroyed that hope came at last: a group of Fairy magicians rode down from the North, defeated the enemy's army, and chased the spirit back to its lair in the plains.

And so it was at last made well by the Northern Folk so Fair
But the cost was high for lives were lost and fertile lands laid bare
And still this spirit lurks and plots, this Ravager of men
And Lydia sits alone and grieves: she'll never love again

All throughout the song, the tavern patrons were silent and still. When the last note of the ballad gently trailed off, there was a moment of complete silence as the townsfolk looked in reverence at Ara. Then, almost without transition, a great cheer rose up and the people laughed and drank once again, shouting her name in praise. Ara, blushing, stepped quietly off the table and worked her way to her own corner of the room, receiving congratulations with every step. Landyn, minstrel of Freehold, stood upon the table, a wide smile upon his face.

"I fear I have been outdone! Unfortunately, mine is the act which must follow hers, and it will be the final act of the night. Thank you all for coming out. I trust you will all be safe and well."

He began to strum his lute masterfully, and with his voice he wove a grand tale of the days of old. His ballad was long and glorious and sometimes tragic, and it told of the High Kings in Eglak when they were still strong and their empire reached across the entire known world.

No fear of men had Prince or King
Nor fear of sorcerers vile
Their line was strong, their lives were long
They ruled nobly without guile

It was a great performance in all respects, but the celebrants were beyond caring if the performance was great or poor. They went on cheering and laughing, even through the sad and tragic parts of the tale. Many of them had passed out by now, and some areas of the room were stained by vomit.

As for Alec and Sarah, they hardly listened to him. When Ara sat down beside them, they showered her with praise.

"Oh, come on. I just sang a little song my mother used to sing to me."

"Nonsense. You were remarkable," said Alec. "I never heard anything like it."

"Mother, you really were great. You could be a bard!"

"Well, let's not get carried away. I just sing songs; I don't play the lute and I don't write tales. And I'm perfectly happy running my shop. Which reminds me: I'm expecting a merchant from Freehold early in the morning. We should get going as soon as this Landyn finishes his song."

"Mother, can't I stay with Alec? It's still not too late."

Ara leaned over to her daughter's ear. "It's past midnight, girl. I know why you want to stay, but you can see Alec on Sunday."

Again, Sarah glared at her mother indignantly. "What makes you think I have any interest in that…that *baker?*"

"I have eyes, don't I?"

Eventually Landyn's song was done. He said goodnight and hurried on his way, bidding the townsfolk to come see him perform at the Goblin's Foot if they were ever in Freehold. Alec noticed Ara staring at the minstrel. She didn't take her eyes off him until he was out the door. Even then, she sat motionless with a dreamy look on her face.

Sarah noticed her mother's behavior as well. "Mother!" she scolded. "Put your eyes back in your head. You don't want to get involved with a minstrel: they're good for entertainment, but I've heard most of them are scoundrels."

Ara shook herself out of her trance and gave Sarah a stern look. "Look here, Sarah Mills, I can look at whomever I like. I haven't been interested in a man since your father, my dear Matthew, died seven years ago, Grok rest his soul. Besides, Landyn lives in Freehold. I'm sure I'll never see him again." She sighed once more and turned to Alec. "Sarah and I need to be going. We have an early day tomorrow. Good-bye, Alec. I'll see you on Sunday."

"Good-bye, Ara. Sarah, it's been fun."

"Maybe for you," she replied. "I'll see you later."

Alec watched the two women leave. When he was a boy he had a serious crush on Ara, and now he was starting to notice the resemblance Sarah bore to her mother. He felt something like desire rise up in him, but he quenched it with another drink of ale.

Me and little Sarah. What an absurd thought!

There was more drinking as the night wore on, but slowly people began to drift out of the tavern and to their homes. Alec sat at the table for another hour, thinking about the wonderful night he'd had, and the wonderful company he kept. Then, happily, he nodded off.

"Alec Mason?"

Alec's head jolted up from where it rested on the tavern table. The voice was deep and old, and it frightened him. When his eyes focused, he saw the old man who had been sitting in the corner. When Alec looked around, he noticed the tavern was nearly empty now. Besides tavern employees and overnight guests, only those who had passed out remained. None paid any attention to Alec or his strange visitor.

"Yes, I'm Alec. What can I do for you?"

"My name is Salin. I'm a collector of rare goods. Antiques, jewelry, artwork, items of this sort. I've been looking for a particular item for some time, a rather valuable trinket, and I heard perhaps you could tell me where it is."

Alec just stared at the old man, uncomprehending. "I'm sorry. I don't know who would have told you that, but I'm just a baker. I don't have anything of value."

Salin was undaunted. "The object I seek is a steel disk about the size of your fist with diamonds set around it. Carved into its face is the image of a sun. It may hang from a golden or platinum chain. Have you seen such a thing?"

"No. Never. Diamonds? Why would I have this thing?"

Salin shook his head and smiled. "My source must have been mistaken. I'm sorry to have troubled you."

Salin rose and began to walk away. Then he turned back to Alec, who was already sliding back into unconsciousness.

"Oh, Alec. I'll be in town for several days. I've been traveling for many months and I need a rest, and this is such a quaint, peaceful village. I've rented a room at the tavern and I'll be here for the rest of the week. If you remember anything about the item I described to you, I'd appreciate it if you got in touch with me."

Salin leaned closer to Alec and whispered, "I'm prepared to pay you one thousand gold for it. It's much more than it's worth, but as a collector I'm afraid I'm quite obsessed. When I hear of something unique, I simply must have it. Well, good night Alec."

As Salin left the common room, Alec finally realized what he had said.

"One thousand *gold*? I've never seen one *hundred* gold! I've never seen one hundred silver! I must be dreaming."

The barkeep, Derik, heard Alec rambling and walked over to him. "Yeah, well, dream somewhere else. I've got to close up."

"Close up?" questioned Alec. Drink and weariness had muddled his mind and he couldn't comprehend the simplest of concepts. "Thousand gold. That's a lot of money."

"There isn't that much money in the whole village, Mason. Now get your sorry self home to bed."

"Bed. Good idea. Need sleep. Need gold. Need…"

Kraig helped Alec to the door and pushed him out. The night air woke Alec up enough for him to navigate the half mile to his hut. He knew nothing about a steel, diamond-studded disk with the image of a sun carved into it, but for a thousand gold he sincerely wished he did.

Soon he was in his bed, and thoughts of Salin and his offer were replaced by dreams of Jordi Luppis singing *The Battle of the Hill*. And soon those dreams were replaced by the image of Alec locked in a passionate embrace with Sarah. And they kissed, and gold seemed utterly irrelevant.

And Alec slept.

CHAPTER 2

The Hermit

When the next day dawned, life returned to normal in Barton Hills. Farmers tended their crops, craftsmen practiced their crafts, and Alec baked. As he expected, his muscles were sore from his exertion the day before, but he was glad to be back at work in the bakery. It was not hard work, but it was delicate and precise and he was very attentive to it. There was an art to making the various types of bread, the special cakes people enjoyed as desserts, and Alec was determined to master this art. He took pride in his work.

Still, he could not wait for the week to be over. Bard's Day had been Tuesday, and he found himself looking forward more and more to Sunday. He tried to convince himself he was anxious to help Ara, but he knew the chance to spend time with Sarah was the real reason he felt excited.

From time to time as he worked, Alec thought of the strange, somewhat disturbing man from the tavern. Did he really offer Alec one thousand gold coins for a piece of jewelry? Alec had begun to believe it was all a drunken delusion. Why would anyone think a simple man from Barton Hills would have anything so precious? *Yes,* thought Alec, *I drank too much and my mind was playing tricks on me. One thousand gold indeed!*

The fact was, Alec had only seen gold coins a few times in his life. It was the currency of the largest and richest of cities and was seldom used in small towns. Alec had heard in southern realms it was exchanged more freely, but he didn't believe it. There was little use for gold in towns like Barton Hills, where a few silver coins could buy everything the town had to offer.

But gold was not important to Alec. After all, he was given room and board by his master, Stan, and when Alec became the master, he could trade his bread for everything he needed. His life was planned out for him. He would be the baker of Barton Hills, and that would be enough. *Almost enough*, he thought, waiting anxiously for Sunday to arrive.

And at last Sunday did arrive. He awoke early, bathed in the stream, and dressed in his brown tunic and pants. Running his hand through his sandy hair, he ran down the road toward the Dragon's Den Curiosity Shop. He shouted greetings to the people he passed on the street, but took no time to engage in conversation. Before long, he arrived at the shop. It was a large building of wood and mud, and a red sign hung above the door, telling all comers they were entering the Dragon's Den, a place of curious wonders. As a child, Alec had spent a great deal of time wandering around the shop, exploring oddities not seen anywhere else in Barton Hills, but for the last few years his visits had been infrequent and brief.

But now he was here, and he joyfully entered the shop. As he took in the sights, he was reminded of his youthful fascination with the place. There were shelves and tables and cabinets filled with strange and marvelous items: colorful silks from far lands, bone tools of unknown purposes, metal statuettes of women and dragons and castles, pottery of intricate and foreign design, delicate glass trinkets, and (reputedly) arcane devices once used by insane magicians. Dusting a strangely empty table at the center of the room, Ara looked up and greeted Alec with a friendly smile.

"Alec, you're just in time. I'm making space for the merchandise from the basement. Sarah's down there now, getting some of the smaller things together. She'll show you what to bring up."

"Thanks, Ara," he said, smiling. "You know, it's great to be in here again. I hadn't realized how much I missed visiting every week."

"It's about time you came to your senses. I hope this means you'll stop by more often, even when I haven't hired you to move boxes up from the basement."

"Count on it. Things have been busy lately, but I'll make time to stop by."

Alec headed down the stairs. The staircase was short but dark, and the temperature dropped several degrees as he reached the bottom. The basement was large and filled from wall to wall with countless treasures and trinkets. The room would have been cast in complete darkness were it not for a single brass lamp casting faint luminance onto the dirt floor and stone walls. The lamp sat on a table at the center of the room, and near it stood Sarah, putting some silk garments in a wooden crate. She looked up as Alec entered and smiled warmly. Then, as if remembering she wasn't supposed to like him, she grimaced and said, "My mother's paying you twenty silver, Mason. The least you could have done was been on time."

"Sorry, Mills," he grinned, "but the thought of seeing you nearly kept me away."

Sarah gave him a hard look, but the corners of her lips turned slightly upward in humor. Then she turned away and pointed to a large chest which sat nearby.

"Think you can handle that one, Alec? Or should I find someone a bit more—physical?"

Alec looked at the chest and shrugged. "Just give me some room. It doesn't look that heavy."

Sarah watched as the young man evaluated the chest. He knelt down, gripped its sides, and with a grunt, lifted it. Before he had taken three steps, his arms shook with the effort. Sarah laughed aloud, but it was a good-natured laugh.

"Let me help you with that. I filled it with some heavy jewelry."

"Just testing me, Sarah?"

"Yes," she said, taking one side of the chest. "I wanted to see if you bakers were as strong and powerful as everyone says you are."

They laughed together as they carried the chest up the stairs. And they continued laughing throughout the day, sometimes sincerely, sometimes slyly, as they alternated between friendly conversation and jeering insults. The day passed swiftly as they worked. Ara continued cleaning and rearranging the shop, while Sarah and Alec gathered things from the basement and brought them upstairs. Alec couldn't believe how much had been hidden away, apparently for years, below the shop. There were old paintings and sculptures, hourglasses and clocks, gems and jewelry, foreign coins of gold and silver, and a wealth of items Alec could not identify. He looked at the vast inventory and shook his head in awe.

"By Grok, Sarah! If your mother lived in a larger town she could be a rich woman! I'm sure that in Freehold or Valaria there would be collectors and merchants willing to pay a great deal of gold for some of these things. And this jewelry! What wealthy noble wouldn't want to give his wife such gifts?"

"Oh, stop dreaming, Alec. My mother doesn't want wealth. What would she do with it? She wouldn't leave Barton Hills for any amount of gold. This shop, it's very important to her, but not because of the money it brings in. In some way, it gives her purpose and allows her to honor the memory of her grandfather. After all, most of this stuff was his. And these things, however trivial they may seem, tend to bring joy to the people who buy them. I think that alone keeps her here, selling her wares to people who wouldn't be able to afford them otherwise."

Alec nodded in agreement. "She's always put other people first. You really admire her, don't you?"

"She's my mother. She's also one of the finest people I've ever known."

And so the day continued, and by dusk the work was nearly done. Sarah was helping her mother arrange the items she and Alec had brought upstairs, and Alec was in the basement making sure nothing was forgotten. The room was nearly empty now, containing only empty chests, cabinets, and shelves. Alec was about to ascend into the shop when he noticed an old wooden chest shoved under the staircase. It was practically hidden from view, and it was covered thickly with dust and cobwebs. Apparently it had been resting in the corner for quite some time, completely forgotten. Inquisitively, Alec withdrew the chest from its nook and carefully opened it.

Alec gasped in wonder and awe. A golden glow filled the chest and illuminated the area around it. Resting within the chest was a beautiful circle of gold, perhaps a headpiece of some sort. Beside it sat a gold ring, in which was set a shimmering amber stone, the source of the golden glow. And hanging from a peg set in the side of the chest was a strangely familiar Talisman. It was a flat circle, perhaps four inches in diameter, made out of glimmering steel. Set all around its circumference were small but priceless diamonds, and on the steel itself an image of a fiery sun was delicately graven. It dangled from a brilliant chain of pure platinum.

For a moment Alec could not move. His thoughts went awry, unable to make the connection between what he was seeing and what the images meant to him. Then a sudden snap of recognition caused him to jump to his feet and cry out.

This was the very artifact the old man in the bar, Salin, had asked Alec about! This bauble was so desired by Salin he had offered to pay Alec a full one thousand gold coins for it. Alec couldn't believe what he was seeing. He reached for the Talisman and pulled it from the box.

As he did so, the room went dark. The glow which had been shining from the ring vanished, leaving in its wake a cold emptiness, as if something precious had been offered and then suddenly denied. At the same time, Ara came down the stairs, followed by her daughter.

"Alec? What is it? I heard you cry out."

Alec looked up blankly, at first unable to recognize the faces before him. But his thoughts were coming together, and in a moment he was able to answer.

"Ara. I was just looking around to see if I missed anything and I ran across this old chest. I found this." He held the Talisman toward her.

Ara looked at it and shrugged. "I don't think I've ever seen it before. That old chest has been here since grandfather bought the building sixty years ago. We could never get it open, so we just shoved it in the corner. I'd completely forgotten about it."

"It opened easily enough for me. Anyway, there are two other things here: a ring and a gold circlet. But this charm is what interests me. Ara, Sarah, let's go upstairs and sit down. There's something I need to tell you."

The three of them went up to the shop and sat around a small table in the back room which served as Ara's office. Alec related his mysterious experience at the tavern, making sure to include every detail. Ara listened intently, her features tensing in concentration.

"It doesn't make any sense. A thousand gold is an unthinkable amount of money. One could buy enough grain to feed this entire town for a year with that much coin. And putting the money aside, how would this Salin have known you would come across the charm?"

"I don't know. It's unbelievable, but it's all true. Salin made the offer. Somehow, I've found what he wants. The only question remaining is, what do we do now?"

Suddenly Sarah jumped up. "What do you mean, what do we do? It's obvious isn't it? On the market, this charm could pull in twenty gold, thirty at most. Knowing Mother, she'd let it go for less than ten. But here's a man who wants to give us a thousand gold coins for it. A thousand! Even split among the three of us, it would be a small fortune. Think of all the things we could do with the money."

Ara smiled at her daughter, but shook her head. "What would we do with it, really? We have all we need. There's little else Barton Hills has to offer and I certainly have no wish to leave. And even if I did, a thousand gold coins wouldn't take us far. Oh, I know it seems like an enormous sum to the two of you, but you've been sheltered in this small town all your lives. In the city, a thousand gold would purchase only a year's rent and meals, and perhaps a few frills along the way."

"Nevertheless," said Alec, "Salin's offer stands. Why turn him down? You say we have little need of the money, which is true. But we have even less need for this charm, beautiful though it is. Why, you could use your share to expand and improve your shop. And I could use mine to visit the nearby cities. I've always wanted to see the grand bakeries of Freehold, Valaria, and the other cities of Tyridan. This could be my only chance."

Ara nodded. "I didn't know you were so ambitious. Very well, Alec. Find this Salin and sell the charm. If he's foolish and rich enough to pay the thousand gold, so be it. We'll split the money evenly, although I still don't see what need I'll have for it."

Alec smiled. "You won't regret it. I'll have to go to the inn tonight. He may not be in town much longer."

Sarah motioned Alec to the door. "Well, hurry, then. Even if my mother can't think of a way to spend her share of the money, I'm certain I can. Now get lost, Mason!"

"Right away, my lady," Alec laughed over his shoulder as he ran for the door, Talisman in hand.

Alec reached the Silver Shield twenty minutes later. The night was deepening in the sky and the moon cast an eerie glow across the village. As Alec entered the tavern, a feeling of apprehension tugged at his heart. The night seemed darker than usual, the tavern more sinister. But he thrust such thoughts aside as he made his way to the bar and sat down.

"What brings you here on a Sunday night, Alec?" asked Derik, the barkeeper.

"Business. Do you know a man named Salin? He's been staying here since Tuesday, I think."

"Of course I know him. Old, leathery fellow. Very mysterious, too, I might say. He doesn't talk much and he won't answer any questions about himself either. And he has a hard look in his eye. Devious. I wouldn't trust him. What business would you have with the likes of him?"

"Private business, Derik. Pour me an ale, please."

"Now that's business I understand."

Alec looked around the large common room. Sitting by the door was Kraig, the huge peacekeeper and protector of the Silver Shield. From his chair Kraig surveyed the rest of the sparsely populated commons. Alec followed the burly man's gaze and noticed the lack of activity, an obvious contrast to the revelry demonstrated earlier in the week. A few farmers and townsfolk sat quietly with their drinks, some playing card games or speaking quietly, but the room was largely empty and still. When Derik brought his ale, Alec asked, "Business is a little slow tonight?"

"Very. Apparently, people are still recovering from Bard's Day. I haven't seen such a party since old Granduk Thorfolly's funeral, twenty years ago. Still, there's business enough to keep me going. Why, there's one fellow here tonight who's been buying enough ale to wash away ten men's sorrows. Look over there."

The barkeep pointed toward the secluded alcove where Salin had been sitting on Bard's Day. There sat an ordinary looking man, perhaps forty years of age. He was dressed in a dusty white tunic and baggy pants and had short brown hair resting flatly against his head. His face was cleanly shaven, revealing features so plain they seemed unusual. He sat still, staring into his drink as if therein lay the deepest secrets of the world.

Strangely enough, Alec recognized the man. He had seen him three or four times before, here in the tavern or walking in the wooded groves on the outskirts of town. Alec had heard the man was named Michael, and he lived in seclusion in a small hut in the woods. No one knew more of the hermit, save he had lived there for many years, longer than Alec had been alive.

"What's he doing here?" whispered Alec. "He hardly ever ventures into town."

Derik shrugged. "Who can guess what old Michael is up to? Maybe he just got tired of sitting out there in the woods all alone. I'm not complaining, mind you. As long as he keeps buying drinks, he can stay here as long as he wants."

Alec nodded. Changing the subject, he asked, "Could you do something for me? I don't see Salin anywhere. Could you let him know I'm here?"

"Sure. I'll send Kist up to fetch him."

Derik yelled to Kist, a stubby boy who ran errands for the bartender. The youth ran up the stairs to deliver the message. When he was gone and Derik had gone about his business, Alec took the Talisman from his pocket and looked at it in the dim tavern light. The diamonds caught the scant light and cast it back at the walls, dotting them with dancing pinpoints of brilliance. Again Alec wondered what significance the charm had to Salin, and why he would be willing to pay a fortune for it. He was lost in his thoughts, staring at the Talisman as it turned on its chain, when a voice startled him.

"How did you come by such a relic as that, my boy?"

Alec spun on the barstool to face the speaker. His surprise deepened as he saw the old hermit, Michael, standing only scant feet from him. Something about the hermit made Alec uncomfortable, and he squirmed in his seat, attempting to back away from Michael's dull, gray eyes.

"Relic? I'm afraid I don't..."

"That charm you hold in your hand," elaborated the hermit. "Where did you get it?"

Suddenly Alec grew angry. He didn't like being questioned, especially by an eccentric hermit who was probably drunk and perhaps half mad as well. Instinctively, he shoved the charm into his pocket.

"I don't see how it's any business of yours. It's nothing but an old piece of jewelry and I stand to make quite a profit from it. So if you'll just go back to your table..."

"Profit? You're going to sell it? There's not enough silver in all of Tyridan to equal the worth of what you hold in your hand."

"Is that so? Look, Salin will be here in a moment and I don't want you here when he arrives."

The hermit's uncannily plain face stretched in a grimace of surprise. "Salin? By the Seven Laws, Alec Mason, he must not acquire the Talisman!"

Alec was about to shout for Kraig, to ask him to show this madman to the door, when suddenly he saw something in Michael's dull gray eyes. Something urgent yet calm, confused yet lucid. Something that urged him to listen.

"How...how did you know my name?" he said more calmly.

"There is no time for questions now, Alec. We must leave this place. If indeed you have sent for Salin Urdrokk, we must not be present when he arrives."

"But he'll pay gold for this charm! I don't know what you want, Michael, but there's no harm in making a profit. He's just a harmless old collector."

"A collector? How do you know this?"

"He told me," answered Alec.

Michael shook his head, his grimace growing taut. "May the Seven save me from fools. You must not give this thing to Salin Urdrokk. You will come with me. Now."

Again Alec caught the passive urgency in the stranger's drab eyes. This time it could not be refused. Regretfully, and to his own surprise, he followed the virtual stranger out of the tavern.

"I don't know why I'm doing this," said Alec, his eyes downcast. "I had an opportunity to be rich."

The hermit walked briskly, turning north toward a wooded hill that lay only a few hundred yards from the tavern. "You had no such opportunity. Salin may have granted you the price he promised, but his coin is tainted with blood. You would derive no wealth from it. Come. We must hurry, lest he sees us and pursues."

Alec followed Michael without understanding why, although he did so of his volition. The strange, divided look in the hermit's eyes demanded faith. There was a sadness in those eyes which Alec could not fathom, but beneath it was wisdom and a keen perception. Such eyes could not be refused.

Soon they climbed the wooded hill and passed the boundary of town. They walked briskly for a time. When Alec realized his companion had no intention of stopping, he halted, placed his hands on his hips, and shouted after Michael.

"You owe me an explanation. I'm not going any further until I've gotten one."

The hermit spun and looked at him urgently. "When we arrive at my home, I'll explain everything. We will be safe there, for a time."

Alec shook his head. "No. I've gone far enough. I feel like a fool for coming here. If you don't tell me what's going on, I'm going back to the tavern."

"You must not! Listen to me well, boy. Salin Urdrokk is not some innocent old jewelry collector; he is a powerful sorcerer and a servant of darkness. This Talisman he would have from you will give him the power to corrupt that which has been pure since the world was young. With its might he could conquer realm after realm until all the world knelt before him and his dark master. This trinket you bear is the Talisman of Unity, the greatest of all the works of Faerie."

Alec frowned and backed away, shaking his head in disbelief. "You're as mad as they say. Dark sorcery! Fairy magic! Tales for children! To think I nearly believed you. Grok's beard, I hope Salin hasn't left town yet; I still may be able to convince him to buy this thing."

Michael looked urgently at Alec for a brief moment. But then he cast his sad eyes toward the ground, all tension draining from his thin frame.

"So be it. I cannot hold you against your will, nor will I attempt to wrest the Talisman from you. I set aside my trials long ago. I was a fool to intervene in affairs which no longer concern me. Go. Do what you will. It matters not to me."

With that, Michael turned his back and walked slowly into the woods. To Alec he looked like a man who had lost something precious, thought he had found it again, and realized he was mistaken. For a moment he considered going to the hermit, trying to make sense out of his strange words, but then he thought the better of it. Perhaps there were such things as magic and sorcery in the world, but if so, they were far away from Barton Hills. Here, there was only farming, baking, and cooking. There was only simplicity and clean living.

The people of Barton Hills were simple folk. Their ways were all Alec had ever known, all he had ever wanted to know. It was the life he was born into and the life he would live. The gold he would soon have would not change him. It would just make life fuller, allow him to expand the bakery and do more for his friends and neighbors. He would sell the charm to Salin, and nothing bad would come of it. Nothing bad ever happened in Barton Hills. It was as simple as that.

Purposefully, he headed back toward town.

CHAPTER 3

Flight

The night had grown deep and black by the time Alec reached the Silver Shield. When he entered, he was surprised to find the tavern empty, except for the bartender and Kraig, who were talking quietly to one another near the bar. Derik wore a worried expression on his usually jovial face, and the burly peace-keeper's muscles bulged with tension. At the sound of the door opening, they looked up in worried anticipation.

"Alec Mason!" cried Derik. "Where did you go? That Salin fellow is off looking for you."

As Alec walked to the bar, he replied, "The strange hermit, Michael, wanted a word with me in private. I don't know why I bothered with him."

"I don't know why you bothered with *Salin*," said Kraig, beckoning Alec closer.

"What do you mean?"

Kraig looked hesitantly at Derik, who said, "I don't think you know what you've gotten yourself into." Both men looked almost frightened as Derik continued. "Salin came down here looking for you. When he didn't see you, he asked me where you had gone. I told him I didn't know. He asked if you had some sort of charm hanging from a chain, and I said, yes, I saw you pull it out of your pocket just before he came down. When he heard that, he laughed. It was an ill laugh, my boy, gleeful but black. Then he stopped laughing and cursed. 'Where is he?' he asked again, this time shouting at me. I told him not to raise his voice to me, which only made matters worse. He turned away from the bar and screamed a curse. Everyone dropped what they were doing to stare at him, not because he was a stranger or because he had shouted, but because they were scared. So scared that when he shouted again, most everyone fled. Even Kraig backed away into the corner for a while."

Kraig looked slightly ashamed, and as if to justify his fear, he said, "I can't explain it. His eyes...his voice. He terrified me. It was unnatural."

Then Derik continued. "He turned on me again and in a low, gravelly voice, he said, 'Where does Mason live? If he will not see me here, I will pay him a visit at his home. The foolish boy cannot evade me for long.' I wanted to keep my mouth shut, Alec, but a terrible fear was on me. I was afraid of what he might do if I didn't tell him. Then he turned and stormed out, his big gray cloak billowing out behind him."

Alec's eyes were wide with dread. What manner of man was this Salin who could terrify grown men with a glare and a shout? And now he was going to Alec's home, which was adjacent to the bakery and his master's residence.

"Grok! I've got to get over there. If he hurts Stan or Matilda it will be on my head."

Derik reached for Alec's arm. "I wouldn't go, if I were you. You'd just feel the fear, too, boy. Maybe if he doesn't find you there, he'll give up and leave town."

"I doubt it. He seems to want this Talisman pretty badly. Maybe the hermit was right about him. I've got to go."

"Wait!" exclaimed Kraig. "I'll go with you. If he's as dangerous as he seems, you may need my help."

Alec accepted Kraig's offer with a nod. The peacekeeper seemed determined to atone for his earlier cowardice. He and Alec left the tavern and made their way through the night toward Alec's home. The darkness around them was close and heavy, and the moon's dim glow seemed only to make the shadows deeper. A silence covered the town; not the peaceful quiet of most nights in Barton Hills, but a dead stillness that filled them with dread. Neither Alec nor Kraig spoke, for even the soft padding of their feet upon the road seemed too loud in the terrible quiet. There was no sound from the houses to either side of the road, nor were there any animal noises from the fields or woods. Even the wind was silent. A scent wafted through the air, a scent like something burning. It was strange and familiar at the same time, and although it reminded him of the smell of a wood fire, Alec fancied it was the smell of fear. In such unnatural darkness and silence they walked, until they stood only yards away from Alec's small hut. Or what was left of it.

"Grok's wounds," muttered Alec.

The door had been cleft in two, one half swinging slowly on the single remaining hinge, the other leaning askew in the doorway. The stone and wood surrounding the door were smashed and burned, and the thatched roof over the entry was scorched. Alec pushed the swinging half-door aside and ran into his home, followed by the big peacekeeper.

Inside was worse. The small one room interior had been torn apart. The table and chairs had been broken and scattered, the mattress of Alec's bed slashed open, his chest emptied, its contents strewn around the room. He gaped, unable to believe what had happened to his home and his few belongings.

"Salin," he whispered. "He must have been looking for it. If he had only waited for me…"

"What is this thing he wants so badly?" asked Kraig, his wide eyes scanning the wreckage.

"I don't know. I don't know what it is."

Suddenly a woman's shriek cut through the night. Kraig was the first to react, dashing through the doorway, but Alec followed quickly, his heart pounding with fear and urgency. The cry had come from the house next door, where Stan Kulnip, the Master Baker, and his wife Matilda made their home. Alec tried to catch up to Kraig as he ran for the Baker's door, but the big man was faster by far. He gained the door a full ten strides before the unathletic youth. As he pushed it open, a fiery white light exploded outward, dropping him to his knees. Alec turned away and covered his eyes as the light poured over him. For an instant night was banished, and heat washed over Alec's flesh. For a long moment he stood there, his back to the brutal heat, until at last the cool dark night re-imposed itself around him. When he turned back to the house, he saw the front had been reduced to rubble, fanned outward by the blast. Kraig knelt in the middle of the debris, his head bowed forward and his hands covering his face. His body shook. Slowly, Alec approached the muscular man.

Only darkness came from the house now. He looked around to find the source of the blast, but the night was still. Kneeling on the ground before the peacekeeper, he said, "Kraig?"

The burly man looked up, his eyes blank. "Alec." His voice shook. "I can't see. The light. I can't…" He buried his head in his hands and was still.

"Stay here. I've got to see if Stan is all right."

"Don't go in there," muttered Kraig. "It's sorcery, Alec. Pure evil."

Alec hesitated, but he would not let fear stop him. Stan and Matilda were like his parents, and he had to know if they were alive. If they weren't…

He stepped from twilight into darkness. He walked slowly, waiting for his eyes to adjust. He stumbled over broken stones and wooden debris as he made his way deeper into the blasted house. Soon he was guided by a low whimper. Someone nearby was in pain.

The walls were still warm from the blast, but they were for the most part undamaged. He felt along the wall for the oil lamp he knew hung near the door, and finding it intact, he lit it. Dim light flickered on the walls and drove the shadows from the corners. On the far end of the room was an open door which led to Stan and Matilda's bedroom. The muffled sobs came from there. Alec took down the lamp and made his way toward the back room.

Entering, he nearly cried out in horror. Stan's twisted body lay in the corner like a discarded doll. His unseeing eyes were wide with terror and blood dripped from the corner of his mouth. His head hung at an unnatural angle. He was certainly dead.

Before Alec could scream, a broken voice shook him. "Alec. Oh, Grok, Alec. How could this have happened?"

His head turned slowly, as if in a dream. Then he saw Matilda, blood covering her broken form. He rushed to her side, tears streaming down his cheeks.

"Matilda. Matilda. What happened? Oh, Grok."

"Alec," her voice shook. "He was terrible. It was you he was after. He knew you were like a son to us. He thought you left it with us. But it's not here."

"No. No, I have it. If I'd have known, I never would have…never could…"

"Listen to me, boy," said the old woman as her blood, her life, seeped from her wounds. "He told us what he sought. He said you had offered it to him, then fled before he could claim it. But you can't go back on your offer, he said. He'll find you and get it from you. He'll go through everyone you care about if he needs to. But he'll get it.

"Alec," she whispered, her eyes fluttering. "Get away. He won't let you live now. Don't let him have it. Don't…"

She closed her eyes and was still. Alec bowed his head over her, his body racked with sobs. He had been as close to the Kulnips as to anyone. They had raised him from a boy, taught him a trade, cared for him like parents. Now they were gone. Gone because of Salin and his mad desire for the strange Talisman. Gone because of Alec.

"NO!" he cried, shaking his arms in the air. But anger and grief would do him no good. His passion could not bring them back. He knew he had to get away or he would share their fate. But as he waded through his grief and made his way toward the door, a though struck him. Matilda had said, *He'll go through everyone you care for if he needs to.*

Grok's wounds...Sarah!

He ran out of the house, paying no heed to the debris threatening to trip him. He was thinking only of Sarah and her mother, knowing Salin had seen them with him at the tavern. Would he have connected them to the Talisman as well? After all, if Salin had known Alec would run across it, he might have known it was hidden in Ara's shop. Alec's heart pounded at the thought of Sarah in danger and he nearly ran straight into Kraig, who was standing just outside the door.

"Kraig...Sarah's in trouble!" he cried urgently. "We can't help the Kulnips, but maybe..."

Kraig reached blindly toward him. He had forgotten the peacekeeper couldn't see.

"Alec, the flash. I can't see anything. I'm no help to you. Go on without me, but be careful."

"Oh, Grok! Grok's bloody wounds! Stay here. I'll send someone to help you if I can."

At once, Alec was running again. As he ran, thoughts and questions swam in his head. Did Salin cause the flash of light? If he had been in the house as they approached, why hadn't he seen Alec? Or, for that matter, why hadn't Alec seen *him*? Why did the flash which reduced the front of the house to rubble leave Kraig virtually unharmed, save his blindness? *Who was this Salin?*

In minutes, he arrived at Sarah and Ara's home. It was quiet and undamaged. Without knocking, he threw open the door and barged in.

The room was illuminated by the faint glow of an oil lamp. Sarah sat alone on a large pillow, her hair covering her face as she bent over a book. She was dressed in a long, white robe, appropriate only for bed clothing. At the noise of Alec's entrance, she looked up in surprise.

"Alec! What on earth are you doing here? Don't you knock?"

"Sarah," he panted. "Where's your mother?"

"What? At the shop, taking inventory. But what..."

"There's no time to explain. By the wounds of Grok! We've got to get out of here. It's Salin. He's after me. He may be after you, too."

She stared at him dumbly. "After me? But why? Didn't you sell him the charm?"

"No, but I'll explain later. Look, he's already killed the Kulnips. We could be next!"

"Killed!" she screamed. She jumped to her feet. "I've got to get some clothes on."

"No! Just grab a cloak. We've got to get Ara and leave town. Maybe we can lie low in Riverton for a while, until things calm down."

Sarah grabbed a heavy cloak from a hook on the wall and wrapped it around her shoulders. It was inappropriate for the time of year, but it was the only thing she could cover herself with quickly. She followed Alec as he left the house and hurried toward the shop.

The Dragon's Den was only several hundred feet away, just over a low hill. As they crested the hill and the shop came into view, a low rumble filled the air. Despite their exigency, they paused to listen to the sound. It seemed to be coming from the ground near the shop. Then the building began to shake, the wood split apart, and an explosion of light burst from within. With a mighty groan, the wood tore itself apart and scattered across the hill. Alec gaped in agony. Sarah cried out.

"No," muttered Alec. "Not Ara, too."

But before the light died he was moving again, dragging the crying Sarah along behind him.

"He won't get you, too. I swear it."

She was looking back at the house, her mouth locked in a grimace of horror, tears streaming down her face. "Mother. *Oh, wounds! MOTHER!*"

Alec was in no shape to be running long distances. His flabby sides ached and his heart pounded, but he forced himself onward. For all he knew Salin was right behind him, playing a sick game, stalking him like a wolf stalks its prey. The Talisman, whatever it was, would soon be in the sorcerer's hand. And Alec would not be a thousand gold richer; he would be dead.

The noise had finally roused some of the town's citizens. Lights were lit in the houses and huts surrounding the shop; heads peeped out windows and doors. But Alec did not stop. He couldn't endanger anyone by staying nearby. He was heading out of town, but on his way, he saw Kraig standing in the middle of the road, arms waving helplessly.

"Alec? Alec? Is that you?"

"Kraig!" he said, slowing at the big man's side. "Can you see?"

"Just shapes. You're just a black blur on a black wall, but I can follow you now. Who's that other blur?"

"Sarah. I...I don't think Ara made it. The shop's gone."

That was all the time he was willing to spare for explanation. He was off again and Kraig followed, hardly hindered by his damaged sight.

"Where are we going?" Sarah asked through her tears. "Riverton is to the south. We're heading north."

"Were going to pay a visit to Michael, the hermit. He got me into this mess. He owes me an explanation, at the very least. At best, he might be able to help. He knows something about the Talisman and about Salin."

They ran in silence. Soon they reached the woods, a place they would normally avoid after dark. At times wolves roamed the wooded hills and snakes lurked beneath rocks and fallen branches. But now the woods offered some semblance of safety. At least they were no longer in the open and would be harder to track. Vaguely, Alec hoped he could find the hermit's hut. He knew it lay in the woods directly north of town, but he had never actually been there. In the dark, he could pass within a hundred feet of it and miss it entirely. Still, being lost in the woods was better than the alternative.

Kraig began to fall behind. Unable to see, he could not navigate among the trees. After running headlong into three, he slowed to feel his way along with his hands. When Alec finally turned to look behind him, he saw the peacekeeper heading off in the wrong direction.

"Wounds," he gritted in frustration. "Stay here, Sarah." He did not want to shout out and give away their whereabouts, so he ran to intercept Kraig. When he reached the big man, he took his hand and pulled him to where he had left Sarah. Then the three, hand in hand, made their way slowly through the darkened woods.

By now everyone in town will be wondering what's going on, thought Alec. After the explosions and flashes of light, the people of Barton Hills would be more than curious. They would be scared. Never in the history of the town had such a display been seen. Sorcery was the stuff of legends, unpleasant ones to boot. Even those few people who had traveled to other towns and cities in Tyridan had found no evidence of magic, so most people in the village believed it only myth. Tonight such misconceptions had been shattered, at least for Alec.

The woods were growing thick around them and Alec wondered if they had passed Michael's hut long ago. His knowledge of the geography outside of town was sparse, but he knew the woods became a true forest a few miles to the north. He had been south to Riverton a few times, and east as far as the Grundeye Inn, but never had he ventured this far into the Northwood. He thought if he cut west he might come to the Wyndsway, the road leading to Freehold. Yet along the road they could be easily followed, and this thought horrified him.

Just hours ago he had happily gone to the tavern to do business with Salin; now he fled from the old man's fiery wrath. So he kept running northward, pulling Sarah and Kraig along with him, trying not to think of those already slain by the sorcerer.

A wolf howled. Sarah whimpered in fear and Kraig mumbled something about the knife he wished he hadn't left at home. Alec pulled them forward, more afraid of Salin than wolves. But his heart raced faster, all the same.

He felt they had been running blindly through the woods for over an hour. His chest was heaving with effort and Sarah was stumbling with weariness. Only Kraig seemed unaffected by the run. They had nearly slowed to a walk when Alec saw a light through the trees. He pointed toward it and Sarah nodded in agreement. They headed toward it.

Soon they were near enough to see the light more clearly. It was streaming from the window of a small, wooden hut. Smoke came from a hole in the hut's straw and mud roof. Hope leaped in Alec's chest as he led his companions to the door. When he reached it, he nearly fell to his knees. He could go no further.

"Where are we?" asked Kraig. "I see light."

"A hut," said Alec. "Michael's, I hope."

"I still don't see what you want with *him*," Kraig said, confused.

"I'm not sure yet, either," answered the baker.

He knocked on the door. In a moment, it opened, and Michael stood in the doorway, a look of mild curiosity on his face. He was still dressed in the same ragged white tunic and baggy brown pants. With little inflection, he said, "Mason. And you've brought friends. Come in." He stepped back and beckoned them inside.

There was hardly enough room in the hut for the four of them. A fire blazed in a small hearth in one corner and a straw bed sat in another. A round table with two chairs sat in the room's center and a modest chest sat on the floor beside it. Bread, cheese and a pitcher of water were lain out on the table. Otherwise, the hut was bare.

"I hadn't thought I would see you again, Alec Mason," said the hermit. "You seemed intent on returning to Salin. But, as you and your friends are here, why don't you join me. I was about to sit down to my evening meal. It is no feast, but there is enough for all of us."

"No, thank you," Alec said, although he eyed the food regretfully. He hadn't eaten in hours. "I didn't see Salin. By the time I returned to the tavern, he was gone. Apparently he thought I had changed my mind, that I wasn't going to sell him the Talisman. I guess he thought I saw him for what he was. He decided to take it by force, although he didn't know where to find me. And so far he's killed three people who are very dear to me. You know something about all this. What by the Wounds of Grok is going on here?"

Sarah, who had been staring blankly into the fire, turned toward Michael, her face a mixture of fear and rage and grief, and cried, "He killed my mother!"

The hermit looked shocked at first, then sad. He lowered his head as if in mourning. But when he raised it, his pale face had again gone blank.

"I'm sorry," he said dispassionately. "I'm sorry about your trouble, but there's nothing I can do. Salin is sly and powerful and I am nothing. My advice to you is to run far and fast. Keep heading north, through the forest. If the One is with you, you may make it to Bordonhold. There you may find men bold and pure enough to aid you."

"Bordonhold!" cried Alec. But that is a world away!"

"It is not as far as your limited knowledge would make it. With haste, you can be there in less than a week."

It was Kraig's turn to speak up. "Look, hermit. We have no food, no water, and we don't know the way. I'm nearly blind and Mason is too flabby for a long journey. Now, he tells me you know something about all this. I suggest you do more than give us some useless advice." Clenching a fist, he towered threateningly over the gaunt hermit.

Michael looked up at him blankly. Then he sat down at the table and began eating a block of cheese. "I said there's nothing I can do for you."

"But you were willing to help me before!" exclaimed Alec. "You were demanding to help me! You said I had to keep the charm from Salin and you were going to help me do it!"

"And you refused."

"I'm not refusing now."

"I was mistaken to get involved. When I saw you in the tavern, when I saw you had the Talisman, I thought...but no. Once I believed in purpose. Once I believed there was a pattern to life, a meaning. I thought I had a place in the order of things. I was foolish. The world moves on without my interference, for good or ill. Flee while you can. You may find others more willing to help than I."

Unexpectedly, Sarah shouted and violently overturned the table. *"He killed my mother!"* she screamed.

Michael looked into her eyes and again his features flirted with grief. He rose and placed a hand on her shoulder.

"You are too young for such sorrow. You all are. I have no power to assist you, as I have said. I'm just a man, trying to live out my years in peace. Yet I would not see such youth and beauty sullied by the dark power of Salin Urdrokk. I know the forest well and I can guide you to Bordonhold. There, perhaps, your needs may be met."

Alec sighed with relief. He was torn with heartache at having to leave his home, especially in the wake of a disaster he helped bring about. But he knew flight was the only answer. And with a guide, they had a chance to get through the forest to Bordonhold. He was not entirely certain he could trust Michael, yet the hermit was certainly more trustworthy than Salin.

"Alec," Sarah whispered softly through her tears. "Do we really have to go? I've never been outside of Barton Hills."

"We really have to go. It's me he's after, but I can't leave you behind. He may hurt you to get to me. Besides, I can't let you wander around in the woods alone, with wolves and all. Kraig here's blind; he'd be no help to you."

The peacekeeper shrugged uncomfortably. "You're right. And I'd be a hindrance to you along the way. I'll stay behind. Maybe in the light of day I'll be able to see well enough to make my way back to town."

"No," said Alec. "You're coming with us. If your sight doesn't come back, you'll die out here. I won't have anyone else die because of me."

Michael, who had been gathering some items from his chest into a sack for the journey, turned and looked at Alec. "No one died because of you. They died because of Salin's greed. He can appear calm as death, but when his lusts drive him his wrath is terrible. You have done right in not giving him the Talisman. It is terrible that people have died, but many more would perish were he to gain what you carry. We must leave at once to give their deaths purpose. We must carry the Talisman where he cannot find it."

"Where is that?" questioned Alec.

Michael shook his head, dismissing the question. "Later. Others will take you there. I am only going as far as Bordonhold."

The middle-aged hermit opened the door and went out into the night. Hesitantly, the others followed. Tears still clung to Sarah's cheeks, but she seemed calmer, more resolved. Kraig still felt his way blindly, yet he moved with more confidence. And Alec felt better to have a destination, a purpose. And he felt better having a guide, even if it was Michael.

The hermit walked into the night and did not look back. He didn't seem to care if they were following or not. But Alec wasn't concerned with Michael's apathy. He was only concerned with getting to Bordonhold. Once there, there would be time to deal with the future. And they had a week to travel. In that time, he would get answers from Michael, even if he had to pry them from his sealed lips. He wouldn't walk as blindly as Kraig from danger into danger.

Together, silently, they walked northward into the dark, imposing forest.

CHAPTER 4

Into the Woods

The night was nearly gone before Michael allowed them to rest. Alec was stumbling, his body heavy with weariness. Sarah, too, was near the point of exhaustion, and even Kraig seemed in need of rest. Michael, however, appeared not the least bit tired. When he stopped, he turned and looked to the others, saying, "We will camp here for a time."

The spot he had chosen was a small clearing guarded heavily by tall trees. Thick moss and fallen leaves covered the ground, making for a soft, if slightly damp, place to rest. Alec let himself collapse to the ground, watching Sarah do the same. Kraig sat down, his back to a large oak. Michael bent down and opened his sack, removing a large bundle wrapped in paper and a thick, empty waterskin.

"There is a stream near here," he said. "I will go to fill the skin. Take some bread and dried meat from the package, but eat only a little. The food must last us until we reach Bordonhold, unless one of you has skill in hunting." He turned swiftly and disappeared into the woods.

Sarah turned her head toward Alec. "Can we trust him? That's the first he's spoken to us all night. For all we know, he went off to lead Salin to us."

Alec shook his head. "No. He seems sincere enough when it comes to his dislike of Salin. What ever he has planned for us, it's not Salin."

Kraig, despite his blindness, seemed to be watching over his younger companions. "I don't like this tramping through the woods all night. But I don't like stopping any better. Even if Michael isn't in league with Salin, Salin could still catch up to us here. I don't feel any safer than I did back in town."

"I feel less safe," said Alec. "We're deep in the Northwood, now. I've never heard of anyone from Barton Hills traveling through these woods. I've just heard rumors of large, black wolves and bears, hungry for human meat."

"Grok, Alec, I'm scared enough as it is," said Sarah. "Don't speak of things like wolves and bears."

"Sorry," he said. He kept quiet, not having anything to say which wouldn't upset her further. Despite her bravery, he knew inside she was shattered at the loss of her mother.

Kraig was not content with silence. "The thing I don't understand is, why is he taking us to Bordonhold? Freehold's closer. And safer, if you believe the stories."

The stories, thought Alec. Bordonhold was barely within the northern border of Tyridan, practically on the edge of the explored world. Only legends and grim stories spoke of the lands which lay beyond, sprawling on forever into dark and evil territories. Bordonhold was originally a fortress built to guard against the invasion of ogres and their like from those black lands, but it expanded and became just another city when it became evident no attacks were forthcoming. Still, many stories spoke of Bordonhold as a city where bargains were struck with dark powers and villains stalked the streets at night. Merchants traveled there to peddle their goods, but most other folks avoided it.

"Maybe he doesn't think Salin will follow us to Bordonhold," offered Alec. "And maybe that's a good assumption. After all, Salin probably knows we wouldn't go there on our own. And he won't know we've taken up with the hermit."

"Still," said Kraig, "it seems suspicious to me."

There was a silence for a time. Unexpectedly, Sarah rolled over on her stomach and faced Alec, and said, "Do you think my mother is really dead? We didn't actually see her die."

"I don't know," answered Alec. "Perhaps she wasn't even in the shop, or maybe she got out in time, escaped from Salin. I hadn't thought of that...but it's possible. Ara's a strong, smart woman. There's hope." In his heart he didn't believe it, but he didn't want to say anything which might crush Sarah's new-found optimism.

To his surprise, she smiled. "If anyone could have made it through, she could have. Thanks, Alec."

"For what?"

"For giving me hope."

But he hadn't given it to her. It had been within her all along. Seeing her smile, Alec felt a great weight lift. If she could go on without grief, then so could he. He moved closer to her, lay on his back, and looked up at the stars.

Soon Michael returned with the water. They had a quick meal and drank enough water to wash it down and slept the few remaining hours of the night. With the dawn, however, they were moving again. Michael roused them with barely a word and said less as he briskly walked northward, never looking back. Alec felt not at all rested by the too few hours of sleep, and within an hour he felt a cramp in his side. For the first time in his life he regretted not exercising more, letting rolls of fat build around his stomach. He sweated and gasped for air but did not complain about Michael's swift pace. He would not slow them down when danger might be close behind. But his sides hurt, his chest heaved, and his weak legs trembled as he walked.

The sun climbed high as noon approached, and despite the density of the forest, enough light filtered through the trees to brighten their way. The day grew hot and Alec saw Sarah wearily wipe the sweat from her brow. Her heavy cloak was making her too hot, but she had nothing else to wear. She should have been in light summer garb, not a sleeping robe covered by a winter cloak. At least her sandals were appropriate to the season.

As the day wore on, Kraig had less trouble following them. In the light, he could make out their shapes better; he claimed some of his sight had returned. Alec began to hope the peacekeeper would soon be able to see as clearly as ever. He knew he'd feel safer if the big man regained his full vision and confidence. Kraig had protected the Silver Shield Tavern for years, and Alec would be glad to have such protection for himself and Sarah. If they ran into trouble, Kraig might be the only one of the group who had the strength and skill to deal with it.

Two hours past noon, Michael allowed a brief halt. They sat, nibbled on some bread, and drank mouthfuls of fresh water. Michael, drawing his knees up to his chest, munched a piece of hard bread in silence. Alec decided it was a good time to question the strange hermit.

"Michael. You've kept pretty silent since we left your hut last night. But you owe us some answers. I want to know why we're going to Bordonhold rather than somewhere closer, safer. But first I want you to tell us about Salin. And about how you seem to know so much about him. What does he want with the Talisman?"

Michael's face was as bland as ever. "You have a lot of questions, my boy. And many of the answers you do not need to know. Not yet. Still, I suppose I do owe you something. I will tell you about Salin Urdrokk, although what I have to say will frighten you. You have seen only the smallest part of his power, and yet his own might is nothing compared to the creature he serves."

Michael paused and looked up at the sky, gathering his thoughts. He tore another hunk of bread from the hard loaf he carried and took a bite. He reached for the waterskin and Kraig handed it to him. He drank deeply and wiped his chin.

As the others continued their meal, Michael began his tale. "Centuries ago, war ravaged all the lands north of Riglak Nord. Tyridan did not exist then; this region was unsettled and unknown. But south and west of here, great armies met upon blood-soaked fields to battle for the fate of the world. The dark army of Mul Kytuer was made up of ogres and goblins and men who had been perverted to the cause of evil. It was lead by Groshem the Dark, a barbaric warrior whose might was unsurpassed. They fought under the flag of Vorik Seth, the shadowy Lord of Mul Kytuer, the very incarnation of evil upon this world. On the other side fought noble men and women from all the free lands north of the Desolation and west of the Sea, and with them fought the magic-wielding Fair Folk, inhabitants of the legendary land of Faerie. They were led by a young warrior whom the High King of Eglak had recently appointed First Bladeknight, the highest rank in the King's army. This man was a warrior of such promise the king put the fate of the known world in his hands. And the name of this warrior was Salin Urdrokk."

"What?" interrupted Alec. "How could he be the same Salin?"

"Be silent, Alec," said Michael. "Just listen, and you will see." He cleared his throat and continued. "Now at this time, as the armies marched to battle, three wanderers came to Varnya, the grand city where sat the Throne of Eglak. They sought audience with the King, and since they were known to him, the audience was granted. The King said to the Three, as they approached his throne, 'What brings you to my realm, now that war is upon us? I have seldom seen you in recent years, although need for your counsel has been great. Never before have the three of you come together!'

"'King Preytur,' the First of the Three replied, 'We have been away in far lands, where men are weaker and less able to resist the powers of night. There we have counseled their lords and tribal chiefs, so when Vorik Seth's power reaches into their lands they will be prepared.'

"'We have granted them magic,' said the Second. 'Arrows that burst into flame, swords that carve metal like flesh, staves that hurl lightning. We instructed them in their use so they could fight the army of Groshem the Dark.'

"'We suspected Groshem would seek to crush those weaker lands first,' said the Third, 'before attempting Eglak and the surrounding realms. It seems our judgment was in error. Still, even without our aid, your forces could triumph. You are strong and on your home ground, and Vorik Seth's arm is not as long as it once was. But you, too, have erred. And I pray we are not too late to set the error aright.'

"'I have erred?' said the King. 'I have built an army of such might even Groshem's ogres tremble before it. Would I were younger so I could lead them myself against the horde of Vorik Seth. But in my absence, I have named a champion, and he will lead my army to victory. For he is the greatest of warriors, pure of heart and strong of body, and his swordsmanship is unsurpassed. Salin Urdrokk, whom I have named First Bladeknight of Eglak, will lead them to victory.'

"The Three bowed their heads, for grief was upon them. 'This is how you have erred,' said the First. 'For over a year has the Voice of Vorik Seth spoken to Salin Urdrokk, whispering corruption into his willing ear. Promises of power and dark knowledge were made and a pact was sealed. Already Salin seeks to betray you. He leads your army not to victory, but to slaughter.'

"As the King strove to deny the charges against his champion, the Second said, 'He was corrupt from the start. But he wore the face of innocence to gain your trust, for his desire was to gain power within your realm, to use and abuse as he would. But now a greater lust drives him: the Seth has promised him more than you ever could. He has promised him vast might and virtual immortality. And all Salin has to do to prove his worth is to lead your army into a trap. They will be surrounded and slaughtered in Zarrana Canyon, eighty miles to the south.'

"The king gaped and then lashed out in outrage. 'This is not true! Salin is brave and noble! You come spreading lies!'

"The Third said, 'It is the truth we speak. If you do not heed us, Vorik Seth will stand victorious this day.'

"'If it is true,' said the King, 'how do you come by this knowledge?'

"'There are many things we can see,' said the First. 'A man's corruption is as visible to us as his face is to you. Salin is easy to read. He wishes for power to control others. He is pleased by the thought of slaughter. We have seen into his heart, and there are none blacker, save only his master in Mul Kytuer.'

"The Three had long been trusted in the realm of Eglak, although no one knew of their origins, and the King knew their words were true. But it was too late to recall his army and there were none swift enough to carry warning to the field of battle. He said, 'There is nothing I can do. I leave it in your hands.'

"The Three nodded, and without a word they left the king. They knew even they could not reach the Canyon before Salin's trap was sprung, but they would do what they could. They rode their swift horses across the miles, and when they reached the canyon, they beheld blood and violence. The King's army was surrounded and half of the warriors had already fallen. Ogres and goblins swarmed like insects, cutting men and women down like helpless children. It was as the Three had suspected. Salin had led his people into a trap, and, joining with Groshem, began butchering them. Groshem's army was strong and unyielding and the forces of the King swiftly weakened. Soon, they would fail completely.

"It was then the Three, joining their hands and mingling their power, cast flame into the canyon. Most of the King's folk were protected from the roaring wall of fire by the foes surrounding them, but the ogres and goblins on the outskirts of the canyon were consumed utterly. In the chaos that ensued, the Three entered into the fray, power flashing from their hands and words of encouragement shouting from their mouths. The people of Eglak and their allies rallied around these beings of wondrous power, their spirits again strong and hopeful. And so it was the armies of Groshem were beaten back, and Salin fled with them.

"But there was little to be celebrated. The victory was too costly to be considered a victory at all. Fully three quarters of the King's army had been lost, nearly fifteen thousand of the finest men of Eglak, Margon, and Riglak Nord. Although they had severely damaged Groshem's forces, Vorik Seth had many other servants at his command and it would not take him long to raise a new army. And worst of all, Salin was a traitor.

"Of the Three little more need be said. Strange wanderers all, they separated and went into the world to pursue their own secret purposes. King Preytur spent his few remaining years trying to rebuild what had been lost in the battle. The lesser lords of the surrounding realms tried to build their own armies to defend against future attacks, but without much success. And so the great Realms of old were made less than what they were, in part due to Salin's betrayal.

"Salin himself went to Mul Kytuer, to the tower of his new master. There he learned the forbidden arts of dark sorcery and became one of the Seth's most powerful servants. His dark power has sustained him throughout the centuries, and though he has become old in appearance, his power has grown. A hundred years after his betrayal at the canyon, he replaced Groshem as Vorik's greatest captain. He led armies throughout the lands, conquering the realms of Margon and Middle Estron. The once great Eglak had been split by civil war and the weaker Northern Eglak fell swiftly to his power. He sent plagues into the cities, slew children with his bare hands. His lust for murder and destruction could never be sated. He assaulted the King of Northern Eglak in his castle. He demanded the monarch bow to him. When he did, Salin cut off his head. From that day forth, all the Western Realms belonged to Vorik Seth.

"Salin lived for many centuries, exercising his might against the weak, serving his dark master with violence and lust. But about a hundred years ago, he disappeared. Many hoped him dead. But now he has resurfaced with a new goal in mind. He seeks to obtain the Talisman of Unity, so he may control the Fair Folk, who have never been conquered. He seeks you, Alec Mason. And he will find you, unless you flee far and fast, to a realm even he may fear to enter."

At last Michael ended his tale. He looked each of his companions in the eye, lingering on Alec. Alec felt uncomfortable under the hermit's gaze, but he did not look away. He hadn't understood much of what Michael said; in fact, the tale raised more questions than it answered. He wanted to say something, ask one of the questions on his mind, but there were too many, all jumbled in his head. Before he could organize his thoughts, Sarah sighed and looked at the hermit seriously.

"You seem to know a lot about ancient history. But it all seems like madness to me. After all, no one lives hundreds of years. And these places you talk about, I've never even heard of them. Even if all this were true, how would someone like you know about it?"

Michael looked at her blankly. "Someone like me? A madman who lives alone outside of town? Suffice it to say I was not always what I am now."

"That's not an answer!" cried Sarah.

"It will have to do, for now. We must be on our way."

"What about the Three?" asked Alec. "If they were as powerful as you claim, why didn't they do something to stop Salin? What were they doing while Salin was storming those kingdoms?"

Michael did not meet his gaze. He looked into the woods and said softly, "The Three are not what they were. Either they could not stand against Salin's new power, or they would not. Now let it pass. We must continue our journey or Salin may yet find us. If he does, we will surely meet our ends."

As they resumed their journey through the woods, Alec realized Michael had not answered his most important question. Why were they going to Bordenhold? But now Alec's mind was full of words and images from a lost time, and he found he could wait before he asked his question again. There was much to ponder in the meantime. Were these tales of the past true, or were they some fiction from the mind of a madman? And if they were true, what did they mean? Who was this Vorik Seth, who Michael named the incarnation of evil upon the world? Did he still live? Had Michael's "Three" survived all these years as well, and if they had, where were they? These questions, and dozens of others, buzzed through his mind as they tramped through the forest.

As the afternoon melted into evening, the forest grew thicker. They walked mostly in silence, watching the trees, small animals, and birds as they passed. Alec felt a strange sense of peace, as if he were out for an evening stroll, as if danger was left far behind. But the illusion was shattered as twilight became night and wolves' howls echoed with the rising of the moon. Suddenly Michael stopped and looked to his right, motioning the others to stillness. After a moment, he turned toward them and spoke quietly.

"Something has stirred the wolves tonight. There is something in their howls…something I have not heard since…"

His eyes became unfocused as his voice trailed off, as if his thoughts had drifted to a far away time or place. Alec and the others looked around nervously, thinking wolves were bad enough without something else "stirring" them. Finally Alec's anxious impatience got the better of him and he blurted out, "What do you mean, Michael? We're following you blindly, Grok knows why, and all you can say is something mysterious about the howls of wolves."

"I did not mean to be mysterious. It is just there are some things I cannot explain to you. Not now. We must keep moving. These wolves will hunt us."

He didn't wait to make sure they were following him. He cut westward, away from the sound of the wolves, and began to walk more briskly, more urgently. Alec's muscles were sore and his chest heaved as he struggled for air. Kraig was nearly dragging Sarah along, even though sweat poured from his brow as well. When he stumbled on a root and nearly fell, he cursed and shouted to the hermit.

"We can't keep going like this! You are driving us like cattle. Why aren't you as exhausted as us?"

Michael didn't even stop. "Do you want to live?"

A wolf howled, as if on cue, closer than before.

"Why do they follow us?" asked Sarah, eyes wide with fear.

This time Michael looked back. "Because Salin commands they follow us."

"What?" cried Alec. "That's just…"

"Be silent, fool. Conserve your strength. We must flee!"

Faster into the night they ran, blindly through the trees. Wolves were moving among the trees, their voices ringing closer and closer. Alec struggled to keep up with Michael's gray form as it continued forward, seeming to gain ground on the rest of the group. Kraig surged on ahead, Sarah in tow, both crying for Alec to keep up. He looked over his shoulder and saw, not far behind, glowing yellow eyes following quickly, winking in and out through the trees. He pushed himself faster, but his body was working against him. His muscles cramped as he pushed them too far. He could run no longer. Grasping at his chest, he fell to the ground.

A wolf jumped from the trees and landed directly in front of him, its head lowered to stare Alec directly in the eye. Sweat poured from the young man's brow and his face contorted in a mask of fear. Three other wolves emerged from the trees, slowly surrounding their prey. Alec could not pull his eyes away from the wolf which held his gaze. Behind him, another beast coiled, preparing to pounce.

Suddenly a cry cut the night. Kraig was running toward the wolves, a flaming branch in each hand. Michael was not far behind, waving another burning branch. The wolves around Alec jerked their heads toward the newcomers, and seeing the fire, withdrew quickly into the trees. Alec could still feel their presence, lurking just out of sight.

"Get up!" cried Michael. "They fear the flame, but it will not hold them back for long. There is a place nearby where we will be safe."

Alec climbed to his feet and followed them as quickly as his weary body would allow. He found Sarah standing with her back pressed against a tree, trying to make herself blend into the bark. As they ran past her, Kraig handed one of his flaming branches to Alec and grabbed the girl's hand.

"Where can we go?" asked Alec. "We are miles from anywhere and these wolves won't give up."

"I said I would take us to a safe place. You must trust me."

Alec heard Kraig snicker at the suggestion. Alec himself wondered if they could trust the hermit. Everything the man did or said seemed to be madness to Alec. Still, if it was a choice between him or Salin—or wolves—then he chose Michael.

Without warning a wolf leapt from the underbrush straight at Alec's throat. With a yell, Kraig tackled the youth and the wolf flew overhead, missing its mark. But the beast's hunting-mates were not far behind, and soon a dozen wolves circled the group, nearly invisible in the darkness but for their glimmering eyes. Kraig jumped to his feet and waved his branch. Michael ran toward the nearest wolf bearing his own makeshift torch. As Alec rose he saw Sarah take a step back, two wolves stalking the unarmed girl.

"Sarah!" he cried, leaping toward her. Even as he reached her a wolf leapt and Alec thrust his fiery brand toward it. The animal's jaws clamped at Alec's arm, but he jerked back out of the way and the wolf chewed air. Alec brought the branch down on the animal's back and the wolf howled in pain as fur caught flame.

Out of the corner of his eye, Alec caught a glimpse of Kraig and Michael. Both were backed against trees. Three or four wolves surrounded each of them, barely held at bay by the burning branches. It was only a matter of time until the fire went out and the wolves could advance freely.

Alec turned just in time to confront a pair of huge wolves running at him over a small, bald hill. He waved his branch and they hesitated, but barely. Two more of the beasts ran toward him from his left, and yet another pair from his right. Spinning, he saw two more completing the circle, surrounding him. There was no hope of escape. To his horror, he saw Sarah trapped in the circle as well.

Suddenly the girl screamed, tears streaming down her face. In fear she thrust her arms forward, vainly trying to ward off the nearest wolf. But with her scream came a light, a yellow fire encircling her body and her outstretched arms, a fire that stabbed forward and encompassed the charging wolf. Instinctively Alec dropped flat against the ground as Sarah's fire grew, roaring outward in every direction. Each wolf in its path was encompassed and burned. Each wolf howled in agony as it died in flame. The remaining wolves fled in terror from the unnatural flame.

And then the fire died. Sarah stood gasping for air, her breasts heaving. Her face bore a bewildered look and a golden glow settled upon her right hand. Alec's own wonder increased as he noticed, for the first time, the ring upon her finger, glowing as it had when he had first found it. It was the ring he discovered in the chest along with the Talisman of Unity, a ring he had forgotten until this moment. By the time he rose to his feet, the light around the ring winked out and the night was again complete and silent.

Michael was the first to reach Sarah, a shocked, almost angry look upon his face. "What did you do, girl? Where did you get that ring?"

Sarah looked at him, her eyes wide and scared. "I…I was afraid! I didn't do anything."

"The fire, girl! You made fire!" He grabbed her shoulders and shook her.

"Wounds, Michael, leave her!" cried Alec, pulling at the man's shoulder. "We'd be dead if she didn't…" His words trailed off. He didn't know what she did.

Michael made a visible effort to calm himself. Slowly, he said, "The ring you wear is of Faerie make. At first when I saw the fire, I thought you were Shaping. But this ability is so rare in humans I…But it's the ring. A Faerie ring! By the One, where did you get it?"

"I found it," said Alec. "It was in the chest where I found the Talisman."

"I just thought…" Sarah began. "It was just a ring. Gold, valuable. But just a ring. I took it after Alec took the Talisman."

Michael shook his head. His former anger was replaced by a confused wonder. "A Faerie ring made for Shaping flame. Locked in a little chest in Barton Hills. Well, I suppose if the Talisman of Unity itself had been hidden away in an obscure farming village, why not a lesser artifact? At any rate, we cannot ponder it here. You have bought us a brief respite, Sarah, but the wolves will be back in greater numbers. And it is likely they will report to Salin. We must keep moving."

They walked onward and Michael again mentioned a place of safety. "I know we must rest," he said. "A friend of mine has a secret place in these woods, a place the wolves cannot reach. Salin and his servants will not find it."

Looking scared and frail, Sarah looked up at the hermit. "How did I do what I did? You say it was the ring, but how did I use it? I didn't even know what it could do. I didn't try to bring up the fire."

"I don't know, child. In theory, you should not have been able to use the ring without knowing something of the fundamentals of Shaping. At the very least you should have had to know what the ring was, and then made a conscious effort to use it. But you Shaped fire from air, not even knowing what you were doing. If there were time, I would study how this happened, and why. Perhaps this particular ring is triggered by fear, or need. Tools of the Fairies are strange and powerful, but never too reliable unless you know everything about them. We cannot count on it working again."

Alec was nodding, but was getting more confused the more the hermit spoke. "What is Shaping?" he asked.

Michael smiled. "It's what you farmers sometimes call magic. It's the art of shaping reality as you would have it, bending the world to your will. Changing air into fire, fire into water, a boot into a fish. Reality is fluid, and those who know how can Shape it as they will. This is one of the Seven Laws they who Shape follow."

"Do you Shape?" asked Kraig.

Michael frowned at the man, his face caught between grief and anger. "Would that I could, peacekeeper. Would that I could."

They walked on in silence for another hour. At last they came to a place so thick with foliage it became almost impossible to continue, yet Michael led them through hidden ways where the thick growth could be passed. A green web of vines and underbrush intertwined thickly between the trees, creating a maze of flora which confused the eye and puzzled the mind. Yet Michael led them onward with confidence, as if he knew the way by heart. To Alec's surprise, the light in the overgrown maze was brighter than in other parts of the forest. It almost seemed the thick vegetation was glowing dimly in the moonlight, lighting their way.

"Where are we?" asked Kraig. "Am I seeing more clearly now or am I going mad? What manner of place is this where vines and bushes seem to make green walls?"

"This is the safe place I spoke of. This is an Addingrove, a place where the spirit of the wood is strong. Seldom are men allowed to tread here, but the Addin knows our need is great."

"The Addin?" Alec asked. He had heard more Fairy tales recently than he preferred, but at least some of them had been proven true. He prepared himself for yet another.

"A woodsman. The Addin, Horren by name, is the master of these woods. He knows me. We may take shelter in his home tonight."

The maze ended abruptly and they stepped out into a vast clearing. The ground was covered with plush green grass, and a soft, silvery glow illuminated the area. The air smelled of clean soil and fresh flowers. A massive tree stood in the middle of the clearing, and wide natural stairs spiraled around it, up its trunk to be lost in the thick canopy of leaves high above. The tree seemed to radiate health and vitality, if that were possible. Small trees and bushes surrounded it and a garden of flowers spread around its base. An archway of flowers and vines framed the foot of the great stair.

Alec's eyes were wide with wonder. The Addingrove was like something out of one of Jordi Luppis's songs, yet here it stood, less than two days' journey from home. He looked at his companions, who stared in disbelief. All but Michael, who appeared to be growing impatient.

"Come. We must go up. Horren will want to see us."

Walking on the grass on the way to the tree made Alec feel light, as if he were walking on a cushion of air. The grass was thick, firm yet buoyant, unlike any grass he'd come across before. In other circumstances he would have laughed with joy, and even now he felt a strange comfort. A path led through the garden, toward the flowery arch. It was made of packed dirt, yet even so it had almost the same buoyant quality as the grass. His eyes darted with amazement between the arch, the grass, the garden, and the tree itself. There were many gardens in Barton Hills, but there were none like this.

As they passed under the arch, a strange chill went through Alec—strange, but not unpleasant. He knew he was being watched, his intentions being measured. He stopped for an instant, unable and unwilling to ascend the stairs. Then, something changed, and the pleasant sensation he'd experienced while walking in the grass returned. He followed the others up the stairs, the warm comfort remaining as he climbed.

Up they went, around and around the huge tree, climbing the wide stairs. There was no railing, but Alec had no fear of falling. He had a notion the tree would not let him fall. He touched its thick, rough bark, and again the impression of health filled him. This tree was a thing alive, not in the normal way, but in a conscious, spiritual way. He nearly laughed at the thought, but awe cut off any laughter.

Through the canopy they climbed and Alec reached out to touch the big, green leaves. Every one of them was pure of color and perfect of shape. They were smooth and moist and each was far larger than any leaf back home.

When they broke through the thick layer of leaves, Alec's eyes popped at the most incredible sight yet. A mansion formed of living wood rested upon a web of limbs, each twice as thick as the trunk of a normal tree. It was shaped like a dome with windows and had three towers which continued up into a second layer of leaves. It was covered in bark, but its bark was thinner and lighter than the rest, and was carved in intricate, beautiful designs. Not carved, Alec realized. It had grown this way.

"It's so beautiful, so unreal, I..." said Sarah, her voice trailing off. Alec understood. There were no words.

"Let us go in," said Michael. "We are expected."

"Expected?" asked Kraig.

Michael eyed him with a hint of a smile. "If Horren did not know we were here, or if he desired to keep us away, we would have never made it up the stairs. Indeed, likely none of you could have passed the arch. Not alive, anyway."

Alec thought of the way he had been unable to pass through the archway until the tickle in his mind had gone away. *What kind of power are we dealing with? Can we trust this Horren? And how does Michael know him?*

They walked along a massive branch which led straight to the open door of the mansion. Alec realized, despite his exhausting journey and the long climb up the stairs, he hardly felt tired at all. This place was somehow refreshing, rejuvenating. In some way, its health was rubbing off on him, and the others, by the look of it.

And then they were inside. Alec hardly had a chance to look around before a thick, low, booming voice broke the silence.

"It's been a long time, Elsendarin. Too long. And who are these guests you bring?"

Alec turned. And what he saw shattered his every conception of what was real.

Grok's Wounds! Not a Fairy-tale after all! Wounds!

CHAPTER 5

The Addin

"Greetings, Horren Addin," said Michael, bowing lowly, formally. "It has indeed been a long time, many years too long. May the leaves of the Addin-grove shelter you and its bark forever nourish you."

"And may the light of the sun warm you and fill you with life, as it is with the Green. But enough formality! You must introduce me to your young companions."

Alec could not pull his eyes off the Addin as he spoke. He was twice as tall as any man Alec had ever seen, and far broader. His muscles bulged with strength, making even Kraig look like a babe not fit to leave his mother's arms. The man was dressed in a coat of bark and leaves, and his pants were made of vines, grass, and flowers. His beard and hair were shaggy and stiff, the strands thick and gnarled like old roots. His face was dark and in it sat eyes of icy blue. His huge, thick hands rested on his knees as he sat on a massive stump, smiling broadly at his guests. Alec had never really believed in Fairies despite the histories he read and he certainly never believed in giants. But the presence of the creature before him gave him no choice.

"These are children from the village of Barton Hills, where I have been living for many years. I would not have brought them here but our need is great. We are hunted by the wolves of Salin Urdrokk."

The woodsman's large mouth twisted into a grimace and his eyes grew fierce. "Urdrokk! I swore if he ever passed into my forest again, I would grind his bones to powder. Elsendarin, if you know where he is, tell me and I shall rend him limb from limb!"

"Be calm, my friend," said Michael, holding his hands out before him. "I do not know where he is. I think he would be following us if he knew what path we took, but he had no way of knowing I would take these children into the woods, toward the uncharted regions. Instead, he sends his wolves to seek us. I fear they found us and will report back to their master. So we have come to you. We seek a night of safe shelter and in the morning we will continue to Bordonhold. There I hope to find someone to guide them to safety."

"Hmm. Salin Urdrokk; a name I have not heard uttered for many years. Perhaps it is for the best he does not enter here. I would crush him into a fine paste, you know, but trees might be damaged in the battle. It is for the best he does not come."

Alec sensed relief in the huge man's voice. Perhaps he was not so anxious to pit his strength against the dark sorcerer as he claimed.

"Yes, it is certainly for the best. This is why I will be gone from here as soon as possible. Yet, I have pushed my companions to their limit and beyond and have promised them rest in a place of safety. May we stay here, in the Addin-grove, for the rest of the night?"

Horren lifted his hands and smiled warmly. "Do you even need to ask, my friend? I owe you more than I can ever repay; a night's shelter is the least I can do. I will provide food as well, and I dare say it is far more nourishing than travel rations, and tastier. But I will have the names of your companions and the story behind this little journey. People from Barton Hills rarely leave their homes and never do they venture this deeply into the Northwood."

Michael bowed again and then turned to Alec. Alec gave him a questioning look and Michael gestured toward the Addin. Feeling weak and inadequate, the youth stepped slowly toward the giant.

"I am Alec Mason, great Addin. I am a baker."

"A baker!" roared Horren, erupting into laughter. Alec was almost offended. "I mean no harm," he chuckled, holding out a huge hand. "Generally speaking, bakers do not go tramping through the woods chased by sorcerers. A mystery indeed. But before we discuss that, who is this beautiful young girl cowering behind you? Is she your mate?"

At that Sarah stood up, pushing Alec behind her. "Mate? I wouldn't marry Mason if he were a prince! I am Sarah Mills, a shopkeeper in Barton Hills. Or at least, my mother is. I help her. I...Grok, you're huge!"

As Sarah backed away, half embarrassed at her outburst, half scared of the tree-like man before her, Horren laughed again. "You humans are quick to take offense. I merely wondered why you follow this boy into danger. Or perhaps you are the one bringing on the danger. Or the big fellow? Who are you?"

Kraig had been standing in the back, his arms folded over his big chest. His eyes were wide, but his demeanor remained calm. Perhaps he still could not see well enough to understand what he faced, or else he had even more self control than Alec thought.

"My name is Kraig, Horren Addin. I keep the peace at the Silver Shield, finest tavern in Barton Hills. I am here to protect my young friends from danger." His stance showed he was not convinced Horren himself was not dangerous. What he would be able to do against the Addin; Alec could not begin to guess.

"And I, as you know, am Horren, the Addin of these woods. This is Addinheart, center of the Addingrove. No one may come here except at my bidding. Not even Vorik Seth himself, may he rot on his throne."

Michael stepped toward the Addin, a worried look on his face. "Please, my friend, do not speak that name. Not even here. His power grows in the world outside and soon he may be able to influence events even here, especially if you draw his eye."

"Just by saying his name? Are you getting superstitious in your old age, Elsendarin? Even he has never been able to corrupt an Addingrove, just as he could never touch the hearts of the Fair Folk. Some things are stronger than evil."

"I hope you are right. But the reappearance of Salin, long hoped dead, proves he is gaining strength again. Much of the world has lain under his shadow for centuries, especially since the sundering of Eglak. And the shadow continues to spread."

"Not here, I say! Never here." His face twisted in anger as he spoke, but after a moment he forced himself to soften. "Not today, at any rate. Here. Sit! I will prepare food and then I will hear your tale. And then you must rest, for you all look weary. Even you, old friend."

The Addin rose from his stump. Alec stepped back a pace, marveling at his size. He had known Horren was huge, but seeing the Addin standing was still a shock. The big man moved gracefully, opening a cabinet full of large, leaf wrapped packages. He put one down on a central table and opened it, revealing a strange mixture of nuts, dried fruit, leaves, roots, and bark. When his guests looked quizzically at the mixture, Horren laughed.

"Nutritious in the extreme, my friends, and far more delicious than you can know. Eat! You need the food, by the look of it."

Kraig was the first to go to the table. Alec thought the man's vision was indeed still lacking, for he scooped up a handful of the mixture and put it in his mouth! Chewing, his eyes grew wide with delight. Around the mouthful, he mumbled, "It's delicious!"

Skeptically, Alec approached the table. He took a small piece of root and chewed it. It was tough and rubbery but tasted unexpectedly sweet. Pleased, he grabbed a fistful of the mixture and began eating enthusiastically.

Horren again laughed his deep, roaring laugh. "How surprised you are to find my food to your liking! I often forget your people are so bound to their ways, their traditions and customs. Especially you village folk. Well, there is much you might learn from old Horren, much indeed beyond woodsman food."

Alec was on his second handful of the mixture when Sarah reluctantly approached the table. It was not long before she was eating as eagerly as the others. Michael approached last and nibbled on some nuts and bark, eating slowly and matter-of-factly as if he had eaten this kind of food all his life. Horren himself had a huge bowl of a thick jelly composed of the same ingredients as the mixture, folded into a clear, viscous sludge. Eyeing the dripping ooze, Alec was glad he was eating the dry version of this woodsman food.

"Well, now," said the Addin after they'd had ample time to ease their hunger, "Tell me everything. What grand adventure brings three young folk from their tiny village, accompanied by none other than old Elsendarin?"

"Why do you call him that?" asked Alec.

"Call who what?" asked Horren, a puzzled look crossing his face.

"Michael. You call him Elsendarin. Michael, is that your family name?"

The hermit looked up and shook his head, his expression bland. "No, Alec Mason. Some people, for reasons of their own, take different names during the course of their lives. Elsendarin is a name I went by years ago."

"It wasn't all that long ago," laughed Horren. "Not by the way I see time, at any rate. Young Alec, your friend here was once a good friend of the Addins, often invited among us on those rare occasions when we gathered. He was one of the few of your kind who understood the Green, and cared for it. Without his help, we might already have…But perhaps I should say no more. What the Addins discuss in secret must remain secret. Besides, I would hear your story. What interest does black old Salin have in you folk?"

Alec looked to Michael, unsure of how much he should say. The hermit nodded at him, signaling that it was safe to speak before the Addin. He told the tale in full, explaining Salin's visit to the Silver Shield and how he had offered

Alec one thousand gold coins for the Talisman, and how he had found the relic in Sarah's basement. He left out nothing, but nearly choked when he spoke of the death of Stan and Matilda, and of the destruction of Ara's shop. He looked over at Sarah as he spoke of her mother, but the girl betrayed no emotion. It was more likely than not that Ara Mills was dead, but Sarah held on to hope. If she still felt any fear or grief, she had buried it. Alec finished the tale, telling about the attack of the wolves and of Sarah's mysterious ring. During the story, Horren kept his wide eyes fixed on Alec, nodding at certain parts, chuckling at others. He seemed to find the smallest details interesting, while taking for granted such things as the fire-Shaping ring. When Alec finished, the big man laughed aloud. He seemed to find almost everything humorous.

"A grand tale indeed. Surely someday a bard will sing of your journey, fleeing from danger into danger, carrying with you the great Talisman of Unity, the most powerful creation of the Fair Folk. What do you mean to do with it?"

"Do with it?" asked Alec. "I…I don't know."

"We hadn't thought about it," said Sarah. "I haven't though about much other than getting as far away from Salin as possible."

"Why don't you ask Michael," said Kraig, giving the hermit a suspicious look. "He hasn't seen fit to tell us much of anything, other than he's taking us to Bordonhold. From there, apparently, we're on our own."

Michael turned his even gaze on Kraig for a moment as everyone sat awkwardly. Everyone except the Addin, who seemed to find the situation mildly amusing. Then Michael looked at the woodsman and nodded.

"Obviously the Talisman must be hidden from Salin. With it, a sorcerer of his power could control the minds of the Fair Folk. If they are corrupted, the few regions of the world not yet fallen to Salin's master will not stand long against him. I'm bringing these children to Bordenhold. I know a few people there whom I trust, and I'm hoping one of them will be able to lead them through the uncharted regions, to the land beyond."

Horren still smiled but no longer laughed. "A dangerous journey. Especially for a group of children unskilled in the ways of the world. Few folk have passed northward through the uncharted lands. Uncharted, at any rate, by humans. Others have mapped those fearful lands."

Michael nodded. "Indeed, but the point is moot. We have no access to Fairy maps, not unless the Addins still can Commune."

Horren shook his head, not sadly, but with a far away look, as if remembering something lost. "Communion is a skill we no longer have. We have learned much during our time in the world, but some doors once opened are now closed. Still, we are not here to discuss ancient history. I would know more of your plan, Elsendarin. You are going to leave the fate of this Talisman in the hands of another? Once, you would not have done so."

"I'm done with causes," said the hermit, his eyes as dead as ever. "I was a fool once, a fool to believe I could do anything to stem the tide of evil slowly consuming the world. I'm tired. I want to live out the rest of my years in anonymity and peace. Let others fight the great war."

"You have changed. And yet, here you are, involving yourself in the struggle you seek to avoid. It seems your ideals are not as dead as you would have others think."

Michael straightened and sighed. "They are dead, Horren. I could not let these children be taken by Salin. That's the only reason I left my hut. Once they are safely away, I'm going home. If I never leave again, it will be too soon."

Horren frowned, but there was still a gleam in his eye. He even went so far as to wink at Alec, as if to say he didn't believe a word of what Michael had just said. Then he stood up again and set himself to preparing some bedding for his guests. He lined a corner of the room with clean hay and straw he gathered from a high shelf and then set many thick blankets and fluffy pillows down upon the makeshift bed. As he worked, he talked, his mood lightening once more.

"It's been a long time since I have had guests. Oh, the woodland animals are good company, but not many remember the Addinspeech anymore. I used to have an old wolf come by now and then, not one of those dark wolves who serve the enemy, but a friendly fellow called Feets. Feets spoke Addinspeech, but he said most of the wolves in his pack no longer bothered to learn. Another lost art. The animals are keeping to themselves more and more, those who haven't gone over to the enemy. It's a shame, but the world is changing, they say."

Alec, again, was filled with wonder. Talking to animals? Two days ago he would have thought it madness, but now, he wasn't sure. So much of what he thought he had known of the world had proven untrue, and so much he had thought only stories had proven fact. And this woodsman, this Addin, he had not even heard tell of in the most fantastic of stories.

"Horren Addin," he said, "Why are you here? I mean, what does an Addin do, exactly?"

Horren had just finished getting the beds ready. He took his place on the big stump, chuckling softly to himself. "What does an Addin do? That's a question I could spend days answering, if you had days. As it is, there are only a few hours left in the night, and if I know Elsendarin, he'll have you moving while the morning is still young. You should be off to bed, young ones, and yet children always like a little bedtime story."

Alec frowned. He was getting tired of Horren and Michael constantly referring to him and his friends as "children." He was about to say as much when the Addin cleared his throat with a low rumbling cough and answered Alec's question. Sort of answered it, anyway.

"An Addin is one who lives in the woods. For this reason we are often called woodsman. Well, you know that much already. There were never very many of us and now there are less than a hundred scattered all over the world. We rarely meet anymore; in fact, the last time the Addins got together was, oh, let's see now…the Spring of the Last Hero? No, it must have been during old Kazkond's reign. No…well, it doesn't really matter. It's been a long, long time. As to our purpose, Addin means 'watcher' in the old tongue of the Fairies. Actually, 'watcher' is a bad translation. It's more of someone who waits. And watches. And guards."

Horren paused and looked at the roof. It seemed he wasn't much of a storyteller, and Michael gave a small smile at watching his friend struggle. Kraig, who had been lounging quietly on the floor, seemingly uninterested, said, "What is it you wait for? What are you guarding?"

The Addin looked at the peacekeeper as if it were obvious. "We wait for the time to come when the things we guard will be needed. Some say the time has come and gone, and yet we still stand watch. This, I believe, is why we can no longer Commune with the Fair Folk."

Alec shook his head, puzzled. "What do you mean, Commune?"

"I mean talk, Alec Mason, as I do with you now. Only without words, and over great distances. It was once the way of the Addin to join in Communion with the Fairies from time to time, to give and receive information of the world. It was through certain Shapings the Fairies performed that we obtained the ability. I think they took it away from us when they grew angry we would not allow them to have what they themselves had given to us to guard."

"But what do you guard?" asked Sarah. "You seem to be staying clear of that subject."

"Do not be to eager," scolded Michael. "Perhaps it is best if the tale ends now. Such knowledge is not for your ears. Even I know only a little of the Addins' secret."

Horren laughed, slapping his knee. "You always were one to spoil a good time, my friend. 'Such knowledge is not for your ears,' indeed! Perhaps I cannot give away all my secrets; after all, mystery is what makes me interesting! But this much I can tell: Hundreds, no, thousands of years ago, only a few centuries after humans first walked in the world, the great Fairy King of the time called the first Addins from the Lost Home. They weren't called Addins then, of course, nor was the Home lost. The first Addins had no bodies, so the Fairy Shapers formed crude ones from earth and root and leaf. Modern Addins are, of course, much more human looking than our ancestors, having improved with time. At any rate, as the Fairy King explained to the first Addins, the Fair Folk had recently discovered a long time friend and teacher of theirs was in fact a Seth. That is, a being of pure evil, stronger in sorcery than any twenty Fairies put together. Apparently there had been numerous Seths early in the world's history; however, all save one were slain in wars they fought amongst themselves. This one was cunning as well as powerful, and he waited while the others destroyed one another. He even went so far as to befriend the lowly Fairies, teaching them to harness their natural ability to Shape. He took the name Vorik, which means 'wise', or perhaps 'wisest.' Eventually, soon after the coming of humankind, his true nature became known, and just in time. He had made the Talisman of Unity, you see, as a gift for the Fairy King. Or so he said. In reality, he intended to use it to control the Fair Folk, to bend the entire race to his will. Human nations were growing all over the world, and with an army of Fairy Shapers he could conquer them easily. But the Fairies had grown wise to him. Seizing the Talisman, they were able to cast him out of their land.

"Soon after, they summoned the Addins. It seemed one of the Fair Folk had had some sort of vision. Vorik Seth would come again, they said. He would eventually bend nearly all of humanity to his will, although it would take far longer without the Fairies behind him, and then he would have enough power to take the land of Faerie for his own. The vision also revealed a greater Destiny for Vorik Seth, although what this Destiny was none could say, other than that by fulfilling it he would stamp out all traces of good from this world and all worlds beyond. Quite a stark vision, if I may say so. The Fairy King told the first Addins it would be their task to gather certain relics of the humans and keep them along with the knowledge of how to use them. It seemed the Fairies believed their own Shaping abilities would no longer be effective against their enemy, but the humans had things which might be. Why did the Addins need to take these things from the humans? Well, for one, to keep them out of the Seth's hands. Secondly, the humans seemed to be forgetting much of the lore they once knew, such as what their own relics were and how they were used.

Only the Addins could preserve the knowledge, to be used when the need arose.

"The Addins went out into the world and performed their task. They performed it well. Because they were clothed in the raiment of the forest, they came to love the wooded lands. They made their homes in the forests, taking on as a secondary purpose the protection of those lands and learning the ways of the spirits of the wood. Addins took forms both male and female, and thus were able to conceive children in the way of Fairies and humans. And so through the years we've lived, serving the purpose the Fair Folk gave us as well as purposes of our own. We have waxed and waned over the years, but lately we have only waned. There are few female Addins, now, and our race is nearly at its end. Perhaps with help from the Fairies we could grow into a mighty race once again, but they no longer help us."

The Addin grew silent, his eyes unfocused, lost in the past. Alec was thinking about what he had said, wondering what these relics of humanity could be. Some kind of powerful tools or weapons, it seemed, the existence of which was all but forgotten. But one thing interested Alec even more. "Why do the Fairies no longer help you, or…Commune with you? You served them once, and well, it seems."

"Too well!" said the Addin. "When Salin Urdrokk first fell under the influence of Vorik Seth, it seemed the ancient vision was coming true. The Fairy King of the time decided it was time to use the artifacts we had guarded for so long. But when the Addins met in council, we decided the time had not yet come. The old relics of humanity were too dangerous to use except at the last, when all other hope was lost. And we knew hope was not lost. The Fair Folk were still strong, holding the Talisman of Unity, and the humans had evolved into a bold and noble race. The power of the One was still strong in the world, and of course the Three walked the land. Yet the Fairies were angered by our unwillingness to surrender to them the artifacts they gave us to guard, so they disowned us. No longer could we share in the gift of Communion and no longer would they give us aid and friendship. And so it has been through the centuries, until today. We have lost so much, and yet life is good here in the Addingrove. I tend to the forest, as do all the other Addins, rarely thinking of our true purpose. Even we have all but forgotten the use of what we guard. And perhaps this is for the best after all."

Horren looked at the ground, folding his hands in his lap. For a long moment no one spoke. It seemed appropriate to observe silence after the story of the Addins, for although it was told in brief, Alec got the impression it was a vast history full of loss and sadness. He didn't ask why there were now few female Addins, or why the race was dying out. He didn't even care what the artifacts of the early humans were. He thought instead on the different sides of Horren. He hardly knew the Addin, but already he saw him in moments of lighthearted glee and in flashes of distant melancholy. The Addins derived great joy from the forests and from life, it seemed, and yet they were deeply saddened by their estrangement from their creators.

"Well, then," said Horren, breaking the long silence, "I suppose you had better get to bed. I hope you find the accommodations comfortable." He smiled, his dark mood dropping from his face as if it were never there. He rose and walked to a ladder on the other side of the big room. "I sleep on the roof, exposed to the open air, as all Addins do. We can't stand to be cooped up very long indoors; even a night is too long. Good night, Alec. Good night, beautiful Sarah. Sleep well, Kraig. And you, Elsendarin. Especially you, my friend. I have a feeling there is much work ahead for you, despite what you say." He looked knowingly at his friend. "You can't hide from what you are."

Michael frowned. "Addins don't know everything. I'm no one special."

"As you say," said Horren, climbing the stairs. When he reached the high ceiling, he pushed open a heavy trap door and climbed onto the roof. Saying one last good night, he closed the door, leaving his guests to fend for themselves.

Sarah had already settled herself into her bed, pulling the blankets around her. Kraig was still standing at the table, making no move toward the straw bedding, and Michael was looking out a large window on the far side of the room. Alec walked to the bed and lay down near Sarah, crawling under some blankets. He was not quite near enough to touch the girl, but back home sleeping even this close to a woman would be enough to cause a scandal. Still, Alec did not feel uncomfortable and Sarah didn't seem to mind.

"Alec," she said, "this is all so…unreal." Her eyes scanned the huge one-room mansion, from the tall, light brown walls grown from living wood, to the high central table, to the several chairs far too large for human comfort. "This place is like something out of a Fairy tale, and Horren…well, I can't even think about him without my mind doing somersaults. These kinds of things aren't supposed to exist!"

Alec knew what she was talking about. "If you listen to most of the old folks talk back home, nothing exists but farms and cows. Oh, sometimes they talk about the Fairies or magic, but only in jest, repeating a silly bard's story. They'd never believe any of this."

"I don't know," answered Sarah. "I have a feeling things have changed since we left. Who knows what they're talking about, now that they've seen sorcery at work?"

Alec shrugged. "Maybe. But maybe they'll just explain it away. Lightning struck the houses. A fire burnt them down. Better to think that than a sorcerer destroyed them with magic, even if they did see it happen."

Sarah considered it and then shook her head. "I don't care what they think. I just want to escape the sorcerer and forget this whole thing ever happened. And I want to find out if my mother is still alive. Grok, Alec, she has to be!"

"I hope so, Sarah. Wounds, I hope so."

Sarah turned away, but not before Alec saw a tear running down her cheek. She was stronger than she looked and she held on to hope, but she was still hurting. Alec wished he could help her, but there was nothing he could do. He couldn't even help himself. All he could do was run, following a man he had no reason to trust, and hope for the best. Hoping they were as safe here as Horren and Michael seemed to think, he closed his eyes. Despite his anxiety, his body quickly remembered its exhaustion and he slept like the dead.

The others were already up and about in the bright light of day by the time Alec awakened. Michael was talking with Horren as the woodsman pulled small packages from his cupboards and stuffed them into a large sack. Sarah was looking out a window, admiring the beauty of the Addingrove in the daylight. Kraig was bending over a tub of water, splashing it over his face and bare chest. He looked at Alec and smiled.

"So you're finally awake, are you, baker boy?" he said almost jovially. "We've already had breakfast and washed. It's nearly noon!"

"I'm surprised Michael didn't have us traipsing through the woods by now," said Alec. "Why are you so happy?"

"I guess things look better by the light of day," answered the big man. "It really is beautiful here, and it seems to lift the spirit, just being here. And Horren's food is incredible. Besides, I can see. I can see as well as I ever could, Alec."

Alec threw his blankets aside and forced himself out of bed. His muscles hurt and his joints were stiff, but the sleep had refreshed him. He stretched and yawned, and walked over to the wash basin, rolling up his sleeves. As soon as Kraig was out of the way, he plunged his arms into the cold water and began scrubbing them, and then he went to work on his face and hair. The cold water stung him into alertness and even took some of the stiffness out of his joints.

"Good morning to you, Alec Mason," laughed the Addin, tying together a bundle of roots and nuts. "I hope you slept well. No unpleasant dreams, I hope?"

"No, Horren Addin," said Alec. "No dreams at all. I slept very well."

"Good," said the Addin, walking over to sit on his stump. It seemed he liked to be seated while talking with the humans so he didn't have to look down at them. "Here in the forest, at least in the Addingrove, the spirits of the woods bring peace. Even a person's dreams are serene. For this reason, among others, the forest is precious and worth protecting. I've set some fruit out on the table for your breakfast, although the others have picked over the best of it. There are still a few scraps left for you if you hurry."

Sarah walked over to Alec, a smile on her face. Her eyes looked red, though, as if not too long ago she had been crying. "It's wonderful here, especially since the sun's up. I wish we could stay. And despite what Horren said, we didn't eat everything. There are so many apples and berries on the table even Kraig couldn't put a dent in them." She gave the Addin a stern look, but then smiled to show she was only joking. He laughed right along with her.

As Alec stood at the table and ate, Michael tied shut the large sack Horren had filled with packages of his strange food. He looked at Alec and nodded, the smallest smile touching his lips. "Horren was kind enough to provide us with food for our journey. Despite being a long winded blowhard, he is a generous friend. He offered to have us stay another night, but we must be moving on. I mean to leave within the hour."

"I wish you would consider staying," said Horren. "I seldom have such pleasant guests, and the black sorcerer would not dare to enter here. There is safety here, warmth and peace and good food."

"Do not be too sure your defenses are proof against Salin. His power comes from a more ancient and stronger source than your own."

"Bah! I was eating sorcerers for dinner long before Salin was born!" Seeing Sarah's eyes grow wide, Horren laughed. "I mean that only figuratively, child. Addins don't eat meat of any sort."

Kraig, who had not trusted the Addin the day before, laughed aloud. In spite of himself, Alec laughed, too. He wished they could stay in the Addingrove. After only two days of travel, Alec decided that long journeys through the wilderness were not for him.

Soon they descended the long, winding stairs to the grassy garden below. Horren escorted them down and stood by his gate as they prepared to leave. He had carried a sack with him and as they said their good-byes he opened it.

"I don't like to see my friends walk into danger unaided, so I thought I'd provide you what small help I could. I'd go with you, but I must not leave my home. If I leave here, the power of the grove would be diminished and evil could enter freely. But I've gathered such items as may be of use."

Reaching into his sack, he drew out a small glass bottle, stopped with a cork. It appeared to be empty. "Young Sarah, this bottle is my gift to you. Inside it is a great tree spirit who once lived in an old oak grove which burned in a fire long ago. I could not save the grove, but I saved the spirit by giving it a home in the bottle. The spirit is old and has lived a full life and wishes to end its time on this world. And yet, it wants to perform one last task against the servants of evil, who have little love for the woods. When you face danger at its worst, and you have no other recourse, uncork the bottle. Freed, the spirit cannot live long, but it will assist you as it can."

"Thank you, Horren Addin," she said softly, taking the bottle. Alec couldn't help but wonder if there was really anything in the bottle. Some things were just too unbelievable to be true.

"Kraig, for you I have something you may, unfortunately, have a use for." The Addin pulled a massive, double bladed axe from the bag. "A horrible thing, made for chopping heads as well as trees. I don't know which is worse. Years ago, some fool thought to chop trees in the Addingrove. He imagined gaining great wealth by selling the wood from my special trees. I had to teach him a…severe…lesson, and of course I took away his axe. I felt foul touching it, so I stashed it away where I could forget about it. But now I'm glad I had it, for you may need such a horrible tool before you are done."

Taking the axe and surveying it gravely, Kraig said, "I thank you. I hope I never have to use it, but it might scare off trouble."

"That it might," said the Addin, "or it might not." Without transition, he turned to Alec. "Alec, you carry a great burden. The Talisman of Unity is a mighty tool and you must see it to safety. For you I have a gift that may give you hope when the burden grows too heavy." He reached into his sack and pulled out a silver box. He opened it and a white light shown from within. "This is a box of Fairy make. For you, its purposes might be twofold. First of all, once it has attuned itself to you, no one else will be able to open it, not unless they are a master Shaper, perhaps not even then. A perfect place to hide the Talisman. Also, bathing in its light will strengthen one's resolve and empower one's spirit. When you lose all hope, look to the light."

Accepting the silver box, Alec nodded and said, "I will use it well, great Addin."

Horren turned his gaze on Michael. The hermit said, "I need no gift, my friend. Your generosity is gift enough, and I fear you have nothing I would be able to use."

"Quite the contrary, Elsendarin," said Horren in a scolding tone, waving a big finger at the man. "You, perhaps, need my gift most of all." He pulled a hefty book out of the sack and threw it at Michael, who stumbled back as he caught it. "There are things you would do well to remember. About your-self…and about the world. You have turned your back on something grand. There is still time to go back to it, old friend. Still a little time." His normally jovial face bore no humor now. He gave Michael a grave look which seemed to carry all the importance in the world. Michael returned it as a blank stare. If the hermit was at all moved, he didn't show it.

"Reading a book is not going to help me, Horren."

"As you will. But keep it with you, as a favor to me. You're not hopeless yet, old friend. That I refuse to believe." He paused, taking them in. Smiling deeply, he said, "Good bye, my friends. The world is strange and sometimes its fate can be changed by a small thing. One would never think three children from a small farming village would be wrapped up in one of the greatest stories of this time. And yet, it may prove so."

"Grok, I hope not," said Alec. "I just want to get this over with."

The Addin nodded. "Stories are fun to hear and tell, but not always fun to be in. I sympathize. Walk well, my friends, and may you always find warmth in the Green."

"Walk well, friend Horren," said Michael.

With one last smile, the Addin turned and walked among the trees of his grove, disappearing into the dense foliage. Michael, holding his book to his breast, began a brisk walk across the garden to the maze leading back into the forest. Alec shared a quick look with Sarah and Kraig, wondering what the hurry was. Shrugging, he followed.

And so they began the third day of their journey. It was uneventful, even pleasant. It was warm and sunny, and again Alec had the impression he was taking a Sunday walk through the woods, perhaps going to Riverton to trade some pies for a new bread knife. To his surprise, he saw the others were smiling as well, enjoying the day. Eventually, he found himself smiling at Sarah, hold-ing her hand as they walked. *What am I doing? This is no time for romance.* But he didn't let go. Their time was far too precious to waste. Soon the sun began to set and the sky grew dim. In the dusk, a wolf howled.

CHAPTER 6

The Minstrel

Landyn, son of Gordon, minstrel of Freehold, hadn't expected to return to Barton Hills so soon after his last visit. He didn't mind visiting the small farming villages dotting the countryside on occasion, but he much preferred the hustle and bustle of the city. There was always something going on in Freehold, always some wealthy merchant or noble to perform for, always a card game to join at one of the local taverns. The men of villages like Barton Hills, Riverton, and Lockguild were appreciative of a good song, of course, but not so generous with coin as city folk. And they rarely gambled. And the women were either married or too young, or, to be truthful, too homely.

No, Landyn hadn't planned on returning to Barton Hills until the next Bard's Day, if then. It was a three day journey from Freehold, and that was riding fast and stopping only for the night. The road was smooth most of the way and it wasn't an unpleasant ride at this time of year, but Landyn hadn't wanted to make the journey again. Yet he had to.

Riding on his gray stallion Luck, he leaned down to check his saddlebags again. They were firmly tied and there wasn't any danger of them coming loose, but he checked them several times a day. They held plenty of gold coin, not to mention his food, wine, clothes, and extra strings for his lute. He had lost a good sum of coin and an expensive jug of wine to some bandits a few months back, and he had been all the more careful with his possessions since then.

A warm summer wind was blowing, pleasantly streaming through his long, light brown hair. He almost smiled in spite of himself. The bright green leaves of the roadside trees rustled in the wind and the grassy fields beyond whispered lightly. A beautiful, pleasant day for a ride. The minstrel would have stopped for a moment to admire the bright day, but he had other things on his mind, and Barton Hills was only a few miles away.

Landyn had begun his journey back to Freehold the day after Bard's Day, anxious to make his next performance at the Goblin's Foot. Three times larger than the Silver Shield, it boasted a large patronage of wealthy merchants and artisans. Of course, no one of noble blood would frequent such an establishment, but there was plenty of money to be made, both performing and gambling. He had arrived there three days later and performed that night to a house full of generous patrons. After the show, Nerid, a high servant of Penndryn, Lord of Freehold, approached him with an offer he couldn't refuse.

"Landyn," said Nerid, patting him on the back with a familiarity Landyn wasn't comfortable with. He had never liked the man. "Next month is our Lord's fiftieth birthday, as you know. The Lady Shanna asked me to prepare a celebration of such magnitude it will never be forgotten. There will be food and entertainment beyond anything you can imagine!"

"That's grand, Nerid," said Landyn, hurrying toward the door. "I hope I'll be invited."

"Ho, ho, you are such a jester, Landyn. Much like your father, Lars rest his soul. I'm here to ask you to provide the main entertainment. You and the woman you sing with, Jessina d'Evanwing."

Landyn stopped in his tracks and looked down at the little man. "Me? If anything, I could be one of the side attractions. I'm a simple minstrel, not fit to play in the palace."

Nerid laughed aloud. "Humility doesn't suit you, Landyn. You know your talent with lute and song is unsurpassed here in Freehold. The only reason you are not the official court bard of Lord Penndryn is your unreasonable refusal to kiss royal behind! Now, there is plenty of coin to be made in this and I won't take no for an answer."

Landyn bowed his head. When Nerid put his foot down, it was impossible not to do what he wanted. He was high servant to the Lord of the city and was not to be refused. "Fine. You've got me, but I'm afraid Jessina won't be joining me. We had a…falling out a few months ago. I think she moved to Valaria to entertain there, but I'm not really sure. I don't really care."

"You'd best care," said Nerid, leaning in close. "I've got a hundred nobles to entertain, and although you're good, you alone aren't enough. I want song! Dance! Sweeping romantic duets!"

"It's impossible. There's not another woman fit to sing with me in all of Freehold, or even in…"

"I will not hear it. If we can't have Jessina, then what about Lucia, daughter of Mava?"

Landyn winced. "I can't work with her."

Nerid reached up and grabbed the taller man's shirt near the collar, his face tight with anger. "You will perform for our Lord's birthday festival. You and a suitable female singer. She has to be good and she'd better be beautiful. Find one. I'm used to getting what I want."

Landyn pulled back. To be talked to so by a servant! But Nerid was no common servant. He was in charge of all palace affairs and had a free hand in running things. He could bully around almost everyone in town, except for the nobles and the richest merchants. If he refused Nerid, he'd have to answer to Lady Shanna herself. "All right," he said. "I'll perform for the festival, and I'll find somebody to sing with. But this had better be well worth my while, Nerid."

The high servant smiled. "Oh, it will be, Landyn. It will be."

The next morning as he sat over his hot tea, Landyn thought long and hard of all the female singers he knew in Freehold and the surrounding towns. There were very few and none were fit to perform at the palace. If only there were someone, both beautiful and graceful, with a voice like a nightingale and knowledge of how to behave in court…

Suddenly he jumped up, running to pack some things for a journey. He remembered a woman, someone he had seen perform on Bard's Day. At Barton Hills, of all places. Ara Mills, he thought her name was. She was a shopkeeper in the farming village, seemingly intelligent and very pretty. With some work, she could be beautiful enough for Penndryn's taste. And her voice, it was fantastic, almost better than Jessina. If she knew little of court etiquette, so what? He'd have time to train her.

With little preparation, he left his apartment and set out for Barton Hills. He hoped this Ara would agree to his offer. He was prepared to give her as much as thirty percent of whatever he was paid…perhaps thirty-five. She would have to agree. That had to be more money than she had ever seen in her little village. And a chance to visit with nobility, who could refuse?

Well, I could, he thought, crossing the last mile to Barton Hills. He couldn't stand their attitudes and their haughty airs. That was the only thing keeping him out of the court. That, and the freedom being a common minstrel gave him. He wasn't tied to one town; he could come and go as he pleased. Let others dance and sing for Lords and Ladies; the common folk showed their appreciation more freely. And that was what he lived for.

The first huts of the village came into view and he saw farmland on the rolling hills surrounding them. He could make out people in the fields, harvesting the last crops of the summer and preparing the land for the next planting season. Several people walked on the streets, going about their jobs. All in all, a very normal day in Barton Hills. Or so it seemed at first.

The closer he came to the town, the more he got the impression something was wrong. The people moved stiffly, fearfully. When he passed them, they did not greet him but averted their eyes. Eyes filled with confusion, and sometimes sadness. Wondering what could be the matter, he continued toward the tavern.

Before he reached it, he passed a row of huts, some small and some large. One had the sign of a bakery hanging by its door. Several of the huts were in ruins, hollow shells of blackened wood. There was a fire here recently, it seemed. Perhaps this was what had put these people in their dark mood. Only, he had seen buildings burnt by fire, and fire didn't account for everything he was seeing now. Pieces of wood were in splinters, fanned out around the buildings. It was as if they had been shattered by a giant fist.

But this was not his concern now. He guided Luck faster toward the center of town and eventually came to the Silver Shield. He hitched his mount to the post outside and went in. Few men were seated in the common room, as he would expect at this time of day. The farmers were in their fields until after dark and the craftsmen would be hard at work in their shops. But Landyn wasn't interested in talking to the locals. At least he wasn't if the innkeeper could give him the information he needed.

He saw the innkeeper behind the bar, polishing glasses and plates. He was a fat, balding man, wearing a wine-stained apron. Darrel his name was, or Darren. Something like that. He approached the man, smiling warmly. Darren did not return the smile.

"I'll have a pint of your best ale, Barkeep," said the minstrel. "You may remember me. I am Landyn, son of Gordon, minstrel of Freehold."

"I remember you," said the fat man, pouring the ale. "You sang on Bard's Day. Not a bad performance, from what I could tell. I was kept rather busy all night."

"Indeed," said Landyn. *Not a bad performance! This fat fool wouldn't know a good performance if it kicked him in his blubbery rump!* "I thank you, good Darren, for your compliment. But I haven't come all this way to discuss Bard's Day.

Well, other than to ask about a woman who sang then. I wonder if you could tell me how I might be able to contact Ara Mills."

The innkeeper was shocked at first, eyes growing wide as he took a step back. Then his eyes narrowed and he said softly, almost threateningly, "Why do you want to know?"

"I only want to ask her to sing with me. There's no need to get upset."

"No need? I can't help you find her, Landyn son of Gordon, because she's gone. Dead, as far as anyone here knows."

It was Landyn's turn to be surprised. "Dead? In the fire?"

"Fire? Maybe. But I don't know about any normal fire, no matter what the town council is saying. Normal fires don't cause houses to blow apart in great bursts of light, throwing the bits all over the place."

Landyn rubbed his chin, thinking about what he had seen. "What could it have been, then? Sorcery?" He nearly chuckled to himself. He had seen magicians at work before and knew magic was real, but the simple folk of these farming villages didn't believe in it, even if they saw it.

"Sorcery," the barkeep said gravely. "Indeed it was."

The minstrel tilted his head and raised an eyebrow. Perhaps these folk were not as backwards as they seemed. Still, Landyn wondered what a sorcerer with enough power to destroy a row of huts would want with a little town like Barton Hills. "But who would do such a thing?" he asked.

The innkeeper appraised him. "I don't see any reason not to tell you. I think it was a fellow by the name of Salin. He was after some piece of jewelry the baker's apprentice had and he went a little crazy when he couldn't get it. Several folks died that night. I'm sure it was Salin's doing. My own peacekeeper ran off that night and I haven't seen him since."

"An unfortunate turn of events," said Landyn. Just as unfortunate for Landyn. He wasn't totally unconcerned for the townsfolk; this obviously was a hard experience for them. But his first concern was for his own well being, and if this Ara Mills was gone or dead, he'd have to find someone else to sing with for Lord Penndryn's festival.

He finished his ale and got up to leave the tavern. Since he had no other business here, he decided to explore the rest of the town. Perhaps someone else knew more about Ara. Besides, his curiosity had gotten the better of him. Sorcery, greed, and murder were the stuff of epic tales, and what was of more interest to a storyteller?

"Good day, Darren. I hope things go better for you in the days to come."

"I hope so, too," the barkeep answered, barely looking up from the plate he was wiping. "And my name is Derik."

"My apologies, good Derik," said Landyn, bowing deeply. He strode out the door, his dark green cape flowing behind him.

He walked through the town, stopping people he passed. No one wanted to talk to him about what had happened, other than to say there had been a fire. One old man complained the baker was dead and his apprentice gone, so there would be no sweet cakes for desert for a long while. Anyone could bake bread, he said, but Stan Kulnip's sweet cakes were something which would be sorely missed. A woman nodded her head sadly when he asked about Ara, saying her shop had been one of the few pleasures of life in Barton Hills. Ara had been a good woman, she said, always willing to sell things for less than they were worth.

Finally he came to where the shop had been. It had sat alone, situated at the base of a low hill. There was really not much left of it. Wreckage fanned out around a central ruin, which was black and jagged and full of holes. The sign out front was curiously whole, the only evidence of what the place once was: The Dragon's Den, a Place of Curious Wonders. Landyn frowned. If Ara was in there when this happened, she was surely dead.

"'Tis a shame, what's happened to the shop," someone said at his shoulder. The voice was high and old and cracked as it spoke. He turned to see an old blue-haired woman, short and hunched and wearing a white shawl pulled around her. She leaned heavily on a twisted cane.

"Yes, a shame," said Landyn, quietly. What a waste, he thought. The Ara woman was beautiful and talented. He would have been saddened by her passing even if he hadn't needed her. "Did you know the woman?"

"Know her? Yes, you could say I knew her. She used to give a poor old widow a few silver a week for dusting her shelves. I don't know how I would have gotten by otherwise, with my husband long dead and my children moved away."

"So she was your friend?"

The old woman nodded. "Yes. We were friends. What is your interest?"

Landyn told her of his plight, and how he had remembered Ara from Bard's Day. He didn't know why he went into detail with the old woman. Perhaps he felt the need to talk to someone willing to say more than a few words, or perhaps he felt sorry for the old lady, so obviously alone in the world. Whatever the case, she nodded when he was done.

"I doubt she'd go with you, but perhaps you can be of some use. I think you'd better come with me, young minstrel."

She began to walk away and he stared after her questioningly. Did she mean Ara was alive? When she turned and saw he wasn't following, she said, "What are you waiting for? I'm too old to waste time. Come, I don't bite."

He followed her to a small hut, furnished only with a small table, chairs, and a low, wooden bed. She sat in one chair, grunting with the effort, and motioned for him to take the other. She slid a small parchment which rested on the table toward him.

"She told me to give this to someone I can trust. Well, I guess I trust just about everyone in town, except maybe old beady-eyed Doc Hamlick, but no one would be willing to go traipsing off on some fool adventure. Except maybe a minstrel from the big city. I hear you folk live for adventure."

Landyn read the parchment, frowning. It was written hurriedly by a nervous hand. It read: *There are dark powers at work here. My grandfather told me stories of such things when I was a young girl, stories I thought he had made up. He was well traveled and I shouldn't have dismissed his knowledge. He told me about the wars they always had in the south and the west, and of the Fair Folk and their Fairy magic. But he told me about darker magic and the sorcerers who used it, servants of a dark master who lived far, far to the west. One in particular he told me about, a bogey man who ate little girls who didn't obey their parents. Salin, his name was. If only I had remembered before I let Alec go to him to sell the amulet! The name sounded familiar when he said it, but I thought nothing of it. Not until the fires and the explosions. Alec is gone, and my daughter Sarah with him, and I can only hope they escaped the hands of that foul murderer. I must leave, for Salin may return here if he cannot find them. He might come after me again, since he thinks I know something about that amulet he wants. I do not care for my own safety, but if I die I won't be able to help my daughter.*

I will give this letter into the hands of Cindra Verdan, a woman I know well enough to trust with my secret. I want it to be generally assumed I am dead. It is my only advantage. I will be in Riverton for a time, waiting for someone to come who can help me find my daughter and young Alec. I have to know they are well. And I have to do what I can to protect them. If you can help, come to Riverton. I will be going by the name Renda Collins. Seek me out at the Gray Horse Inn. Please. Help me.

Landyn raised an eyebrow and looked at the old woman. "Cindra, is it? Very intriguing, I must say, Cindra. Without a doubt the makings of an epic. A magic amulet, two youngsters running to keep it out of the hands of a foul villain, the diligent mother in hiding, hatching a plan to save her child. But why confide in me? You know nothing about me."

Cindra grunted. "Because I'm old, you fool. I may keel over in my soup at dinner tonight and no one would have ever gotten the message. The folk here in town are good folk, but they know little of the world outside Barton Hills. They aren't worth much against black magic. Maybe you aren't either, but I'll wager you know a thing or two about the world. I imagine a rogue like you has to."

"Rogue?" he said, "I'll have you know…"

"I know your type. Behind your fancy face and your charming ways, you'd just as soon pick a rich man's pocket as sing a song."

He was offended, but he said nothing. He'd much rather sing a song, but at times the temptation of a fat purse had overtaken him. He wondered what made this old woman such a good judge of character. "If I'm such a rogue, that's reason not to trust me."

"There's a difference between a minstrel who sometimes picks a pocket or two and a raving, murderous magician. I'd be willing to bet you would go out of your way to help a lady in trouble. Maybe you even know some others who would help."

Landyn stroked his beard in thought. "But surely there must be someone else. Her husband…?"

Old Cindra shook her head. "No, minstrel, Matthew's been dead nigh on seven years now. There's no one else."

Landyn raised an eyebrow. "A widow? My, this *is* intriguing."

The minstrel wasn't one to put himself in danger. But maybe he would seek out Ara. If he recorded her story, put it to song, perhaps he would go down in history as one of the great bards. He smiled for a moment, imagining his name in the history books beside Ottis Brachnitter. This might be his last opportunity for greatness.

"You know, Cindra Verdan, perhaps I will go to Riverton after all. Thank you for putting your faith in me."

"Faith? Bah, I'm too old for faith. I do things out of need. Now get on out of here; I'm older than Grok and I need some rest."

With his most formal bow, he swept out of the hut and made his way back to the Silver Shield. He rented a room for the night, telling Derik he would be on his way in the early morning and would need a supply of travel rations. He rested for the remainder of the day, already turning over poetry in his mind. It had been a long time since he had written anything, but the words were not long in coming, and a tune not far behind. He only knew the very beginning of the story, but it was enough for a start. He was only vaguely aware that already he was envisioning himself as a central figure in the tale. After all, if he were to chronicle the story from first hand experience, he would have to be there, perhaps even taking a hand in its outcome. Besides, Ara was a beautiful woman. The more he thought of her, the more he remembered her beauty above all else.

Beautiful enough to replace Jessina? He quickly got that thought out of his head. He didn't even know this Ara, and no one could replace Jessina d'Evanwing. She was a true lady, raised in a minor noble house of Freehold. Her style and grace could not be equaled. She could sing like no other, her dancing was unmatched, and she had skill in other areas that made Landyn sweat just thinking about it.

Enough! He had other things to think of now: helping Ara, learning more about this Salin and the amulet he was after. It would make a grand tale when it was done and telling it would make Landyn famous. If he lived through it.

Of course he would live. It probably wasn't nearly as dangerous as these farmers made it out to be. They were a simple folk and any little display of power would awe them. Landyn was a skilled and knowledgeable man and he thought he could well end up being the hero of his own tale. A silly thought, he knew, but enticing. Especially with Ara being grateful to him.

As night fell, he put away his writing tools and lay in bed, trying to put the excitement and uncertainty out of his mind. Tomorrow he rode for Riverton. It would be a long day.

CHAPTER 7

The Watcher

Alec twisted, trying to get comfortable on the rocky ground. Two days had passed since they had left the Addingrove, and he still longed for the safety and comfort of Horren's home. From what Michael said, it was still at least two more days to Bordonhold, and Alec had already had it with sleeping outdoors. The forest ground was dirty and damp, and in places filled with large stones and sharp rocks. It seemed like Michael always chose a rocky place to camp. Alec could see the reason the hermit chose the spots he did. They were secluded spots, surrounded by large rock outcroppings or well hidden by trees. Certainly they were safer spots than sleeping out in the open, but Alec didn't understand why the safest sites were also the least comfortable.

The night after they had left the Addingrove they were pursued by wolves again. Somehow they had avoided being seen by the creatures, who always seemed to be just a little bit behind the travelers. Just when it seemed the wolves would find them, the wind changed, blowing their scent away from the beasts. The howls became more distant then, as the disoriented wolves ran off in the wrong direction.

The next day had passed quickly, and was much the same as every other day of the journey. It was sunny, warm, and pleasant, although Alec started to wish he had a change of clothing. From the look of Sarah, so did she. She was still in her night gown and cloak, which had snagged on some bushes and ripped in several places. Kraig's open-chested black shirt and his brown pants had gotten torn and dirty as well, but for some reason it only seemed to enhance his rugged good looks. Michael's plain clothes were as unscathed as he himself was, not marred by stain or tear. Nothing seemed to affect him.

The nights were much less pleasant than the days. Fear seemed to press in on them from the blackness between the trees, urging them onward when they should have been resting. If a wolf howled in the distance, Michael pushed them faster. It was almost as bad if they didn't hear a wolf; silence was more oppressive and just as terrifying. In those silent moments, Michael muttered that Salin had servants other than wolves, who were more discreet in their pursuit and more horrible when they caught their prey. Alec couldn't imagine what could be more horrible than ending up in the belly of a wolf, but the thought kept him moving.

Now, as he lay, he hoped they had lost the pursuit for good. They hadn't heard any wolves tonight, so Michael let them stop a little early. Even he seemed optimistic they had lost pursuit, at least for the time being. He seemed to think their pursuers still would not expect them to go to Bordonhold, especially since Freehold still lay closer. For a while, until it became plain they made for Bordonhold, they would be relatively safe. Or so the hermit said.

Alec lay near Sarah, as he had taken to doing, and as he struggled to get comfortable, he said, "These blasted rocks make for poor pillows. I wish we were back home, or at least at Horren's place. My back will never be the same."

Sarah turned to face him, propping her head on her hand. "You always were pretty soft for a man, Mason. I kind of like this camping out. The ground isn't so bad."

Alec grimaced. "That's because I always let you have the least rocky piece of land in our Grok forsaken camp sites! Grok's beard, Sarah, I hope we reach Bordonhold soon, and in one piece. What I wouldn't give for a bed and a bath."

"Soon enough, Alec. I'm looking forward to those things, too, as well as a little safety. I imagine once we get there, things will be easier. Michael has friends there. Maybe they'll take the Talisman off your hands and put Salin off our trail."

"And on to someone else's. Can I do that to somebody?"

Sarah rolled her eyes. "You're no hero, Alec. Michael's city folk friends will know what to do with it."

Alec shrugged. "Maybe. But Michael never talked about giving the Talisman to someone else. He's been saying he's going to find someone to lead us to a safe place. Maybe that's what our lives have come to, fleeing from place to place, hoping we find safety. After all, Salin wants me as much as he wants the Talisman. He thinks I deliberately robbed him of it."

"You're not important to him, silly. If he gets this piece of jewelry he wants so badly, he'll forget all about you."

"But you're missing the point," said Alec, shaking his head and frowning. "We *can't* let him get it. If what Michael says is true, that much is clear. I guess our only hope is to get it to someone as powerful as Salin, someone who can…Shape…as well as him. And I don't think we're going to find someone like this in Bordonhold."

"I hope we do. I want this over as soon as possible so we can go home. I've got to see if…everything's okay there."

Alec knew what she meant to say. She wanted to see if her mother was alive. The fact that she couldn't say it made it obvious she was still hurting. She hid it well, better than Alec thought he could have. He had lost the Kulnips, two people he had cared about deeply, but they were not his parents. Turning again so the sharpest rocks didn't press into his back, he tried to sleep.

Early the next morning, they were moving again. It was the fifth day since they had left Barton Hills and at least two more until they arrived at Bordonhold. Alec's muscles were achy and stiff, but the pain had receded into the background enough for him to ignore it. The forest was still thick around them, although there seemed to be more light filtering through the canopy of leaves. Alec watched a squirrel scamper up an old spruce tree to rest on a branch high above. He almost wished he was a squirrel, with no problems and no responsibilities other than gathering nuts for the winter.

Later, Sarah grabbed his arm and pointed to a family of deer, running gracefully though the trees. They had seen many smaller animals during their journey, but nothing like this. In Barton Hills, surrounded as it was by miles of farmland, deer were rare. Occasionally a few might wander out of the Northwood, but seeing a whole family like this was a delight for Alec, Sarah, and Kraig.

"Look at them," said Sarah. "So beautiful, so free. They belong here, unlike us. They certainly don't have our problems."

"Oh, I don't know," said Alec. "Wolves hunt deer, too."

"Wolves, yes," said Michael. Alec hadn't known he was listening. "But not Salin Urdrokk. We must waste no more time."

Alec wanted to strangle the man. He couldn't let them forget for one minute they were fleeing from deadly peril. He couldn't take a moment to admire something beautiful or chat about something pleasant. He was obsessed. If he hadn't also been right, Alec *would* have strangled him.

They walked on into the afternoon, and Alec heard the sound of running water. Soon the woods opened into a clear area. At the bottom of a hill, Alec saw a wide river of clean, clear water, running slowly from east to west.

"The Fourpoints River," said Michael. "At least that is what it is called around here. I've been anxious to reach it. We should be able to cross it near here, where it's shallow. It is my hope crossing the river will throw those wolves off our trail for good."

"The Fourpoints," said Kraig. "I've heard of it. It touches four major cities in four different countries; that's how it got its name. In Tyridan it passes through Freehold."

"Yes," said Michael. "In Margon it cuts through Mar'Ridden, and in Estron it touches Estron City. It also serves as the boundary of Northern and Southern Eglak, flowing through the once grand city of Madygoth. The waters flowing through this river have seen much history, from the battles in which evil conquered Margon to the civil wars which tore Eglak apart. But for now our only concern is getting to the northern bank. Come; let us go down to the water. I have been here before, so I can find the ford."

They went down the hill and stood near the river. It seemed shallow, and it was clear enough to see the bottom. Many flat rocks broke the surface of the slow-moving water. Alec thought it would be possible to cross right here, but Michael seemed intent on finding the perfect spot. They walked westward along the bank for several minutes, until the hermit nodded his head.

"This is the place. See those markings on that rock?" Alec looked to a cluster of rocks near a big willow tree by the edge of the water and indeed saw some strange markings. "That shows this is a safe ford, marked by the woodsmen years ago."

"You're sure it's safe?" asked Kraig, eyeing the water warily. "It's shallow enough to walk across?"

"Yes," said Michael, already stepping into the slowly flowing river. "You can see the bottom. It will not rise above your waist."

Kraig backed away, shaking his head. "I don't know about this."

Alec saw fear in the burly man's eyes. "Kraig, this is no deeper than the river back home. And the current's slower, too. We all went swimming in that river as children."

The peacekeeper shook his head. "I didn't. I never had time to learn how to swim. I've never set foot in water, except to bathe, and then only in shallow pools or a tub. Never in a river."

Alec couldn't believe what he was hearing. He didn't think Kraig was afraid of anything. After all, for years his job had been stopping fights and tossing troublemakers out on their behinds, often dealing with men even larger than he himself was. That he would have been afraid of something as common as a river, a *shallow* river, mystified Alec.

"Come on," he said, smiling. "Look. You really can see the bottom, and it's no more than three feet deep. Sarah and I will be close by."

Sarah nodded in agreement. She was smiling at Kraig, too, suppressing a chuckle, Alec thought. Apparently she found the situation rather amusing.

Kraig took a deep breath. "All right. Let's get this over with."

The three of them took a step toward the river, Sarah and Alec surrounding Kraig. Michael was already half-way to the far bank. Just as they touched the water, there was a high-pitched cry from the woods behind them. Something long and straight flew by Alec's head, nearly nipping his ear, and splashed into the water only a few paces in front of him. Kraig, forgetting his fear, pulled Alec closer to his side.

"That was a spear! Run for it!"

But it was impossible to run quickly through the water. Alec splashed forward, twisting his body to look behind him. In the trees he saw a group of short, greenish-gray creatures doing some sort of wild dance. They wore only loin-cloths and waved spears nearly as long as themselves above their heads. Their eyes were huge and yellow, and each had a coarse tuft of green hair atop their heads. They all began to shout a high-pitched wail and one aimed his spear toward Alec.

"Wounds! Goblins!"

Alec had never seen a goblin. He had, of course, heard stories of the mischievous creatures, hunting the night to steel sheep and kill cattle, and carry little children away from unsuspecting mothers. Michael had also spoken of goblins, fighting in the armies of Vorik Seth. Again, Alec was overwhelmed by myths coming true.

If he had never believed in goblins before, he decided now was a good time to start. Otherwise, he might well end up skewered by a child's tall tale. A spear flew toward his head, and he quickly dived under water to avoid it. When he surfaced, he saw Kraig jumping out of the way of another shaft, pulling Sarah along with him. Alec wanted to help them, but he could barely figure out how to help himself. He called for Michael, but the hermit was far ahead, swimming to the other side, oblivious to the attack.

A second group of goblins appeared out of the trees, screaming and performing their mad dance as they dashed down the river bank and jumped into the water. Alec dived again, intending to swim to the far bank without surfacing, if he could.

He pulled himself through the water inexpertly. He hadn't really gone swimming in years, but he remembered the motions. If only his muscles didn't ache after a few strokes, and his chest didn't pound, demanding breath. By the time he was about half-way across, he broke the surface, gulping air.

A group of small creatures were paddling toward him, splashing loudly and laughing uproariously. They were having fun! Beyond them, he could barely see Kraig and Sarah, clinging to one another, jumping to avoid yet another spear.

The little beasts were nearly upon him. Alec turned and began swimming furiously for shore. He felt a hand grabbing at his ankle, but he managed to kick it away and keep swimming. The goblins were catching up quickly. Furious splashes caught his vision on either side now as they began to surround him. They laughed as they swam, enjoying their game. Small hands clamped around his ankles, this time firmly. Something sharp sliced into his side, and he cried out, taking in water. Then, as he reached forward, his wrist was caught in a firm grip.

He thought he was done for. But then, the hand which had him by the wrist pulled him upward, out of the water. The hand was bigger than a goblin's, and white. He blinked the water out of his eyes and stared into Michael's plain face, which showed as little emotion as ever. The hermit grabbed Alec's other hand and yanked him onto the bank.

Alec had made it to the far side. The goblins lost their grip on him as he struggled up the bank, and he crawled quickly to the nearby trees. Three creatures popped up out of the water, screaming anger at having lost their prey, running toward him.

Before they could take three steps, Michael swung a long, sturdy branch he had grabbed from the ground, striking the three goblins in the chest. They flew backwards screaming, two of them colliding with others trying to climb up the bank. The result was a pile of goblins falling back into the water, thrashing and gibbering madly.

"Come on," said the hermit, grabbing Alec's arm. "That will not delay them long."

"But Sarah! And Kraig, we can't leave them!"

Michael was already pulling Alec into the trees. "They will have to fend for themselves. They should be all right; you are the target."

Alec took only a few steps before the pain in his side made him crumple to the ground. He grabbed his side, and felt warm blood welling from a fresh wound. Michael tried to pull him up, but then noticed the crimson slash.

"A knife wound. Why did you not say anything?"

"When did I have time, with you pulling me along?" he grunted.

Some of the goblins had taken to fighting one another. The goblins who had been knocked back into the water by their falling companions were biting and clawing at them, furious at being nearly drowned. Those not engaged had managed to pull themselves out of the water and were racing for where Alec had fallen. Michael still had his sturdy branch, but this time it looked like he would be overwhelmed. No fewer than a dozen of the little demons were running toward him, some clutching long knives and others waving spears.

Suddenly the nearest goblin fell backwards, clutching an arrow which appeared in its chest. Then another grunted as a shaft impaled him. Alec saw a third arrow soar from the branches above, skewering a goblin through the eye.

Two goblins had gotten past the hidden archer, but Michael thrashed at them with his make-shift quarterstaff, sending one rolling down the bank and flattening the other with a decisive crack to the head. While arrows picked off another three, the remaining four closed in around Michael and Alec. They ran straight for the hermit, bearing deadly, curved knives. Looking up from the ground, Alec realized the hermit would not be able to stop all four.

There was a flurry of movement in the branches above, and a large, dark form dropped through the canopy of leaves and landed lithely between Michael and his attackers. A longsword flashed from a black sheath, and in a single stroke two goblin heads tumbled through the air. One creature threw its knife at the swordsman, who caught the weapon in his gloved fist. As the wide-eyed goblin turned to run, the swordsman threw the knife expertly and impaled the creature between the shoulders. Almost simultaneously, he parried the last goblin's attempted stab, and cleanly took off its grayish head.

Alec looked up as the swordsman turned to face him. The man was very tall, if not as broad as Kraig. He was dressed in tight black leather, with tall, hard boots, and long, studded gloves. A longbow and quiver were strapped to his back. His bearded face was hard and cold, but his eyes seemed to smile mysteriously. His long, slick black hair was tied in a short tail. Michael evaluated the man before putting his staff aside and extending a hand in welcome.

"I thank you, stranger. I doubt we would still be here if it was not for your intervention."

The dark swordsman smiled. "I would have been here sooner, but I had to help your friends first."

For the first time, Alec noticed Kraig and Sarah, still making their way to shore. At least ten dead goblins floated in the water behind them, most with arrows sticking out of their backs. The rest had large, bloody gashes in their chests, or were missing their heads. Kraig was holding his axe, blood dripping from its blade. He did not look pleased.

"That big fellow is untrained, but his strength makes up for it. Still, the axe is a crude weapon. I prefer the bow, but the blade comes in handy in tight spots, wouldn't you say?" His smile grew wider, showing straight, white teeth. "I am Tor. A watcher."

"Under the circumstances, we are pleased to make your acquaintance. I am Michael, and this is Alec. Over there are Kraig and Sarah. If you will excuse me, I have to see to the boy's wound."

As Michael bent over him, Alec looked at Tor. Watchers were the personal guards of the highest lords of Tyridan. This explained his almost supernatural skill with the blade. But what was one doing here, in the middle of the forest, where no lord was likely to set foot?

Michael applied a salve from his pack to Alec's side and wrapped it with several layers of thin, white cloth. Almost at once the pain subsided and Alec was able to stand. Kraig and Sarah came to shore and introduced themselves to Tor, and then they walked over to Alec.

"I thought we were dead for sure," said Sarah, "until arrows started coming from nowhere, killing those horrible things. Are you all right?"

"I'll live," said Alec. "I hope I don't slow us down even more than I already have. Michael's ointment seems to have killed the pain, but I feel like if I move too much I'll pull the wound open."

"You'll be all right," said Kraig. His shirt was covered with goblin blood. He held up his axe and shook his head. "I can't believe I had to use it already. Still, it's not like I had to kill any people. Just those little green…goblins."

"Goblins," repeated Sarah, shaking her head in disbelief. "Right out of a child's storybook."

Michael came over to where the three of them were talking. "I've been speaking with Tor," he said quietly. "He's agreed to come with us as far as Bordonhold. I've taken him up on his offer. We can use his talents, especially if we run into another ambush. Still, do not be too free with your tongue around him. Do not speak of the Talisman, or of Salin. I have told him we simply are traveling to Bordonhold to see some friends, and we thought cutting through the woods would be faster."

"You don't trust him?" asked Alec.

"I cannot afford to trust anyone I do not know, at least not until my trust is won. This Tor appeared at a most convenient time. Perhaps it is coincidence, and perhaps not. For now, we need him, so he comes along. But we do not know him, so be wary."

Michael walked back to where Tor was standing, looking out over the river as the goblin corpses drifted away. Kraig's face looked grim as he shook his head and said, "Be wary, he says. I still don't trust *him*." He walked over to where the two older men stood talking. Alec and Sarah followed.

"We don't usually see much goblin activity this far north," Tor was saying. "They occasionally raid in the forests below Valaria, but even that has nearly been stopped. I wonder what this hunting party was doing in the Northwood."

"A strange race," answered Michael. "Prone to mischief and evil. Who can say why they act as they do?"

"Who can say, indeed," said Tor, smiling. Even smiling, his face looked hard as rock, his eyes cold as ice.

Without another word, Michael led them northward. Tor walked at his side, and the others followed a few paces behind. They were still more than a day from Bordonhold, but Alec hoped the danger was over. With luck, they had left the wolves on the other side of the river, and the goblins were dead. At least, he *hoped* they were all dead. Could there be more? Michael had said Alec was the target, but the baker hoped it had just been a random attack, a hunting party that thought they had spotted some easy prey. But Michael hadn't been wrong about anything so far. So, more likely than not, the goblins were working for Salin. The thought made his blood run cold. The sorcerer would surely catch up to them shortly if any of his servants reported their whereabouts to him. Shivering, Alec prayed they had managed to kill all the goblins.

They spent the rest of the day walking in silence. The afternoon and evening passed uneventfully as they traveled quickly northward. The light and warmth filtering through the trees felt good to Alec as it dried his clothes and hair. He hadn't had time to notice before, but the river water was quite cold. At dusk they came to clearing, a ring of trees surrounding a dry, leaf-covered circle, and Tor suggested they camp for the night. It was not a spot Michael would have chosen, but he nodded in agreement to the muscular swordsman. If Alec hadn't known better, he would have thought Tor had taken over leadership of the party. The way he carried himself and the cold set of his eyes boasted a self-confidence Michael did not seem to have, despite his resolve. The black-garbed man had a presence you could feel, a dark charisma that made you want to follow him. At least this was the impression Alec had gotten in the few hours he had known the man.

They laid out the blankets around the center of the clearing and settled in for the night. As darkness fell around them, Alec wished they could have a fire, if only to push back the night weighing heavily upon him. He knew it could put them in danger by pinpointing their camp for any onlookers, and besides, it was too warm for a fire. He took some comfort from the fact that their journey was taking place in mid-summer; in the winter, it would be a difficult, uncomfortable trek. He settled in beside Sarah, said goodnight, and closed his eyes.

He was not certain how long he had lain asleep when a noise at the edge of the camp woke him. He peered into the darkness, and caught a glimpse of a black shape moving through the trees. He turned to wake companions, all of whom still slept soundly. All except Tor, who was nowhere to be found.

Before Alec could get out of his blankets, the dark figure stepped from the woods. A ray of moonlight fell across it, revealing the dark swordsman.

Tor smiled at Alec's look of panic. "No need to be afraid, young man. I'm just making sure none of those goblins are still about." He walked over and sat in the dirt beside Alec. "Michael wanted to take the first watch, but I insisted. After all, I'm much more experienced in securing a camp than any of you, I think."

Alec wondered why Michael let this stranger stand guard alone after telling them not to put too much trust in Tor. For himself, Alec had as much faith in Tor as he did in the hermit. After all, Tor had saved them from the goblin's attack at the risk of his own life. If he wished them any harm, he could have let the goblins do his work for him.

"You just startled me," said Alec. "You can understand why, with all we've been through in the last few days."

"Indeed. You folks should have stuck to the road. Cutting through the Northwood makes the trip no shorter, and adds an element of danger. Even discounting the goblins, packs of wolves hunt these parts."

"I have…heard tales of the wolves," Alec said, carefully. "We even heard some howling close to our camp the other night. I suppose you're right; the road would have been a better idea. Well, goodnight, Tor." Alec lay back down on the hard packed dirt.

Tor made no move to resume his guard. "I must say, the four of you make an unlikely group. You and the girl do not look cut out for long journeys, not on foot through the woods. And Kraig and Michael hardly look like they travel in the same circles. How did the four of you end up together?"

Alec sat up, somewhat irritated. What could he tell Tor if not the truth? "Well, we are all from Barton Hills, of course. A few folk we know from Freehold moved up to Bordonhold a year or so back, and we haven't seen them since. True, the four of us aren't all that close, but since we all have friends in Bordonhold, and since long journeys can be dangerous, we opted for safety in numbers."

Tor raised an eyebrow. "Your Bordonhold friends must be very special to warrant such a trek. It is not often people undertake such an expedition for a social call."

"Yes, they're good friends. Good night." Alec lay down and turned his back to the swordsman.

"Still, you could not find horses, a carriage, perhaps? It is a long way to travel on foot."

Alec bolted upright, sure his irritation was showing on his face. He was *very* tired. "I don't know what you're used to in Valaria, but not every one in Barton Hills can afford a horse. It's a simple, farming village. Now I hate to be rude, but the day's events have left me weary. If you'll allow me to get some sleep…"

"Of course, Alec. Just one more question." Tor leaned close enough that Alec could feel the man's breath on his face. "Where have you hidden it?"

Alec's heart jumped into his throat. "Hidden it?"

"The Talisman, boy! I've searched the camp, but I cannot find it."

"I don't know what you…"

Tor grabbed his shirt and pulled him closer. He was as cold as ever, showing no anger or urgency. "Do not play the fool, child. Salin is paying me well to find it and bring it to him. I have no quarrel with you. I wish you no harm. You are quite lucky I found you before the sorcerer; he would burn you to cinders and search your remains. I simply want to get paid. Once more, where is it?"

"Michael!" cried Alec. No one stirred.

"They will not awaken for many hours yet. I know a trick or two of sorcery myself. I allowed you to awake prematurely when I couldn't find the Talisman."

"But…you saved us from the goblins. Why?"

"Salin employs many sorts of agents. Many he does not trust. Goblins are good at tracking, but they are not good at delivering merchandise. I followed them until they found you, and then eliminated them so I could get to you myself. Now, I am a very patient man, but I can use less pleasurable methods of persuasion if pressed. We have all night, but wouldn't you rather do this quickly and painlessly?"

Alec's mind raced. How could he get out of this? While he hesitated, Tor dragged him away from the camp, forcing him to kneel before a small sack. It contained food, and one other thing. Tor held on to him with one hand, and with the other withdrew a small, silver chest from the sack.

"I could not open this by strength or sorcery. Now, I imagine I know what it contains. Would you care to open if for me?"

It was the silver chest Horren had given Alec. Apparently the Addin's claim no one but Alec could open it had proven true. It hardly seemed to matter now, however. The watcher—or what ever he really was—had Alec at his mercy. If he didn't open the chest, he would probably die.

Alec took the chest. Again, he hesitated. If Salin got the Talisman, more towns would suffer as Barton Hills had. Likely, they would suffer a far worse fate.

"No? Ah, well, I'm sure Salin can open it. His sorcery far surpasses my own. But I am afraid I will have to kill you and your friends. Lack of cooperation must bring penalties, you know."

As he began to draw his sword, Alec cried, "Wait!" Salin probably could open the chest. He would have the Talisman, and Alec and his companions would be dead. This way, there would still be hope. If Tor kept to his word and let them live. "I'll open it."

Alec turned the front of the chest toward the swordsman. There was no latch, no lock. It was simply sealed shut for all hands but his. Slowly, he pulled the lid backwards. Tor leaned eagerly forward, his hand still resting on his sword.

A shaft of white brilliance shown forth from the chest. Tor leaned back and made to shield his eyes. Alec threw the chest the rest of the way open, and the night was filled with white fire. The main shaft of light was focused directly forward, into the face and eyes of the swordsman. He cried out and stumbled back, throwing his arms in front of his eyes, too late.

Alec slammed the chest shut, taking advantage of Tor's temporary blindness. He lifted the chest into the air and then brought it down hard upon the watcher's skull. There was a crack, and Tor fell to the ground, motionless. Alec grabbed his sack and began to make his way back to the others. As an after-thought, he turned back and carefully pulled Tor's sword from its sheath. Then he ran back to the camp.

He knelt beside Michael and began to shake him. He slapped the man, shouted in his ear, but he wouldn't wake up. He tried again with Kraig, and with Sarah, but with no success. He resigned himself to crouching down near the camp, where he had a clear view of the swordsman's still form. He held the sword awkwardly, but prepared to use it if Tor even flinched. He prepared him-self to spend the rest of the night in that position, or at least until his compan-ions awakened. Michael would know what to do with the so-called watcher. At least, Alec hoped he would.

Alec felt a hand on his shoulder, shaking him awake. As his eyes opened, he cursed himself for falling asleep while watching Tor. His hand still gripped the sword, which he brought upward to defend himself. He stopped himself just short of impaling Kraig.

"Alec! What are you doing? Isn't that Tor's sword?"

Alec looked toward the edge of the clearing, seeing Tor's form still laying there. *Thank Grok! If he had awakened first, we'd all be dead!*

"Look," he said. "That's Tor over there. He knows about the Talisman; he's working for Salin! I managed to knock him out, but we've got to do something before he wakes up. We've got to wake the others."

Kraig nodded, taking it all in stride. Within moments, they had shaken the others awake and explained the situation. Michael shook his head gravely, sug-gesting a practical and final solution to the problem.

"Kill him!" cried Alec. "But that's murder. I thought we could some-how…detain him. Hand him over to the city guard once we reached Bordon-hold."

"Whether you like it or not, we are fighting a minor war against Salin," said Michael. "That's how you have to look at this. Tor knows where we are headed and will report to Salin if we allow him to live. You should have killed him as soon as you had the advantage. If you will not, give me the sword. I will do what must be done."

Filled with horror, Alec handed the sword to Michael. Killing wolves and goblins was one thing, but this was a human being! Sarah covered her eyes; even Kraig looked sick. Michael started walking toward the edge of the camp, where Alec had pointed. Then he turned and faced the baker, a grim look on his face.

"Where did you say you left him?"

"Right over there, where you were headed. Don't you see him?"

Michael looked again, and then threw down the sword, shaking his head.

Alec walked over to the hermit, looking to the spot where the swordsman had fallen. Only crushed leaves and a small pool of blood marked the spot where he had lain. They were still alive, and the Talisman was safe for now, but Salin would be informed of their location and their destination.

Tor had escaped.

CHAPTER 8

Bordonhold

The forest began to thin as Michael bent their path slightly westward, toward the Wyndsway, the road which would take them into Bordonhold. He explained they would intersect the road a few miles outside the city, so they would look like normal travelers when they reached the gate. Four strangers coming out of the woods would raise more than a few eyebrows. They would raise eyebrows, anyway, Alec thought. They were filthy, obviously not clothed for travel, and carrying few supplies. Even if people assumed they came from the nearest village, an overnight journey at best, there would still be questions.

Late in the afternoon, Alec asked Michael a question he'd been pondering since morning. Michael had told them not to trust Tor, and yet he had let the man watch over the camp while the others slept. How could he have put that kind of faith in a man they had only known for a few hours? Michael stiffened and answered in a harsh tone, although his face retained its habitual emotionlessness.

"He used what is known as the *Charin-ta*. It is a subtle form of influence, Shaping the perception of others to see what one wants them to see. In retrospect, I am aware I had been influenced, but while experiencing the *Charin-ta*, I thought I was making my own choices. Once, I would not have been fooled so easily."

Alec nodded, not really understanding. Another magic trick, he supposed. "I guess we were all taken in by him. I didn't trust him, but I was prepared to do anything he said. Until he demanded the Talisman, of course. Then I was too scared to listen to him."

"This is one of the flaws of the *Charin-ta*. It does not allow one to make outright demands, only subtle suggestions. Used over time however, it has been known to make kings into slaves."

Sarah had been walking a step or two behind them, beside Kraig. She jogged forward a few steps, until she was beside the hermit. "Michael. How is it you know so much about all these things? Magic, history, the Talisman. This…Kren-ta thing."

"*Charin-ta*," corrected Michael. "As I have said, I was not always a simple hermit. I was a…a student. And at another time, a teacher. The world is a fascinating place for a young man, and I was eager to learn everything about it. Unfortunately, I learned too much. I discovered things no man should have to know, to bear. It was then I realized how futile the struggle against evil always was, this battle against impending doom. It was then I gave up my roles as student and teacher and settled down to live out my years in solitude and peace…until I happened to be in the wrong place at the wrong time and got tangled up in this young man's affairs." He pointed to Alec.

"You didn't have to say anything," said Alec, somewhat angry. "You probably wouldn't have, if you weren't sitting in the tavern, half drunk. If I had just sold the Talisman as I had agreed, none of this would have happened."

"Perhaps not. And perhaps nothing would, for a few years, at least not in the simple town of Barton Hills. But eventually, Salin would turn the Fair Folk into virtual slaves by the might of the Talisman. Using them as his army, he would decimate your land, conquering the world city by city, country by country. The Fairy Shapers would throw fire at the great armies of the east, and cause hail to rain down upon them. Simple human beings would not stand a chance, especially with Eglak divided. Half the world is already under the shadow of Salin's master. The rest would fall easily if the Talisman were in that fiend's hands."

Alec shook his head. "So you keep saying. Maybe it's all true, but I don't want to talk about it anymore. Once we get to Bordonhold, I want to put this mess behind me."

Michael nodded. "Pray it is possible. Once I contact some of my friends in the city, I will leave you in their hands. Perhaps they will be of greater help than I have been. Know that you can trust them as you trust me."

Alec chuckled, inside. "Great," he said. *Some comfort.*

By the time they camped for the night, they were within a few hours walk of Bordonhold, according to Michael. They sat and talked for a short while and ate some of the roots and nuts and berries Horren had given them. The night was cool and particularly dark, and for once Alec found a comfortable spot to lie. Kraig sat nearby, propped against a tree, taking the first guard of the night. Michael would be next, then Alec. He missed being able to sleep through the night, especially with the permanent ache which had settled into his bones.

Over the past few nights, Sarah had been moving closer to him as they slept. Tonight, when she settled into her blankets, her shoulder touched his. He looked over at her, and she smiled sweetly. For a moment he felt a swelling desire kiss her, but then he silently chastised himself instead. *Fool! She's just looking to me for comfort. I'd be an ass to take advantage of her.* He managed a smile, and then drifted into an uneasy sleep.

Too quickly, they were walking again, the sun fully in the sky. The night was blessedly uneventful, but far too short, especially for Alec who had to watch over the camp in the last dark hours before dawn. His eyes had kept darting through the shadows, searching for any sign of wolves, or goblins, or Tor. Or even Salin. But there was no trouble, and at dawn Alec breathed a sigh of relief.

Before noon, they came to the Wyndsway. The forest suddenly opened up, and there was a wide, flat road in front of them. It was obviously well traveled, but also well maintained. The Wyndsway was the highway of Tyridan, going through most of the major cities and many of the smaller towns. It passed within several miles of Barton Hills, lying west of the town, and Alec had walked its path before. Not nearly this far north, however. In another hour or so, they crested high a hill, and the towers of Bordonhold came into view. Alec nearly fell over. His eyes widened, but they still hardly sufficed to take in the sights. His jaw dropped, but words failed him. Kraig, likewise amazed, summed his feelings up nicely.

"Grok! It's so damned *big*!"

"Welcome to Bordonhold," said Michael, allowing himself a small smile.

The city spread out before them like a huge island in a sea of trees. Paved streets ran between buildings taller than Alec had ever seen. Each and every structure was larger than the Silver Shield, the biggest building in Barton Hills. And they were so close together! Alec wondered how anyone could breathe squeezed so tightly between buildings. And there were high watchtowers, one on each corner of the wall surrounding the city. Truly this place had been built as a fortress. In the center of the city, Alec could make out a huge building made of polished stone, with white towers surrounding it, banners waving atop each. A castle.

Michael sighed as he saw the three villagers staring awestruck at the city. "Come. I know it is a staggering sight if you are not used to large cities, but we must hurry. We are on the road now, exposed. Anyone in those towers could have been watching us for hours. Besides, this is only the third largest city in Tyridan. If this were Valaria, I don't doubt you would have fainted and I would be dragging you to town."

Sarah was the first to recover. She gave the hermit a sidelong glance, and smiled slyly. "Was that a joke? Boys, I think the solemn hermit just made a joke!"

They laughed, and even Michael's smile widened, despite his concern. Soon they were walking down the hill quickly; Alec, Kraig, and Sarah anxious to experience their first real city. As they reached the bottom of the hill, the buildings and streets disappeared behind a massive stone wall, and the two closest watchtowers seemed to grow taller and taller. The wall filled their field of view, vanishing into the woods on both sides of the road. A large, iron gate was set in the wall, and above it was a small guardhouse. The gate was open, but a small group of armored guards stood to either side.

"Act as if there is no reason for the guards to be suspicious of you, and they will not be," said Michael. "If they ask any questions, I will answer them."

"What about this?" asked Kraig, pointing to the axe that he had strapped to his side. "Will they question why I'm walking into the city armed? And what about your sword?"

Michael, who had kept Tor's sword and now wore it hanging from his belt, said, "It is not uncommon for travelers to be armed. One must protect oneself from bandits along the road."

Sarah laughed again. "Or from goblins in the woods. But what about my clothes? Don't you think they'll wonder why a girl is taking a trip dressed in nothing but nightclothes covered by a winter cloak? In the summer?"

"They will think it strange, but they will not question it any more than they will the weapons. Stranger things happen in a city of this size. Besides, we are no threat, and they will see this."

Before long, they came to the gate. One guard from either side came to stand before them, each holding a halberd, blunt end resting on the ground. They wore chain-link armor, and across their chests they wore a red silhouette of an ogre's head, the grim symbol of Bordonhold. One of the guards mumbled a speech he was obviously forced to memorize and had probably spoken to hundreds of visitors.

"Know you are about to enter Bordonhold, the last bastion of civilization on the edge of a savage wilderness. We hold the line between order and chaos. Know that Lord Revel Ducard commands here, with the blessing of our good King of Tyridan, Arynn the Fourth. Know while here you must obey the law of Bordonhold, as set forth by Lord Ducard. You may bear weapons, but you may not use them except to defend your lives, nor may you bear them in the presence of Lord Ducard or any of House Ducard, or any of the noble houses recognized in this city. You may not steel, nor rape, nor plot against this city or its Lord. You may not…"

The speech went on for several minutes, and Alec tuned it out. At the end of it, they were asked if they agreed to these terms, and answering yes, they were allowed into the city. Kraig shook his head in wonder.

"I'm glad I don't live here. If I had to hear this speech every time I came into the city, I think I'd go mad!"

"It is much shorter than it used to be," said Michael. "Once, three guards took turns delivering a single speech so they would not lose their voice over the course of the day. As for living here, citizens of the city are given a pass; they need not hear the speech every time they must go through the gate. Visitors have no such luxury. Now, before we look for my friends, there are a few things we need to take care of: a room, a bath, a good meal, some new clothes. I think we have enough time and money for these simple things."

"Thank Grok," said Sarah. "That's the most sensible thing you've said since I've known you."

Alec laughed, but his mirth was cut short as he looked around him. If he had been impressed before, seeing the city from the hill, he was even more so now that he was within the city walls. The streets were paved with flat, white stones, aligned carefully so as to make a carriage ride smooth. Crowds of men and women jammed the street, just milling about or striding purposefully. Some had stopped at one of the many merchant's booths or carts lining the streets. The merchants called out, advertising their goods, selling apples or carrots, bread or wine, jewelry or trinkets or shoes, or just about anything imaginable. Many stood out front of tall buildings they owned or rented, shops containing more of their fine goods. It was a loud, bustling marketplace unlike anything Alec had experienced. So many voices filled the air: shouting, laughing, greeting friends, even singing. And so many scents wafted by! He smelled roasting meats, exotic perfumes and flowers, oils from a nearby tannery, raw fish being sold by a street vendor, smoke from a blacksmith's forge. So many things were happening at once it threatened to overwhelm him. Glancing at his companions, he saw they felt the same way, except Michael.

"Grok, look at this place," said Kraig. "How do they keep any sort of order with so many people around?"

"The town guards are good at what they do," said Michael. "And most of the people keep themselves from trouble. Of course, in a city this size, there are always those who remain outside the law. Thieves, assassins, and brigands of every sort stalk the shadows here. It is said they are even organized in guilds, or clans. Their impact is not so great as to affect the lives of normal folk, yet it pays to be cautious. You are not in Barton Hills any longer."

"Oh, look!" exclaimed Sarah. "A dress shop! I need some new clothes."

"We all do," said Alec. "But you most of all. I suppose getting something to wear should come first. After all, it would be a shame to take a bath and then put these filthy rags back on."

Michael nodded. "I agree. More importantly, we need to blend in with locals. I'll take Sarah into the dress shop; you two can find something appropriate for yourselves. Do not go far, and meet us back here in one hour. Then we must find an inn."

They pooled their money, which turned out to be a rather paltry sum. Michael doled out ten silver each for clothing, and put the rest in his pouch. He claimed that if they found an inexpensive inn, they could live on what they had for nearly a week, and they certainly didn't intend to remain here that long. And then they separated, Alec and Kraig heading further into the city.

"I don't know if this was such a good idea," said Alec. "I could get lost here easily, or what if…what if Salin should find us?" He said the last in a whisper.

"Relax, Alec," said Kraig, smiling. "If we keep to this main street, all we need to do to get back is turn around. And if Salin were here, which isn't likely, he'd be hard pressed to find us in this crowd. And if he did, then what? Attack us in bright daylight, in front of all these people? Surely even he wouldn't risk that."

"I suppose. Maybe I just don't like leaving Sarah alone with Michael. I mean, we've been traveling with him for a week, but we still don't know him. We don't know anything about him, except that he knows things he shouldn't. Who *is* he?"

"I don't know. But we have no choice but to trust him. He's better than Salin."

They had been walking through the town as they talked, slowly milling through the crowd. No one seemed to pay them any heed, for which Alec was thankful. Soon they came to a shop with a bright orange sign reading, "Chaun's Garments, for Men." Kraig pointed, and they entered.

The shop was not very large, but it was clean and contained wooden racks filled with shirts, pants, stockings, and light jackets and cloaks. A shelf held several different styles of hats, many unfamiliar to Alec. Equally unfamiliar were the strangely cut shirts and bright, silky pants filling the shop. Luckily, he managed to find a plain, brown, wool outfit like he was used to wearing at home.

"How much for these?" he asked the stocky shopkeeper, who was sitting behind a counter reading a book.

"Twelve silver," said the man, barely looking up.

Alec's jaw dropped. At home, he could have gotten three of the same outfits for as much. "That's outrageous. I'll give you six."

The Shopkeeper laughed. "I will starve, boy, if I sell my wares so cheaply! But I like you. Ten!"

"I've only got eight," Alec lied.

"Nine!"

"Deal!" said Alec, pulling the coins out of his pocket. He took the simple shirt and pants from the rack, and paid the man. Kraig found a low cut gray shirt and baggy black pants, and ended up paying his full ten silver. Alec stuffed their clothing into his sack, and they made their way back up the street to where they had left the others. Michael and Sarah were waiting for them.

"You should have seen some of the dresses in there," said Sarah excitedly. "All different colors and materials…nothing like what we have in Barton Hills. I couldn't afford what I wanted, but I managed to get something nice. I can't wait to put it on."

"We did well, also," said Kraig. "What about you, Michael? We can show you where we got our clothes."

"I'm fine, for now," said the hermit with a hint of a smile. He was fine, too. Of all of them, his clothes remained the cleanest and the most intact. They didn't even seem to retain the faint body odor the others, unfortunately, had.

"Well, I'm all for getting to an inn," said Alec. "I need a bath, a meal, and a bed."

The others agreed, and Michael led them deeper into the city. Soon they came to a street where the crowds were thinner. The shops were replaced with houses and taverns, and inns dotted every other corner. Some inns were larger than others, their outsides well maintained. They kept walking until they came to a more quaint section of town, where the buildings were smaller and older.

Fewer people walked the streets, and there was a sense of quiet. There was still far more activity than was the norm in Barton Hills, but at least it was calm enough to let Alec's head stop spinning. By the time they stopped in front of a small, homely looking inn, they had been in the city for more than three hours.

"Things have changed greatly," said Michael. "It has been many years since I have been here. But if memory serves, this district has the least expensive inns in Bordonhold, yet the accommodations are quite acceptable. I think we have found a temporary home." He smiled, pointing to the sign above the inn's front door. It read, simply, "Home."

Michael pushed open the old, rickety door, and they followed him into the common room. An aroma of food and ale filled the large room, which made Alec's stomach rumble. The common room was similar to the one at the Silver Shield, with wooden walls and rafters supporting the high ceiling. Oil lamps hung from fixtures on each wall, providing subtle illumination. Small round and large rectangular tables were arranged throughout the room, and at many of them sat men and women engaged in conversation, card games, laughter, and, in some cases, solitary contemplation of their drinks. The bar was situated near the left wall, and before it, polishing an ale mug, was a tall, thin, long-haired barkeeper. Near the bar a flight of stairs climbed upwards, presumably where the bedrooms were. A door in the far wall led into the kitchen, and serving maids constantly streamed in and out, carrying hot plates of food to their customers.

"Well, this place sure reminds me of home," said Kraig. "It's bigger, but I can almost imagine I'm back in the Silver Shield."

"I will see about securing rooms," said the hermit. "You three find a table and keep to yourselves."

As Michael walked toward the slim barkeeper, Sarah mockingly said, "'Keep to yourselves!' Honestly, he must think we're children."

"You are," said Kraig, who was at least five years older than Alec. The burly man smiled. "Don't be offended, Sarah. There's nothing wrong with being seventeen. Come on; let's sit down."

They found a table in the corner and made themselves comfortable. Alec watched Michael talking to the barkeep, wondering if the little money they had would be enough to rent rooms. Just as he was about to comment on their lack of funds, a serving maid blocked his line of view.

"Hello. I am Glinda," she said. "What do you desire?"

Suddenly Alec thought he desired Glinda. Her blond hair fell down around her shoulders, highlighting her big blue eyes, small, soft nose, and full, sensual lips. Her tight dress and low cleavage accentuated her firm, round breasts. For a moment he forgot he was supposed to have feelings for Sarah.

"Uh…desire?"

Kraig looked over at Alec and smiled knowingly. "She means food and drink, Alec."

Sarah, realizing what Alec was staring at, gave him a hard kick under the table. Her glare was equally painful. "Cool it, baker," she quipped. "Your bread is rising."

If Glinda had noticed the interchange, she kept it to herself. "A pint of ale is a silver, and a plate of hot fowl and beans is two."

Kraig frowned. "Do you have anything less expensive?"

"Watered down wine is a silver a jug," she said distastefully. "Meat stew is a silver a bowl. I'd stay away from that, personally," she confided.

"We have little silver," said Kraig. "Bring us a jug of your worst watered down wine, and four bowls of stew."

"As you wish," she said. As she walked away, she gave Kraig a wink. Sarah turned her wide eyes to the bearded man.

"I guess she likes you. Sorry, Alec."

Shortly the hermit joined them. "I rented two rooms for one night, at four silver a room. At this rate, allowing for food, we have money enough for four days."

"I thought you weren't planning on staying," said Alec.

"I am not," said the hermit. "Not any longer than it takes to locate one of my contacts who is capable of dealing with your particular problem. At any rate, there is a bathing room upstairs, which you can all use in turns, and then you can retire for the night. I will go out into the city to find my friends."

Kraig leaned over the table, toward Michael, and said in a low voice, "Is it safe here? What of Tor? Surely he will tell Salin where we were headed, or come for us himself."

Michael shook his head. "There is nothing to be done about that now. We must trust fate. We are the ones with the advantage. We are in a large city, and tracking us down will be difficult. Salin cannot use his wolves and goblins here. We will be safe enough until I find someone to lead you to a safe haven."

"Lead us?" said Sarah. "I thought we were done with running. The plan was to get someone to take this stupid Talisman off our hands, wasn't it?"

"That may not be enough," said Michael. "Salin wants you, or at least Alec, as much as he wants the Talisman. And I have come to suspect there may be a deeper connection…ah, I can say no more on this now. I must go."

"Deeper connection to what?" asked Alec, intrigued.

"There is no time to explain now," he said, rising.

"But wait," said Sarah, "we ordered you food!"

"You split my share," he said, already walking away. "I will have the last of the travel rations." He walked out the door, and was gone.

"I don't like this at all," said Sarah.

"Neither do I," said Kraig, "but we don't have many options. We've trusted Michael this far. We might as well trust him a little further."

They sat mostly in silence until Glinda brought their food and wine. There was little point in discussing their problem further, and small talk seemed too trivial given the situation. But after they began eating the dark, warm stew and drinking the cool wine, their moods brightened a little and conversation turned to the small comforts of the inn.

"This food isn't so bad," said Alec, spooning a chunk of some unidentifiable meat into his mouth. "Not after eating Michael's rations and Horren's nuts and berries for the last week."

"I can't wait to bathe and change into some clean clothes," remarked Sarah.

"And I'm looking forward to sleeping in a bed for once."

"Speaking of beds," Alec said hesitantly. "We're going to have to sleep two to a room. At any rate, I wouldn't want to leave Sarah alone, but it isn't exactly…appropriate that one of us should sleep with her."

"Well I certainly don't want Michael in my room!" said Sarah. "It's okay, Alec. We're not in Barton Hills anymore. I trust you to keep to your side of the room and keep your eyes away from me while I undress for bed."

I wish I trusted myself as much, thought Alec. It was one thing sleeping near each other outside on the rocky ground, but in a bedroom? Alec's face grew warm, and he hoped he wasn't blushing. Kraig's growing smile showed him he was. Sarah opened her mouth to comment.

As if to save Alec further embarrassment, there was a loud commotion on the far side of the room. A huge man, the inn's peacekeeper, was grabbing a slightly smaller man by the shirt and hoisting him up from a table. The smaller man had long, dark hair and a scraggily beard. He staggered as he rose, obviously drunk. He dropped his mug, its contents sloshing across the table and onto the floor.

"How many times has Bertrand told you, if you can't pay, you can't drink!"

"But my good peacekeeper," said the drunk in deep voice he struggled to control, "it is only the drink that sustains me! Why, my brother…"

"Your brother forced you into this sad, pathetic life. Yeah, we've heard it all before. Let's go, Lorn."

He dragged the disheveled man to the door and thrust him out. The drunk's protests could still be heard through the door, but the peacekeeper stuck his head out and said something that made the fellow stop talking. Satisfied, the big peacekeeper walked back into the room and took his seat next to the bar.

"I like to see the job done well," said Kraig.

"He's even bigger than you are," Alec commented.

"I could take him."

They finished their meals, spirits rising with every bite. By the time they decided to go up to their rooms, darkness and danger seemed far behind them. They asked the innkeeper, the tall, thin man named Bertrand, to show them to their rooms, which he did almost silently. The rooms were simple, but comfortable, each having two small beds with thick, brown blankets, a wall mounted lantern, and a small writing table and chair. Alec stashed his belongings under his bed, including the silver chest which contained the Talisman, and announced he was off to the bathing room.

When he entered, he was surprised and embarrassed to find four of the six large tubs occupied, two by women! One was an old, white haired matron who smiled at him as he entered. The other, however, was a slim young beautiful girl, relaxing with her eyes closed. Covered to the neck in water and foam, she was as good as clothed, but Alec still felt uncomfortable.

"Uh…I'm sorry…I didn't realize…"

The old woman smiled. "You're from out of town, aren't you? There's no need to be uncomfortable. All the bathing rooms in Bordonhold are communal. And you don't have anything I haven't seen on my six sons, youngster. But there's a privacy curtain you can draw, if you like.

Sure enough, a curtain surrounded each tub, suspended from hooks on the ceiling. Alec hurried to a tub and pulled the curtain all the way around, making sure there were no cracks before stripping off his old, filthy clothes. He felt nervous until he stepped into the hot, foamy water. But then he was in heaven. He sighed as his body absorbed the warmth, as the water soothed his aching bones. After a few minutes he scrubbed the filth from his body with a coarse sponge, feeling clean for the first time in days. After almost half an hour, the water started to cool and he regretfully rose from the tub. Wrapping a thick towel around his body, he opened the curtain and made his way back to his room. An attendant, waiting outside the bathing room, quickly went in to drain the tub and prepare it for the next bather.

In the room, Sarah had already stripped off her clothes and was wrapped in a big, furry towel.

"Grok," said Alec, his face once again growing red, "why are women taking off their clothes everywhere I turn?"

"What are you talking about, Mason?"

"The bathing room is communal. There are men *and* women in there."

"Grok's beard!" said Sarah. "Isn't there any decency in this city?"

Alec smiled. He was glad he wasn't the only one having trouble dealing with life away from Barton Hills. "Relax. There are privacy curtains. Although I was the only one in there who was using one."

Sarah walked past Alec to the door. She gave him a long look as she passed, staring at his exposed chest and stomach. "It looks like the week you spent walking paid off. Why, I'd say you've lost at least ten pounds." Smiling, she walked out of the room and down the hall.

Alec looked down at himself. He hadn't thought of it, but he *had* lost quite a bit of the fat around his stomach. He had never been very concerned with his belly, but seeing it shrinking somehow pleased him. Still, he had a long way to go if he ever wanted to look like Kraig. Which he didn't. Not really.

Alec put on his undergarments and crawled into his bed. It was still early evening, but with all he'd been through recently, going to bed early was appealing. The mattress was somewhat lumpy, but after a week in the wilderness it felt like the most comfortable bed he'd ever slept in. It wasn't long before his eyes closed, and he drifted into a heavy, dreamless sleep.

Night was falling, and Michael was starting to get frustrated. Things were not going according to plan. For the last few hours he had been walking the streets of the city, visiting the homes of his old associates. Or rather, their former homes.

Sometimes I forget the passage of time.

It had been more than twenty years since he had been through Bordonhold, since he had last seen Charnak Grad or Bekka du Raven. Those Shapers had been old even then; if Michael had thought about it, he would have guessed they had long since passed away. Maddok had been young enough, but given the warrior's lifestyle, it was not surprising he had died as well. Michael had only one hope left, and it was a slim one. Shad Flynt had been in his forties the last time the hermit had seen him, but given his dangerous profession, it was doubtful he had survived. If he had, it was more than likely he had ended up in some noble's dungeon. Shad was a notorious thief. In his prime he had been like a shadow, able to slip into a guarded fortress and escape with whatever riches were to be found. He was equally adept at stealing a good woman's virtue.

An unlikely alley, but a useful one. If he was still around, he would certainly be able to take the children where they needed to go. And then Michael could return to his life of seclusion.

But why? thought the hermit as he crossed over the wide, paved street. *Why not go with them? I have started something and I should see it through. Once, I would have done so without question.*

But then he shook his head, cursing himself for a fool. *That's not who I am any more. If I had to face Salin again, I'd fall to my knees in quivering terror. I'm no longer even a match for a child like Tor.*

But what if Shad was dead, or imprisoned, or simply gone? Would Michael leave the children to fend for themselves? He resolved not to think about it until he had no other options. Instead, he hurried into the eastern quarter of town, where the poor folk and the riff-raff made their homes.

Michael felt somewhat nervous as he passed the street dividing center city from the eastern quarter. Almost at once he felt dark eyes upon him. Dusk had embraced Bordonhold, a dangerous time to be in this part of the city. The hermit put his hand on the hilt of his sword, attempting to look like he remembered how to use it. Once, he could have passed through here unarmed in the dead of night with all the confidence in the world. Now, it was all he could do to keep moving down the dark street.

He had learned to live with his fear. Fear had caused him to assume the life of a hermit. Fear coupled with apathy. Strange bedfellows they were, his fear of his incapacity to save the world and his inability to care. For years, they had rendered him useless. And since he had met Mason, and agreed to lead him here, his fear had grown. Salin Urdrokk had resurfaced, and instead of hiding like any other sane, impotent human being, Michael was staying close to the exact thing the sorcerer was searching for. He must have gone mad.

Lost in his musings, he almost didn't notice when he reached the little shack that had once been the home of Shad Flynt. It had not changed in all these years, except it appeared a little more weather-worn. The hermit knocked four times on the door in a pattern that had, many years ago, been his signature knock; the secret knock of their circle.

After a long moment, he heard someone shuffling slowly toward the door. There was a clang as a deadbolt drew back and the door opened a crack. The face peeking out was old, creased, and scared. Gray eyes squinted in suspicious caution and then widened in recognition.

"By the Seven! When I heard the knock, I couldn't believe…but now! Michael, come in! Come in!"

"Shad?" questioned Michael. Nothing about this old, broken man reminded him of his old associate. He was thin and hunched, his gray hair thin and unkempt. When he walked, he limped, heavily favoring his right leg.

"That's me," said Shad. "Although I go by Jak now. Old Jak, they call me. Wounds, it's been forever. What brings you here? I expect it is no social visit."

"I fear not, old friend," said Michael. Shad groaned as he lowered himself into a hard wooden chair which sat next to a plain table. Michael sat across the table from him and looked around the room. There was no decor on the walls or floor, and besides the table and chair there was only a small woodstove in the room. An open doorway led to a tiny bedroom.

"As I expected. But please, humor an old man. What have you been doing all these years? You haven't changed at all."

Michael shook his head. "Nothing at all. It all became too much for me. The constant planning, fighting a war we could never win. Falling out with my brothers."

"You shouldn't have concerned yourself with what they thought. They were high and mighty, pompous fools. What ever became of them, anyway?"

Michael shrugged. "I do not know and I do not care. You know we hardly spoke even back then. But what of you? What have you been up to?"

Shad smiled sadly. "For the last fifteen years I've just been sitting in this shack, growing older. Before that, I was at the height of my career. Then I…took a fall off a balcony. The leg's never been the same. Later, a case of Red Fever took my health. Shad Flynt was dead and gone then. I changed my name to Jak hoping all the enemies I've made over the years wouldn't be able to track me down with a new name. It either worked, or they decided an old, pathetic man wasn't worth the trouble, because I'm still here."

Michael smiled sympathetically. Inwardly, he winced. This old man could not help him. Yet, he still owed Shad an explanation for his visit. "I have a problem, Shad. I have come from Barton Hills, bringing three children with me. One of the children, Alec Mason, bears the Talisman of Unity."

"By the One!" exclaimed Shad, his gray eyes bulging.

"That is not all. A dark sorcerer covets the Talisman, and with his minions has pursued us here. That sorcerer is Salin Urdrokk."

Shad's mouth moved, but words did not come. His hands, folded on the table, began to shake. As with Michael, the years had robbed him of his courage. "Salin. Salin. Legends become real. Demons live again. The world grows ever closer to falling to the Seth."

"I wish I could comfort you, but I share your fears. I had hoped to find someone here to lead the children to the only place they and the Talisman could be protected from Salin. But you are the only one left of our old circle. And you are…" he trailed off, not knowing what to say.

"Not up to the job. I understand your disappointment. And I understand why you are unwilling to go yourself. There are few Shapers left who are a match for Salin Urdrokk. So say the legends, anyway; that sorcerer has never before surfaced in my lifetime."

"You are wise to trust the legends. Take me at my word: there are *no* Shapers left who can match his sorcery. Even among the Fairies you will not find his equal. Only his master is greater."

Shad placed his hands flat on the table to stop their shaking. His eyes met Michael's, and he steadied his voice. "I know where you mean for the children to go. I cannot help you, but I know of one who can. There is one man in this town I trust, and he knows the way. If there is anyone who can get them there ahead of Salin, it is him. He's quick and clever, and he's good with a sword."

"Who is this man?"

Shad rubbed his eyes, as if he was hesitant to say more. "I must warn you, he has been going through a bad time. Many see him only as the town drunk, a fool to be laughed at or ignored. But he has been my friend for several years, and I know there is more to him than is readily apparent. I know little of his past, but I know his skills. And I know his heart. If I can talk to him, get him away from the drink, I know he'll be able to help us."

Michael wasn't so sure. A drunk? Once, he would have trusted Shad's judgment implicitly…but now…? "His name, Shad. Let us start with his name."

"He is called Lorn."

CHAPTER 9

Lorn

The next morning, Alec awakened early. Looking across the room, he saw Sarah still sleeping in her bed. He looked at her for a time and a feeling of affection rose in his chest. She looked so beautiful lying there, her youthful face at peace, her chest slowly rising and falling under the blanket. Alec smiled and got out of bed, still somewhat stiff but feeling well rested. He hurried into his new clothes, appreciating the feeling of the clean, new fabric upon his skin. Then he gently shook Sarah, who smiled at him as she woke.

"Is it morning already? I felt so wonderful sleeping in this bed. And safe, too."

Alec softly touched her cheek. "It was a good night. But we need to get up now. It's early, but I'm sure Michael will want to tell us what he's been up to. With luck, we can put this whole thing behind us this morning."

"I hope so, Alec. Grok, I hope so."

Alec took his small, silver chest from under the bed, placed it in his sack, and then covered it with his old clothes. Then, heading for the door, he said, "I'll see if they're up yet. Then I'll wait out in the hall while you dress."

"Thanks," she said, climbing out of bed. Alec hurried to avert his eyes, but still managed to catch a glimpse of her in undergarments. He quickened his pace and left the room before she could see him blush.

Kraig was in his room, sitting on his bed and pulling on his boots. "Good morning," he said as Alec came in. "Michael's already downstairs. Apparently, he's found some folks who can help us. He wants us to go down to meet them right away."

"Good. I'm ready to see the end of this."

"So am I. The sooner I get home, the better. Why, I bet old Derik is lost without me. I doubt there's anyone in Barton Hills who is qualified to be the tavern's peacekeeper."

Alec laughed. "There sure isn't anyone as big as you are."

When Kraig was ready, they went into the hall to wait for Sarah. She joined them shortly, looking beautiful in her new dress. It was long, but not bulky: a traveling dress. Its colors were conservative green and brown, but its neckline was lower than the norm in Barton Hills. Still, it was not nearly so revealing as the dresses worn by Glinda or many of the other women Alec had seen in the city. At any rate, Sarah seemed more than pleased with herself as she twirled to show off her new attire.

They went down the stairs and entered the common room, which was empty but for a few of the inn's guests eating breakfast. At an isolated table in the back of the room, Michael sat with two men. One was old and bent, his gray hair thin and long. Alec thought he recognized the other man, a tall, muscular man with long black hair and rough but handsome features. Then it struck him: it was the drunk who had been thrown from the inn the previous night!

"I don't believe it," he said, pointing. "The drunk. Remember?"

Sarah rolled her eyes, and Kraig frowned. "What's going on here?" he muttered.

Unable to answer, Alec silently led the way to the table. Michael waved them closer, motioning them into chairs. When they were seated, he introduced his companions.

"I trust you slept well, my friends. This is an old associate of mine, Shad Flynt. He has just introduced me to his friend Lorn, who has agreed to guide you to a safe haven."

Kraig pounded the table with his fist. "I'm tired of your games, Michael. We aren't prepared to go running off again, especially not with some drunken fool! This Lorn fellow was thrown out of the inn last night, obviously full of drink he was unable to pay for."

The man known as Lorn shifted uncomfortably. "I am not proud of my actions last night. I have not been...well, lately."

"Not been well," snarled Kraig. "I've seen your sort too many times to be taken in by such utter..."

"Please!" shouted Michael, his voice loud but conveying as little emotion as his face. "Allow Shad to speak. I have known him long and trust him completely. If he will vouch for this man, then so will I."

The old man nodded. "Thank you, old friend. Now, young ones, Michael has told me you bear a precious burden. It is imperative we keep it away from Salin and take it to the one place it can be protected from him…and the one place where it can be used properly."

"And where is that?" interrupted Alec.

Shad looked at him quizzically. "Why, Faerie, of course! It is a long way, through dangerous territory, but Lorn can lead you there."

"Faerie!" cried Alec. "Lead us? Grok's wounds, we can't go to Faerie."

"But you must, you see," said Shad. "The Talisman of Unity belongs to the King of the Fairies. In his hands, it will unite the Fair Folk and restore them to their former greatness. It was a sad day for the Fair Folk when the Talisman was lost, and they will rejoice to have it restored to them."

"All well and good," said Sarah. "Why don't you take it to them?"

"Look at me and you will know the answer. I am old, and unfit for such a perilous journey. But even if I could take it, you would have to go as well, both for your own safety, and for other reasons. Unless things have changed greatly, evil cannot enter the forests of the Fair Folk. The Fairy Shapers protect their lands with powerful enchantments even the Seth cannot yet break. Salin will hunt you down wherever you go, whether you still possess the Talisman or not. He believes you have cheated him, and he will not rest until you pay the price for your actions. Only in Faerie will you be safe."

Alec nodded, believing Salin was capable of holding such a grudge. "You said there were other reasons."

"Indeed, but I am not free to speak of all I know…or suspect. Just know this, Alec Mason. It is no accident that it was you who discovered the Talisman. Such artifacts do not just fall into someone's hands at random. Throughout history, it has been shown time and time again that the most powerful artifacts of magic place themselves into the hands of people who can do the most good with them. The Talisman chose you, Alec."

Alec laughed. "That's ridiculous."

"Is it indeed?" said Shad, smiling. "Tell me, how did you find it?"

"Well, in a chest. In the basement of Sarah's mother's shop, when I was helping them bring some things upstairs."

"And did you know this chest was there, Sarah?"

The girl tilted her head and frowned. "Well, yes. My mother pointed it out to me once when I was just a child."

Shad smiled. "And were you never curious what was inside?"

"We couldn't open the chest. My mother once said she had the blacksmith try to crack it open with his hammer, and even that would not work. She shoved it under the stairs and forgot about it."

"Interesting. And yet Alec here comes along, and just opens it right up."

Alec wanted to shake his head and deny it, but he couldn't. That was just what had happened. But the Talisman *choosing* him? Choosing *him?* Inanimate objects could not make choices, of course, but if they could, why him?

"All right," said Alec. "Suppose I agree I have to go to…to Faerie. Why would I follow this Lorn, who I don't know at all?"

Shad looked at his younger companion and grew serious. "I have known Lorn for several years now, and I would trust him with my life. He is a fair swordsman and a good pathfinder. Besides, he has been to Faerie before."

Alec, Sarah, Kraig, and even Michael turned their heads to the grim looking man in disbelief. Lorn bowed his head when he saw so many eyes upon him, unable to meet their gaze.

"It is exceedingly rare to find a human who has entered the Fairy lands," said Michael. "If this is true, then I cannot imagine a better guide."

"Well I can," said Kraig. "Look at him. The way he holds himself. The way he can't look into our eyes. Without a bottle in his hand, he cannot even function."

With obvious effort, Lorn raised his head. His eyes focused on the wall beyond Alec's head, and his jaw trembled as he spoke. "It is true I have nearly ruined myself with drink. Through it all, only Shad has stood by me. He has always had faith in me, even though I no longer have faith in myself. But would you not be the same as me if you had walked the paths I've walked?

"Nearly four years ago was I cast out of my home by my own brother, banished from my country and forced to walk the lands as a pauper. It seemed a curse was upon me, for I could find no friends, no job. In these dark times strangers are looked upon with suspicion, especially strangers with no silver, no possessions, no friends or family. I wandered hungry and tired for years, until finally I came to Tyridan. Here, in one of the few lands that have not yet felt the Seth's dark touch, I finally found a home. A few friends. But my despair grew still, and only ale and wine could ease my pain. And so I drink…but my money runs out…and I…I despise what I have become." He buried his head on the table, unable to finish his tale.

Shad looked sadly at the others. "When we first met, he had just come into town. He was too thin, starving, and I felt pity and took him in. With food and friendly companionship, he grew strong and his sadness lessened. He found my old sword and began to practice with it. He has a knowledge of the old forms, the forms the old sword masters once used. Lorn will not speak of where he learned such forms, but I must say they have come in handy a few times. There are rogues who walk these streets, you know, and an old man like me is an easy target. But not when I walked with Lorn.

"But then, a year ago, Lorn heard some news which broke his spirit. Do not bother asking him what the news was; he has never revealed it even to me. But it cast him back into his old despair. He began drinking, lost his job. His other friends abandoned him. He had never been truly happy, but I thought we were making progress. I thought he could be saved." He looked at Lorn with pity and affection. "I still believe it is so."

Lorn lifted his head and took a deep breath. Alec could almost feel strain pouring from the man. It took vast effort for him to face them and speak.

"After I left here last night, Shad and your Michael found me passed out in the street. They talked to me long into the night, badgering me to take you to Faerie. Shad believes it is my last hope at redemption. I for one do not believe in redemption, not for one who has fallen so far as I have. And yet...I cannot stay here. This life I have attempted to build for myself has failed. And I cannot refuse the wish of my last friend. I will lead you and protect you with my own life."

Alec didn't know what to think, but Kraig was not at all convinced. "Excuse me if I don't feel sorry for you. Everyone has choices in life. You didn't have to become a drunk, no matter what terrible news you heard. So your brother cast you out of your home. Were you not man enough to build a new home for yourself? Or take a stand and demand justice? I look at you and see only weakness."

For an instant, Alec thought there would be a fight. Lorn met Kraig's gaze for the first time, his eyes alight with fire. His shame had suddenly become burning passion, and his eyes gleamed hotly. His posture, slack and indifferent, became firm and strong. His hands curled into fists and slammed the table.

But as suddenly as it had come, the passion was gone. The fire died, and Lorn's eyes became gray, his body limp and powerless. "Weakness? Yes. I have become weak. Yet I was not always so. Once, in my youth, I proudly journeyed to Faerie with my father and my brother, to meet the Fairy-King as emissaries from our country. We braved the wild lands with no fear and entered into the magical forest of the Fair Folk with our heads high. I have fallen far indeed, but I still know the way to Faerie. If anyone can get you there, I can. I beg you. I have no purpose in my life. My dreams are shattered. Allow me to be your guide. If you do not…I will return to my ale and my wine. As you say, I am weak."

There was a long moment of silence and Alec glanced at his companions. Kraig sat stone-faced and silent. Michael's thoughts remained hidden behind his calm, pale face. But Sarah's eyes betrayed pity and her mouth frowned sadly. A tear rolled gently down her cheek.

"Lorn," she said. "Kraig is right about one thing. There are always choices. I guess you've been making the wrong ones up to now, but I want to help you turn your life around. You know how dangerous leading us will be, yet you ask to join us. I don't call this weakness at all. I call it courage. I want you to be our guide to Faerie."

Alec looked at her with wonder and admiration. He'd always felt Sarah was a good judge of character, and she saw something worthy in this Lorn. In her compassion, she had taken a chance on the man. That was enough for Alec.

"Then I, too, think you should join us. As long as you understand there will be no time for drinking or feeling sorry for yourself. A powerful sorcerer is after us…after me, and what I carry. We'll have to hurry if we hope to survive."

Lorn, surprisingly, smiled slyly. "I'm afraid of a lot of things, but sorcerers do not frighten me."

Alec, confused, said, "This one should. Why do you not fear…?"

"You two have lost your minds!" exclaimed Kraig. "I can't believe you feel for this man! He as much as admitted he's a weak-willed fool. If he doesn't betray us, he'll abandon us when things get rough."

"It appears you are outvoted, peacekeeper," said Michael. "Alec and Sarah have agreed to travel with Lorn. After all, Shad knows him well…"

"Does he? Very well, Shad, tell us more about your friend. Where did he come from?"

The old man opened his mouth, but after a moment, he closed it again. He lowered his eyes and said, "I do not know. Lorn has not been forthcoming about the details of his past."

"I see," said Kraig. "You don't know where he comes from. You don't even know if Lorn is his real name. What was his job before he came to Tyridan?"

"Well, he has stated he was an emissary of some sort, and his skill with the sword suggests…"

"It suggests he could be a pirate, a thief, a hired killer. As for being an 'emissary,' that could mean almost anything. He could be a representative of a powerful lord or a guild of assassins."

Shad turned to Lorn for help, but the long-haired man buried his head in his hands and said nothing. Kraig nodded triumphantly, but Michael would not let him have the last word.

"Nevertheless, no other choice remains before you. I cannot go any further, nor can you find Faerie on your own. You cannot remain here, and rest assured Salin will find you where ever you may go. I very strongly suggest you take Lorn up on his offer."

Kraig stood up in a rage, knocking his chair onto the floor. He pointed a heavy, accusing finger at the hermit. "I don't take orders from you. I don't *trust* you. You're as much of a mystery as Lorn. I will *not* be a part of this anymore! Good luck, Alec. If you choose to trust these madmen, you're on your own." He turned quickly and stormed out of the room.

Alec watched him go, and then turned to face Sarah. Her brow was creased with sadness. "He can't mean that," Sarah said. "He can't leave us."

"He won't," said Alec. "He'll see there's no other choice, and he'll come around."

"I wish I could be sure," said Sarah.

Alec also wished he was sure.

Lorn slowly raised his head. There were tears in his eyes. His voice quivered weakly as he spoke. "His concerns are justified. But I cannot speak of my past. The past is dead to me. If I drudge up old memories…even just to relate my story…I will break down again. I have said too much already. I am Lorn. I have no family, no past. I have no loyalties and no hidden agenda for which I would betray you. There is no more about me you must know. If you will still have me as a guide, we must leave as soon as you are ready. As I understand it, this Salin is eager to get his hands on you, and one of his servants knows where you are. We must flee quickly, in a direction they are not likely to suspect."

"Yes," said Michael. "They may realize your intention to go to Faerie, which lies through the wilderness to the north. They will not think you would risk traveling westward, toward regions closer to the influence of Vorik Seth."

Alec said, "Fine. We will gather our things, and then head west. I can't say I fully disagree with Kraig's reasoning, but I fear there are no other options for me."

Shad breathed a sigh of relief. "I believe with your choice you may have saved your own life, and Lorn's soul, and quite possibly this entire land. I fear you still do not know the importance of that which you carry."

"May he never need to find out," said Michael. "Now, if all is decided, I will go rest. I have had a difficult night."

Michael and Shad excused themselves and left the table. Lorn, too, got up to leave, telling Alec and Sarah that he would meet them here in an hour, prepared for the journey. Alec looked at his companion, who met his gaze sadly.

"I'm worried," she said. "Shad seems nice, and Lorn sounds sincere, but what if Kraig is right? What if Lorn is like that awful Tor, and is using the *Charin-Ta* on us? What if he works for Salin, too?"

Alec shook his head. "I don't think so. Shad's known him for quite a while, and Shad and Michael are old friends. Michael's given us no reason not to trust him, and if he can vouch for Shad Flynt, then I think we can trust Shad's judgment. I have to believe Lorn won't betray us."

"Now if only we can convince Kraig."

Alec put his hand on Sarah's. She grasped it tightly and smiled warmly at the baker. He couldn't help smiling back. They rose together and went upstairs to their room, hand in hand, to prepare for the journey ahead.

Kraig had been brooding for nearly half an hour, walking the streets around the inn called Home. He was conflicted over his decision. After doing some more thinking, he had realized there was no choice for Alec. He had to go with Lorn. Kraig cursed himself for choosing to abandon Alec and Sarah, but what else could he do? Since the beginning of this horrible affair they'd had to trust people of dubious virtue. First the mysterious and infuriating hermit and then the imposing Horren. Then they made the mistake of trusting the so-called Watcher named Tor; now they were being asked to trust Lorn. It was quite possible he would lead them directly to Salin. And if not, even if he was sincere, he was a weak fool. He would most certainly fail them in their time of need.

But there was another alternative. Kraig did not have to abandon his friends, and he did not have to trust Lorn. He didn't like this new possibility, but it seemed to be the only other option.

I can't believe I'm thinking this.

Quickly, with renewed purpose, he marched back to the inn. Once there, he jogged up the stairs to the room he shared with Michael, and forcefully threw the door open.

The hermit, who had been sleeping on his bed, sat up quickly, his eyes wide with uncharacteristic surprise. It was only a second, however, before his face resumed its neutral expression.

Kraig's face was hard, filled with controlled anger. His hands were in fists. He suspected Michael could read his emotion. He hoped he could.

"Michael. No more secrets. No more games. Let's talk."

An hour had passed. Alec and Sarah had gathered their few possessions and had returned to the common room of the inn. Lorn was there already, a worn leather backpack over one shoulder and a chipped long sword hanging at his side. He had tied his long, dark hair in a pony-tail, which made him appear slightly less wild. Because of his unkempt beard, however, Alec thought he still looked somewhat mad. On the table in front of him were two bulging water-skins and a large package of trail rations he had obtained for the journey. When he spoke, he exhibited more confidence than before, but he still would not meet Alec's gaze.

"Just the three of us, then? I am sorry your friend could not be convinced to trust me. Still, each man must go his own way."

Alec shrugged. "I just didn't expect him to go his own way so quickly. Just a moment ago I checked his room, and neither he nor Michael were anywhere to be found. I suppose they were both serious about putting this journey behind them."

Lorn looked around the room warily. "And now we must put this town behind us. If you are pursued as you say, you have been here too long already."

"Agreed," said Alec. "Lead on, then."

And so they left the inn and headed toward the west gate of Bordonhold. Alec took the opportunity to take in the sights of the city one last time. It was still early in the day, but already the hawkers were out on the street, crying out the benefits of their fresh bread, fish, and milk; their wool, silk, and cotton; their fine capes and peasants robes. Shops and homes lined the streets, as well as many taverns, from which wafted the tempting smells of cooking meats. They even passed a large bakery, and Alec stared after it longingly. He could smell fresh bread and sweet cakes baking within. He thought of his master, Stan Kulnip, and longed to return to his simple life and his chosen craft. But there was no returning. Stan was dead and Barton Hills was a week's journey behind him.

They progressed into the western quarter of town, which Alec immediately guessed to be a poorer section. The streets became cracked, and soon were no longer paved at all. The houses became smaller, less well built, and the shops and inns vanished entirely. Loud, boisterous noise spilled out of the occasional tavern, sometimes laughter, but just as often sounds of fighting. Lorn stiffened at the sound and quickened his pace.

"Here can be found some of the most unsavory elements of Bordonhold. I would not walk these streets alone, and never at night."

They walked onward quickly, and within an hour they reached the west gate unmolested. Lorn had resisted an earlier attempt by Sarah to begin a conversation, and since then they had walked in silence. As they progressed through the western quarter, Lorn had grown more and more agitated, looking over his shoulder time and again. His face was drawn in worry. When they were within a few hundred feet of the gate, he spoke.

"I think someone is following us. I caught a glimpse of a shadowy figure…but perhaps it is only my mind…drink has shattered my nerves, my capacity to think. I do not know if what I see is real anymore." He stopped walking and hid his face in his hands.

"Wounds, Lorn!" said Alec, annoyed their guide was falling back into his self-pity. "We have to assume what you think you've seen is real! Get a hold of yourself; we need you!"

With effort, Lorn lowered his arms and looked toward the gate. "We must make haste," was all he said.

Alec and Sarah could barely keep up with the pace he set. Lorn shouted to the gatekeeper, who opened the gate without a word. Apparently, there was no speech upon leaving the town as there was upon entering. A small thing, but Alec was grateful there would be no delays. They passed through the gate, and started down a slender dirt trail leading immediately into a dense wood.

"Only tiny villages and outposts lie along this road," said Lorn. "Few people live this far north, outside the borders of the city. After we are well away from the gates, we will turn northward toward the wilderness. Far to the north lies the land of Faerie."

The trees grew tall around them, seeming to bend over them threateningly. The leafy canopy overhead closed off much of the sunlight, and the forest grew increasingly darker. Alec thought he could hear something in the wind, like the sound of many voices moaning in agony. It sent a chill through him. Sarah shivered as well, wrapping her arms defensively around herself. She moved in close to Alec as they walked, and he put his arm protectively around her. The voices in the trees became clearer.

"There's something out there," whispered Sarah.

"It's only the wind," reassured Alec, uncertainly.

As if to confirm Sarah's whispered fear, Lorn came to a halt, his hand going to his sword hilt. "Something is not right here."

"What is it?" asked Alec, his eyes wide with fear.

"The noises of the forest are wrong. The trees speak...with fear. It is the sound of..."

Lorn never finished his sentence. He leaped back, just as a spear lanced the ground where he had been. He stumbled back, unable to maintain his balance. Falling, he launched himself at Alec and Sarah, pulling them to the ground as three more spears passed over their heads.

"Grok!" cried Alec, just as Sarah shouted "Wounds!"

The moaning of the wind raised in pitch until it became the falsetto cackle of goblin laughter. Suddenly a score of the ugly little creatures leapt from the trees, laughing and shouting their blistering war cry. Many had spears and several held long stone knives. Alec's heart threatened to burst from his chest as fear overwhelmed him. He was weaponless and surrounded. He looked to Lorn, but the tall man was still on the ground, cowering behind upraised arms.

Two goblins raced toward Sarah while the others surrounded them. Alec cried out and leapt to his feet, throwing himself in front of the helpless girl. The first goblin reached him and stabbed outward with his knife. Alec swung the sack he was carrying and batted the knife aside. Then he brought the sack around a second time, the silver chest within cracking the second goblin on the skull, knocking it down. The first creature readied its knife for a second pass. Alec saw the goblin out of the corner of his eye, but was off balance and unable to bring the sack around for another parry.

Sarah's leg jutted outward in front of Alec, into the path of the charging goblin. It tripped and screamed, its knife flailing uselessly through the air. Alec took advantage of the moment Sarah had gained him, and slammed his boot down on the fallen goblin's head. Disgust welled in his stomach as the skull cracked, but it was coupled with relief.

The relief lasted only a moment. The circle of goblins tightened around them, and more dropped from the trees. Then the circle parted, and a much larger, more muscular goblin entered the circle. He wore chain mail and carried a heavy mace. The gold necklace and earrings he wore designated him as a clan chief, a rank which only the strongest and smartest goblins attained.

"Salin will pay us well for your head, boy!" grunted the creature. He twirled his heavy mace easily, and closed in on Alec and Sarah.

"Lorn!" cried Alec. But a quick glance showed him the man had curled up on the ground, shaking in fear.

A cry rang out beyond the circle of goblins. Suddenly blood sprayed through the air, and two goblin heads thunked as they struck the ground. An axe flashed again before the stunned creatures could recover, and Kraig brought down another, cleaving a mighty gash in its chest.

On the other side of the circle, the bright, rune-emblazoned sword which had belonged to Tor cut a swath through the goblins. Disbelief overwhelmed Alec as four of the creatures fell to Michael's wrath in the blink of an eye. The hermit, his eyes cold and dead, expertly knocked spears aside with his blade and effortlessly parried flashing knives. The goblins lost interest in Alec, Sarah, and Lorn and turned to face their unexpected attackers.

All except the chief. He would not be distracted from his prize. He advanced on Alec, leaving his minions to their fate. Alec bent down and picked up a knife, fearing he would be no match for the goblin chief. He glanced around quickly and saw he would not be receiving any help from Michael or Kraig. More goblins had converged on those two, threatening to overwhelm them with shear numbers.

"Come on then," said Alec. "I won't go down without a fight."

But Sarah must have known it was a fight her companion could not win. She ran back to where Lorn lay and began to beat on him with her small fists. "Get up! Grok, that thing will kill us all. To hell with you, you coward! Kraig was right about you! Kraig was *right!*"

Alec saw Lorn look up, his eyes red with tears. But then he was forced to turn away, for the goblin chief was upon him. The thing laughed as it brought its mace down toward Alec's skull. The baker leaped aside and the mace struck the ground inches to his left. He lashed out with his knife, but the goblin backed away from the blow. Impossibly fast, it brought the mace around again, forcing Alec to stumble back. But the mace came around too quickly, and struck Alec's outstretched arm. Pain surged through him, and the knife few from his hand. The force of the blow knocked him to the ground. Pain filled his arm, and his side burned as his old wound nearly reopened.

Through tear-filled eyes, Alec saw his end coming. As if in slow motion, the big spiked head of the mace fell toward him. A laugh erupted in his ears, and all his vision was filled with the dark form of the goblin and its mace. Then another dark form, larger than the goblin, entered his line of sight. It smashed the goblin-form aside, and the mace never landed.

He rubbed the tears from his eyes, and his vision cleared. Lorn stood over him, his eyes red with grief and rage. His chest heaved with effort, with anger. "Rise, goblin," he said, his voice hard and cold. "I have something to prove here."

"You wish to prove your blood is red?" cried the goblin chief, leaping to its feet. "Then let us dance!"

And to Alec it appeared they did indeed engage in a dance, for there was a raw beauty to the goblin's movements, and an elegant grace to Lorn's. The heavy mace whirled through the air, sometimes from right to left, sometimes from high to low. One solid blow against an unarmored man would be fatal, yet not one blow did land. Lorn ducked and spun out of the way, moving with a grace Alec had never before seen. And his sword flashed time and time again, sometimes turned by the goblin's armor, sometimes missing its mark due to the goblin's own quickness, but occasionally drawing some blood.

For a full minute the dance lasted, until Lorn leaped over a low swing, thrusting his blade forth while the goblin was in mid-swing. His sword passed easily through the creature's soft neck. The heavy mace dropped to the dirt, and the goblin slid wetly off the long blade, dead before it hit the ground.

Sarah had cowered against Alec. "Look!" she cried, pointing off to the left. He pulled his amazed eyes away from Lorn, and saw Kraig still battling several of the little beasts. A pile of dead goblins was stacked up around him, but now it was apparent his blows were weaker and slower. He was nearing his limit. Soon, a spear or knife would find its mark.

Michael was likewise occupied. Only three goblins still threatened him, but it was clear he could not reach Kraig in time.

Lorn leapt with incredible speed toward the peacekeeper. His blood-stained sword arced outward, carving open two of Kraig's attackers. The remaining three creatures turned their twisted faces toward the new threat, allowing Kraig to stumble back out of harm's way. Two spears thrust toward Lorn, but he knocked them aside with a flick of his blade. With a low sweep of his leg, he caught the nearest two goblins behind the knees, sending them gracelessly to the ground. Two quick slashes opened their necks. The last goblin turned to flee, only to have his head spit by Kraig's axe.

Alec's heart pounded madly. He turned his attention to Michael, and saw him sitting calmly on a fallen log, cleaning his sword with a piece of cloth torn from a goblin's shirt. The ambush had been thwarted. No goblins had escaped.

"Grok's wounds," whispered Alec, relief pouring through him. "We're alive."

Sarah sighed silently, but did not let go of his arm. Her head was buried in his shoulder. She had nothing to say.

Alec put his arms around her and held her for a long moment. He closed his eyes and imagined he was far away, surrounded by green fields, alone with Sarah. But his illusion was fragile and was soon shattered by a hand on his shoulder. He looked upward to see Kraig staring down at him, a sad half-smile on his face.

"I thought you weren't coming," said Alec.

Kraig breathed deeply and ran his hand through his hair. "I couldn't let you go through this alone. It's a good thing we caught up with you when we did."

Alec stroked Sarah's hair as he held her, his compassion for her growing. *I wish I could protect her from all this.* "What about Michael? I thought he was gone for sure."

The burly man shrugged. "We had a little talk about responsibility. I managed to get him to see things my way."

"Thank Grok!"

Lorn had joined them, his bloody sword sheathed. His eyes still held the fire sparked by the attack, by Sarah's hard words. He looked Kraig in the eye, and for a long moment they held each others' gaze. No words needed to be said. Alec knew they had silently come to terms with one another. At last Lorn turned away. He walked toward the fallen goblin chief and said, "We had best be on our way. Likely this is not the only trap Salin has lain for us."

Alec got up slowly, helping Sarah to her feet. He touched her under her chin, and lifted her face to meet his. A few tears were drying on her cheeks.

"It's over, Sarah. We are safe."

She bowed her head. "No we're not. These horrible…*things*…keep finding us. It's only a matter of time before…but that's not it. That's not why I'm crying. I'm scared I'll never see Mother again, even if she is alive. I'm afraid our lives, as we've known them, are over. What futures can we ever have now?"

"It will be all right. When Lorn gets us to Faerie, this will be over. The Talisman belongs to the Fair Folk. They'll know what to do with it. And then we'll be free."

"I don't know. Will we ever be free of Salin?"

Salin. Alec wished to Grok he'd never heard his name. The truth was, he didn't believe the sorcerer would ever give up his vendetta. But he hoped the magic of the Fairies was equal to his sorcery. It was the only way he could think of that he would be able to return to his village, resume his life. He had to return. He was the baker of Barton Hills now.

Wounds, that's all I want out of life. Just to go home and master my craft. And Sarah. Grok help me, I want Sarah.

Alec took Sarah by the hand and led her toward the others. Lorn had removed the chain armor from the goblin-chief and was draping it over his own torso. Alec's stomach churned when he thought of taking anything from the goblin corpses, but he overcame his disgust to grab a couple stone knives from the ground. One he gave to Sarah, and one he placed in his belt.

"Just in case this happens again," he muttered.

Kraig wiped his axe on a goblin's body and slid the handle under his belt. "Let's go," he said.

As they headed westward down the trail, Alec looked over his shoulder. Michael was still sitting by the tree, staring at his sword. Alec was about to tell Lorn and the others to stop and wait, but the hermit rose and followed them at a distance. He made no effort to catch up to them, and he avoided eye contact.

"Why is Michael so...distant?" Alec asked Kraig.

"I think he's ashamed of his behavior before. He was ready to abandon us to our fate. He started us down this path, and I made him see if he didn't see this thing through, then he was as much of a coward as I thought Lorn was. He always talked about how important it was to keep the Talisman away from Salin. I told him if it fell into Salin's hands, it was his fault. If he abandoned us. I think I finally got through to him."

"He didn't seem to care before."

"No. But the way he talks, the things he knows...they led me to believe he was *someone* once. Someone important. Someone who cared. I think I found a little piece of that person inside him. Enough, anyway, to convince him to come with us to Faerie."

Alec was impressed. "I didn't know you were such an expert in human nature," he said, smiling.

Kraig laughed softly. "There's more to being a peacekeeper than cracking heads."

And so they trekked onward, following Lorn through the forest. The long-haired man rarely spoke or acknowledged his companions, but he stood erect and strode with confidence. The fire slowly left his eyes, but some spark of it remained in the way he moved, fluidly and surely. It seemed the Lorn they had met in Bordonhold was gone, at least for the present. For this, Alec was glad. But still great uncertainty troubled him. He was worried about Sarah, and he wondered if she was right.

Will we ever be free of Salin?

Tor felt his stomach twist itself into about a hundred little knots. He always became ill when he had to report a failure to his master. It was only three days ago he had returned to Quintin Flat with the news he had been thwarted in his first attempt to retrieve the Talisman. After a rigorous and painful punishment, he had been sent out of the farming village Salin had taken over to set ambushes all around Bordonhold. The journey was not long, as Salin had chosen Quintin Flat due to its proximity to Mason's probable destination. And so Tor had assembled his stupid goblin troops and set them near each of the four gates of Bordonhold. Surely thirty goblins at each gate would be enough to stop a naive fool like Mason and his companions.

But it was not enough. When Tor had come across the slaughter beyond the west gate, he had to clench his fists to keep them from beating against trees, hurling little corpses through the air. Somehow, the fat little baker had escaped the goblins.

No. Not escaped them. *Massacred* them. By the Seth, who was he traveling with?

He could not dwell on the question now. Salin had come to Bordonhold, and Tor had to deliver his report.

Tor pushed people out of his way, forcing his way through the throng. The streets were packed with city-folk, and the warrior didn't have the time or patience to walk at their slow pace. The glares of the weak men he shoved or the old women he pushed down amused him. If the situation hadn't been so urgent, he would have been enjoying himself.

Soon he came to the inn where his master was staying. The Old Bull was huge, reputedly the largest inn in the northern district. It was rumored to be a favorite haunt of thieves and ruffians, but that didn't stop it from being a center for entertainment and revelry. Always crowded, it was a perfect place for Salin to hide. Despite his occasional outbursts, he was a master at blending in with a crowd. Tor, on the other hand, preferred to work with smaller groups. His greatest weapon was his mastery of the *Charin-ta*, which worked best when only a few victims were to be influenced.

He entered the building and was surprised the common room was nearly empty. Despite the fact it was nearly dinner time, only a handful of patrons sat around the tables. The corner of the room, usually reserved for minstrels, poets, or other entertainers, was bare and silent. At the far end of the room, a dusty gray cloak pulled over his spotted flesh, sat Salin Urdrokk.

The knots in Tor's stomach wound tighter as he forced himself to slowly saunter toward the sorcerer. He held his head high and stood erect, but his hands kept curling into fists. Droplets of sweat began to form on his brow by the time he faced his master.

"I thought you would never arrive," said Salin.

"I came as quickly as I could. They left through the west gate."

Salin's frown showed Tor the sorcerer guessed what had happened. "The ambush was not a success, I take it."

"No, master. I fear Mason has found skillful companions."

"Sit down, Tor."

Tor hesitated a moment, knowing a calm Salin could be more dangerous than an angry one. Then he pulled out a chair and sat across from his master.

"You know," began the sorcerer, folding his hands in front of him, "I fear I have made mistakes in dealing with this Alec Mason. I thought him to be a fool, easily intimidated by my show of power at Barton Hills. I should have sought him out quietly, slew him in secret, and taken the Talisman. But sometimes I grow angry, Tor. You know that, don't you?"

Salin's mirthless grin filled Tor with fear. "Yes, master."

"And when I am angry, I must destroy things. And slaughter people. It is my one vice, I fear, but one I can live with. When Mason didn't bring me the Talisman like he had promised, I am afraid I just couldn't control myself. I dislike when people break promises."

Tor's heart jumped to his throat. "Of—of course."

"Did you not tell me you would bring me the Talisman? Did you not assure me…*promise* me…the ambush would be a success?"

His knuckles grew white from grasping the arms of his chair. "I…I did, my master."

Salin breathed deeply, closing his eyes as he exhaled slowly. "Then you must make sure your *promise* is kept. They cannot have gotten far. I will accompany you to the woods to the west. I suspect they are still on foot, so with our horses we should be able to quickly overtake the fools."

Tor didn't realize he had been holding his breath until he loudly exhaled his relief. "As you desire," he said, breathlessly. "Shall I recall what remains of the goblin force?"

"No," said Salin. "They have proven their worthlessness. I will have them killed. I have sent out a Call to summon other help from the North."

"The North?" asked Tor. "But they head west."

"Not for much longer, my short-sighted friend. Why would they flee this far north unless they intended to go further? They seek to place the Talisman beyond my grasp. They seek the land of Faerie."

"Faerie? They will never make it through the wilderness, my lord."

Salin shook his head. "Perhaps. But if they do survive and enter the land of the Fair Folk, it will…inconvenience me. We must double our efforts. I would rather catch them before they reach that hated realm. Let us waste no more time. Get our horses and meet me at the west gate."

"At once, master," said Tor.

Tor quickly left the inn, his relief swelling as he strode further from his master's presence. For many years he had been Salin's agent, but he had grown no more comfortable around the sorcerer. Now he had additional reason to fear him. Salin was not particularly tolerant of failure. At least he had given Tor another chance.

Unfortunately, Salin meant to accompany Tor. This put a sour edge on his relief. When Salin had originally summoned him from his home in Valaria, his instructions were to meet a goblin tribe in the west of the Northwood beyond Barton Hills, and search for Mason and his Talisman there. Salin himself was searching the eastern regions, and later they would rendezvous at Quintin Flats. Apparently Salin's wolves had reported Mason's general location, but were not able to determine the direction in which he traveled. Separate search parties were necessary to cover all possibilities.

But now the direction—and the destination—was clear. There was no need to split up. So Tor, to his dismay, was to travel with Salin himself.

He quickened his pace and tried to remember who he was: Tor of Valaria, once Watcher to the High-Lords, Master of Arms of the Third Legion, a man who feared nothing. A man who had been on both sides, never compromising, never looking back. He had made his choices. Regret was not an option. Nor was fear.

He would not fail. This Mason had nearly cost him his life. He would cut out the fool's heart and hand his master the Talisman of Unity.

And damned be the consequences.

CHAPTER 10

The Trackers

The warm summer breeze gently tossed Ara's shoulder-length hair as she gazed out across the clearing. Her gray mare shuffled her feet, and Ara patted her neck to calm her.

"It's all right, girl. We'll be on our way soon." She turned to Landyn, who sat silently on his own horse. "When do you think they'll be back?"

The minstrel shrugged. "It shouldn't be long now. If Kari and Jinn haven't picked up their trail by now, then it can't be found. We may as well head back to the camp."

Ara reluctantly pulled her gaze away from the horizon and turned her mount back toward the East. "I suppose waiting for them here won't make them come sooner. Grok, I pray they're able to find something—just a hint of Sarah and Alec's trail."

"If anyone can do it, Kari can," assured Landyn. "She's the best tracker in Tyridan."

"I hope so."

Ara watched Landyn's back as they headed toward the camp. He was maddeningly handsome and more charming than anyone she'd ever known. And in the few days since he found her in Riverton, he had been very supportive and sympathetic. Tales of minstrels made them out to be scoundrels or rogues, but Landyn didn't seem like anything of the sort. In other circumstances, Ara might have fallen for the man.

But now, concern for her daughter was foremost in her mind. During the night of terror in Barton Hills, Sarah and Alec had vanished. After the horror of her own brush with death had subsided, Ara deduced their disappearance had something to do with the collector, Salin, and the strange charm he desired. She hadn't stayed in town long enough to discover much more—only that dark sorcery was to blame for the destruction and death in Barton Hills. And at its heart was Salin.

Since her shop had been destroyed, most people had assumed she was dead. She did nothing to correct the misconception. She wasn't sure who she could trust, save old Cindra Verdan, and besides, she would rather Salin believe she was dead. If he sought her out again, she might not be so lucky as to survive the encounter.

And so, in secret, she began to carry out a plan to find her daughter.

She crafted her note and gave it to Cindra. Then she fled to Riverton under an assumed name and waited. She didn't know what else to do, for she was frightened Salin might discover she lived and use her as leverage against Alec and Sarah. Yet the waiting proved agonizing. She had no way of knowing in only a week, Landyn would come to her rescue. Against all odds he came, bringing with him a plan to track down Alec and Sarah.

"There are two scenarios," he had said. "The first is that they have already been abducted by the sorcerer. In this case, the charm is in his hands, and your daughter is probably dead. The second scenario is that she and this Alec Mason fled into the woods, escaping him. We have to assume they fled and are still one step ahead of him. If this is the case, we can find them. I know people who can find the tracks of the smallest creatures in the worst conditions. With their help, we will find Sarah and her friend."

For some reason, she immediately trusted the minstrel. Maybe it was his charm, or maybe it was because she had no choice, but she had no second thoughts about accompanying him to the trackers' camp.

The "camp" itself was actually more like a small village. When they had arrived the previous day, Ara was surprised to see a cluster of log houses, a small tavern, a supply shop, and a smithy. About half the size of Barton Hills, Markway huddled among the trees some twenty miles north of Riverton. It was too small to appear on any maps, and so secluded that very few knew of its existence. A few people occasionally migrated to Markway, people who preferred the unspoiled wilderness to towns and farmlands. The only others who sought out the camp were people who wished to acquire the services of the trackers.

Ara had never heard of Kari du Sharrel or Jinn Alyndra. Kari was a tall, muscular woman unlike anyone Ara knew, with flowing dark hair, deep brown eyes, and sharp, chiseled features. Jinn, in contrast, was a short, slim, blond man with icy blue eyes and snow white skin. Strangely, though, his facial features bore the same chiseled look as Kari's: thin and pointed, but not gaunt. They were vastly different, but oddly alike. And exotically attractive.

Kari, who seemed to be the leader of Markway, had listened intently as Landyn described Ara's plight. She seemed distant, almost cold, and Ara thought she would refuse to help. But she did not refuse; instead she announced she and her companion Jinn would set out at once. All she needed was something which belonged to Sarah or Alec, something one of them had recently touched.

Luckily Ara had just the thing. She had brought with her a small book of poems which Sarah had loved, and used to read from every night before going to sleep. Kari had taken the book and casually tossed it to Jinn, who began to sniff it and rub it all over his body. Ara thought this strange enough, but when he licked its cover, she angrily snatched it out of his hands.

"What do you hope to accomplish by doing that?" she exclaimed.

Jinn smiled mischievously. "I be like the hound, my lady. Ruff ruff!! I be sniffin' out your daughter's tracks so my mistress can find her. Her smell, you see, is what I need to begin the search. Her smell, her taste, her touch. Ah, yes, to touch the lovely girl, to taste her sweet…"

Ara almost took a swing at the little man, but Kari stepped between them, holding out her hands.

"Enough, Jinn. Forgive him, Ara. He speaks such filth all the time, but he is harmless. And he can pick up her scent. Once he leads me to her trail, I can follow it to the edge of the world."

Ara had nodded and backed away. She wondered why the trackers had agreed to help them so quickly, when she had little to pay them. Later Landyn explained the trackers at the camp were always starved for entertainment. He had agreed to provide them with a week's worth of song and storytelling. Also, he believed, they relished any task which could truly test their abilities. In their field of expertise, there was little that challenged the trackers.

Now they returned to the camp, to wait for the trackers. Kari and Jinn were to return as soon as they locked on to Sarah and Alec's trail. Then, she and Landyn would join the trackers, hopefully to reach the children before Salin did.

Despite the small population, the camp was bustling with activity. Children were playing in the dirt path connecting the few buildings. Hunters, newly returned from their morning's expedition, carried freshly killed rabbits and other small game, as well as a small deer. A small area had been cleared for planting vegetables, and a handful of women worked the plot. Others prepared to skin and cook the food brought by the hunters. Young boys took care of the horses and livestock, and old men worked leather into shoes and clothing.

It was a simple way of life, one Ara found quaint but appealing. She had always thought life in Barton Hills was simplistic and rural, but seeing the way things were done in Markway gave her a whole new perspective. The people of the camp had chosen to embrace an older way, one practiced before civilization had taken hold of the world, before kingdoms had risen and united to form the Eglacian Union. Barton Hills sat mostly apart from the rest of the world, but never so wholly as Markway.

"Let us go rest at the tavern," said Landyn, dropping down from his horse's back. He held out his hand to help Ara down, an unnecessary gesture, but one she accepted graciously. A tall stable boy was waiting nearby to take care of their horses. Landyn handed him the reigns. "Thank you, son," he said. The boy nodded and led the beasts off to the stables.

They entered The Boar's Head, a tavern roughly half the size of the Silver Shield. A few farmers sat within, nursing mugs of ale, and two old women sat in the corner chatting and cackling loudly. A young, pretty bar maid in a long, brown dress busily wiped down the tables.

"Brynda," said Landyn, bowing to the maid, "you are as lovely as ever!"

"Why, Landyn," she said, smiling shyly. "I heard you were in the camp. What brings you by this time?" She dropped her rag and drifted toward the minstrel as she spoke, her eyes lighting up while her face flushed. Ara knew how she felt.

"I need Kari's help with a problem. But right now, what I need is a mug of ale. And one for my friend Ara, as well."

Brynda curtsied briefly, locked eyes meaningfully with Landyn, and hurried to the bar. Ara felt a pang of jealousy. She knew it was unwarranted and it made her feel silly, but she just couldn't help it.

Landyn had taken a seat at a nearby table. When Ara sat across from him, he smiled at her, and she felt her heart quicken. Before she could blush, she turned her thoughts to other matters.

"That Jinn is a strange fellow. Can he really track someone by their scent?"

The minstrel chuckled. "It seems unlikely, does it not? Yet stranger things happen all the time. The world is full of magic: some dark, some light, and perhaps some to make a man's nose as keen as a hound's. Of one thing you may be sure: whatever their methods, Kari and Jinn seldom fail to find their quarry."

Ara still wasn't certain about Jinn's claims, and she definitely disliked the little man's mannerisms. Still, Kari seemed like the kind of person who would not tolerate much nonsense. She would keep her companion in line.

"Those two certainly are strange. Where do they come from?"

Landyn shrugged. "I've known them many years, but only since they've lived here. They do not speak much of their past. They certainly hail from a distant land. I myself believe they migrated from away south, beyond the boarders of the Eglacian Union, where it is warm year 'round and the land is strange."

"Well, as long as they help us find my girl I suppose it doesn't matter where they're from. Grok's beard, I hope they return soon."

"They've only been gone a short while. You must have patience, Ara."

Brynda brought their drinks, hovering over Landyn as long as she could without being obvious. She gave Ara a carefully neutral look, which Ara returned just a little more coldly.

Landyn seemed oblivious to the exchange. He turned his perfect smile on Ara and said, "Tell me more about yourself. How did you come to run your shop in Barton Hills? Surely a woman as sophisticated and talented as yourself could have been successful anywhere, say in Freehold or Valaria."

"I grew up in Barton Hills. I thought it a wonderful place to raise Sarah. I never even considered leaving, even after my Matthew passed away. But I've been talking about myself and my problems since you came to Riverton the other day. I want to know more about Landyn, Minstrel of Freehold."

He sat back and laughed heartily. "Now the storyteller must tell his own story. It is not as interesting as you may think, my lady. I was born and raised in Freehold, the son of an aspiring bard and a talented singer. My father had been trying for years to win the interest of old Lord Wynnburn, the lord of Freehold at the time. He spun tales and verse that were quite good, but too common for nobility. He had a certain mastery of rhythm and form, but his works failed to attain the lofty, flowing feel of true poetry. He never rose beyond being a simple entertainer, but as a child I thought he was a master of his art. He and my mother inspired me to become what I am today. I learned much from them in my early years."

Landyn took a long draught from his mug before continuing. "When I was sixteen, I left home and traveled the land with a caravan of merchants. I wanted to see the world and I wanted the world to see me. You see, I thought I had become quite an entertainer, a virtual master of song, and I wanted to make a name for myself. I performed in all the major cities of Tyridan, and in some beyond our borders. It was during this journey I first came to Markway and met the trackers. The camp was in its youth then, consisting of a few huts and a tiny farm. Of course, it has remained small, by design rather than chance, but you should have seen it then. It truly was a simple camp.

"I returned home soon after my twentieth birthday. I had seen many grand cities and scores of tiny towns. I had lived in the Grand City of Doshan for nearly a year, a place filled with enough wonders to occupy a lifetime. But the more of the world I saw, the more I realized I belonged in Freehold. It was a large city, but not so large one became lost in the crowd. I had proven I was a good minstrel, for I was well received where ever I went, but, like my father, I had failed to catch the eye of the high lords and ladies. I still had more to learn if I were ever to become a true bard."

Landyn shook his head and sighed. His eyes had a far away look as he resumed his tale. "And so I returned to Freehold and practiced my art. And then one day, by chance, a man named Nerid saw one of my performances at The Goblin's Foot. He approached me after the show and told me how impressed he was. He was the head servant in the court of Lord Penndryn, the newly raised lord of Freehold. He invited me to play before the court. And thus I had surpassed my father: I was to perform for nobility.

"The next week, I performed with many other entertainers in a grand ball held at Castle Freehold. Lord Penndryn and Lady Shanna as well as many other nobles were in attendance. I was well liked, especially by the Lady, and of all the entertainers they asked only me and two others to return for more private performances. I was convinced that soon I would be the official bard of Freehold.

"Alas, it was not to be. Although my skill upon the lute as supreme, and my lyrical voice could melt the coldest young maiden, my own compositions were little better than my father's. A man named Eric Valase was chosen over me. His verse, I must admit, more closely approached the likes of Ottis Brachnitter than mine, but with his rough voice and mean skill at the lute, he should never have been offered the position. All is water under the bridge now, as they say. Eric is still the official bard at court, but these days I am invited to play at most formal functions as well. I refuse many such offers, for I have grown fond of my station. The common folk are a far more appreciative audience than the nobility, who have always been more concerned with their haughty affectations than with art.

"The years passed, and while Eric remained official bard, I became considered the city's official minstrel. I held forth nightly at The Goblins Foot, the largest inn in Freehold, and one of the largest in all of Tyridan. The place was packed night after night, as people from all over the city and surrounding countryside came to see me. Through it all, I remained as humble as I could, yet it gave me a certain confidence I would not have had otherwise. And then, perhaps ten years ago, at the height of my popularity, I met Jessina.

"Ah, lovely Jessina d'Evenwing. She was a minor noble visiting from Valaria. But she was not like the other ladies I had met; she retained a quality of humility and wholesomeness usually only found in women of lower station. I think I loved her from the first moment she spoke to me. And when she sang, it was like her voice was sent from the heavens, soaring among the clouds, whisking about the mountain peaks, and sometimes showering gently across a calm, green meadow. We became a team, she and I, and performed together for common folk, nobility, even royalty. Our careers grew together as did our love, and poor Eric the bard was all but forgotten.

"Yet because of my lack of ability in the composition of verse and song, Lord Penndryn refused to name me bard. I believe it had much to do with Nerid, who held, and holds, much influence over the lord, and who has some sort of strange loyalty to Eric Valase. Still, over the years I have continued my studies, and now believe I am able to compose great tales in the sweeping high verse of the bards of old. Yet, my ambition has cost me much. I fear in my zeal to master my craft, I neglected poor Jessina. She has recently left me to return to Valaria, where, rumor has it, she currently performs for the King and Queen of Tyridan."

For a moment, Landyn's eyes became unfocused, and a shadow of grief fell upon his face. But then, he smiled, and banished his sadness with a wave of his hand. "Water under the bridge. I keep myself so busy I barely miss her. This is one of the reasons I accepted the invitation to host the Bard's Day celebration at Barton Hills. And the fact that, traditionally, it falls to the bard of Freehold to host the celebration there, and I am not him. All in all, I have no regrets. And now, I have a chance to craft the tale of Ara, and her heroic search for her daughter. It could be an epic which will win me a seat beside the great bards of Tyridan."

Ara chuckled. "I doubt my story will be the stuff of epics. But I'm glad you're here." She sobered, and reached out to touch his hand. "I'm...sorry about Jessina. You must have loved her."

"I did. But I have always lived for my art and I always will. But enough history. For now, let us drink, eat, and forget our troubles. There is nothing more we can do until Kari returns."

Landyn called Brynda over to order food and more ale. She hurried to the kitchen, and soon returned with a plate of hard bread and cheese, and fruit from the garden. They talked as they ate their midday meal, Landyn telling more of his journeys and Ara telling tales of keeping her shop, and raising her daughter. As she spoke of Sarah, an ache swelled in her breast and a lump filled her throat. Yet, she drew strength as well as grief from thinking of her daughter. Somewhere inside, she knew Sarah was alive. There was still hope.

Ara lost track of time as they spoke, becoming lost in Landyn's tales and her own thoughts. But when the door banged open and the trackers burst in, her head spun toward them and her thoughts focused on the matter at hand. Kari strode into the room, a cold confidence issuing from her tall, muscular form. Jinn followed behind her, a devious smile upon his lips and a mischievous spring in his step. Kari bowed to Landyn and nodded to Ara.

"They head deeper into the Northwood. Jinn followed the girl's scent to a clearing many miles into the woods. There we saw signs of conflict. There were wolf corpses strewn about, some charred and blackened as if by flame. I found four sets of tracks leading away from the battle, all human. The size and style of shoe of one of the sets of tracks seemed to point to a female. Jinn confirmed by scent they are the tracks of your daughter."

Ara's heart soared. "Oh, thank Grok! They're alive!"

Kari shrugged. "The tracks are several days old. A lesser tracker would have missed them entirely. We cannot assume from an old trail that whatever made it still lives. The only way we can know they're alive is to follow the trail to its end."

Kari's pessimism annoyed Ara, but before she could respond, Landyn said, "Then we will do just that. Let us take a few minutes to gather supplies, and then be on our way. I'll get our horses from the stable, Ara."

Ara nodded as Landyn bowed deeply and rushed out. Kari went into the kitchen to gather some rations, and Jinn followed at her heels like an obedient dog. Ara was left to herself, and doubts began to creep into her mind. To chase them away, she decided to take a walk around the camp.

The day was growing hot as the sun reached its peak overhead. Activity had slowed in the camp as residents went indoors to eat their midday meal. Ara made her way to the stables, stopping to admire the ordered simplicity of the log buildings around her, from the store which sold only the necessities of life, to the smithy who made horseshoes, farming tools, arrow and spear heads for hunting, and knives for preparing food. She marveled at this self-contained community, which rarely needed to trade with the world outside. They had few needs they could not meet on their own.

Except entertainment, she thought as she saw Landyn leading their horses from the stables. Her smaller gray horse she had named Lucy, after a silly character from an old song. His much larger horse, called Luck, was a darker shade of gray. She hoped the stallion brought with it the good fortune its name suggested.

"Are you ready to travel?" asked Landyn. "Kari will drive us at a hard pace. There will be little time for rest."

Ara took Lucy's reigns and patted the horse's neck. "I've had more than enough rest lately. Just set me on the path, and I'll outride you all."

"Excellent," said Landyn. "I admire your resolve."

He helped her into her saddle and then leaped fluidly into his own. After a moment, Kari rode up on her massive black stallion, followed by Jinn on a sleek white pony.

"Let us away," said Kari. "The day is half gone already, and we have much ground to cover."

"Lead on, then," said Landyn.

And so they rode forth from Markway. Kari led the way, setting a brisk pace. Jinn rode close behind, followed by Ara, while Landyn brought up the rear. Soon they rode through the clearing where Ara and Landyn had ridden earlier, and then they passed into the thick forest beyond. Kari was soon forced to slow her pace so she did not lose the others among the trees.

Ara felt glad to be traveling again. Her secret trip from Barton Hills to Riverton had been blessedly uneventful, but fear and loneliness had weighed heavily upon her. Her short journey with Landyn from Riverton to Markway had given her a spark of hope. Now things were finally falling together. A slim hope had against all odds become a real chance of finding her daughter, and she grasped desperately at the chance. She had no idea what she would do when she found Sarah and Alec, especially if they had run afoul of Salin, but she put the thought out of her mind. The important thing now was to find them. When she did, she would worry about what came next.

They rode onward for hours, mostly in silence. Kari did not speak at all, except to consult with Jinn now and again about the path ahead. Jinn occasionally made small talk with Ara, often rude and suggestive, but a cold glare from Kari was all it took to silence the imp. Landyn filled some of the time with silly songs or trivial tales of his past adventures. Ara was glad of his lighthearted banter, for her own thoughts remained dark despite her newfound hope.

Sometimes she turned her gaze and her thoughts to the forest itself. In places where the trees were thick and the leaves blotted out the light, the forest could be oppressive and frightening. But in more spacious areas where the trees parted and grew less densely, light shined through, illuminating the true beauty of the woodlands. The light played on shades of green and brown, making the leaves and bark come to life. Mosses growing on tree trunks and on the forest floor glimmered in the sunlight with a beauty of their own. Woodland creatures small and large, from rabbits and squirrels to the occasional deer, could be seen running, hunting, and resting. It was comforting to Ara to know the same world which produced evil like Salin was also capable of creating such simple serenity. She wondered why she hadn't realized before what a wondrous place the forest could be.

By day's end, they reached a small clearing. Kari dismounted and bent to the ground. A south-blowing wind brought a stench like rotten meat to Ara's nose, and she grimaced in disgust. Then she saw the source of the smell. Wolf carcasses filled the clearing, half-eaten by scavengers and insects.

"Here are their tracks," said Kari, touching the ground. Ara looked at the forest floor and saw nothing. She heard sniffing noises, and turned to see Jinn breathing the stench-filled air deeply. He let out what seemed to be a sigh of delight. Ara winced in disgust.

The exotic, dark-haired tracker turned to Landyn. "We should continue before we lose the light. As I have said, these tracks are old. Already they become obscure, even to me. I would like to follow them as far as we can tonight."

Jinn sniffed the tracks and nodded his agreement. "The scent is weak as well, my lady. By tomorrow, perhaps the next day, my skills will no longer be of use."

"Then let us go," said Landyn. "I would not wish to remain long in this place of death, anyway. Ara?"

She nodded in hasty agreement. "Let's go."

They pushed through the clearing, over the dead animals. On the far edge of the clearing was a blackened ring, as if fire had burst outward from a central point, charring all in its path. Ara had to look away from the twisted, burned wolf-shapes dotting the black circle. She could not imagine what strange power could have caused such destruction.

Except sorcery. Could Salin have done this? Oh, Grok...Sarah!!

"Are you all right, Ara?" asked Landyn, riding up beside her. She had nearly collapsed in her saddle, and was holding her head in her hands.

"Wounds," she gasped, recovering. "There are no human bodies here. Right, Landyn? You haven't seen any?"

"No, my lady, only wolves. Sarah and her friends did not perish here. See, Kari follows the tracks onward, beyond the ring of ash."

He clasped her hand for a moment, and then fell into his place behind her. Feeling steadier, she urged Lucy ahead to close the gap between her and Jinn.

I have to be stronger than this. I have to see this through.

After they had ridden a few more miles, the sun had set and the forest was dark. They stopped and set up camp for the night. Kari and Jinn pulled blankets from their saddlebags and tossed a few to Landyn and Ara. Then Kari passed around some dried meat and hard bread, and they sat in a circle and had their dinner. The night drew close around them. When they spoke their voices seemed too loud; thus silence filled their small camp, and soon they went to their blankets.

"I will stand guard first tonight," said Kari. "Jinn will take the second shift. We need little sleep."

Ara was glad she would not have to take a shift. The day's travel had made her weary, and she needed a full night's rest. She saw Landyn wrap himself in a blanket and close his eyes. She couldn't help but smile as her gaze lingered upon him. Then, she found a comfortable, mossy spot and lay down. Before long, she drifted into a deep, peaceful sleep.

The next day, Kari roused them early. After a quick breakfast of bread and cheese, they mounted their horses and began the day's journey. The day was again bright and warm, and Ara quickly forgot the eerie oppression of the forest night. She breathed the fresh air deeply and relished the feeling of the wind against her face.

Every so often, Kari stopped to examine the tracks more closely. Jinn would sniff the air, and sometimes put his nose to the ground where Kari pointed. Late in the morning he shook his head and frowned. He announced the trail was too stale and he could no longer follow the scent. Luckily, Kari was still able to pick out signs of passage. She remained confident she could follow the trail to its end.

The morning wore into afternoon, and the sun began its decent into the west. To Ara's surprise, the forest abruptly changed, becoming more dense with underbrush, more tangled and confusing. It was almost as if the trees had purposely twisted themselves into walls, creating a maze to confound those who would go further. Kari motioned for them to stop, her eyes wide with shock.

"By the Seven!" she exclaimed. "Their tracks lead directly into the Addingrove!"

"The what?" questioned Ara.

"An Addingrove," said Landyn. "I had heard there were several within the Northwood, but I never expected to be so near one. Ara, the Addins are a strange race of giants who tend the world's forests. I believe they are in some way kinsmen to the Fair Folk."

"Not kinsmen," corrected Kari, her naturally cold eyes chilling further, "although they have had dealings with the Fairies in the past. They are betrayers, and are not to be trusted. Unfortunately, your daughter and her friends passed into the grove. No tracks lead out again. If they left this place, they left by another path. We must…we must follow, if we are not to lose the trail."

For the first time, Ara read reluctance in Kari's words and actions. Reluctance and perhaps a touch of fear. What manner of creatures were these Addins?

They made their way slowly through the maze of trees and bushes. Ara thought they would certainly have become lost if they were not following in Sarah and Alec's footsteps. For a moment she panicked, wondering if the children had become hopelessly lost, and had perished while wandering the maze. But then her fears softened as they at last emerged into a vast field of thick, healthy grass. In the middle of the field stood the single largest tree that she had ever seen, surrounded by a marvelous garden.

"It's…it's beautiful," she whispered.

"Indeed. Never in all my travels have I seen…" Landyn shook his head, unable to finish his sentence. There were no words.

Kari was not moved. "I wish to be away from this place. Come, the tracks head off toward the…"

Suddenly a horrible cacophony arose away to their left, just beyond the edge of the clearing. The trees and bushes rustled, and leaves flew outward as a horde of greenish gray creatures burst from the forest. They were short and ugly, with blunt snouts and gnashing teeth, and they made Ara wince in disgust. Then fear gripped her, for the creatures were rushing straight toward them!

"They're going to attack us!"

"No," said Kari. "Listen to their screams. They are terrified of something."

"Goblins," muttered Landyn. "Disgusting."

The trees shook again, this time with greater violence, and three massive monstrosities burst into the clearing. They were eight feet high, muscle-bound, and covered in gray flesh. Their short hair was thick, bristly, and black. Their faces were almost human in appearance, save for a thick ridge above the eyes and an exaggerated lower jaw. Each wore fur pants and a hide vest, and each held a massive, spiked club. For their size, they moved quickly.

"Grok's wounds!" shouted Ara, grabbing Landyn's arm. "What are those?"

"Ogres," answered Kari. Her face betrayed disbelief. "I have not seen them this far south since…" Her voice trailed off and she shook her head.

The panicked goblins ran in all directions, some directly toward their attackers. The ogres violently clubbed the little monsters, smashing their skulls wide open. The three attackers split up then, and chased down their confused prey. Blood spattered the fields, and bits of flesh and bone flew through the air. The ogres were covered in gore as they crushed the goblins, and they reveled in it, laughing aloud. Ara watched the mad slaughter, the frenzied chaos of move-ment and sound. She wanted to look away, but she was transfixed. Apparently her companions were as well.

"I've never seen such…such brutality," said Landyn.

"We should stop this," said Kari.

"Why?" questioned Jinn, licking his lips lustfully. "I like it."

For once, Ara agreed with Jinn, if not for the same reasons. "What do you mean, 'Stop this?' They would kill us! We should go back, hide until this is over. Let them kill each other."

"Each other?" said Kari, turning a stern look on Ara. "The goblins stand no chance. I have no love for their kind, but we cannot let ogres run free in our land. We must stop them."

"You must have gone mad, Kari," said Landyn. "Look at those things!"

Before Kari could answer, the ogres shouted a victory cry. The last goblin lay dead on the grass, gore spilling from what remained of its head. Almost at once the gray-skinned monsters turned their eyes, and their bloodlust, upon Ara and her companions. The ogres roared, and raced toward them with clubs held aloft.

"Fist of Lars!" cried Landyn. "We must flee!"

"Get behind me," said Kari, her voice cold and firm. She rode her stallion forward and lifted her right hand. She spoke some words Ara could not make out, and suddenly a whirlwind sprang from the air before her. Translucent cords of air whipped forward, entangling the nearest two ogres. Kari raised her hand higher, and the wind howled loudly, lifting the thrashing creatures into the air.

The last ogre rushed her, unharmed by her mystic attack. Club at the ready, he launched himself at her.

"Kari, look out!" cried Landyn.

Her mind elsewhere, she could never have reacted in time. But suddenly Jinn leapt forth, his small body vaulting high into the air, coming down upon the ogre. He howled in a rage, and as he fell upon his enemy he changed. His hands grew long, his fingers becoming knife-like claws. His face became elongated and savage looking, his mouth opening impossibly wide to unveil razor-sharp teeth. He fell on the ogre, becoming a blur of slashing arms and gnashing teeth. Blood spewed from the gray giant, and it dropped its club, arms waving wildly. It cried out, but it its agony it managed to grab Jinn with both hands. Jinn struggled, but could not break free of the ogre's crushing grip.

Meanwhile, Kari closed her right fist. One of the ogres she had entangled grabbed its throat and began to thrash wildly. Its eyes bulged grotesquely, and its face grew red. Blood oozed out of its ears, nose, and mouth. It convulsed one final time, and then went limp.

The other ogre, however, managed to put its feet on the ground. With a roar, it burst free of Kari's whirlwind, and charged her. She reached for the knife at her side, but it was too late. With a sweep of a massive arm, the ogre knocked her from her horse and continued running toward Landyn and Ara.

Landyn pulled his short sword from his belt, riding his horse forward to protect Ara. Sweat poured from his brow, and his arm shook as he lifted his blade.

He's going to die! she thought.

Suddenly the grass beneath them sprang up, growing two feet in less than a second. It entwined the ogre's legs, and he fell forward onto his face. The grass grew up over his struggling body, holding him fast. But the creature was strong, and flexing his back, he began to pull the grass out by its roots.

"Foul creature! You dare to bring your evil here? *HERE?*"

Ara looked up from the struggling ogre, and what she saw nearly made her fall off her horse. Standing before her was a towering man, with hair and a beard like gnarled branches, and muscles like tree trunks.

"The Addin," whispered Landyn, dropping his sword.

The grass withdrew, releasing the ogre. The creature rose to its full height, its eyes red with rage. The Addin towered over it. With a single blow of his fist,

- the Addin turned the ogre's face into a bloody pulp. The ogre crumpled like a discarded doll and lay on the ground, unmoving.

Silence filled the grove. Ara looked beyond the Addin for a moment, and saw Jinn sitting on top of the ogre corpse he had attacked, licking his claws. Somehow he had wriggled free of the beast and had managed to kill it. Despite his awful behavior, she was glad he had survived.

But that was all the attention she could spare him. Her gaze was drawn back to the towering Addin. His eyes were glazed with rage, and his massive fists curled and uncurled in an attempt at control. He looked around, confused for a moment, and then seemed to calm when he saw that the ogres were all dead. The fire left his eyes and the tension drained from his huge body.

He turned to survey his visitors. He considered Landyn and Ara briefly, but he let his gaze linger longer on Jinn. His eyebrows raised in curious surprise. Then he turned to Kari, who had picked herself up and was standing proudly, even coldly, before the Addin. He regarded her in much the same way he did Jinn, but with even more wonder in his eyes.

"It has been long since I have beheld one of your kind," he said. Ara was shocked as he knelt humbly before the tracker, bowing his head to the ground.

"My name is Horren. How may I serve you, good Fairy?"

CHAPTER 11

The Ravager

Alec shielded his eyes from the blazing sun as he at last stepped out of the Northwood. He had grown accustomed to the relative darkness of the forest, and the light hurt his eyes. Squinting, he looked out across the plain of brown grass spread before him. Far to the north, beyond the plain, he saw a range of tall, rocky mountains.

Lorn stood a few feet before Alec and the others, gazing toward the mountains. "Behold the Gravescorn Mountains, beyond which lay the forests of the ogres. Few humans have passed into this fell domain, and far fewer have returned to tell the tale. Away beyond the ogre-lands, the Fair Folk live in their woodland cities. The way before us is long and dangerous, but with stealth and good fortune we may come to Faerie unharmed. The grassland between here and the Gravescorn, known as the Plain of Naar, holds dangers of its own. Watch where you step, for many breeds of snakes, scorpions, and all manner of small but deadly creatures hide in the tall grass."

Kraig walked up beside their guide, brushing back his long bangs. "There is something else I don't like about this grassland. We'll be out in the open, exposed to anyone who might be following us. It will take days to cross on foot; we will be vulnerable the entire time."

"Unfortunately, there is no other way," replied Lorn. "If we quicken our pace, we can reach Gravescorn by tomorrow night. Once there, we can hide ourselves among the crags and crevices of the mountains and travel virtually unseen."

"Then let's not waste any more time," said Kraig. "For all we know, Salin could be right behind us."

Alec turned to find Sarah standing at his shoulder. She hadn't spoken much since the last attack outside Bordonhold, and her mood remained dark. Alec's attempts to lift her spirits had met with small success, but he refused to give up. He offered her his hand, and together they followed Kraig and Lorn. Behind them, in grim silence, trudged Michael.

It was the second day since they had left Bordonhold. Soon after the goblin attack, Lorn had decided their ploy to travel westward had already failed, and they turned north toward their true destination. At the end of the day, as they camped, Lorn reminded them to be more careful than ever. Tyridan was behind them now and the untamed wilderness lay ahead. Alec silently laughed: he hadn't exactly thought of the Northwood as "tame."

Of course, the Northwood extended beyond their country's border. Although he could see or feel no change in his surroundings, a strange sense of nervous wonder filled him. He had never been outside of Tyridan before.

Throughout the night and the next day, Michael remained withdrawn and silent. When addressed, he spoke brief answers and then walked away. Alec wondered what had brought on the change in the hermit: was it shame, or perhaps fear? Or maybe he was sulking because he wasn't in charge anymore. The party's leadership now seemed to be shared between Lorn and Kraig. Lorn made suggestions, and Kraig either approved or vetoed them, seldom consulting the others. The two had developed a mutual respect, despite their rocky first meeting. Alec was glad they were getting along, but he somewhat resented being left out of the decisions.

They started across the plain, wading through the knee-high grass. Alec followed close behind Kraig and Lorn, hand in hand with Sarah. Again Michael fell behind and followed from a distance. In this way they traveled for a few hours, and the forest slowly shrank into the distance behind them. As they walked silently through the brown grass, Alec grew accustomed to the sunlight and the feel of the warm wind on his face. It lifted his spirits, and by the time the sun began to fall into the west, he had renewed his determination to coax Sarah out of her black mood.

"You know, I'm actually feeling pretty good right now," he said, smiling sincerely. "Being out of the forest, in the open air and the sunlight, reminds me of home."

Sarah looked at him blankly. "The land here is flat and covered in ugly grass. Where are the green, rolling hills we have at home? Where are the farms? And tell me, where are our friends, our families?"

Alec shook his head. This was going to be harder than he thought. "Well, the sky is blue and sunny, and the air is clean and fresh, just like Barton Hills. And you are among friends, Sarah. I mean, I always considered you a friend, but now…I think going through something like this can bring people closer together. Everything—every problem, every ordeal—has a bright side. Maybe the bright side here is we were brought together." He looked into her eyes for a moment and was filled with her beauty. His heart pounded faster, and he bent as if to kiss her. Then his face went red with embarrassment, and he straightened, pulling away from her.

"I…I mean, we were brought together as friends. You, me, Kraig, and the others. All of us."

Sarah looked up at him. Her eyes were wide and her lips flirted with a smile. "I suppose."

"And remember where we're going, Sarah. Faerie! Why, two weeks ago I wasn't even sure there was such a place, and now we're actually going to see it. To see the Fair Folk, to meet legends! Grok's beard, how many people have been so fortunate? Sure, it's been a dangerous trip, and likely there's more danger ahead. But Michael and Lorn are here to protect us, and Kraig can hold his own in a fight. We'll make it to Faerie, and then our troubles will be over. The Fairies will know what to do with the Talisman, and they'll take care of Salin."

Finally she smiled. She squeezed his arm and pulled him close, resting her head on his shoulder. "Well, I am excited to see Fairies. I wonder if they look like they do in the stories."

Alec nodded, a feeling of awe swelling inside him. "I hope so…ten foot tall beings of pure light, reflecting the beauty of the gods."

"Well, I was thinking of the stories which said they were four inches tall, with little pointed ears and butterfly wings."

Alec laughed out loud. "I never heard *those* stories!"

She squeezed him again and joined him in laughter. He liked the feel of her body against his, and he felt disappointment when she broke away from him. She quickened her pace, looking back at him with a playful grin. He returned it and jogged forward to catch her. At last she had broken free of her gloom; he was not about to let her sink back into it. He reached out and grabbed her around the waist. Lifting her up, he swung her in a circle. She squealed and giggled, and he laughed heartily.

Kraig looked back and grinned. "No time for that now," he scolded. "We've got a lot of ground to cover." His face showed his reprimand was not entirely serious.

Alec put Sarah down. "Sorry, Kraig. We wouldn't want to have any fun on this trip, would we?"

Lorn stopped and looked at the three of them. He did not share in their light-hearted fun. "Do not forget, danger may craw through these blades of grass. It certainly follows behind us, how near we cannot know. Do not forget caution."

As Lorn turned to resume his brisk march, Sarah turned her grin back at Alec. "What an old stick in the mud," she muttered.

Alec chuckled. "He certainly is, but I guess he's right in this case. Let's be more careful where we step. But keep smiling, Sarah. It makes you look even more beautiful."

Her eyes lit up with surprise and delight. "You've never called me beautiful before. Getting soft on me, Mason?"

To cover his embarrassment, Alec said, "You wish, Mills."

They said little more for the remainder of the day, and they took more care where they stepped. But each time they locked eyes, Sarah smiled warmly. Alec smiled back, glad he had been able to pull her from her gloom. They walked onward as twilight fell, and he felt contented, if only for now.

Ara stood at the edge of the Addingrove, her mouth hanging open in amazement. As if goblins and ogres weren't enough—as if this giant, this Addin, wasn't more than her mind could accept—she now had to contend with the fact that the giant was bowing to her companions. And he was calling them Fairies.

Fairies? Grok's beard, what madness have I fallen into?

The Addin had looked like a god filled with righteous anger when he had stood over the dying ogre. Yet, when he saw Kari and Jinn he humbled himself, falling to his knees in deference. His eyes twinkled, and he smiled as if his bowing to them was more playful than reverent, but he seemed sincere. Now Kari, arms folded and face stern, grunted irritably at the Addin.

"Enough of this," she said. "I will not have some Addin kowtow before me in a mockery of respect. Why do you, a betrayer, bow to one of the betrayed?"

Hurt spread across the giant's rough-skinned face. "Betrayer? We have never considered ourselves as such. We only sought to execute our duties, the very duties given to us by your people, as best we could. We have always acted out of love, love for the Fairies and love for the world. Love for the One. Please, come to my home. Let us try to find a way to heal the hurts that have been between our people for hundreds of years."

"I fear such healing is impossible," said Kari coldly.

"Then at least let me assist you as I can," he said, rising to his feet. "It is plain you are in search of something. Perhaps I can help. I know these parts well."

Kari seemed to consider for a long moment. "Very well. Lead us to your home. Maybe you have seen those whom we seek."

"Maybe I have," said Horren, his eyes smiling.

They walked toward his house, situated high in a great tree at the center of the grove. Ara took in the garden, the lush green grass, the flowery archway. She smelled the freshness of the grove, from the scent of moist loam to the subtle perfume of flowers. She couldn't help but smile as the Addin lead them up the stairs to his mansion, round and round the giant tree. Before she knew it, she was inside.

Awestruck, Ara looked around the vast mansion. It was large and clean, with walls of light brown wood and a great, domed ceiling. Horren took a seat on a stump toward the far end of the wide floor, bidding the others to come near. Both Kari and Jinn were hesitant, almost fearful now that they were in the heart of the Addin's domain. Landyn hesitated not at all, visibly thrilled at finding himself in the middle of a bard's song. When they were gathered around the Addin, Horren grinned broadly and spread his thick arms in welcome.

"Now, my friends," he said in a hardy voice, "what is it you seek, and why has your search brought you to the Addinheart?"

Kari, still eyeing their host suspiciously, said "We are following the tracks of this woman's daughter. The girl travels with three companions, probably all male. Her name is Sarah, and one of her companions is a boy named Alec Mason."

Horren threw back his head in laughter. Ara wondered what he found so amusing. "So," he said, "the tale of the young baker and his intrepid friends continues! Ah, yes, your Sarah is a beautiful young girl. It is quite obvious Alec Mason thinks so, too."

"What?" cried Ara, forgetting for a moment she stood before a creature out of myth. "Were they here? What happened to them?"

Horren continued to smile amiably as he answered. "They came by here nearly a week ago, traveling with another villager named Kraig and my old friend Elsendarin. Michael, some call him."

"Michael," said Ara. She recognized the name but couldn't place it. Then she remembered the strange hermit who lived on the outside of town, a few years older than she herself was, yet as eccentric as a crazy old man. "Michael! What were they doing with *him?*"

Horren raised a mossy eyebrow. "He was helping them, of course. He is a very wise fellow, my friend Elsendarin, and can be very helpful to those in need. And I assure you, those children were in grave need. Old Salin Urdrokk was after them."

"Yes, I know," said Ara. "Salin razed half of Barton Hills and destroyed my shop. He very nearly killed me! I have prayed on every night since then he hasn't gotten to Sarah yet. Why does he want them? Why didn't Alec just give him the silly piece of jewelry and be done with it?"

"Slowly, slowly!" cried Horren. "One thing at a time." He paused to smile and shake his head at Ara. "Your concern for your daughter is clear. But getting overly excited won't help her. She is in good hands now, perhaps the best hands given the current circumstance. She and Alec were lucky to fall in with Elsendarin, for he knows the sorcerer's ways better than anyone, I think."

Ara wasn't at all convinced. "All the same, I'd feel better if I knew where she was. I don't like this Michael. He's always skulked around on the outskirts of town, rarely speaking to anyone, always keeping to himself. He's a crazy hermit and I don't trust him to lead Sarah and Alec to safety."

The Addin shook his head. "You simply do not know him as I do. The man you know as Michael is not the man I knew as Elsendarin. Elsendarin was a wise man, a councilor, a powerful ally. But the burdens laid upon him were heavy. He saw the world falling piece by piece under the shadow of a dark enemy, and he knew despair. His despair drove him to abandon his task, a task he grew to see as hopeless. This is why he turned inward and lived alone near your quiet village. This is why he became Michael, the simple man, the fool, the hermit. But he has not changed as much as he thinks. He is not as foolish and powerless as he leads himself and others to believe. For this reason I have given him the book, so he might…ah, but I digress. You don't care about all this history. You simply want to know where your daughter is."

Ara gazed up into his eyes hopefully. "Do you know? Can you tell us where she is now?"

Horren shook his head slowly. "No, my lady. I do not know where she is. But I can tell you where she's going. Elsendarin will take her and Alec to the only place that might be safe from Salin Urdrokk."

"Where?" she questioned, hope leaping into her heart. "Where is safe?"

"The realm of Faerie, dear lady."

"Faerie!" cried Ara. Her already tenuous hold on hope began to slip away. "Does such a place actually exist?"

At the mention of the Fairy homeland, Kari's eyes widened and her stance grew stiff. Jinn crouched down on all fours and began to growl softly.

"Oh, yes, Ara Mills. Faerie certainly exists," said Kari. "I have not seen my homeland in more than twenty years. I swore never to return, not after Martyn…" She stopped herself in mid-sentence and breathed out heavily. For a moment she looked sad and thoughtful, but then her eyes regained their habitual icy glare. "Are you certain this Michael is taking them there?"

"He said as much," said Horren. "Although he himself did not intend to go. He intended to find a guide for them at Bordonhold. Of course, things change, and I believe he may change his mind about accompanying them to Faerie."

"How can he know the way?" asked Kari. "Few humans do."

"Do not tell me that you, a Fairy Shaper, have not heard of Elsendarin!" exclaimed Horren, genuine surprise coloring his face.

Kari shrugged. "I have heard tales of such a person, but your friend cannot be the same one! Why, that would make him older than…"

"I know of only one Elsendarin," said Horren, closing the subject with a wave of his hand. "Now, what should we do about you folks? It is obvious, Ara, you intend to follow your daughter's trail to its end. Have you considered how dangerous this could be?"

Ara nodded. "I have. But Landyn has a wealth of knowledge about the world, and Kari and Jinn have shown they can do more than follow a trail. I, too, am in good hands."

Horren smiled and pointed at the Fairies. "Yes indeed. This woman is a cold one, thinks she's above mere humans. But Salin's a human, and he could roast her like a pig on a stick without so much as breaking a sweat. And this little Jinn, well, he might be a match for a singular ogre, but put him up against a group of Salin's slaves and he'd be just so much meat. Your friend Landyn may know a bit about the world, but not enough to help you against sorcery. No, perhaps you should just return home and wait. Forces are at work here beyond your capacity to influence."

Kari leapt toward the Addin, rage flaring in her eyes. "How dare you! How dare you presume to know what I think about human beings! And you know nothing of my power! The ogres took me by surprise! If I'd had but a moment to prepare myself, I could have…"

"You could have perhaps taken two instead of one. But regardless, Salin is a more dangerous foe by far. Even his minions hold power beyond your understanding. I've been alive far longer than you, and I can only begin to comprehend their might. I have killed many sorcerers in my day and picked my teeth with their bones, but Salin is another matter. His might is second only to the master he serves."

"I'll not abandon my daughter," said Ara. "I'll not sit at home and wait."

Horren sighed. For a moment, he looked sad. "Then there is only one thing to do. I cannot in good conscience let the four of you go chasing down black old Salin on your own. I would be sending you to your deaths." He looked up gravely, his big eyes sorrowful but resolved. "As much as I am loathe to leave my beautiful Addingrove, I will accompany you."

Kari shook her head. She thrust her fist toward the Addin in a defiant gesture. "I will not stand for it! I will not travel in the company of one of the betrayers."

All humor drained from Horren's face. Ara thought she had never seen anyone look so sad. "Then you will die."

Kari turned and stormed away. "I do not have to listen to this!"

Ara looked from her companion to the hulking Addin and back again. Although Kari often seemed cold and untouchable, Ara had grown to trust the woman's knowledge and abilities. If Kari did not trust the Addin, perhaps he was not worthy of trust. But Horren appeared genuinely concerned and somewhat knowledgeable with regards to Salin Urdrokk. Moreover, he knew where Sarah and Alec were headed. For these reasons alone he could prove to be a valuable companion on the road. If only Kari could be convinced.

Ara looked to Landyn, who hadn't moved since they entered the Addin's home. He stood still and focused, as if he were concentrating on memorizing every detail of his surroundings. If he had noticed the exchange between Kari and Horren he gave no sign.

Ara crossed to him, passing by a fuming Kari and an amused Jinn. The minstrel saw her coming and grinned.

"Just like in the stories," he said.

"I don't care about stories right now," she said. "Haven't you been paying attention? The Addin seems to think we're doomed if we continue to track my daughter. With Salin out there somewhere, I'm afraid he might be right."

Landyn looked at her seriously. "Of course I've been paying attention. Kari and Jinn are Fairies and Fairies don't like Addins. I've just got other things on my mind, like how I'm going to capture this moment in song."

Ara felt like screaming. "Forget your Grok forsaken song! Horren has offered to come with us. I have a feeling he'll be a useful companion on the road, especially if we run into trouble. Someone has to convince Kari, though."

Landyn nodded. "I agree. I would *love* to have an Addin...an *Addin!*...with us on our journey. I've known Kari for quite a while; she respects my judgment. I'll see what I can do."

Landyn walked over to where Kari stood, her back turned to the others. Jinn joined them in a moment, the mischievous grin never leaving his face. Ara stood away from the group, more interested in how the Addin was taking all of this. He was sitting on his stump quietly, rubbing his gnarled beard, his eyes lost in thought. She wondered what was on his mind.

Landyn, Kari and Jinn talked for quite some time. Ara couldn't make out what they were saying, but at last Kari threw her hands up in frustration. Jinn began to laugh aloud and Landyn nodded his head. The tall, brown-haired Fairy made her way over to Horren's stump.

"Addin," she said slowly. "I have no love for your kind. My people brought you into this world, gave you substance and purpose, and you betrayed us. But...the minstrel has convinced me Salin Urdrokk is a worse evil by far." Ara could see Kari was fighting with herself, struggling with each word. "Your strength and knowledge will be...a boon to us as we travel northward. If your offer to join us still stands, then I...I accept."

Horren's smile was so wide it appeared to cover his entire face. His big white teeth shown brightly under his brown, rough lips. "Good Fairy, I would be honored to accompany you in your quest."

"Just stay out of my way," muttered Kari as she briskly marched away.

Ara breathed a sigh of relief and Landyn smiled in satisfaction. Jinn gripped his stomach and rolled on the floor, laughing gleefully.

They spent the night in the Addinheart and followed the trail onward at first light. Horren shed a tear, saying a long good-bye to his grove as he left it behind. He explained later the Addingrove would wither without his power to sustain it, and evil would be able to enter freely into his domain. If and when he returned, he might find his home gone, either assimilated into the woods around it or destroyed by creatures of shadow, who always looked to assail places of goodness when they were unprotected. Yet, the Addin had no second thoughts. He had found an opportunity to serve the Fairies again, and he held it was his divine responsibility to do so.

Kari was, if anything, appalled by the prospect. Horren had sworn loyalty to her, but she didn't want anything to do with him. Yet, since there was nothing she could do other than allow him to follow behind her, awaiting her orders, she coldly accepted his presence in their party.

Landyn was ecstatic to have him with them. As the minstrel rode his gray horse Luck, the Addin walked beside him and the two talked constantly. Horren listened at length to Landyn's tales of the world, both old and new. He was especially interested in the current events of nearby countries, for he received no news in the Addingrove except the little he learned from passing animals. And Landyn listened for hours as the Addin talked of old times, hundreds of years in the past. The minstrel asked many questions, logging all the information in his mind to be used in songs and stories he claimed he would compose sometime soon. "You are a wealth of information!" he exclaimed to the Addin late in the afternoon. "Praise Lars we ran across you. With your knowledge of history and my talent with song, I will compose ballads to rival even the works of Ottis Brachnitter!"

Ara smiled at the comparison. She liked Landyn for many reasons, and his ambition to be the next great bard was one of them. She had no idea if he was as talented as he claimed, but it amused her when he compared himself to the Great Bard. From another man such words might seem arrogant, but from Landyn they just seemed enthusiastic. His enthusiasm complimented his charm and his good looks to make him irresistible.

And so it was the five of them continued on their way, Kari continuing to follow the tracks carefully northward. Horren respected her wishes and kept his distance, but little by little Ara sensed the tension between them dwindling. Landyn and the Addin were constant companions, and Ara was mostly left with Jinn for company. Strangely, the little Fairy's spirited, sometimes rude mannerisms didn't bother her half as much as they once did.

Perhaps we all are growing more tolerant of the differences between us.

When night fell they made camp and prepared a small meal, and Ara reflected back on the last few days. She felt more confident with the Addin in their little company, and she began to think everything would be all right.

Surely they were growing closer to Sarah and the others. Surely they would find them safe and sound.

Wrapped in her blankets, she closed her eyes. Her last thoughts were of her daughter and the reunion they would soon share. She drifted into a sound sleep and passed the night in dreams thankfully devoid of sorcery and darkness and Salin Urdrokk.

Alec and his companions had progressed roughly a third of the way to the mountain when they stopped to camp for the night. They spread their blankets out, crushing the long grass beneath so they could lie down without being swallowed by it. Alec said goodnight to Sarah as she lay down to sleep, and she answered with a small smile before closing her eyes. Lorn stretched out several yards away, and Kraig sat nearby, taking the first watch. Michael sat on his own blanket, separated from the others by twenty feet of the high grass. He rested his hands on his knees and stared blankly into the distance. Alec shook his head silently and then took his place by Sarah's side.

For twenty minutes he lay there, tossing and turning, his mind continually returning to the hermit. Michael's silent sulking had been bothering him nearly as much as Sarah's depression. He resolved he would at least try to breach Michael's wall of silence. Perhaps he could find out what was wrong with the hermit and could help in some way.

He got up and waded through the grass until he came to Michael's blanket. The hermit sat with his legs crossed, a closed book resting before him. His eyes blankly stared at the thick tome while his fingers traced the edge of its cover. He did not notice Alec until the baker loudly cleared his throat. Then he looked up, his eyes filled with pain. He said nothing.

Alec sat down facing him. "Is that the book Horren gave you?"

Michael nodded, his eyes dropping to the book's cover.

"What is it about?" asked Alec.

The hermit sighed. Without looking up, he said, "It is about the past, a past long dead and best forgotten. It is also about the Laws."

"The Laws?"

Michael met his gaze and held it weakly. "The Seven Laws. I have spoken of them before."

Now that he had gotten Michael talking, Alec was not about to let the conversation lose momentum. Besides, he was genuinely interested in anything the hermit had to say.

"The Seven Laws. They have something to do with magic, right?"

Michael nodded. "Shaping, yes. The Seven Laws define the basic principles of Shaping reality to one's needs. They are central to every Shaper's early training. Without a full understanding of and belief in the Laws, what you call magic could not exist."

Alec nodded. "And it's all in your book, is it?"

Michael shrugged. "Not that it matters to me. I know the Seven Laws by heart, yet I cannot Shape. Knowing them is not enough. One must have utter faith in the Laws, and complete confidence in oneself. I have neither."

Michael started to turn his back, a sure sign the conversation was over. But Alec spoke up before the hermit could get away.

"So what else is in the book? You said something about the past."

With a slow nod, Michael said, "It is a history text. It tells the tales of the great Shapers of old, both fairy and human. It speaks of the power of the Three, whose brilliance outshone all other Shapers before or since, save the One from whom they derived their strength. It tells of many who followed the Seven Laws, most of whom belong to a glorious, but long dead, past. It also mentions the sorcerers; corrupt men and women who twist the world into an evil Shape. Sorcerers like Salin Urdrokk."

"Salin. It always comes back to him. He really is a master of Shaping, isn't he?"

"No! Call it sorcery, if you call his dark art anything at all. For those who practice sorcery follow only six of the Laws. The First Law, the law they shun, is the most important of all: 'All things, living and not, and all energy, are a part of the One. The One is pure and good, and thus nothing done with his power shall be done for the sake of evil.' As sorcery corrupts, it breaks this First Law and thus is not true Shaping. Shaping is creative, sorcery destructive. Shaping is defensive in nature, sorcery is aggressive. Both bend the fabric of the world, but sorcery coerces while Shaping gently coaxes. It is said that some who fail to grasp the concepts of Shaping turn to sorcery in frustration: it is easier, and seemingly more powerful. It is seductive, but false. The true way lies always with the Seven. And with the One."

Alec sat back, stunned. Michael had for a moment forgotten his grief and had allowed himself to embrace a hidden passion. His eyes burned red as he spoke of sorcery, and his voice was filled with contempt. It was a side of Michael Alec hadn't seen before, and it frightened him, but at least it showed he cared about something. If Alec could force Michael to channel his passion, make use of it somehow, he could perhaps bring the hermit out of his despondent mood once and for all.

First Sarah, now Michael. What am I, the party priest?

"You seem to know a lot about this book. But I haven't seen you open its cover once since Horren gave it to you. Have you read it before?"

"I never read it, but I have heard much of what it contains. It is the most complete history of Shapers and Shaping ever to be compiled. It is known as *The Book of the One.*"

"Why did Horren give it to you?"

Michael shook his head and raised his eyebrows. "He believes it will help me. I have not walked under the face of the One for many years. Horren thinks this book will remind me of the man I once was, the man he thinks I could become again."

Alec leaned in close to the hermit, his expression grave. He felt he was getting close to something. Softly, he asked, "And just who were you, Michael? Who are you?"

His only reply was a cold, iron silence.

Alec shook his head and grimaced. "All right," he said. "Have your little secret. It doesn't matter who you were. Who you *are*. What matters is you are here, helping us. Something terrible went wrong in Barton Hills, and you're helping to set matters right. You can pretend not to care as much as you want, but the fact you're here, with us, proves you do care. Tomorrow, why don't you join us? I mean walk by our sides, talk to us, offer your advice like you used to. So you can't Shape…I've never met anyone who could. You know more of the world than anyone I know, and your wisdom has gotten us this far. Without you I'd be dead by now and Salin would have the Talisman. We need you, but not as some sulking tag along. We need *you*."

Michael hesitated, his eyes uncertain. Then, he pressed his lips together and nodded decisively. "So be it. I will offer whatever help I can. Thank you, Alec. I doubt any of the others have as much faith in me as you seem to. Now, go. You need sleep and the night is wasting."

Alec nodded and meaningfully held Michael's gaze for a few seconds. Then he rose and walked to his own blanket. Looking back, he saw the hermit open Horren's book and bend to read it by the light of the moon. Alec lay down and was able to drift into a deep, satisfied sleep.

Kraig gazed out into the dark and silent night. From his perch upon a fallen log he had a clear view of the camp and the area surrounding it. Sarah was wrapped in her blankets sleeping peacefully and Alec was off talking to the hermit. Lorn was lying down nearby, but Kraig could tell the warrior was not asleep. He kept turning over and over, and occasionally he would run his hands through his hair or over his beard and mumble something to himself. It was not the first time Kraig had noticed the warrior acting strangely, especially at night when he thought no one was watching. Lorn looked afraid and worried, emotions he effectively hid from the others during the day. At night, though, in darkness, he could not suppress the fears and nightmares which threatened to overwhelm him.

Kraig was concerned for Lorn, but he was more concerned for what would happen if the warrior's fears crippled him. Who would guide them to Faerie? Michael? Kraig was still not ready to put his faith in the hermit; after all, Michael hadn't been much more than sulking dead weight since Bordonhold. They were depending on Lorn, and if the warrior fell back into his old ways, they would most likely never reach their destination.

Rising purposefully, the peacekeeper made his way over to where Lorn lay. He knelt down beside the warrior, who jerked upright when he noticed he was no longer alone. His face was covered in sweat, his eyes wild with fear.

"Lars," he said after a moment, calming himself with deep, slow breaths. "You startled me. I must have been dreaming."

"You weren't dreaming," said Kraig. "You were awake. I was watching you. What's going on with you, Lorn?"

Lowering his head, Lorn asked, "What do you mean?"

"Since our battle with the goblins outside of Bordonhold, you've been steadily improving. I mean, you seem to be carrying yourself with more confidence and you're not afraid to voice your opinions. I might not like the choices you made before we met you, the choices which led you down the neck of a bottle, but I respect you for trying to climb back out of that bottle. You're doing well. What's more, I've never seen anyone fight like you. With all the progress you're making, and with all the skill you obviously have, what in Hell are you so afraid of?"

"Afraid?" he asked. He lowered his eyes to where his fists lay in his lap, tight with emotion. "I am afraid of just about everything. Most of all, I am afraid of failure. I am ashamed at what I have become, and I fear I will never be able to break out of the cage of impotence I have erected around myself. Ever since I left my home four years ago, ever since the life I had been prepared for was torn from my grasp leaving me with nothing, I have had no sense of purpose or value. I even started to believe some of the terrible things they said about me."

Lorn's answer only provided Kraig with more questions. "Lorn, I won't pretend I understand what you're talking about, but none of it matters. What ever you did, or what ever they said you did, is in the past now. You spoke before of your brother casting you out of your home. Forget him and move on. Build a new home, a new life, and let the past die. Concentrate on the here and now. We're all counting on you to get us to Faerie."

"It is not so easy," said the warrior. "You do not know how serious the accusations against me were, or what my brother hoped to gain by casting me out. Somehow he convinced our father to turn against me, and I fear what else he can accomplish by bending our father's ear with his lies. In our youth we were the best of friends, but he has changed, become dark and greedy, and I know not why. And there is more. Recently I have heard he has married my old love. This is what sent me into my most recent fit of depression and drinking. She swore to remain faithful to me forever, even in my exile, and now she is his."

"I'm sorry, Lorn. But we need you."

The warrior pushed back a stray piece of long hair which had fallen out of his pony-tail. He lay back down and turned on his side, dismissing Kraig.

"Leave me be. I will not let you down, but in the night you must leave me to my sorrow. I must deal with it in my own way."

The peacekeeper wasn't convinced of Lorn's promise not to let them down, but he took some comfort in the fact there was no ale or wine on hand. He was sure the warrior would never be able to resist the temptation. But he was too frustrated to go on arguing, so he left the man to his fears and demons and went back to his post. He hoped in the light of day Lorn would be able to shut his weakness away as he had over the last few days. He didn't want the others to know their guide was not as strong as he tried to seem. They had enough to worry about already.

The next day the mountains loomed closer, and the forest had vanished entirely into the distance behind them. The sun was bright and hot for most of the morning, but before noon gray clouds blew in from the east and blotted out the light. For the first time since they set out from Barton Hills, the weather turned gray and threatened rain.

Alec looked up into the overcast sky as the cool, crisp wind blew over him. He was certainly not pleased by the prospect of rain, but the wind brought welcome relief from the summer heat. He breathed deeply, the fresh sting of the whipping wind filling his lungs. He found the change in the weather strangely delightful, even somewhat exhilarating. He had not felt so good, so alive, in quite a while.

Even physically speaking, Alec's condition was much improved. His muscles had gotten so used to constant abuse he no longer felt their pain. The ache had become an intrinsic part of his being, not worth any more consideration than breathing. He could travel further now without rest, and he could keep up a brisk pace with little effort. The exercise and the meager rations he had been forced to live on for the past eleven days had done him some good. His belly still jiggled as he walked, but not half so much as it had before.

Michael, who had been walking beside Alec and Sarah, surveyed the thickening clouds above. "A storm gathers. I fear we'll find no shelter from it here."

"Oh, what's a little water," said Sarah, whose black mood was all but gone, replaced by her usual playful sarcasm. "What, are you afraid of melting?"

Michael raised an eyebrow, his mouth considering a grin. "Quite the contrary, dear child. I enjoy the rain. Still, we may find ourselves wishing for shelter. Out here on the plains storms can reach raging proportions, with mad winds and furious downpours."

"More good news," muttered Alec.

Kraig and Lorn walked several yards ahead, tramping a trail through the grass. When the first drops of rain began to fall, they stopped and turned to the others.

"I think we should quicken our pace," said Kraig. "In the mountains ahead, we may find shelter from the storm. We could reach them in a few hours if we hurry."

Michael shook his head. "Our pace is fast as it is. Running will only tire us, and this storm may not last long enough to make a forced march worthwhile. Let us continue as we have been, and hope for a short, light rain."

"Lorn?" said Kraig, turning to the long-haired man.

Lorn evaluated the distance between where they stood and where the mountains sat in the north. "Regardless of speed, we will not reach Gravescorn before this weather takes its toll on us. Best to conserve our energy so we might better face the storm."

Kraig nodded. "Then let's go. A slow march is better than standing still."

And so they trudged onward as the rain came down harder. It was not long before Alec saw lightning dancing on the peaks of the Gravescorn and heard thunder tearing the air. The west-blowing wind howled in his ears, tossing buckets of water at him and his companions. The grass whipped in the wind and was bent low to the ground. He lifted one arm to shield his face, and with the other he pulled Sarah close to his side. Her long blond hair was tossed by the wind, and she squeezed her eyes shut against the rain. Her green and brown dress clung to her body, completely soaked through.

"Well, this certainly is unpleasant!" she cried over the wind. Squinting up at him, she managed a smile, and Alec couldn't help but laugh.

Ahead, Lorn gazed out through the downpour, his hand shielding his eyes from the rain. As he stopped and scanned the area carefully, a curious look covered his dripping face. "There is something ahead, a hazy blur rising from the plain. It appears to be a low structure. I remember passing through several settlements when last I traversed these plains, but that was many years ago, and I had heard they were abandoned. Even so, it might provide us with sanctuary from this gale."

They followed Lorn onward, and it wasn't long before Alec saw the structure. It seemed out of place on the otherwise desolate plain: a long, short building constructed of white stone. As they grew closer Alec noticed the outer walls were rough, and many shuttered windows were evenly spaced along the building's side.

When they reached the building's long, southern face, Lorn led them around the side when it became obvious there were no entrances there. When they reached the northern wall, Alec saw a sturdy wooden doorway set in its center. Other than this, the north-facing wall was identical to the south.

With the raging wind and the torrential rain obscuring his vision Alec could not be certain, but he thought he could make out other structures nearby. They were smaller and oddly shaped, jagged as if they were unfinished or had been damaged. It appeared someone had made a home in these plains, but whether they were still here remained to be seen. He also wondered what sort of people these plain-dwellers were and if they would be sympathetic to a band of strangers.

Lorn rapped on the door. He waited a moment, and when there was no answer he shoved it open with his broad shoulder. He peered in briefly and then entered. Kraig went in next and Alec followed carefully.

Alec had no expectations, but he still felt a little disappointed by what they found inside the building or rather what they didn't find. There was nothing there save some broken stones, some gravel, and a few decrepit pieces of furniture. A rectangular table, long and decayed, was overturned in the center of the elongated hall. Toppled and broken chairs lay around the table, and on the walls were paintings and tapestries so faded they showed not a sign of the art which once graced them. Some scant light shown through the shutters, but for the most part the hall was dark.

"A meeting hall of some sort, or a dining area," said Lorn. "I was very young when last I crossed this plain, and my party did not pass through this region, but I had met other plain-dwellers on the journey who lived in similar villages to this one. Apparently they are gone now, but we may shelter here while the storm rages."

A thought struck Alec. "But what about Salin? I doubt he'll stop for rain or wind. What if he *is* nearby and catches us here?"

"We will stay only a short while," said Lorn. "If it does not let up within a few hours, we will have to brave the storm. But I would rather not risk it. Long exposure to weather like this can take a great toll on a person's health, and we cannot be burdened with illness. And there are other dangers. The rain awakens the creatures I mentioned, and the grass will be crawling with them. At any rate, I believe Salin is yet far behind us. We will reach the relative safety of the Gravescorn before he is upon us."

"I hope you are right," said Michael. "I would rather face a scorpion's sting than Salin's wrath. Yet I, too, have traveled this plain and am aware of the dangers. We should wait out the rain, if we can."

Kraig nodded, but began to pace nervously. "I don't like standing still. We'll wait if we have to, but I want to march long into the night to make up for lost time. Try and get some rest now. I'll stand guard."

Alec didn't feel tired, but nevertheless he located an area relatively free of debris and lay down. Sarah lay beside him and used his belly as a pillow. As she snuggled against him, he became far too aware of her presence. She had been sleeping near him for the majority of their journey, but she had never before been *this* bold. He closed his eyes and tried to still the feeling rising inside him.

He lay still, listening to the rain beating on the roof. He concentrated on the sound, managing to steer his awareness away from the sleeping girl cuddled next to him. But as he listened, he heard voices muttering nearby. Lorn and Michael were speaking softly, obviously not wanting the others to overhear. They must have thought Alec was asleep.

"Yes," said Michael, "I have heard of him. But what makes you think he still exists?"

"I do not know if he still lives, or if he remains in the plains, but we must be wary. What else could have brought such destruction upon this village?"

"Many things. The weather, sorcery, or just men with their petty wars. A devastated village is not a sure sign the Ravager still wanders the Plain of Naar. Besides, this village was abandoned long ago. Just look around!"

"I am simply saying we must give the Ravager consideration. The plainsfolk used to live in constant fear of the beast. I remember the stories they told. They said he brought storms like this one to destroy their crops, flood their homes, make them vulnerable. Fire poured from his eyes, consuming all who met his gaze. He fed upon their children!"

There was silence for a moment, and then Michael's voice spoke calmly. "Tales have a way of growing in the telling, Lorn. I believe there was a Ravager at one time, if only because so many tales speak of him. But he has rarely been seen outside of Naar, and there have been no new tales of the creature for many, many years. If indeed he was responsible for the destruction here, he has long since moved on."

"You are probably right," admitted Lorn. "But I fear these plains. The Ravager is only one of the dark legends of Naar."

"This place has spawned many evil tales, as have the Gravescorn Mountains. You were wise not to mention your fears to the children. They have had too much darkness to deal with already."

"Then we will keep this between ourselves. There is, of course, a great chance we will pass through the plain and over the mountains without incident. We have come this far and have had no encounters. I hope our luck holds."

"As do I. I am all for caution, but do not let your fears run wild. Remember, you were young when you passed through here and heard these fell tales. Perhaps it is only your childhood fancies you fear."

"Perhaps. And yet..."

The conversation was cut short by a banging noise. Alec sat up sharply, knocking Sarah off his stomach. The door had been thrust open, and standing in the doorway stood a bent old man, framed by the gray fury of the storm. His hair was short and white, matted down by the rain. His wrinkled face was covered in a scruffy beard, and his eyes were gray and tired. He wore brown rags and leaned on a stick. At his side he carried a small brown bag.

"Who's there?" he questioned, peering into the dim hall. "What are you doing in my home?"

Lorn's sword was suddenly in his hand, as if by magic. "Who are you?" he said, taking a threatening step toward the newcomer.

"Who am I? Why, I think I should be the one asking the questions. You are the intruders here. This is my home!"

Sarah, who had jarred awake when Alec jerked up, was staring at the old man with a sleepy curiosity. Alec looked from her to Lorn, and then to Kraig, who was pulling his axe from his belt while glaring at the stranger. Michael stood calmly beside Lorn, seemingly unconcerned.

"No one has lived here for an age," said Lorn. "You lie." He advanced menacingly.

"N...no!" cried the old one. "I do live here. I...I am the only one left. The other villagers—and all the plainsfolk, as far as I know—perished years ago. Only I survived."

Lorn lowered his blade, but not his guard. Kraig took a few steps closer to the old man, his eyes filled with danger. The man backed away, preparing to flee back out into the rain.

"This is foolish," said Michael. "Let him come in. Keep him under close guard if you wish, but do not send him out into the rain. If he lives here as he says, then he is a harmless old man. If he is an enemy, it is best to keep him close where he can do no harm. At any rate, I am curious to find out what happened here and he is our only source."

"Very well," said Lorn, taking a step back. The old man cowered as Lorn led him into the room. He clutched his small bag to his chest.

Sarah leaned toward Alec and whispered in his ear. "After Tor, I can't help but be suspicious of anyone we meet on this trip."

"I suppose he could be one of Salin's spies," said Alec, "but I doubt it. I'm not half so worried about him as I am of something I overheard Michael and Lorn talking about."

Sarah tilted her head quizzically. "What did you hear?"

Before he could answer, Michael walked up to them and said, "You two might as well join us. We are going to question our friend, here."

Alec pushed himself up and helped Sarah to her feet. They followed Michael to the center of the room, where Kraig arranged several chairs in a semi-circle, a single chair facing them. Lorn pushed the old man down in the lone chair and stood guard over him. Alec joined the others as they took seats in the semi-circle. Michael leaned forward, casting his passionless gaze at the old man.

"What happened out here, and how did it come to pass only *you* managed to survive? It seems very unlikely, and quite suspicious, especially since you claim to have survived alone out here for a number of years."

"I swear, it is the truth," the stranger gasped. "Look, this is what I live on these days."

He pulled open his sack and emptied its contents onto the floor. Alec's gut squirmed at the sight of the tangled mass of small snakes lying dead upon the floor.

"I pick them out of the grass. They are quite easy to find, especially when the rain drives them from their holes. This breed is not poisonous, and they are very nutritious, even though they taste like dung. It is not hard to survive alone in this land, if you know how to harvest what the plains provide. I may be old, but I am no cripple, not yet.

"As for how I came to survive the…tragedy which destroyed the village, this is not so easy to explain. I'm not sure I understand myself."

When he paused, Lorn placed a hand on his shoulder and squeezed. "Try to explain."

The old man wrung his hands. "For years, the people of the Plain of Naar led simple lives. Our fathers were a nomadic folk, explorers from Madagon and other countries in the north of Eglacia. They set out from their homes to blaze new trails northward, hoping to establish a new country to call their own. They found these plains and settled them. The land was hard to work, and the grass-land was inhabited by all manner of dangerous creatures, but they were a hearty folk and would not let their dream die. You see, the founders of Naar were driven by their passion to tame wild lands; they could not go back. The kingdoms of the Eglacian Union, under the dominion of the High King in Eglak, were too quiet, too civilized. The plains provided them with what they needed: a challenge.

"Many villages were established across the plain, so spread out there was lit-tle communication between them, and almost none with the land they left behind. By my generation, the lands to the south were but a legend to us, as we must have become to the people there. We heard of Tyridan, of course, as it was our nearest neighbor, and occasionally a party would pass through on the way to the Fairy-land, but this was the extent of it. The villages were self-suffi-cient. We kept mostly to ourselves.

"But, as I said, life out here could be hard. It was difficult to grow crops in the hard soil of Naar, and few large animals were to be found for food. Occa-sionally, ogres would come from their lands in the north and raid our villages. And, of course, the villages had differences with one another, and often resorted to battle to settle them. But of all the horrors of the plains, the greatest was the creature we named Ravager."

Alec saw Michael and Lorn lock eyes grimly. It was almost too coincidental that the old man had brought up the very creature they had been discussing just moments ago. Yet they said nothing, and the stranger continued his tale.

"It was whispered among the people that the storms were caused by the Ravager and that the crops died because the Ravager willed it. When people disappeared or died mysteriously, it was the work of the Ravager. As a young man, I thought such stories were ridiculous, tall tales to scare children by the fire at night. But as I grew older and wiser, I learned to believe."

As the old man told his tale, his anxiety vanished and an excitement filled him. He seemed to have forgotten he was practically their prisoner, taking the role of a fireside story-teller instead. His eyes grew wide as he spoke, and his hands waved melodramatically.

"Many times throughout the years the Ravager worked his evil. I heard rumors from distant villages that the beast had carried off half their women in the night, or that twenty men were found beheaded in the fields, or that their homes blew apart in the midst of a storm. And in our own village, people grew scared. Once, hideous laughter filled the air, and the next day our fields lay burnt and ruined. Another time, a figure was seen running from home to home, and later each home he touched collapsed while the residents were inside. Most were killed instantly. And in this very hall, where the village council met, the Ravager himself appeared and killed all of the council with fire from its eyes. It was not long after the final attack came, the one which tore apart the village and slaughtered everyone but me."

He paused for a moment, his excitement dying. His eyes teared and his body shook. He cast his eyes down toward the floor, and said, "I remember very little of it. I was visiting my daughter and her husband, sitting outside their home playing with my granddaughter. Then I looked up and saw the skies grow dark. Lighting came from the sky and the loudest thunder I had ever heard shook the land. I rose and ran through the village, screaming as fiery hail dropped from the sky. And then…the next thing I knew, I lay in the street, naked and bloody. Many slashes, like knife wounds, covered me, and an arrow pierced my leg below the knee. Yet, my wounds did not bleed and I felt little pain. I surveyed the village, horrified. Bodies, torn limb from limb, were scattered in the streets, and the homes and shops were blasted and broken. But for myself, there were no survivors.

"There is not much more to tell. It took days, but I gave the villagers a proper funeral, burning the bodies as is our custom. I cried over my daughter and her girl for hours. I wandered in grief for days, but then I became determined to survive. I was too scared of death to do otherwise. Being too old to travel, I lived here as a hermit for many years, gathering these snakes for food, hiding from the predators which sometimes come in the night. I have had no visitors until you came, and I expected none, for no one passes this way anymore. Even the Ravager himself seems to have gone away. Now, there is only me, sad old Druga."

When it became obvious his tale had ended, Michael nodded. "Druga, is it? I wonder why you were left alive when all your folk had been torn apart. And how do you account for the knife wounds and the arrow? Surely this Ravager has no need for such weapons."

"I cannot say how I came by those wounds. I do not remember anything!"

Michael rubbed his clean shaven chin, his eyes looking through the man called Druga. He sat still for a moment, and Alec wondered what thoughts consumed him. Suddenly he rose and walked over to the old man.

"There are creatures which exist outside our world, beyond our limited knowledge. Sometimes these beings can be brought here or can come here on their own. But they have no form, no shape of their own, for here they exist only in spirit. They must enter into a body of some sort, sometimes a construct and sometimes living flesh. I believe your Ravager is such a creature. I believe he entered into you, took control of your body, and used it to raze this place. That is why you had the wounds—your fellow villagers were trying to slay you, for you were slaughtering them and destroying their homes! Druga, you were the Ravager."

Druga's jaw dropped and he shook his old head in horror. "No! What you say cannot be! The other villages, I never visited them. They were attacked as well!"

"The Ravager could have possessed another. If he was as powerful as your tale makes him out to be, he could have leapt from body to body many times over the years. At different times, the Ravager could have been different people, spread out all across the Plain of Naar, and perhaps beyond."

Alec peered at Druga, fear, pity, and disbelief filling his heart. Could such a tale be true? If it were, poor Druga had to live with the knowledge of what he did to his village! The baker turned his gaze to Sarah and saw compassion in her eyes. Then he turned to Kraig, whose face was twisted with doubt. Lorn retained his cold poise over the man and Michael paced in front of him.

"It is possible, though unlikely, this spirit known as the Ravager still exists within you. These beings seldom wish to return to their own world, and if there was not another host near-by, he would have clung to you. Perhaps he could leap to another body as far away as the next village, but if he already slaughtered everyone there, there would have been no body to which he could return."

"What about its previous host in that village?" offered Kraig.

"He could have died from wounds inflicted during his rampage, or simply not had Druga's will to survive. Or the very power of the Ravager could have consumed him from within. Few survive such a possession. From what I understand, Druga is in the vast minority. Just the fact that he still lives leads me to believe the Ravager still resides within him, saving him for some further purpose."

Druga jumped up and waved his hands wildly. "This is absurd! I am not the Ravager! I am no killer! Get out of my home!"

"What should we do about him?" asked Lorn, pushing the man back into his chair. "If he is this creature as you suspect, we cannot let him run free."

Michael shrugged. "We can do nothing. I will not take this man's life, for he is not to blame for the evil within him. I cannot drive the spirit from him, but I have heard there are Fairy-shapers who can do so. As they called the spirits forth who became the Addins, so can they force such beings back to their own worlds."

"Are you suggesting we bring him with us?" asked Kraig.

"It may be the only way," answered Michael.

"I will not go anywhere!" cried Druga. "I must wait here for...*for the master!*"

Suddenly his eyes glowed red, and he launched himself forward at Michael. Effortlessly, he pinned the hermit to the ground and bent his head as if to bite Michael's neck. Lorn ran at Druga, but the old man swung his arm around and sent Lorn flying across the room.

"*You fool! Vorik Seth will not allow his Ravager to be cast from this body, from this world. He has plans for me yet...I have plans!*"

"Vorik Seth?" grunted Michael.

Suddenly Kraig shouted, his muscles bulging as he raised his mighty axe into the air. He brought it down violently, burying it deep in Druga's back. The Ravager howled using the old man's mouth, and turned its gaze on the peacekeeper. The axe still in its back, it leapt at Kraig and wrapped its hands around his neck, throwing the big man to the ground.

Before he could question his sanity, Alec ran to where the Ravager was strangling Kraig. With a swing of his boot, he kicked the creature in the face, breaking its nose. When it looked up, Alec kicked again with all his might, and knocked Druga onto his back. The axe blade struck the floor and pushed up through the old man's chest. He grasped the slippery red blade with his shaking hands, coughed up thick blood and lay still.

Alec looked down at Druga's wide-eyed death-glare and fell to his knees, shaking. "Wounds. Is it...is it dead?"

Michael, just recovering, stumbled over and looked down. "If he is dead, he took the Ravager into death with him. Such a creature dies when its host dies, unless it manages to jump free of the body first."

Suddenly the ground shook and the storm outside raged harder. The body before Alec lifted into the air, righted itself, and was surrounded by a dark, purple light. The eyes glowed red again and the mouth twisted in a sinister grin. A whirlwind, centered on Druga's floating form, knocked Alec and the others back.

Hideous laughter filled the air. *"For the Seth I ravaged the Plains of Naar, and for him I will travel southward and raze those lands if they will not join in his cause. I have been waiting...waiting for a new host strong enough to make the journey. And now fate has provided!"*

His hands twisted into his claws, and the room was bathed in a blood-red glow. The light in his eyes intensified, and a blast of flame shot directly toward Alec!

"NO!"

The cry had come from Lorn, who had seemingly come from nowhere to position himself between Alec and the fire. He threw up his arms and turned his head away as the fire enveloped him, crackling as it licked his flesh. But when the fire died, Lorn stood unharmed. The big man smiled when he saw the Ravager's confusion and without transition was upon the beast.

Alec was confused, too. Did he not just see Lorn consumed by flame? And yet the man had no evidence of burn or boil. Rather, he had leapt high into the air and pulled the Ravager down to the floor, beating him fiercely with his bare fists. Druga's face was bloodied, and again he lay still. Lorn pulled out his sword and laid it across the old man's neck. His muscles tensed to deliver his death blow.

"Wait!" cried Druga. "It's me! The Ravager has fled!"

Before Alec was able to assimilate what was happening, he heard a loud slam behind him. He turned to see the door had been thrown open. Lighting cracked directly outside, illuminating the dark figure in the doorway.

"I have found you at last," said Salin.

CHAPTER 12

Flight to the Gravescorn

Three hours earlier it had just started to rain, and Tor felt his heart sink further. It was not bad enough he had to endure Salin's continual mood swings, ever fearing the sorcerer would turn on him in a fit of rage. And even the band of loud, smelly ogres who had joined them just north of Tyridan was not the last agony he had been forced to bear. This was a journey of horrors, and this downpour was just the icing on the cake.

He rode onward following his master, his depression deepening with every mile. He longed to find Mason, slit his throat wide, capture the Talisman, and ride homeward. Preferably alone. Working for Salin Urdrokk had provided him with many rewards, but he began to wonder if riding along side the demon was worth any reward. Especially now that the stench of twenty wet ogres continuously assaulted his nose.

Tor continued to be surprised by the resources at Salin's command. Only a few hours after the sorcerer had sent out some sort of telepathic message, they were joined by a group of ogres nearly thirty strong. The huge creatures must have had lairs nearby, although in general ogres lived far to the north, and there had been no sightings in Tyridan for many years. Salin must have called for them previously, keeping them in waiting until they were needed. Ten he sent on a goblin hunt, for when he had said he would have the little creatures killed, he had not been joking. The rest he bade join him and Tor to assist in the chase.

Of course, the call he had sent out would reach other ogres as well. It would be heard as far north as their forest home beyond the Gravescorn, and even now they would be racing toward the Plain of Naar in force. Mason and his friends would be caught between a virtual army of ogres and Salin's fury. They didn't have a prayer of reaching Faerie.

And Salin's influence did not stop with the likes of goblins and ogres. He had many, many agents as his command, agents who, like Tor, had once been good men and women corrupted by the power of Salin's promises. Two of them, sisters named Stiletta and Gwendolyn, had joined them at Bordonhold. Tor was not fond of either of them, for although they were as beautiful and seductive as any women he'd ever met, they were cold as steel and filled with hate. Stiletta was a master of small weaponry, such as daggers and throwing knives, and Gwendolyn was a sorceress with a certain mastery over ice. She could freeze a man's heart with a glance, literally.

Luckily for Tor, those two kept mostly to themselves. Unfortunately, this left him with Salin for company. As they rode through the rain, he forced himself to turn toward his master.

"Are they near?" he shouted over the sound of the wind.

Salin grinned, his yellowed teeth showing through cracked lips. "Yes. There is a presence close to us, a strong mystic power throbbing at the edge of my consciousness. It must be the Talisman. We grow ever closer to it. Soon, the fool Mason will be dead, and the Talisman of the Fairies will be mine!"

Good. And then this will be over.

"When we find them, leave Mason to me," said Salin. "You can have the rest if you can beat the beasts to them."

Tor wondered if Salin meant the ogres or the women. He felt a pang of regret, for he would have liked to take some of his frustration out on Mason, the child who had blinded him with his cursed light and knocked him senseless. But what Salin wanted, Salin got.

Lightning flashed through the air and thunder rumbled nearby. The storm was growing. Tor checked to see that his equipment was adequately protected from the downpour, especially his new sword. He cursed himself at losing his old one, for it had been enchanted with mystic runes of power, making it truer than a normal blade, and unbreakable. Yet his skills far surpassed those of most master swordsmen, and even without magical aid he had defeated some of the most renowned Bladeknights of Eglak. The only thing surpassing his skill with a sword was his unbelievable accuracy with a bow. He prayed he would be blessed with an opportunity to use his talents.

After enduring the rain for hours, they came to a demolished settlement. Salin, laughing and rubbing his hands together in anticipation, said, "They are here! The cretins have taken shelter in that large hall just ahead. Tor, order the ogres to surround the building. Tell Gwendolyn to stay with them, and you and Stiletta come with me. I wish to give Mason and his friends a little surprise."

Tor delivered the orders, and then dismounted to follow Salin toward the building. They found the door, and he and the woman waited for their master's command.

"I feel…great energies being expended inside. Something is happening. But no matter. Our goal is here…my destiny is upon me!"

He kicked open the door with a grace and power no man his age should have possessed. Lightning flashed and Tor heard his master say, "I have found you at last."

Alec was stricken with panic. Behind him, Lorn grappled with a being capable of razing entire villages. Before him stood the terror he had been fleeing since he left Barton Hills. There was no escape. One way or another, death had found him.

An explosion of almost instantaneous events erupted around him, but they took on a dream-like quality, slow and somewhat blurred. Alec was part of the dream, his sluggish muscles unable to respond to his fear. He saw Salin, grinning wildly, pull his bejeweled long sword from its sheath. The blade radiated a crimson light which pulsed in rhythm with Alec's pounding heart. Vaguely he was aware of motion around him: Kraig leaping forward with axe in hand, a panicked Michael fumbling futilely with his sword, Sarah reaching out for Alec's arm. Salin ignored everyone but Alec. He aimed his blade at the baker's chest, and a sizzling blaze of crimson lightning stabbed forth.

If Alec hadn't leapt aside in panic when the sorcerer raised his sword, the blast would have torn him apart. As he crashed to the ground, the lightning struck the far wall and blasted it into slivers of white rock. The jagged hole left by the bolt was larger than Alec himself. Salin raced toward him laughing, a ball of flame gathering in his left hand.

Out of the corner of his eye, Alec saw Kraig go flying backward, his axe torn from his grip by some unseen force. Michael had managed to draw his sword, but in his panic he dropped it to the floor.

The baker tried to move out of the way of the sorcerer's onslaught, but it was far too late. Alec moved as if through quicksand, and Salin was lightning itself. Alec said a quiet prayer to Grok as the sorcerer lifted his hand to release the ball of flame.

Without warning a blood-red glow enveloped Salin. He froze in his tracks, his fire vanishing and his eyes bulging in shock and rage. Anger twisted his face as he shouted, "Get out of my mind! Do you not know who I am?"

The voice of the Ravager roared through the room, coming from everywhere and nowhere. *"I do not know you, sorcerer, nor do I care who you may be! There is a great power within you, and I would call it my own!"*

"Damn you!" raged Salin. "Get you gone from this place, spirit! You have no prayer against me, but you delay my victory!"

Salin dropped his sword and grabbed his head with both hands. His old face wrinkled in pain and he began to scream pure fury. Taking advantage of the situation, Alec leapt up and ran toward the hole Salin had blasted in the wall. He grabbed Sarah's arm and shouted to the others.

"Run while he's down! It's our only hope!"

Kraig and Michael followed quickly, both having retrieved their weapons. Lorn had been standing over Druga all along, unwilling to let the man free even after Salin had burst in. Now he jumped up and shouted, "Come on, old man! It is obvious the Ravager no longer has use for your feeble flesh."

As they escaped through the splintered tear in the wall, Alec risked a glance over his shoulder. To his shock, Tor was running through the door, accompanied by a woman. The two paused, confusion plain on their faces when they saw the thrashing sorcerer.

Then Alec turned and ran as hard as he could, his companions only a few steps behind. The rain still pounded the plains, but he no longer spared it a thought. He did not watch where he was going; he did not care as long as it was away from Salin. When the towering, gray form suddenly appeared in front of him, he cried out in horror.

"DOWN!" cried Lorn, leaping through the air toward him. Alec ducked and the warrior flew over his head, sword flashing. Black blood rained down on Alec as a huge gray body toppled beside him.

"Ogres!" shouted Lorn, pulling Alec up by the arm. "Stay behind me."

Alec's mind was suddenly devoid of all rational thought. There was only room for fear. Salin, Tor, and now ogres—there could be no escape from so many terrors. He was not even aware of his feet working, padding through the wet grass at a crazed pace. Vaguely his mind registered countless gray hulks, some before him, some behind, all converging on his position. He followed a shape which might have been Lorn. He heard many shouts, and also many clangs and thunks that he barely understood to be axes and swords slashing and chopping. The storm raged ever harder, drowning out sight and hearing, and panic erased all thought. Soon there was only movement, movement inspired by a terror which threatened to tear open his heart.

Where were the gray hulks? What about the smaller shape he had been following? Where was the hermit, the peacekeeper?

He stumbled forward and fell, blackness reaching out to take him.

Sarah?

Tor had no idea what was happening. He had seen his master's rage before, but he had never seen anything like this. Salin was throwing himself against the wall, pounding his head with his fists. He was shouting out curses, screaming in agony. Tor could not pull his gaze away from his flailing master until he felt a hand grip his arm.

Stiletta turned to him, her face painted with urgency. "Look! They are escaping!"

He turned his head and saw a hole in the far wall, and through it he witnessed their prey running into the distance. But one of the runners, a pathetic old man whom Tor did not recognize, had fallen just beyond the opening and was unable to rise. He drew his sword and ran toward the hole.

First blood. Even if it is a helpless old nothing.

"OUT!" cried his master. "Return to whatever pit you call home!"

Tor felt cold, as if a chill wind had blown through him. Ignoring it, he ran out into the rain and lifted his blade above the fallen man's neck. Before he could strike, the old man turned his head toward Tor and smiled. His eyes gleamed with a deadly red glow.

A blast of flame took the former Watcher by surprise, and he fell back screaming, his body on fire. He dropped to the wet grass and rolled, the moisture dousing the flame before it could do much damage. He rolled onto his belly and looked back into the hall. The old man was running, almost floating, toward Salin.

"If I cannot claim your mortal flesh, then I will destroy it, as I have destroyed this land of Naar!"

Tor thought he saw Salin smile. "Come, then. I relish a challenge."

And then Tor saw no more, for the hall exploded in a flash of light and flame, and fiery death spread outward in every direction across the plain with a fury unmatched by any storm.

Wrapped in darkness, Alec felt a pair of hands shaking him. Painfully, he forced his eyes open and tried to make out the blur in front of him. Before long, a grim-faced Michael came into focus. Alec glanced about and saw dark stone walls surrounding them, dampness seeping through the cracks.

"What...where are we?"

"In a watchtower a few miles outside of the village. You stumbled just before we came to this place. Kraig carried you here."

"Kraig did? Did...did everyone make it?"

Michael backed away, and Alec saw Sarah and Kraig sitting against the far wall. The girl was wrapping a makeshift bandage around the man's muscular stomach. Already blood was seeping through the cloth.

"Grok. What about Lorn, and the old man Druga."

"Druga's gone, I think. Lorn is downstairs, keeping watch. I believe the ogres have perished, but Salin could not have been slain so easily. We must go as soon as you and Kraig are fit to travel."

Alec rested his head in his hands, trying to remember what had happened. "The last thing I remember is fleeing from Salin. There were monsters in the storm. Lorn was fighting them."

"We all were, although if it weren't for him, we would have surely perished. There were at least a dozen ogres, and I only managed to take down one. Kraig beheaded two with his axe and Lorn claims five kills. As for the rest, I suspect they died in the fire."

"Fire? What fire?"

"There was a battle of incredible power fought upon the plain. Such a display of unbridled sorcery has not been seen in the world for hundreds of years. Remember what was happening when we fled? The Ravager was attempting to take control of Salin's body. I believe Salin fought him off and he possessed someone else. Perhaps it was one of Salin's companions, or perhaps the spirit returned to Druga. Then they fought, and one of them unleashed a fire which tore across the plain, reaching out in all directions for nearly a mile. The ring of flame died only a few steps behind us, but the ogres we fought were caught within. If not for the rain, the fire would have spread across the plain, and we would have been killed as well."

"Grok's wounds," muttered Alec, shaking his head. "I cannot believe it. Maybe we are lucky, and Salin and the Ravager have slain each other."

"No. I know Salin's power. The Ravager is a mighty spirit of evil, but the sorcerer is greater still. Otherwise he would not be among the highest of Vorik Seth's generals."

"The...the Ravager mentioned Vorik Seth. Does he serve him, too?"

"It is possible. The Seth employs all manner of creatures to spread his evil across the world. Yet, I would not want to give anything that spirit said too much credit. It is also likely it came to this world on its own, and only used the name of the Seth to give its lust for death a cause. But we have other concerns now. The storm has subsided, and we must flee to the mountains before Salin resumes his pursuit. Once there, we will be harder to track."

Michael turned away and descended a flight of stairs spiraling downward in the center of the room. Sarah, who had just finished with Kraig's wounds, turned to Alec and offered him a weak grin.

"How are you?"

He shrugged. "Better than Kraig, I guess. You carried me? With that gash in your stomach?"

The peacekeeper nodded. "I didn't even notice I was wounded until we got here. I didn't have time to think about it. When you fell, about four ogres were ready to jump on you. I scooped you up, threw you over my shoulder, and kept running. We gained some ground on the creatures, and then the fire came. I swear it stopped right under me. I felt the heat of it on my back and under my feet, and then it was behind us. The ogres didn't have a chance, though. I heard them scream. Grok, you should have seen it, Alec. It was like…it was like what happened in Barton Hills, tenfold. I can't imagine anything surviving it."

"Michael says Salin did."

"I'll believe it when I see it. Although, I hope not to see it. Just in case, I think we'd better continue on toward Faerie. There are other dangers out here. Lorn said ogres live in the forest north of here; they could be after us as well."

"North. That's just where we have to go," said Sarah.

Alec nodded. "Well, we'll just have to take things as they come. We've survived wolves, goblins, Tor, and Salin himself. What are a few thousand ogres?"

They laughed, and Alec felt the strain of the last day lighten. He was amazed at their growing ability to face great danger and come away laughing. Perhaps it was impending madness, but he believed it was just them adapting to a difficult situation. To allow themselves to feel the full weight of their danger was the true path to madness.

Sarah rubbed Alec's shoulder and said, "You should eat something. While you were unconscious we had some of the bread and dried beef we brought from Bordonhold."

"I am a bit hungry. We *never* seem to eat on this journey."

Soon after Alec began to munch on a loaf of stale bread and a strip of salty meat, Lorn stuck his head up through the opening in the center of the floor.

"We had better go. I saw some movement on the horizon. Something is heading this way and I doubt it is friendly."

They gathered their things, and Alec took a moment to make sure his silver chest was secure in his pack. Then they descended quickly. The level below them was a watch area, with small windows set in the brick walls. It was here Lorn must have stood watch, for from the windows one could see for miles in every direction. They continued spiraling downward through a few floors of barracks and guard-stations, and eventually came to the ground floor. They rushed out of an open gate and set a fast pace toward the Gravescorn. Alec looked back, but could see nothing moving in the distance. Lorn saw his worried glance.

"They were only visible from the tower. They are still far behind us, but they are moving quickly."

No one spoke as they marched swiftly through the wet grass. The sky was still overcast and the air was damp. A cool wind blew over the plain, but not nearly as violently as before. It was well into the afternoon, and the clouds would make darkness come early. Alec urgently hoped they would reach the mountains before then.

Lorn's pace was faster than any he had set before, and the baker almost had to run to keep up with the taller man's strides. Sarah was struggling as well and despite her best efforts was falling behind.

"We have to slow down," said Alec. "We're already exhausted. This pace will kill us!"

"*Salin* will kill us," answered Lorn. "He is coming fast, Alec Mason, and we must keep ahead of him. Move, if you want to live."

"It's all right," said Sarah. "I can make it."

"That makes one of us," muttered Alec.

Every so often, he glanced back to try to get a glimpse of their pursuers, but for a long while he saw nothing but damp grass and gray sky. Then, after hours of brisk walking, when they were about half way between the ruined village and the towering mountains, he spotted several forms on the horizon.

"There they are," he said, pointing.

"Yes," said Lorn. "I saw them more than half an hour ago."

"We must run," said Michael. "It is surely Salin who follows us. I can feel him."

"Feel him?" questioned Sarah. "You must be imagining things. Why are you so afraid of him? After all, it's not you he wants."

"That is only because he has yet to discover who I am. If he were to recognize me, I fear he would take great pleasure in my torture and murder."

"Why?" asked Kraig, who was easily matching Lorn's steady gait. "What's your connection with Salin?"

Michael shook his head dismissively. "Later. If there is time. For now, concentrate on reaching the mountains, for there we might lose him among the rocky crags. It is a slim chance, but it is our greatest hope."

He began to run, setting a pace even faster than Lorn's. It was not a sprint by any means, but Alec knew he could not match his speed for long. Beside him, Sarah's face grew red with strain. Lorn, Kraig, and Michael ran with little effort, which caused the struggling Alec no little frustration. If he had known his life would depend on a long run over a plain, he wouldn't have let himself grow so flabby. But, by Grok, how could he have known?

When he saw the still far-away forms growing larger and taking on discernible shape, he forced himself to continue running. But in spite of their steady run, their pursuers were gaining ground.

"I just don't...understand," he gasped. "How did...they survive the fire? It looks like they...managed to save their horses, too."

Lorn looked over his shoulder. "Yes. There are at least four of them, all on horseback. It is difficult to understand the ways of sorcery. If the histories are accurate, Salin has survived worse."

"On that point, at least, they are accurate," muttered Michael.

"At least their horses will be slowed down in the mountains," offered Kraig.

"Therein lies our hope," said Lorn. "We will be faster on foot."

Sarah was gasping, her strides slowing. Alec knew how she felt. Suddenly, with a small cry, she collapsed to the ground and did not rise.

"Stop!" cried Alec. "It's Sarah!"

The three men in front of them came to a halt. Kraig bent to the girl and put his hand gently on her head, his face tight with worry. "Grok. Sarah, are you all right?"

Her eyes fluttered and she murmured, "Too...tired. Can't...go on."

The peacekeeper lifted her into his big arms and drew her to his chest. "Then I will carry you," he said softly.

Almost immediately they were running again. Kraig made running with Sarah in his arms seem as effortless as running unburdened. If anything, he pushed them even faster. Behind them, the horsemen were gaining ground. Before them, the mountains loomed closer, yet still too far away. Alec was gazing at the Gravescorn, wishing it was closer, when suddenly he became aware of many large shapes running down the mountain's slope. Apparently, Lorn had seen them, too.

"Fist of Lars!" cried the warrior. "Ogres!"

"By the Seven," grumbled Michael. "There have got to be hundreds of them."

Panic arose in Alec's chest. The mountains they had looked to for salvation were infested with savage ogres! Trapped between the sorcerer and this new threat, all hope seemed shattered. Looking back, he imagined he could see Salin's face clearly, drawn in a grin of malice and victory. Tor was there, too, and further back a pair of women rode with them. The riders would be upon them soon, and would crush them against the wave of ogre barbarians.

"We are lost," said Lorn.

Michael looked back, and then gazed toward the west. "Perhaps not. I know a place…where we might hide."

"NO!" cried Lorn. "I know what place you mean. That way lies a darkness from which few mortals have the strength to emerge. Death is all we will find there."

"A death more certain than the one we face here? No, that way lies our last hope."

"Lars. If there was time, or another option, I would argue against this choice. But we cannot fight a thousand ogres and Salin besides. Run for the west! We must sprint the rest of the way!"

Alec could not make his legs move any faster. Lorn saw him lagging behind, so he turned back and scooped the smaller man up in his arms. Grunting under the baker's weight, he began to run again.

"This is absolutely humiliating," muttered Alec, holding on to Lorn as the tall man sprinted onward.

Like a wind they flew north-westward, still toward the mountains but away from the massing ogres. Sweat poured from Lorn and Kraig, and faint perspiration dotted even Michael's face. The thick grass no longer hindered them; they crushed it beneath their boots as though it were nothing. Fear drove them, and need, and it seemed to Alec no human being had ever run with such speed.

So it was they reached the Gravescorn in advance of Salin and his party, and far west of where the ogres gathered. Perhaps a mile behind them, four horses brought their riders forth at a fierce gallop. Eastward, the ogres leapt and crawled quickly through the mountains. It would be perhaps two minutes before their foes converged on them.

The grass ended about a thousand feet from the mountain wall, turning to rock and mud. Here, the towers of the Gravescorn were sheer and rocky, and far too steep to climb.

"What now?" questioned Alec. "You brought us to a wall!"

"Where is it?" asked Lorn, gazing at the towering stone before them.

"There," said Michael, pointing westward. "The entrance to the Fairy tombs."

Just to the west, Alec saw a wide stairway carved of stone leading up the face of the mountain toward a massive set of double doors. On either side of the doors, serpentine statues curled around stone pillars. Above the doors, carved in the mountain rock, was a sun-symbol identical to the one on the Talisman of Unity. It seemed to radiate a gentle, serene light all its own.

"Behold," said Michael, "the tomb of Faryn-Gehnah, wherein lie the great kings and queens of Faerie long dead, lain to rest in ages past. It will be difficult for Salin to track us within its labyrinthine tunnels."

Alec wanted to protest, for if the sorcerer would be unable to follow them, wouldn't they also become hopelessly lost in the tomb? But he scarcely had a chance to open his mouth before Lorn dashed toward great stair, carrying Alec along with him. As they reached the foot of the stair and he gazed at the awesome gate towering high above them, he heard a malicious cry not a hundred yards away.

"I have you now!"

The voice of Salin Urdrokk.

As the sorcerer's black steed raced toward them, Salin's eyes filled with red rage. It seemed a shadow gathered around him and his companions. Blue lightning danced about him.

They bounded up the stairs as Salin's blue power stabbed from the sky, rending the ground asunder just behind them, heaving chunks of rock and mud as big as boulders into the air. Lightning broke the stairs to rubble just a step behind Alec and his companions. They reached the massive entry, and dropping Alec and Sarah to the ground, Lorn and Kraig threw themselves at the doors. Muscles straining, the two large men forced the double entry open a crack, just enough to squeeze through. They quickly ushered their companions inside, and followed just as a ball of flame broke against the unyielding stone.

"Push the door shut!" cried Lorn.

Darkness surrounded them, broken only by the thin shaft of light stabbing inward from outside. When Kraig and Lorn heaved against the doors, the shaft became a sliver and quickly diminished to nothing, and shadow swallowed them entirely as the doors thudded shut.

"Help me turn this wheel!" cried Lorn in the darkness. "It will lock the gate!" There was a loud squeak, as if some mechanism long idle was being moved, followed by a series of clangs. Then, for a moment, there was silence.

In the darkness, Alec heard Lorn gasping for air. "It…is done. The great locks are in place. They cannot be undone from without, nor from within save by a team of men of tremendous strength, or by powerful magic."

"You mean we're trapped?" asked Sarah.

Before anyone could answer, there was a thunderous pounding at the door. A terrible force raged against it, but it did not give.

"Even Salin's magic cannot open this gateway from the outside," said Michael. "Perhaps he could tear the very doors from the mountainside, but doing so would cause tons of rock to bury this tomb, and all within it, forever."

"That's not so good for us," said Alec.

"Nor for Salin. It would put the Talisman of Unity beyond his reach forever."

The pounding at the door stopped, and Alec breathed a sigh of relief. It appeared they were safe for the time being.

"We need some light," said Kraig.

"I have a torch here somewhere," replied Lorn.

"No, wait," said Alec. "I have a better idea."

Fumbling around in the dark, Alec reached into his sack and drew forth the silver chest. He opened it, and bright silvery light shone forth, dispelling the darkness of the tomb.

He gasped as his eyes adjusted to the light. They stood in a vast chamber, its high, arching ceiling held up by massive pillars of black stone. The floors and walls were plated in gold, as were the myriad statues placed at intervals among the pillars. The statues were masterfully crafted images of exotically beautiful men and women, all with sharp features and high, strong, cheekbones. On the far side of the room, a tunnel led into darkness.

Alec could not pull his eyes away from the beauty of the statues. "Who…who are they?"

"Fairies, of course," said Michael. "Crafted in likeness of ancient royalty, all of whom are buried here within Faryn-Gehnah."

Kraig and Sarah were speechless, obviously as impressed as Alec. Lorn, his face stern and his manner stiff, was not so moved.

"We must move on. Many are the corridors that twist under the rock of the Gravescorn, some natural and some made by the Fair Folk when they built this shrine. Perhaps we can find our way through to the far gate, which opens onto the northern slopes of the mountain. Many dangers bar our way, if the legends speak true, from traps to discourage grave-robbers to restless spirits who refuse to depart this world. Of course, even if we reach the other side we might find Salin waiting for us."

"Perhaps," said Michael. "But the mountain cannot be crossed here, and the paths to the east barely accommodate horses. Salin will have to return to the pass and cross on foot, leading his mounts if they will follow at all. His road is long, while ours is more direct. If we survive the tomb, we should emerge far ahead of our foe."

"But how will we find our way through?" asked Kraig. "You and Lorn speak of this place as if it were a maze."

"In my youth I had studied maps of this place," said Lorn, "as a required part of my schooling. I remember some of what I learned."

"Some?" questioned Sarah. "Is 'some' good enough?"

"I may be able to lead us where Lorn's knowledge fails," said Michael. "I have walked these paths before, long ago."

"Grok," said Alec. "Is there anything you don't claim to have done? Anywhere you haven't been? You're not *that* old, Michael."

Lorn shook his head gravely. "The boy has a point. How do you come by all the knowledge to which you lay claim?"

Michael shrugged as he began walking toward the far tunnel. "It matters not. Follow me, or do not."

Lorn rubbed his unkempt beard for a moment and then set off after the hermit. "Come, Alec. We need your light."

Alec walked beside Lorn, holding his chest so the light spilled forward into the tunnel. Sarah followed and Kraig brought up the rear to guard their backs. Michael paused for a second to allow Alec to catch up and nodded approvingly at the silver chest.

"It is fortunate Horren gave you such a gift. A rare and useful magic it contains."

"This is the second time it has saved us," said Alec.

Michael nodded. Silently, they walked side by side into the dark corridor. Alec felt the shadows closing in upon them, and he fancied he heard a deep moaning from afar, echoing softly down the corridor. A chill ran through him, and his heart began to race. In these rough-hewn tunnels lay kings long dead, perhaps sleeping, some, perhaps, not.

As they walked deeper into the darkness, he prayed the dead were resting peacefully. He hoped they would reach the far gate safely and not find Salin waiting. To keep his mind from panic, he thought about reaching the open air and traveling without incident the last few miles to Faerie. Soon, they would be safe. Soon, they would be at long last beyond the reach of spirits, ravagers, and sorcerers.

Soon.

Tor shuddered as Salin raged against the massive stone doors with his fists, screaming hatred. The old sorcerer had been foiled and Tor feared the repercussions. Behind them, Gwendolyn and Stiletta waited with cold patience.

Do those fool women fear nothing?

"Banes of Lars!" cried Salin. "I could tear this Seth-forsaken mountain down on their thrice-cursed heads, but then the Talisman would be lost! They have engaged the ancient locks of the Fairy-shapers, and I cannot undo them. Not from this side."

Rage filled him, and purple light sizzled about him. For a moment Tor thought he would blast the gate to rubble, sacrificing the Talisman in favor of revenge. But the fiery power subsided as Salin regained some semblance of calm.

"We will have to go around and travel through the mountain pass to the east. They will make for the far gate, and we can catch them there if they survive the tomb. If they perish within, all the better. We will simply have to find their corpses and I will have my prize."

They descended the broken stairs and mounted their horses. As they raced silently eastward, Tor was again filled with awe at their miraculous survival in the blazing fires that consumed miles of grassland during Salin's battle with the Ravager.

When the spirit found it could not possess Salin, it fled back into the old man's feeble body. It summoned its full sorcerer's might and engaged Salin in a horrifying conflict of magic. They hurled fire at one another, and called lighting down from the sky, and their might caused storms of flame to roar across the plain. The ogres and the wild beasts of the plain burnt and perished, and the grassland was lain to waste, but through his great might Salin somehow shielded Tor, the women, himself, and even their mounts from the destruction.

Tor had felt the flames raging over his back, and he was burnt and scarred, but he survived. Obviously, Salin still had some use for the swordsman.

The so-called Ravager was not so lucky. Its body burned and the spirit trapped therein was destroyed. When the fire finally died, Salin seemed none the worse for wear, save that his anger had grown tenfold. The Ravager's interference had put his prize further from his grasp.

Then, as if nothing had happened, the sorcerer commanded them to their mounts, and they raced northward in renewed pursuit. And just when they had caught up to their prey and victory seemed assured, Mason and his companions stunned them by entering where the Fairies themselves now fear to tread.

Either this Mason is far braver than I thought, or he is as stupid as I guessed. Perhaps both…often courage and ignorance go hand in hand.

And so the pursuit continued, and Tor's trials were prolonged. Soon, he told himself, they would have Mason and the others, and he would finally be rid of Salin's maddening company. Soon, this would all be an unhappy memory.

Soon.

Far to the south, in the ruined village, a blackened corpse lay prone upon the dead earth. A single raven had lit upon its charred head and was pecking at its open eye. Suddenly the bird flew up in panic, for its meat, so obviously dead, had moved. The corpse jerked upright, its joints grinding painfully as it rose from the ground.

Flakes of black skin fell from the Ravager as he lifted his arms toward the sun, feeling some semblance of unlife flowing through the corpse it still possessed. All aspects of its host's mind had been burned away, and all that was left was hate…a pure, burning hate for all who lived.

As the Ravager began shambling across the plain, hungering to bring fire and death and madness to the realms of men, it found the joints and muscles of its host were all but useless. It stumbled and fell to the ground and was unable to rise again. The spirit survived, but the body was finished. Still, the Ravager clung to the ruined flesh as long as it could. It could not leap free unless there was another host close enough to possess, not unless it was willing to perish.

It held on. Soon, it told itself, something would come this way: a wanderer, an animal, a snake, a bug. *Something* had to have survived the fire. Soon, the Ravager would leap free of this useless flesh and live again. Soon, it would be free to visit destruction upon the kingdoms of men.

Soon.

CHAPTER 13

Journey in Darkness

The sound of silence rang loudly in Alec Mason's ears. Whenever they stopped walking, the dead blackness around them, unbroken by noise and barely diminished by the silvery light from Alec's box, seemed to close in like a thing alive. No one spoke, for even the quietest whisper echoed far too loudly through these halls of the dead. As Alec walked beside Michael, a nervous sweat formed upon his brow. He held his silver chest tightly in his hands, letting it spill its light on the path ahead. Resting at the bottom of the chest, the Talisman of Unity reflected and magnified the light, causing a broken pattern of luminance to dance upon the smooth stone ceiling. Even so, the darkness pressed inward, consuming the light like a hungry demon.

They had been walking slowly and silently down a straight corridor for what might have been minutes or hours, for all Alec could determine. His eyes kept being drawn toward the strangely smooth walls. Carved as they were through the mountain rock, he had expected the surfaces to be rough or jagged, but the floor and walls were like polished opal, almost like glass to the touch. If not for the black shadows moving across the walls where they shouldn't and the eerie silence filling the place, Alec would have been filled with wonder at the strangely and expertly constructed passage.

Eventually they reached a fork in the tunnel. A branch sloped slightly downward to the left and a corridor bared right. Here Michael stopped and rubbed his clean-shaven chin. He turned to Lorn and quietly broke the silence.

"One of these paths should lead to a series of ancient tombs, the other to newer ones. Through the newer tombs may the far gate be reached. Yet something is amiss here. This passage is not as I remember it."

Lorn peered down both corridors, his eyes straining to pierce the shadows. "This is odd. The maps I have studied clearly showed two sets of stairs here, both leading higher into the mountain. Maps can be wrong, however."

"Lorn, it was long ago when I walked these dark ways, and my memories are dim, yet I too remember stairs. Something has changed here."

"How could that be?" questioned Kraig. "Look at the ground here. The stonework is smooth and continuous. There are no signs of more recent construction, and certainly there would be signs if stone stairs had been chiseled or somehow blasted away."

"No signs indeed," muttered Michael. "I fear we are not looking upon normal stonework or excavation. It would take powerful magics to do what has been done here. Come. Let us take our chances down the right branch. The other descends deeper into the earth, and the exit is up higher."

"Or at least it was," said Lorn.

They walked onward and soon came to a four-way intersection. Michael chewed his lip, his eyes darting down each of the three dark ways before him.

"By the One. There should be only two choices here. It seems the very mountain is against us now."

"The left tunnel should be the one we want," said Lorn, "if any of my old knowledge holds true. The maps did not show a straight passage here, but the left is still open to us."

Alec's confidence in their guides continued to drop as they turned down the left path and found themselves on a downward slope. The stone-hewn hall narrowed and sloped more steeply as they progressed, and Alec thought he could hear a low, quiet moan echoing from below.

"What was that?" he whispered, grabbing Michael's arm.

"I do not know. Often in old tunnels such as these there are sounds which cannot be explained. Usually they are nothing to be concerned about. Still…perhaps it would be safer to turn back and try another way."

"No," said Lorn. "I am still confident this is the right way. Besides, we must choose a path and stick with it. If we continue to second guess our choices, we will be wandering these dark paths forever."

The corridor leveled off and came to yet another junction. To the left, the path dropped quickly into darkness. To the right, it widened and descended at a gentle slope. Michael chose the right, and soon the passage opened into a high, wide room. Alec's silver light illuminated only the nearest end of the chamber, but as he gazed into the shadows he had the impression the room was vast, larger even than the entrance hall of the tomb. He could make out dark rectangular shapes on the floor at the edge of the light."

"Caskets," said Lorn.

"Yes," said Michael. "They are small and not ornamented with the gold and finery that would denote a royal burial ground. This appears to be the first in the series of old tombs, in which are buried the minor nobles of ancient Faerie. Here rest the lords and ladies of the houses of Rehyn-Tylle and Hahn-nah-Shamyn, and the ancestors of the small but important house of Krah-Fallyn. I do not believe the exit lies this way."

"Can you be certain?" asked Alec. "With everything not as you remember, can you be sure this is the tomb you think it is?"

"No. I cannot be certain."

"Then let us press onward as I have suggested," said Lorn. "There is little point in turning back until we are sure."

"I don't like this at all," whispered Sarah, who was walking directly behind Alec.

"I don't like it either," said Alec. "But as much as I'm beginning to doubt Michael and Lorn's knowledge of this place, I don't have any better ideas."

Slowly they entered the vast chamber. Caskets lined the floor in a circular pattern, spiraling in toward the center. The caskets nearer to the center sat upon raised stone platforms and were more decorative, and further inward they became even more ornate, the platforms higher still. Slim pillars slightly taller than Alec were spaced around the room, set with torches dark for centuries. Again he heard a low moan, and this time it was louder and closer. He shuddered, for this time it seemed to him he could hear words in that moan.

Soon they passed near the center casket. It was crafted of silver and carved with suns and flowers. Four stone pillars decorated with carvings of vines and blossoms held the sarcophagus aloft, and elaborate candelabra stood at each of its four corners. Alec admired the silver works before him, thinking in a place other than here they would seem beautiful. In the darkened tomb they seemed only cold, like distant moonlight.

"This is the grave site of someone rather important," said Michael. "I didn't expect to find something like this here. Perhaps one of the highest lords of House Krah-Fallyn rests here, surrounded by his vassals and servants."

"I'm not much interested in whose corpse is in there," said Kraig. "I just want to get out of here."

As they moved past the elegant sarcophagus, the moaning sound again rang in Alec's ears. He froze where he stood, shivers racing along his spine and over his flesh. This time, he was certain the moan was a voice, and the voice spoke with words.

Alec glanced at his companions, who had stopped as well. Michael stood straight, his head turning from side to side, as if trying to pinpoint the source of the noise. Lorn's sword jumped into his hand and Kraig reached for his axe. Sarah clutched Alec's shoulder nervously.

"The dead speak," whispered Lorn.

"Hurry," said Michael. "We must leave this place."

They turned to flee they way they had come, but dark shapes were moving toward them through the shadows. Michael cursed quietly and led them further into the burial vault.

Sounds of shifting stone and creaking wood filled the room, and Alec looked back in horror to see caskets slowly opening and lids sliding from sarcophagi. With a brilliant flash, every torch in the chamber burst to life, flaming brilliance upon the high stone walls.

Voices raged through the air—screaming, crying voices growing louder as more caskets opened and ancient death broke free. Corpses in various states of decay rose from their long rest, pushing themselves out of their caskets with rotten limbs. Some were wrapped in preservative rags which had worked to varying degrees, and others wore no flesh at all, grinning skulls on skeletal frames. The horrors shambled slowly toward the terrified companions.

"The rumors were true!" cried Lorn. "The dead of Faryn-Gehnah no longer sleep!"

"The Fairies have abandoned their ancient burial ground for a reason," said Michael as he raced forward. "This place has been cursed!"

There was no more time for discussion. They fled across the tomb, past slowly opening sarcophagi. A decayed arm reached out of an opening coffin for Alec's leg, and he leapt over it with a brief cry. Even in the midst of such horror, he could not help looking back over his shoulder at the massing dead.

The light grew more brilliant around the central sarcophagus. A twisting funnel of air formed beneath it and lifted it from the pillars. Energy flashed through the funnel and, like a stroke of lightning, shattered the stone coffin. As stone splinters rained to the ground, a huge mummified corpse became visible, floating where the sarcophagus had been. Horizontal at first, its arms crossed upon its chest, the thing righted itself and spread its arms outward. Its silver robes rippled in the unnatural wind and its gold crown gleamed in the harsh torch-light. The now familiar moan emanated from the mummy as it flew toward the companions.

With a shout of warning, Alec increased his pace and raced by his companions. Around him, the dead were rising, some stumbling forth on skeletal legs and others shambling from their caskets on limbs of decayed flesh. Alec leapt over a coffin on the outskirts of the room just as its lid flew open and a rotting body jolted up. As he neared the far end of the chamber, he saw two archways leading into different passages. He gave no thought to which one might lead them to daylight. Fear overwhelmed all other considerations, and he raced through an arch at random, hurtling down the corridor as fast as he could run.

He did not stop until he heard tormented howls rolling up the hall toward him. Peering into the darkness, he saw hunched shapes trudging toward him. He turned to look the way he had come and saw Lorn and Sarah running from the tall mummy, who had advanced to the front of the ranks of the dead. The thing was wreathed in a fiery glow, and it moaned a low, anguished cry as it floated quickly, effortlessly down the corridor. It pulled a glowing short sword from a sheath that hung at its side and pointed it directly at Alec.

"Grok!" he screamed, stumbling back as the thing advanced. Sarah and Lorn caught up to him, but Michael and Kraig were nowhere in sight. Alec grabbed Sarah's hand and began to run away from the mummy, but he stopped again when he saw Lorn was not with them.

Their guide had fallen back, his sword held at the ready as the flying mummy approached. Alec's eyes grew wide as the creature and the horde of dead things closed in on the lone warrior.

"Lorn! Come on!"

"No! I must hold them here lest they overrun us all! Run, Mason, or all will be lost!"

But there would be no easy escape. The shapes moving in the passage before them became visible in Alec's silver light, more skeletons and zombies like the ones following behind. Alec turned to Sarah, who was shivering in complete terror.

"Listen to me," he said, struggling to keep his voice steady. "We can't give up. Michael is sure to be here any second; he'll know what to do. He's got to be…"

But as he looked back, he realized there was no hope of the hermit or Kraig joining them soon, for the passage was choked with undead. The mummy, its sword in hand and its crown glowing with power, descended like a falcon upon Lorn. The warrior raised his sword, and there was a great flash of light as steel met steel. The mummy pressed forth, screaming a dead scream, slashing with such speed Lorn was kept on the defensive. Then the masses of the dead swarmed around the combatants, some stopping to surround Lorn and others pressing toward Alec and Sarah. Alec lost sight of Lorn in the crushing mass of dead flesh.

"We're cut off from the others," he said quickly, trying to keep panic at bay. His hands shook as he grabbed his stone goblin knife. "We have to make a stand."

As the creatures crawled up the corridor in front of them and closed in behind, he placed his glowing chest on the ground and grasped Sarah's hand. She was shaking, but she nodded gravely and pulled out her own stone dagger. Perhaps it was a futile gesture, but silently they agreed they would not give up without a fight.

And then the first of the horrors were upon them. Skeletal forms of long dead Fairies reached forward, and Alec slashed out with his blade. Sharp stone struck ancient bone, and the hand of the closest skeleton was severed at the wrist. The hand fell and broke into dust as it smashed against the hard, smooth floor. As the thing came closer, Alec struck again, his blade slashing through the brittle bone of its neck. Severed skull and flailing body fell in separate directions, breaking to pieces as they hit the ground.

Inspired by his initial success, the baker tried a new tactic. When the second skeleton neared him, he kicked it hard in its midsection. His leg broke through the thing's brittle spine and it crashed to the ground in pieces. The undead pressed ever closer, but Alec turned to face them feeling not so hopeless as before.

"These things are fragile, Sarah!" he cried. "One good kick and they break apart like a stale loaf of bread!"

Out of the corner of his eye, Alec saw the girl solidly kick a nearing corpse in the knee. The lower part of its leg snapped off, and the unbalanced creature teetered for a moment before falling to the ground and breaking apart. Sarah grimaced with the effort, but Alec thought he saw grim satisfaction in her expression as well.

Onward flowed the masses of the dead, and Alec knew, unless help came soon, their bold efforts would be for naught. He and Sarah continued to kick, punch, and stab at the corpses and many went down, but those among the dead who still wore flesh held together better when struck. Those Alec found he could knock back, but he could not destroy them. Stabbing them drew no blood and caused them no pain, and they came at him with more force each time he thrust them away.

His fear grew again as several of the fleshed monsters drew close, their decayed arms outstretched. They formed a ring around him and Sarah and closed inward at an alarming rate. Desperately Alec's mind raced for a way out. Fighting, he knew, was an option that could only end in death. Then he thought of the chest at his feet, still spilling its silver light in a circle around him. Perhaps its sacred light could be used to fend off these unholy creatures. He bent quickly and grasped the chest, turning it to bathe the zombies in its blinding, purifying light.

To no avail. The argent light served only to illuminate the oncoming horrors, detailing their dread features more clearly. Horren's gift had proven invaluable in the past, but now it had failed him.

And yet I was not the only one to receive a gift from the Addin!

"Sarah!" he cried. "The bottle Horren gave you, the one he said contained a tree spirit. I think you'd better open it!"

She nodded and reached into the pouch she had taken to wearing on her belt. She fumbled through its contents and finally pulled forth the small, glass flask.

But she had taken too long. Distracted with hope, Alec didn't notice the dead thing until it wrapped its rotten fingers around his neck. Alec grabbed at the zombie's arms as it squeezed mercilessly, but he could not pry free of the thing's vice-like grip. Other undead pressed in around him, forcing him to his knees, and he saw several grab Sarah as well. She screamed and dropped the bottle, which rolled along the floor and became lost among the shuffling feet of their attackers.

The last thing Alec saw as a black cloud engulfed his vision were four zombies carrying Sarah down the corridor. She was calling his name, thrashing and screaming in a mania induced by utter terror. His grip on the zombie's hands failed, and for lack of air his eyes fluttered shut and saw no more.

Kraig turned to look behind him and was shocked to see Michael alone was following.

"Wounds!" he cried. "Where are the others?"

Michael slowed as he caught up to the peacekeeper and joined him in scanning the corridor down which they had just been running. In the fading torchlight of the burial chamber they had just left they could see dead shapes lumbering slowly toward them, but of their companions there was no sign.

"By the Hells," cursed Michael. "Somehow we managed to get separated. We must go back for them."

"But how?" questioned Kraig, pointing back toward the large chamber. Ranks of undead were advancing, clogging the corridor and dashing all hope of returning to the chamber.

"They must have gone down the other corridor," said Michael. "If any of my knowledge of the tomb's former structure holds true, these two corridors merge before they reach the next burial chamber. We can catch up with them at the juncture."

Kraig just grunted, no longer convinced the hermit knew what he was talking about, at least where it concerned this tomb. As he turned to run down the corridor, he realized they no longer possessed any source of light. Michael, apparently, had anticipated the problem, for he drew a short torch out of his pack. Before they had taken ten strides in darkness, he had it alight.

"It always pays to carry a light source," said Michael. "Unfortunately this is my only torch, and it will not last much more than an hour."

"Well, if we don't find the others by then, chances are we never will, regardless of light."

"Always the optimist, I see," said the hermit.

They hurried down the stone passage, putting some distance between themselves and their pursuers. The corridor twisted and turned, and in a few minutes it had narrowed considerably. Soon only one of them could squeeze through at a time, and Michael took the lead. The sounds of the dead had faded to silence and the oppressive darkness had returned, swallowing the dim light of the torch.

A thought occurred to Kraig, a thought that forced him to squash a feeling of panic as it formed in his stomach. What if this tunnel didn't connect with the one their companions had taken? It would be nearly impossible to go back and catch up to the others with the ranks of the dead barring their way. With clenched fists and a solemn grimace, Kraig resolved not to think about it. Alec and Sarah were with Lorn, and he had proven himself a worthy protector. But with ghastly undead things at every turn, how could he possibly...

No! They will be fine. We will meet again.

Michael held the torch above his head and led Kraig onward. The peacekeeper thought for a moment about the mysterious hermit and his transformation from apathy, to self-pity and grief, to newfound confidence and, perhaps, purpose. Kraig was glad for the latest change in the hermit, and he hoped it would last. He had been feeling overburdened with the leadership of the party, even though he had shared it with Lorn. He certainly liked the feeling of being in charge, but he knew he was out of his depth in these circumstances. Better that Michael resume his role as leader and councilor.

But, he asked himself for the hundredth time, who exactly *was* Michael? In spite of himself, Kraig found he trusted the middle-aged man more each day. Yet they still knew nothing about him, save he had lived alone outside Barton Hills for more than two decades, occasionally dropping by the Silver Shield to drink. How did he come by his vast knowledge of the world and its history? And where did he learn to use a sword with nearly the skill of a Bladeknight? By Grok, who *was* he?

They had been walking for what seemed an hour but might have been only minutes, when the tunnel abruptly opened into a small room, perhaps twenty feet square. Hewn from the mountain rock, its dark walls were as mysteriously smooth and shiny as the rest of the tomb. In the center of the room, stretched out on the floor as if asleep, lay a lone gray figure dimly illuminated by the light of Michael's torch.

They entered the room slowly, carefully, and more light fell upon the figure. It was not a corpse, or at least if it were it had not decayed in any visible way. It was a young looking woman, fair of face and lithe of form. Kraig gasped as he gazed at her pure beauty. She wore translucent gray robes spread loosely on the floor about her, draped clingingly over her breasts and thighs. Her hair was long and dark, and her face, in contrast, was a pale and perfect white. Her nose was thin and somewhat sharp, and her ears were slightly pointed, but these strange features only enhanced her beauty. If she had stood, she would have been as tall as Kraig himself.

Michael looked at her. If his breath was taken away as Kraig's was, he gave no sign. "She is of Faerie," he whispered reverently. "She is not dead, but she is not alive as you understand living. She has passed into the *fey-non-morte,* the sleep which is not sleep, the death which is not death. This is how a Fairy may endure years or even centuries of grief and awaken when the time of grief has ended. As human beings, we cannot understand the Fairy-sleep or the reasons they find it necessary."

Kraig nodded, unable to pull his eyes away from the beautiful creature. "But why is she here, of all places? Why go into this…this trance in a place as dangerous as this?"

"I do not know. Let us ask her."

"Ask her? How?"

"From this deep and lasting sleep a Fairy may communicate with one who knows how to reach into her mind. I had this skill once; perhaps I can remember how it is done."

"Is it magic?"

"No. Merely a technique practiced among the Fair Folk, a mental exercise. Anyone can learn to do it with time, patience, and a good teacher. Now, I will attempt this thing. Perhaps she can tell us why this tomb is not as I remember it, and why the dead are so restless."

Michael knelt beside the slumbering Fairy and placed his hand upon her chest. With his other hand he pushed the hair back from her forehead and kissed her gently. Then he lowered his face to her ear and began to whisper to her, slowly chanting words Kraig couldn't make out. He clutched her hand, which lay limp upon the floor, and he pressed harder on her chest so that his fingers nearly dug into her, through her clothes and into her flesh. For a moment Kraig thought the hermit might hurt her, but he knew in this state she was beyond pain. But still, to bruise that pale, perfect flesh…

Michael's voice grew louder as he spoke secrets into the Fairy woman's ear, but still Kraig could not understand a word. Then, suddenly, a soft feminine voice filled the small chamber.

"I hear you, human. Why do you disturb my sleep?"

Her lips had not moved. Indeed, the sound did not seem to be coming from her body at all.

"I am Michael. Elsendarin. You may know of me."

The hermit spoke aloud now, not into her ear but to the ceiling, his neck stretched upward and his eyes pressed shut. One hand gripped her thin hand tightly while the other dug into the flesh between her breasts.

"I know you, Elsendarin. Your name is spoken fondly in many of the houses of my people. I will speak to you, but only for a short while. I require the peace of the *fey-non-morte*."

Michael wasted no time. He began questioning the sleeping woman at once. "Who are you, and how came you to this place, which the Fair Folk so long ago abandoned?"

"I am named Landrya ma'Hahnenshey, and I am the Keeper of this Tomb. Do not believe the Fairies ever abandon that which is theirs. Still we hope to reclaim this place of horrors and sanctify it, hallow it, and purge it of darkness. Listen now, and I will tell you how the Tomb of the Fairies fell into shadow.

"Two hundred years ago the powers of darkness descended upon Faerie, seeking to enter our forests and corrupt or destroy us. We were yet a strong people, and by our enchantments we repelled the shadow from our woodland home. But the forces of the Seth would not be foiled entirely. Unable to corrupt our home, they still managed to foul something of Faerie. They entered this tomb, cursing it, desecrating it with their darkspawned souls, awaking those who should have slept for all eternity. We felt their corruption even as far north as our home, and we were grieved by what they had done. We set at once to the task of making things right.

"But almost immediately we learned how deeply the damage went. Evil had been fused with the very rock of the mountain! Corruption polluted this place beyond even the abilities of the Elders of Nom, the most powerful Shapers of Faerie, to purify. Whosoever entered this place was greeted by the living dead, creatures who envied and despised living beings. It was a grave blow to us, for our loved ones and our ancestors, placed here at the time of their deaths with love and tenderness, were now corrupt souls of evil whose only thought was the destruction of the living!

"And yet the tomb was ours. It belonged to Faerie. We would not so easily give up the battle to purify this place, to make it sacred again. And so was created the Order of the Keepers of the Tomb. Thirty-three of our strongest Shapers took up residence in the tomb, using their magic to send the restless souls back to sleep, Shaping the walls and tunnels of the tomb so evil would pour from them, like sand from a sieve. The evil they collected and trapped in special receptacles, and buried it deep, deep beneath the earth. For one hundred years they continued their work, and for a long time it seemed they made great progress. But of course you know much of this already, for you are Elsendarin, the wise one."

Michael grimaced. "The translation is somewhat inaccurate," he said, "but flattering. If knowledge in itself were wisdom, I would perhaps be wise, but there is so much more to it than that. So much more. But yes, I knew of the Keepers of the Tomb, and I knew something had corrupted these once sacred halls, but much of your tale is new to me. I never considered how or why corruption fell upon this place, although I suspected the hand of the Seth. And I do not know you. You say you are the Keeper of the Tomb. Where are the others of your order?"

"Dead," came her soft, elegant, disembodied voice. "All dead, long dead. I am the last. Listen, wise one, and learn.

"A century ago the Elders came to me, pleased with my progress in the study of Shaping. I had mastered and accepted the Seven Laws, and I was one of the strongest Shapers to rise through the ranks in many years. They asked me if I would join the Order of the Keepers, and of course I accepted at once; it was an honor! I quickly learned my duties and joined the other Keepers, now numbered at nearly fifty, inside the tomb. For ten years we continued our work, everything progressing as it had for a century. We felt the evil of the place lessening, and the dead slept for longer times without awakening. Within another hundred years, we thought, the tomb would be purified, ready to be the holy place it was made to be.

"But something terrible shattered our expectations. Something horrible was working against us. One day, and on many days after, we heard a dark laugh echoing through the tomb as we performed one of our purifying rituals. Each time this happened, one of our number would fall sick and often would die. Sickness and death are rare among Fairies, who usually live out a life span of five centuries or more in perfect heath, so these multiple deaths caused great concern among the Keepers. Our numbers declined, and the work we were doing slowed nearly to a stand-still. We begged the Elders to send more Shapers to become Keepers, but they told us none were yet ready for the burden. The evil of the tomb began to grow again, and the dead stirred more and more often. We were afraid, but being Fairies we would not give up, not if but one of us were left alive.

"And slowly, more of us died. Twenty years passed, and in that time a like number of Keepers had fallen to the illness. We felt evil seeping out of the walls, out of the burial chambers, out of our own flesh! The laughter came more often, and we were deathly afraid. Still we would not leave the tomb, save a few at a time to report to the Elders and bring back supplies.

"Within ten years, it was not only the sickness that reduced our number. The dead had broken free of our control, and occasionally they would claim one of us before we could force them to sleep. It seemed the curse of the Seth's minions was stronger than we had thought, and we were not equal to the task of breaking it.

"Call it courage or call it folly, but fifty years ago, fifty years after I had become a Keeper, the remaining twenty of us performed a grand ritual, a last ditch attempt to stem the growing tide of evil once and for all. We poured all our power into the walls, the floor, the very rock of the tomb, attempting to push the evil out of the mountain and into the air, where it might dissipate as does a cloud of smoke. But for all our power, we could not break the curse. On the contrary, it fed on our power! It blackened it and threw it back at us tenfold. Oh, how we burned and screamed, how the others threw themselves before me to protect me, for I was the youngest and the strongest, and they considered me their best hope! They all perished in the black flame, consumed by the evil they sought to destroy.

"And then I was alone. I knew I could not stand alone against the shadow, and I knew I could not leave the tomb without at least one Keeper. And so I took the only option left to me: I would not provoke the dead or the curse by fighting, but I would remain here, passive, a constant reminder to the shadow that we will never wholly cease the fight, never truly abandon the tomb. I first unlocked both gates of the tomb so others might come to stand against the darkness, and then I lay down to sleep my long sleep. And in sleep, I remained vigilant.

"For I could still see, and I could cast my sight about and survey the entire tomb. As long as they were undisturbed, the dead continued to sleep, though not deeply. But the curse, which throbbed still in these walls, continued to grow slowly and silently.

"Occasionally, some few humans or Fairies would walk these ways, as you have done in the past, Elsendarin. Quietly they would come, but a few at a time, and thus the dead did not notice. Never did anyone linger here, or pray, or lovingly visit the dead as they once did, but rather they used these tunnels only as a faster way through the mountains. Evil bit at their heels and hurried them on their way. The old glory of the tomb was all but forgotten. The curse and the dark legends it spawned were all that were remembered.

"And at last, the evil grew too great. No one would set foot here. The shadow grew and ate at the tomb until it bent the very stone, changing the paths and stairs and chambers until nothing remained as it was. Finally, the curse had won. This was no longer the tomb of the Fairies. They had, it seemed, abandoned it for good.

"And yet I remained. I will not awaken until the curse can be shattered. At that time, I will live again and resume my role as the Keeper of the Tomb. I will help to purify these walls, quiet the dead, and return to Faerie one of its greatest achievements."

Then the voice fell quiet, and Kraig was suddenly saddened by its absence. He looked at the still form of the Fairy, and at Michael, still poised over the woman. The tragic tale had touched Kraig as few things had, and the woman's beauty moved him. He wished there was something he could do for her, but he was just a man, and he knew nothing of curses or magic. Besides, he had other, more urgent concerns. Michael echoed those concerns with his next question.

"You say you can see everywhere in the tomb? Where are our companions? Can we continue down this pathway and meet with them before we reach the next burial chamber?"

There was a silence, and Kraig thought Landrya would not answer. But then her voice sang softly from the walls, the air.

"Your friends battle for their lives. The dead surround them. The warrior with the sword is mighty. He may prevail. The others...I have lost sight of them. They are carried away in a wave of the dead."

"NO!" cried Kraig. "We've wasted too much time, we should have...!"

"They may yet be saved," said Michael. "How can we get to them?"

The voice of Landrya answered, "Keep going as you were. As you guessed, this corridor connects with the one they are in before it reaches the next vault. But make haste, for even there the dead are stirring, awakened by the sounds of conflict. You must pass through that tomb, and another, before you escape this place. Always choose the path which climbs higher, save at the great stair, where you must plunge into darkness. Only through darkness may you again come into the light."

"Our thanks, Keeper," said Michael. "When we reach Faerie, we will tell the Elders you remain vigilant. One day your people will reclaim this place."

"Good-bye, Elsendarin. It has been good having someone to talk to. And farewell, handsome Kraig."

Kraig gaped. She had not addressed him before, and he couldn't understand how she knew his name.

And handsome? He almost blushed like an inexperienced boy.

Michael pulled away from the woman, breaking off the connection he had made with her mind. Kraig felt a strange silence fall around him, as if a door to another world had been closed. The hermit stood, shaking, and wiped the sweat from his forehead. Saying nothing, he continued down the dark pathway.

It would have been difficult for Kraig to get the Fairy out of his mind if there hadn't been such urgent matters at hand. Her plight moved him. How she loved this tomb, and how she despised the curse that had profaned it! But for now, he thought mainly of Alec and Sarah, and he prayed he and Michael would find them in time.

Alec opened his eyes. He couldn't have blacked out for more than a few minutes, for he was still in the hands of the zombies, and they were still carrying him down the corridor, for what purpose he didn't wish to consider. A few still had a grip on Sarah, who had passed out from exhaustion or terror. Alec remained still, wishing his captors to think he was still unconscious.

Down the tunnel they slowly trudged, through near-darkness. A faint light came from somewhere ahead, casting the shambling dead in dark silhouette. With a panic Alec realized he had dropped the chest containing the Talisman of Unity, and he nearly cried out. They had so far succeeded in keeping it out of Salin's hands, but losing it here seemed almost as bad. He had to deliver it to Faerie! Michael had convinced him of this. Somehow, he had to live, to break free, to regain the Talisman. His mind raced, and his body ached to act, to twist out of these foul creatures grasp and to race back the tunnel in search of the Talisman.

But instead he lay still in their arms. He could not break free of their iron grip. And if he could, how far would he get before they caught him again, perhaps this time breaking his neck or snapping his spine? No, better to wait for an opportunity. Maybe they would put him down before deciding to rip his heart out.

Have to stop thinking like that. There has to be a way out of this. Where is Lorn?

He forced his body to stay limp, hoping Sarah would not awaken. She might panic, forcing him to act before he was ready. He tried not to look at his captors, tried not to gaze at their dead eyes or their blackened, gaping flesh. He tried not to feel their disease-ridden fingers about his arms and legs. He looked at the ceiling passing by, trying to focus all his attention on the smooth stonework.

Grok, I can't take this!

Finally, after what seemed ages, they came to another burial vault, not quite as large as the first but filled with many caskets and sarcophagi. They were all open, and a ring of skeletons and zombies stood in the center of the room, facing inward. His captors walked to the center of the ring and dropped him on the ground. Soon Sarah was placed beside him.

He lay on the cold floor as the zombies joined the circle. The dead stared at them silently, and Alec wondered what he would do. His chance, it seemed, had come, and he had to act quickly before they decided to kill him and Sarah. But how could he break from this circle of death?

Ghastly wails echoed in his head. Like the moans he had heard earlier they carried words, but this time he could understand them. The dead were speaking to him.

"Living flesh, we love you."

"Yes, we hate you…"

"Lust you…"

"Love…"

"Must have you."

"Desire…"

"Stay with us."

"…want you to stay."

"…no living flesh may stay, so we must…"

"…must rend bite suck kill kill *KILL*…"

"…die, my love, die for us…"

"…and stay."

"NO!!" he cried, leaping to his feet. "You'll not have your way with me, demons!!"

He stood defiantly, wanting to launch himself at the perverse horrors standing before him, but unwilling to leave Sarah undefended. His face twisted in near madness, and his hands curled into fists. They came at him, closing the circle.

The first to reach him was a skeleton, and he smashed its ribs with his fist. As it fell, he grabbed a section of its leg and began to beat upon the other creatures with it. The dead advanced, and he smashed them one by one with the leg bone. The skeletons broke to pieces under his brutal assault, and the zombies fell back upon one another. Some did not rise again, especially those whose skulls he had crushed.

He had never been filled with such rage, such visceral horror at the things the voices told him. The things these unnatural creatures wanted to do to him. And to Sarah.

TO SARAH! he cried as he bore down upon a zombie's soft skull. Its dark blood splashed him and stained him and he did not care.

One by one he quieted them, and still they came, unwilling or unable to pause in their assault. Then the bone he was wielding snapped, and he pummeled the things with his bare fists, bloodying his hands as the sharp bones of the skeletons cut his knuckles and fingers. He didn't feel the pain. Only the horror. The rage.

But he was no warrior. He had not trained to endure such punishment, such exertion. His blows grew weaker and slower, and still they came. Finally one of the zombies struck him across the face with a mighty backhanded blow, and he toppled to the ground. Dizzy, he tried to get up and found he could not. Blackness threatened to overwhelm him again.

"Alec?" said a soft voice. It was Sarah.

He saw her rise, confused. She looked around at the circle of the dead, now crushing inward. They reached out toward her, spotted gray hands grabbing at her clothes, her flesh. She screamed. She had finally remembered what was happening.

And then he couldn't see her. They fell upon her, covering her, consuming her. She screamed bloody death, and Alec closed his eyes against tears of rage and sorrow.

And then there was a sound, the raging sound of roaring flame. Light burned through his eyelids, and heat tore at his flesh. He opened his eyes and saw the dead surrounding him, stumbling madly as they burned, fire raging over their dry, decayed flesh and bone. Fire burned the air itself, and the chamber was filled with it. Alec hugged the floor, and the flames rolled over him, heating his skin but leaving it untouched. But the dead burned to ash, screaming in agony, thrashing wildly, sent at last to a final rest.

At the center of it all was Sarah, crying tears of anguish, holding her fists aloft, sending fire outward from herself. Her Fairy ring blazed with power, and her passion made it grow to a conflagration. She was Shaping, turning the very air, the very rock of the tomb, to fire. She looked like a goddess standing there, a ring of flame causing her hair to glow like the sun. Alec forgot his anger and gazed at her in awe.

But only for a moment. The dead had already been consumed, but she did not stop. She caused more of the rock to turn to flame, and Alec could not breathe because she had changed all the air in the chamber to fire! And still she did not stop, could not! The fire was flowing into her, burning her, and she screamed in pain. Her hair and clothing caught on fire, and her flesh began to blister. She could not stop it, could not turn off the flow of the power.

Alec didn't hesitate. He leaped into the fire and knocked her to the ground. In pain, he grabbed her wrist and smashed her hand to the ground. He grabbed the ring and yanked it from her finger, clutching it tightly in his fist.

At once, the fire was gone. Air flowed into the room with an audible clap, like quiet thunder. He rolled Sarah on the ground, dousing the few flames still clinging to her, and then he patted out the flames licking his shirt. He was only lightly burned, and to his surprise, Sarah was not much worse. Her dress and hair were blackened, and she had some blistering on her flesh, but she seemed otherwise all right.

"Grok's wounds," she muttered, tears streaming down her face. "I couldn't stop! It wouldn't let go of me!"

"It's all right," said Alec, pulling her close to him. "They're gone, the fire's gone, and we're still here. We're still whole and alive. It's all right." He stroked her hair and kissed her head.

"I can't take any more of this, Alec. Things like this don't happen. They don't! I want my mother, our shop. I want my old life back!"

"It's all right," repeated Alec, wishing he believed it. "It will be over soon."

He held Sarah a moment longer, until she was strong enough to pull away. She looked him in the eye and wiped away her tears, showing him she was ready to move on. Looking at her, Alec knew she would get over this. She was strong. No one could swallow as much horror as she had and not feel some pain, but it would not break her. The fact that she hadn't fallen to her knees screaming told him this. She took a deep breath, and it was clear she had regained control of herself.

"Now what?" she said.

Alec considered. "Now…I don't know. Maybe we should…"

He broke off as he saw Lorn stumble into the chamber. The warrior's clothing was torn, his armor damaged. His right hand clutched his sword, which was broken just above the hilt. He had a gash on his forehead, and blood covered his face and hair and seeped from fresh wounds on his torso. He held something under his left arm, clutching it close to his body. He was gasping for air, and upon entering the room he leaned heavily on the wall.

"You dropped something back there," he said.

Alec's eyes grew wide and his hope was renewed as Lorn casually tossed the package he was carrying to the floor. He had recovered the silver chest. The Talisman of Unity was safe!

Then the warrior reached into his pocket and pulled forth a small glass vial. He reached out to Sarah, saying, "And I believe this belongs to you."

She ran up to Lorn and accepted the vial, the gift from Horren she had dropped when the undead grabbed her. Then she looked at Lorn and concern shown from her eyes.

"How badly are you hurt?" she questioned.

"I have had worse wounds than these. They will heal." He looked around the room, noticing the scorched walls and the piles of ash which had once been walking corpses. A grimace of confusion spread across his face.

"What is this? How did you…?"

"Don't ask," said Alec. "Not now. We have to get out of here before more of those things find us. How did you manage to defeat that mummy?"

Lorn frowned, his eyes dropping to his useless, broken sword. "I didn't. I destroyed many of its minions, but the most I could do against the mummy was to wound it, to slow it down. It was far too strong. My blade broke against its mighty sword and I was forced to flee. I fear it still pursues us. We should make haste before it catches us."

"Then let's go," said Alec, picking up the silver chest and opening it so that its light brightened the flame-scorched chamber.

"Wait," said Sarah. "What about Kraig and Michael?"

Alec and Lorn both looked at Sarah, and then at each other. Alec was unsure of what to say. They certainly couldn't wait here with the mummy and the other undead at their heels. And yet how could the abandon their companions?

The dilemma was resolved when Michael entered the room, holding aloft a sputtering stump of torch. Kraig hurried in behind him, smiling at the sight of his friends. The hermit acknowledged the others only with a nod.

"Thank Grok you're alive," said Kraig. "To tell the truth, I feared the worst." Before Alec could say anything, the peacekeeper went on. "Listen, we know the way out of this place, but we must hurry. We saw that big mummy stumbling this way; twenty or so of his creatures were with him."

Sarah ran up and threw her arms around Kraig, crying out in joy that he was alive. Alec stood there smiling, more reserved but equally overjoyed. Now that they were together again, he was certain they could make it out of this horrible tomb.

"Time for reunions later," said Lorn. "We must hurry away."

"I agree," said Michael, "but we must go carefully. We must pass through another of these burial vaults before we are free of this place, which means we will likely face more of these undead monstrosities. If we are alert and quick, we can evade them. They are slow, and for the most part, weak."

Then there came the sounds of shuffling feet, and Alec heard the moan he knew belonged to the huge mummified monster. Wasting no more time, they fled from the chamber into the hall beyond. Quickly but with great care, Michael led them into the darkness. The sounds of the dead followed behind them, not fading, but thankfully not drawing nearer.

Alec looked at his companions as they marched and knew at once they were all the worse for wear. Lorn's chain-mail was torn in spots, links ripped out by claw and blade, and his sword was broken and useless. Worse, blood stained his clothes from gaping wounds beneath. Sarah was burned and blistered, and just watching her as she forced herself to walk was painful. Alec knew she was enduring greater pain than he, and he was glad she no longer had the ring. He knew it had saved both their lives, but he was glad he now had it in his pocket where it could cause the girl no more harm. He turned his gaze to Kraig and Michael, who seemed the least affected by the trials they had faced. They were not wounded, yet both looked somewhat shaken. Alec wondered what they had seen while they were separated that had disturbed them so.

Alec himself still felt the heat of Sarah's fire on his skin. The bruises and cuts he had gained while fighting the dead caused him significant pain as well. But these things no longer troubled him, not really. This journey was making him harder, stronger. He would never again be the simple country baker he had thought he'd always be. Somehow, knowing this pleased him and saddened him at the same time.

There was more danger in the tomb ahead, of this he was certain. And out there in the world waited Salin, ready to claim the Talisman or pry it from Alec's dead hands. But Alec couldn't let himself be daunted by these thoughts. He had to survive. He had Sarah to think of, after all. Sarah, the Talisman, the Fate of the World. It was quite a lot to ask of a simple baker from a rustic village, he thought.

But he would survive. He would prevail. He repeated these thoughts again and again. He didn't believe them, but thinking them helped him ignore the sound of the dead as they gathered behind him and before him.

CHAPTER 14

The Search Continues

Ara sat silently as she sipped her hot tea. The common room was thankfully quiet; she wasn't in the mood for the boisterous atmosphere typical of taverns. Of course, they had chosen the Dark Helm for its relative quiet and had not been disappointed. Landyn was well traveled, and of all the inns and taverns in Bordonhold, he knew this one was the least frequented. Its unpopularity was partially due to the fact that it was located at the northern tip of town, furthest from the central markets and the commonly used gates, and partially because of the widespread rumor its owner watered down the wine and ale to the point of tastelessness. Ara had found that rumor to be true, but she didn't care. She was more in the mood for tea anyway.

She looked across the room to where Jinn was pestering a young waitress, his eyes fixed upon her deep cleavage and his hand continually slapping her behind. For some reason, the girl didn't seem to mind the impish Fairy's advances. Actually, she seemed to appreciate his attentions. Ara supposed there was no accounting for taste.

Yet, as much as she hadn't liked Jinn at first, she had come to realize he had some redeeming qualities. He was completely loyal to Kari and was more than willing to help anyone in need. On more than one occasion he had asked Ara if she needed anything, and he hurried to cater to her if she did. She was suspicious of his motives at first, but he never asked for anything in return. He still had a habit of being lewd and suggestive, but she was finding it easier to ignore him.

Kari and Landyn had gone off into the town in search of some friend of Landyn's, leaving her and Jinn to fend for themselves. Horren was waiting for them in the forest outside the town. His presence here, he maintained, would cause too much of a stir. He was twice the size of a human and somewhat alien in appearance, so Ara was forced to agree with him. Few people knew of the Addins, and those who knew would still most likely faint upon seeing one, especially one wandering the streets of a city. Of course, Horren had no desire to enter a city. Only among the trees did he feel comfortable. It was with great regret he left his own grove to accompany them.

It had been a week since they'd left the Addin's home. They knew Alec and Sarah's probable destination, but not their route, so Kari insisted on following the tracks as closely as ever. If Sarah's party ran into trouble before they reached Faerie and got sidetracked, Ara and the others might miss them entirely if they just blindly traveled northward. Ara agreed, but the slowness of following the tracks had frustrated her to no end. They might as well have been on foot for all the progress they made.

But they had continued on at a steady pace, eventually coming to the gates of Bordonhold. After hearing the city watch ramble on about "you shall not do this, you shall not do that" for twenty minutes, they were allowed into the city. Ara had been to Freehold once or twice in her life, but she was amazed once again at how different from her country home a city could be: the huge, multi-level buildings and towers, the castle rising high at the center of the city, the rows of shop after shop that made her Dragon's Den seem small and insignificant. She looked around in wonder at the people crowding the streets and the vendors hawking their wares. Kari and Jinn ignored their surroundings, and Landyn sauntered confidently, back in his element.

"Obviously, I cannot follow a trail in a place like this," said Kari. "Unless they climb walls, though, their trail should lead out from one of the city gates. Later, I will try to pick it up again."

"Let us make for an inn I know in a quiet section of town," said Landyn. "Once we're settled, I will go look up a few friends of mine who always have their ears to the street. It might pay to acquire a little information. Perhaps someone has seen Sarah and her friends, or maybe some word of Salin's activities is spreading through the streets."

They walked from the southern gate to the far end of the northern quarter, which took them nearly two hours. They finally came to the Dark Helm Inn, and Landyn rented them rooms for the night. After a quick bath and a quicker meal, Landyn and Kari set out to look for the minstrel's friends and try to pick up the Sarah and Alec's trail again. Ara wandered around town a bit until evening fell and then returned to the inn to sit in the common room and sip some tea.

As she reflected back on her travels, she wondered if she was doing the right thing. Probably Horren was right; she could do nothing to help Alec and Sarah, not against Salin. But she couldn't sit back and do nothing. This quest of hers was the only way she could think of to stay sane. And besides, Salin might be a powerful and cunning sorcerer, but his magic had failed to kill her the first time.

Her survival had been luck, really, but she couldn't help smiling as she felt the outline of the golden circlet she kept with her other belongings in her waist-pouch. She hadn't told the others about the headpiece yet, not even Landyn. Not that she meant to keep it a secret or anything; she simply had so much else on her mind she had nearly forgotten it. She had taken the gold circlet Alec had found in the chest along with the ring and the Talisman of Unity. Sarah had already claimed the gold ring set with the amber stone, and Ara didn't dispute it. Why should she? There was enough merchandise to sell that she could afford to let her daughter have a gold ring.

But the circlet caught Ara's eye. She had been studying it the night Salin came, trying to estimate its value. She was sitting in her shop, running her fingers across the thin circle of gold, wondering at its seamless construction, when she heard a voice.

"I have to kill you. Nothing personal, you understand. Just sending a message to your dear friend Mason."

She turned toward the voice, but there was no one there. The shop began to shake and the air became hot. In a panic she ran for the door, but she only made it two steps before a ball of flame burst outward from the center of the room, roaring deafeningly and consuming all in its path.

But Ara was not consumed, nor even touched by the fire raging around her. The gold circlet she clutched so tightly in her hands seemed to vibrate, sending tingles through her body. It glowed intensely as the flame surrounded her, and an amber light radiated from it and enveloped her. The fire broke upon the amber glow like a wave upon the shore, and although the fire tore the shop down around her, she was unharmed. She didn't even feel warm.

Of course, it was pure luck that debris falling from her blasted ceiling didn't crush her, but the circlet protected her from the primary danger, the fire. She wondered if the ring Sarah kept had similar properties. Thinking of Salin's sorcery, she hoped it did.

She had fled then, seeking to take advantage of the fact that Salin, and nearly everyone else, thought her dead. The element of surprise. That was her advantage. That, and the magic circlet.

She was still lost in thought when Landyn came through the door. Behind him came a similarly dressed man, and like Landyn he sported wavy brown hair and a well groomed mustache, but he was not nearly so handsome as the minstrel. Landyn smiled when he saw Ara and led his new companion to the table.

"Ara, this is Luke. He is a minstrel here in Bordonhold, one I've worked with in the past. He is a good friend. He can be trusted."

"Pleased to meet you, my lady," he said, taking her hand and kissing it gently. It was amazing how like in mannerism he was to Landyn.

"Pleased to meet you, Luke."

Landyn and Luke took seats at the table, and Landyn said, "Minstrels do a lot more than play songs, at least the ones I associate with. You know what I mean, Ara. We are not a wholly noble breed of person."

"Really?" she said sarcastically. "And here I thought you were my white knight."

Landyn smiled widely. "We are always on the lookout for information we might be able to use to our advantage: what lord is fornicating with what lady, or better yet, what common girl; who is plotting to kill whom; which rich merchant is passing through town at what time, and how many guards he has. We have to make our living somehow, and singing in the tavern isn't always enough. To keep up our standard of living, many of us are forced to indulge in the buying and selling of information, perhaps a little blackmail, or even picking a pocket or two. You understand, we are not thieves by nature. We never take much at a time, and never from someone who really needs the money. But, it is hard not to use the skills you have."

Ara smiled. "I think I understand."

"Good. Luke here has many contacts throughout the city. He has managed to discover a few things you might find interesting."

Luke leaned toward Ara conspiringly. "Normally, of course, I would have to charge you for this, but since I owe Landyn a favor, this one's on me. My sources tell me some people fitting the description of your daughter and her friends stayed a night at an inn called Home, in the eastern district of the southern quarter. They must have had a falling out, because the girl and a young man left earlier than the other two, who followed after an hour or so later. They headed into the western quarter, and presumably left through the western gate. Such an event would have hardly warranted the interest of my source if the girl and the boy hadn't left with the drunkard, Lorn."

"What?" exclaimed Ara. "Drunkard? What are you talking about?"

"Lorn is sort of a joke around these parts. He's been in town a couple of years, had a few jobs but failed miserably at them. Turned to the bottle. He only has one friend, who's as much of a joke as he is, a fellow by the name of Jak. Actually, few people remember this, but Old Jak once went by the name Shad Flynt. He was reputedly a master thief, so skilled at his craft the law could never prove anything against him. But he got old and silly, became a dotard, lost his skill. Now he's a pathetic old man who lives alone in a little hut, all the wealth he obtained thieving squandered away in his youth. He and Lorn deserve each other.

"Anyway, your daughter left with Lorn. Why he would put down his bottle for a journey through the wilderness I couldn't say, and why the girl and her friend would take up with such a fool I just don't know. Seems to me like he'd be more of a hindrance than a help on a journey."

"Grok," said Ara. "I don't like this at all." If she had not liked them being in the company of Michael, she hated the sound of this Lorn. And they had separated from Kraig! She had been pleased they at least had the big peacekeeper for protection, and now he might no longer be with them.

"There's more," said Luke. "Landyn tells me they are pursued by an old man named Salin. He's been here, too, only a few days behind your girl. He met up with some big warrior and a couple of frightening looking women. He stayed in town a day or two while he sent the warrior off on some task, then they set out together, through the west gate. As they were on horseback, I'd say it is fairly likely they have caught up to your daughter's group by now, if they were good trackers or knew where the others were headed."

"Oh, no...oh, Grok, no..."

"Calm down, Ara," said Landyn. "He's just speculating. We don't know all the facts. Anything could have happened out there. Michael and Kraig could have caught up to the others. Salin could have been delayed. We don't even know for certain if he knows their destination. Maybe this Lorn is not what he seems. They could be safe now, laughing about all this."

"I don't think so," she said, tears forming in her eyes. "But thank you. You're right. This is no time for despair. I think at first light we should head for the west gate and get back on their trail."

Landyn nodded his agreement. "Of course. I am sure Kari has found it by now. But there is one more thing I'd like to do this night. Luke, you've piqued my curiosity about something. Would you care to accompany me into town?"

"As you wish, my friend."

They rose, and each tried to outdo the other as they bowed to her with exaggerated formality, both using their cloaks to embellish the bow even more. Somehow, Landyn looked elegant and dashing while Luke looked awkward and silly. Landyn bid her good evening and then rushed out into the night with his friend.

She sat there a moment longer and realized Jinn had disappeared. So had the waitress he had been making friends with. Ara chuckled to herself, wondering if the girl knew what Jinn was. She supposed it didn't matter. Ara had not known at first Jinn and Kari were not human. She supposed all the parts under their clothes looked as human as the rest of them.

Imagining what Jinn had under his clothes made her feel slightly ill. Banishing the though from her mind, she finished her tea and retired to her bedroom for the evening.

"Are you certain this is the place?" asked Landyn, looking at the weather-worn old house.

"Of course I am," said Luke. "But I still don't see what you want with Old Jak. No matter what he was, he's just a foolish old man now."

"You said he is Lorn's only friend. Perhaps he can offer us some insight into why a drunk would take up with a couple of youngsters tramping through the wilderness."

Luke moved his head to the side and nodded, eyes focused upward, as if to say "Oh, good idea, hadn't thought of that." Landyn moved passed him and sighed as he knocked on the door.

Luke had always been a good friend, and he was excellent at acquiring information, but Landyn always found him a bit of a dolt. When they met years ago, Luke was just starting out as a minstrel and hadn't found an image for himself. All minstrels had an image, a combination of what they wore and how they carried themselves. Landyn befriended the young man, taught him a few things, and told him how he himself developed his image. Luke, not being very creative for a minstrel, attempted to copy Landyn's image to the letter. Landyn should have been angry, and he was a little, but he decided to accept Luke's infringement as flattery. After all, being in different cities they were not in competition with one another, and even if they had been, Landyn would win out every time. Luke just couldn't pull off the dashing, gentleman-rogue act the way Landyn could. Because for Landyn, it wasn't really an act.

The door opened a crack and a bent old man peaked out. "Who's there?" he said with a crackling voice. "I don't want any trouble."

"You'll find none here, good sir," said Landyn. "I am Landyn son of Gordon, Minstrel of Freehold. I am here to ask you a few questions about a friend of yours, a man named Lorn. He was last seen in the company of two people whom I seek, and I would like to ask you a few questions."

At that the old man's eyes grew wide with horror. "Lars protect me!" he cried, slamming the door shut. Through it, his voice rang out. "You can kill me if you like, but tell your master Salin I spit on him! I'll never tell him where they're going! Never!"

Landyn was taken aback. "No, no, old man! Open up! I'm not with Salin. I'm helping Ara Mills, Sarah's mother. She's trying to find her daughter."

The door opened and the old man looked out suspiciously. "Not saying I believe you, but since you could kick in my door any time you choose, perhaps you should come in. If you're going to kill me, I can't stop you, door or no."

He opened the door wide and Landyn entered, followed by Luke. "I know you have reason to doubt us, but we simply want to know why Lorn has accompanied the children. We know they are going to Faerie. Horren, the Addin, told us as much."

"Horren," said the old man, relaxing a little. "If you heard it from him, then chances are you are not Salin's ally. All right, I suppose I will tell you about Lorn. I assume, since you're here, you already know who I am. Most call me Jak, but my real name is Shad Flynt."

"Yes, so Luke has told me," said Landyn, indicating his friend. "I do not intend to take up much of your time, but I must know about this Lorn. I have heard he is nothing but a drunken fool. Why would he go off on a possibly dangerous trip with two young folks he hardly knows? Why would they have him?"

Shad spread out his hands and smiled. "He went with them because I asked him to. They accepted him because they had no other choice." He paused for a moment, and Landyn motioned for him to go on. "Michael, an old friend of mine who was traveling with Alec, Sarah, and Kraig, came to me and asked if I could recommend someone to guide them to Faerie. He did not wish to go himself, although I thought he would be the best man for the task. The only other person I knew who could act as their guide was Lorn. Most people know him only as the town drunk, the town fool, but this isn't truly who he is. He was once someone great, I think, at the very least a mighty warrior. And he has been to Faerie before. I know little about him, but he told me this much. It was difficult, but I made him stop drinking, at least long enough to guide Alec and Sarah to their destination. I convinced him to go. It was harder to convince them to accept him, but they finally did. I'm not sure if their other companion, Kraig, ever accepted him. I also don't know if Michael decided to go with them or if he returned home as he claimed he would. But know if they are with Lorn, they are in capable hands. I know he is more than he seems. I'm sure he can get them to Faerie safely. That is, if he can keep them ahead of Salin."

"That's the trick, isn't it?" said Landyn. "So this Lorn is now their guide, and Michael and Kraig might no longer be with them. I'm not sure if I'm pleased by this news or not. Ara led me to believe Michael isn't a trustworthy person, but Horren has been trying to convince us otherwise."

"Believe me, I know Michael well and there's no one you'd rather be with if you were in danger. I pray to Lars he's with them still."

"Shad, tell me one last thing. Who is Michael? If I am to believe Horren's stories, he is the greatest man who ever lived and we should all be bowing down before him and showering him with praise. But Ara says for as long as she can remember he's been an eccentric fool, as much of a joke in her home-town as Lorn is here. How could he have fallen from the pillar Horren puts him on to the pit Ara's seen him crawl out of?"

"I'm afraid, my friend, you don't have the time to hear that tale. Suffice it to say Michael has been around for a long, long time and has seen too much darkness. He fought it for many years, but he fell into despair because he couldn't stop it from growing. He couldn't win the war, so he surrendered. Perhaps now he is ready to fight the war again. Lars, for the sake of the world, I hope he is."

Landyn wasn't at all satisfied with Shad's answer, but he let it go. If he really wanted to learn more about the enigmatic hermit, he could always ask Horren later. "Very well, sir, I will not take up any more of your time. Thank you for your information; you've been quite helpful. I pray Lorn is as competent a guide as you seem to think. Ara is quite concerned about her daughter, Sarah, and I have taken it upon myself to help her find the girl, preferably alive and safe. Farewell, Shad Flynt."

"Good-bye, Landyn of Freehold. I also pray you find them safe and alive. You may not understand it, but it could be the fate of the world rests with those children."

"Now that would make quite a song!" exclaimed the minstrel as he bowed deeply, flourished his cape, and exited gracefully.

Luke, following behind, said, "Do you know what he meant about the fate of the world?"

"Not really. I've been so caught up with tracking Sarah and the others that I haven't given much thought to why Salin would want them. I know it has something to do with some piece of jewelry Alec found, but I don't know its significance. Perhaps I will ask Horren. He's bound to know."

Half way back to the Dark Helm, Luke bade Landyn goodnight and went on his way. Landyn continued his journey alone, keeping his hand on the hilt of his short sword. Bordonhold was not the safest town to be in after dark, and he remained alert and ready for trouble. At the back of his mind, however, thoughts he could not quiet fought for his attention. Something was going on here that was deeper than he knew. Perhaps it was a mistake for him to have gotten so involved in it. But he couldn't back out now. He couldn't disappoint Ara. As much as he tried not to admit it to himself, he was falling for her. She was not at all like Jessina, except for her angelic voice, but he was growing fond of her in spite of that, or, perhaps, because of it. He had loved Jessina for so long he thought he would never find pleasure in another woman's company. But he enjoyed being with Ara, even in this situation.

And then there was his plan to write the greatest ballad of his time. The fact that there was more to this situation than met the eye scared and thrilled him at the same time. He was afraid he was out of his depth, but, oh, the song this would make!

He hoped he'd be alive to write it. And he prayed it would have a happy ending.

Fist of Lars, I must be getting old if I'm having such thoughts.

He reached the inn at last, glad to be sleeping in a bed for once. He went to the room he was sharing with Jinn and found the diminutive Fairy was not there. He hardly gave the imp's absence a second thought as he undressed, crawled into bed, and drifted into a deep, dreamless sleep.

The next day they gathered early at the stable, mounted their horses, and rode toward the west gate. Kari announced she had picked up the trail again. It went westward for a short time, she said, and then turned north.

"It appears they ran into some trouble not far out of the gate," she said. "Goblins. I saw about thirty of their filthy little bodies strewn around. They look similar to the ones we saw before, near the Fourpoints River, possibly from the same tribe. At any rate, there were no human bodies. Five sets of tracks lead away from the combat—the four we have been following and one more."

"That one more would be Lorn, their new guide," said Landyn. "But you bring us good news. We thought Sarah and Alec had gotten separated from the others. It seems they are all together again."

"That is what the tracks seem to indicate," said Kari.

Ara breathed a sigh of relief. She still had her doubts about the hermit, but she was glad Kraig was still there to protect her daughter.

Soon after they left the town, they were rejoined by Horren. He was smiling and there was a spring in his step.

"Ah, these forests are wonderful! Why, just a few miles to the west is a place which would make a fine Addingrove. It would take years to grow the grove to my liking, but perhaps I will settle here when our journey is over. I mean, if my current home is no longer suitable for me." This seemed to sober him, but only for a moment. When he looked again at the forest around him, the smile returned to his face.

They passed the area where Sarah's party had the skirmish with the goblins, and Ara looked at the little creatures with disgust. She had seen them twice before, at the Addingrove and at the Fourpoints, where Sarah, Alec, and the others had first run into them. The sight of them, even dead, still made her shudder. They were horrible little things!

"It's a shame," said Horren, looking at the goblin corpses.

"What is?" questioned Landyn.

"That they're all dead. It might be fun to toss a few goblins around."

"You have a strange idea of fun," replied the minstrel.

Horren laughed. "I suppose. It's just that I haven't had to fight anything in so long I would relish a good battle. The ogre I killed hardly counts. One ogre against an Addin is terribly unfair, I'm afraid."

"Then I gather these goblins wouldn't be much of a challenge either," said Ara.

"Do not underestimate them. They are small and stupid, but they usually attack in large groups. Together, they can defeat the strongest warrior, overwhelming him by sheer numbers. I would be challenged by, oh, a hundred or so."

Jinn, who was riding beside Kari, turned and flashed a toothy grin. "I would pay to see that, Addin."

Horren rolled his eyes. "You sprites are all alike."

Jinn laughed uproariously until Kari gave him a deadly look.

They rode on until dusk, falling into the traveling routine they had established before reaching Bordonhold. Landyn and Horren exchanged stories all day long, and Kari rode silently in the front, stopping often to check the tracks. Jinn alternated between fawning over his mistress and making small talk with Ara. Not all of it was crude, and Ara was finding it harder to dislike the small Fairy. Sometimes he seemed genuinely concerned for her well-being.

It had been close to two weeks since Alec, Sarah and Kraig had fled into the woods and Ara had left for Riverton. It seemed so much longer. Their lives had been uprooted and entangled with powers Ara couldn't begin to comprehend. As they rode on, she said a prayer to the patron god of farming, fertility, and simplicity, whose wounds bleed forever upon the soil of the land, making wholesome things grow in abundance.

Grok, she prayed, *let us find them soon. Let us all reach Faerie together, and start our lives anew. Keep Salin away from them, I beg you!*

After they had made camp for the night, Ara looked up at the stars for a long while wondering if the gods really listened to the prayers of mortals. She hoped so. If she ever needed divine intervention, she certainly needed it now.

Luke couldn't see who had grabbed him from behind, but fear surged through him when he could not wriggle free of the massive arms that held him. Someone huge and powerful carried him into an alley, and a rough voice muttered, "You shouldn't be prowling the streets this late at night, minstrel. It can be dangerous."

The powerful arms threw him to the ground, and he banged his head against one of the buildings which formed the walls of the alley. He turned, touching his head and feeling blood flow from a gaping wound. Squinting through his pain, he gazed at one of the largest men he had ever seen looking down at him. It was a black man with short dark hair and yellow teeth, wearing a tight blue shirt and baggy black pants. He hovered menacingly over the minstrel.

"Who were those people asking questions about Mason? What do they know of Salin Urdrokk?"

Luke shook his head, confused. "What? I don't know…"

"Don't be stupid," said the black man. "You're not the only agent Salin has in this town. He made it quite clear anyone asking questions about Mason or anyone traveling with him was to be killed."

"Well, I…"

"Shut up. Don't you know how to follow orders? You must not disobey Salin. Why didn't you kill them, or if they were too strong for you, why did you not call for help?"

Luke shuddered. Salin had promised him great wealth if he would serve him. He offered him women, a chance to be held as the greatest minstrel in Tyridan, perhaps in all of Eglacia. All he had to do was keep an eye out, be a spy. Salin had never said anything about killing until recently. Luke never intended to kill anyone, but he couldn't tell Salin that. You could never say no to Salin.

"You don't…understand. Landyn…he is my…friend."

The black man laughed. "Old loyalties and friendships die when one swears fealty to Salin, fool! You have proven yourself worthless in the Great One's eyes. You must pay the price."

"No! I…I…But Salin is not here! He cannot judge me if he is not here."

"He does not need to judge you personally. I am empowered to act is his place." He bent closer and showed the minstrel his true face. Luke began screaming in fear. "Now do you know who I am?"

Luke nodded, screaming all the while.

The dark Fairy shaped. Luke's head erupted in a fountain of blood, bone, and tissue.

Drakkahn Shynagoth howled with delight as he licked the spattered blood from his lips. Assuming his natural form, he climbed the city wall and went out into the forest to hunt.

CHAPTER 15

The Lord of the Dead

More than an hour had passed since Alec, Sarah, and Lorn had reunited with Michael and Kraig, and still it seemed they were no closer to escaping Faryn-Gehnah. The corridors twisted and branched, but now Alec perceived renewed confidence in Michael. The hermit was choosing their path without hesitation, always taking paths sloping upward or remaining level. They moved quickly through the shadowy ways, spurred on by the sounds of the dead behind them. The mummy and its minions were constantly at their heels, just out of sight in the darkness behind them, but they kept their lead by moving quickly and not daring to stop for a rest. Alec walked side by side with the hermit, the silver light from his chest continuing to illuminate their way. Apprehension gripped him whenever he thought of the burial vault that still lay ahead. If the dead in the vault had awakened already, he had no idea how they would manage to fight their way through them.

The corridor bent sharply, narrowing until they had to walk single-file. The walls continued to grow closer until Alec had to turn sideways to fit through, and even then his shoulders and stomach brushed the smooth stone walls. He wondered if the corridor would narrow until they could no longer squeeze through, but after a minute of shuffling along sideways with their backs pressed up against the wall, the hall widened enough so they could walk comfortably. Before long, Alec was able to resume his place beside Michael, and the space continued to open up around them until three men could walk abreast. The open space relieved some of Alec's anxiety, but the sounds of the still pursuing dead behind them caused his panic to rise again. He shivered, hoping they would find the tomb's exit before the undead overran them.

Without warning the walls to either side ended, and they found themselves standing in the entry of the final burial vault. As his light fell across the stone floor, Alec could make out caskets and sarcophagi resembling the ones he had seen in the previous vaults, save that these were arranged in neat rows and were raised off the floor upon stone platforms decorated with silver trim. Most strikingly, all the caskets were open and empty.

Just at the edge of the light, beyond the first few rows of caskets, dark forms waited in the shadows. Some stood absolutely still, but others swayed back and forth hypnotically. A few began to shuffle forward, decayed features revealed as they stepped into the light. Quiet voices murmured: the muddled, gravely voices of the dead.

Alec's heart pounded faster. The mummy and its followers were nearly upon them, and the way forward was blocked. Suddenly fear clutched his heart. They had fought their way through the tomb only to be trapped here at the last to become a bloody feast for the dead. Hopelessly he turned toward Michael, who was standing beside him evaluating the rows of creatures barring their way.

Michael acknowledged the baker with a brief nod. Then he turned to the peacekeeper and said, "Kraig, you and I must try to forge a path through these creatures. Alec, you and Sarah follow close behind. You'll have to cover the rear, Lorn. I fear you are the only one with the skill to stand against the mummy."

Lorn nodded gravely. He quickly considered the broken stump of sword in his hand and cast it aside. Reaching into his pack, he pulled out a torch and some flint and steel with which to light it. As he quickly worked to set the torch aflame, Alec wondered what kind of weapon the torch would make against the mummy. Old rags and dry flesh and bone should go up in flames easily, he thought, but this mummy had some sort of magic. Would it be protected in some way from fire? And it was more than possible Lorn would never be able to land a blow. The creature was huge and fast, and its sword was deadly.

Alec turned his back to Lorn as Sarah grabbed his hand. Michael and Kraig, sword and axe at the ready, locked eyes. The hermit gave a nod, and the two raced forward into the shadow, toward the lumbering shapes blocking their way.

Alec and Sarah ran several strides behind them. The light he carried cast an eerie glow on the ranks of undead, lighting decayed faces frozen in expressions of pain, rage, and horror. Creatures of bone and monsters of flesh reached out as they approached, deadly claws bared to grab and rend and choke.

Kraig was the first to reach the line of undead. The muscles of his powerful arms bulged as his axe flashed in a wide arc. Like lightning striking a tree, the axe splintered bone and sent the remains of no fewer than three skeletons skittering across the floor. Kraig pressed deeper into the mass of the dead, screaming fury as he slashed open the zombies pressing in around him.

Michael was only a step behind the peacekeeper. His rune-engraved sword seemed to give off a dim blue glow as he hacked at the corpses. Skeletons broke to pieces as his blade mercilessly carved through rib cages and split skulls, and zombies went down in droves as he separated their heads from their shoulders.

Alec ran into the opening in the wall of corpses his companions had cleared, pulling Sarah along behind him. There were more undead here than he had thought when gazing at them through the shadows, and as they closed in from the sides he began to despair. Michael and Kraig had become fighting machines, but even they could not clear a path quickly enough. They would all be crushed as the hordes of the dead pressed inward.

Suddenly a loud cry rang out behind Alec. He spared a glance over his shoulder and saw Lorn grappling with the terrifying mummy. Lorn had dropped his torch, which sat upon the ground near him, flickering uselessly. His right hand was down at his side, holding the mummy's left wrist, trying to push the creature away from him. His left hand was raised over his head, desperately gripping his assailant's sword arm as the mummy tried to bring the blade down upon his skull. The warrior's muscles shook and his face was drawn with effort. It was clear he could not match the mummy's incredible strength.

Lorn faltered, and the mummy managed to pull its left arm free of the warrior's grip. It reached across its body and struck Lorn hard across the face with the back of its hand. Lorn staggered, his head wrenching sideways with the blow, but somehow managed to maintain his hold on the wrist of the monster's sword arm. His muscles shook more fiercely, and Alec knew the warrior's strength was waning quickly. The instant it gave out, the mummy's jeweled short sword would split his skull in two.

Alec could not let that happen, not without trying to help. Without giving himself time to consider the insanity of his actions, he pushed Sarah toward Michael and Kraig and launched himself back through the collapsing walls of the dead to help Lorn. His heart was nearly bursting with panic, but he could not let the warrior die alone.

He threw his weight against the mummy and managed to knock the creature back a step. Lorn, taken totally by surprise, released his grip on the thing's wrist and stumbled in the opposite direction. The mummy brought its sword down, slicing only the air. But it recovered at once, regaining its balance instantly while Alec's momentum sent him sprawling to the ground.

The baker looked up just in time to see the horror's gleaming blade poised above him, ready to hew Alec's head from his body. Eyes wide, he rolled out of the way as the sword came down, still clutching the open silver chest against his body.

The sword struck the floor and astonishingly cut a deep gash in the stone, sending blue sparks flashing into the air. The mummy's eyes glowed red with rage and hatred as it raised its sword and moved toward Alec. The other undead closed in around him. Unable to gain his feet before the nearest skeleton was upon him, Alec clutched at the only weapon at hand, the small silver chest. Holding it by the lid, he swung it forcefully. The solid chest smashed through the old brittle bones with a sound like breaking glass, and the pieces of the skeleton flew in all directions. But as the chest completed its arc, the Talisman of Unity flew from it and skittered across the floor, stopping at the mummy's feet.

Alec cursed, knowing he must not lose the Talisman here. He leapt to his feet, madly pushing his way through the groping undead gathered around him, and dived with outstretched arms for the Talisman. Something grabbed at his feet and pulled him down. He reached out as his body slammed against the floor, his grasping fingers inches from the Talisman.

Looking up, he saw the mummy staring down at him. Strangely, the thing had lowered its sword and held it limply at its side. It made no move against Alec. Its eyes moved from Alec to the Talisman of Unity and then back to Alec. The red glow left the thing's eyes and was replaced by a dull gray light. It motioned slowly toward the other undead, who were poised to descend on Alec like vultures on carrion. At the mummy's command, they backed up slowly, giving Alec room to move. Keeping his eye on the mummy, he inched forward and grabbed the Talisman, which at his touch began to glow brightly.

When nothing attacked him, he carefully rose to his feet. He held the Talisman at arms length, letting it twist and turn as it dangled from its chain. Its glow spread outward to fill the vault, lighting the walls with dancing sparkles of gold. The mummy took a step away from Alec, and then, to the baker's utter surprise, knelt before him. Alec was so taken aback he forgot the fear which had consumed him only moments ago. Looking around, he saw the other undead were following the mummy's example, all bending knee before Alec and the radiant Talisman.

With the dead bent low, Alec could see his companions. Lorn had been fighting his way toward Alec, somehow managing to send countless skeletons and zombies back to their eternal rest with only his bare hands. Michael, Kraig, and Sarah had nearly gained the far side of the vault, but at the last they might not have made it. A ring of the dead surrounded them, all now kneeling before the glowing Talisman. Kneeling before Alec.

His companions, even Michael, bore a look of total confusion. They were frozen in battle stances, not believing the dead had ceased their assault. Eventually they noticed the glow and they turned toward Alec. They saw the Talisman, its light bathing Alec in a majestic glow, and their eyes filled with wonder. It seemed to Alec they gazed at him as one might look upon a god.

And then the mummy looked up from where it was kneeling and its eyes locked with Alec's. It opened its mouth, and in a voice like a whisper from the grave it began to speak.

"Welcome, Cursebreaker, to Faryn-Gehnah. I am Azdach shah'Gazoth, Lord of House shah'Gozoth of Eastern Faerie. Since the time of the curse, I have ruled the dead of Faryn-Gehnah. Our lusts drive us to take life. The Powers of Evil fill us as they fill this place. I bow to you in the hopes you can free us of the Curse."

Alec gaped, unable to find any words. Finally, he managed to say, "Me?"

The mummy stood, but did not approach Alec. "You are the Cursebreaker. You hold the Talisman. We have awaited you for centuries."

"The Talisman of Unity? You've waited for someone to bring it here?"

"Not *someone*," spoke the mummy. "*You*." He pointed at Alec's chest.

Alec shook his head. He had no idea what was going on. He didn't know how to break the curse. He didn't know why the Talisman had begun to glow when he picked it up. He certainly didn't understand why the dead, seemingly mindless before, suddenly worshipped him and spoke to him. He opened his mouth but could find no words.

"I can see your power," said the mummy. "Only you can break the curse. Only with the Talisman can you lay the dead to rest and cast the evil from this place. Act now, Cursebreaker, for soon the urge to kill will overwhelm me again. Even now as I smell your blood I desire to bathe in it. I can perhaps hold back my lust a little longer, but the others are far weaker than I am. They refrain from taking your life only because my will holds them. It cannot hold them much longer."

Alec didn't know what to do. Perhaps some fluke had bought them some time, but he couldn't break the curse of the tomb. Michael had told the story of the Keepers of the Tomb. If such powerful Shapers were unable to cast the evil from Faryn-Gehnah, how could a simple baker from Barton Hills?

"I…I cannot do what you ask," he said. "I don't know how."

The mummy stared at him and then bowed its head as if saddened. "You are the one. I cannot be mistaken about this. But you are not ready. Flee this place, Cursebreaker, before I am forced to slay you. But grant me your oath you will return one day when you are ready. Grant me your oath you will return to break the curse and send us to our final rest. Speak this oath to the Lord of the Dead."

Alec was not one to make an oath lightly. He knew he would never return to this place if he could help it. Yet, his survival and the survival of his companions depended on this creature's misconception he was someone special. If they couldn't get out of here with the Talisman, perhaps the world's survival was at risk as well. Biting back his fear at making an oath he had no intention of keeping, Alec looked the mummy in the eye and spoke.

"Azdoch shah'Gozoth, Lord of the Dead, I promise by all I hold holy I will return to this tomb one day and attempt to break the curse. I will do all I can to grant you the peace of eternal sleep."

Azdoch looked up and met Alec's eyes. Then the mummy turned its sword and offered it hilt first to the baker. "Take this as a symbol of my loyalty to the Cursebreaker. It is Flame, the greatest treasure of House shah'Gozoth, powerful among the weapons of Faerie. It cannot be broken, and can carve stone and steel as easily as flesh. It has other powers as well, but these each user must discover for himself."

Alec took the sword and bowed. "You honor me," he said, feeling sick he could not earn the gift he had been given. "Farewell, Lord shah'Gozoth."

"Farewell, Cursebreaker. Go quickly! I feel my grip on the minds of the dead slipping. Soon they will forget who you are and attempt to slay you. It happens now! Flee!"

The corpses began to move, slowly rising from their knees. Alec turned away from the Lord of the Dead and began to run, stooping only to pick up the chest he had dropped when diving for the Talisman. He shoved the chest under his left arm and gripped his sword tightly in his right hand, feeling slightly more confident wielding the new weapon. He passed Lorn, who fell in behind him, and in seconds reached the far end of the vault where the others were waiting. Together, the five companions raced from the chamber while the dead clambered to their feet. In seconds they were running down the smooth passage. Their way was illuminated by a strange mix of gold and silver light shining from the Talisman and the chest. The shuffling sounds of the dead followed close behind.

"I do not know what you did back there, Alec Mason, but it may have saved our lives," said Michael as they ran.

"It seems there is more to our friend than meets the eye," added Lorn.

A feeling of frustration swelled in Alec's gut. "I didn't do anything! I didn't make the Talisman glow and I don't have the power to break the curse of this tomb! That mummy was mistaken. Death must have rotted its brain as much as it rotted its body!"

"As you say," said the hermit, increasing the pace.

The dead were slow, and the fact that they were recovering from the influence of their master's will made them slower still. Alec and his companions pulled away from their pursuers until the shuffling footfalls faded into the distance. Only then did they dare to slow their pace to a brisk walk.

Minutes passed. The corridor snaked and curved but did not branch off or intersect another path. Finally they found themselves in an open area, not nearly as large as the burial vaults but wider than a normal passage. At the far end of the open area there was a wide staircase leading up high into the mountain. The stairs climbed higher than they could see, twisting up into unknown passages far above. It seemed obvious to Alec this was the path they were to take, and he raced for the stairs.

"Wait!" cried Michael. "That is not the way." He pointed to an area to the right of the grand staircase. "There lies our path."

Alec looked to the right and saw only a dead end. Then he cast his eyes downward and saw a large hole in the ground, leading into utter darkness. It appeared the ground here had collapsed, for the area around the hole was cracked and broken and sloped downward. He had no idea what Michael was talking about.

"Are you mad?" he exclaimed. "You would have us jump into a pit? Look, these stairs must lead to the exit."

"Michael's right," said Kraig, who had been bringing up the rear with Sarah. "The Keeper of the Tomb told us we must descend deep into the earth when we found the great stair. This is it. The exit is near!"

Sarah looked down into the hole and echoed Alec's concern. "And how do you suppose we get down there? We don't know how deep it is. We can't just leap in and hope for the best."

"No," said Lorn. "We cannot. Here." He reached into his pack and found a length of sturdy rope. "Like torches, you should never travel without rope."

He bent down and said, "If there is a place to secure one end…ah!" Luck was with them, for he found an outcropping of rock near the hole. Alec thought it fortunate the terrain here was not smooth like the rest of the tomb, but he supposed it only stood to reason. The collapse which had created the hole must have caused the rock around it to rupture and crack, creating a new and different landscape.

Lorn expertly fastened the rope to the outcropping and tossed the other end into the hole. He looked at the others and shrugged. "I will climb down and see if the rope is long enough to reach the bottom and to make sure it is safe. I will shake the rope as a sign it is safe to come down."

Alec eyed the rope hesitantly. "I'm not much of a climber."

Kraig patted him on the back. "We can tie the rope around you and lower you down. I think I'm strong enough. Besides," he said, eyeing Alec's shrinking belly, "I don't think you're as heavy as you used to be."

"There is little time for talk," said Michael. "Go ahead, Lorn."

With a nod, Lorn grasped the rope and lowered himself into the pit. Alec and the others looked over the edge until the warrior was lost in darkness. The baker examined the knot, hoping it was as sturdy as it looked. It did not seem as if it would give way or slip off the rock, but still nervous sweat formed upon his brow. If the rope did not hold, it could well mean the end of Lorn.

But the rope did hold, and after a full minute of anxious waiting, movement traveled up its length until it reached the knot. Lorn was shaking the rope, signaling it was safe for the others to come down.

"Alec, you should go next," said Michael, beginning to pull up the rope. "Kraig and I should be able to lower you down easily, and then we will lower Sarah."

Alec nodded and waited for the hermit to finish gathering the rope. He wished there was a faster way to escape the tomb, for he knew the dead were not far behind them. They had gained a few minutes, but those minutes were quickly dwindling away.

Michael pulled the end of the rope from the hole and fastened it securely around Alec's waist. Then he and Kraig grabbed the rope tightly, giving Alec a few feet of slack. Giving a quick smile to Sarah, who regarded the baker with concerned look, Alec lowered himself into the pit.

The walls of the pit were rough, and jagged rocks jutted out at strange angles. The rope bit into Alec's waist as he slowly descended, and he grunted in pain. He wished he could grab onto the rope and pull himself up slightly to take some of the weight off his constricted midsection, but he was gripping the sword and holding the chest and was not able to free a hand. He gritted his teeth and bared the pain, keeping his eyes on the walls as he twisted round and round.

The pit was not nearly as deep as he had thought. In less than a minute he saw an area of dim light and made out the familiar form of Lorn. The warrior was standing at ease, looking up at Alec. In another twenty seconds, Alec had his feet securely on the ground. The warrior helped him untie the rope, and he shook it to let the others know they could draw it up.

"Look down that passage," said Lorn, giving a small smile. "Look at the light."

Alec looked into the dim light coming from the low passage leading from the bottom of the pit. It did not seem like the light of a torch or lantern.

"Grok's beard," he said softly. "Daylight."

"Daylight," repeated Lorn. "I think we have found the far gate. We have nearly escaped the tomb."

For a brief moment Alec felt relief. He almost forgot the pain of the rope burn that had set fire to his waist. But the relief was short lived. He would be glad to put the horrors of Faryn-Gehnah behind him, but there were worse terrors in the world outside. He prayed they had managed to keep ahead of Salin and his minions.

It wasn't long before he saw Sarah descending into the pit, being lowered in much the same way he had been. She had both her hands around the rope, however, saving herself some pain. She was being lowered more quickly than Alec had been, and she had a worried expression on her face. When she touched bottom, she fumbled with the rope, urgently trying to untie the knot around her midsection.

"Help me!" she cried. "The dead have almost caught up to us. We heard them coming, their shuffling feet and their horrible moans!"

Lorn grabbed at the rope and undid the knot with a few flicks of his wrist. He gave it a shake, and then turned to Sarah.

"How close were they? Did you see them?"

She shook her head. "No, but the voices sounded close. Grok, I hope Kraig and Michael can make it down in time."

All they could do was wait. Alec looked up into the darkness, feeling his pulse pounding in his temples as the silence grew thick around him. He was looking for some sign his companions were coming, but nothing moved in the darkness above. He wrung his hands, unable to keep them still. Sarah pressed up against him. He felt tension pouring from her body. They were all worried about their friends.

Finally the rope jiggled. Someone was coming down. Out of the shadow came Kraig, descending carefully hand over hand as quickly as he could manage. When he looked down and saw only ten feet remaining, he let go of the rope and dropped to the ground, landing easily on his feet. He did not waste time shaking the rope; instead, he called up, "Michael, I'm down! Come now!"

Lorn put his hand on the peacekeeper's shoulder. "What is happening up there?"

"The dead had just entered the chamber when I started down. I tried to make Michael go first, but he refused. They've got to be on him by now; Grok's wounds, I wish I could have stayed to help him!"

"That would have been foolish," said Lorn. "Michael seems capable of taking care of himself. Besides, it was necessary to go one at a time. The rope could not take the weight of two men at once."

The sounds of the dead echoed down the pit. There were screams and moans and scraping sounds which made Alec's blood run cold. The rope began to shake, and he grew hopeful Michael was on his way.

And then the rope dropped. Its length fell down the pit, coiling at the bottom. Horror filled Alec's mind. The rope had been untied or cut! There was no escape for the hermit.

A shape plummeted through the darkness. Alec made out Michael's baggy brown pants and white shirt, and he saw his plain face contorted in an expression of, strangely enough, anger. Michael did not cry out, but spread himself out as if accepting his fate.

Kraig leapt forward, pushing Alec out of the way. He braced himself beneath the still coiling rope, and held out his well-muscled arms to catch the hermit.

Grok! They'll both be killed!

Michael plummeted into Kraig's massive arms. The impact knocked the peacekeeper back, and he landed hard on the rocky ground. Michael's limp form was somewhat cushioned by Kraig's body, but all the same he bounced a few feet into the air and landed hard upon the ground. Kraig lay still on his back for a moment, an expression of pain contorting his face. The hermit lay where he landed, unmoving.

Alec bent down to Kraig, who sat up, holding his back and wincing.

"I'm all right," he grunted. "Just got the wind knocked out of me. See to Michael!"

Reluctantly Alec turned away from his companion. He joined Lorn, who was already bent over Michael. He looked over at the warrior, who wore a grave expression.

"He is alive, but his breathing is labored. I cannot tell if anything is broken, but it would be a miracle if nothing was. He fell from at least thirty feet."

"We've got to get him out of here," said Alec. "Those noises are driving me crazy. I wonder if those creatures can get down here somehow."

"I do not wish to find out. Help me move him. Carefully!"

Alec slid his sword into his belt and closed the silver chest, slipping it into the pack he wore on his back. He took Michael's legs while Lorn lifted the hermit gently under his arms. Alec was surprised at how light he seemed. They began walking down the corridor, toward the source of the light.

Sarah had been bending over Kraig, making sure he was all right. He was bruised and sore but insisted he was fine otherwise. He walked with a bit of a limp however, wincing with every few steps.

As they made their way down the tunnel, Alec noticed the walls had become rough and jagged, quite unlike the majority of the walls of the tomb. This area more resembled the great hall they had come into when they first entered the tomb, for the construction of that area was rough in comparison to the deeper sections of Faryn-Gehnah. The light was growing brighter, giving Alec hope that around the next corner awaited the exit they sought. He longed to put the horrors of this place behind him. His mind had been forced to grow larger in the last few days, for previously it could not have encompassed such things as Addins and sorcerers and goblins and Fairies. But, by Grok, living dead were still too much for him to accept. He had seen them, fought them, even spoken with them, but their existence was still beyond his capacity. He fled from them not only because he feared them, but also because seeing them again, being forced to acknowledge they were real, might have been enough to drive him mad.

They rounded the bend in the corridor and saw an open area before them. It was a chamber much like the one on the south side of the tomb, decorated with marble statues and ancient tapestries and golden candelabra. Light was streaming through an ornamented gateway made of thick iron bars set in the far wall. It was wider than ten men and taller than many trees Alec had seen, and swirling waves and clouds fashioned of metal decorated it. It was closed, but the massive bar serving as a deadlock was raised so the gates could be opened easily from either side. They made their way to the gate, and Alec breathed a heavy sigh of relief to see the light of day again.

"Put Michael down, carefully," said Lorn. "I will open this gateway, if I can."

They lowered the hermit to the floor, and the warrior leaned his strength against the center of the gateway, pushing outward. Slowly and with a great grinding noise the gates parted, swinging outward as Lorn's muscles bulged. He pushed the gates until they stood far enough apart for a man to comfortably pass, and then motioned for Alec to help him with Michael. They lifted the hermit and, followed by Kraig and Sarah, exited the tomb.

Alec breathed in the evening air. They had emerged into a lightly wooded area, cool and damp after the storm. Grass and moss grew on the rock of the mountain, and some vines twisted around the bars of the gateway. The growth here seemed green and lush compared to the brown grassland south of the Gravescorn. They were on the outskirts of a forest. According to Lorn, this area was home to the ogres. The thought made Alec cringe. They were away from one danger, only to enter the realm of another. At least, he thought gratefully, there was no sign of Salin.

Lorn paused and looked into the sky, toward the sun setting in the west. "By the position of the sun I judge we were in that foul tomb for nearly five hours. We will soon lose the light. We had best put as much distance as we can between ourselves and the mountains before it is too dark to go on. I have no idea how quickly the sorcerer is capable of crossing the Gravescorn, but I know ogres can leap quickly over rock and crag. Those who pursued us on the other side might soon find us here."

As they marched on, Kraig said, "But isn't this forest the ogre's homeland? How can we avoid them if we just walk right through the middle of their territory?"

"Ogrynwood Forest, whose southernmost reaches we are now passing into, is the largest forest known to humankind," said Lorn. "The ogres have crude villages spaced out over this vast land, and rarely do they stray far from their homes, except when they are called to war by a higher power. Or when a leader rises among them and rallies them to raid the lands to the south. I think, except for the ogres Salin has bent to his cause, they will not go out of their way to hinder us. Years ago when I traveled these lands I was taught where the ogre villages lie. I will keep us far from their homes as we travel to Faerie."

"How far is Faerie?" asked Sarah, still helping the limping peacekeeper.

"Five days' walk, perhaps a week," said Lorn. "Ogrynwood is wide, but it stretches less than sixty miles northward. Beyond the forest is an area of gentle hills, much like your home, and beyond the hills lie the glades of Faerie."

Alec looked back as the northern gate of Faryn-Gehnah receded in the distance. His eyes widened with a start, for several of the dead stared out with cold gray eyes, glaring hatred and dark lust at the escaping humans. Then their dark, rotted fingers grasped the bars of the gate and pulled it shut. They slowly backed away until they were lost in the darkness of the tomb.

"Grok's beard!" he cried. "Look!"

He nodded toward the tomb and the others turned, but the dead were gone. The closed gate, however, was a testament to their persistence.

"At least they cannot follow us out here," said Lorn. "Their spirits are tied to the tomb, thank Lars. There are few undead spirits who can wander where they will. The vast majority must haunt the place of their death or their burial, forever or until the curse which binds them is broken."

"Undead spirits," muttered Alec. He still couldn't accept it.

"There are other creatures like these?" asked Sarah.

"Oh, yes," said Lorn. "In graveyards across the lands, or in homes where people have died, the dead sometimes walk. It is an evil thing, always a curse which has called them back from their final rest. It is rare, to be sure, but it happens. Some say it is the will of Vorik Seth that causes the dead to rise. Others say it is the need for revenge against someone who did them evil in life, or perhaps murdered them. Some believe Sharnna, goddess of the dead, sends them back for some purpose. I do not know."

"Well," said Kraig, "it seems Vorik Seth or his servants are responsible for the curse of *this* tomb. At least that's what the Keeper told us."

"It may be so."

They walked on in silence until the night closed in around them. Then they made camp among a tight grove of pine, spreading their blankets over fallen pine needles and soft earth. Kraig carefully placed the unconscious Michael among some blankets so the night air would not chill him. Alec looked down at the hermit, silently praying he would recover soon. As they prepared for sleep, Lorn announced he would take the first watch, leaving second and third to Kraig and Alec. The baker lay on the ground, relieved to finally get some much needed rest. He placed Flame, his new sword, by his right hand so it would be ready at a moment's need. His left arm he curled around Sarah as she lay next to him, her head upon his chest. He smiled. He could live with days filled with danger and uncertainty when this was his reward. He kissed her head and drifted into a deep, pleasant sleep.

It seemed like only minutes had passed when Alec was awakened by a soft nudge from Kraig. He looked up at the peacekeeper and rubbed the sleep from his eyes.

"Your watch, Alec," said the big man.

"How are you feeling?" Alec asked as he pushed himself up.

"I'm fine. The bruises still hurt a little, but I've had worse at the Silver Shield."

"What about Michael?"

Kraig shook his head. "No change. His breathing is fine and he hasn't gotten worse. But he hasn't woken up yet either."

Alec nodded. "I guess that's not the worst possible news."

Kraig smiled. "I guess not. I need to get some sleep. Don't forget your sword."

"I won't. I need all the help I can get."

As Kraig lay down, Alec picked up his sword and walked over to a row of trees at the edge of the camp, the place were he could best watch over the camp and the surrounding area. He sat on a rock, his back to a big pine tree, and thought about the journey. It had been only twelve days since they had set out, yet it seemed like forever. And Barton Hills seemed a world away.

The remainder of the night passed quietly. When the dim light of dawn peaked over the horizon, Alec took a moment to watch the sun rise. The coming of day filled him with new hope. Perhaps with the tomb behind them the most dangerous leg of their journey was over. Maybe they were far ahead of Salin and would reach Faerie with no further trouble. His gaze fell to his new sword and he picked it up. He felt safer now than before, but he was still glad to have this new, supposedly magical, weapon. He knew it would pay to remain cautious as they traveled, so he would keep the blade at the ready always. He held the sword before him, admiring the gems set in the hilt and the runes running along its blade.

"Mind you do not poke your eye out with that blade, boy," said a voice behind him.

Alec turned with a start to find Lorn looking down at him, a small smile touching his normally grim face. He was rubbing his bearded chin thoughtfully.

"Lorn, you startled me! You're right, though. I don't know the first thing about handling a sword. I was just thinking about how glad I was to have it, but I probably couldn't do much good with it. Perhaps you had better take it to replace the one you lost in the tomb."

As Alec offered the sword hilt first to Lorn, the warrior shook his head and waved away Alec's offer. "That sword was a gift to you from the Lord of the Dead. It would be wrong and perhaps dangerous for me to take it. Besides, I have no love for short swords. I have trained long and hard with all manner of blades and have found my style of fighting is much better suited to long swords. I prefer the longer reach and the heavier feel of long blades. No, you keep your sword. But before you think to wield it, you would be wise to consider training. Without the proper knowledge and skills, your own weapon could be more of a danger to you than a foe's."

Alec shook his head. "When do I have time to train? Anyway, I'm a baker. I have no desire to learn swordsmanship."

Lorn's face became stern. "We have days yet until we reach Faerie. I will lead us there by the safest paths I know, but I cannot promise total freedom from danger. You may need to bloody your weapon before the week is over, and you had best know the blade from the hilt."

Alec was somewhat taken aback by Lorn's insistent manner. But the warrior's words made sense. "All right. I suppose some training would be useful. But when do we have the time?"

"In the evening, when we first set camp. There is time enough then before sleep. And we could begin right now. It is still early, and the others will be sleeping for another hour. It is still to dark to travel, but light enough to train. I can give you some pointers and introduce you to some basic techniques."

"Fine," said Alec, standing up. He brushed the dirt from his clothes and held his sword outward. "What do I need to know?"

Lorn backed up a step. "First, do not wave that thing so freely in my face. It is magic, or so the mummy claimed, and we do not know what powers it may have. And even if the blade has no magic at all, it is still deadly. Always have a care when you handle a sword. Respect it. Here, hand it to me and I will show you the proper grip."

Lorn demonstrated the grip and then gave the sword back to Alec. It felt awkward in his hands, the grip unnatural. But Lorn insisted holding it any other way would make it easy for an enemy to disarm him, or even make the sword slip from his hand in the heat of combat.

Once Alec felt more comfortable holding the blade, Lorn showed him a basic thrust and parry. It took Alec the entire hour to perform the two maneuvers to Lorn's satisfaction. After countless repetition of the same strike and the same parry, the youth's entire body was sore and covered in sweat. When Lorn announced the lesson was at an end, Alec dropped his sword to the ground and doubled over, gasping for air.

"Grok, that sword is heavier than it looks!"

Lorn's hard expression broke into a smile. "After an hour of what I just put you through, a bread knife would seem heavy. But you have made progress. I wouldn't pit your skill against more than a goblin or two at this point, but at least you will not fall on your own blade while you walk."

"That's reassuring," Alec replied. "I still feel awkward just holding this thing. Those moves, especially the parry, make my muscles ache in places I didn't even know I *had* muscles."

Lorn began to walk toward where the others still slept, and Alec followed. "It will be hard at first. Your mind will be challenged as much as your body as I teach you some more advanced maneuvers and we begin work on the forms. The Bladeknights, the elite guardians of the Lord of Eglak, know more than three hundred forms for attack and defense and can instantly determine which one is suitable for any given situation. I will teach you as many as I can before we arrive at Faerie."

Alec nodded, wondering how anyone could master so many different forms. Then a thought struck him. "The way you fought those goblins and ogres...are you a Bladeknight, Lorn?"

The warrior grinned at the suggestion. "No. But I've bested Bladeknights in combat. My father taught me the art of the sword." He seemed to be lost in a memory for a moment, but then shook his head sadly. "That was a long time ago. Come, we must wake the others and move on."

When they reached the campsite, Alec leaned down and gently shook Sarah while Lorn went to check on Michael's condition. She opened her eyes and smiled up at Alec. He would never grow tired of looking into her eyes, he thought.

"Good morning. It's time to go."

"Morning, Mason." Suddenly her face wrinkled in a wince. "What did you do, go for a five mile run? You're sweating like a dog and you stink to high heaven!"

"Lorn was teaching me how to use a sword. Grok, it's more exhausting than I'd imagined!"

"Well, go find a river and dunk yourself in it for about an hour. Then come back and we'll talk."

Alec laughed and shook his head at her. He looked over to the peacekeeper, who had already been awakened by his and Sarah's banter. Before he could say anything to Kraig, he heard a voice from not far away."

"Seven! How long have I been unconscious?"

Alec looked over to see Michael sitting half way up, Lorn kneeling down beside him. He breathed a heavy sigh of relief to see the hermit awake.

"Only since early last evening," said Lorn.

Michael shook his head, as if trying to remember what had happened. "The corpses! Those foul things cut the rope. I should not have let them. I should have been stronger, faster. I should have…argh!"

He had been trying to rise as he spoke, but as an expression of agony twisted his face he lowered himself back to the ground. "Still…a touch of pain…in by back. My legs."

"It seems more than a touch, my friend," said Lorn, putting his hand on Michael's shoulder. "Rest easy. You took quite a fall and it will take time to recover. And do not be so hard on yourself. There was nothing else you could have done. We were all lucky to escape with our lives."

Michael muttered something Alec couldn't hear. The hermit rose to his feet, more gently this time, fighting his way through his pain. Alec and the others gathered around him, concern written plainly on their faces.

"What?" he snapped. "I will be fine. Come, gather your things. The day is wasting."

As they packed their belongings, Sarah rolled her eyes and said, "Show someone a little concern, and you get your head bitten off. That's just like a man."

"Don't be too judgmental," said Alec. "His self-esteem is fragile as it is. It makes it worse when he has to depend on anyone else."

"We all have to depend on each other," she replied.

"I know. But Michael…I think he's used to being in control. Losing control, I think, is what made him become a hermit. He wants to be able to do everything himself."

She shrugged and finished her packing. After a few bites of stale bread and dried meat, they set out once again. As they tramped onward, the woods grew denser around them. Michael managed to set a brisk pace despite a limp and constant pain. Kraig seemed to have recovered entirely. Alec was weary from his training, but he surprised himself by the ease at which he was able to keep up. Lately he always felt tired, yet at the same time he knew his body was growing stronger. If he survived this journey, he would surely be the better for it.

And so they walked, leaving the Gravescorn far behind them. At the crest of a hill, Alec paused to look back. He could make out the rocky face of the mountain through the trees, and it suddenly struck him how far from home he was. In less than two weeks he had traveled far beyond the border of his homeland, beyond what was generally considered the known world. He became lost in thought, longing for home and yet excited by what lay ahead. Then he felt a soft hand clasp his and he turned to see Sarah smiling at him. As she pulled him away from his reverie, he returned the smile. They followed the others down the hill, passing deeper into the beautiful but dangerous forest of Ogrynwood.

Tor groaned in effort as he led his horse up the steep, rocky path. Salin had driven them without rest all the way to the eastern pass through the mountains, nearly a day's journey from the entrance of the Fairy tomb. They had ridden hard all the way there, Salin spurring his horse on to greater and greater speeds. The sorcerer would not speak; he was completely focused on his pursuit. In his eyes burned a fiery passion at which Tor could not bare to look. Salin's eyes were the eyes of hate.

When they had at last reached the pass, which climbed high over the mountains and descended into the ogre's homeland on the other side, Salin had turned his burning eyes to his followers and spoke. Gwendolyn and Stiletta sat coldly astride their mounts, as if Salin's anger wasn't worthy of their concern. Tor, on the other hand, knew Salin better. These women would learn to fear him…if they lived long enough.

"We must make haste over the Gravescorn," said the sorcerer, his voice grim and full of ire. "We will stop for nothing. If they survive the tomb, it is possible they will be ahead of us when we reach the other side. I have minions to the north, but without a way to send word to them, they will not know to capture Mason and his Seth-cursed companions."

"Can you not send out the Call?" asked Tor, referring to Salin's ability to send messages mentally over vast distances.

Salin waved a fist in front of Tor's face, and for a moment green energy crackled around him. Tor wished he had kept quiet, fearing his careless question had brought on Salin's wrath. But Salin lowered his fist and the energy dimmed and vanished. His eyes, however, still burned a hateful red.

"The Call can communicate only need, not specific instructions. I can Call my servants to my side at need, summoning them from as far away as the Desolation, but I cannot issue commands. Only the Fair Folk can Commune; sorcerers are denied that power." His face contorted and he growled harshly, his whole body tensing. "Damn them! Damn the Fairies and their pure white souls! I must have the Talisman so I may bring them to ruin!"

He yelled to his horse and spurred the beast into motion. Tor waited until his master was a good distance along and then followed slowly.

For more than an hour they had made slow progress up the path, until finally the rocky ground became too steep and precarious for riding. They were forced to dismount, and now Tor sweated and cursed silently as he trudged upward. He listened as Salin began to mutter to himself.

"If they reach Faerie, I will have to bring all my resources into play. The Dark Folk will have to step up their timetable; the revolt will have to begin sooner than planned. Still, it could work, if only…"

He ceased his muttering as a great howl echoed across the mountains below them. Tor turned and saw a massive, horrible shape clawing its way toward them, navigating the rocks quickly and with ease. He would have been terrified if he hadn't known what the shape was. Salin had servants of many kinds; not all of them were human.

When the grotesque monstrosity was before them, its many limbs and gnashing fangs began to shift and change, melting away as the creature shrank to a less imposing size. At last Tor had the satisfaction of seeing the two sisters lose their poise; obviously they had never seen the Lord Shaper of the Dark Folk in his true form.

After the transformation was complete, a muscular black man stood in the creature's place. He smiled from ear to ear and said, "Hello, Tor. It's been quite some time. What do you think of my human shape?"

Tor shrugged. "I prefer your fair form, but this shape is better than the one you were just wearing."

The black man flashed one more toothy grin at the warrior and then turned toward Salin. He bowed deeply and reverently and said, "My master, I have come as you required. What is it you wish of me?"

Salin motioned for him to stand. "Your timing could not have been better, Drakkahn Shynagoth. I was just thinking about you. We need to move ahead with the plan. It is sooner than anticipated, and all the pieces are not yet in place, but urgent need drives me. I may have to enter into the realm of Faerie."

Shynagoth raised his eyebrows. "That will take some doing. The webs of enchantment which keep enemies at bay are still strong. I will need time to prepare counter-magics."

"Then go," said Salin. "There is just one thing more. The one I seek may have made it to the other side of the mountain. If we can catch him, there will be no need for me to enter the Seth forsaken Fairy-land. If you spot him on your journey northward, detain him for me—or kill him, I care not which. If you do not run across the cursed fool, be sure to alert our allies in Ogrynwood. They are stupid, witless creatures, but I am certain they can handle Mason."

"I understand, my master." said Drakkahn Shynagoth. "I will pass on your message and continue to Faerie, if I do not find Mason first. A glorious day is dawning for us, Great One."

Tor could not believe it when he saw Salin grin. "A glorious day indeed. Go with the Seth, Lord Shaper."

"Go with the Seth, Great One."

So saying, Shynagoth's form bent and twisted, and in a moment he resembled a giant, malformed bird. Beating great, leathery wings, he lifted into the air and soared over the mountains to carry out his master's commands. Tor watched him go, wondering what it would be like to have the power of shape-changing. Although all Fairies were said to have the ability, very few could harness it in any useful way. None he had seen could match Shynagoth's facility with the talent. There was a reason Drakkahn Shynagoth ranked highest among the dark Fairies.

"Let us go," said the sorcerer, his yellow grin fading. "We cannot fly like Shynagoth, but we can still make good time if we push ourselves. With luck, we will catch those fools long before they reach the hated Fairy-realm. The Talisman *will* be mine!"

Tirelessly, Salin plodded onward, leading his big black horse over the rocks. Tor, not immune to weariness as his master appeared to be, toiled after him. Behind him came the ever silent Gwendolyn and Stiletta, content to follow the sorcerer and serve him without question like the cattle they were.

Tor hated them. He hated Salin. But most of all he hated Mason and Michael and all their companions. It was their fault he was in this unbearable situation. He would see them dead. By the Seth, he would have their heads if it was the last act of his life.

CHAPTER 16

Ogrynwood

"Gently, Alec, gently!" said Lorn as he watched Alec thrust his sword into the air. "Relax, flow though the forms. You are trying too hard."

Alec cursed under his breath as he wiped the sweat from his brow. It was the third evening of his training, and he had yet to evoke a positive comment from his tutor. He had so far learned six basic thrusts, three different swings, and seven defensive maneuvers. Lorn had also taught him four of "the forms," which combined the individual thrusts, swings, and parries into flowing sequences. Practicing the forms over and over proved to be one of the most exhausting things he had ever done. And his mind was challenged as much as his body, for remembering the sequence of moves in each form took his full concentration. Each night, at the end of a two hour long session, he fell into his blankets and slept like the dead.

Sarah sometimes would watch as he practiced, amused as he fumbled his way through the forms. That night she had lost interest half way through the session and had gone to sleep. Sometimes Kraig would watch, too, but more often he wandered the perimeter of the camp or went to bed early to be rested for guard duty. Michael had taken to sitting alone in the evening, intently pouring over the book Horren had given him. He approved of Alec's training but took little interest in watching the sessions.

Alec took a deep breath and forced himself to be calm. He ran through the form in his mind, lifting the sword to begin again. He began with a short swing and flowed into a high parry. This became two thrusts, one high and short and the other low and deep. Two more parries, one to the left and the second low and to the right, passed immediately into a lunging attack. He twisted his body, sidestepping an imaginary foe, and thrust straight outward with the killing blow. He held the final stance for five seconds, as Lorn had instructed, and then let the point of his blade drop to the ground. His body quivered with exhaustion as he stood at ease.

He prepared himself for more of Lorn's harsh criticism. The warrior scratched his bearded chin as he seriously regarded his student. Then he broke into a grin and gave Alec a nod of approval.

"Good. You finally learned not to hold your sword like you fear it. You seemed more relaxed and confident, so the form flowed well. Another night like this, and I will teach you something more advanced. By the time we reach Faerie, you might be ready to spar with a live opponent."

Alec wore a surprised expression. "You know, that's the first compliment you've given me since you started teaching me."

"It is the first compliment you've deserved. Now get some sleep. You have last watch again tonight."

Alec groaned as he made his way to his blankets. He had not had to stand watch the previous night, as Michael had recovered enough to take a shift. But now it was Kraig's turn to sleep the night through, so it was back to work for Alec.

He lay down next to Sarah, who was already deep in sleep, and gazed at the leaves blowing in the wind high above. The Ogrynwood Forest was not nearly as dense as the Northwood, and he could make out some of the stars glowing in the heavens. The last few days had been peaceful and pleasant, and thoughts of danger were tucked away in the back of his mind, not forgotten, but not haunting him either. They had seen no ogres, nor any other living creatures except birds and small animals. The days since leaving the tomb had passed quickly, and he had enjoyed them as he would enjoy a walk in the groves surrounding Barton Hills. He had learned to take his pleasure where he could find it, and the moments of peace spent walking beside Sarah were all it took to make him happy. He wished the peace could last forever.

Now they were more than half way through the Forest, and Faerie lay only a few days away. He didn't know what to expect when they reached the mythical land, but he was confident his troubles would be over when they did. He would be glad to give the Talisman over to the Fairies, for it belonged with them. They would put it to good use, he was sure, and perhaps it would give them the strength to capture or kill Salin Urdrokk. Then Alec, Sarah and Kraig could return home and put this nightmare behind them. He could resume his role as baker, then, and practice the craft for which he was born. He was sad for a moment, thinking of Stan Kulnip, the master baker and the man who had raised him. Because of Salin's greed, Stan and his wife Matilda were dead. Ara was probably dead, too. Alec wondered sadly if the sorcerer had killed anyone else in his rampage.

He forced his thoughts down a happier path. When he returned home, he would be the baker of Barton Hills. At least, he hoped he would. He'd been gone more than two weeks, and he would not be returning for much longer, so he feared he might be replaced. After all, how long could a town go without a baker? And yet there was no one else to take his place, unless they called in an apprentice from another village. This was unlikely, as few people desired to leave their home town. Feeling Sarah's warmth beside him, he finally dosed off and dreamt of working in the bakery, dressed in his white baker's grab and pulling golden bread from a hot oven. It was the best dream he'd had in weeks.

The night was too short and before he knew it he was serving his watch again. To pass the time, he took his sword in hand and rehearsed the forms Lorn had shown him. He thought he was progressing well, but without the warrior's comments and criticisms Alec wasn't confident he was performing the forms accurately. Soon he gave up in frustration and simply paced for the rest of his shift. The three hours until morning passed slowly, but at last the sun rose, and with it his companions awoke. He was weary as usual after guard duty, but his spirits rose as they ate a small meal, even if it was only crusty old bread and salty, dry meat.

As they pressed onward through the forest, he chatted with Sarah. They made small talk, discussing their past in Barton Hills and their hopes for the future. Kraig joined in their conversation, admitting that he, too, was homesick.

"Anxious to get back to the tavern to keep the peace, Kraig?" asked Alec.

"Very. If there still *is* a tavern. Without me there preventing fights, the whole place could have been torn apart by now. Poor Derik! I hope things are all right." He was silent for a moment and then he smiled. Lowering his voice, he said, "But do you know what I really want to do? Someday I'd like to open a tavern of my own. In a way I suppose I'm Derik's apprentice; maybe I'll take over the place when he retires. Or I'll build a new tavern, bigger and better than the Silver Shield."

"I never knew you had any interest in being a barman," said Sarah.

"I can't be a peacekeeper forever. Someday I'll be too old to throw drunken brawlers out onto the street. Besides, it's wearing thin already. As much as I like working for Derik, I want something more."

Their talk died down as they passed through grove of oak and maple. Before long they heard the sound of gurgling water, and they entered a small clearing where long grass grew near a bubbling pond.

"At last," said Lorn, gazing at the water. "I feared we had missed it. This is Fresh Spring, at least that is what my father called it. Underground springs feed the pond, causing bubbles to burst on the surface. This is the only place I know of in Ogrynwood where we may fill our waterskins, unless we march into an ogre village and ask to use their well. Drink your fill; the water is clean and pure. We will rest here for a time."

Alec realized it was nearly noon and he felt his stomach rumbling. He hadn't thought much about water, but now he realized in another day or so their supply would have been exhausted. He was glad Lorn had taken such things into consideration. But as for food, their rations were quickly dwindling. Lorn claimed to be a proficient hunter, but they could not spare the time to hunt game. Besides, they had no weapons appropriate for hunting. One needed a bow and arrows; you could not expect a deer to stand still while you attacked it with a sword. Alec supposed they would have to travel the last few days to Faerie on reduced rations. The thought made him all the more hungry.

He followed the others down to the spring. The water was crystal clear and he could see a bed of stones at the bottom. Some larger rocks broke the surface near the bank. Tall, healthy grass grew around the pond, and on the far side a single weeping willow bent to the water. Alec knelt in the grass, and cupping his hands he took some water from the spring and drank deeply.

"Grok's beard! I forgot how wonderful cold water tasted!"

Sarah drank greedily beside him. "This is amazing. We've been living on a sip of water here and there. I just sort of accepted it, but this is the way people are meant to drink."

Lorn, who was drinking to Sarah's right, nodded in agreement. "The body craves water. We have been busy enough to ignore it, but we could not have gone on much longer without it. We might have reached Faerie, but we would have been parched to the point of illness by then."

They said nothing more until each of the companions were satisfied and had filled their waterskins. Then they sat down to a small meal of dried meat and stale bread, washing it down with more of the cold, fresh water. They talked a bit, trying to keep the conversation light, but eventually darker matters arose.

"We have not heard or seen any sign of Salin since before the tomb," said Michael. "Yet I grow worried he is not far behind. We gained some time, but he is swift and has many servants."

Lorn nodded his agreement. "He has much influence among the ogres. This makes it doubly important we stay clear of the villages. Still, if we press on as we have been, I do not see how he could catch us. Not on foot. Remember, he could not have taken his horses over the mountain, not unless he went far out of his way to the eastern pass."

"True," said Michael. "But you do not know him as I do. He is never without a plan. We must make haste or he will surely find us."

Alec grew somewhat irritated they were discussing the very matter he was trying to forget. "I wish we could just stay here for a while. It's peaceful, and the water is delicious."

"We dare not stay for long," said Lorn. "Even putting the danger of Salin aside, many beasts come here to drink. They would perhaps leave us alone, but then again they might not. Just because we have not seen any bears or wolves do not think this forest is tame. And sometimes ogre hunting parties stop here for water. We must press on shortly."

Alec sighed. "I guess I'll take one last drink before we go, then."

He went down to the water and drank until he was full. The others did the same, and then they shouldered their packs and left the clearing. Lorn led them northward through clusters of spruce and pine, and soon the sound of the boiling springs faded behind them.

Despite being reminded danger was all around them, Alec felt good. The water was refreshing and it had rejuvenated him more than he would have though possible. He was no longer tired, and he walked briskly with ease. Suddenly he realized he couldn't remember the last time he had felt the dull pain in his muscles which had been his traveling companion for so long. He had been tired, certainly, but the pain from constant activity was all but gone. Maybe the exertion of training with Lorn had conditioned him against the lesser weariness and pain of marching. He looked down at his stomach and noticed for the first time just how small it had become. Where once there were rings of flab hanging from his waist there was now only a small paunch. He had never thought he would be so thin. Still, looking at Kraig, he knew he was far from fit.

As the afternoon wore on into evening, they wandered into an area thick with tall pine. Crickets chattered loudly around them. The ground was carpeted with brown pine needles, and thick moss grew on the bark of many trees. It was a comfortable place, Alec thought. It brought him a sense of quiet peace. He looked up as the pink twilight filtered down through the trees and his feeling grew stronger. He took a deep breath and smiled.

"What are you so happy about?" Sarah asked playfully, giving him a curious look.

"Look around. This place is remarkable."

Sarah glanced around the woods, her gaze lingering on the pink sky. "It really is a beautiful sight. It's a shame we're not on this journey for pleasure. It would be nice to sit here under a tree and watch the sky until it was dark."

"Well, we can enjoy the scenery while we walk. This journey is really opening my eyes about certain things, Sarah. My perspective about what's important is changing. All the wonderful and terrible things we've seen have made me realize the simple things are what make life worth living. This," he motioned at the forest around them, "makes life worth living."

They walked on in comfortable silence until Lorn motioned for them to stop. He was gazing into an open area filled with small bushes and a tall, forked tree.

"I know this place. The ogres sometimes gather here when different tribes must meet. A few miles from here the forest thins out, and beyond the trees there is a wide ravine that cuts through the land. It is deep and dangerous, and it stretches far to the east and west. Going around it would take days."

"How can we cross it?" asked Kraig.

"There is a bridge. We will have to pass more closely to an ogre village than I would like, but there is no other easy way to cross the ravine."

"Do the ogres use the bridge?" asked Alec.

"Sometimes. But if we are stealthy we can avoid them. We will be able to see the bridge while we are still hidden among the trees, and they should not be able to see us. And unless Salin has somehow gotten ahead of us, the ogres will not be expecting us. At any rate, we will not reach the bridge until tomorrow. It is late and we must find a place to camp."

It was not long before they came to a small clearing protected by a ring of trees. As twilight faded to night, they spread their blankets on the ground and made camp. As usual, Alec trained for two hours while Lorn looked on sternly. The warrior taught him nothing new, but insisted Alec endlessly run through the forms he had already learned. As he worked, Alec realized he could now flow through the easiest of the forms without thinking. The harder ones he still fumbled through, but he knew he was improving.

He could scarcely believe how comfortable he was becoming with the sword. When Lorn had begun training him several days ago, he had thought he would never get used to the feel of the hilt against his palm. Now if felt almost natural, as if the weapon belonged there.

"Good," said Lorn as Alec finished a form. "A bit stiff at the beginning, but your last few strikes were flawless."

Alec wiped the sweat from his brow and smiled. "So I'm getting better?"

"Better, yes, but do not grow overconfident. Any soldier worth his salt could still slip a sword between your ribs in his sleep. But you are improving. To be honest, I did not expect you to be such a quick study. Others have taken weeks to progress as far as you have in days."

"Stan always did say I was a fast learner."

"Stan?" questioned Lorn.

"My old master, the baker of Barton Hills. He was a good man." For a moment a pang of grief overwhelmed Alec. "Salin killed him." He bowed his head sadly.

"I am sorry," said Lorn. "But he was right about you, Alec, you are a fast learner. Just remember, swordplay is not like baking. It is a skill that could save your life. It could also get you killed, but if you are going to carry a blade you must know how to use it."

Alec nodded his understanding as a single tear ran down his cheek. Embarrassed, he wiped it away with the back of his hand. "I know. I just wish it wasn't necessary."

Lorn's face softened and he put his hand on Alec's shoulder in an uncharacteristic display of compassion. "I know exactly how you feel." He held Alec's gaze for a moment, and then backed away, resuming his grave expression. "But we still have half an hour left. Move on to the third form."

In spite of his weariness, Alec lifted his sword and went back to work.

The next day they set out early. Alec had slept dreamlessly all night, and he felt refreshed. The sun was bright and warm, sending shafts of golden light down through the branches. Soon the trees thinned out, and the companions stepped into an area of rocky ground where forest growth was sparse. They continued walking until they reached a steep downward slope. The ground was covered in rock and stone and was devoid of any growth except small, dry brush. At the bottom of the slope the ground fell away forming a massive chasm, half a mile across and hundreds of feet deep. Alec looked off to his left and right. The rift stretched on further than he could see.

A little to the east, a wide wooden bridge crossed the ravine. Alec was amazed such a thing could have been built. It must have been a grand undertaking, crossing a rift so wide and so deep. The bridge was fashioned of plain wooden planks and supported by great pillars of stone. Lengths of thick rope tied around wooden posts formed a rail along each edge of the bridge to keep the unwary traveler from falling. It seemed sturdy and safe. But as he gazed along its length, he saw a black spot toward the center of the bridge. Something looked wrong to him, but he was too far away to know what.

"Ogrynwood Bridge," said Michael. "Built by ogre hunters long ago to allow them to seek game in the northern reaches of the forest. It is fortunate they built it, for going around the ravine would take us days out of our way."

Lorn was gazing at the bridge, scowling and rubbing his thickening beard. "Something is wrong. Look, the bridge has been damaged." He pointed to the black section Alec had seen.

Michael cursed quietly. "It looks like a section of the bridge is missing. If the gap is too wide…"

"I pray to Lars it is not," said Lorn.

"Talking about it will get us nowhere," said Kraig. "You two are always telling us we have to keep moving. Let's go down there and take a look at it."

Raising an eyebrow, Lorn regarded the peacekeeper. "Getting impatient? All right, let us go."

They made their way down the slope, taking care not to stumble on the rocks. Alec helped Sarah over some of the steeper areas, where rocks jutted precariously from the hillside at strange angles. Half way down, a stone Alec stepped on gave way. He gave a yelp as he began to slide down the hillside, pushing small stones down in front of him. Just as he was about to collide with some sharp rocks, a strong hand reached out and grabbed him around the wrist. He looked up to see Kraig smiling reassuringly.

"Are you all right?" asked the peacekeeper.

"Just a little bruised."

From then on, he tested each rock before stepping on it. The going was slow, but eventually they reached the bottom of the hill and made their way across the dry land until they stood before the bridge.

Up close, the bridge was even larger than it had seemed from the hill. It was wide enough for ten men on horseback to ride abreast. The wooden planks were wide and thick, and Alec guessed it would take at least five strong men to lift them. But the ogres, being far larger and stronger then men, probably had little trouble lugging around tree-size wooden planks.

Alec looked out across the chasm, toward the ruined middle of the bridge. He realized now the blackness he had seen was an area where the bridge had been burned. Beyond the burned area, charred, jagged splinters jutted out where something, presumably, had struck the bridge, tearing it apart.

"This does not look good," commented Lorn. "Wait here."

Without another word, he ran out across the bridge. He shrank into the distance, stopping when he reached the charred hole. He paused to consider the damage and then ran back. When he stood before the others, Lorn shook his head slowly.

"A twenty foot section of the bridge has fallen away," he said. "By the look of it, it was struck by lighting. Or a power like unto lightning."

Kraig groaned. "What can we do? Go around?"

Michael shook his head. "No. It will take too long. Salin will have more time to catch us. No, we must take the other bridge."

"Other?" questioned Sarah. "I thought this was the only one."

Lorn took a deep breath. "No. I was loathe to mention the second bridge. It is not a sturdy piece of work, barely held together by old rope and wood. But this is not why I wanted to avoid it. The second bridge is located within an ogre village."

"Wounds," muttered Kraig. "That's all we need."

"Right," said Sarah. "What are we going to do, march right in and say, 'Hello, may we use your bridge?'"

No one seemed to have an answer for her. It appeared they were all in silent agreement that the situation was impossible. Even Michael shook his head grimly, unable to offer any viable suggestions. Finally Kraig, growing impatient, looked to Lorn questioningly.

"You're supposed to be our guide, Lorn. What do you propose?"

For the first time since before they reached the Gravescorn, the warrior looked uncertain, even worried. Alec thought he saw a hint of the old Lorn, the Lorn filled with shame and impotence they had met in Bordonhold. He was looking down at his feet, biting his lower lip, and rubbing his unkempt, scraggly beard. Finally he looked up, but his eyes showed fear and uncertainty.

"We cannot fight our way through a village of ogres," he said. "Perhaps there is another way, but I do not know if I can...no, I am not the man I was. They will not know me." He turned away in shame. "Michael, you will have to see us through this. I cannot."

The hermit marched to Lorn and spun the larger man around. "There is nothing I can do, Lorn. As you say, we cannot fight a whole village. If you know of a way to get past them, you must tell us. Lorn, you've come a long way since you joined us in Bordonhold. You can handle this. You must!"

Lorn took a deep breath and exhaled slowly, visibly making an effort to calm himself. He shook his head at Michael, keeping his eyes lowered. When he looked up, some of his confidence had returned.

"All right," he said softly. "This is my plan. A long while ago, when I passed this way with my father, we spoke at length with an ogre chieftain. My father, a great councilor and mediator, was able to favorably settle a dispute between the ogres and the Fair Folk, thereby gaining the trust and friendship of both races. I will talk to the ogres. With any luck they might remember my father. If so, they might remember they owe him a favor. Even being ogres, they might honor the debt."

"That's a lot of 'mights,' Lorn," said Alec. "And what if these ogres are working for Salin?"

The warrior shrugged. "Let us hope they are not."

Alec was far from reassured by Lorn's answer. The warrior started off toward the east and the others followed. Michael walked beside him, consulting him quietly.

"You remain a mystery to me, Lorn. Who is your father that he has done favors for the ogres? Very few humans have had discourse with their breed."

"Ogres are not like goblins," replied Lorn. "They are not evil by nature. They are warlike and territorial, but not evil. The shadow of the Seth has perverted many of them to the cause of darkness, but there are still those who remain free."

"I know," said Michael. "But all the same, they are not overly fond of humans. What was this dispute between the ogres and the Fairies your father helped settle?"

Lorn looked at the hermit darkly. "I will reveal my secrets after you reveal yours."

Michael looked away, clamping his jaw shut. He walked away stiffly, not turning toward the warrior again.

"Some pair they are," Sarah whispered into Alec's ear.

Alec gave a small smile, but he felt little humor in Sarah's remark. He was tired of the enigma of Michael, and he was growing more curious about Lorn. Lorn was no simple soldier. His father must have been a person of some influence. A wealthy merchant? A minor noble? He wondered. Grudgingly, he admitted to himself such mysteries were not important. Not now, when there were bigger things to think about. But after they reached Faerie, after they were safe, he would know the truth, about both Michael and Lorn. They couldn't keep him in the dark forever.

They had been marching eastward for two hours when they reached the village. The terrain had been rocky, but to Alec's relief the ground was flat. The slope to their right remained steep, but they were able to avoid it. Above, beyond the slope, the forest looked darkly down upon them, causing Alec to wonder if there were eyes watching them from between the shadowy trees. To the left, the ravine had narrowed somewhat, but the sheer cliffs plummeting to its floor remained unclimbable.

The village itself huddled between the steep slope and the chasm. Huts of stone and wood rose haphazardly from the rocky ground, as if constructed hastily and given little care. One hut, larger than the others, stood by itself on an outcropping of rock that jutted out over the ravine. Before it sat a curved row of rocks, facing the door of the hut.

"This village," said Lorn, "is unique among the habitations of the ogres I've seen in that they use so much stone. Since they live where there is more rock than wood, they have learned to use it in construction. Elsewhere, they rely only on trees to provide building material. Look, the leader lives in the big hut. The stones out front are where the villagers sit when their chief calls them to meet. Just beyond the village is the bridge I told you about."

Alec cast his eyes further and saw the bridge. Any hope of a simple crossing fled immediately from his heart. The thing was a simple rope-and-wood construction which rocked back and forth in the wind, creaking. There were no supports, and it sagged heavily in the middle.

"Grok," said Alec. "We're going to cross on *that*?"

Before anyone could respond, two large ogres emerged from a hut and locked eyes with the companions. One shouted something in a guttural language, and six other ogres emerged from the nearby forest, looking with curiosity and suspicion down the slope toward the humans.

"Here comes the welcoming committee," said Kraig.

"What ever you do," said Lorn, "make no motion toward your weapons. I will do the talking." Whatever fear he felt at the prospect of dealing with ogres he hid effectively under a steely facade.

The two ogres approached, each wielding a great club. The others descended the hill and positioned themselves behind the humans. They grunted and jeered and talked to each other in the ogre tongue. The largest of the creatures, one of the first two, took a menacing step toward the companions, holding his club aloft.

Lorn held up his hand in a calm gesture of greeting. "*Achnag, jech lyhben Lorn, schun do den Chen do Eglacha. Nuse vachog crux den Hyche.*"

The ogre hesitated, his eyes narrowing. Obviously he was as surprised as Alec was when Lorn spoke the ogre tongue. The creature lowered its club, but the look in his eyes made it clear he was not ready to accept the companions with open arms.

"*Achnag, Lorn. Jech lyben Grazog, sug-batchen do Farch. Jech vachog getch Grod, nu batchen. Gu shak nu slugie.*"

The big ogre turned and walked toward the large hut while the others pressed in around the companions, their weapons at the ready. Alec turned to Lorn, and voiced the question he knew must be on everyone's mind.

"So what did he say? What's going on?"

Lorn paused a moment before answering, watching the ogre go into the hut. "I told him who I was, hoping it would mean something to him, and said we needed to use their bridge. He said his name was Grazog, the sub-chief of the village of Farch. He's going to consult with Grod, their chief. He made it clear that until further notice, we are their prisoners."

"That doesn't seem very encouraging," said Sarah.

"It is as much as I had hoped for," said Lorn. "At least we are to have an audience with the tribe's chief. The best most humans who enter an ogre village can hope for is an audience with the inside of a cook-pot."

"Why didn't you tell us that before we agreed to come here?" asked Alec.

"Because then you would have feared to come, and this is our only hope."

They stood in anxious silence for long minutes until at last Grazog came out of the chief's hut and walked back over to where they waited. He towered over them, his muscles rippling under his gray skin. He smiled an unreadable grin, showing sharp, twisted teeth that had seen better days.

"*Batchen Grod nel scan gu.*"

"The chief will see us," translated Lorn.

They were led toward the big hut resting on the outcropping of rock. The ogres who guarded them stayed crushingly close, and Alec felt as if he was trapped in a tight ring of tall trees. He looked at Sarah, who trembled slightly under a mask of bravery. He then turned his gaze to Kraig, whose hand clutched and unclutched, as if he longed to reach for his axe. Beside the peace-keeper walked Michael. As usual, the hermit was unperturbed.

They reached the hut and were forced to stand in a semi-circle, near the stone seats. One ogre stood near each of them, their enlarged brows furrowed ominously.

The wooden door of the large hut thrust open, and out stepped an ogre far larger and more muscular than the rest. A crown of leaves encircled his thick spikes of black hair. A bear-skin robe was draped over his shoulders, the creature's only garment save short pants of brown fur. He bore a heavy broadsword in his right hand. His voice was low and guttural, but he addressed them in the human tongue.

"You claim to be Lorn, son to one who is known to us. How can we know your claim is true?"

"Few know what my father did for your people. Through his negotiations with the Fairies, your *Krydchenclek* was returned to you. A war was avoided which might have destroyed you."

Grod considered them for a moment, his gray eyes looking at each of them. His eyes lingered longest on Alec, who cringed under the chief's gaze. Then the ogre turned its eyes back on Lorn.

"Few humans know of the *Krydchenclek*. If you are not who you claim, you have studied well. I offer you this choice. You may pass over the bridge, but you must pay us with something of great value. What have you to add to the treasure horde of Grod?"

"We carry little of value, great *Batchen*. Some silver, a few coins of gold. I offer you all we have."

The ogre shook his head. "Not enough. What of that weapon the human boy carries? That looks valuable. Maybe magic, too, if those runes mean anything."

"That was a gift to him, strong one, and it holds meaning beyond its physical worth. Take our silver, and I pledge on our way back I will bring you great wealth. You have my word, as the son of my father."

The chief leaned down until he was nose to nose with the warrior. "If you lie, we will hunt you and kill you. Ogres are the best hunters, you know. We never fail."

"I do not lie," said Lorn, softly and seriously. "My word is my oath."

"As is mine, small one. Very well, I accept your offer. All your silver and gold, plus great treasure later, for passage over our bridge."

Lorn reached into his pack, pulling out a small sack of gold and silver coins. He emptied it onto the ground and instructed the others to add whatever coins they might have to the pile. Once they had made a meager pile of gold and silver, Lorn bowed before the chief and turned to walk away.

The others followed him, their ogre guards now content to let them go. Alec breathed a sigh of relief as he started toward the others. He had never guessed it would be possible to bargain with ogres.

Before he had taken two steps, however, he felt a big hand grab his shoulder and pull him back. He cried out as he felt the massive hands of the ogre clench around his shoulders, pinning his arms to his sides. Lorn turned around, confused anger in his eyes.

"What is this?" he said. "I thought we had a deal!"

Grod's lips curled in a toothy grin. "I said only that *you* may cross the bridge. I said nothing of your companions. This one," he said, pointing at Alec, "I will keep. The others you may have."

"Fist of Lars!" cursed Lorn, striding back to the towering chief. "You owe my father a debt! Is this how you repay your debts, ogre?"

"Your father is highly regarded among my people," said Grod, "but older loyalties bind us. We were told by the shape-shifter to watch for this boy, to keep him and his possessions for the sorcerer."

"The sorcer..." began Lorn.

Horror clutched Alec as strongly as did his ogre captor. The sorcerer. These ogres were pawns of Salin after all!

Grok, this is it! Oh, Wounds, Salin's won!

"You would betray us to Salin?" cried Lorn. His eyes were wild with fear, anger, or both. "Think! If you do this, and he gets the power he is after, your people will be nothing but slaves! You think there will be a place for you in the new world he will build for his master? You will live as slaves and fodder in his army, and then you will be cast aside when you are no longer useful."

"Bah!" exclaimed Grod. "The sorcerer gives us gifts of wealth and power! If he turns against us in the end, we will crush him easily, for none are mightier than ogres."

"You are fooling yourself. Let the boy go."

Grod looked down at the warrior, anger flaring from his eyes. "I will not."

Lorn clenched his fists and gazed into the chief's gray eyes. Sweat formed on his brow, and he began trembling as his facade of fearlessness cracked. "This is your final word?"

"It is."

"Then...then you must die."

Ignoring his growing fear, Lorn launched his body forward and smashed forcefully against the ogre. Surprised, Grod stumbled back, losing his footing. He fell backwards to the ground, and Lorn landed on top of him. The big creature screamed in rage and grabbed Lorn in an iron grip. Its hands dwarfed the warrior, who struggled in vain to free himself.

Everyone, both ogre and human, was stunned by the turn of events. But Kraig was the first to recover, and he cried out and ran toward the ogre who held Alec. The ogre turned to face his attacker, but it was too late. With a thunk, the axe buried itself deep in the creature's chest, and as the ogre fell back its grip slipped from Alec's shoulders. Blood pulsed from the wound in spurts as the peacekeeper yanked his axe from the thing's chest.

The other ogres were already reacting. There were seven more besides the chief, and they were closing in swiftly, spiked clubs in hand. Yards away, Alec saw Michael draw his rune-graven long sword, standing forward to protect Sarah as two ogres ran toward them. Kraig was leaping toward the chief to keep him from snapping Lorn in two, leaving Alec to face the remaining five ogres. They circled around him, faces drawn in grimaces of lust.

Arms trembling, he drew his sword. He struggled to remember the forms, but nothing he was taught would come to him. The sword felt as awkward to him as if he had never touched it before. It was all he could do to keep from falling to his knees.

The first ogre closed in. Red fire flared in its eyes as raised its club above its head. The light was blotted out as the massive beast bore down upon the baker, its club descending toward Alec's soft skull.

Where his mind failed, Alec's body took over. He had repeated the swing so many times it just happened. The sword flashed, and the hand holding the club flew into the air, severed cleanly from the ogre's wrist. The club tumbled through the air, landing harmlessly several feet away.

In awe, Alec watched the ogre stumble back, clutching its wrist as blood pumped out. It had been effortless. It shouldn't have been so easy to cleave through all that muscle and bone. He hadn't felt any resistance at all.

The sword was glowing, giving off an orange light which was brighter around the runes. Alec remembered. He wielded Flame, the magic sword given to him by the Lord of the Dead. The mummy had claimed it could cut through steel with ease, but Alec had thought until now his words were exaggerated.

He pressed forth, his training coming back to him in a rush. He thrust, driving his blade deep into the stomach of the ogre he had already wounded. Effortless. The thing slid back off the sword with a wet sound, dead before it hit the ground. The second ogre came at him in a rage, but Alec brought his sword around, and what was meant to be a simple parry took the creature's arm off at the shoulder. Using a movement from the first form, he continued sweeping his blade in a full circle, reaching upward and severing the monster's head.

Effortless!

A fire had ignited in his gut. A rush of emotion he could not control took hold of him, and he desired nothing more than to kill the remaining ogres. It was so easy, so very satisfying! Flame was a godsend. With this sword he had nothing to fear. Even the threat of Salin seemed insignificant.

The last three ogres rushed him at once. Something tugged at his mind, something telling him he should be concerned, but he ignored it. Flame would not let him fall to these foul beasts! As they neared, he brought the glowing blade around in a circle, the first maneuver of the third form, and sliced open the closest ogre's stomach. Alec laughed as he saw the gore pour out, the stupid beast trying to hold in its guts with its bare hands.

Then he felt a club smack the back of his head and he fell forward. Flame fell from his hands, and suddenly the fire inside him winked out, leaving him cold and empty.

Blackness swam in his head as he hit the dirt, threatening to overtake him. He was appalled at the emotions he had been feeling. He had wanted to kill! He'd had a taste of blood and had found killing all too easy. And he had liked it.

But now, as a club came down at him again, he remembered what Lorn had said about becoming overconfident. He wished he had heeded the advice.

Kraig leapt at the ogre chief, his axe held in both hands above his head. He screamed out, chopping downward with all his might toward Grod's skull. The ogre, who had been intent on crushing Lorn, looked wide-eyed at the axe falling toward it and rolled out of the way. Kraig's axe buried itself in the dirt, inches away from the ogre's head.

Lorn took advantage of the moment. The ogre loosened its grip as it rolled, dropping its broadsword. Like a serpent, Lorn wriggled free of his captor's grasp, and in the same movement sprang to his feet. He kicked the weapon away before the beast could recover it, and danced quickly back, out of harm's way.

The ogre was enraged. It leapt up with a speed something so huge shouldn't have possessed, and launched itself at Kraig. The peacekeeper's muscles bulged as he tried to pull his axe free of the rocky ground. The thing bore down on him with blood in its eyes. Kraig knew if he couldn't free his axe in less than a second, he was dead. With all his strength, he yanked the axe handle, veins popping from his rippling arms. In a shower of dirt and stone, the axe ripped free, and Kraig hurled it at the approaching creature. It spun through the air, blade over handle, again and again as it flew toward its target.

There was a massive *THUNK* as the axe blade buried itself entirely in the ogre's chest, the momentum knocking the creature to its back. Its hands went to the handle as its eyes rolled back into its head. Then, as blood began to spew from its mouth, it managed to sit up.

"I will…take you with me into death, human!"

Kraig nearly stumbled in shock as the beast rose to its feet, its eyes focusing one last time. Weaponless, the peacekeeper fell back as the ogre approached. Its hands reached out, massive and strong even at the last.

It never reached him. Lorn came out of nowhere, swinging Grod's own broadsword at the ogre's stomach. He slashed it open and Grod fell to his knees. Then, swinging mightily, Lorn chopped half way through the ogre's neck. It took him two more swings to relieve the creature of its head. The body fell forward against the ground, driving the head of Kraig's axe completely through its back.

"You should have bargained with us, Grod," said Lorn, giving the body a kick.

Kraig's gaze was drawn by the noises of battle further from the hut. "Lorn, look!" he cried.

Alec was in trouble. It looked like he had managed to kill three ogres, but now he was disarmed and lying on the ground, blood pooling around his head. Two ogres stood over him, one poised to strike the baker with a spiked club.

"Get your axe," ordered Lorn. Wielding the broadsword, he ran toward Alec and the ogres.

Kraig bent to pull his axe free of Grod's body, praying Lorn would get to Alec in time.

Alec tried to push away the darkness. His head was hurting and he found it harder to keep his eyes open. Soon, he wouldn't have to worry about it. The club was falling. When it struck, it would all be over.

But it didn't strike. The dark shape he knew to be the ogre fell back, a silvery blade piercing its stomach. Sunlight fell upon Alec, trying to bring him out of the shadow. Droplets of blood spattered his face, his clothes, falling like rain from above.

He shook off the darkness and forced himself to sit up. Lorn was standing above him, holding the sword he'd taken from the ogre chief. He had already killed one of Alec's attackers and was standing his ground before the second. Alec could do nothing but watch, for his head still swam from the blow he had taken.

The ogre Lorn faced was the one he had first spoken to, the sub-chief Grazog. Grazog swept his club outward, but Lorn danced back gracefully, avoiding the blow. He waited for the ogre to charge. In a rage, the beast brought its club downward, and Lorn easily sidestepped the blow. As he did, he held his sword outward, and the ogre's momentum carried it into the edge of the blade, which Lorn raked across its stomach. The warrior spun, now striking the ogre across the back, sending it to the ground. He thrust the point of his blade into Grazog's neck, and the ogre died gurgling.

Alec's gaze turned to Michael, who had been holding off two of the beasts. Now, somehow, three ogres were dead at his feet while three more had backed him and Sarah against the side of a stone hut.

"I knew there had to be more of them hiding somewhere around here," commented Lorn, running to Michael's aid.

Lorn roared as he leapt at the nearest ogre, his sword poised to strike its neck. All three of the beasts turned to face him, but they were not fast enough to stop the warrior from slicing open his target's neck. The ogre fell to its knees, clutching its throat, its eyes wide with shock. The other two raised their clubs and, together, rushed Lorn. He was able to dance backwards out of the way, but working in unison they had put him on the defensive. He dodged side to side and ducked their blows, but he could not find an opening to strike.

He did not need to. Kraig appeared to Lorn's left, his axe flashing outward, hacking wet chunks of meat from an ogre's chest. And the last ogre fell forward as Michael impaled it on the point of his blade. The three men stood still for a second, breathing heavily as dark blood pooled around them. They looked at one another silently for a second, eyes wide, and then Lorn began to laugh.

"What's so funny?" blurted Kraig, face still flushed with adrenaline.

Lorn wiped his face with his hand, smearing blood into his beard. "All that time we spent trying to bargain with them, and it came down to this. I wanted to avoid fighting. I did not think we would have a chance! And yet, look how it turned out. So much for the mighty *Batchen* Grod and his people." He stifled another burst of laughter.

Michael looked at him seriously. "Get a hold of yourself, Lorn. Obviously we were lucky. Not everyone who abides in this village is here, or we would have been hopelessly outnumbered. I do not know where the rest are, but we had better cross the bridge before they return."

Chuckling, the warrior said, "As you wish. Let me gather the coins we gave to Grod and then we can head to the bridge."

"Wait!" cried Sarah, who ran past the men toward Alec. "Alec's bleeding. He hurt his head!"

Alec shook his head, confused. He was in pain, but he hadn't noticed he was bleeding. He put his hand up to the back of his head. It felt wet.

"Wounds!" he cried. His hand was dripping and red. Suddenly he felt dizzy.

Sarah knelt down and put her arms around him. Without her support, he would have collapsed. Soon Michael was there, inspecting his wound, cleaning it with a damp cloth.

"There, there, young Alec," he said, soothingly. "It looks far worse than it is. Head wounds tend to bleed a lot, even when they are minor. The ogre dealt you only a glancing blow. You have nothing to worry about."

He wrapped a long cloth around Alec's head, binding the wound tightly. Then he helped him up, making sure he was securely on his feet before stepping back.

"Thank you," said Alec. "I feel better already. Except…I'm still shaky. Not from the wound. From the fight. The way I felt. The way…oh, never mind. It's over now."

Michael gave him a strange look, and then glanced briefly at the short sword at Alec's side. He looked almost worried. But he let the matter drop and cast his gaze at the rickety bridge.

"We had best go now, if you've gathered our silver, Lorn."

"I have," said Lorn. He had regained his composure, but with blood streaking his face and beard he looked like a madman. "I think it would be wise if we crossed two at a time. Kraig, you take Sarah and go across first. Once they pass the half-way point, Michael, you and Alec follow. I will guard the rear and cross last."

The others nodded in agreement. They walked past the dead chief's hut and stood before the bridge. Here the chasm was far narrower than at the other bridge, and yet it still seemed too far to the other side. The bridge creaked as Kraig stepped upon it, and he held the rope railing nervously. The thin wooden planks lashed together with hemp swayed in the wind, and Alec wondered if the peacekeeper would have trouble keeping his footing. But he continued onward and motioned for Sarah to follow. She gave Alec an uncertain glance and then stepped out onto the old bridge.

With Lorn and Michael, Alec watched his companions make their way slowly across the ravine. Sarah stayed a few steps behind Kraig, who looked back every twenty seconds to make sure she was still following. As they neared the center, the sagging bridge seemed to groan under their weight.

Alec took a look around the village. He hoped the other ogres weren't on their way back, or worse yet, still hiding in their homes. A thought struck him. "I wonder where the women are."

"What do you mean?" asked Lorn.

"The female ogres. Aren't there any in this village?"

Lorn and Michael looked at each other. Lorn broke into a wide grin and the hermit gave a small smile.

"What?" asked Alec. "Did I say something funny?"

"In a way," said Michael. "There were females among the ogres we fought. They are nearly impossible to tell from the males."

"At least when they're clothed," commented Lorn. "And you wouldn't want to see one *unclothed*, believe me."

"Ogre females are as strong and brutish as the males. They are perhaps even fiercer fighters. The only difference is they bear the children. Only when pregnant or taking care of very young children do they distance themselves from hunting or fighting." He paused and looked out over the ravine. "They are near to the other side. It is time for us to go, Alec."

Just as they started across, there was a cry from the far side of the village. Spinning, Alec saw a group of ogres returning from the hunt, carcasses of large animals slung over several of their shoulders. They had spotted the humans, and were throwing down their prizes and reaching for clubs.

"Lars!" cried Lorn. "Get over that bridge!"

Alec did not have to be told twice. The bridge wobbled as he stepped upon it, but he didn't have time to care. Much more quickly than Kraig had dared, he shuffled along the planks. Michael came swiftly behind him.

"Faster," said the hermit. Alec walked briskly, constantly adjusting to the bounce and sway of the bridge. He felt as if it might twist and hurl him over the edge at any time.

Behind them, the bridge pulsed a fast rhythm. Alec glanced past Michael to see Lorn coming, running confidently toward them as the bridge tried to throw him off his feet. The ogres had gathered by the edge of the bridge and were debating whether to follow.

Ahead, Sarah and Kraig had reached the other side. They saw what was happening and began to shout encouragement to the others. Both looked worried, especially when the bridge began to sag tremendously, the old wood creaking as if it were about to give way.

Lorn was catching up to Alec and Michael, putting more dangerous weight toward the middle. To make matters worse, Alec saw two ogres stepping onto the bridge. They were either too stupid to realize the groaning structure would never take the added weight, or they didn't care. These humans had murdered members of their tribe, including their *batchen;* they would have revenge at any cost.

The creaking continued until it became a constant cracking. By the time Alec was three quarters of the way to the north side of the ravine, he knew the bridge would give way soon. He wanted to run, but the movement of so many people was causing the bridge to sway, bob, and buckle, and it would throw him if he let go of the roping. He struggled along at a steady pace as sweat matted his hair and dripped into his eyes.

A third ogre stepped onto the bridge. The two who had pursued first were half way across now, only yards behind Lorn. Alec spared one last look behind him and then made for the north side. He was only yards away.

Relief washed over him as he stepped onto solid ground. Sarah embraced him, and Kraig patted him on the back. Michael was only a step behind. But as the hermit stepped off the bridge, it began to cry out in agony. Alec pulled away from his friends and they all looked toward the center of the bridge, where the sounds of cracking wood and tearing rope filled the air.

The ropes snapped. The boards broke. The bridge collapsed, breaking apart in the middle. The south side fell away until it slapped against the south wall of the ravine, and the north side swung toward the north wall. Two ogres fell into the ravine, crying out in terror. The last held on to the flimsy bridge, still barely connected to the anchors that fastened it to the northern side.

"Grok! Lorn!!"

Looking down, Alec saw the warrior holding on, twenty yards away, ten yards ahead of the ogre. He was working his way up, hand over hand. He was coming quickly, but the creature behind him was coming faster. Still, with luck, he could hold his lead until he was out.

The bridge shifted. The rope was fraying, and the anchors were pulling from the rocky earth. The entire structure dropped about two feet. Michael cursed, Sarah screamed, but there was nothing anyone could do. They waited as they watched the rope tear, little by little.

Lorn's muscles were straining. He was only yards away, but he could barely pull himself up. The ogre was almost close enough to grab his ankle. It was agonizing to watch, but Alec could not turn away. Lorn's strength was about to give out, and he reached upward, hand extended, clutching at empty air.

At the last instant, Kraig leaned over the edge and clasped Lorn's hand. Simultaneously, the ogre grabbed at the warrior's ankle. Alec shouted a warning, but there was nothing to be done.

And then the bridge gave way. The ropes snapped, the anchors ripped from the ground, and the entire structure plummeted into the pit. Roaring frustration, the ogre fell backwards, arm still reaching for his prey.

Straining, Kraig pulled the warrior up. Lorn struggled over the rocky edge and crawled a few feet from the ravine. He collapsed to his side, exhausted.

"Fist of Lars," he breathed. "That is about the closest I have ever come."

Relief poured over Alec. They were safe. On the other side, the rest of the ogres leapt into the air and waved their fists in rage. They had been robbed of their revenge. He looked at them, but was too far away to hear their cries. For this, he was grateful.

When Lorn was ready, they continued northward. They talked little, for there were no words to express how they felt. Alec was emotionally drained, tired, and invigorated all at once. He was still concerned about the ecstasy he had felt in the heat of battle, but he let it drop for now. They had faced death yet again, and had come away with only minor wounds. With every mile they put behind them, it grew more likely they would reach Faerie before Salin caught them. Then, at last, they would know peace.

They passed from the rocky land into the northern reaches of Ogrynwood. The rocks gave way to dirt, the dirt to rich soil. Weeds became bushes; bushes, trees. Once again, the forest was thick around them. There were few ogre villages on this side of the ravine, Lorn told them, and in another day or two they would leave the Ogrynwood altogether. Then, there was nothing left between them and the land they sought, save a thin band of green, grassy hills. There was nothing left to fear.

Nothing but Salin, thought Alec. *Grok protect us.*

CHAPTER 17

Arrival

Two days later, they left Ogrynwood. The woods had been thinning all morning, and by the time the sun was at its noontide peak, they had reached the region of pleasant hills north of the forest. Alec stepped onto the grassy earth, enjoying the buoyancy of the soft loam beneath his feet. This, and the unfiltered sunlight shining on him, brought a wide smile to his face. He breathed the fresh air and was reminded of the land surrounding Barton Hills. This place was like home.

He could tell Sarah was feeling it too. She was beaming, her eyes flicking from the green grass to the clear blue sky. She turned to Alec and her smile widened.

"Look at this! So open, so fresh. The forest was all right for a while, but this is more like home."

Even Kraig was moved. "Barton Hills could be right here, just past those hills. Those woods back there could be the Northwood."

Looking back over his shoulder, Lorn chuckled. "The lay of the land might be similar, but this is not Barton Hills. There is no civilization between here and Faerie. Humankind has never settled these northern lands. Few humans have ever visited here and no maps exist to show the way. These gentle hills roll on for miles; it is perhaps a day's march until the woods surround us again. But the woods to the north are different than any you have seen. Those are the woods of the Fair Folk."

"I'm in no hurry to return to the woods," said Kraig. "I want the sun. Feel the warmth!"

Michael, who had been looking out over the grassy hills, turned his head toward the others. "When you see the woods we are heading toward, you will change your mind." He began walking over the short, thick grass.

When Lorn joined the hermit, Alec and the others followed. The woods faded into the distance behind them as the day wore on. The hills were not at all steep, and the day's march was easy and peaceful. A few bushes and small trees dotted the hills from time to time, but largely the only vegetation was healthy, green grass. Alec occasionally saw some small birds flying overhead or nesting in trees, and brown and white rabbits sometimes hopped through the grass nearby, but there were few other signs of life. It was obvious this way was seldom traveled by man or beast.

As he had taken to doing in quiet times, he held Sarah's hand. He looked at her, stunned more and more by how beautiful he found her. The burns she had suffered in Faryn-Gehnah had mostly healed, and her flesh was nearly as smooth and perfect as ever. The only visible remnants of the blaze were the dark streaks where fire had burned her hair. Oddly, the black wisps of hair mixed in with her blond served only to make her more attractive.

Alec's own wounds were healing as well. The cut in his side where he had been stabbed by a goblin knife hadn't hurt for days, and only a long, white scar was left. As for his head, he had been able to remove the bandage that very morning. There was some scabbing on his scalp, but there was little pain, and his hair covered the wound. Thinking about his injuries only made him smile more. Considering what he had been through, he must have had the luck of Grok to have escaped with such little damage.

But the trouble was nearly over. As early as tomorrow afternoon, they would reach the woods of the Fair Folk. He could scarcely believe it. They had been stomping through woods, over plains, and under mountains for almost three weeks now. He could hardly wait for a rest in a safe haven. And his heart leapt at the idea of meeting Fairies. Living ones, this time, of course.

The rest of the day passed quickly and quietly. The weather remained warm and sunny all afternoon, but early in the evening some clouds rolled in from the west. Alec hoped that there would not be another storm. Under the gathering clouds they spread their blankets and made camp for the night.

As usual, Alec spent two hours training with Lorn. Since the battle at the ogre village, he had taken the training more seriously. Each time he drew the sword and practiced the forms, a strange amalgam of emotions swept through him: anger at the circumstances which had caused him to take up arms, grief at the lust for battle he had felt during the confrontation with the ogres, pride at knowing how quickly he was picking up the skills Lorn was teaching him, and ecstasy at the thought of using his newly learned skills. This last emotion he tried to stifle every time he felt it. He did not want to kill again. And yet at the same time, he could not wait for the chance to wield Flame in battle.

After two hours of intense work, Alec was too exhausted to feel any emotion. He ended his work-out by running through the six forms he knew back to back, and when he finally finished his muscles were quivering. He looked up at Lorn, who was shaking his head and smiling.

"You need to improve your upward thrusts, and you are still using too much force in your parries, but otherwise the forms look good. I never would have thought you had the coordination to get through the Estronian Series so smoothly."

Lorn was referring to the sixth form, a sequence of movements based on fighting techniques used in Estron. The movements seemed more foreign to Alec and more demanding on his muscles than the other forms and techniques he had learned. And yet, Lorn said, they would be more deadly when mastered. As great as the soldiers of Eglak had always been, the deadliest and most elite warriors came from Estron.

Alec smiled half-heartedly. "I feel like I'm improving, but there's just so much to learn. I feel differently toward my training now. Before I was doing this because I had to; now I'm doing it because I *want* to."

"Good," said Lorn.

"No, you don't understand." Alec shook his head. "I feel driven. Ever since the battle with the ogres. It…it awakened something in me. I want to learn to fight not because I might be forced into battle at some point along the way, but because I *hope* to get into a battle."

The warrior stroked his beard, considering. "I would not be concerned about it. It is natural for a young man learning the ways of the sword to want to test his skill against a real opponent. You are learning fast, and the weapon you wield is far more potent than most, but I would not be so hasty to test your skills in the heat of combat. You fared well against the ogres, better than I would have thought, but you still have much to learn. Your passion is good; keep it focused. But keep it under control."

Alec nodded seriously. "I will." He sighed. "If we're done, I'm off to bed."

Turning toward his own blankets, Lorn said, "Yes, we are finished for now. Goodnight."

Alec lay down in his place next to Sarah, pulling his blankets up to his neck to keep out the evening chill. Clouds gathered in the night sky, blotting out the light from the stars and the moon. It had been hard to see during his training, and now there was almost no light at all. Alec hoped Michael, who had the first watch, would be able to see well enough to know if something approached their camp. Looking into the dark sky, he let such thoughts slip away and tried to go to sleep.

Michael couldn't see a thing. It was the darkest night since they had set out from his little hut weeks ago. He tried focusing his mind on the Seven Laws, tried bending the forces of nature to his will to create just a little light, but it was no use. Study as he might, he could not perform even the simplest of Shapings. He hadn't been able to Shape for decades, not since he had come to understand the futility of the struggle against evil. Not since he had lost his faith.

He tried once more to will little charges of electricity to form a ball above his hand, creating light from darkness. Failing, he sat back in frustration and turned his thoughts on other matters. He was very concerned about Alec. The boy was far more than he seemed, far more than Michael had anticipated. Ever since Alec was born, the hermit had known he was more than a common peasant. Michael had always been drawn to the boy, always felt the need to keep an eye on him. He had never known why. From the shadows, he had watched Alec grow up, witnessed the little triumphs and tragedies which made up his life. The hermit had never understood why this common boy interested him so.

The night Salin struck, the night Michael first spotted Alec with the Talisman, Michael had gone to the tavern because he *felt* something was about to happen. He couldn't explain it then and it still mystified him now. Something inside him, a vague voice or a strange urging, guided him to the tavern. Was it the voice of the One? Was it the Talisman itself calling out to him? He couldn't say. All he knew now was that Alec was not the simple baker he appeared to be. The fact that the Talisman of Unity had chosen him proved as much. Michael had guessed the boy had some latent ability to Shape buried deep inside him, probably a very minor ability, but one the Talisman was able to sense. For this reason it allowed Alec to discover it. Michael believed it had chosen Alec to bear it back to Faerie to be reunited with its true master, the King of the Fairies.

But Michael had not expected the so-called Lord of the Dead in Faryn-Gehnah to bow down before Alec, convinced the simple baker was a Shaper with the power to break one of the most potent curses lain since the beginning of the world. This put a new spin on things. Not only did they expect this "Cursebreaker" to come one day to the tomb, they expected him to have the Talisman of Unity. The mummy could have been mistaken, or insane, but Michael had seen enough of the world to know things like this usually meant something. They usually meant something big.

And now Alec was training with Lorn, learning the sword faster than should have been possible. Even someone with an aptitude for swordplay usually took longer to learn the things Alec had nearly mastered. Michael wondered how much of it was Alec's natural ability and how much was the sword. The sword was what worried him the most. Magical swords were dangerous tools, often enhancing a person's skill beyond their natural capabilities. Such magical enhancements were never without price. Perhaps the lust for battle Alec had apparently developed during the recent conflict with the ogres could be attributed to the sword's influence. Such weapons, useful though they were, often corrupted their user.

Michael did not want to see Alec corrupted. Especially if there was hope for him to learn the Seven Laws and become a Shaper. There were too few Shapers left in the world, and too many dark sorcerers. Salin was only one of many, although he was far and away the most powerful. If only there were still potent Shapers to stand against him.

There might be, in Faerie.

This thought alone drove him on. The Fair Folk had remained strong over the years, and as far has he knew, none had ever turned to evil. If they still were powerful, if they still protected their lands with the ancient Shapings even Vorik Seth could not foil, there was hope. The Fairy King, with the Talisman returned to him, could perhaps end the threat of Salin Urdrokk. He could perhaps build armies to challenge even the Seth.

This Michael doubted. As much as he wanted to, he couldn't regain his faith. No one but Michael himself understood the truth. He had learned the horrible truth decades ago and it had shattered any hope he had ever had of victory against the darkness.

The lords of the heavens sided with Vorik Seth. The gods themselves sided with evil.

He shivered with the futility of his life, of his sacred mission. Even what he was doing now was futile. He grabbed his book, his gift from Horren, and held it against his chest. It was small comfort against the coming storm, but it was all he had. Having no faith of his own, he tried in vain to find comfort in the faith of others.

The next day, they rose early and continued their journey over the hills. The weather was cooler than it had been, and an overcast sky provided a gray light. The air smelled of rain, reminding Alec of many a rainy day back in Barton Hills. They depended on frequent rainfall, being a farming community. Even though they had built a primitive irrigation system over the years, bringing water in from White River North, there was no substitute for a good, steady rain. Looking at the sky and thinking of how little rain there had been lately, he hoped the clouds would soon release their storm over Barton Hills. But here, over these hills, he hoped the rains would not come. Remembering the storm in the Plains of Naar, he decided he didn't at all enjoy traveling in the rain.

They marched briskly through the morning, Lorn leading the way, Kraig and Michael following, and Alec bringing up the rear with Sarah. They talked little, for after weeks of travel they had run out of small talk, but occasionally Sarah commented on her expectations of Faerie. She was excited that they were so near their destination. Like Alec, she was anxious to see a place where magic was common, and to gaze at the Fair Folk themselves. Legends spoke of them, but few could agree on what they were actually like. They had seen statues of Fairies in the tomb, but it was not the same as seeing the Fair Folk in the flesh.

By early afternoon, Alec could see clustered trees in the distance, stretching across the horizon. The grassy hills were coming to an end, which meant they were within mere miles of their destination. His heart leapt with joy. Surely Salin couldn't catch them now. They marched onward, quickening their pace. Excitement electrified the air around them. Every member of the party was anxious, expectant. As they came closer to the trees, Lorn addressed them without slowing down.

"From the time we set foot in those woods, we will be watched. We will not be able to see those who watch us. Do not attempt to address them; they will reveal themselves to us when they are ready. When they do, let me do the talking. They know me, or at least they know of me. Unless things have changed greatly, I will be welcome here. And therefore, so will you."

The others, except Michael, nodded in agreement. The hermit said, "I am known here as well, although it has been a long time since I passed into the Fairy land. I agree that Lorn should speak for us. I may not be as well received as I would have been once."

Soon they were within a few hundred feet of the forest, and Alec could hardly believe what he was seeing. He glanced at Sarah, whose eyes were also wide with wonder. She met his gaze, and they both smiled widely, unable to express their awe any other way. Then they each looked back at the wonderful, magical trees growing ever closer.

The trees were tall, although no taller than some of the trees of the Northwood. But they were healthier than any of the trees in Tyridan, more vital than even the trees of the Addingrove. The leaves were large and green, deep green and bright green but no shades of red or brown. Each leaf was alive, pulsing with a health Alec could somehow sense. The branches were a deep, rich brown, as if the very life of the earth reached up from the loam below and filled the limbs with vitality. The trunks were old and thick, solid and strong, filled with ancient power and wisdom. Of course, Alec didn't understand how a tree could be filled with wisdom, but this was the impression he got looking into the forest.

As they stepped into the woods, Alec thought he saw a silver glow around the leaves of the trees, but when he looked directly at them the glow was gone. But a sense of the glow remained: an invisible light he could see with his heart, and it was silver and beautiful like the moon. The glow filled him, the beauty stole his heart, and he felt he could walk under these trees forever and never want for anything more.

Fingers snapped before his face. He shook his head, blinking his eyes as if awaking from a marvelous dream. Lorn was looking him in the eye, studying him carefully. When he saw Alec's eyes focus, he smiled and patted him on the shoulder.

"So, you have already encountered one of the dangers of Faerie. This place has a magic of its own, and it can enchant those who enter unwarily. Its beauty is surely something to behold, but keep your purpose in mind at all times. Many men and beasts who have wandered here have died simply because they were so mesmerized with the beauty of this place they forgot to eat. They simply sat down, looking up at the trees for days or weeks, until they died smiling. It is the Fair Folk's first line of defense."

"How can something so beautiful be so dangerous?" questioned Sarah, who was still staring wide-eyed at the surrounding wonders.

"Often beauty can be deadly," said Michael. "The Fair Folk are beautiful themselves, but it is hard to imagine more lethal foes. Warriors, bowmen, Shapers of the highest order. And most as resplendent as the heavens themselves."

"Most, yes," said Lorn, "but not all. The sprites in particular can be strange to look upon."

"Sprites?" asked Kraig.

"Shape changers," said Michael. "Actually, all Fairies are shape changers, but sprites are masters of it. In their natural form they are rather short, with sharper features than other Fairies. Many can track someone by smell alone, like a bloodhound. Some have very unpleasant personalities."

"I hope we don't meet any of those," said Sarah.

Lorn laughed. "We may or may not. They are relatively rare. But come, we are in the woods of Faerie, but we have a long way to go before we reach Faerie proper."

"Are we safe from Salin?" asked Alec.

"We should be," said Michael. "Webs of enchantment encircle these woods. The webs can read one's intent, much like the archway we had to walk through at Horren's home. If a person's intent is evil, or if they would bring harm to the Fair Folk, the webs will keep this person out. If the intruder persists, forcing his way through the web, he will die. As far as I know, even Salin is not strong enough to break the magic of the web. Thousands of ancient Fairy Shapers, stronger than any who live today, forged the web, many sacrificing their lives to give the enchantment the necessary strength. It is perhaps the greatest and strongest act of Shaping that has ever been performed."

Alec nodded, relieved. At long last they were beyond the reach of Salin Urdrokk. He looked over at Sarah, surprised to see a tear running down her cheek. She reached for Alec's hand and leaned her head on his shoulder.

"Grok, Alec," she whispered, "I can't believe it. I can't believe it's over."

He just smiled and put his arm around her. It really was over. They were safe.

Hours passed, and they continued deeper into the Fairy wood. Alec had to keep his mind active, or he found himself slowing his pace to gaze absent-mindedly at the majesty of the trees surrounding him. They pulled at his heart, and he wanted nothing more than to spend the rest of his life here, dancing under their full, glorious branches. But then he thought of his life at Baron Hills, how he longed to return there to serve as master baker, and he was able to look away from the trees. Or, he had but to look at Sarah, concentrate on the feeling of her hand in his. As lovely as the forest was, it failed to compare to her smile.

Twilight fell, but the absence of the sun barely darkened the forest, which seemed to glow with a strange, invisible silver. The trees appeared to give off a light of their own, pure and soft, but at the same time it seemed they only reflected light which was already there. But if this were so, Alec asked himself, where was the source? Magic, he supposed.

Suddenly, a form dropped from a tree and landed before them, making almost no noise. Startled, Alec stopped in his tracks, his eyes saucers. It was a man who stood before them, tall and slim, with long blond hair and chiseled features. His ears were slightly pointed, his cheek-bones strong and his face thin. His skin was nearly as light as his hair. He wore a low-cut brown tunic, skin-tight pants of deep green, and high, black boots. A very long and slim sword was in his hand, pointed directly at Lorn, who was in the front of the party.

"What have we here?" asked the Fairy, a sly half-smile curling his lips. "Travelers from the south? Humans? Perhaps to offer themselves as servants to King Elyahdyn? What do you think, brother?"

"I think we should kill them now and ask questions later."

Alec spun to face the source of the second voice. To his surprise, numerous Fairies surrounded them, some with bows, some with knives or swords, some without any weapon at all. Some were blond and blue-eyed, some were dark of hair and eye. But all were tall and had sharp features, and all were beyond beautiful.

"Do not be quite so hasty, friend Rhyan," said the first Fairy. "Perhaps we should hear them out before we run them through. What say you, humans? None may come unbidden into the Fairy-lands."

Lorn raised his hand in a symbol of peace. "I am Lorn of Eglak, known to the Fair Folk in years past as Lorn *Narnsahn*. These people come to you in great need, and I am their guide. We request an audience with your King."

The Fairy raised an eyebrow curiously. "An audience with the King? Well, that is quite a presumptuous request, especially for such poorly dressed humans. I know of the *Narnsahn*, of course, but as I have never seen him I cannot be sure you are him. Tell me, '*Narnsahn,' hyn eyst uhra pacta?*"

Standing straight, looking the Fairy, Lorn said, "*Muhra pacta eyst ny Narn o Egla, kyhn a rah sa Breyden Faryn-Lahdyne.*"

The Fairy looked at him cautiously for a moment, searching Lorn's eyes. "You speak our language. This alone is no proof you are who you claim, but it is enough to save you from the point of my blade. You may well be the *Narnsahn*, but these are dangerous times and I fear we must err on the side of caution. You will come to our village under escort. Once there, we can discuss your fate in more detail."

Lorn nodded, showing that he accepted the conditions. "And what shall I call my captor, good Fairy?"

"I am known as Vyrdan. Follow now and try not to make so much noise."

Surrounded by tall Fairies, the companions followed Vyrdan. They tramped through the forest in silence for half an hour before coming to an area where the trees were sparse. Spread among the trees were simple wooden buildings, some tall and some squat, some large and some small. There were houses built in the trees themselves, high up in the branches and accessible only by rope ladder. Here and there were people going about common chores: buying and selling necessities, gathering nuts and berries from the forest, taking care of children, feeding livestock, carrying water from a central well. To Alec it looked like any other rustic village, except the people were all tall, slim, and lovely. Alec had expected there to be visible magic all about, something spectacular and wonderful, but these Fair Folk appeared to live simple, humble lives.

Vyrdan turned to one of his companions, the one he called Rhyan. "Send word ahead to Lady Devra. Tell her we bring five human guests for her to read."

"As you wish, my lord."

Rhyan and three other Fairies rushed off toward the center of the village and vanished in the trees. Vyrdan turned to Lorn and grinned knowingly.

"If you are the *Narnsahn*, we will know soon enough."

"Indeed," said Lorn. "Your Lady Devra need not use her magic to read us; she will surely know me by sight."

"The eye can be fooled. Devra's inner sight cannot."

They passed the center of the village, where a group of children were playing along a wide dirt path. Several adults regarded the humans suspiciously. It obviously had been a long time since outsiders had passed through here.

Finally they came to an old tree which dwarfed those around it. Its trunk was massive and it is branches stretched upward far beyond the reach of its neighbors. Its old roots clawed into the dirt beneath it, reaching outward from the trunk like thick, gnarled fingers. High in its branches was a tree house, larger than any of the others Alec had seen. A rope ladder led up to the house, swaying gently in the breeze.

"This is the Lady's mansion," said Vyrdan. "Follow me up, and remember you are watched."

Not waiting for a reply, the Fairy lithely raced up the ladder. Lorn followed more slowly. Alec went next, talking each rung even more carefully than the warrior. He found it difficult to climb a ladder made of rope, for the steps sagged underfoot causing his arms to do more of the work. He was grateful for the stamina he had gained through the journey and his training, for three weeks ago the climb would have exhausted him.

He reached the top, and pulled himself up through a trap door onto a wide wooden platform. Ahead, under a wooden roof, he saw some elegant wooden furnishings. A long table with tall chairs sat in the center of the platform, and to their right was a curtain leading into another room. Beyond the table was a sitting room, where deep padded chairs were arranged around a brick fireplace. In one of the chairs was a woman so beautiful Alec's breath caught in his throat.

She stood and moved gracefully toward where Lorn and Alec stood. Alec was vaguely aware that Rhyan and a few other Fairies stood in the sitting room, but he couldn't take his eyes off the woman. Elegant brown hair fell to her waist, and her amber eyes caught the light and sparkled perfectly. Her skin was white, and her gown was pale green. When she reached the edge of the sitting room she smiled and beckoned the newcomers.

"I am Devra, Lady of Lehnwood. By the grace of our King and Queen I govern this village. Welcome, Lorn *Narnsahn*. It has been a long time. Come to me."

"Wait here," Lorn whispered to Alec. He strode across the platform until he stood face to face with the Fairy. He dropped to one knee and bowed his head before her. She placed a slim white hand upon his head and closed her eyes. In a moment, she opened them and smiled sincerely.

"You are truly the *Narnsahn*. Welcome back to Faerie, friend Lorn."

He rose and smiled as he met her eyes. "My Lady, you are as lovely as ever. It does my heart good to see you again. My companions and I have faced many trials on the path to the Fairy-wood. We come to you in great need."

"We shall have time enough to speak of need, *Narnsahn*. As I have read you, so must I look into the minds of your friends. These are suspicious times, and we must all take what precautions we can against the shadow."

"I understand, my Lady. These are indeed dark times."

Alec looked behind him and saw the others had arrived at the top of the platform. He had been so mesmerized by the sight of Lady Devra he had not heard them come up. Vyrdan, who had been standing off to the side, motioned for them all to approach the Lady.

Devra's eyes grew wide when she saw Michael. She motioned for him to come to her, and he obeyed silently. As Lorn had done, he knelt before her and allowed her to touch his head. She closed her eyes for several seconds, and when she opened them she looked sad.

"Rise, Elsendarin. By the One, I cannot believe it is you. It has been…a very long time, old friend."

Michael regarded her with a somber expression. "Why do you look so sad? Have you seen the blackness in my heart? Have you seen the reason why I have stayed away so long?"

Leaning down to him, Devra placed a hand on each of his cheeks. "You have lost much, Elsendarin."

"Only my faith. It is nothing."

"It is everything. Why did you not return sooner, my love? Here, there are those who could help you, those who could…"

"You can do nothing. None of you can. But this isn't about me, Devra."

She looked close to tears. Alec couldn't understand what was going on. She obviously knew Michael, but why was she so sad? Had she really called him "my love?"

"No," she said, "I saw in your mind it is not. You are here because of the human boy. What need has driven you to bring him here?"

She backed up, allowing Michael to rise. He was not quite as tall as she was, and he had to bend his head back to look her in the eye. "We have been pursued by the sorcerer, Salin Urdrokk. He desires something which young Alec possesses. It is imperative we speak to the King as soon as possible."

She looked at the hermit quizzically, unasked questions visible in her eyes. She touched his arm, obviously wanting to talk to him more. Instead she looked past him into Alec's eyes.

"Alec? Come to me."

He could not resist. He glanced back at Sarah and Kraig, both of whom where as confused and mesmerized as he was. He went to Lady Devra and, following his companions' example, knelt before her. He felt her hand upon his head, and a moment later, a fire burned within him. It tore through his mind, opening his thoughts to her as if he were a book. She read him, read things from his book which even *he* did not know. He felt it. Secrets poured forth from his mind like water from a cup. Then the fire was gone. She removed her hand from his head.

Looking up, he saw her stumble back, a surprised expression on her face. "The Talisman of Unity! It was lost…and you found it! And the mummy, in the tomb, calling you Cursebreaker. By the One, you honestly don't know, do you?"

"My lady?" Alec said, getting off his knees. "Are you all right? I don't know what?"

"No, I must be wrong. What I have seen, it cannot be true."

She looked as if she might faint. Vyrdan and the other Fairy guards were rushing toward her, but Michael was faster. He grabbed her, steadied her, and looked with concern into her eyes.

"What is it, Devra?" he asked. "What is it that you saw in Alec?"

She shook her head. "A mistake. It happens from time to time, when I am tired. Please, do not ask me to speak of it. What I saw about the Talisman is what is important. This is true, isn't it?"

"Yes," Michael said, nodding. "He found the Talisman of Unity in his home town of Barton Hills. The sorcerer somehow knew of the discovery and sought to take it for his own. He would have succeeded, had I not gotten to Alec first. This is why we must see your King. We must deliver the Talisman into his hand so he might use it to restore the ancient glory of Faerie."

"If I had but known…why did you not simply tell me about the Talisman? Why did you not tell Vyrdan as soon as he found you?"

"As you told Lorn, these are suspicious times. I know the Fair Folk have never been corrupted in the past, but the shadow of the Seth is spreading out over all the lands, Faerie included. Perhaps his shadow has at last tainted the purity of some of your people. I know that no Fairy would be able to use the Talisman for evil, but a corrupt Fairy would struggle to keep it out of the hands of the King. I wanted to keep it secret until we stood before the King. I should have known such a secret could not be kept from a reader."

"Indeed, you of all people should have known that. What else have you forgotten over the years, Elsendarin? Have you forgotten the mysteries of the spirit world? How it feels to touch the One? Have you forgotten how to sing the song which Shapes the world?"

"I remember the song, but it no longer holds meaning for me. My voice is too harsh for singing these days."

A great sadness filled the deep pools of her eyes, making Alec's heart ache. He didn't understand what was happening, but he knew she was hurting. She was hurting for Michael, feeling a pain he was too numb to feel for himself. She turned to Vyrdan and waved him away.

"Go. And take these humans with you. I have no strength to read the others now. Treat them well, for they are our honored guests. All who travel with Lorn and Elsendarin are to receive the consideration we would grant visiting nobility. Provide them with food and drink and a place to rest. Send word to King

Elyahdyn that the *Narnsahn* and the Wise One seek an audience with him, and tell him Lady Devra humbly suggests he accommodate them as soon as possible."

"At once, my Lady," said Vyrdan. He ushered the humans from the sitting area and led them to the rope ladder.

When they were gathered together on the ground, Vyrdan led them to a large hut near Lady Devra's tree. He pushed aside a wooden door and motioned them inside. It seemed like a comfortable living space, complete with simple bedding and a table for dining. Burning oil lamps hung from the walls, casting a warm glow about the room. Upon a shelf were many books, and beside the shelf sat a comfortable chair and a reading lamp.

"These are our guest quarters. It is not much, but you will find the beds comfortable. Feel free to read any of the texts you find here. Some are in the tongue of Eglak, but others are in our native language. I suppose only the *Narnsahn* will be able to take advantage of those volumes." He smiled. "I apologize for doubting you, Lorn *Narnsahn*. You are always welcome in the forests of Faerie."

"Thank you, Vyrdan."

"I will see that food and drink are brought to you at once. Rest here if you will or walk at your leisure through the village. I will return when I have news from our King."

The blond Fairy bowed deeply and left the hut. Alec fell down on one of the beds, suddenly realizing how tired he was. Sarah followed his example, and Kraig and Lorn each took chairs at the table. Michael sat down in the plush chair and began examining the books on the shelf.

"What was that all about?" asked Kraig. "It seems like you are both acquainted with Lady Devra. What is all this about 'reading'?"

Michael was engrossed in the books, reading titles off their spines as they sat upon the shelf, so Lorn answered Kraig's question. "All Fairies have magic in one form or another. Some are true Shapers, some express their talents in other, subtler ways. Some of those, like Devra, are readers. By touching a person, they can look into their thoughts. Usually the talent is used to determine a person's intentions, or to verify the truth of a person's claims. Sometimes a reader can see more deeply into a person's soul. They can see things even the one being read is not aware of."

"Like when Lady Devra was reading me," said Alec. He frowned, worried about her reaction to him. "What could she have seen in me that would have frightened her so?"

Michael looked away from the books, his face grim. "It must have been something of great import, something unexpected. I have never seen Devra react is such a way when reading someone. Alec, I have suspected there is more to you than you know, and now I am sure."

"That's ridiculous," said Alec. "Whatever she saw was a mistake. You heard what she said."

Michael shook his head. "She was lying. Whatever she saw shocked her so much she could not discuss it. I must go to her later and speak with her privately."

Lorn studied the hermit carefully. "What exactly is the nature of your relationship with Devra? From the way she addressed you, it seems you know her well. Very well, perhaps."

Michael turned back to the books. "Years ago, we were friends. Very close friends. But that was long, long ago."

It was obvious Michael didn't want to discuss his relationship with Devra, and Lorn let it drop. Michael pulled a book off the shelf and began to read as the others sat in silence. Before long, Alec drifted into a light sleep.

He awakened to the sound of shuffling feet. Vyrdan had returned with several other Fairies carrying trays of food and drink. Alec watched as they set the table with plates of steaming meat, bowls of fresh fruits, warm loaves of bread and trays of cooked vegetables. His stomach roared at the sight of such a feast. He had not eaten a meal like this since before he left Barton Hills. Actually, he thought, he had not eaten such a feast since last Yule, when Stan roasted a huge boar.

"If you require anything else, just call on Bree," said Vyrdan, pointing to a young-looking woman who had helped bring in the food. "She has been assigned to cater to your needs. She will be nearby."

Bree bowed, her dark hair falling in front of her slim face. "My home is next door. You can find me there, should you need me."

"Thank you," said Lorn. "All of you. The meal looks wonderful. The hospitality of the Fair Folk has not been lessened by the passage of time."

Vyrdan gave one of his deep bows and led the other Fairies from the hut. As soon as they were gone, Alec rushed to the table and began filling a plate with food. The others quickly followed suit. The meal was marvelous. The meat and vegetables were hot and delicious, the fruit was cool and fresh, and the bread was the best he had ever tasted. Alec wondered if he would have a chance to find the town's baker and pry some secrets out of him. If he learned to make bread like this, any village would be quick to welcome him.

After the meal, Alec stretched and lay down on the bed. Now that his stomach was full, he felt even more tired then before. Sarah lay down on the bed closest to his, lying on her side and smiling. She looked happy. He knew exactly how she felt. They had come a long way in the last month and had been through more horror than anyone should ever have to face, but at last it was over. Neither Salin nor his minions could enter this forest. At long last, they were safe. The thought overwhelmed Alec, and a pleasant, warm glow filled him. He gave Sarah a long look, holding her eyes with his. He hadn't admitted it to himself before, but he knew there was no denying it now. He was in love with her.

He forced himself to look away from her so he wouldn't blurt out his feelings. Now was not the time. Besides, he could barely keep his eyes open. He felt sleep coming upon him quickly, and with a yawn, he let it take him.

Devra stood alone, gazing pensively out a large window in the side of her mansion. She wondered if she was doing the right thing. The only thing she wanted was to do what was best for Faerie, but she was no longer sure of what was best. She knew the old King was weak and her people were suffering because of it. The Fair Folk were dwindling, their power declining, because the royal bloodline had been diluted over the years. There were those among the Fairies, not of the royal blood, who still retained the power of the ancients, the power to Shape the world and command others, to lead them to greatness. Someone sure and strong had to take command of the Faerie, or the land would continue to weaken until at last it succumbed to the shadow. The old fool had to be replaced.

It was treason, of course. Her very thoughts were treason. If the King possessed the Talisman of Unity, he would instantly know if one of his people was plotting against him. The thought made her shiver. If she expected to maintain her charade as the King's loyal servant, she would have to arrange an audience for Michael and the others. To do otherwise would arouse suspicion. Elsendarin and Lorn *Narnsahn* were respected among the Fair Folk; there would be no good reason to deny them their request. Only, they would present the Talisman to the King and all her planning would fall to nothing.

Still, she was a reader, and as such she had the power to shield her thoughts. Perhaps she could keep her secret for a time. She didn't know how long she could do so against one who possessed the Talisman. She had not yet been born when last a king held the tool, and she knew too little about it. In all her three-hundred years she had never learned much about its powers.

And yet, even discounting the Talisman, new fears stirred her. Those she plotted with wanted to dethrone the King for intentions less noble than her own. She knew they were using her, just as they knew she was using them. She feared what they would do if she allowed them to gain the upper hand. But more than that, she feared Alec Mason. She didn't completely understand her vision of him, but she felt something inside him…something dark and powerful and waiting to be released. His soul was different from anyone else's she had ever read. It was bigger. Much bigger.

She was not sure what this meant. She had never thought of souls in terms of size before. The souls of the Fair Folk burned more brightly and purely than those of most humans. Human souls were gray, but solid and strong. Shapers, both human and Fairy, had shining white souls. Sorcerers had souls black as night. But size was not an issue.

Alec's soul was black. Not black like the shadows of night, but black like an utter void and vast as the heavens. She was almost swallowed by it, lost forever in his eternal darkness. She had never, ever felt anything like it. A sorcerer's soul was like the light of the sun compared to Mason's.

And yet she had felt the good in him. He was a simple man, a baker's apprentice, and he longed for nothing except to lead a simple, quiet life. He bore no ill will toward anyone, save perhaps Salin Urdrokk. Yet somehow there was a darkness inside him as big as the world. She shuddered, thinking perhaps this was all the more reason to go ahead with her plan. That someone like Alec Mason would come now, at so critical a juncture, was a sign of some sort. She knew how to read signs.

She spun at the sound of soft footsteps upon the wooden floor. It was Rhyan. He stood at ease, his hand resting gently on the hilt of his sword. He was grinning.

"What is it?" she said.

"The time has come," he replied. "In perhaps a week, no more than two, all of our plans will be set into motion."

"Why now, so soon?" she asked, knowing the answer full well.

"Because of our guests. We will have to play our hand early before the Talisman of Unity can attune itself to the King, before he learns to use it."

"What of our ally? We have been working with him out of necessity, but you know as well as I he cannot be trusted. This situation with the Talisman casts a whole new light on things."

"I agree, but we must press on as planned. He has sent a message to inform us we must not delay. The timing is more critical now than ever. Once the King is dethroned, we can deal with our friend. Remember, this is our place of power, not his. If he thinks to betray us, he will spend eternity regretting it."

Devra nodded. "I know you are right. I just was not ready for this. What will we do with the Talisman? Certainly we must keep it out of *his* hands."

Rhyan raised an eyebrow. "Of course. We will simply have to keep it safe until a new King is named…someone strong who can return Faerie to greatness. Someone with power. In his hands, the Talisman will forge our people into the mighty race we were meant to be."

She regarded him carefully for a moment. There was something in his smile she did not like. He was right, though. They had to act soon or all would be lost. "Very well. Tomorrow, our guests will have their audience with the King. Next week, there will be a revolution. I hope Elsendarin and the others are safely away from our land by then."

"They will not go. They fear Urdrokk and will want to remain here because they think it will be safe. You must not warn them otherwise. It would be detrimental to the plan."

She frowned. "Yes, secrecy is of the utmost importance. I will have to find a way to keep them from harm."

"Do not lose focus of the plan for a group of humans. Remember, what we do is for the good of Faerie."

She felt her cheeks flush with anger. "Do not presume to tell me! You are getting too full of yourself, Rhyan. I am still the Lady of Lehnwood, and you are under my command. Go now, and trouble me not until morning. I have much to think upon."

"Yes…my lady."

With a grin that seemed close to a sneer, he bowed and left. Devra wondered what had gotten into him. Rhyan hadn't always been like that. She supposed it was the stress of plotting treason. That, coupled with the knowledge of just whom they were plotting with.

If she regretted anything, it was that Elsendarin wouldn't have approved of what she was doing. He would never understand. She loved him, and if Fairies and humans were permitted to mate, she knew he would have been hers long ago. But, despite being older than she herself was, Elsendarin was human. She knew if his seed had ever mingled with hers, she would have committed an infinitely greater treason than the one she was now contemplating. Treason not only against Faerie, but against the One himself. A young Fairy had been hanged for mingling with a human woman during Devra's lifetime, the only time in a thousand years the Fair Folk had executed one of their own. The crime was serious, for the consequences could be dire.

She returned to looking out her window, wondering how she would live with herself after the next few days. Especially if anything happened to Elsendarin or even Lorn. She would have to find a way to keep them out of the way, somewhere where they would be safe and could not interfere. In a way, it was a blessing Elsendarin had lost his ability to Shape. If he had not, he would certainly have tried to stand in her way. As it stood, he was powerless to stop her. She would commit treason. She would save Faerie.

The One help me.

Night closed in over Faerie as Michael walked alone under the stars. The trees glimmered with the silver glow which made it clear beyond doubt this was a place of magic. Seeing this land at night almost brought a tear to his eye. Even jaded as he was, he could not help but be moved by the sight of magic made visible. The stars were brighter here too, the sky clearer. He felt like he had come home.

His heart yearned like it had not yearned in years. He had been numb, almost emotionless, for as long as he could remember. It was the only defense against the horror in his heart. But now, seeing this land, seeing Devra, had opened him to his emotions. He felt joy again, and longing, and pain, and horror. Faerie had a way of opening one to deep emotions; for this reason above all others he had wanted to avoid coming here. He knew it would break his heart.

Seeing Devra, the love he could never have, broke his heart. Seeing the beauty of Faerie, knowing someday it would fall before the Seth, tore him apart. This was the only place in the world evil had never touched. But its day was coming.

A voice behind him made him turn.

"I have been looking everywhere for you," said Lorn.

He stood there, his long dark hair removed from its pony-tail and falling gracefully about his shoulders. He had shaven his face, and Michael was surprised at how different he looked. He was a strikingly handsome man, with dark skin and firm, strong cheekbones. Michael would have been more surprised if he had not known good looks ran in Lorn's family. Good looks, and much, much more.

"How are the others?" questioned the hermit.

"Asleep. Kraig wanted to stand guard, but I convinced him there was no need. They all need sleep. So do we, come to think of it, but I wanted to have a few words with you, in private."

"I thought you might."

Lorn searched Michael's eyes for a long moment. "You know who I am." It wasn't a question.

"Yes. You were careful to protect your secret, except when you were talking to the ogres, and later the Fairies. Of course, I had my suspicions from the time we fought the Ravager back on the Plains of Naar. The creature hit you with a blast of fire which would have flattened an elephant. The ability to Shape is exceedingly rare in humans. Immunity to the effects of Shaping is far rarer still."

Lorn grinned without humor. "My immunity is why I have little fear of Salin or other sorcerers. They can call down lighting from the sky or throw firestorms at me all day long, and I will not even feel it."

"Sorcery itself cannot harm you," said Michael, "but it can still affect you indirectly. If Salin lifted a mountain with his magic and dropped it on your head, you would die. The lifting was magic, but the mountain itself was not."

"I know," said Lorn, "which is why I still have to be careful. But the immunity native to my bloodline gives me a great advantage."

They were silent for a moment and then Michael said, "You assumed no one in our party but you could speak the language of the ogres, or that of the Fair Folk. You spoke of your heritage right in front of us. I did not say anything before, because I knew you wished it to remain a secret."

"You have to admit it was a fairly good assumption none of you spoke ogre or Fairy. After all, the Fair Folk use our language almost exclusively in their dealings with humans, and the tongue of the ogres is known to but a few. But I underestimated you. I knew you had been to Faerie, but I thought that was the extent of it. The way Devra talked to you taught me otherwise. Who are you, Michael?"

The hermit looked at the stars. "One who knows too much. One who has seen too much. But my secrets I will keep, for now. What of you? How did you fall from what you were to become a drunkard, a fool?"

"It is an evil tale and a longer one than I want to tell tonight. As I said, I am tired, and I believe I will turn in for the night. For now, suffice it to say I was betrayed by my brother, framed for crimes I did not commit, and sent away by my father."

Michael's heart skipped a beat as painful memories filled his head. "I, too, have been hurt by my brothers," he said softly.

Lorn frowned, appearing unsure of what to say. He offered Michael a sympathetic look and then walked off toward the hut they shared.

The hermit looked back up at the sky. The tree tops shined bright in the moonlight. He let himself admire the beauty, the magic, tracing the web of enchantment with his eyes, a web few could perceive. The web kept evil out for now, but how long would it last? Certainly not many more years, not with the power of the Seth growing in the west.

But it would last a few more months at any rate. Time enough deliver the Talisman to its rightful master and have this journey over with at last. Time enough for the Fairies to unite and bring Salin low. They might not be able to do anything against Salin's master, but the sorcerer himself would be no match for them once they were united by the Talisman.

Michael yawned, suddenly realizing he was tired, too. With a last glance into the night sky, he made his way back toward the hut.

CHAPTER 18

Revelations

Alec swung the blade through the air, completing the fifth form. The others had not yet risen, but Alec had awakened before sunrise and found it impossible to go back to sleep. He was restless, excited to meet the Fairy King and present him with the Talisman. The only thing he could think of to help him wait was to pick up his sword and practice the forms.

They were coming easily to him now. His body felt good moving through the form, and Flame felt comfortable in his hands. It felt right. He hungered to learn more and was surprised to realize he regretted missing his training session the previous night. Practicing with the blade gave him a release he needed. He knew he was learning quickly, and this made him feel good. He never would have suspected that he had any natural talent in swordplay, but it gave him satisfaction to be good at something besides baking. Even if it was something which had no practical use in his life.

He smoothly performed the sixth form, sweat flying from his hair as he spun around, lashing outward with his blade. When he was finished, he stopped to catch his breath and saw Lorn leaning in the doorway of their hut. The warrior looked different. His appearance was striking, handsome and confident.

"You shaved," said Alec. "I like the new look."

"Actually, it is my old look," said Lorn. "I've had that beard for too long. It made me look a little wild."

"Yes, it did."

It wasn't just the beard, though. He looked like a new man. His dark hair was clean and full, falling past his shoulders down to the middle of his back. He was dressed in a fine leather shirt and tight black pants, clothes Alec had not seen before. He looked almost fit for a banquet at a noble's castle, Alec thought.

"Well," said Lorn, nodding at the sword, "now you are practicing on your own time. And you look fairly good, too. I knew I could make a warrior out of you."

Alec laughed. "I doubt it. I just needed to kill some time until the rest of you got up. I couldn't sleep. With all we've been through, I'm anxious to see this resolved. And today, it ends."

Lorn rubbed his clean chin pensively. "Not really. Salin is still out there somewhere; someone will have to deal with him."

"Well, it ends for me. Once the Talisman is out of my hands, I'm through with adventure. I suppose Sarah, Kraig and I will have to stay here awhile, until things are settled with Salin, but after that I'm going home. I'll have little use for this sword training then, but maybe I'll use it as a form of exercise. It certainly is the most tiring thing I've ever done."

"It is excellent exercise, for the mind as well as the body. It teaches discipline. But for now, other matters take priority. We have an audience with a king today and we must prepare ourselves."

"Lady Devra sent word of us to the King, but are you certain he agreed to see us so quickly? I mean, we only arrived yesterday, and I imagine kings are busy people."

Lorn smiled. "Devra urged the King to see us. She is one of the greatest readers among the Fair Folk and her word is trusted. He will see us today."

Alec nodded. "I had better get cleaned up, then."

There was a water basin in the hut which Alec used to wash his hair and face. He was about to put on his old clothes when Lorn threw him a soft package.

"What is this?" he asked, catching it in both hands.

"New clothes. I went for a walk last evening, and Fendehl, one of the clothiers, offered to give us some appropriate attire for our audience with the King. I told him I had nothing to pay him with, but he gave them as a gift."

Alec unwrapped the package and found a leather shirt similar to the one Lorn wore, and a pair of forest-green pants. He dressed quickly and examined himself in a small mirror which hung over the bookshelf. He nodded with satisfaction. The cut of the shirt hid what little fat he had left, and the pants were not too tight or too loose. He had never been dressed so well.

The others were shortly up and about, and within the hour they were dressed in their new clothing and ready to go. All the clothes were similar, except for Sarah's. She wore a gown of deep browns and reds, just modest enough for decency, but cut properly to tastefully display her blossoming womanhood. Alec had no idea how Lorn had found clothes to fit them all so well, but he was glad to have something new to wear.

It was still early, but the village was already alive with activity. As the Fair Folk of Lehnwood went about their daily routine, Vyrdan came with Rhyan and a few others to summon the companions.

"Lady Devra awaits at the stables. She has ordered the stablemaster to prepare ten fine horses so we may journey to the palace. The Lady, Rhyan, Dyllahn, Landah, and I will accompany you."

"Is it far to the palace?" asked Kraig.

"No, not far. Faerie is a large land, but Lehnwood is near the Palace of the King. It is perhaps a six hour ride."

Accompanied by the Fairies, the companions made their way to the north side of the village, where the stable sat at the edge of a wide meadow. Upon the grassy clearing ran a group of horses, watched over by several grooms and trainers. Vyrdan explained that the meadow was cleared and maintained to provide a place for the horses to graze and exercise. The Fair Folk never used saddles or bridles on their horses; they treated them as friends and cared for them as they cared for their families. The horse trainers communicated with the beasts through some sort of empathy which human beings could not understand. The grooms had ways of knowing a horses needs and providing for them perfectly. A bond of friendship was formed so the horses would carry a rider willingly and gladly and no reigns were needed to guide them.

Alec was impressed, but not entirely convinced. He was no horseman, and he doubted he could ride a horse without bit, bridle, and saddle. The horses he saw running in the meadow were large, muscular, and somewhat intimidating. Still, he could not help but admire the powerful animals. Like everything else here, they were filled with an intangible health that set them apart from others of their kind. He wondered if he was worthy to ride astride such wondrous creatures.

They neared the long wooden structure which housed the stables. It was a nondescript building, but well made and clean. The wide double doors were flung open, and Alec could see it was equally well kept inside. When they entered, he was surprised none of the odors normally associated with stables assaulted his nose. He wondered at first how a place where horses were kept could smell so fresh and look so clean, but then he remembered where he was. It seemed magic had more uses than he had imagined.

The stalls of the stable were larger than any he had seen before, although his experience was limited to the little stable-houses of Barton Hills, Riverton and the Grundeye Inn. The horses were not confined to small boxes where they could not move around; they were given room to be comfortable. Large windows let in the radiant daylight, dispelling shadows even from the corners of the room. Near one of the stalls, petting the nose of a beautiful white horse, was Lady Devra.

"Welcome, friends. I trust you slept well."

"We are well rested," said Lorn, "and ready for our audience with King Elyahdyn. I am quite anxious to see his majesty and his beautiful queen again after all these years."

"As am I," said Michael, "although when last I left this land it was not under the best of terms."

"Think nothing of it," said Devra, waving his concern away. "It was a long time ago even by our reckoning. With the gift you bring to our King, he certainly can bear you no ill will. It has been generations since a king of Faerie has worn the Talisman upon his breast. But enough delay. Vyrdan, show them to their horses while I take Snowmane out into the meadow."

She spoke a word in her own tongue and motioned amiably at the white horse, which left its stall and proudly followed her from the stable. Vyrdan then led them each to a horse and then went to his own.

"All you have to do is sit upon the horse and hold on to the mane. They will bear you safely because we have instructed them to do so. They know the way to the Palace, so you will not have to guide them."

"How do they know that's where we're going?" asked Sarah.

"We have told them."

One of the Fair Folk, the one named Dyllahn, helped Sarah and then Alec onto the backs of their mounts. The other three companions managed on their own. Soon, the horses marched out of the stable and, heads held high, trotted into the meadow. They caught up to Lady Devra, who was stroking Snowmane's neck and looking to the north.

"The Palace is miles to the north-east, in the city of Fairhaven," she said for the benefit of Alec, Sarah, and Kraig. "It will take us all morning to get there.

There is no path, and the way is confusing to humans. Simply follow me, but if we should become separated, do not worry. Your mounts will find the way."

She started off into the woods at the north end of the clearing, and with no urging from their riders, the other horses followed. Alec rode beside Rhyan, who kept a careful eye on him. Alec wondered what the Fairy was worried about. After a few minutes of feeling self-conscious, he turned to look Rhyan in the eye.

"What is it?" he said. "Why are you looking at me that way?"

Rhyan's eyes narrowed. "How is it that someone like you, a human farmer with no magic, comes to possess one of the great artifacts of Faerie?"

Alec shrugged. "Not much of a story, there. It was in a chest in the basement of my friend's shop. I opened the chest, and there it was."

The Fairy shook his head. "Unbelievable." The way he looked at Alec clearly stated he *didn't* believe it. In fact, he seemed more suspicious than ever. He rode on ahead, passing Michael, Lorn, and Vyrdan to ride just behind Lady Devra.

Alec looked back at Sarah, Kraig, and the two other Fairies who brought up the rear. He gave his two friends a questioning glance.

"Did you see that?" he asked. "I don't think he likes me very much."

"Rhyan doesn't seem very friendly," Sarah commented, softy enough so the Fairies behind her couldn't hear. "I like Vyrdan and the others, but something about Rhyan doesn't sit well with me."

Kraig grunted. "I think they're all a bit stuck up."

Alec grinned a crooked half-smile. "You just don't like that they're all better looking than you."

"Who isn't?" added Sarah with a quiet giggle.

"Why, you little…" began the peacekeeper. He clenched his fist and tried to growl menacingly at Sarah, but started laughing instead.

It felt good to be able to laugh so freely again. Despite being in such an unfamiliar place, they were finally letting go of the anxiety which had been heavy upon them for the majority of the journey. If the Fair Folk were a little odd, at least they were not a danger. In the embrace of this beautiful and pure land, the companions were safe from Salin and his evil.

The forest remained bright and vibrant as they rode deeper into its heart, a far cry from the dark oppression of the Northwood. The trees were spaced rather far apart, letting sunlight dapple the forest floor. The magical, invisible glow burned strong in Alec's mind and heart, filling him with peace and warmth. He truly could remain here forever.

They rode quickly through the forest, keeping a pace Alec wouldn't have thought was safe. But the horses navigated through the trees unerringly, never stumbling, never endangering the riders. Lady Devra's horse seemed to be the leader of the group, for where she went, they followed loyally. The brisk trot went on all morning and the miles fell away quickly. Alec was enjoying the forest so much he didn't realize when the morning was gone and afternoon was well underway. He was surprised when the Lady called a halt and turned her horse to face the others.

"We are here. The city of Fairhaven lies just out of sight, beyond a dense maze of trees. Those who do not know the way could never pass through unaided. Come now, the King and Queen await."

As they progressed, Alec indeed saw the forest growing thick around them, branches forming tangled walls as the trees pressed close against them. There were many false paths through the impassible walls of trees and vines, lined with beautiful flowers and grass. The place was filled with a deadly beauty, for Alec knew Devra had spoken the truth: unaided, he would have walked these paths in confusion until he died.

It took twenty minutes to get through the maze. When the sunlight fell full upon them once again, Alec found himself gazing at a glorious city. A city of silver, gold, and magnificent trees. A city of light.

This was closer to what he had expected of Faerie, yet it was wondrous beyond his expectations. The city sprawled grandly hundreds of feet below, in a valley surrounded by forested hills, walled by the maze of foliage they had just come through. There were no tall towers like there were in the cities of humans, unless one considered the giant trees themselves. The buildings, constructed of the finest wood the forests could provide, were ornamented with silver and gold decorations. Clean streets paved with flat stone ran through the city, bustling with activity. While not as large as Bordenhold, the city was grand in other ways. The whole place was alive with magic, a magic Alec could feel with his heart.

In the center of the city, a great wooden mansion was constructed in the boughs of four mighty trees, standing together as the corners of a massive square. Held aloft by branches the size of lesser tree's trunks, the mansion's shear size inspired awe. It far larger than any building in Bordonhold, larger even than the house of Horren Addin. Alec shook his head in wonder, unable to pull his eyes from the sight.

"The Palace of the King," said Lady Devra, pointing at the mansion.

"It's incredible," whispered Sarah.

Even Michael was smiling subtly. "Indeed it is. It has been so many years…"

Michael's voice trailed off to silence, and the party looked in awe at the radiant city and the palace at its center. Even the Fairies looked at the place with wonder in their eyes. Alec supposed they seldom came here, their duties at Lehnwood keeping them busy the majority of the time. Devra alone seemed to take in the sight with a matter-of-fact attitude. Silently, she urged Snowmane down the hill into the valley of Fairhaven, and the other horses followed obediently.

Soon they reached the foot of the green hill and passed into the city. There were countless tall, thick trees throughout the city, many of which supported grand houses. The structures on the ground, to either side of the shiny white streets, were equally magnificent. Fair Folk greeted them with wonder, many bowing to Lady Devra as she rode passed. Alec could see some whispering and pointing, Fairies wondering what a group of humans was doing here, escorted by a Fairy noblewoman. Devra held her head high, but offered a friendly smile and wave to those who greeted her. Vyrdan and Rhyan rode to either side, slightly behind her. Vyrdan was given a few bows himself. He was obviously a person of some import, although not as high as Devra.

They passed homes and shops, inns and taverns, and eventually came to the base of the trees supporting the Palace. Six tall men in robes of deep red stood guard at the foot of a great spiral stair winding its way up between the trees. They bore the distinctive look of the Fair Folk, but their faces were drawn in hard expressions. They carried no weapons that Alec could see.

"The Lady Devra and her guests," spoke one in a deep but unexpectedly soft voice. "You are expected. King Elyahdyn and Queen Mahv await you in the audience chamber."

"Thank you, Brother Marn."

Once the man she addressed as Brother Marn helped her down from her horse, she motioned for the rest of the party to dismount as well. Then she patted Snowmane's head and said, "Off to the stable with you, girl. Take the others. The grooms are expecting you and will take good care of you."

Alec couldn't suppress a chuckle as he watched the ten horses prance proudly down the street, riderless. "I've never seen anything like it."

Kraig shook his head. "Every time we see something new on this journey, I say the same thing. Those are ten smart animals."

They didn't have time to watch as the horses continued around the corner, for the others had already started up the stairs. Alec felt suddenly nervous as he passed the robed guardians, who eyed him coldly as he began his ascent. He leaned toward Kraig, who was only a few steps behind him.

"I wonder why the Palace guards don't carry weapons. Maybe they're powerful Shapers."

"I wouldn't doubt it, Alec. This is the heart of Faerie, after all. If you believe the legends, it's the most magical place in the world."

"How can we not believe the legends now? Some of the things we've learned go far beyond the legends. Even the most wild of Jordi Luppis's songs seems tame compared to what we've seen."

"Alec, someday you'll have to explain to me this obsession you have with Jordi Luppis. He's a fine minstrel, but I have heard better."

Alec rolled his eyes. "There are none better, my friend. Someday, Grok willing, you'll see the light."

Kraig chuckled and patted his friend on the back. They continued around the spiral, heading upward between the massive trees until they climbed through a hole in the floor and into the entrance chamber of the palace. The others were already waiting, as were six more robed guards. The room itself was large, the walls covered in beautiful tapestries of many colors and designs, the floor carpeted in red. Elegant golden poles were spaced evenly about the room, the tip of each glowing with a magical light. Beyond the entrance chamber was a massive golden gate, open wide to grant guests access to the halls of the palace. A large skylight was set in the ceiling, through which Alec could see the tops of the trees spreading overhead. The size of the pane of glass in the skylight mystified Alec. He had not known that glass could be worked in such a way.

One of the robed figures was bowing before Lady Devra, who returned the bow slightly.

"Honor to the Lady of Lehnwood," said the robed Fairy.

"Honor to the Order of Nom," she answered. "May your guardianship of the Royal Family never falter."

"May the King continue to guide us as only he can."

She smiled and looked him in the eye. "Brother Zahn, how good to see you again."

"And you, my Lady, but there is no time for small talk. The King said to send you and your guests in as soon as you arrived."

"Then we will make haste to the audience chamber."

Accompanied by three of the robed guards, they passed the grand gates and walked down a wide corridor. The way was lighted by more golden posts, and there were large doors of dark wood set on either side down the length of the hall. The hall ended in a set of golden double doors, which swung open when one of the robed Brothers waved his hand.

The room beyond was vast and round. The floor gleamed like pure silver. Set in the walls were large windows which looked out at the city, and on the high, domed ceiling hung several large chandeliers of crystal, glowing warmly with magical light. Several Fairies dressed in white robes stood silently toward the room's center, near a raised platform. Upon the platform itself rested two thrones, fashioned of solid gold and set with diamonds and rubies. A figure sat on each of the thrones, one male, and one female: the King and Queen of Faerie.

The King was dressed in golden robes and crowned with a simple circlet of gold. He was tall and straight, and the silver hair sweeping past his shoulders remained full to his waist. His face was unwrinkled, but his eyes spoke of an age measured in centuries. He was as imposing and handsome a man as Alec could imagine.

If he was handsome, the Queen radiated beauty. She, too, seemed to hold the wisdom of hundreds of years in her eyes, but her face and body looked perfectly youthful. Her hair was dark and straight, her eyes a stunning streaked brown, her skin tan and smooth. Her dress was silver and clung tightly against her perfect from. She was crowned with a circle of small leaves.

Lady Devra fell to her knees and touched her head to the floor. When Alec saw Lorn and Michael following her example, he bowed, too. He had never been in the presence of royalty before and his heart pumped with wild excitement.

"You may rise," said a voice, both deep and commanding. "Lady Devra of Lehnwood, High Reader of Faerie, who have you brought before us this day?" The introductions were a formality, of course; the King would not have granted an audience unaware of who was to come before him.

Devra rose first, Alec and the others standing soon after. She swept her arm back toward the companions, looking up to face the king.

"Your highness, I bring before you some you know, and some you have not yet met. I present to you first the *Narnsahn*, Lorn of Eglak. He has come far to guide his companions to us, for their need is great."

King Elyahdyn raised his hand in greeting. "We are pleased you are among our people again. How is your father, who is to us the most beloved of your race?"

Lorn took a step toward the King, but lowered his head. "I have not seen him for many years. When I left him, he was healthy and still strong in his commitment to the Fair Folk."

"I would know the reason you are no longer by his side, but there will be time for such tales later. Who else comes before the King and Queen?"

Devra bowed again and said, "Elsendarin, the Wise One, long friend to our people."

The King raised an eyebrow as his eyes fell upon Michael. "Ah, Elsendarin, the human who predates even the King of Faerie. Sometimes a wise advisor to our people, sometimes a protector, sometimes a bringer of doom. You left us suddenly, many years ago. By the things you said at the time, by the anger between us, I never thought to see you again."

Alec could see something burning fiercely in the King's eyes. The Queen only smiled, putting her hand upon his.

"Be still, my love," she said. Her voice was rich and soft, feminine yet powerful. It was calming, sensual, yet perhaps even more commanding than the King's. "Let not old enmity stand in the way of reason. If the Wise One is here again, he must have an urgent purpose."

"As ever, my Queen, your wisdom outshines even your beauty. Wise One, speak your reason for coming where you are no longer welcome."

Michael looked into the King's eyes without acknowledging the harsh greeting. Standing proudly, he said, "Salin Urdrokk has returned, my nemesis of old, and yours. He seeks my young companions, for they carry something he greatly desires. I have brought them here to you so you may council us in our need. We come also to offer you a gift."

King Elyahdyn looked up and rubbed his chin. "You, the one we named wise, seek council from another? And you offer me a gift. There is only one thing I do not possess which I desire, and even you cannot bring it to me."

"Do not be so certain," whispered Michael.

Devra stepped before him, putting a hand on his chest. "My King, I also bring before you three human children from the kingdom of Tyridan: Kraig, Sarah, and Alec Mason. It is Alec who carries the prize sought by the sorcerer. It is Alec who will present you with a great gift." She turned to Alec. "Now is the time, young man. Approach the King."

Alec was unprepared for this. He had no idea how to address a king! He hesitated, not knowing what to do, but when he saw that all eyes looked to him expectantly, he nervously took a few steps forward. He bowed deeply, held the bow for several long seconds, and then stood to face the king.

"Your highne.. uh.. your majesty…um, Great King of the Fairies, I am Alec Mason, a humble baker from Barton Hills. Um, that's in Tyridan, my lord. As Michael has said, we had to flee from Salin because I found something, and, well, I think it belongs to you."

The King laughed. "Young human, there is no need to be frightened. I am not going to order you beheaded if you say the wrong thing. It is no crime that you have not been taught how to behave in court; I am sure there is no need for etiquette where you were raised. Let us dispense with formality. Tell me, Alec Mason, in plain words, what is it you bring to me?"

Alec forced himself to relax. He straightened, trying to face the King with as much confidence as Michael had shown. "I bring you this," he said.

When he had dressed this morning, Alec had taken the Talisman from the silver chest and hung it from its chain around his neck, slipping it under his shirt. Now he pulled the chain over his head, and the Talisman of Unity was revealed for all to see. He held it out toward the King, and it turned on its chain, sending forth its pure golden light as it had done in the tomb. Alec felt the warmth of it circling his hand, filling his being. In a way, he was almost sad he was about to give it up. But the Talisman belonged to the King, and it was in his hands that it could do the most good.

A shocked look spread across the face of King Elyahdyn. The Queen gasped and put a hand to her breast. The white-robed Fairies' eyes grew wide and some stumbled back in disbelief. There were gasps and mutterings and oohs and ahs as every eye fell upon the brightly glowing disk.

The King broke into a grin. He no longer looked like a king, but more like an eager child. He laughed out loud, and the Queen smiled as she looked at him. Then, the King seemed to remember who and where he was, and with great effort he regained some of his composure.

"By the One! The Talisman of Unity! Do you know how long ago, how many centuries gone, the Talisman was lost? It was my great-grandfather who last held it and carried it into battle against the horde of Vorik Seth, losing it when he lost his life to the demons which ravaged the land now called Tyridan."

Queen Mahv reached out and took her husband's hand. "The people of Faerie thank you, child, for returning to us what is ours," she said. "You do not know how much we have suffered without the Talisman of Unity. For the Fair Folk, it is natural to unite our minds and purpose as one so we may more effectively stand against the darkness. Together, our magic is mightier than the lord of Mul Kytuer himself. Without the Talisman, we cannot unite as wholly as we must. Without the Talisman, we have each of us stood alone."

"My wife speaks true. Now, we shall rise again to be a true power in the world, a force for good united under my will. Approach me, child, and bring me the Talisman."

Alec did as he was asked. The glow filled him, shining brighter than ever before, as if the Talisman knew it had come home. Heat poured through him, and he knew he, too, was glowing with the brilliance of the Talisman's magic. It felt good. It felt right. As he neared the King, sorrow gripped him that he would have to give this feeling up. But the Talisman was not his. He had no right to it. He slowly climbed the steps until he was face to face with the King of the Fairies, and he placed the Talisman in the King's outstretched hand.

And the glow was gone. Suddenly the lighting of the room, which had seemed so bright and warm before, seemed insufficient to provide for the chamber's needs. It was like a cold darkness had fallen upon them where once there had been light, an emptiness where once there was something grand. In the King's hand, the Talisman had become nothing more than a dead hunk of metal on a chain.

Elyahdyn looked at it for a second, a mystified expression on his face. Then steam began to rise from the Talisman and the flesh of his hand sizzled, and he cried out and tossed the steel disk aside. He waved his hand in the air as smoke rose from his burned flesh, his eyes wide with disbelief.

"It can't be! It rejected me! The Talisman rejected the true King of Faerie!"

No one in the room knew what to do. The Queen gazed in wide-eyed sorrow at the King, and the other Fairies stood by in disbelief. Joy had been turned to confusion and horror. Alec looked back at Michael, hoping the wise hermit would know what was going on. But Michael looked as mystified as everyone else.

Darkness pulled at Alec's heart. Now that he had bathed in the radiance of the Talisman, he felt he could not stand the absence of its light. He reached down to the ground, where the Talisman sat at his feet. As soon as he picked it up, the glow returned. It filled him and then spread out across the room, wiping the looks of horror from the faces of the people.

King Elyahdyn's jaw dropped. "How can this be?" he whispered. "The Talisman rejects me in favor of…a human child. How can this be?"

A tear dropped from the Queen's eye. "What hope is there for us now?"

Suddenly the King rose, his face becoming stern. "Leave us now," he commanded, sounding like a king again. "Everyone. Elsendarin, Lorn *Narnsahn*,

Lady Devra, even my trusted advisors. My Queen and I would be alone." Alec turned to go. "Alone with Alec Mason."

"With m…me?" stammered Alec. "I don't know what's happening here, but I'm sure there's a reasonable explanation. H…here, take the Talisman, it will work for you this time. It has to!"

"We will speak to Alec Mason alone!" ordered the King. "The rest of you will go. *Now!*"

There was a flurry of movement as the white-robed advisors and the other Fairies hurried to leave. Alec turned to his companions, but they were being rushed out of the room by Devra and Vyrdan. Apparently the Lady knew when the King spoke so forcefully, he was not to be contradicted.

The doors slammed shut. There was no one in the room save the King, the Queen, and Alec. He dropped to his knees, feeling very, very small. The glow around him faded and flickered out.

"Now, Alec Mason," said the King, leaning toward him menacingly. "Who are you, really?"

Michael felt panic pushing upward from his gut. He was being forced out of the room, leaving poor Alec at the mercy of the King, and there was nothing he could do about it. He didn't understand what was going on, and he wasn't accustomed to not understanding. There was no reason this should be happening. Alec was just a human being; the Talisman should not be responding to him so strongly. And Elyahdyn was the rightful and true King of Faerie! The Talisman of Unity was made to be used by his family! Its rejection of him was inconceivable. It was impossible!

They were lead to another area of the palace, a large waiting room filled with comfortable chairs and elegant decor. Red-robed guards were placed outside the door, elite Shapers from the Order of Nom. They said they were there to see to the needs of their guests, but Michael suspected they were stationed there to prevent anyone from interfering while the King questioned Alec. The doors were shut and Michael collapsed into a chair helplessly. Sarah and Kraig paced nervously, and Lorn simply gazed at a painting on the wall with his hands behind his back. Devra, Vyrdan, and the other three Fairies who had accompanied them from Lehnwood sat silently on plush couches.

Michael sat there for long minutes, casting his mind uselessly from thought to thought. Why did the Talisman reject the King in favor of Alec? Alec might have had some potential as a Shaper, as Michael had originally suspected, but he was a human after all. If there was more to Alec, Michael had no way of knowing. He could not see into Alec's soul.

Suddenly he jumped up. "Devra!" he cried. "Devra, I need to speak with you. Now."

"Elsendarin, I know you are concerned for Alec, but the King is wise and just. Your young friend is in no danger."

"Be that as it may, we need to talk."

She came over to where Michael was standing, and he took her arm and drew her away from the others. His companions and hers had curious looks on their faces, but he ignored them. He spoke quietly so no one could hear but Devra.

"What did you see when you looked into Alec's soul?"

"I told you already, what I saw was a mistake. I misread him."

"You forget who I am, beloved. I know you. Lesser readers have been known to make errors, but you never have. When you see something, it is always truth you see. It is not by chance you were named High Reader of Faerie."

She looked at him with sorrow in her eyes, defeated. She knew he would tolerate no more lies. "All right," she said. "I was only trying to protect you and young Alec.

"I have never seen a soul like his," she continued. "Blacker than a sorcerer's, far blacker, and as big as the world."

Michael looked at her in disbelief. "Big? You've never spoken in terms of size before."

"I know! That is what frightens me, even more than the darkness. I could never judge a soul by size before; it is not something readers do. Souls aren't supposed to exist in a way which can be measured. Size, weight, volume, these words had no meaning when describing souls. Until now. His spirit is vast. I nearly became lost in it."

Michael considered this for a moment. "Then he is something you have never seen before?"

"Yes."

"Tell me: what is his potential for Shaping?"

"I do not know. I feel the potential in him—not the way it lies dormant in some humans, to be realized only by intensive training and study. And not a potential like all Fairies have, a set strength in magic fully realized at birth. He has a combination of these traits, but how this can be, I do not know."

Michael covered his mouth as the ramifications of what he was hearing washed over him. It was simply staggering. "One forgive us," he breathed.

Then he shook his head and said, "Devra, that is the answer! Mercy of the One, I must tell the King!" He ran for the door. "Brothers of Nom, open this door! I must see the King!"

The explanation he had come up with made little sense, but that was the point. It wasn't supposed to make sense. It wasn't supposed to make sense because it wasn't supposed to happen. Ever. But it did happen. And somehow, the Talisman had sensed the potential power of this new being and had bonded itself to it. The Talisman was no longer a thing of Faerie. All bets were off.

"Open this damned door!" cried Michael, pounding upon it. The Brothers had locked them in. It figured.

The door opened slowly and four red-robed Fairies peered at him seriously. "What do you want?"

"I have urgent news for the King. I must speak with him at once."

The guards looked at one another. "No one is to disturb the King and Queen until they have finished speaking to Alec Mason."

"Fools!" cried Michael. "Do you not remember who I am?"

"You are Elsendarin, the Wise One. But even one with wisdom must wait on the word of the King."

Michael gritted his teeth in frustration. "The Wise One. Seth be cursed, why is it no one remembers the true translation of my name?" He stood up straight, a fierce light burning in his eyes. "I am Elsendarin! I am the Wizard, not the Wise One, the Wizard! I am the Second of the Three, and only a fool would refuse to do as I say. Take me to your King at once!"

The Brothers of Nom looked at each other nervously. "But...but...you are him? The Wizard? Ah...yes, very well then, follow me." They cowered, deferring to Michael. He marched out, ignoring them. He was in no mood for games.

The world was changing too fast. A sign of the end had come. The gods would soon have their way, using the Seth to spread evil over the face of the world. Not even the One could help them now.

"Wha...what do you mean, who am I really?" stammered Alec. "I'm Alec Mason and everything I've told you is the truth."

The King leaned back, his eyes narrowing with suspicion, but his anger cooling. "The Talisman has bonded with you. It will not accept the touch of another. The Talisman does not bond with humans, save those able to warp it with great sorcery. It bonds only with Fairy shapers."

"Your majesty, do I look like a Fairy? I know nothing of magic or sorcery, except that I fear it! I've been running from it for nearly a month. Please, you must believe me."

"I will judge what I must believe."

Queen Mahv put a calming hand upon his arm. "Elyahdyn, this boy has been read by Devra. She would have told us if he intended us harm, if he intended to use the Talisman against us. He would not have come before us only to intentionally betray us. Look at him; he is as confused as we are."

"I do not know, my Queen," he muttered. For a long moment he looked at Alec, and the baker felt those cold eyes piercing him. Then the King seemed to relax, forming a steeple with his first fingers as he rested his elbows on the arms of his throne. "I suppose it could be as you say. Alec Mason, you are a mystery to me. What ever are we going to do with you?"

Alec wanted nothing more than to find a place to hide from those eyes. "I'm sure there's a way to, um...*unbond* the Talisman from me. I mean, I don't know what to do with it. I don't want it. I want to give it to you, to make the Fairies strong enough to beat Salin."

"There is only one way I know of to remove the Talisman from one to whom it was bonded. That is to kill him."

"No!" cried Alec. "There has to be another way! I'm not ready to die!"

The Queen sighed. "We would not kill you, Alec. If we had to, we could easily wait until you died naturally. Our life spans are many times that of your short-lived race."

"Unfortunately, the Talisman would be useless during that time period," said the King. "Although it has bonded to you, you have not the strength to use it. You could not unite our people under your mind."

"Grok's wounds, I wouldn't want to! No, I'm sure there's another way. You have Shapers, users of magic. Surely one of them could find a way."

"Perhaps," said the King. "We will think on it. Until such a time as we reach a conclusion, you will stay in the palace as our guest. You will want for nothing. You will be treated as a visiting lord."

Alec couldn't help but feel he was more a prisoner than a guest. Still, he supposed things could have turned out worse. He knew there had to be a way to break the bond between himself and the Talisman.

Suddenly the double doors that lead into the room were flung open, and Michael came striding in. Four Fairies in red strode after him.

"Elsendarin!" boomed the King. "What is the meaning of this intrusion?"

"Intrusion?" said Michael, his voice as commanding as the King's. "I fear I must remind you of who I am. Although there has been enmity between us, I have been one of your greatest allies throughout your long reign. I bring you wisdom when you have none of your own. Now is such a time, Elyahdyn. I know why the Talisman has chosen to bond with Alec Mason over you."

The King's face was red with barely controlled anger. "Very well then, Wise One. What is the answer to this mystery?"

Michael paused, muttering something under his breath about translations. He, too, seemed filled with unspoken wrath. "Alec Mason is of Fairy blood."

"What?" cried the King and Alec in unison. Alec fell to his knees, unable to speak. Michael had gone insane!

"You are mad," said the King, echoing Alec's thoughts. "Look at the boy. He is unlovely as any human I have ever seen. He has not the look, the grace, or the power of the Fair Folk."

Michael spread his arms and grinned darkly, showing teeth. "He is also of human blood."

The Queen put her hand to her head, looking as if she might faint. The King's rage drained and his face became bone white. The silence and tension in the air was unbearable. Alec felt walls pressing in on him and was unable to draw a breath. He couldn't have gotten off his knees even if he had considered doing so.

"Seth take us," whispered the King. "Seth take us all."

"It is what we have been warned against," said Michael. "If the union of a Fairy and a human ever bore fruit, a new being would be born, a being who would have the power to destroy us all."

"A being of evil," said the Queen.

"Evil," said Alec. He was at last coming to his senses. He took a breath and rose to his feet. "Look at me! I am a baker, for Grok's sake! I come from Barton Hills. I have no ambitions save mastering my craft. I've never hurt a soul...well, not until this journey, and not if I had any other choice. I don't have an evil bone in my body!"

"Not necessarily evil," said Michael. "Perhaps not evil at all. I do not know. The old texts warned us against such a being, but the old texts are not prophecy. There is no such thing as prophecy. The ancients simply had more knowledge than we do now, and they knew there was a danger in conceiving a human-Fairy hybrid. Something new has been created, and it is natural to fear something new. But until we know more, let us put fear aside."

Alec had heard enough. "Excuse me, but I am here in this room! Stop talking about me as if I weren't. I am not a *something*, a *being*, or a *high bridge* or whatever you just said. I am a person. Just a person, nothing more."

Michael walked to Alec, calming at once. He put his hands on the boy's shoulders and shook his head. "I am sorry, Alec. You are right, of course. You are a person. But you are a very special person, and I was not aware just how special until a few moments ago. Listen to me. I think one of your parents was a Fairy."

Alec looked at the ceiling and took a deep breath. "No, that's impossible. My parents were both born in Barton Hills. My mother died when I was only six, and my father vanished soon after. But they were both human!"

"How do you know the people who raised you until you were six were your true parents?" questioned Michael. "You cannot know."

The King, face still white with horror, whispered, "How old are you?"

Alec was confused by the question, but he said, "Twenty. I'll be twenty-one next month."

A long silence hung heavily in the air. Finally, the King said, "That is when it happened. Twenty-one years ago."

"When what happened, your majesty?" asked Michael.

King Elyahdyn took a deep breath. "A young Fairy named Martyn left our land as part of a *Tynn*, a party of scouts we send out every decade to gather information of the outside world. Martyn's *Tynn* was exploring the region near Barton Hills when Martyn became enamored of a human woman. I cannot say why he would have taken a liking to a human when there were many Fairy-maidens who desired him, but at any rate he courted this woman. They lay together as lovers. Another member of his *Tynn* discovered his treachery and brought him back to Fairhaven in shackles. He was executed. The Captain of the *Tynn* claimed he had killed Karlyn, Martyn's human lover. But Captain Correth's heart was always soft. Perhaps he lied about killing her."

Darkness swam before Alec's eyes. He swayed and nearly fell over. "Karlyn...my mother's name was Karlyn."

Michael placed a hand on Alec's shoulder to steady him. "King Elyahdyn, I think Alec has been through enough for now. There is obviously much to be discussed, but I believe for the present we all need time to think and rest. I would like to take the boy to a room so he can lie down."

The King hesitated, but the Queen's face softened and she spoke. "Of course, Elsendarin. If this one is to destroy us, he will not do it this minute. Later we will meet in council to discuss what must be done."

"Thank you, my Queen."

As Michael pulled him toward the door, Alec's world rushed away from him and blackness rushed in. His knees buckled, his stomach heaved, and everything went dark.

There were swirls. Colorful swirls. Then, the swirls came into focus. He was looking at a painting. It was a painting of hills, and trees, and birds flying through the trees. He was lying down, looking at a mural painted on the ceiling. Suddenly a head came in from the side and blocked his view of the mural.

"Alec? We've been so worried about you!"

The face was the most beautiful thing he had seen in ages. Blond hair fell toward him, tickling his face. He put a name to the face.

"Sarah." He shook the cobwebs from his mind and jerked up. "Sarah! What's going on?"

She was standing beside a big bed, which he was just noticing was extremely comfortable. Standing right behind her left shoulder was Kraig. His face was crinkled in concern.

"You've been unconscious for hours. Michael brought you in here and then came to get us. He…he told us what he thinks you are."

"We don't believe it, Alec," said Sarah. "What he was saying about you being half a Fairy, it's just madness."

Alec chuckled half-heartedly, feeling somewhat mad himself. "The King spoke the name of my mother. Karlyn. Karlyn was the lover of one of the Fair Folk, twenty-one years ago. Some coincidence, don't you think?"

"Yes," said Kraig. "But that's all it is. Karlyn is a rather common name in Tyridan. Besides, I remember how things were when you were just a baby. I used to help your father, Brok, on the farm. I remember Karlyn. She loved him. She never would have gone with some Fairy."

"Maybe," said Alec, pulling his knees up and resting his head on them. "I don't know what to believe anymore. Ever since Salin came into my life everything's gone mad. I don't think things will ever go back to the way they were. Maybe I am just some bizarre half-breed."

Sarah threw her arms around him and squeezed him tightly. "I don't care what you are, Alec Mason. You're my friend and nothing else matters to me."

He felt her arms around him and some of the grief lifted from his heart. He returned her hug and kissed her lightly on the cheek. "Thank you, Sarah. You mean the world to me."

They held each other for a long time, until at last Kraig said, "Um, would you like me to leave?"

Sarah broke away from Alec with a little giggle. A tear was rolling down her cheek. Alec couldn't help but smile, even though confusion still tore at his soul.

"No, that's all right," said Alec. "I need both of you right now."

Suddenly the door swung open and Michael leaned in. "Sorry to interrupt, but we have to go."

"Go?" asked Kraig. "Where?"

"To the Grand Hall of the Council. There is much which needs to be resolved."

"Resolved?"

Michael looked grim. "I'm sorry." He looked infinitely weary as his grieving eyes fell upon Alec. "The Council meets to decide if Alec lives or dies."

CHAPTER 19

Betrayal

The Grand Hall of the Council was as large as the reception room in which Alec had met the King and Queen, but it seemed less spacious than it was since it was packed from wall to wall with people. Alec could scarcely believe his eyes when two Brothers of Nom led him and his companions into the room. Long rows of semi-circular wooden tables faced a grand marble table in the front of the room. At the wooden tables sat scores of Fairies, many dressed in red robes and a few dressed in white. Sitting behind the marble table, between more of the red and white robed Fairies, were Lady Devra, and in the center, the King and Queen. To Alec's surprise, Michael took the last open chair at the front table.

The Brothers ushered Alec, Kraig, and Sarah to a smaller table near the front, where Lorn sat waiting for them. The handsome warrior wore a worried expression. When they were all seated, he leaned in toward Alec.

"A fine mess you've landed in now, Alec Mason. I never would have guessed you were half Fairy."

"I'm not!" Alec replied.

"For your sake, I hope not. According to the oldest books of knowledge, crossing human and Fairy blood would produce a being of incredible power and an unrelenting capacity for evil. They will have to kill you if it proves true."

"Grok!" cried Alec. "This is insane. What power have I ever displayed? What evil? To think I fled from Salin into the hands of these lunatics."

"This is Michael's fault," said Kraig, his hands balling into fists. "He put this ludicrous idea into their heads."

"Do not judge him harshly. Not yet. Let us wait to see how this plays out."

Suddenly the King raised his hand and the murmurs of conversation throughout the room went silent. He gazed with iron eyes at the people seated in the room. When he spoke, his voice was rich with authority and power.

"My trusted advisors and councilors, Brothers of Nom. Today we are here to sit in judgment of one known as Alec Mason, one who has come to us bearing the one artifact which can save our people from the shadow, and one who very well may hold the power to destroy us all. He claims no knowledge of such power, just as he claims that had he power, he would not use it for evil. But our ancestors warned us against the coming of one such as he, one with both Fairy and human blood. For he is the son of Martyn of Faerie, and Karlyn of Tyridan, a human woman. At least, this is what the evidence indicates.

"First we must decide if Alec Mason is what we think him to be. Then, we must decide if he poses a threat. Lastly, we must decide what to do with him. Lady Devra, you have read this one. The Council would hear your thoughts first."

Lady Devra stood and bowed to the King. She looked at Alec sadly, and perhaps a little fearfully. "My King, councilors and Brothers, I have looked at the intentions of this child. He came to us with no thought other than to bear the Talisman to the King. He fully wished to give it into the King's hands and be done with it. He feared the sorcerer who had hounded him across the miles. He not only feared for his own life, but for the lives of his friends. For the lives of anyone whom Salin might harm. Believing himself powerless against the sorcerer, he nevertheless risked his life many times to keep the Talisman from the hands of evil. His courage shines pure, as does his heart. I saw no evil within him.

"But I have looked into his soul and have seen horror there. I perceived a vast darkness like I have seen in no other being. He cannot be human and he cannot be Fairy. He is something entirely new, something I have never seen in all my years as High Reader. He has potential for Shaping, both in the way a Fairy does and in the way rare humans might. He has both innate ability and potential to strengthen his ability through study and practice. No one should have both. He breaks the rules. I believe the only way this could be true is if he were of mixed blood. He is a hybrid of Fairy and human."

There were gasps and mutters throughout the room. Alec heard one voice cry out, "Kill him now!" The King raised his hand again and all fell silent.

"I will now hear the wisdom of Councilor Syndar, First Advisor to the Throne."

A tall, white-skinned Fairy, even slimmer than most, stood. He had been sitting at the head table, to the right of the King. He bowed slightly and turned a harsh look on Alec.

"The ancients were wise beyond our comprehension. The old texts were written by them as proof against an age when their wisdom would be forgotten in the deeps of time. We no longer know how they came by their knowledge, and we do not understand their reasoning, but we know what they wrote in those texts. A passage in those texts explains in no uncertain terms that mixing the blood of the Two Races would produce a hybrid with the power to destroy us. The power to destroy us! They say such a being would hold a dark magic, the magic of death. I can interpret this in no other way: the one who stands before you is evil! An abomination! We must waste no time. I speak for the Council when I say that he must be put down before he can do us harm."

Alec's strength was draining from him. Everything was happening so fast. They wanted him dead!

King Elyahdyn thanked Syndar for his wisdom and then said, "Father Sang, high commander of the Order of Nom, what is the word of the Order?"

A red-robed Fairy with extremely dark hair and skin leaned forward. He was broad and tall and was as powerful a presence as the King himself. He did not stand, but simply folded his big hands in front of him. He smiled, showing a row of perfect, white teeth.

"To preserve Faerie, he must die," was all he said.

Alec's heart gripped in panic. The King rose.

"I have heard the judgment of my reader, my advisors, and my protectors. I fear there is little more to be said. I grieve for you, Alec Mason, for I understand you do not know what you are. I grieve for your friends who will miss you. But for the good of Fairy, I must pronounce this doom upon you: At dawn, you will d…"

"Sit down, Elyahdyn."

All heads turned to see who would address the king in so disrespectful a fashion. There were gasps of horror from all corners of the chamber. Alec turned, too, and saw Michael standing, fists on the table, anger burning in his eyes. Alec had seen Michael angry once, when he was discussing the evil of sorcery, but he had never seen him like this.

"*What did you say!*" roared the King.

"I. Said. Sit. Down." uttered Michael with controlled rage. "You know me as Elsendarin. I am the Second of the Three. I am called by some the Wizard. I hold a place on this Council, as do my brothers, and I will be allowed to speak."

"You are no longer welcome in our land, Elsendarin. I suffered you to sit at this table in respect of our old customs, but your voice will not be heard. And you will not speak to me without the respect due to me."

Michael pounded on the table. He looked wild with rage. "My respect must be *earned*, Elyahdyn! You have earned it in the past, but today you play the part of the fool! I do not respect fools. You claim to respect old customs. If this is the case, you must hear me this day. Remember, your station as King requires you to follow the strict protocol of Faerie. Failure to do so is grounds for removal. Certain members of this council are empowered to remove you from your station, at least until you surrender to protocol."

"What? You speak treason!"

"I speak *Law!* The First Advisor, the Father of Nom, and the First of the Three are all empowered to remove you. In the absence of the First, the power falls to the Second. It falls to me."

The King was seething. He spoke slowly, deliberately, barely controlling his rage. "Protocol. Very well, then, Wizard, you may speak."

Michael grinned viciously. But when his eyes met Alec's, he sobered. "Your Majesty, councilors, if you kill Alec Mason, you are all utter fools."

Gasps of horror and rage rang out. This was scandalous!

"I have traveled far with young Alec," he continued. "I have seen what a special young man he is, courageous and filled with good will. I have seen him leap into battle with the dead of your Faryn-Gehnah, against impossible odds, to save our companion Lorn. He had no chance against those undead horrors, but he did not even pause to think of his own life. He was prepared to die to save Lorn.

"But he did not die. Instead, the dead bowed to him."

There had been murmured reaction at the mention of the Fairy tomb, but Michael's last revelation caused gasps of disbelief.

"Yes! Those sad creatures in the tomb which you avoid at all costs bowed to Alec! They named him the Cursebreaker, saying he alone could break the curse and restore the sanctity of that once-hallowed shrine. Kill Alec, and you will never regain your most precious burial ground.

"But that is the least of it. Consider the words of the old texts. I have read them many times. 'Avoid a coupling of one of the Fair Folk with one of the newcomers, the humans. For out of such a union will be born one with the power to destroy us, one who holds a dark power, the magic of death. The mingling of the blood of the Two Races brings forth the doom of our people.'

"These words are vague. They represent knowledge lost to us, lore we no longer fully understand. Remember, however, the ancients, though wise, could not see the future. They say the new being will 'have the power to destroy us.' They do not say he *will* destroy us. They tell us he has the magic of death. I, too, have magic which can bring death. So does each and every Brother in the Order of Nom. The text says he 'brings forth the doom of our race.' The word 'doom' carries connotations of darkness and death, but this is not what the word means. It means destiny. This one could lead the Fair Folk to their destiny. If he is dead, he certainly cannot do so.

"And remember this above all: the Talisman of Unity chose to bond with him. The Talisman has, in the past, *always* chosen to bond with the most pure, most powerful, and most glorious of the Fair Folk. It has always bonded to your king. Those with less than pure intentions it rejects, as it rejects those without the power to use it properly. Salin, had he captured it, would have been able to force the Talisman to accept him, since he derives his power from Vorik Seth, who had a hand in creating it. But Salin is the exception to the rule. Any other who sought to do the Fair Folk harm, or guide them with evil purpose, would never be bonded to the Talisman.

"It has chosen Alec. It has a mind of sorts, a will, as do all the greater artifacts of Faerie. It can read a man's heart and soul, much like Lady Devra. And like the Lady, it cannot be fooled. Since it has chosen Alec, we can rest assured he will not bring us to evil. If he brings anything at all to the Fair Folk, it will be only your destiny. And destiny, my friends, is unavoidable in any case."

He paused and took his seat, his anger and passion gone. He turned his gaze toward the king and sat silently, awaiting a response.

The King remained silent for a long while. He whispered something into his Queen's ear, and she nodded and whispered in his. At last he turned toward Michael and spoke.

"We are forced to acknowledge there is wisdom in what you say. But if we are not to kill him, what should we do with him?"

Michael smiled. "It is simple. We must train him. He is bonded with the Talisman, but he has not the knowledge nor power to use it to unite the Fair Folk. He can lead us to our destiny, and a great one it may be, but he cannot lead us if he does not know how. I will guide him in the Seven Laws, along with any other Shapers who wish to participate in his training. King Elyahdyn, you and the councilors should school him in the ways of government, so through him you may justly guide your people's hands and minds. You are the King, and you must continue to rule, but you cannot guide your people to their destiny, not alone. You need Alec."

The King stared into the crowd, a blank look on his face. Without turning, he said, "First Councilor Syndar, what say you to the words of Elsendarin?"

The Councilor stood. "He speaks wisely, your majesty. You should consider his words."

"Father Sang?"

The burly Fairy tensed under his robes. "I do not trust this Elsendarin. He abandoned us decades ago. I still say the boy dies."

The King, looking somewhat torn, again whispered with the Queen. Alec had the feeling, although King Elyahdyn ruled, he valued his Queen's opinion above all others, even, perhaps, his own. Alec liked Queen Mahv, but he wasn't sure he trusted her with his life.

The King rose, motioning that everyone else should rise as well. Everyone did. He spoke in his deepest, most commanding voice.

"This, then, is the judgment of the King of Faerie. This judgment is final. On this day, Alec Mason is proclaimed a citizen of Faerie. He is to be treated with the kindness and respect you would give to any of our people. He is to be taught the Seven Laws so he may learn to harness his natural ability to Shape, and he is to learn the ways of a ruler so he may kindly and justly bring our people into union with one another by the power of the Talisman of Unity. We will teach him so he might, one day, teach us. He represents our destiny."

There was some scattered applause, a few cheers, and many moans of disagreement. Father Sang pushed his chair back in disgust and strode away from the King, the other Brothers in tow. As he passed by Alec's table, he spared him one last, disdainful, look. His eyes made Alec's guts writhe.

He looked over at his companions to see them smiling at him. Sarah, especially, wore a wide grin. She leapt out of her chair, ran over to him, and threw her arms around him.

"Oh, Alec, this is wonderful! Not only will you live, but they are going to teach you marvelous things! They've practically made you one of them!"

Her arms felt wonderful around him, but nothing else about the situation pleased him in the least. "Sarah, this is horrible! I'm glad they're not going to put me to death, and I'm eternally grateful to Michael for what he said up there, but I'm going to be like a prisoner here! I have a feeling I'm not going to see home for a very long time."

She pulled away, her smile vanishing. "I'm sorry, Alec. I thought you'd be happy to stay here a while."

Lorn leaned toward him, placing a reassuring hand on his shoulder. "Alec, you have an opportunity very few people have. You are going to learn to be a Shaper. By Lars, boy, do you know who you are going to be trained by?"

"Well, by Michael. That's what he said."

"Yes!" exclaimed Lorn. "By Michael! By Elsendarin, the Second of the Three."

"The Three," whispered Alec. It was just registering in his mind. He remembered Michael telling them the story of Salin Urdrokk's fall from grace, centuries upon centuries ago, when he betrayed the King of Eglak and led his army into a trap. They were in a canyon, surrounded by the forces of Vorik Seth, and would have perished but for the intervention of the mighty Shapers known as the Three.

The revelation filled Alec. He couldn't believe it. "Wounds," he breathed. "How old is he? When was Michael born?"

Lorn shrugged. "A thousand years ago? Two? No one knows much about the Three. It is said not even they remember their origins. It is whispered the Three were placed in the world by the One in order to stand against Vorik Seth. If not for their intervention, he would have taken us all long ago."

Alec had about a thousand more questions, but before he could ask even one of them, Michael stood before him. So did King Elyahdyn and Queen Mahv. It was the Queen who spoke to him first, a warm smile upon her perfect face.

"Alec, we are more than honored to have you as one of our people. Thank Elsendarin, for his wisdom saved us from making a grave mistake. If there is anything you need, come before my husband and me and we will see it is provided."

The King sucked his bottom lip, as if reluctant to speak the words he had to say. Finally, he forced a smile and said, "As the King, I seldom have to admit when I am wrong. Truth be known, I am seldom wrong. But today, I would have sentenced you to death if not for the wisdom of Elsendarin. His name might mean 'Wizard,' but I believe the title Wise One fits him just as well. He, like you, will always be welcome among our people."

Michael straightened, and Alec saw him standing proudly for the first time since he'd known him. The former hermit turned to Alec and said, "You have much to learn, young one, and here, in Faerie, there will be plenty of time for your schooling. I have other matters to attend to for now, for I have been away from this place for many years and must reacquaint myself with some of these folk. I would especially like to have a talk with Father Sang. Take the rest of the day and all of tomorrow to relax and recover from your journey. The following day we will begin your training."

He walked off, and the King and Queen followed. There was quite a commotion as the room cleared out, and before long, he was sitting alone with Sarah, Kraig, and Lorn.

"Oh, Alec," said Kraig, slapping his younger friend on the back. "Out of the frying pan and into the fire, as they say." He laughed.

"Well," said Alec, "I guess it's better than being executed. Besides, when they find I have absolutely no talent for magic, they'll let me go. I'm still sure there is a way to break the bond between me and the Talisman." But as he looked hopefully at the Talisman dangling from its chain about his neck, he wasn't as sure as his words implied.

Lorn got up and stretched. "Perhaps you're right, Alec. But you had better at least try to learn something about this Shaping nonsense, or the King might change his mind about hanging you. For now, though, I could use a bit of exercise. What about you? Bring that sword of yours."

Alec smiled. "So I get to continue my training with you, too?"

"Of course. I have nothing better to do right now, and you still need a lot of training before I'm convinced you won't poke your eye out with that thing."

Laughing, Alec said, "Well, then, we have some work to do."

He excused himself, hugging Sarah and patting Kraig on the back. He raced out after Lorn, feeling somewhat giddy with relief. He was alive, and he was going to stay that way. He went to his room to retrieve his blade, looking forward to the work-out ahead.

"Are you ready to begin?" asked Michael.

Alec was standing with Michael in a wooded park near the palace of Fairhaven. They were both dressed in simple brown robes which Michael had borrowed from the Order of Nom. Trainees of the Order wore brown robes, Michael had told him, because red was reserved for those who had mastered the art of Shaping.

It was the morning of the second day since their audience with the King. The previous day, Alec had walked through the city with Kraig and Sarah, the three of them filled with wonder as they explored. The Fair Folk were equally impressed that a group of young humans had come to visit their city. Many of the younger Fairies had never seen humans and had many questions. Alec was especially fond of a boy named Gryn, who by appearances seemed several years younger than Alec, but in reality was nearly sixty years old. Among the Fair

Folk he was still an inexperienced child, and he was awed when Alec told him the story of his journey from Barton Hills to Fairhaven. Gryn walked with the companions most of the day, showing them the sights. By the time he lay down to sleep, Alec felt as exhausted as he had during his days of tramping through the wilderness.

Today he had been awakened early by Michael, who gave him the robe and took him out into the park. This was the day he was to begin his training. He laughed to himself at the prospect of learning magic. The sword was one thing, for even a humble baker could learn a few tricks with a blade; this was quite another.

He sighed, feeling absurd dressed in the flowing robes. "I suppose I'm as ready as I'll ever be. What do we do first?"

Michael patted him on the shoulder and gave him a subtle smile. "First, we walk." He began to head off through the park.

Alec trotted to catch up. "Just walk? I thought I'd have to, you know, do some concentration exercises or something. Learn to feel magic."

Michael laughed. "You already can feel magic, Alec. You can feel the difference in the air between this place and anywhere else you've been, can't you? You can feel the health of these woods."

"Well, sure I can, but can't everyone else?"

Michael shrugged. "To an extent. Magic this strong can touch even the hearts of those who have little or no talent for it. But you can feel it more strongly. Your Fairy blood is attuned to the One."

Alec nodded, although he didn't understand. He still wasn't convinced about this business of him being part Fairy. "So we're just going to walk? What is *that* going to accomplish?"

"It is a pleasant day, and I thought perhaps a walk might serve to clear our minds. There is much I must teach you, and we do not have to be sitting in some stuffy room for your lessons. We can achieve as much out here as anywhere."

"All right," said Alec. "What am I to learn first?"

"Eager to begin? Very well, then, the first thing you must become familiar with are the Seven Laws. Learning the Seven laws is the first step. Believing in them is the second. The third and hardest step is believing in yourself. Once these steps are accomplished, you will be well on your way to becoming a Shaper.

"Even before you set upon the path of the Seven Laws, however, you must accept the One as your guide and master. Only by the power of the One is magic made possible."

A puzzled look crossed Alec's face. "You've spoken of the One before, but you've never really explained what it is. Is the One a god?"

Michael shook his head. "Not in the sense your Grok is a god. The One is at the same time more than a god, and less. The One is all around us. Everything we see is a part of the One, everything that grows or lives upon this world is an extension of the One. The plants, the trees, the animals, and the birds are all the flesh of the One. The rocks, the soil, these are his bones. Water and air are his lifeblood and fire is his passion. Even the Fair Folk are part of the One."

"What about us?" asked Alec. "I mean, humans?"

Michael frowned. "Humans alone upon this world are separate from the One. I do not understand how this can be so, but mankind stands alone. We are not of the One, yet we can accept the One as our guide and learn to feel and use his power. In fact, the few humans who have the potential to become Shapers can become more powerful than any of the Fair Folk. An extreme few, like me, can become far more powerful."

"How can that be true? If Fairies are part of the One, they should be stronger."

"A Fairy's spirit resonates in sympathy with the spirit of One. Since this is so, a Fairy can become no stronger in Shaping than the resonation of his spirit will allow."

"What?" Alec was mystified.

Michael chuckled. "Compare it to the strings of a lute. Say you have two lutes but they are tuned differently. The first string of each lute should play the same note, but they do not. The notes resonate differently, creating dissonance. Understand?"

"So far."

"Imagine the first lute is a Fairy and the second is the One. Some Fairies are very out of tune with the One, and they can Shape only weakly. Some are closer in pitch, more in tune with the spirit of the One. The closer the Fairy is in pitch to the One, the better he can Shape. No Fairy ever resonates exactly in sympathy with the One. If this were to happen, the Fairy would be of equal power to the One, virtually all-powerful. Nothing would be able to overcome such power."

Alec nodded his understanding and Michael continued. "Now, Fairies cannot change the pitch at which their spirits resonate. What they are born with is what they have for life. Thus, a Fairy whose pitch is far out of tune with the One will never be a strong Shaper, no matter how much they train. A Fairy who resonates more closely with the One can learn to be a mighty Shaper with only minimal training. But their power is set at birth. They can never improve.

"Humans are not like Fairies. Since they are not of the One, not tied to the One in any way, their spirits do not resonate in sympathy with the One. We are like lutes so severely out of tune we don't sound like lutes at all. But here is the difference: humans are not tied to the One, so the pitch at which our spirit resonates is not set in stone. Like a lute, we can be tuned. Through study and practice, we can tune our spirits to become closer to the One, so we may borrow his power, so we may Shape. And through study and practice, we can continue to tune our spirits until we resonate in sympathy with the One *even more closely than the strongest of the Fair Folk!* This is what the Three are: human beings who have learned to resonate almost in unison with the One. The closer a human can tune his lute string to the lute string of the One, the more powerful a Shaper he can become.

"Of course, there was one other race who walked this world, before the time of humanity, who resonated almost perfectly in tune with the One. This was the race of the Seths. It is said they were born of the One to be the shepherds of the world, to guide the lesser race of the Fairies to do the work of the One. The Seths were nearly all-powerful, able to Shape the world, the One, as no one else could. But something went wrong. Instead of kindly guiding the Fair Folk, they became corrupt, hateful, filled with greed and lust. They made war on the Fair Folk and on each other. The Seths ended up slaughtering one another, and when each Seth died, his killer absorbed his power. When at last there was only one, he held the power of every Seth who had ever lived. Vorik Seth is the last of his kind, and his spirit resonates so closely in pitch with the One no living thing has the power to stand against him. He is the antithesis of the One, the Enemy. In this world, he is truly the source of all evil."

Michael's eyes went out of focus and he stopped walking. Alec waited for a moment, thinking about what Michael had said. The Fair Folk could all Shape, but their power depended on how closely their spirits were tied to the One. They could not change their spirits. Humans could not naturally Shape, because their spirits were not tied to the One at all. But with practice, they could come closer to the One. Unlike the Fair Folk, humans had the power to change their own spirit. They could learn to be closer to the One, and could eventually come closer than the Fair Folk themselves. And the most powerful of all were the Seths, who were made to be closer to the One than anyone. Now there was only Vorik Seth, with the power of all those who came before him. It was truly staggering. How could anyone hope to stand against one with such power?

Finally Michael began talking again. "But you are different, Alec. You have human blood and Fairy blood within you. Like a Fairy, your spirit is strongly tied to the One. But like a human, you can learn to change your spirit so you might resonate even more strongly with the One. Conceivably, you could become the strongest Shaper in history. Who knows what can be accomplished by the combination of these traits? This is why you are feared: because you are something new. A new idea, with an unheard of possibility of power. This is why the Talisman of Unity bonded with you. This is why you must be trained."

Alec ran both hands through his hair, trying to absorb it all. Everyone around him was delusional! "All right," he said. "I'll let you train me. We'll see what happens. But I assure you, Michael, even if my father was a Fairy, I'll never understand anything about magic. I understand bread. I'm a baker."

"Fair enough," said Michael, chuckling. "I thought you would feel this way. But I am glad you have chosen to humor me and allow me to teach you about the Seven Laws."

They continued to walk through the pleasantly wooded park, occasionally passing some Fairies out for a stroll. Alec saw lovers walking hand in hand. He saw parents taking their children out to play. For a moment Alec wished his own life could be so carefree. Michael soon went on and Alec focused on what he was saying.

"I have told you before that Shapers follow the Seven Laws. Now listen to me closely Alec, for this is of the utmost importance. By following the Seven Laws, by accepting them totally, a Shaper can do marvelous things. By accepting the fluid nature of everything around you, you can do almost anything your mind conceives, bend reality to suit your needs. You can change common rocks into gold. You can make the air glow and bring light to the darkness. You need never be concerned about hunger again, for you can turn dirt into rice or a shoe into a loaf of bread. You can turn air into fire. Mud into iron. A sword into water. Anything your mind can conceive, as long as the scale of it is within your power, you can accomplish.

"Here, then, is the First Law of Shaping: 'All things, living and not, and all energy, are a part of the One. The One is pure and good, and thus nothing done with his power shall be done for the sake of Evil.' The exception to this rule, as I have already told you, is the human race. Humans are not part of the One, but when using his power, they must obey this law. If this Law is broken, the power being used is not Shaping, but sorcery. Sorcery is an aberration, foul in the sight of the One. Sorcery derives from Vorik Seth. This Law alone is ignored by sorcerers, for even they must understand and obey the next six.”

They continued walking as Michael spoke and Alec tried not to be distracted by the beauty of the park or the people walking through it. But before he had a chance to assimilate the First Law, his instructor moved without pause to the Second.

“The Second Law of Shaping: ‘Reality is fluid, not set in stone as most believe. The particles of reality are always moving, flowing, and those who understand how can control the flow.’ It is by controlling the flow of the tiny particles which make up all things that Shapers work their magic.”

Alec opened his mouth to ask a question, but Michael, oblivious to the confused look on his student’s face, continued his lecture. “The Third Law of Shaping: ‘Energy is simply material in another form. Energy, too, whether it be lightning, fire, light, or heat, is under the dominion of the Shaper.’ These forces of nature we see around us, the light and heat of the sun, a burning flame, lightning from the sky: they, like matter, are made up of particles we can control. They, too, are a part of the One.

“The Fourth Law of Shaping: ‘The power of Shaping derives from the world around you; it is not a part of your being. The forces of nature are bound together as One, and everything touches everything else.’ The power comes from outside us. It is not really a part of us, but rather we use what is all around us. Everything is tied together, so anything you do with Shaping affects everything else. Everything and everyone in the world can be affected by Shaping. There are a very few exceptions to this Law.”

“Exceptions?” asked Alec, turning toward Michael as they walked. “What Excep…”

“The Fifth Law of Shaping: ‘All living things have a spirit. By perceiving our own spirits, we may perceive the spirit of the One. When we perceive the One, we perceive all things, for all things are the One. And perceiving all things, we may control them.’ By getting in touch with our own spirit, we can see and feel the spirit of the One. The closer in pitch we resonate with the One, the better we can see him. By knowing the One, you can actually see how the particles which make up all things fit together. Knowing this, you can learn to arrange the particles as you desire. We call this Shaping. And by the way, sorcerers replace the words ‘the One’ with ‘the Seth’ when stating this rule.

“The Sixth Law of Shaping: ‘Control of the fluid reality is done by a perfect union of the spirit, body, and mind. Without perfect union, Shaping is not possible.' There are three parts which make up every living being. We all have spirits, minds, and bodies. With our spirits we perceive the One. With our bodies we contain the vitality that allows our spirits to soar. And with our minds we understand how everything fits together. When all three are strong and united in perfect harmony, we are then able to Shape."

Michael turned to Alec and searched the youth's eyes for comprehension. "I've given you much to ponder, Alec. I fear this is all I can teach you of the Seven Laws for now. Think on them, for until you understand them you cannot progress to the next stage."

Alec stopped and put his hands on his hips. "But that was only six! What is the Seventh Law?"

"The Seventh Law cannot be put into words. It is a concept too high for language. The Seventh Law is energy and matter fused into one; mind, spirit, and body perfectly unified. The Seventh Law is power itself. When you fully understand and accept the first six, when you learn to feel your own spirit and through it perceive the One, when you feel the particles that make the world flowing through the fingers of your mind, then you will know the Seventh Law. Knowing it, accepting it, will grant you the power of Shaping."

"But how can I accept it if I don't know what it is?"

"As I said, you will know when you master the first six. Now, I have taught you all I can for today. I will put the first six Laws to paper so you may study them this afternoon and evening. Think on them. Tomorrow I will show you how to meditate so you might come to a greater understanding."

They continued walking until they reached the far end of the park, and then they went their separate ways. Michael said a friend of his at the Temple of Nom was expecting him, and Alec had been invited to have the mid-day meal with Gryn. He was glad his lesson had ended early enough so he could make his appointment. He walked leisurely down the streets of Fairhaven, smiling at the bright day. Perhaps living for a time in this magical land wouldn't be so bad. He was making friends and learning new things. When he at last returned to Tyridan, he would be one of the most knowledgeable and well-traveled young men around. He would be admired. When people talked about the town baker, they would talk with respect. Alec thought his future looked bright indeed.

Michael breathed deeply as he walked along the white streets of Fairhaven, relishing the fresh, healthy smell permeating the city. It had been far too long since he had visited the Fair Folk and their marvelous forest cities, and his heart soared to be back among them. Of course, part of his joy stemmed from having a purpose again, having a worthy student to whom he could impart his knowledge. If Alec was reluctant to accept who he was and what he could do, at least he was full of youthful vigor and a desire to learn new things. If the boy set his mind to his studies, he would do just fine.

But there was more on Michael's mind than Alec's training. He had been reading a lot lately, especially from *The Book of the One*, the text Horren Addin had given him in the Addingrove. The book was filled with facts and histories, philosophies and wisdom. Some of the wisdom, Michael thought, was of a rather dubious nature, but at the same time it made him think. It made him think about who he was, who he had been in the past, and what he and his brothers had done and could do. After all, a large part of the book dealt with the Three, of which Michael himself was the Second.

Michael thought of his brothers: Vor, the First, who was known as the Magus; and Siv, the Third, often called the Enchanter. Strange it had been so long since he had really thought about them, and so many years since he had actually seen them. He had no idea where they were or what they were doing, but up until recently he hadn't cared. Many years ago they'd had a falling out over what their purpose was, what they could possibly do to save the world from the power of the Seth, and after a heated debate in which many regrettable things were said, they separated and never spoke again. Michael had never really gotten over it, but the sundering from his brothers was not what finally crushed his faith, taking away his ability to shape. That came years later, when through dangerous and arcane rituals he sought wisdom from the gods and discovered their true nature. The gods, who sit above the world in judgment of all, whispered into his ear their plan for all of creation.

"In the end, the Seth will claim all. He is the death of all things, and it is his Destiny to return everything to the darkness from which it came. When the world is at last dark and cold, and nothing lives but the Seth himself, he will be rewarded with glory the like of which none have ever known. This is the Destiny we have proclaimed for the Seth and the World, and it was for this Destiny he was created."

In that instant Michael's faith was gone. He had always believed it was the mission of the Three to stand against the power of Vorik Seth, to eventually cast him down and end his evil for all time. But the gods had other plans. These entities of vast, unfathomable might desired the destruction of the world! Only the One remained true, but the One was not a god. The One was the spirit of the World itself, and as such was a creation of the gods. It was the

One who brought Seths and Fairies into the world, intending them to live in peace as teachers and students. Apparently the gods had other plans.

Still lost in thought, Michael found himself at the golden door of the Temple of Nom. He had reached his destination. Ever since he had come to Fairhaven, he had wanted to visit his old friend, Elder Toros. Toros was old and wise among the Fair Folk, and if anyone could offer Michael advice in his time of trouble, Toros could. He often had insights which surpassed even Michael's own.

He entered the temple, nodding to the Brothers and students he passed as he crossed the vast, golden meeting room. He progressed into a hallway in the back of the temple, where members of the Order had their rooms. Toros was expecting him, as Michael had earlier sent word of his visit. When he found the proper room, he knocked and went in.

Toros was seated at a desk toward the back of his small office, which was the first in a series of rooms belonging to the Elder. Most of the Brothers had only small rooms, but the respected Elders were afforded some luxury.

"Elsendarin!" exclaimed the old Fairy. "When I heard you were in town, I could scarcely believe it. It seems dark circumstances surround your return, old friend."

"Indeed they do," said Michael, crossing the room and clasping his friend's shoulders. "Yet this place gives me hope. How are things with you?"

Toros smiled, revealing straight teeth as white as his short hair and beard. "I have been busy in my studies, as you might well have noticed by my absence from the recent meeting in the Grand Hall. I have been trying to revive some of the Lost Arts and my efforts are near to bearing fruit. Father Sang has hindered my progress somewhat, thinking my time would be better spent in more practical pursuits."

"I am not pleased with this Sang, lately." said Michael. "He is short-sighted, and in my opinion not at all the leader your Order deserves. You would be far better suited to the post."

Toros chuckled. "Then I would really have no time for my studies! But come, let us talk about you. I know there must be a reason why you have come to see me, besides to visit socially."

Michael's smile faded. "As usual, you are right. You may have heard I…I am not what I was. I can no longer touch the spirit of the One. What faith I once had has been destroyed."

Toros nodded gravely. "I have heard as much. But you know, it is not uncommon for a Shaper to experience a crisis of faith. In times of trouble, a person may lose faith in the One or in himself. Through study and meditation, through learning how the One works his magic in the world, this lack of faith can usually be overcome."

"Of course, Toros," said Michael. "But not for one such as I. I have learned too much about the world, and I know there can be no victory against the Seth. At least, this is what I have come to believe. I was hoping against hope you would be able to shed some new light on the matter of faith."

"My wisdom pales compared to yours, my friend. What advice could I possibly give?"

"You are familiar with *The Book of the One*, are you not?"

"Of course. What Shaper has not read that ancient text?"

"I hadn't, until recently."

"Well," said Toros, "that is understandable. After all, you predate the book. By the One, you are *in* the book!"

"Yes, although it presents a much romanticized version of the Three. We can do anything, if the book is to be believed. Still, the unknown author of the text was wise in his way. He claims the words came to him, as in a dream, directly from the One himself. Of course, others have made such claims, but by the brilliance of the author's wisdom and the depth of his knowledge, I find it hard to disbelieve his claim."

"Indeed," replied the Elder. "Never has there been such a work in all the history of the world. As a history and an inspirational guide to Shapers, there is no other book like it."

"That is why it was given to me, I think: to inspire me. I have read it from cover to cover, now, and for the most part I am left cold. Yet, there is one passage which lingers in my mind, as if it were a message especially for me. In this passage the author claims: *'For when your faith is at its lowest ebb, and you are troubled by thoughts of futility, even if these thoughts are like unto prophecy, remember that the One provides for all eventualities. There is a purpose for all, even that which seems evil, and this purpose is guided always by the hand of the One.'* You know very well I do not believe in prophecy, but some things are so certain they might as well be prophecy. That each of us must eventually die is certain. Also, the plans of the gods will certainly come to pass, for no being within the world has the power to hinder the will of the gods. I have gained wisdom 'like unto prophecy' that in the end the Seth will be victorious, and he will bring an end to all light and life. Nothing the One has provided can stand against this eventuality. Even the Three, who are said to be the One's agents against the Seth, cannot approach his vast might. Others may believe it so, but as one of the Three I can say with certainty we are not his equal. Even our combined power does not come close."

Elder Toros looked at his friend sadly, but then a smile brightened his face. "If the Three are not equal to the task of defeating the Seth, then such is not their purpose. They are not what the One has provided to stand against the Source of All Evil."

"Then what is? There is nothing else. No human being is that strong, and even the greatest Fairy Shapers pale under his vast shadow. What else has the One provided?"

"What else, indeed," said Toros, smiling. "Who is to say? Can you claim to possess all knowledge of the Mind of the One? Perhaps, even now, he is seeking to provide for us. It was by the hand of the One the Fairies were given life, and the Seths as well. We are all a part of his magnificent being. He still provides for us, day in and day out, giving us food to eat, air to breathe, and a world in which to live. Would he let the Seth take all this away?"

"Not if he had the strength to stop him. But we cannot know for certain he does, especially when there are other Powers at work, Powers we cannot begin to comprehend."

"You speak of the gods," stated Toros. "Have faith in them as well, especially in the Crafter, for we have always known those who sit on high to be benevolent."

Michael frowned. "Then you do not know all I know." He grasped his friend's shoulders and then headed for the door. "Thank you for speaking with me. There is much else I must do today, so I will leave you to your studies. You have given me much to think about."

Toros smiled warmly. "And do think on it, Elsendarin. In your wisdom you may find something you have not yet considered. Once, you had faith in the One. Embrace him again."

Michael nodded once and walked out. As he left the Temple of Nom and headed toward the palace, his mind turned over the things he had read in the book and the things he had discussed with Toros. His thoughts were dark and hopeless, but he could not get that passage out of his mind: *"The One provides for all eventualities."* Could it be true?

He shrugged. If the One was providing something or someone to be set against the Seth, Michael could not see it. Without faith or hope, he continued on his way.

The next few days passed quickly for Alec. Each morning, he studied with Michael, learning the meditation techniques which would supposedly bring him closer to understanding the Seven Laws. On some mornings, Michael would give him long lectures on individual Laws, explaining in detail what they meant and how they worked. Sometimes he tried to guide Alec toward perceiving his own spirit. Alec tried as hard as he could, but the concepts seemed beyond him. Half the time, he didn't understand a word of what Michael was telling him.

The afternoons he liked better. He spent two or three hours each day training with Lorn, continuing to improve his swordsmanship and learn more of the forms. By the fifth day after their audience with the King, he knew twenty forms and had mastered a dozen of them. Each one seemed easier than the last. Sometimes he would spar with Lorn or some of the Fairies, using wooden practice swords. He found he was far clumsier with the practice swords, often tripping over his own feet or forgetting certain moves which came easily to him when he held Flame. He lost every sparring match, but Lorn seemed pleased with his progress nevertheless.

His evenings he spent with his friends. He, Kraig, and Sarah would go for long walks, visit some of the Fair Folk who they had become friends with, and sit outside talking and laughing for hours. Gryn, and some of the other young Fairies, joined them more often than not. Alec was getting used to life here, enjoying it, and he no longer felt like a prisoner.

On the third day in Fairhaven, Alec had spoken at length with Lady Devra. He liked her a lot, and she told him many of the legends of the Fair Folk. In return, he told her, in great detail, the story of his journey. She was especially interested in the golden ring which had allowed Sarah to Shape fire on two separate occasions.

"I would like to see this ring," she said. "Such items are very, very rare. And Sarah must herself be a rare person to have made the ring work. Perhaps, with training, she can learn to use the ring without danger to herself or others. It would be interesting to me to teach her something of Shaping with the aid of artifacts. Aside from reading, magical artifacts are my specialty."

He showed her the ring and she studied it for a long while. She said it was a Rage Ring, a rare and undependable tool triggered by strong emotion, especially fear and rage. With proper training, however, one could learn to bring the power of the ring forth at will.

Thus, Sarah, too, began training in the ways of Shaping. Lady Devra said Sarah was a *Nahl-Shyfir,* one who could wield magical artifacts but could not

Shape without their aid. She did not need to learn the Seven Laws, or learn to perceive her spirit or that of the One. She simply needed to learn to understand and control the workings of the Rage Ring. Within a few days, she could occasionally bring forth small flames from the ring. More often than not, she could not make the ring work, but Alec was proud of her anyway. He was also a little jealous his own abilities did not appear to be forming so easily.

Kraig, too, seemed to need something to occupy his time. He befriended an old Fairy named Gorah who claimed to be an expert at wielding a battle-axe. The peacekeeper spent many an hour learning the techniques of axe fighting from Gorah.

The days were full and they passed quickly. Before he knew it, Alec had been training with Michael for a full week. Any attempt to actually Shape met with failure, but sometimes he thought, while meditating, he could feel his own spirit. Michael told him that was good; he was progressing well. Alec thought it just might have been his imagination, though. After all, he didn't know what a spirit was supposed to feel like.

One day, Alec looked up at Michael and said, "Sometimes they call you the Wizard, now. What does that mean?"

Michael smiled. "Wizard is my title. It is a very, very old word which means someone who can wield magic. It is no longer used, except to describe me. It is especially ironic now, since I can no longer Shape."

"And why not? I can understand why you couldn't before, when you had given up on everything, but you seem to be over that now. Why can't you Shape?"

Michael bowed his head. "I have accepted who I am now. A councilor, a teacher. One need not Shape to do these things. It is too hard for me, Alec. Remember when I told you the third step in Shaping is to have faith in yourself? I have no faith. My lack of faith does not bother me anymore, for I have found other purposes to make my life worth living, but there is simply no way I can find my faith again. Not with the things I know."

"What things?"

Michael lifted his head, and laughed. "What, you would have me shatter your faith as well? Then where would we be? Come now, Alec, let us get back to your exercises."

On the morning of the tenth day since he had begun his training, Alec went to Michael's room and found him sitting on the edge of his bed, talking to

Lady Devra. They had all been given rooms at the palace, small rooms by palace standards, but larger than the old hut Alec used to live in.

Devra looked at him from where she stood near Michael's bed. "Good morning, Alec."

"I didn't know you were here. Sorry to interrupt." He started back out into the hall.

"You are not interrupting, Alec," she said. "I was just telling Michael I would like to speak to you all together. There is something I would like to show you this morning, something I think you should all see."

"I have not been able to pry any information out of her," said Michael with a grin. "But if I know Devra, this should be interesting."

"Sounds intriguing. I'll get the others and meet you downstairs."

Downstairs meant outside, at the base of the spiral staircase leading up into the tree palace, and it wasn't long before the five companions stood together with Lady Devra. Sarah still looked sleepy, and Kraig looked as if he had just been exercising. Lorn was dressed in fine leather garb, the broadsword he had appropriated from the ogre *batchen* hanging at his side in a fancy new sheath. Michael and Alec were clothed in the brown robes they wore during Alec's lessons. Everyone was more than curious what the Lady had in mind for them that morning.

"Follow me," she said, leading them into the street.

"You're being very mysterious, Devra," said Lorn, catching up to her.

"Keeps things interesting," she replied, a sly look on her face.

She led them across town, waving to the crowds of Fairies already jamming the streets. It was now well known there were humans in Fairhaven, honored guests of the King, no less, so Alec and his companions got many friendly waves and bows as well. It was strange to see these magical beings, whom until a short while ago Alec had thought were legends, smiling and greeting him as if he were an old friend. He just waved back and continued following the Lady.

Soon they came to a large stone building toward the east edge of town, surrounded by trees and overgrown with tall grass. There were not many people around, for most activity took place toward the center of town. The only other buildings nearby were the small, humble homes of the common Fairies. To Alec "common Fairies" seemed a contradiction, but of course not everyone of their race could be a lord or lady.

"There is something in here the King wanted you to see," she said. "This is where we store some of the magical artifacts we no longer use. It is a museum of sorts, very interesting if you have not seen it before."

"You store them here?" asked Michael. "I thought they would be kept somewhere more secure."

Devra laughed. "Secure? There is no theft here, no crime. Elsendarin, I think you have been away from Faerie for too long."

"I think you are right, Devra. Speaking for myself, I would be quite interested in seeing these artifacts."

She opened to door to the stone house and ushered them inside. Alec looked around, expecting to see tables and shelves full of wondrous items. What he saw, instead, was an empty room built of cold stone.

Michael turned, a questioning look in his eyes. "Devra, what…"

The door slammed shut. The light of day was shut out, and in the darkness, Alec could hear a deadbolt sliding shut. Everyone stood for a moment in shocked silence. Kraig was the first to recover his wits.

"Devra! What are you doing?" He shook the door, but it wouldn't budge. "Let us out of here!"

"I cannot believe this," muttered Michael. "Why would she lock us in here?"

Lorn muttered something Alec couldn't understand. There was silence for another moment, and then Michael spoke.

"Wait…someone is Shaping. I can feel it."

To his surprise, Alec could feel it, too. It was like the air around him was charged with electricity. He felt as if his hair should be standing on end.

"I don't feel anything," said Sarah.

"You wouldn't," answered Michael. "Someone is putting a shield around this room. Even if we could get past the locked door, we wouldn't be able to get past the shield."

"Shield?" asked Kraig.

Michael grunted. "Yes. Who ever is out there is making the air around this building hard. Essentially, they are building an invisible wall around us."

"Why would Devra want to keep us here?" questioned Alec.

"I have no idea," answered the former hermit, "but when we get out of here, I am going to find out."

There were no windows to let in light, and Alec collapsed to the floor in total darkness. He heard Kraig testing the door, ramming it with his big shoulder, but soon the muscular man gave up. His shoves accomplished nothing.

Alec could think of no reason why Lady Devra would trap them here, unless she had gone insane. She was one of the kindest, friendliest women he had ever met. She hadn't given them any reason not to trust her. Why, then, had she imprisoned them in a stone house on the outskirts of the city?

He decided not to think about it anymore. Eventually someone had to find them. It was only a matter of time before they were set free. And then, he would discover the answer. He knew there was some logical reason why Devra had locked them in here. There had to be. He listened to Lorn and Michael muttering their disbelief and Kraig cursing under his breath. Alec himself chose to sit with his back to the wall, waiting silently.

As Devra nervously made her way to the Royal Inn, she fretted over whether she was doing the right thing. All her planning, all her scheming, was coming quickly to fruition. She had gotten the word early that morning. The revolution was upon them.

She knew the King had to be deposed. She had read him, years ago. His soul was weak and shriveled; all trace of what had made the royal bloodline great was gone. No wonder the Talisman of Unity rejected him. He was no more powerful a Shaper than the lowest born of Faerie. Even with the Talisman, his will was not strong enough to unite the Fair Folk under him. If he was allowed to remain in power, Faerie would fall to the shadow of the Seth.

And yet doubts nagged at her. Few of her coconspirators could be trusted. Those dark Fairies from the far north especially made her nervous. They had always been a mysterious people, always keeping themselves apart from the rest. They were Fairies, of course, and as such were under the dominion of the King of Faerie, but even so they seemed to be a people unto themselves. The few who came to the south, ambassadors and traders mostly, rarely socialized with local Fairies any more than they had to. But since the whispers of revolution began, many of them had flocked to be a part of it.

What really bothered her was the terrible timing. If it could have been any other time but now, a time when Elsendarin and Lorn *Narnsahn* were not among them, when young Alec and his friends were somewhere far away, she would have felt better. She did not like having to lock them away, having a Brother shield the building, but it was for their own protection. Even though this was to be a peaceful coup, there was a possibility of bloodshed.

She prayed it would not come to that. The Shapers were to disable resisters without harming them, letting the warriors rush in without having to kill anyone. The King and Queen were to be taken prisoner but not harmed. The thought of holding them in a dungeon broke her heart. She liked Elyahdyn and Mahv, but they were not the rulers Faerie deserved. When a new King was in place, they would be released and restored to a position of dignity and wealth. They simply would not be allowed to rule.

She reached the Inn and entered the common room. The only people inside were Rhyan, Landah, and four of the dark Fairies who had joined the cause. As she approached the table, her eyes were drawn to Gothra l'Uarach, the dark Fairy who seemed to be the leader of their little group. She was tall and slim, and her skin was slate-gray. Her eyes were like opals, and her hair black as night. Devra supposed men would find her beautiful. Devra only found her cold and disturbing.

"Glad you could make it," said Rhyan as Devra took her seat. "We were about to begin without you."

"I still say we should have waited until nightfall," said Gothra in a voice cold as steel, or moonlight. "My people work best under shadow of night."

"You know as well as I do why we must strike during the day," said Devra. "The palace's gates are locked at night, and the Order of Nom reinforces them with powerful shields. I know there are mighty Shapers among us, but even they could not tear down the Brothers' shields."

"Very well," said Gothra. "We strike now. Five hundred of my folk wait in the forest beyond the city, fifty of them Shapers."

Devra nodded. "Our people are placed all around the city. They only wait for the sign. But remember, there is to be no more bloodshed than necessary. And no harm is to come to the King and Queen!"

Gothra grinned sardonically but said nothing. Rhyan sighed and said, "You take the fun out of everything, my Lady." Devra didn't like the twist he put on the words "my Lady."

"Give me ten minutes to get back to the palace," she said. "Then give the sign. There is no backing out now."

"As you wish," said Gothra.

Devra marched quickly from the inn, glad to be away from Gothra. The more she thought about it, the more she regretted inviting Gothra's people to take part in the revolution. It had been a necessary evil, though. Without the forces the dark Fairy brought, Devra didn't have enough people on her side to ensure success. And she had to succeed. The future of Faerie, perhaps of the world itself, depended on it.

When she was safe in her room at the palace, Devra stepped out onto her balcony and looked at the people below. They milled about, unexpecting of what was to come. She felt sorry for them, in a way, for they did not know that what was about to happen was for their own good. She wondered how many would be killed. As much as she preached about a peaceful revolution, she knew some fools would throw their lives away defending the King. She prayed the Shapers could keep those fools at bay, for their own protection.

Suddenly fire erupted in the sky, a mighty flash which exploded high in the air and rained sparks down upon the streets of Fairhaven. The sign. People cowered or looked up in shock, not knowing what was happening. They did not know the display signified the beginning of a new era.

There were screams as Devra's people leapt into action, pushing through the crowd, toward the palace. Shapers acted in secret, magically throwing bystanders against the sides of buildings, clustering them together and throwing shields up around them. A flood of dark Fairies appeared out of nowhere, running threateningly at the people with swords and bows at the ready. The people of Fairhaven fled and Devra sighed in relief. As long as they kept running, no blood would be spilled.

But what was this! The dark Fairies loosed a rain of arrows upon the fleeing people, spilling their blood upon the white paved roads. Swords were drawn on both sides, and people locked in combat. Fires raged from the hands of Shapers, burning innocents as they ran. It was not only the dark Fairies who screamed hate and spilled blood needlessly, but Devra's own people as well!

Upon her balcony, she cried out in horror. What was going on? By the One, what had she done? As utter chaos erupted on the street, she ran from her room and hurried down the hall, toward the stairs leading outside. People were already rushing around the palace in a panic: servants, visiting nobles, councilors and sages, Brothers of Nom. She had to get down to the street and somehow stop this. This was not the way it was supposed to happen.

She flew down the steps, knowing she had been betrayed. She had trusted the wrong people, taken too much for granted. Why had she not read more of her fellow revolutionaries? Why had she not even thought of it? She should have at least read Gothra. Or that other dark Fairy, the one who had come to her first. Where was he?

Seeing the death in the streets, seeing the battle raging as Fairy killed Fairy for the first time in history, she screamed in horror. There was nothing she could do! She hid her eyes and felt sanity slipping away.

CHAPTER 20

Loss

They had been sitting in darkness for five minutes when a small flame appeared, casting a bit of light around the room. Alec looked over and saw Sarah holding a little ball of fire in the palm of her hand. She grinned with satisfaction.

"This is about all I can do with the Rage Ring," she said, "but at least we can see each other's faces now."

"Devra has taught you well," said Michael. "She told me you were a *Nahl-Shyfir*, one who can Shape with the aid of enchanted items. But I still think this particular ring is too dangerous to use. Rage Rings are too undependable; they never should have been made."

"Oh, Michael, you always have something negative to say," grumbled Sarah. "A flame this small can't do any harm."

"I suppose you are right. Unfortunately, a flame will not help us get out of here."

Lorn muttered something under his breath about a sword.

"What was that?" asked Alec.

"I said, 'It is too bad Alec doesn't have his sword.' When Michael said 'flame' it reminded me of your sword. That blade might be a help to us now."

Alec leapt up. "I *do* have it, Lorn! I've taken to wearing it under my robes. I don't know why, but I just feel naked without it lately. I don't see how it could help us now, though."

"Don't you?" asked Lorn, jumping to his feet excitedly. "Let me see the sword."

Alec lifted his robe enough to pull Flame free of its new ivory scabbard. He didn't like the idea of anyone else handling the blade, but he reluctantly gave it over to Lorn. He wondered what the warrior had in mind.

Lorn took Flame over to the bolted door and held it aloft. With a shout, he brought the blade down, carving into the stone of the door. The magic of the sword enabled it to pass through stone with ease, and when Lorn had hacked at the door three times, a triangular chunk fell away. A bit of light shown through the hole. Lorn grinned. He leaned over and reached through the hole, feeling around for the deadbolt on the other side. Alec heard it slide sideways, unlocking the door. Lorn stood, pushed the door open, and walked back to where the others waited.

"Your sword, Alec," he said, presenting the hilt to the speechless baker.

"Aren't you forgetting about the shields?" said Kraig. "I mean, it's great the door is open, but Michael said there are magical barriers in place around this house."

"Magical barriers?" said Lorn. "They mean nothing to me. You four wait here. I'll bring someone, one of the Brothers, maybe, to undo the shield."

He walked outside. Alec felt a shock run through him as Lorn passed the area Alec knew contained the shield of solid air. Kraig, curious, got up to follow, but ran head first into an invisible barrier and fell back onto his behind, rubbing his forehead.

"Ouch! How in the name of Grok did he get through that?"

Michael walked outside and put his hands on the invisible wall. Alec thought he looked like a mime.

"Lorn is a rare person. He is one of the very few people to whom the effects of Shaping mean nothing. Magic cannot affect him in any way."

For a minute Alec remembered when Lorn had leapt in front of one of the Ravager's balls of fire, saving Alec from incineration. He had wondered why Lorn hadn't been killed then, why he didn't even seem to have been singed. He was still puzzled, though, how a man could be immune to magic.

"Look," said Kraig, still on the ground with his hand on his head. "What's that?" He was pointing to the sky.

There was a fire somewhere, a large one by the look of the clouds of smoke billowing skyward. Alec stood with the others just outside the stone house, looking silently at the smoke, and listening. Far in the distance, he thought he heard screaming.

"Something is happening here," said Michael. "Listen. Those are the cries of death."

They stood waiting several more minutes. The cries grew louder and closer, and Alec began to hear the clash of steel against steel. "Grok! There's a battle going on here!"

"That is impossible!" exclaimed Michael. "Simply...unthinkable."

Sarah clung to Alec's side apprehensively. "Wounds, Alec, just when things were going so well...do you think it's...him?"

Alec looked into her wide eyes. "Salin? No, he couldn't get through the enchanted webs around Faerie."

Sarah swept her hand in front of her. "Lorn got through this one."

No one had an answer for that.

As the cries grew stronger, Lorn came running back, a red-robed figure coming quickly behind him. Alec recognized him as Brother Zahn, one of the Brothers of Nom who guarded the palace.

"War has broken out!" exclaimed Lorn as he ran toward them. "People are fighting...dying...in the streets!"

"Seven!" cried Michael. "How can this be?"

"Stand back," said Zahn. He began waving his hands around, and Alec felt something happening to the air around them. He thought if he turned a certain way, squinted just so, he could see what was going on, see particles of air thinning and separating. But it was just his imagination. He was certain of it.

"By the One, this is a powerful shield," said Zahn. "I can scarcely undo it." He continued to struggle, a sheen of sweat glistening on his face. Finally he fell back, exhausted, but smiling. "It is done," he said.

Michael raced out, followed by Kraig and then Alec and Sarah. The former hermit placed a hand on Brother Zahn's shoulder and asked him if he was all right.

"I will be fine after I catch my breath. Someone much stronger than me put that shield around you. But listen, Elsendarin, you must help us! The Dark Folk from the north have descended upon us in force. Some of our own people fight on their side. Together they slaughter innocents in the streets and lay siege to the palace. The Order of Nom stand against them, but we are too few to hold them back. Please tell me Wise One, what must be done?"

Michael pulled the Brother up and turned to Lorn. "We must get to the King and Queen. They must be protected. We have to root out the leader of this rebellion and put an end to it. You three children stay here, where it is safe."

Kraig laid a hand upon his axe, which these days he never seemed to be without. "I'm coming too."

Sarah grabbed Alec's hand and said, "We all are. Perhaps we can do some good. At any rate, it might not be safe here for long."

Michael rolled his eyes, as if to show he didn't have time for such nonsense. "As you wish. But stay out of the fighting! Let us away."

They ran off toward the fire and the noise, and Alec held Flame tightly in his hand. He tried to fight a feeling taking hold of his heart, a lust for battle, for blood. His sword began to glow orange and the feeling grew. Heart pumping, he ran after the others, thirsty for war.

Gothra l'Uarach, surrounded by her warriors, made her way to the outskirts of the city. When a city guard or unfortunate citizen penetrated her circle of protectors, she cut him down easily with a casual slash of her long sword. She wanted to send her warriors away so she might enter into the fray herself, but she could not put herself at risk. She had to welcome her master to Fairhaven.

When she reached the maze of growth which was supposed to keep Fairhaven safe, she passed into it and unerringly navigated through. She knew the short path, the path only the King and a few others were supposed to know, a path hidden by illusion. She reached the other side in just under a minute. Waiting there were her fifty dark Fairy Shapers, who had stayed behind at her command. They were not needed in the battle. They would have been needed to control the populace according to the wench Devra's plan, but with her warriors striking fast and hard, striking fatally, the Shapers would have been redundant. Besides, she needed them here. They were about to do what was thought impossible.

With perfect timing, her master rode in on a massive black stallion. He wore his fair face, for some reason. Perhaps he was reluctant to let even his own people see him in his true form. They were dark Fairies, too, and had to pull on forms of beauty like they would pull on clothing, but even they might have shrieked in horror to gaze upon the true face of Drakkahn Shynagoth.

"My lord," she said as he dismounted, handing the reigns of his horse to a near-by Fairy. "It has begun. You have arrived just in time to witness our victory. How are things in the south?"

Drakkahn grinned evilly. "Things go well. Stationed every ten miles are fifty of my dark Fairy Shapers, bending back the web of enchantment so the Great One may enter the realm of Faerie and take what is his. The web must be parted here as well, and soon, for he is near."

"My Shapers are ready."

"Then begin."

She turned to her Shapers, sorcerers, really, she supposed, and gave the command. The air was thick with power as they began their work, bending the web which kept evil out of Faerie, opening the way for the Great One.

They worked quickly. The way was opened, and just in time, for charging through the forest, leading his human followers and a pack of ogres, was the Great One himself upon his black stallion. Salin Urdrokk had come.

Blood washed the streets. Swords clashed as city guards and common citizens fought in vain to beat back the invaders. Salvos of arrows fell like deadly hail from the sky, loosed by archers hidden among the trees. Magic flashed from the hands of Brothers of Nom and other Shapers, mostly in defense of the citizens of Fairhaven, but sometimes against them. Alec though he saw a red-robed Fairy casting flame at the terrified people in the street.

"Stay back!" Michael commanded. "Lorn, let us forge a way through to the palace. Brother Zahn, cover us with magic!"

"As you command, Elsendarin," said the Brother.

Lorn drew his sword, which he constantly wore at his waist as if it were an article of clothing, but Michael had to bend to pick one up off a bloody corpse. They raced into the fighting while Zahn threw lightning at dark Fairies who tried to get close to them.

Kraig stood at the ready, axe held tightly in hand. His huge arms bulged with strength, quivering to act. Alec knew the only reason Kraig held back was to protect him and Sarah. Alec, too, ached for action. His sword cried out for blood.

He wondered at his last thought. His *sword* cried out for blood? Alec must have been trying to displace his own blood-lust onto the weapon.

Then there was no more time for thought. Screaming dark-skinned Fairies raced out of the trees, waving swords in the air. They rushed past Alec, toward the palace, pushing him to the side like he wasn't worthy of their notice. He stumbled and nearly fell as more came at him. Glancing over, he saw Sarah shoved to the ground by a dark Fairy as a dozen more raced toward her. She would be trampled!

He didn't think. He acted. Flame burned orange in his hand, and he leapt into the path of the dark raiders. The first one thought to push Alec aside, but instead found himself sliced cleanly in two, diagonally from shoulder to waist. The second and third saw the mistake of the first and swung their swords in unison as they ran past Alec. Alec ducked under the swords and ran one of the Fairies through. The other spun to stab Alec in the back, but instead the baker blocked the blow with Flame, shattering the other blade. The wide-eyed attacker tried to run, but Alec took off his head with a casual swing.

The next three charged him together. He wondered if he could handle three at once, but it turned out he didn't have to. Kraig rushed in from the side, his axe coming down fast and splitting the right-most Fairy's skull. The other two hurled themselves at Alec. In a second, both of their heads were tumbling through the air, leaving streamers of blood behind them. Flame sang with delight.

The last six were more cautious. They formed a ring around Alec and Kraig, closing in slowly. Alec and the peacekeeper stood back-to-back, both breathing heavily.

"A fine mess this is," said Kraig. "I thought it was supposed to be safe here."

"If you can take two, I can handle the rest," muttered Alec. Everything looked red to him. The color of blood.

"What do you…"

Kraig was cut off as the dark Fairies raced at them, screaming. Alec heard the sounds of an axe breaking armor, carving flesh, but he had his own problems. He leapt over a sword as an attacker swung low. He immediately had to dodge as another rushed in to his left. The Fairy had a tall iron shield in hand, which Alec cleaved in two with an effortless swing of his sword. The Fairy stared in disbelief as the two useless halves of his shield fell away and a blade impaled him through the heart.

The others hesitated. It was the only opening Alec needed. Flame lashed out like lightning, hacking swords in half, slicing through armor, opening chests and necks. In the end, the four attackers he had promised to kill lay dead at his feet. He turned to Kraig, who had just finished off the other two.

"Wounds!" shouted Kraig. "That was incredible, Alec. I had no idea you had come so far in your training." His look of awe twisted into disgust as he looked at the bodies around him, at the blood on his clothes and hands. "Oh, Grok, I think I'm going to be sick."

Deep down, Alec knew he should have felt the same way. They were not killing goblins and ogres now, but Fairies. This was, if anything, *worse* than killing human beings. But Alec's spirits soared at the thought of finding some more of these slate-skinned Fairies to slaughter.

"We'd better go see if there are any more of these raiders around. We have to protect the innocent." He thought this was a motivation Kraig would accept.

He was about to race into a fight he saw breaking out less than twenty yards away, when he saw Sarah lying on the ground, sobbing. Suddenly the red tint to his vision was gone, and the orange fire around his sword faded away. He dropped the hunk of cold steel and rushed to his beloved's side.

"Grok, Sarah, are you all right? Did you get hurt during the fighting?"

He cupped her head in his hands and turned her face up to his. She managed a smile through her tears.

"I'm not hurt, Alec, but I don't want you to be hurt, either. You can't go racing off into battle. There are too many of them."

"But if we just stay here, the battle will find us."

"Then let's get out of here. The tavern over there, away from the fighting, let's take shelter there."

"She's right, Alec," said Kraig. "I don't know what good we thought we could do out here."

Alec considered. He looked from his sword where it lay on the ground, to Sarah's face. His decision was made.

"All right. We go to the tavern."

He picked up Flame, and walked arm in arm with Sarah toward the relative safety of the tavern, leaving the raging sounds of war behind.

"This way!" cried Michael, running past invaders as Brother Zahn's lightning kept them at bay. Those few who managed to get close to him he dispatched with an expert thrust of his sword. He felt sorrow each time took one of the Fair Folk down, dark or not, because he knew none of them had started out evil. These dark Fairies had always been strange, but they were always true to their King in times past. The unthinkable had happened at last. The Fair Folk had been corrupted.

Lorn was right behind him, swinging his sword like a master. He was a whirlwind of destruction, a better warrior than Michael had ever been, better than he'd ever seen. Lorn was even better than his father, and that was saying something. But even he would have been swallowed by the sheer number of attackers if it wasn't for Zahn's lightning.

They had nearly reached the palace. On the palace stairs, Brothers of Nom flung lightning and hurled fire at the dark Fairies trying to force their way up. But the enemy had Shapers as well, and blasts of energy took off several of the Brother's heads. To Michael's horror, he saw some of the Brothers turn on their own, joining with the raiders. This treason ran deeply indeed.

The raiders, both dark Fairies and others, swept up the stairs and took the palace. Red-robed Brothers fell from the stairs, clutching wounds which stained their robes an even deeper crimson. Michael tried to force his way through a cluster of people fighting, but he became caught up in it and was swept away down the street. Looking toward the palace, he saw Lorn had made it to the stairs. He looked back at Michael, wondering what to do.

"Go!" cried Michael. "Save the King!" He saw Lorn race up the stairs, leaping over bloody bodies. Then the fighting closed in tight around him, and Michael was lost in its chaos.

He swung his sword. He didn't know who to kill, so he tried to stick to the dark Fairies. They all seemed to be on the side of the raiders. Other Fairies went down before his blade, too, as he tried to hack his way toward the palace, and he prayed he wasn't cutting down innocents. Too many times a blade came close to him and many nicked him as he waded through the fray. Where in Hell was Brother Zahn? The lightning had stopped some time ago, leaving Michael open to assault.

Miraculously, he stepped out of the raging battle, which continued moving down the road behind him, gathering combatants along the way. There were still some minor skirmishes between him and the palace, but he could avoid them. Heart beating quickly, he raced for the stairs.

He never made it. Lightning splintered the stairs, the impact sending him flying backwards. He shielded his face from the rain of splinters falling around him. When he looked up again, he saw men and women on horseback, and ogres running behind them. Several dark Fairies were with them, including a huge one Michael could tell was a powerful Shaper. No. He was a powerful sorcerer.

Glancing up at the men on horseback, he recoiled in horror. One was Tor, the warrior who had gained their trust through the use of the *Charin-ta* and had nearly taken the Talisman. The other man was Salin Urdrokk.

How? How could this be? They could not possibly have gotten through the webs that protected Fairy. And yet, here they were.

Michael leapt to his feet. He could not stop Urdrokk, but he would try to slow him down. If he had to, he would give his life to keep him from Alec. To keep him from the Talisman. Michael knew he had no power to match Salin's, but he could bluff.

He hurried out into the middle of the street, his brown robes billowing around him. He stood tall and tried to remember what it was like to have power, how to look confident, intimidating. He held his sword aloft and shouted as Salin and his slaves approached.

"Hold! In the name of the One, hold before me or be struck down!"

Salin pulled on the reigns, a wide grin on his face as he came to a stop a few feet in front of Michael. "I remember you. Tor, do you remember this worm?"

"Indeed I do," said the dark warrior, pulling up beside his master. "He was one of Mason's companions."

"Yes, I believe you are right," said the old sorcerer, an evil glint in his eye. "Where is your friend Mason, worm? He and I have some business to settle."

Michael felt his courage bending under the pressure, near to breaking. He wanted to fall to his knees and cry. Instead, he said, "Your business is with me. Do you forget me, Salin Urdrokk? When last we clashed, when you brought your army to Riglak Nord, I sent you fleeing from my wrath. Though nearly two centuries have passed, I thought you would remember my face."

Salin's smile faltered, but only for a second. "So. Nul, whom the Fair Folk name Elsendarin, the Wizard, and the fools of Tyridan call Michael. You have changed much, but I can see now it is you. The Second of the Three, who years ago lost his faith and his desire to stand against evil. What has changed now, to bring you here to stand against me?"

"I could not let you have Alec Mason, or the Talisman. I have come back so I might kill you, Salin. Your evil has gone on long enough."

Again, Salin faltered. But then he leaned forward, and Michael had the impression the sorcerer was peering into his soul. After a moment, Salin began roaring in laughter.

As the slaughter continued around them, the sorcerer said, "You have no power! You bluff. I can feel magic, fool, and you have none! Your lack of faith has brought you low. I have no time for worms."

He turned to Tor and the dark Fairy who waited nearby. "Tor, Drakkahn, stay here and deal with the worm. You may join in the raid of the palace when you are through to make sure the King and Queen are killed properly. I have more important matters to deal with."

"Yes, my master," said Tor. The dark Fairy merely nodded.

Then the sorcerer swept past him, and there was nothing Michael could do to hinder him. The two women on horseback followed, as did the ogres who came behind them. Fear blocked out the noises of battle as Tor dismounted and started walking toward Michael.

"Hold him, Drakkahn. This is going to be fun."

The air hardened around Michael, forcing his hand open so his sword fell to the ground. Terror gripped him. He could not move! Drakkahn had trapped him in a shield of air, and he was powerless to break free.

Clutching his sword, Tor approached menacingly.

Devra came awake when she felt a pair of hands shaking her gently. Her head swam, her mind foggy and mired in pain. She remembered coming down the stairs, watching in horror as Fairy killed Fairy in the street. She had stood there, unable to decide what to do, when something hard struck her in the back of her head. She fell forward onto the pavement, surrendering to darkness.

She squinted, and the face looking down at her came into focus. Wide shoulders, red robes, a short white beard…it was Father Sang. She breathed a sigh of relief. He was one of the few of her coconspirators she still trusted.

She looked beyond him and saw they were in the kitchen of the palace. In the halls beyond, she heard people running, fighting. She tried to sit up, but the pain in her head made her lay back down.

"Do not try to move yet," said Father Sang. "I have not yet finished Shaping your wounds closed."

Sure enough, she felt the tingling on the back of her scalp she knew was the feeling of flesh being knitted back together by magic. She felt her swelling go down, and the pain was reduced to bearable levels.

"Sang," she said. "What happened? What went wrong with the plan?"

"The dark Fairies betrayed us. I knew from the moment you introduced me to Drakkahn Shynagoth he could not be trusted. I have always been suspicious of that strange breed."

She sighed. "You are suspicious of everyone, Father. But in this case, I suppose you were right." She paused as she sat up. Her head still pounded, but the wounds were gone. "Did you bring me up here?"

"Yes. I was forming shields to protect the innocent when I saw you fall. I raced through the fighting to bring you somewhere safe. This is the only place I could think of."

"Thank you," she said. She pushed herself to her feet. "We have to do something about this madness. I fear our betrayers mean to kill Elyahdyn and Mahv. You know I never meant for that to happen. We have to get to them, if it is not too late, and get them to safety."

Sang shook his head. "I do not know if it is possible, my Lady. I do not know if it is even wise. I do not want them to die, either, but if we rescue them, the revolution fails. After this, the people will never agree to remove them from power."

"Sang! How can you think about that now? It has all gone wrong, and we must put an end to it! Perhaps knowing their King is safe will rally the people to victory. Our erstwhile allies must be driven out, or destroyed!"

"Think, Devra! Even if we rescue the King, how will the people know? And if we do this, then the revolution will fail, and if it fails, then Faerie will fall. You yourself have preached these very words time and again."

"I do not care. I do not wish to save their lives because it is wise. I wish to do it because it is right. I cannot let them die because of me. Now you may come with me, or you may stay here, but I am going regardless."

She strode past him and stepped into the hall. She heard his footsteps following, a few paces behind.

"I cannot condone this course of action, but I cannot let you go alone. You would get yourself killed out here."

She smiled in spite of herself. At least Father Sang had not betrayed her.

They marched down the hall, past bodies of the dead and dying. In crossing hallways there were people fighting, a skirmish here and there, and the sounds of battle echoed through the palace. Sometimes people ran past them, dark Fairies and palace guards, Shapers and swordsmen. If any got too close to her, Father Sang threw them back with a blast of solid air. Soon they entered the hall which led to the throne room, beyond which lay the chambers of the King and Queen. Screams and clashing steel could be heard from the throne room, and smoke poured from the open double doors.

She raced onward, past Fairies locked in mortal combat, dodging swords and jumping over bodies. Sang was right behind her, his magic hurling to the side anyone who stood in their way. She ran through the double doors, nearly choking on the black smoke filling the room.

Death was all around them. There were a few people still standing, still fighting, but the living were outnumbered by the dead five to one. Dark Fairy invaders lay broken and bloody on the floor, side by side with Brothers of Nom, palace guards, and servants who had taken up arms to defend their King. Small fires crackled around the room, remnants of a contest between Shapers and sorcerers. She and Sang ignored those around them and headed for the doors at the far end of the room, behind the magnificent thrones of the King and Queen. Sang flung his hands outward, tossing the thrones out of the way and throwing open the doors. Unhindered, they ran through, entering the private chambers of Faerie's rulers.

The outer chamber was empty, so they continued on into the back room, the royal bed chamber. Inside, beyond the giant silk-covered bed and the mahogany dressing table, past the dark wooden desk and the wardrobes filled with royal garb, stood King Elyahdyn and Queen Mahv, guarded by two Brothers of Nom and four armored guards bearing long swords. Relief exploded in Devra's chest that they were still safe.

"Father!" said one of the Brothers. "Thank the One. We were worried you…"

His words were cut off as his robes turned to fire and roared to consume his flesh. The guard to his right found his own sword jumping out of his hand and impaling him through the chest. In horror, Devra turned to Father Sang to shout for him to help them, but his face was already drawn in concentration. A sinister smile parted his lips.

"Die!" he cried as fire leapt from his outstretched hands.

The two guards who tried rushing him were instantly incinerated by his blazing passion. Only dark ash marked their passing.

The last Brother held his hands out and lightning flashed from his finger tips. Father Sang only laughed as the lighting forked and passed to either side of his body, never touching him. He closed his fist, and the Brother's head crushed inward with a horrid crunching sound.

The last guard simply dropped dead. Devra didn't know if he died of fear or of some sinister trick of sorcery.

Father Sang laughed aloud as he threw her to the ground before the King and Queen. He took a step forward, trapping them all in impenetrable shields.

"Sang!" shouted Devra. "Why?"

"You will hang for treason, Sang!" shouted the King.

His laughter roared louder. "I will hang? Quite the contrary, Elyahdyn, you weak-willed slug! I will be regarded a hero! When Salin Urdrokk sits upon the throne of Faerie, the Talisman of Unity in his hands, I will be his right hand! I, who slew the fool King while others failed. Thank you, Devra. Without you convincing me to come here, I might have let someone else get the credit for this kill."

"One," Devra sobbed. "Oh, what have I done?"

Sang took his time, savoring his kill. He drew the shields tighter, ever so slowly crushing the life out of his three victims. His eyes were the eyes of a lunatic. How had a man so mad seemed so sane only moments before? How long had he served Salin?

The world started to go dark, a dark tinged with red. Devra was certain it was over. It was all her fault; she had brought the Fair Folk to this. Perhaps she deserved this horrible death.

"Hold!"

The voice rang out loud and deep behind Father Sang, and he spun to face it. A warrior holding a sword was rushing into the room, but raging fires sprung up around him, roaring like thunder, hot as the sun. Grinning, Sang turned back to his victims.

"I said *hold*, traitor!"

The figure stepped out of the inferno, unhurt. Sang's jaw dropped as he spun again. He threw lightning as the warrior rushed him, drawing his sword back to strike. The lightning passed through him as if he were a ghost.

At the last second, Sang realized his error. He motioned toward the desk, which sprung into the air and flew toward the warrior, but it was too late. Before the desk had flown half way toward its target, the warrior plunged his sword into Sang's chest. The desk fell to the ground as blood bubbled from the Father's gaping mouth and seeped from the wound in his chest. He slid back off the point of the blade with a wet sound and slumped to the floor, gurgling. His death was not quick, nor was it pretty. Devra was not the least bit sorry.

Lorn stepped toward her and helped her up. She breathed deeply, free of the shields of air which had nearly squeezed the life out of her. She continued to gasp for breath as the *Narnsahn* knelt before the King and Queen.

"Your Majesty," he said. "My Queen. Are you well?"

"We will survive, thanks to you, *Narnsahn*," said Elyahdyn. "What in the name of the Seven is happening? In all my six hundred years, the peace of Faerie has never been broken."

"I do not understand it either, my lord. But we cannot stay here. More of these dark Fairies are on the way. I must get you out of here."

"Then we will go," said the King. "Just get us to the Hall of the Council, and I will take you through the secret ways leading from this palace to safety."

"As you command."

And so the King and Queen of the Fair Folk, and Devra, Lady of Lehnwood, followed Lorn *Narnsahn* through the bloodied halls of the palace. Around them, the battle roared on, but Lorn's sword, slashing like lightning at anyone who got too close, kept them from harm. Before long they reached the Hall, and the King led them into a secret passage that opened beneath the grand marble table in the front of the room. They descended steep stairs into a dark passage, and the sounds of conflict faded behind them.

Alec never made it to the tavern. Before he, Kraig, and Sarah had covered half the distance, a second group of dark Fairies dropped from the surrounding trees and cut them off. It was as if they had been lying in wait especially for Alec and his companions.

"Wounds!" cried Kraig. "Won't this ever end?" His axe was out before he finished voicing his question.

In Alec's hand, Flame roared to life once again, the orange glow of the blade transforming cold steel into hot magic. At the same time, Alec was filled with the need for blood. He pushed Sarah away and raced toward their attackers.

There were many more than before, perhaps more than twenty dark swordsman in all. They closed in quickly, giving Alec and Kraig no time to react. Alec saw the peacekeeper swinging his axe madly, and blood sprayed from several of the Fairies who surrounded him. For each that went down, however, another filled the gap, and Alec knew his friend could not keep up his onslaught forever.

Alec's own problems were worse. His sword didn't have the reach of Kraig's axe, and at least ten of the assailants were closing in on him at once. Even with Flame in his hands, Alec knew he could not take all of them.

The first Fairy who reached him went down as Alec relieved him of his head. The second met a similar end. The third, fourth, and fifth, however, reached Alec together, and for all his furious swinging and thrusting, they did not go down. They were fast, these Fairies, and they had watched him long enough to be able to anticipate his moves. Alec knew thirty of the forms, but he had mastered significantly fewer, so he had been using the same maneuvers, the ones he knew best, over and over. His opponents were cunning and had already learned how to avoid his best efforts.

Apparently, they still hadn't discovered how to get past his defenses. So far, he hadn't had to use many defensive techniques, so he still could surprise them with his dodges and parries. He was quick, his movements flawless, and whenever his attackers struck, Alec disarmed them by shattering their blades with Flame. Alec silently thanked the Lord of the Dead for his marvelous gift.

But Alec was on the defense, unable to land a single strike. Knowing he could not win, Alec's bloodlust slowly seeped away and was replaced by growing panic. His confidence left him and the sword's glow faded. He began to stumble, barely able to avoid the swords slashing at him from all directions. Then the inevitable happened: a blade slashed Alec across his arm and he dropped his sword. As it left his hand, his concentration was destroyed, and it seemed his body would not respond to the simplest commands. He was suddenly clumsy, an oaf, tripping over the bulky brown robes he wore. He threw up his arms in a vain attempt to ward away the swords. At least six of the dark Fairies closed in on him, and he fell to his knees, defenseless.

"Enough!" cried a rough, old voice. "Stand away from him!"

At the sound of the voice, his assailants immediately backed away, and Alec turned toward the source of the voice. When he saw the old man it belonged to, he wished to Grok the Fairies had finished him off.

Atop a muscular black stallion, dressed in black leather and wearing a flowing dark cloak, sat Salin Urdrokk. His rune-covered long sword hung at his side, and a smile nearly as sharp creased his old, spotted face. His wispy gray hair blew in the wind. He raised a hand in greeting to Alec.

"You have led me on a merry chase, young Mason, but it ends at last. I assume you have the Talisman?"

Alec forced down panic and tried to speak calmly, but his bulging eyes and shaking hands betrayed his feelings. "I...no. No, I don't have it anymore. I...it's gone, I left it, ah..."

Salin laughed. "Let me see. If I were an ignorant, dull-witted young fool, where would I keep the Talisman...ah, yes, I know!"

He lifted his hand, and Alec began to feel something moving on his chest. Of late he always wore the Talisman on its chain under his robes, and somehow Salin had guessed it! The chain snapped, and the Talisman lifted out of his robes and floated through the air toward the sorcerer's outstretched hand. Alec's panic rose to new heights as the Talisman settled into Salin's palm, and the sorcerer slowly closed his fist around it. His eyes flamed with sinister delight and his sneer widened. Then, he raised an eyebrow at Alec, his grin fading.

"It has bonded with you? I am impressed, young Alec! I do not believe I have ever heard of the Talisman bonding with a human, or even with any Fairy who is not of royal blood. Still, it is a situation easily dealt with." He waved his hand over the Talisman and it began glowing, not with the golden light it sometimes radiated when in Alec's hands, but with a sickly, green glow. "The bond is now broken!"

Alec felt something snap inside him. A horrible pain shot through him, and he grabbed his stomach and hunched over, feeling as if he would vomit. In a few seconds the pain faded, but it was replaced with a vast, empty feeling. It was as if a part of him had been torn away. He felt like crying.

Out of the corner of his eye, he saw Kraig on his knees, arms around Sarah, protecting her. Six or seven of the dark Fairies stood around them, swords at the ready. One held Kraig's axe, a trophy, perhaps. Silence fell around them; even the sounds of battle seemed far away and insignificant.

Salin dismounted, his movements quick and sure despite his frail appearance. He made a subtle motion with his hand, and Alec found himself pulled upright. He was lifted into the air, his toes hanging several inches above the ground. Salin chuckled as he slowly walked in a circle around Alec, evaluating him.

"You look different than when last we met, child. Slimmer, stronger. A pity you will not be alive long enough to enjoy your new physique. I would love to stay and chat, but I fear I must cut short my visit. Until I have full control over the Talisman, and thus, the Fair Folk, I do not think they will roll out the red carpet for me.

"And so good-bye, Alec Mason. It has been fun, but all games must come to an end sooner or later. We will not meet again, you and I, unless it is in Hell after my Master achieves his final victory." He pulled his sword from its sheath and rested the point over Alec's heart. He turned to the dark Fairies, and in a cold voice said, "Kill the others. This one is mine."

He pulled back the sword, gave Alec a last smile, and drove it toward the baker's chest.

And then, out of nowhere, an arm as big as the trunk of a tree slammed into the sorcerer, sending him hurtling through the air. Alec looked up in surprise and saw a man twice his height bending down over him. He had rippling muscles which made Kraig's seem withered and fragile. His skin was brown and rough, almost like bark, and his clothes appeared to be made of flowers and leaves woven together with thin vines. His face was etched in an expression of rage, and his fists were clenched in fury.

"Grok's wounds," whispered Alec. "Horren!"

"Be right back," he snarled.

The Addin moved like the wind, his knobby hands reaching out to crush the skulls of any dark Fairy within reach. Swords swung at him, and a few connected, but although they drew thick, sap-like blood, they could not slow Horren's assault. He was fury incarnate, fists like battering rams crushing those who got in his way, huge hands breaking arms and legs and necks like they were brittle twigs. The Addin let out a cry of rage and the few dark Fairies who still stood fled in terror.

Alec looked around, wondering what had become of Salin. The sorcerer sat upon his horse, apparently unhurt, calmly viewing that carnage around him.

"An Addin! Why, it has been centuries since I have been afforded the opportunity to slay one of your kind." A circle of fire ignited around Horren. Salin snarled in delight as Horren shied away from the flame. "Come to me, treeman."

The ring grew thicker and higher, and Alec could feel the heat searing his skin, as far away from it as he was. It must have been nearly unbearable for the Addin. This was no normal fire, but the infernal flame of sorcerer's magic, the merest touch of which was death.

A tear dropped from Alec's eye. He wanted to reach for Flame, to at least try to save the Addin, but he was still hovering inches off the ground, held fast by Salin's magic. He saw Kraig reaching for his axe, but the burly man was hurled to the ground by a fist of air. Salin had total control of the situation. In agony, in frustration, Alec screamed.

Blood flew from Michael's mouth as Tor struck him across the chin. Drakkahn's sorcery was holding Michael still, effectively paralyzing him, and he had no way to defend himself. The stone-faced warrior grunted as he drove his gauntlet-covered fist into Michael's gut. When the former hermit keeled over and spat blood, Tor stepped back and laughed.

"This truly *is* fun! I never thought I would be granted the opportunity to torture and destroy one of the high-and-mighty Three!"

No! cried Michael in silence. *It cannot end this way! But I am powerless...faithless...broken...*

Tor spun, delivering a powerful kick to the side of Michael's face. The former hermit crashed to the ground, tears welling in his eyes. Unbearable pain shot through him, and he was certain that his jaw was broken. The sorcery held him, but he would barely have been capable of moving even if it didn't.

Faithless...broken...The One provides for all eventualities. But what has he provided to be set against Vorik Seth?

"Lift him up," said Tor. "I am not finished."

Drakkahn sighed. "Tor, we have work to do. Finish this game now."

Tor spun to the sorcerer, growling. "I will end it when I am damned good and ready. Lift him!"

Michael felt himself straighten and rise, as if invisible ropes were pulling him up by the shoulders. As soon as he was on his feet, Tor kicked him again, his boot delivering a crushing blow to Michael's chest. At least one rib cracked as Michael flew back, landing hard against the pavement. Blankets of pain wrapped him tightly, trying to push consciousness from him. He cried out in agony.

The gods are laughing at me. They are laughing at us all. Horren's book was wrong! What has the One provided?

This time Tor lifted Michael himself, gripping him by his robes and hauling him up. He took a step back, and then smashed the back of his gauntlet against Michael's skull. Black visions swam in Michael's head, and he felt vomit and bile rising from his stomach. He teetered precariously on the edge of oblivion.

WHAT HAS THE ONE PROVIDED?

As Tor laughed, relishing his victim's pain, Michael struggled to shut out his agony and think. He was going to die—Tor was going to kill him—but just once before he perished he wanted to know faith. *The One provides for all eventualities.* Michael wished he knew what that meant.

When Tor hit him again, Michael fell to the ground, unsure if the wetness he landed in was blood, vomit, or urine. He wondered how many of his bones were broken. Was he paralyzed?

His body was shutting down, leaving his mind to wander in a place where the pain was dull and far away. Again, his mind cried, *What has the One provided to be set against Vorik Seth?* The Three were not equal to the task. No human had the strength, nor did any Fairy. It would have to be something else, a new thing the world had never seen. Something with vast power over life itself, something with vast magic…

Something with the magic of death.

"Avoid a coupling of one of the Fair Folk with one of the new comers, the humans. For out of such a union will be born one with the power to destroy us, one who holds a dark power: the Magic of Death."

As Tor stepped back to observe his brutal handiwork, Michael's heart sang with revelation.

The One provides for all eventualities.

Something new, with the magic of death.

Suddenly Michael understood. In the most unlikely way imaginable, the One had provided. In that moment of revelation, Michael was reborn into faith. Passion ignited his spirit, and he felt the world flowing through the fingers of his mind.

"The One provides for all eventualities," he whispered.

Tor was coming at him, his sword pulled back to finish Michael at last. With a disdainful laugh, he said, "Fool! Is your precious One providing for you now?"

"Oh yes," whispered the Wizard as power gathered around him. "Yes he is."

Before Tor could reach Michael, the ground erupted in front of him, huge chunks of earth and pavement pummeling the dark warrior and sending him flying back. He scrambled to get out of the way before he was buried by raining rocks and dirt.

"Drakkahn!" he cried. "Why in Hell are you doing this?"

The dark Fairy's face was slack with shock. "I…I am not."

A wave of earth followed Tor, and he ran from it. The ground cracked and buckled, spewing its wealth high into the air. Michael's spirit grabbed at the earth and pulled it free, sending storms of rock after the fleeing swordsman.

Without effort, he shredded the magic which bound him and rose to his feet. His bones were broken, and blood covered him, but wrapped in the passion of his magic he could ignore his pain. Tor was getting away, but Tor was by far the lesser of the evils standing before him. This Drakkahn Shynagoth was a sorcerer of no small strength, and as such was an opponent more suited to Michael's skills.

"I fear your luck has taken a turn for the worse," said the Wizard, wreathed in a halo of power and glory.

Drakkahn's surprise had faded and was replaced by grim determination. "We shall see, human. You may have found a little power, but it is nothing compared to mine. I am Drakkahn Shynagoth, Lord Shaper of the Dark Folk."

"And I am Nul, Second of the Three, called by some the Wizard. This day you fall, sorcerer."

Black lightning flared from Drakkahn's fingertips, but it broke like glass against Michael's power. The Wizard roared fury, and balls of liquid fire engulfed the dark Fairy. Screaming, Drakkahn leaped forward, fire searing his flesh, madness ravaging his mind.

Michael prepared to Shape again, but when the charging sorcerer began to change, shock broke his concentration. He had seen Dark Folk wearing their true forms before, but nothing had prepared him for this.

Drakkahn's head grew and elongated, his chin jutting out horribly. Tusks grew from his mouth, and teeth became knives. His body twisted and his flesh darkened, and numerous arms ending in deadly claws jutted from random locations around his body. In the space of two seconds, he grew to three times his original size, veined muscles bulging from his chest and legs. His hands became thin and long, his fingers black daggers. His legs bent backwards like a beast's and he sprouted a long, black tail. His entire body had become one massive, unyielding weapon, and it was headed straight for Michael.

At the last second, Michael dropped to the ground, letting the thing's momentum take it over and past him. The slavering beast which had been Drakkahn Shynagoth stumbled to a stop and slowly turned to face its prey.

Michael rose, again taking hold of the power all around him. Drakkahn screamed hatred, his huge black eyes narrowing as he hurled himself at Michael.

The Wizard flexed his spirit.

In mid-leap, Drakkahn Shynagoth exploded. The beast's massive chest ruptured, and bloody ribs and chunks of meat flew outward in every direction. Claws and arms and legs flipped end over end, propelled high into the air. The thing's head burst, spraying gray brains over the gore-soaked street.

Michael stood amidst the shower of gore, but none of it touched him. He held his arms outward and bent his head backward as the golden glow of his power burned all about him. He was basking in the glory of the One.

Regretfully, he realized he could not bask forever. Sounds came to his ears, sounds of battle, and of death. There was still a war going on, and now he had the power to put an end to it. As the Second of the Three, he could do nothing less.

Fearlessly, he strode into the fray. He was secure in his newfound power, and not even Salin Urdrokk would stand in his way.

Salin's laughter continued to fill the air as Alec struggled against the bonds of magic that held him. Kraig was still sprawled out on the ground where Salin had thrown him, and Sarah sat holding her knees to her chest, overcome by horror. Horren, held helpless by the collapsing ring of flame, stared at Salin in useless rage.

The sorcerer stopped laughing and turned his fierce gaze upon Alec. "Well, boy, it is time to end this game. I have stayed too long already. I have the Talisman, and I must go so I may begin putting it to use. Try not to scream too much while my sorcery crushes you. I am afraid it will not be as quick as the sword would have been." He chuckled and raised his hand. Alec felt ropes of solid air pulling tight around him, forcing the air from his lungs. The ropes continued to constrict, and in a moment he could not breathe at all. His chest was collapsing inward. It would be only moments before his ribs were crushed, the breath of life driven from him forever.

"There they are! Hurry!"

The familiar, feminine voice rang out from the trees to Alec's right. He managed to turn his head toward the voice, and when he saw her his jaw dropped. How could this be? He thought he was delusional, until Sarah's voice rang out in reply.

"Grok!" she cried. "Mother!"

Ara Mills was riding toward them on a gray mare, her beautiful light brown hair flying in the wind. To her right rode a finely dressed man with wavy brown hair and a brown mustache, a cape rippling out behind him. On her left, upon a dark, powerful horse, was a Fairy woman, strong and dark with eyes of cold steel. On a pony behind her rode a small figure, smiling in eager glee.

With them, spread out through the trees, ran scores upon scores of Fairy warriors. Some had swords in hand, and a few sat upon horseback and bore lances. Still more ran with bowstrings pulled back, arrows nocked and ready. They were calling a chilling battle-cry which sent shivers through Alec's body.

Salin gave a quick look at the small army running toward him and decided not to try his sorcery against so many. He gave Alec a last, hateful sneer, and, pulling hard on his horse's reigns, turned and raced into the distance.

Alec couldn't believe it. As soon as Salin was out of sight, the magic holding him vanished. He dropped to the ground, landing clumsily. At the same time, the fire around Horren winked out, and the Addin angrily stepped out of the charred ring. Alec went to stand beside the amazed Sarah and Kraig, the three of them watching agape as Ara's horse came to a stop before them. A look of worry was replaced by a smile of joy as she looked at her daughter. At once, tears were streaming down her face, and she jumped down from her horse and swept Sarah into her arms. They were both crying, holding each other tight.

After a moment, Ara spared a glance for Alec. "Oh, Alec, I'm so glad you're all right." She slowly pulled away from Sarah, laying her hands on her daughter's face. "Sarah, thank Grok. Thank Grok we got to you in time."

"Mother," Sarah sobbed. "I knew it! I knew you were alive."

Alec took a step forward, struggling to get hold of his amazement. "Ara. I can't believe…how did you…what in the name of…?"

"It's a long story, Alec." She looked at her companions. "You might remember Landyn. He's the minstrel who played at the Silver Shield on Bard's Day. He's been helping me. And, of course, we never could have done it without Kari and Jinn, two of the Fair Folk who were able to follow your tracks all the way here."

Alec's gaze passed over Landyn and rested on the two Fairies. The one Ara had called Jinn was short and strange looking, not at all like the Fairies Alec had met so far. Jinn must have been one of the sprites Lorn and Michael had told them about.

Alec looked at the hundred or so Fairy warriors standing beyond Ara's group. "Where did they come from?" Alec asked, waving his hand toward them.

"Them?" asked Ara. "They were scattered on the outskirts of the city, confused after fighting back a few bands of those dark raiders. We came across them, and Kari was able to convince them to join us in looking for you. She didn't have to twist their arms, though, Alec. It seems you three are well-liked around here."

Alec smiled. "We've been here more than a week. We've made quite a few friends."

Horren had been standing silently off to the side, letting his anger cool. Finally, a big smile appearing on his face, he strode over and stood by Alec.

"Well, my boy, you sure know how to cause a stir. At least we chased black old Salin away, and it looks like the fighting is almost over. It looks like everything's going to be all right after all."

For a moment, Alec thought so too. Then he touched his chest. Because of what he did not feel there, he remembered why Salin had come. He knew that things would *not* be all right.

"Wounds," he muttered. "Oh, Horren, you're wrong. Salin got what he came for."

All eyes turned to Alec. "What do you mean?" asked the Addin.

"He's taken it. Salin's taken the Talisman of Unity."

A silence like unto death fell upon Fairhaven.

CHAPTER 21

Decisions and Sacrifices

Tor managed to catch up with Salin a few miles outside of Fairhaven. Despite the fact that the sorcerer clutched the Talisman of Unity safely in his fist, he wore a look of deadly ire. Apparently, something had not gone according to plan. Riding close behind Salin were Gwendolyn and Stiletta, the women who, like Tor, had pledged to serve him. Of the force of ogres which had accompanied them to Fairhaven there was no sign.

Tor dug his heels into the sides of his mount to urge it toward his master. When he rode side by side with Salin, he said, "I see you have the Talisman, master. You must be pleased."

Salin shot Tor a glance which drove daggers into his heart. "I have the Talisman. As soon as we reach my stronghold, I will begin bending it to my will, forcing it to bond with me so every living Fairy will be as a slave to me. The process will not take long. For this alone, I am pleased." He frowned. His ancient flesh wrinkled horribly, but the fiery power in his eyes belied his age. "I did not manage to kill Mason."

"What? How could he have...that is, what happened, Great Master?"

"First," replied Salin, holding up a long, thing finger, "an Addin showed up. That I could have handled; in fact, I *did* handle it. Then, a ghost came riding in on a gray horse with an army behind her. I might have been able to take them all, but I decided against trying. Why risk my life when my goal was in my hand?"

Tor was confused. "A ghost?"

Salin's eyes narrowed. "A woman I thought I had killed. Either she was a ghost or I am getting careless." He paused, turning his face forward and urging his mount faster. "It matters little. Soon, the world will tremble beneath my fist."

"Yes, master. With the Talisman, there is little you will not be able to accomplish." Tor was trying to soothe the sorcerer's anger, but the words he heard himself saying frightened him. The last thing he wanted was for his master to become even more powerful. Salin terrified him enough as it was. He wanted to drop back, to be away from the sorcerer, but his curiosity was getting the better of him. "What happened to the ogres?"

Apparently it was the wrong thing to ask. Salin's back stiffened and rage flared from his eyes. "The resistance was more than I had expected. After I left you to deal with Michael, a group of Fairhaven's illustrious guards intercepted us. They would not have presented much difficulty for us had they not had a few of the cursed Brothers of Nom with them. I refused to be delayed, so I commanded Gwendolyn and Stiletta to take the ogres and engage the guards while I pressed onward. Drawn by the Talisman, I found Mason and his little friends already at the mercy of my dark Fairy servants. I took the Talisman from around the boy's neck. Tor, do you know what had happened? The Talisman had *bonded* with the Seth-forsaken peasant. It was amazing, but I do not expect you to understand such things. It was easy enough for me to break the bond, at least break it enough so I could take the Talisman with no harm to myself. At any rate, I was about to run him through, when a massive arm came out of nowhere and tossed me to the side like a rag doll. I would have been crushed had I not already placed fields of invulnerability around myself. As it was, it certainly hurt.

"It was an Addin! I was so amazed to see the big creature that for a moment I forgot to kill it. It managed to crush the dark Fairies before I could act, but finally I imprisoned it in a ring of fire. I took some time to have a little fun, closing the ring of fire slowly around him. I should have used the time to crush Mason. My little diversion kept me from the satisfaction of my kill, for when I finally started squeezing the life out of our little baker, the Fairy horde showed up with that woman, Ara Mills, whom I thought I murdered back in Barton Hills.

"Oh, Tor, I was not pleased, but rather than risk a conflict I made a hasty retreat. After all, I had the Talisman, and anything else was beside the point. When I found Gwendolyn and Stiletta, they were finishing off the last of the Fairy guards. The ogres were already dead, but they had served their purpose.

The three of us raced out of the city through the secret ways and continued onward. I gave orders to the dark Fairy woman, Gothra, to make sure the King dies if he is not dead already. His will is strong and he would be hard to conquer even with the Talisman. You see, Tor, the Talisman was made to be used *by* the King of Faerie, not *against* him. Those of royal blood have a chance of resisting its mind controlling effects. This is why he must die. For this reason, among others, I gave the reader Devra visions that her king was a weak fool, so she would betray him."

Tor hated it when Salin rambled on. All he had asked was what had happened to the ogres! At least talking things through seemed to calm the sorcerer. Now that Salin was in control of himself, Tor ventured to ask the question which was really on his mind.

"So what happens now, my master? Now that you have the Talisman, you no longer need me. When we at last quit the forests of the Fair Folk, will I be allowed to return to Valaria?"

Salin laughed, truly amused. His mood swings were maddening! "Of course not, Tor! Not yet. You are to accompany me to my stronghold. I have many tasks for you to attend to while I am busy with the Talisman." He turned to look at the sisters who rode close behind them. "As for the women, I think I'll send them back to Fairhaven. It is not that I do not trust Gothra l'Uarach and Drakkahn Shynagoth, but I would feel better if two of my personal agents were there to insure the King and Queen are dead. And it would be best to rid ourselves of the infuriating Order of Nom." Salin paused for a moment, his lips curling into a devilish grin. "But tell me, how did you and Drakkahn fair against Michael? In what horrible manner did you kill him? I want all the details."

Tor's heart sank. He had hoped to avoid the topic, but he should have known Salin would want a report. He uttered a curse under his breath, knowing his failure would enrage Salin. It was possible Drakkahn had managed to kill Michael, but nothing was certain, especially in light of the formidable powers the Wizard had displayed. Tor looked up at his master, who was gazing at him in expectation.

Steeling himself against the wrath he knew his report would invoke, Tor told Salin of his failure.

Less than an hour had passed since the assault on Fairhaven had ended, and yet so much had happened Alec's head was still spinning. As he walked toward the palace in the company of Sarah, Ara, Kraig, Michael, Horren, and a score of others, he listened to the frenzied chattering around him. No one knew quite what to make of what had happened, but everyone wanted to talk about it. Something would have to be done about Salin, obviously, so everyone was headed to the Grand Hall of the Council, where the most important matters were decided. Only, no one knew if the King and Queen were still alive, and no one was sure how many, if any, of the King's advisors survived. There were a few Brothers of Nom scattered around, the oldest and the most powerful being Faerie's acclaimed elders, and in the absence of the King and his advisors, they were the highest authority in the land. It was they who had called a council, and it was they who would preside over the council if Elyahdyn, Mahv, and the advisors could not be found. The unfortunate thing was that the highest of the elders, the leader of the Order of Nom, Father Sang, was still unaccounted for.

Soon after Salin had fled, Alec and the others started toward the palace, intending to help the people of Fairhaven in any way they could. They hadn't gotten far when they realized the invasion was all but finished. It had been a close battle, and only one thing, apparently, had turned the tide in favor of Fairhaven's defenders: Michael. Alec didn't believe it at first, but word had it that Michael had regained his power and had rained devastation upon the invaders. Conflicting stories put him everywhere: in the south quarter of the city, causing dark Fairies to burst suddenly into flame; near the palace, calling lightning down upon those who would lay siege; in the market district, causing bottomless chasms to open up beneath the feet of invaders. When Michael himself had come limping over the battle-field to join Alec's party, he claimed the stories were exaggerated. He had found some small power and had done what little he could to aid the resistance.

Horren, too, was creating quite a stir, since no Addin had walked the forests of Faerie in hundreds of years. Some of the Fair Folk looked at him suspiciously, remembering the tales which made Addins out to be betrayers, but most accepted him with smiles and salutes when they learned how he had fearlessly attacked Salin to save Alec's life. Ara had quite a bit to say about Horren as well, at least when she could pull herself away from Sarah. Mother and daughter walked side by side, tears of joy in their eyes, hardly able to believe they had found one another again. Alec couldn't believe it either. He had heard only bits and pieces of Ara's story, how Landyn had come to her aid, how they had recruited the aid of the trackers, Kari and Jinn, and how Horren had insisted on joining their party.

"We wouldn't have survived without him in Ogrynwood," commented Ara, looking back at the giant as young Fairies, filled with curiosity, surround him.

Alec smiled when he saw his friend Gryn, wide eyed as the rest, trying to get close to Horren. They were firing questions at him faster than he could hope to answer, and he looked amused and somewhat overwhelmed by the attention. Alec chuckled as Ara, an arm around Sarah's shoulders, went on with her tale. "Twice we were confronted by ogre hunting parties, which Horren tore through easily. Of course, Landyn helped, too; he's actually fairly good with that short sword of his. And Kari and Jinn were able to hold their own, she with her magic and he with his…well, you have to see him to understand. I even managed to kill one of those monsters."

"Mother!" cried Sarah. "You could have been killed."

Ara smiled, giving her daughter a fierce hug. "I didn't really have a choice. Everyone else was occupied, and an ogre was coming straight at me. Luckily Landyn had given me a few of his daggers. I managed to put one through the thing's eye.

"At any rate, after the battle we traveled as fast as we could until we were in Faerie. We couldn't ride our horses over the mountains, of course, so Horren ended up carrying me most of the way. And speaking of the mountains, let me tell you, you folks gave us quite a panic when your trail led right up to the entrance of the tomb. Kari told us about that place, and from what she said it didn't look like you'd make it through. We weren't able to relax until we had crossed the mountain and found your trail on the other side.

"Anyway, when we reached Faerie, Kari led us to Lehnwood and spoke with some of the people, who told us you had left for Fairhaven. We borrowed some fresh horses and made our way here. When we arrived the battle had already started, and Horren, always ready for a fight, raced ahead to join the fray. And it was a good thing he did, since Salin was about to run you through when Horren found you."

Alec shuddered at the memory, but couldn't help smiling as well. "Thank Grok he got there in time. And thank Grok you arrived when you did, too, backed up by all those soldiers."

Soon the conversation trailed off, and Alec took the opportunity to look around the city. While it could not be said that Fairhaven was in ruins, the conflict had taken a toll on the city's buildings, streets, and citizens. Here and there the white streets were stained red, and blood dampened areas of thick grass in the parks. Bodies of innocents and raiders, guards and Shapers, lay broken across the field of battle, and groups of Fair Folk were already collecting the dead. Other Fairies were busy putting out fires, Shapers simply making the flames vanish, perhaps changing them into air, and others pouring buckets of water on the smaller fires. Many people were weeping, some over lost loved ones, others simply because the peace of Faerie had been broken for the first time in memory. Others, like the folk who joined Alec's party, were too over-come with curiosity or confusion to feel their grief. Or perhaps they were intent on finding the instigator of the invasion and putting an end to him. Word had gotten around that Salin Urdrokk had been at the heart of the attack, and that he had captured the Talisman of Unity.

When they had nearly reached the palace, Alec noticed Michael staring into the distance, a far-away, somewhat sad, look in his eyes.

"Michael? What's wrong?"

"What?" He appeared startled when Alec addressed him, but he recovered quickly. "Oh, I was just thinking. I was thinking about Devra. I was wondering what she had to do with this attack."

"Lady Devra?" questioned Alec, surprised. "You think she…" Alec trailed off as he thought about Devra locking them in the abandoned building on the outskirts of town. Why had she done that? "She was trying to get us out of the way. It's like she knew something was going to happen."

"Exactly, Alec. She knew. And she did nothing to stop it; she warned no one, and she locked us away where we could not interfere. Perhaps she was trying to protect us, or maybe she just wanted us out of the way."

"Michael, she couldn't have had anything to do with the attack. Salin was behind it. I can't believe she would have anything to do with that monster."

Michael was frowning, his gaze locked on the palace ahead. He was trying to appear calm, even cold, but Alec knew he was hiding something. Michael cared for Devra, and if he thought she had betrayed him, he would be hurting. "We will see," was all he said.

They reached the great spiral stair leading up into the palace and were greeted by three guards and a Brother of Nom. The Brother solemnly ushered them up the stairs, and before long they were walking down the wide corridor toward the Grand Hall. Servants were hurrying about, cleaning blood from the walls, scrubbing the floor, and removing damaged carpets and tapestries. Sev-eral white-robed advisors walked the corridor, conversing in hushed tones with one another as they made their way toward the Hall. To Alec they looked as confused and lost as everyone else.

The Grand Hall of the Council was not nearly so crowded as it had been the first time Alec was there. There were perhaps ten advisors, including First Advisor Syndar, and six Brothers of Nom, two wearing the gold necklaces which designated them as elders. Several guards and soldiers rounded out the crowd, all standing near the back of the room.

Michael led Alec and the others to the second table before progressing to his seat at the front. It took a while for everyone to get situated, but finally they all had taken their seats, and the council was ready to begin. Seated at the front along with Michael were Councilor Syndar, three other advisors, and the two elders of Nom. Syndar sat in the chair next to the King's seat, which was left empty. Raising his hand, he called the meeting to order.

"Fellow Fairies, honored guests. Today there has been a terrible tragedy. In the wake of such devastation, we must decide how to pick up the pieces and make things right. The King and Queen are missing, perhaps dead, and our fair city is in shambles. Worse, I have been informed by Elder Toros that the sorcerer Salin Urdrokk has captured our most sacred possession, the Talisman of Unity. The elders have called this meeting to discuss our choices, and I, as the highest authority in the land in the absence of our great King and Queen, must hear your suggestions and decide. Elsendarin, as you have faced Salin in the past and know him well, we would hear your counsel first."

Just as Michael made to rise, the doors of the Hall opened with a loud bang, and all heads turned to watch the dark-haired warrior stride confidently through the entry. He wore a grim expression, and his hand rested on the hilt of his sword. He surveyed the crowd, and when he was certain he had everyone's attention, he spoke.

"I would not make any decisions," said Lorn, "until you have heard the will of your King."

Lorn stepped to the side, and in strode King Elyahdyn and Queen Mahv, dressed in splendor and majesty, wearing expressions both grave and commanding. They were even more imposing than last time Alec had seen them, and Alec felt the need to back away as they passed, as if the power of their presence would burn him to ash. He was certain he was not the only one who felt this way. They took their thrones at the head table, and after a moment the King's deep and powerful voice broke the silence.

"My people. Today we have been invaded by a dark enemy second only to the Great Enemy who resides in the west. Today, from what I have heard, he has torn away a treasure we had only recently recovered. But this is not all that has happened, not even the worst of it. Today, we have learned the Fair Folk are not above corruption. Many of our cousins from the north, the Dark Folk, now serve Salin Urdrokk. Worse, some of the Fair Folk, citizens of this very city, have turned to Salin. How can this be? How can a people who have been incorruptible since the dawn of the world have succumbed at last to the whispers of evil? I do not know. I can only say it fills me with pain. Pain and great anger. Salin Urdrokk is a foul creature who has brought us great, perhaps irreparable, harm. We are, for the first time in history, a people sundered.

"There is only one thing which might have the power to repair the rift. What Salin has stolen from us we must recover. Only the Talisman of Unity can help mend the damage the fiend has done. If it remains in his hands, he will certainly use it to break us further, to unite us all under a cloak of evil. He will bend us to his will and send us to war under the banner of his master. This is not the destiny of the Fair Folk! We must use any and all means, sacrifice as much as we need, to hunt down the sorcerer and reclaim what is ours. Our greatest trackers must pick up his trail and follow him to the edge of the world, if necessary. One way or another, we must regain the Talisman."

The Kings words were greeted with low murmurs, some in agreement, some questioning if recovery of the Talisman was possible. Alec merely sat there, shaking his head. Maybe it could truly be done, if enough Fairy shapers were sent after him and they found him in time, but he was just glad his part was over.

At the head table, Michael rose and looked to the King. Elyahdyn nodded, giving the Wizard permission to speak. Michael opened his mouth to begin, but instead of speaking, he placed his hand on his forehead and sat back down. Alec noticed he was sweating, and he shook as if in great pain.

"Forgive me," he said. "I was…wounded while facing a dark Fairy sorcerer and have not been able to heal myself fully." He took a moment to master his pain, and then he sat up straight and began to speak.

"I am in full agreement with King Elyahdyn. Salin must be tracked down and stopped. I myself volunteer to follow him and try to destroy him. I…I must go alone, or with Lorn and Horren, if they will accompany me."

There was quiet discussion at that. Elyahdyn nodded, as if he agreed with Michael, but Syndar voiced the question that was in Alec's mind.

"Why alone? Why not take a few Brothers with you? Surely in numbers you will stand a greater chance against the sorcerer."

Michael shook his head sadly. "I fear I cannot take any of the Fair Folk with me, save one tracker, which I will need. We do not know how long it will take Salin to master the Talisman. If he gains any degree of mastery over it before we can find him, any of your people who travel with me will be his to command. Even if my power proves equal to Salin's, I cannot face him and a group of Brothers at once. No, it is a risk we cannot take. I will take no Fairy shapers."

The room was quiet. The Fair Folk might have respected Michael, especially now that he had regained at least some of his former power, but they were not happy their fate was in his hands alone. Still, none could argue with his logic. As long as Salin held the Talisman, they had to stay as far away from him as possible.

Something off to the left caught Alec's attention. He looked across the room, but saw nothing unusual. He was sure he had seen something out of the corner of his eye, a light perhaps, something moving, but there was nothing there now. Shrugging, he turned his attention back to the front table.

Seated to Alec's right, Lorn cleared his throat. "I will, of course, accompany Elsendarin. Salin's magic cannot harm me, not directly anyway. My sword is at your command, Wizard."

The Addin, who was sitting on the floor at the edge of Alec's table, said, "I would like to have a part in crushing black Salin as well. One doesn't toss fire at an Addin and live to tell about it, not for long, at least."

Michael did not smile, but his eyes showed satisfaction, or relief. He was glad he would not be going alone.

"What about me?" asked Kraig. Alec and Sarah both shot stunned looks at the peacekeeper. How could he volunteer to go against Salin? Had he gone mad? "I wouldn't be much good against sorcery, but I can guarantee Salin will be surrounding himself with ogres or the like. My axe and I would come in handy against that sort, you must agree."

Michael looked less pleased than he had when Lorn and Horren offered their aid, but after a moment he nodded grimly. "It is more dangerous than you can know, and yet I cannot turn you away, Kraig. I need all the help I can get."

Again, Alec sensed something, movement or light, to his left. Something pulled his attention that way, but when he looked, his eyes found nothing. This time, however, the feeling did not go away. He peered past tables and people toward the wall, and tried to peer *through* the wall.

"Then we are agreed," said Michael. "All we need now is one Fairy tracker, and then we can…"

"Tracking him will not be possible," said a voice from the doorway.

Alec turned to see the Fairy woman who had come with Ara; Kari, she was called. She stood in the doorway, standing tall, her face drawn in a severe frown. Her strange companion, Jinn, crouched at her feet like a loyal puppy.

"Who are you, woman, that you would intrude on this council uninvited?" asked the King.

Proudly, she announced, "My name is Kari of house du Sharrel, daughter of Manra and Kesh du Sharrel, sister to *Martyn*." She practically growled the last name at the King.

Martyn, thought Alec. *Wasn't that the name of the Fairy who supposedly...*

"I am a tracker of some skill, my King," she continued. "In fact, if I may leave modesty aside for a moment, you are unlikely to find my equal even here in Fairhaven. I have already attempted to track Urdrokk. I tried to pick up his trail, my King, but I could not. There is no trail."

"What? This is not possible!" cried Councilor Syndar, earning a harsh look from the King for speaking out of turn. He coughed and meekly pretended to inspect a spot on the table.

"It *is* possible," said Michael, running a hand through his flat brown hair. "It is an intricate work of magic, but it can be done by a master. He has erased all signs of his passing. I myself have used such a technique, long ago, when I was at the peak of my power. I should have known he would do this. Seven take him! We cannot track him now."

Alec jumped up, unable to sit still any longer while the feeling something was *there* kept nagging at him. Oblivious to the eyes that watched him, he walked to the wall and found nothing. Whatever was drawing him was beyond the wall. He touched the place on his chest where he had worn the Talisman, suddenly knowing what it was he felt.

"Wounds." Spinning to the look at the shocked faces turned toward him, he said, "I can do it. I can track Salin."

It was Michael's turn to look astonished. "You? Alec, how?"

"I can still feel it," answered the baker. "The Talisman. It's still connected to me somehow, and I can feel it...that way." He pointed toward the source of the feeling pulling at him.

"Are you certain?" asked the Wizard.

"Completely. Grok's wounds, Michael, I'm still bonded to the Talisman! Well, a little, anyway. Enough to know where it is and what direction it's headed. I wanted to put all this behind me, and I thought I finally could. But now..." Alec sighed. He could barely bring himself to say the words. "I will go with you. You'll never be able to find him without me. I'll help you get the Talisman back."

There was a moment of silence while everyone gaped at Alec. He saw a wide range of emotion as he scanned the faces before him: concern from Sarah and Kraig, disbelief from some councilors and other Fairies, curiosity from Michael demonstrated by the subtle raising of an eyebrow. The King and

Queen looked at him with unreadable expressions and said nothing. At this point, it was clear they were deferring to Michael's wisdom. At last the former hermit shook his head and spoke.

"Very well, then. It seems, Alec, you are our best, or rather, our *only*, hope. If you can track the Talisman, then you can lead us to Salin. King Elyahdyn, Lord of all Faerie, this, then, is the wisdom I offer you: Alec Mason, Lorn *Narnsahn*, Kraig, Horren, and myself will set out after the sorcerer. We will take back the Talisman by any means necessary. If it comes to conflict, I, myself, will do battle with Salin Urdrokk, even though it may mean my end."

The King spread his hands and proclaimed, "So it shall be. This council is at an end. Go with the peace of Faerie."

It was an abrupt ending to the debate, Alec thought, but then he realized nothing more need be said. He joined Michael and the King and Queen at the front table as the Councilors and Brothers cleared out of the Hall. Sarah and Kraig remained, as did Horren, Lorn, and Ara. The Wizard looked near to collapsing; obviously the battles he had fought had taken a lot out of him. But he had a worried look on his face which had nothing to do with pain or weariness.

"I wonder what has happened to Devra," he said, not really talking to anyone in particular. His eyes darted toward the door as if he expected her to walk through at any moment.

"She was with us, before," said Lorn, placing a hand on Michael's shoulder. "Michael, I fear she...she took an arrow in her shoulder. It was poisoned."

The Wizard's gray eyes widened in shock. "You mean she is...by the One, is she...?"

"She is alive," said Lorn, "but very ill. She is in the care of the healer, Rayannah. We do not know if she will recover. I am sorry, my friend."

The King, too, looked saddened. "I think she was trying to tell me something when we took her to Rayannah. She looked so sad, and she kept mouthing 'I am sorry.' 'Sorry for what?' I asked, but she was taken by delirium and could not tell us more."

"I must see her," said Michael. "I must see her at once, before I prepare to set out after Salin. Lorn, take the others and gather the things we will need for the journey. We must leave this very day, before the sorcerer gets too much of a lead. I will meet you at the stables no later than two hours after noon."

Without another word, he hurried out the door. His movements were urgent, but jerky and pained. Alec wondered how he could possibly be up to a journey when he was obviously injured. Yet his concern for Michael was outweighed by his worry for Devra, who was in a far more dire condition. She had been a friend to Alec and the others since they met, and he would grieve for her if she did not recover.

Sarah, as if reading his thoughts, gave him a tight hug. "She'll be all right," she said. "She has to be. These Fair Folk are strong; a little poison won't put one down."

"Come on," said Lorn. "We have work to do and the day is wasting."

Bidding the King and Queen farewell, Alec, Kraig, and the Addin, along with Sarah and her mother, followed the warrior from the Hall of the Council.

"So what happened then, after you threw her against the wall?" Landyn, minstrel of Freehold, asked the strikingly handsome Fairy sitting across the table.

"Well, I slashed her across the shoulder," said Vyrdan, miming a flicking stroke of the sword, "and she dropped her knife. But, by the One, a dagger leapt into her other hand faster than I would have thought possible, and seemingly from nowhere! I tell you I have never seen someone move so fast." He took a long swig of ale before continuing. "Luckily for me the blade turned on my chain-mail shirt, and I only took a small wound. Her speed surprised me, though, and she got away. I think perhaps she would have been able to kill me, loathe as I am to admit it, but someone was calling her. I think it was Salin Urdrokk himself, summoning her to his side!"

"Amazing," said Landyn. This Vyrdan was an interesting fellow, and by his own estimation a formidable fighter. Talking with him over a mug of ale was certainly more interesting than some dry, tedious council. Ara and the others would be at the palace now, discussing what was to be done about Salin and the Talisman. Certainly their discussion was important, but Landyn could get the details later. Right now, he was interested in drinking and talking with someone who had been neck-deep in the fighting. While any tale about the events of the day would have to include the decisions of the council, the things Vyrdan was telling him were really the stuff of song. Battles and warriors of valor: those were the things which made a great ballad.

"So this woman, she left with Salin? What did you do then?"

Vyrdan finished his ale and motioned to the tavern keeper for another. Landyn chuckled to himself as he watched the silver-haired Fairy race to the keg to fill Vyrdan's mug. It was incredible how quickly he had the tavern open for business after the fighting ended. It seemed things here in Faerie were not so different from anywhere else: even in times of trouble, perhaps *especially* in times of trouble, the tavern was never closed.

"Well, good minstrel, I rejoined the fray at once! Many a dark Fairy fell to my blade and many a citizen were saved by it. As long as Fairhaven was in danger, I could not rest. If only I could have reached the palace to help protect the King." For a moment, the Fairy sobered. "I hope he and the Queen are safe. I have heard no news of them."

Landyn hoped they were safe as well. Not that he knew them, but the last thing he wanted was to be in a land which had just lost its rulers. The turmoil resulting from such a loss would be unpleasant at best. "I am certain they are fine," he said.

"Yes, the Order of Nom would not let any harm come to them." He climbed to his feet, swaying slightly. "I must take my leave of you now, good sir. I have neglected my duties for too long. I must see about the King, and my Lady, Devra of Lehnwood."

"What about your ale?" said Landyn, eyeing the mug the tavern keeper had just set down on the table.

"You have it," said Vyrdan. "I will settle our tab with the barkeep."

"Nonsense," said the minstrel, "let me help with…"

"No, good sir, you are a guest in our land, and it would not be gracious of me to accept your coin. The defenders of Faerie are paid rather well, after all, and I have silver to spare. Barkeep! We have a bill to settle, I believe?"

Landyn chucked as he watched the light-skinned Fairy count out several coins and place it in the silver-haired man's hand. With a final bow, Vyrdan strode out of the tavern. From their talk, the minstrel surmised Vyrdan was as much of a rogue as he himself was. A rogue with a sense of duty and nobility, but a rogue nonetheless.

Landyn surveyed the faces of the Fair Folk who remained in the tavern. There were twenty-odd patrons still downing mugs of ale, drowning their sorrows or celebrating after having survived the attack. Some were soldiers and some were farmers, and still others were craftsmen or merchants or hunters. No one caught Landyn's eye as Vyrdan had, at least not until he spied a young looking, dark-haired Fairy enter the tavern. The fellow's eyes scanned the room for a moment, and then a look of recognition appeared on his face as he saw someone across the room. Landyn watched the Fairy cross the tavern and sit down at a secluded table where a darkly attractive woman sat waiting.

They began to talk quietly, and something about them caused the minstrel to keep an eye on them. They were neither drowning their grief nor celebrating; in fact, they weren't drinking at all. To Landyn's rogue-like sensibilities, it appeared they were conspiring. He pretended to take interest in his mug, the walls, the other tavern patrons, but the lion-share of his attention was focused on the two conspirators.

He tried his best to watch their lips. Reading lips was an important skill he had learned early on; he could not count the times he had been able to profit from the ability. From where he was sitting, it was impossible to catch everything, but he could make out bits and pieces of the conversation. As the dialogue went on, Landyn grew more and more anxious about what was being said.

In a moment, Landyn leapt from his chair and raced for the door. He had to find Ara and the others and find out which of the Fair Folk were in charge, who he could trust. If the King and Queen were still alive and safe, they might not remain that way for long. He committed to memory both the faces of the conspirators and the things they had said. Without a thought for his unfinished ale, Landyn made his way toward the palace.

Michael opened the door to the House of Rest and was instantly assailed by the stench of death. Every bed in the house was packed with the wounded and the dying, and men in white tunics carried the bodies of the people who could not be helped out the back door and onto a wooden cart. Healers and Shapers, mostly older men and women, bent over the wounded, applying salves and ointments, bandages and balms. Some of the Shapers lay their hands upon open wounds, the power of the One knitting them closed with varying degrees of success.

Michael motioned to an old Fairy-woman who appeared to be overseeing the House. She had silver hair and a few creases on her face, the only signs of age the Fair Folk ever showed. She had to be in her fifth century, at least. Another human might have been in awe of such an ancient being, but Michael was older than she was. Existing in spirit so closely with the One, Michael had not aged much in the last seven centuries or so.

"Venerable Fairy, I am Elsendarin, Second of the Three. I seek the healer Rayannah."

The old Fairy grunted. "Then you have found her, I guess. I know you, Elsendarin, and I am honored by your presence, but I have little time for conversation. There is much to attend to here."

"So I see, good healer." The healers more than had their hands full. This wasn't the only House of Rest in Fairhaven, but there were so many people in need of aid that Michael was sure all the Houses were as full as this one. He wished he could spare the time to add his own skills to those of the healers, but he had other matters to consider. Besides, all his energy was focused inward to heal his own wounds. Only a few hours earlier the majority of his bones were broken and he was bleeding inside. Now, he was bruised and scraped and it hurt to move, but he was in no danger of dying.

Self-healing took a tremendous toll, however. He wanted nothing more than to collapse on one of Rayannah's beds and call for one of the healers to help him. If he kept pushing himself, he was likely to pass out before they were on the road after Salin. At the very least, he would be too weary to Shape for days. In his weakened state, there was no way his body was up to fulfilling its part in obeying the Sixth Law.

"Rayannah," he continued, "I do not wish to take much of your time. I must see Lady Devra. I need to know how she is doing, and there is something I must discuss with her."

The healer gave him a harsh look. "She is in no condition for talk. It took all my skill to draw the poison from her wound, and she is still in deadly danger. Without complete, undisturbed rest, and a little luck, she will die."

"I will be brief, my lady. It is of the utmost importance."

Rayannah shrugged. "Very well. She is in one of the private rooms, the second door on the left."

"Thank you, healer Rayannah."

"Brief!" she reminded as Michael headed for the door. He nodded back to her.

He passed the rows of beds, struggling to avoid looking at the dying Fairies. The fact that his faith was restored, at least in part, was not enough to keep his heart from breaking if he looked too long at pain and death. He pushed open the door to Devra's room, entered, and closed it gently behind him.

The room was dim, lit only by a single magic sconce upon the wall. The only features in the room, besides a few decorative tapestries, were a bed, a table, and a shelf of medical supplies. In the bed, Devra lay with her hands at her sides, her eyes closed peacefully. The bandages wrapping her shoulder were already dotted with blood which seeped from her wound. She stirred when Michael approached her bed, the peaceful cast gone from her face as soon as she opened her eyes.

"Oh! Elsendarin!" Tears came almost at once. "What have I done? Oh, One, this is my fault."

"My Lady Devra," said Michael, sitting on the side of the bed and taking her hand. "My love. What was all this about? What kind of game were you playing?"

She grabbed his hand like it was her only anchor to life. She could not meet his eyes as she spoke. "Years ago, I began having visions of the King. Visions of weakness. You know I have never been wrong about my readings before. I saw that his soul was weak, the spirit which made the royal blood special all but gone. With the power of the Seth always growing in the West, I knew it was only a matter of time before it would overcome us. Without a strong king to unite the Fair Folk, we would all die under the power of the shadow. Somehow, I saw this with complete clarity. If the weak king continued to reign, we would perish, and the world would die with us.

"So I began to organize my people, people whom I knew I could trust. There were so few, for most of the nobles and minor lords under me, like my dear Vyrdan, were utterly loyal to the King. I organized who I could, and found allies in the most unlikely of places: soldiers, shopkeepers, even some of the Brothers of Nom. The Dark Folk were quick to answer my call, and under their Lord Shaper, Drakkahn Shynagoth, a great number of them joined the movement.

"I fear I lost control near the end to Shynagoth. I feared him and his people, but I was committed to my path and needed their aid. It was Shynagoth who decided when the raid would take place. He was the one who controlled everything. I see that now. I was never in control, except at the very start."

Michael squeezed her hand. A tear ran down his cheek. "Not even then, my Lady. I fear this was a plot all along. You were fooled, and not by Shynagoth. I believe it was Salin Urdrokk who used you, who used his sorcery to influence your reading of the King. You saw what the sorcerer wanted you to see. Perhaps it was his plan to throw Faerie into a bitter civil war so, like the human land of Eglak, it would break and be easier for the Seth to take. But when he discovered the Talisman, his plans for Faerie evolved into something else altogether. This was why Shynagoth, by Salin's command, called for the revolution to begin now. Salin needed a distraction so he could come for the Talisman."

"This is worse than I thought!" moaned Devra. "I have doomed us all!"

"No. No, you were used. Blame no one but Salin Urdrokk. You are a good woman, only misguided. I know you care about what is good and right, Devra. I know why you sealed me and the others in the stone house before the fighting began. You did not want to see us hurt. I know you did not want to see anyone hurt."

"Yes, it was to be a peaceful revolution, as little bloodshed as possible. But that was not the way it happened; Shynagoth saw to that."

"You need not worry about Drakkahn Shynagoth any longer. I have destroyed him."

"You? But Elsendarin, how?"

"I am restored, beloved. I can Shape."

For the first time, a gleam of joy came into her eye. She smiled briefly, and said, "I am glad." All too quickly, her joy faded. "What of Salin?"

"I am going after him, with some others. But you concern yourself only with getting better. You must recover, for you have many duties to resume."

Her eyes dropped to her chest. "No longer. I am a traitor to Faerie and treason is death. I must submit myself to the King's justice."

Michael felt his heart tearing in two, but he forced back the tears and squeezed her hand harder still. "No, Devra. Your death would be a waste, especially now when your skills are needed. The King does not suspect you in this treason and he will not learn of your involvement from me. Remember, what you did was not your fault! Salin is a master of deception; anyone could have been fooled by him. Even the actions you chose to take were probably dictated by him."

"You would keep this a secret? But justice demands…"

"Justice, or Law? Your death might serve the letter of the Law of Faerie, but it would by no means serve justice. Devra. I must go, for I must be off after Salin, and I also promised the healer I would be brief. Promise me you will be well. Promise me also you will keep our secret. Do not seek your own death."

She squeezed the tears from her eyes. "I promise you, my dear, my forbidden, my love. It is upon your shoulders, now. Please, save us all."

Michael sighed. "I will do what I can. Farewell, my heart."

Seeing her like this, knowing in his heart there might never be another chance, Michael did what he had never done before. He bent to her mouth and pressed his lips gently upon hers. She returned the kiss hungrily and wrapped him weakly in her arms. If she had been well, he thought she would have pulled him down on the bed with her, and damned be the Laws of Faerie. He wanted her like he had never wanted anything in all his years, but now was not the time or the place. She was ill and he had other things to do. Besides, what he was considering was still very much forbidden.

The kiss ended and he reluctantly pulled his wet mouth away from hers. She gazed up at him with eyes full of need, a need he knew was also in his own eyes. Without another word, he left her room and hurried past the beds of the dying.

His face was flushed, and his eyes were red from crying. He feared that the emotions he had repressed for so many years were about to come exploding forth uncontrollably. When water starts seeping through a crack in a dam, it is not long before the rushing river blows the whole structure apart.

He bowed quickly to Rayannah, ignoring her comments that he had taken too long, and rushed out of the House of Rest. Biting back his sorrow, he hurried for the stables.

A crowd had gathered around the stables where Alec stood waiting while Kraig and Lorn spoke to the stablemaster about acquiring horses. Horren, Sarah, and Ara were with him, as well as his friend Gryn and a few other young Fairies. Beyond their immediate circle, soldiers and Brothers stood with several councilors, and beyond them were clusters of curious townsfolk. Alec sighed, regretting that he was becoming quite a celebrity in Fairhaven.

"So you are really going off after Salin?" questioned Gryn, a look of admiration in his eyes.

"Yes, it seems we have to," answered Alec, looking off into the crowd. He wished Michael would hurry. "I have to go, because I'm the only one who can track the Talisman. We've got to get it back before he can start using it to control the Fairies."

Gryn ran both hands through his pageboy-style blond hair. "In classes, I learned about the Talisman of Unity, but I never paid too much attention. Are you saying that with the Talisman, Salin would be master over all the Fair Folk?"

"Exactly. You would all be his to command."

"One," muttered Gryn. "I guess you had better succeed in getting it back."

Ara stepped up and put her hand on Alec's shoulder. "I have complete confidence in you and the others, Alec. You're going to be traveling in good company. To say Horren is good in a fight is an immense understatement, and Kraig can hold his own. Lorn and Michael seem to be more than capable, and they're obviously both quite knowledgeable. If anyone can take back the Talisman, you five can."

"I wish I shared your confidence," said Alec.

"Black old Salin won't stand a chance against the likes of us," rumbled Horren, smiling down at Alec. "I'll grind his bones to powder for the trick he pulled on me earlier."

Sarah, who had been looking at Alec with sad eyes, said, "Just don't get yourself into any danger, Alec. Remember, you're just going along because you can track the Talisman. Let the others do the real work."

"You can count on it," said Alec, a small smile coming to his lips. "Just because I can use the sword a little doesn't mean I'm going looking for trouble." He hoped it was true. In the back of his mind, something red was stirring, looking forward to the possibility of battle ahead. His hand strayed to Flame's hilt, but he stopped it before he touched the sword.

"You've got to come back to me, Alec. That's all there is to it."

"I will, Sarah. By Grok, I will."

She hugged him tightly, and he squeezed back. The two of them had been growing closer, and he began to hope one day they could be more than friends. It was terrible to think of this now, when he was about to ride into deadly danger. He knew he had no right to think of Sarah in that way. Personal feelings had to be put aside while the fate of the world was in jeopardy.

Looking toward the crowd, Alec noticed a lone Fairy woman push her way through the gathered people and make her way toward him. It was Kari, the tracker who had led Ara and her group to Faerie and who had interrupted the council in the Grand Hall. She strode purposefully toward Alec, her face grim.

"Alec Mason," she said. Her voice was thick with emotion.

"Kari, right? What can I do for you?"

For a moment she only looked at him, and then she drew a small glass sphere from a pouch she carried. "This is for you."

"What is it?" he asked, taking the globe and turning it over in his hands.

"A gift. I was...told to give it to you."

He gave her a confused look. "You were told...? By whom?"

Her lips tightened and her forehead creased. Alec saw moisture gathering in her eyes, and if he didn't know better he'd have guessed she was on the verge of tears. "By...by someone I cherished."

He was still confused, but growing curious. "What is it for?"

She shook her head and backed away. Ara stepped forward and called her name, but Kari had already disappeared into the crowd.

"What was that all about?" said Alec.

"I have no idea," answered Ara.

Before Alec could consider it further, the crowd parted and the King and Queen of Faerie, surrounded by red-robed Brothers, strode into view. Radiating majesty, they stopped before Alec. He put the globe Kari had given him into his pocket, focusing his attention on the royal couple.

"Your majesties," he said, bowing deeply. He was amazed at how calm he had learned be around royalty. "I hadn't expected to see you before we left."

"Young Alec," said Queen Mahv, "you and your friends ride forth for the sake of the Fair Folk. The King and Queen of the Fair Folk can do no less than to see you on your way and offer you our undying gratitude."

Alec bowed. "Thank you both. I don't know what to say."

"You do not have to say anything," said the King. "Just know we are proud to have you among our people."

Despite the danger, Alec smiled. And he kept right on smiling until Kraig and Lorn emerged from the stable with the stablemaster and several grooms leading four strong horses. The horses were for the humans; Horren, of course, was far too big for any horse. He claimed he would never need one, though, since his great strides could easily keep up with a galloping horse. Ara had confirmed the Addin's claims.

"Everything is prepared," said Lorn. "As soon as Michael arrives, we can be on our way."

Lorn was garbed in a new suit of hardened leather armor, polished until its black surface shined. A black cloak, hood down, hung to the ground at his back. Kraig was dressed similarly, but his armor was deep brown and his cloak dark green. Alec himself wore black leather pants, high, hard boots, and a soft leather shirt in which metal studs had been fastened. It was heavy, but the armorer had told him the added protection was worth the extra weight.

When Michael arrived, his face was locked in the emotionless expression Alec once expected of the man. Lately, though, his apathetic mien had become more and more uncommon. Why he wore it now, when by all rights he should be feeling the same anxiety as everyone else, was a mystery to Alec.

Michael acknowledged the King and Queen with a small bow and said, "If everything is in order, I suggest we leave at once." He was dressed in a plain white tunic and pants, as unflattering as the clothes he had worn back in Barton Hills. The brown robes had suited him better, Alec thought.

"We've got supplies packed, and the horses are ready," said Kraig. "All that remains, I suppose, is for Alec to point us in the right direction."

"One other thing remains," said King Elyahdyn. "Now that you five are gathered together, I offer you the blessing of all Faerie. May the One guide you with his speed and strength, and may your way be always shown by his light. I grant to you the *Lyll Una*, the blessing only the King of Faerie may grant, and only once in his reign."

Michael's eyes widened slightly. "Elyahdyn, are you sure? You know the consequences…"

"What must be done, must be done. This is for the good of all Faerie. This is for the good of the world." He turned to Mahv. "My Queen, you understand why I must do this."

"We have discussed this already, my Lord." She spoke formally, but there was a glint of moisture in her eyes. "The preparations have been made."

Nodding, Elyahdyn raised his hands and chanted words Alec could not understand. A glow formed above him and light shone from his hands. The light grew brighter, came into focus, and solidified. His body trembled with effort as his hands grasped the now-solid shaft of light, which continued to compress until it was a slim rod, just over two feet in length. Thunder cracked and a sudden wind whipped through Fairhaven.

And then it was over. The light was gone, except for the bright, burning white rod in the King's hands. Elyahdyn fell to his knees and held the rod out to Michael.

"I give to you the *Lyll Una*, the Word of the One."

Michael took the rod and held it tightly in his fist. "I…thank you, great King." His emotionless facade looked near to breaking.

"I only do what I have to do, Elsendarin. Everyone must help in this time of crisis however they can; the King, especially, can do no less. You, above all, know what I have sacrificed this day."

"Indeed I do." A single tear was rolling down his cheek. "I only pray we are up to the task and your sacrifice is not in vain."

"We will succeed," said Lorn. "How can we fail, with the *Lyll Una* bestowed upon us?"

"How indeed," said Michael. He looked to the horses, his gray eyes hiding grief. "The trail grows cold. We must away."

He did not look at the King as he mounted his horse, pulled on the reigns, and rode away from the crowd. Alec frowned, unsure of what just happened. The King looked tired, somehow smaller than before, and he leaned heavily on the guards who led him away. Whatever he had just done had used a great deal of energy.

He said goodbye to Ara and gave Sarah a hug. The crowd around them gazed in wonder at what was happening. It was obvious they, too, had no idea what their King had just done, or why he seemed so weak.

"Oh, Alec," said Sarah as they hugged, "I'll say in one last time: be careful." There were tears running down her cheeks.

"I will." Alec looked up and saw that the others had already mounted. "Sarah, I've got to go."

She did not let go of him. He didn't want to break the embrace, either. Wounds, how he needed her!

"Oh, for Grok's sake," said Ara, "would you two just kiss already?"

They needed no further encouragement. Sarah grabbed his head and pulled it down, pressing her warm mouth to his. Mouths open, passion pounding in their hearts, they kissed deeply, locked in a moment of heaven, a moment far too brief.

"I love you," breathed Alec as they parted.

"Not as much as I love you," whispered Sarah.

As they started to kiss again, Lorn said, "Alec, we have to go."

It was the hardest thing Alec ever did, pulling away from his love and mounting his horse. Giving her a last, longing look, he urged the beast into motion and joined the others as they raced to catch up to Michael.

I have to make it back. Please, Grok, let me make it back. She loves me!

Ara watched Alec's back as he rode into the distance. She was amazed at how much he had changed since she'd last seen him in Barton Hills, only a month and a half ago. His arms and legs, once thin and delicate, were tight with well-defined, if small, muscles. His face had slimmed down, letting his handsome features shine through. But the most obvious, and the most impressive, change was his baby fat was all but gone. Perhaps there was a small ring of fat left around his stomach, but no more than the majority of people back in Barton Hills had. He was harder, stronger, and it showed in the way he carried himself. He was a very different person than she had known, and yet he was still Alec. He had just grown from boy to man.

As Alec and the others passed from sight, she turned toward Sarah, who was still gazing after Alec, sobbing. She loved him and he was gone. Ara took her hand and squeezed it lovingly.

"He'll be back, honey. You'll see."

"Oh, mother!" she cried, throwing her arms around Ara.

They stood there for a moment, oblivious to the crowds still milling around the stable. The advisors and Brothers, and some of the guards, had left with the King, but everyone else was still around, gossiping over the amazing and incomprehensible events of the day.

They continued holding each other until Ara heard someone calling her name. Then she gently withdrew from Sarah's arms, and turned to see Landyn pushing his way through the crowd. He wore urgency as plainly as he wore his cloak.

"Ara," he said, breathing heavily. "Thank Lars. Where are the Councilors? Or the King; I heard he has been found. I was just at the palace and they said everyone was meeting here. There is something I must tell them!"

"They just left," said Ara. "What is so important? Landyn, what's going on?"

He took a moment to catch his breath. "It's the raiders, Ara. They are not finished yet."

"What do you mean?"

"In the tavern, two people were talking. I think one, a woman, was a dark Fairy in disguise. The other, Rhyan, I think, was a soldier from Lehnwood. Salin has commanded them to make sure the King is dead, they said. There are still dark Fairy troops around here, shapers and all. The attack is not over!"

"Oh, Grok's wounds. We've got to warn the King!"

Grabbing Sarah's hand, Ara raced through the crowd toward the palace. Michael was gone, Lorn and Horren were gone, and the King had been weakened by what ever it was he had just done. This was not a good time for another assault.

She took a deep breath. After weeks of searching and hoping, she had found Sarah and Alec. Her thoughts had never gone beyond that point. Now, it appeared she was wrapped up in something beyond the search for her daughter, something deeper than she had imagined. She hoped her feet would carry her to the palace in time to deliver the message, in time to make a difference.

With Landyn running beside her and Sarah clutching her hand, Ara raced through the crowded streets of Fairhaven.

CHAPTER 22

The Tale of Karlyn and Martyn

About a mile outside Fairhaven, Alec felt the pull of the Talisman shifting southwestward. He pulled on the reigns to adjust his course, and the others followed. He was gripping his mount tightly with his legs and clutching the reigns in his hands. He wasn't a very confident rider. Even though the horses of Faerie were more intelligent and better trained than any he'd seen before, he still felt as if the big beast he rode would throw him at any moment. Before, on the path from Lehnwood to Fairhaven, he simply had to sit on the horse's back, since it knew where it was going. Now, he had to guide his mount, and his lack of expertise was showing. It was a constant struggle to keep the beast on course, even though he sensed its intelligence and its willingness to carry him wherever he wished. He doubted he could have controlled a lesser horse at all.

Lorn chucked good-naturedly as he watched Alec's struggle. "It looks like I should have been giving you riding lessons as well as sword lessons. Not to worry, Alec, that horse will not throw you."

"Maybe not, but I might just fall off on my own. I never had much cause to ride back home. Everywhere I ever had to go was in walking distance."

Horren, who was striding at what appeared to be a leisurely pace beside Lorn, laughed heartily. "Ah, Alec, you've gone from being a sheltered villager to a man of the world. You've probably traveled farther and seen more than even the oldest graybeard in your village. I would guess you'll be traveling to quite a few more places that aren't 'within walking distance' before your journeys are through."

"I'm beginning to think so, too," said Alec with a sigh. "I'm never going to be able to go back to my old life, am I?"

After a moment of silence, Michael, from his place to Alec's right, said, "No, Alec, I do not think you will. I think you were born into this world for a reason, and I do not think the reason is to be a baker." His grave expression lightened as he said, "Actually, it was thinking about you and the reason you might be here that helped me regain my faith."

Alec raised his eyebrows in surprise. "Really? I helped you get your faith back? What could this purpose of mine be?"

Michael gave a small smile. "Plenty of time for that later, Alec. For now, just lead us to Salin and the Talisman. That sorcerer and I have an enmity that goes back more years than you can imagine, and I have a mind to put it to rest once and for all."

They rode on in silence for the rest of the morning. At midday they stopped for a rest and a meal, and Alec began thinking of the gift Kari had given him. He took the clear glass sphere from his pocket and showed it to Michael.

"By the Seven," said Michael in genuine surprise. "Where did you get this?"

"From Kari, the tracker. I don't know why she would give me a gift; I hardly know her. What is it?"

Michael shook his head in wonder. "That, my friend, is a Faerie relic called a memory glass. It is tool used to record a person's life magically. Through meditation, one may pass his memories, his life experiences, into the glass. Later, someone else can retrieve those memories and experience the other's life as if in a dream."

Horren laughed. "Fairy-magic is a marvel! I have heard of these memory globes, but never have I seen one."

"Why do you think this Kari woman gave the glass to Alec?" asked Kraig.

Michael shrugged. "There is only one way to find out. Alec, lie down."

"What?" exclaimed Alec. "Why?"

"I want you to try something. Lie flat on your back." When Alec complied, Michael said, "Rest the globe on your chest. Good. Now clear your mind, as you would for one of our Shaping lessons. Feel the glass as it rests upon you. Concentrate only on the glass. If it is meant for you, you will soon fall into a trance and begin to dream. You will dream another person's life."

Alec closed his eyes and tried to do as Michael suggested. He squirmed on the ground but could not get comfortable. He sighed, opened his eyes, and said, "Michael, this isn't going to work! I can't get relaxed here on the ground in the middle of the day! Not with everyone gathered around staring at me!"

Michael laughed. "Try again, Alec. The memory glass will help you, if you let it."

Alec rolled his eyes. "All right, one more try."

Again he closed his eyes and tried to shut out the world around him. He concentrated on the weight of the globe upon his chest. He felt it resting there smooth and firm. And then it began to grow warm. Suddenly it filled his body with a tingling sensation, and its heat flowed through him. He grew strangely weary, felt himself begin to drift away. And then, slowly, as if through darkness and mist, an image began to form in his mind. It was an old image, a memory older than Alec himself. It was a woman…a woman he knew, but younger than he remembered.

Sudden recognition flashed through him. He experienced a pang of sadness, yet it was sweet and comforting. Contentment filled him. He felt he had come home.

Mother!

He embraced the image, was swept away by it, and became lost in an ancient dream of love and pain. A dream of his mother.

A dream of Karlyn.

Ever since she'd been a little girl, Karlyn dreamed of Fairies. It began years ago when old Jordi Luppis came to town, strumming his lute and singing the night away on the hill outside the Silver Shield. His voice was rough and his playing imperfect, but his marvelous tales drew her in, taking her to a world filled with magic and wonder and endless possibilities. He sang of magicians and monsters, of valorous knights and maidens fair. But what mesmerized her, what filled her with longings and passions she barely understood, were his tales of the Fair Folk who lived in the North. Glorious was their history, filled with triumph and tragedy, and beautiful were the enchanted forests they called home. In her mind's eye she could see mighty trees glimmering with magic, and she could see the elegant people who lived among them.

She was in love with the Fair Folk years before she'd ever met one.

When she was a girl her father sometimes scolded her for taking the songs of the old minstrel seriously. "They are only fanciful tales to pass the night, girl," he often told her. "Fairies and ogres! Why, next you'll be believing in goblins and sorcery." He would laugh and pat her on the back, sending her to her chores.

Chores were always an important part of the day in Barton Hills, as her mother never failed to remind her. But as she did the wash or tended the garden or milked the cow, her mind drifted back to the minstrel's songs and dreams of Faerie.

But Karlyn's dreams became dark in the years that followed. When she was only nineteen her parents took ill and passed away, leaving her with nothing but her grief and a meager inheritance. She worked hard in her garden raising vegetables to sell at market, but she earned little and was forced to rely on the goodwill of friends and the charity of neighbors. She was not the most beautiful girl in Barton Hills, and by her twentieth birthday she hadn't received any proposals of marriage. Too early in life she grew weary and sad, and dreams of Fairies were her only escape.

She was rescued from grief and poverty by a kind-hearted farmer named Brok Mason. A small, brownish man in his early thirties, hunched by years of hard labor, he was as caring a man as she could ever hope to meet. He lived on the outskirts of town and often came to the Silver Shield to relax at the end of the day. On these occasions they would talk for long hours, for he, too, had lost his parents at a young age, and he sympathized with her grief. And then one day, he invited her into his home.

"I'm not much for housekeeping, and I'm weary of beans and stew, which is about all I can cook. Now I know what you must be thinking, but believe me, my intentions are entirely honorable. I have an extra room I could make up for you, and I could see that you live comfortably from here on out."

"Why, I don't know what to say," she answered. "Brok, you've been so kind to me, but I don't know if I can…"

"Now don't be silly. I might not be quite old enough to be your father, but you've become very much like a daughter to me. We're both alone in the world. We can take care of each other."

She smiled at him, placing her small hand on his. "All right," she said. "You've shown me more kindness than anyone else, and I do need the work. When can I start?"

As a wide smile lit up his eyes years of toil melted from his face. "Why not today?" he said.

And so for a year she lived with Brok, and they grew closer as time went on. She kept his house clean and prepared meals, and he made sure she was comfortable and had everything he could provide her. Long evenings they would sit together, and they shared many a conversation at their favorite table in the tavern. The people in the town began to talk, wondering if Karlyn and Brok would soon marry. The two of them always laughed about it, telling the others they were just close friends.

But one day Brok approached her as she was fixing dinner, and he spoke quietly and nervously.

"Karlyn, there is something I've been meaning to ask you. That is, um...I wonder if you would consider...if you might wish to..."

She laughed warmly and put her hand on his arm. "Brok, I've never seen you like this. What is it you want to say?"

He took a deep breath to steady himself. "Well, we've been living under the same roof for over a year now, and I've grown quite fond of you."

Karlyn smiled. "I've grown fond of you, too, Brok."

He looked down and paused for a moment before going on. "What I mean is, I care for you deeply. I know I'm not the most handsome man in the world, or the smartest, but I'd be deeply honored if you would...um, if you would...marry me."

Karlyn gasped, her brown eyes growing wide. After her initial shock passed, she sighed and smiled and shook her head. "Oh, Brok. You are so dear to me; you're the sweetest man I know. But marriage? I don't want to hurt you, but I'm not sure I would be a good wife to you. You deserve someone who could love you with her whole heart. I'm just not that person, Brok."

He took her hands and looked at her hopefully. "I know you don't feel the same way about me I feel about you, but we belong together. Over time, you may learn to love me."

She hugged him tightly and was silent for a long moment. "Oh, Brok, you don't understand! I *do* love you, but not in the way you need. I cannot be a wife to you."

"I don't care about that, Karlyn. Any love you have for me is enough. I just need you by my side until I die."

Karlyn pulled away from the hug and saw a tear in his eye. She kissed him on the cheek and stroked his coarse hair, and then he turned and left the room. She did love him and she hated to see him in such pain, but what could she do to help him? She pondered the dilemma as she finished preparing the evening meal, but in her sorrow she could find no satisfactory answer.

The next day she went to see her friend Ara Mills, who had recently opened a shop on the east side of town. Ara was considered wise for her years, and she herself was married to an older man. Perhaps she could offer Karlyn some wisdom.

Karlyn entered the shop, walking past rows of shelves containing Ara's unusual inventory: foreign jewelry, clothing of strange material and design, decorative trinkets and baubles, exotic statues and ornaments. Ara was on the other side of the room, kneeling beside a large chest and withdrawing from it a wooden carving of a horse. She looked up and smiled when she saw her friend.

"Karlyn! You haven't been by for weeks. It's good to see you."

Karlyn managed to smile. "It's always good to see you, Ara. What have you got there?" she asked, indicating the horse.

"Oh, this? You know Mary Roberts and her husband John? Their boy Kraig just turned six today; I'm looking for a suitable birthday gift for him."

Karlyn crossed the room and knelt across the chest from her friend. Looking at the finely carved horse, she said, "I'm sure he'll like this."

Ara nodded in agreement. "The horse it is, then." She rose to her feet and walked toward her office in the back. As Karlyn followed, Ara asked, "Would you like some tea? I still have some in the back from this morning, although it's not very hot anymore."

"That would be fine," said Karlyn. "Thank you." When they were seated at the table in Ara's office, Karlyn took a sip of her tea and continued. "Ara, I wanted to ask your opinion about something."

"Sounds serious," said Ara.

"It is. Brok asked me to marry him."

"Grok's beard!" exclaimed Ara, her bright young eyes growing wide with surprise. "I suppose it had to happen eventually. What are you going to do?"

Karlyn shrugged. "I don't know. I mean, he's a good man, but he's more than a decade older than I am and he's sort of a father to me. I love him, but not like a wife should love her husband."

Ara smiled and touched her friend's hand. "I understand. Once, it was much the same with me and Matthew."

"Really?" asked Karlyn in genuine surprise. Ara and her husband of two years had always appeared to be very much in love.

"Yes. He was in his twenties when we met, and I was just a girl of fifteen. He was like my older brother then, but when I became a woman my feelings for him changed. He began to see me differently, too, and when he asked me to marry him I didn't even have to think about it."

Karlyn nodded, circling her finger around the rim of her tea cup. "My situation is different. I was already a grown woman when I met Brok. Granted, my feelings for him are deeper than they've been for anyone else, but he's just not what I imagined in a husband."

Ara chuckled. "What do you want? A knight in shining armor? There are none of those to be found in Barton Hills. Or maybe...maybe you still dream of Fairies. Just as likely Grok himself will swoop down from the clouds and make you his bride."

"Don't make fun. The more I think about it, the more I think I *will* marry Brok. Maybe my love for him *will* grow. I just don't want to make a mistake about something so important."

"Karlyn, do you really want my advice?" Ara asked seriously.

"Of course."

"Marry him. He's a caring, gentle man, and he treats you like a queen. You know as well as I do men like that are almost impossible to find. Besides, people are talking. A lot of people assume you and Brok...you know, carry on as married folk do."

Karlyn gasped. "You mean they think we..."

"Some people do. After all, you've lived with him for more than a year. Now, most people aren't too judgmental, but some of the older folks look down on it. If you were to marry, that would stop the gossip."

Karlyn was still catching her breath. "I had no idea people thought..." she said, trailing off.

Ara sighed. "Karlyn, in some ways you are still so naive. Marry Brok. You could do a lot worse."

They talked for a long while longer, and by the time Karlyn left the shop, she had made up her mind. Brok loved her and would care for her to the end of his days. She could learn to love him as a wife loves her husband. She would have to. She was going to marry him.

"Yes," she told Brok in the field that afternoon.

"Yes what?" he asked, looking up from his work.

"What do you think?" she said with a grin. "Yes, I'll marry you."

The farmer dropped his hoe and jumped up in joy, laughing as tears rolled down his face. He lifted Karlyn from the ground and swung her about, clutching her close to his chest. They laughed together, and for the first time he kissed her gently on the lips. After a moment, however, he sobered and put her on the ground.

"Karlyn," he asked gravely, "are you certain? You don't have to do this."

She smiled warmly. "But I want to do this. No one has shown me as much kindness as you. I love you."

He hugged her again, unable to stop crying. She felt she was doing the right thing, but in her heart something still troubled her. She hid it effectively, even from herself, but deep down she knew she could never give Brok the love he deserved.

At the same time, a week's journey from Barton Hills, Martyn du Sharrel proudly rode his white steed beside Captain Correth, the leader of his *Tynn*. It was Martyn's second mission with a *Tynn*, the second time he had left his home in Faerie to journey into the world of humankind, and he could not have been happier. Exploring unknown realms was what Martyn lived for. Something had always drawn him to humans, something he could not explain, and he felt strangely at home in their company. This was extremely unusual for the Fair Folk, who considered themselves above humans and kept themselves apart from the lesser race.

The Captain continued with what he was saying, and Martyn forced himself to pay attention. "The town is called Barton Hills. Quaint, don't you think?"

Martyn looked at the light-haired Captain and said, "Indeed. And what leads Father Sang to believe the item we seek is there?"

"The Father of Nom need not share his knowledge with simple soldiers like us. His powers of divination are second to none, and he told us it is somewhere in Tyridan. Other *Tynn* have been sent to search elsewhere in the realm; we are ordered to search Barton Hills and other nearby farming villages."

"It simply seems unlikely it would be here, Correth. And something else concerns me, if I may speak freely."

"You may, old friend."

Martyn looked back, making certain the others in the *Tynn* were not within earshot. "This mission comes to us from Father Sang, and not from the King himself. This worries me. It is normally the prerogative of the King to order a *Tynn*. Does his Majesty even know where we are, what we're doing?"

"Of course he knows of the *Tynn*." Correth paused a moment, and Martyn thought he looked hesitant. Whispering, he said "It is possible, however, the King does not know our specific quest."

"What?" Martyn cried in surprise. "For what reason would Sang hide a quest as important as ours from our Lord?"

"Quietly, Martyn! This is not for the ears of the others. Father Sang keeps this information from King Elyahdyn for the present because he does not know if we will be able to find what we seek. He does not wish to give the King false hope. Sang only wishes to save the King heartache if we fail in our mission, or if Sang's divination is wrong. To give him hope and then to shatter it would be cruel."

"But the King deserves to know the truth."

Correth looked at him harshly. "It is not for us to decide. We depend on our King to lead us with strength and courage; a King with shattered hope cannot do so. For what it is worth, I believe Sang's way is best."

Martyn remained silent but he did not agree. Sang had always been a proud Fairy, too proud at times, and Martyn could not help but be suspicious of his motives. Nothing good could come of keeping the King in the dark. The thing they sought was too important.

As they rode onward, Martyn thought about home in order to keep his mind off his concerns. He thought of his mother and father, how proud they were of him, and he thought of his sister, who somewhat idolized him. He smiled, for he loved young Kari the most, and thinking about her made his troubles slip away. He thought as highly of her as she did of him, for he admired her abilities in tracking and hunting, and he was in awe of her recently discovered strength in Shaping. Although a woman could never become a full member of the Order of Nom, many received training and became powerful Shapers in their own right. With her talent, Kari would go far.

Martyn looked up at the sunlight filtering through the lush trees. He smelled the fresh spring air. Sounds of the forest filled his ears: birds singing, tiny animals scurrying over crunchy fallen leaves, even their own horses clomping along the narrow dirt path. There was no magic in the forest as there was back home, but the lack of magic gave the land a natural, wholesome quality which appealed to Martyn. Surrounded by ordinary, mundane nature, Martyn let go of his concerns.

It would take them nearly a week to reach Barton Hills. Until then, Martyn decided he would relax and enjoy the ride.

The days were hectic in Barton Hills as plans for the wedding went forward. Karlyn ordered a dress from the clothier in Lockguild, and Derik the tavern-keeper planned a great feast. Ara was in charge of obtaining flowers, and Brok assisted Karlyn in extending invitations to all their friends. They were to marry in one month's time in the garden outside the tiny Temple of Grok which stood in the center of town. Most of the townsfolk would be there, for although Karlyn and Brok were close to few of them, weddings were one of the few times when the people of the village stopped work to celebrate. Everyone always took advantage of the opportunity weddings presented.

Karlyn still had her doubts, of course, but she let the excitement of the moment carry her away. It was her wedding, something all girls dreamed about, and she would make the most of it.

One afternoon, however, about a week into planning the wedding, she began to feel restless. Her doubts and fears flooded her mind all at once, and she had the sudden need to escape. She was certain a walk would help her clear her head. Afterwards, she would be fine. A walk was all she needed.

"Ara," she said, for she was sitting on her friend's front porch watching the setting sun when her doubts ambushed her, "I…need to go. All this planning is catching up to me. I've got to get away from it for a while."

"Karlyn," said Ara with concern, "are you feeling all right? You look pale."

Karlyn suddenly found it hard to breath. "I'm…I'm fine. I just need to walk."

She hopped up from her chair and hurried down the road. She soon found herself beyond the edge of town, near the border of the Northwood. She had rarely ventured into the woods, so she was surprised at herself when she entered the forest with little hesitation.

Am I mad? There are wolves in this forest, and worse! But I have to get away from town. Why did I agree to marry Brok? What am I doing?

Breathing heavily, she felt panic setting in. What was wrong with her? She fled into the forest as if it were her only hope, as if she were being drawn deeper into its depths. As if something was calling to her.

Brok is not the man for you, said a voice in her head. *He is a good man, but not the* right *man. Yours is a different destiny.*

"For the love of Grok, what is happening to me!" she sobbed.

She was running as fast as she could, not watching her step, so it wasn't surprising she fell over a raised root and landed flat on her face. The fall knocked the wind out of her lungs, and the shock of it jarred her out of her panic. She lay there for a moment, breathing heavily, when the sounds of numerous horses trotting up the path came to her ears. Slowly, she managed to push herself to her knees just as the riders came into view.

She gasped. For a moment her heart stopped beating.

She knew what the riders were even before they stopped in front of her.

There were perhaps twenty of them, riding two by two on the path before her. In the front rode two men who took her breath away. One was pale of both hair and face; the second had sandy hair and was a little darker. Both radiated power and majesty and carried themselves in beauty and pride. The pale one had an air of command about him, a strength of body and mind a blind man couldn't miss. But it was the darker one who made her feel weak, who caused her heart to quicken beneath her breast. He was handsome beyond belief, and she knew she would never be free of his deep, brown eyes. His long hair swept down past his chiseled cheek-bones to his strong shoulders. His features were both delicate and strong, his muscles sleek and defined.

Once again she found she could not breathe. For the first time in her life, she was certain she was in love.

"F…Fairies," she whispered. "Here…"

"Who are you, woman, and why do you roam these woods?" asked the pale Fairy. "How do you know what we are? Most humans know we are different but do not guess we are of the Fair Folk."

She tried to respond, but she couldn't speak. The tan Fairy was gazing at her, holding her with his eyes, smiling. Suddenly he dismounted and extended his hand to help her from her knees.

"Please, Captain, do not burden her with so many questions at once. It is obvious she is in shock. What human wouldn't be, if they recognized us for what we are."

As she took his hand, he gently pulled her to her feet and continued. "My name is Martyn of house du Sharrel, from the land of Faerie. This is my Captain, Correth, and behind him are the members of our *Tynn*. Pleased to meet you, young human."

She took several gulps of air before she could utter a single word. Collecting herself, she managed to say, "My name is Karlyn…Karlyn Smith. I am from Barton Hills, sir."

The Fairy laughed. "Please, my name is Martyn. It just so happens we are heading to your village. Would you care to ride with me and show us the way?"

She nearly lost her breath again. "Ride…with you?"

Martyn mounted and once again extended his hand to her. She had no choice but to take it, and with a mighty pull he lifted her onto the saddle behind him.

"Martyn," said Captain Correth, "put the girl down. We have business we must attend."

Martyn laughed. "Of course we do, but our business is in Barton Hills. Surely we can take the girl to her home there."

"Very well," sighed Correth. "My lady," he said to Karlyn, "enjoy your ride. Few of your kind have ever ridden with the Fair Folk."

Martyn turned his head and said to her, "Put your arms around me, my lady. I would not want you to fall."

She was shaking as she reached around his waist and held him tightly. As he kicked his mount into motion, his soft hair blew into her face and tickled her nose. It smelled fresh, like spring itself, and she breathed the scent as deeply as she could. With her body pressed up against his back, she felt a sense of longing swell within her breast. She needed this man.

"So what is it you do, Karlyn of Barton Hills," asked Martyn.

She nearly melted at the sound of his voice. "I…I live with a gentleman, a farmer. I prepare his meals and clean the house."

Martyn raised an eyebrow as he glanced back at her. "You are his servant, then?"

"Well," she said, "I don't think of it that way. He doesn't either. We're…good friends. We take care of each other."

"It is good to take care of your friends," agreed the Fairy. "But this man, if you live with him, he should make you his wife."

Too quickly, Karlyn blurted, "Oh, no, that wouldn't work at all. Our relationship isn't like that."

Why did I say that? she asked herself. *Why didn't I tell him we're going to be married?*

You know why, she answered.

"You know," said Martyn, "we are going to be in your town for a few weeks. Why don't you show us around when we arrive?"

She smiled. His friendly manner almost made her forget to be nervous. "There's not much to see. Barton Hills is a small town. What do you want there, anyway?"

Martyn just smiled and said, "You need not concern yourself, good lady. We are merely paying Tyridan a visit."

They rode the rest of the way in silence. Karlyn closed her eyes and concentrated on the hard body pressing up against her own. She continued to breathe his scent. She let everything else slip away.

Too soon they arrived in town, and the townsfolk gazed at these strangers in curious wonder. Karlyn couldn't tell if the surprise on their faces was due to the Fairies themselves or the fact Karlyn was riding with one. None of them seemed to be particularly impressed, though. No one but Karlyn herself realized these visitors weren't human.

She took them to the tavern where they rented rooms for themselves and shelter for their horses. There was barely enough room in the stable to house the twenty marvelous beasts, but the grooms and stablemaster didn't complain. They were happy to have such beautiful creatures in their care. Derik the tavern keeper was a little less enthusiastic about finding room for twenty guests, strangers to boot, but when he saw their gold coins he hurried to accommodate them.

When they were settled in, Martyn said, "Thank you for your assistance, my lady Karlyn." He took her hand and kissed it gently. "We have much work to do today, but perhaps you would join me here for a drink this evening? I would like to hear about life in Barton Hills."

She smiled, feeling her cheeks redden at his touch. "It's not all that interesting, sir…Martyn. But a drink would be nice. Thank you."

He bowed to her and left the tavern with his companions. She gazed after him for a moment and collapsed into a chair. His presence made her weak. When at last she found the strength to rise, she left for home. She still had much to do and the day was wasting.

Martyn gazed around the field, barely concentrating on what Correth was saying. For some reason, he kept thinking about the feeling of the human woman's arms around his waist. He hoped he'd get a chance to ride with her again before their work in Barton Hills was finished.

"And only if you are already facing in the right direction," finished the Captain.

"I beg your pardon?" said Martyn, trying to focus on the leader of the *Tynn*.

Correth sighed in frustration. "What is the matter, Martyn? You haven't heard a word I've said. You are not homesick, are you?"

The brown-haired fairy smiled at the suggestion. "No, not at all. I am sorry; I was simply admiring the farmers' fields. What were you saying?"

Correth shook his head. He hated repeating himself. "I was telling you how to use the glow-wands, Martyn. According to Father Sang, the wands are attuned to powerful magic and should lead us to what we seek. The closer you are to a thing of magic, the brighter the gem on the end of the wand will glow. It will only work if you are within several miles of a source of magic, and only if it is pointed directly in the direction of the source. The wands are not perfect, but they are our best hope of finding our prize. The Father was able to construct only a few glow-wands before we set out; our *Tynn* has but four. I will keep one and entrust a second to you; the third and fourth I will give to Gahn and Aron. We four will lead the others across northern Tyridan, using this village as our base."

Martyn nodded his understanding. "I realize we must start somewhere, but it seems to me we are searching for a pebble on a beach. I wish Sang's divination could have been more specific than 'Tyridan.'"

"The odds are not with us, my friend, but we are closer than we've been in generations to finding that which was lost. Now come, we may as well round up the others and begin the search. Today we will search the town itself, for it is as likely here as anywhere."

Martyn nodded in agreement but said nothing. He was thinking about Karlyn again. She was a plain woman in some ways, but there was something about her…something in her nervous smile, her shy brown eyes, her gentle voice. Hers was a subtle beauty, a beauty any but the keenest eye might overlook. But for the man lucky enough to notice, it was a beauty as fresh as springtime and as new as dawn.

Strange, thought Martyn. *No Fairy maiden has caught my eye as this human girl has.*

He followed his Captain back into town, but his mind was not on his mission. He found himself looking forward more and more to the evening, when he would be able to see Karlyn again. As he crossed the fields of wheat and corn, he thought of her eyes, her smile, and sighed deeply.

They had not been sitting long in the tavern when Martyn suggested they go for a walk under the moonlight. Karlyn's heart jumped at the idea, and she accepted his extended hand and followed him outside. She ignored the looks the other tavern patrons gave her as she passed them. They knew she was engaged to Brok and didn't understand or approve of her keeping company with a stranger. Karlyn didn't care what they thought.

"It is a truly beautiful village you live in, Karlyn," said the Fairy.

"I think so," she replied, "but it can't be anything like your home. From what I've heard, Faerie is a magical place, lovely beyond compare."

Martyn laughed. "It is full of what you call magic, and that gives it a certain beauty and light. But when you've lived among such wonder all your life, it is nice to see a place where the only beauty is created by nature. Magic is a part of our beings; we depend on it for everything, even our beauty. I am in awe of what you folk have built here without the aid of magic. In Faerie, such an accomplishment is nearly unknown."

Karlyn laughed softly. "No one here even believes in magic. If I told them you and your friends were Fairies, they would lock me up."

"It is for the better they do not know. We do not like to cause a stir when we venture into the realm of humans."

"That's probably a good policy."

He turned to her and smiled. She resisted the sudden urge to reach up and trace his thin lips with a finger. He said, "How is it you could see us for what we are? In the past we have found humans cannot tell we are of another race. Unless they are sensitive to magic, of course."

She shook her head. "I don't know how I recognized you. It just seemed so obvious. I've never seen a man as beautiful as you...I mean, *all* of you seem to be...so handsome. Flawless, really."

"It's a kind of magic," he said, winking.

"I don't know how anyone could miss it."

"Your kind generally ignore magic. Magic is simply not in humankind's nature. You, however, are obviously sensitive to it." He paused and gazed into the night sky. "The moon is bright and full tonight. A perfect night for a walk in the forest."

She gasped. "The forest at night? No one goes into the Northwood after dark; it's too dangerous."

"Dangerous? Nonsense! Forests are most lovely under the light of the moon and stars. Come, let me show you."

He tightened his grip on her hand and ran toward the forest, pulling her behind. She had no choice but to run with him, and soon they were both laughing into the cool, refreshing wind. They rushed past the outskirts of town and soon crossed into the Northwood. The forest was dark, but before Karlyn knew it they entered a clearing where the light of the moon shown down brightly. Within a ring of trees, a soft bed of leaves and moss and pine needles covered the ground. It was here they stopped, and Karlyn struggled to catch her breath.

"You see?" he asked, indicating the clearing with a sweep of his arm. "Under the moonlight the forest is a thing of splendor. While you are with me the night predators will not harm you."

She gazed at the trees and leaves glowing silver under the moon, listened to the night crickets chirping nearby. The moss below smelled moist and fresh. Martyn was still holding her hand. She gazed up into his eyes, and suddenly her heart was lost to him. It took every ounce of will she could muster to resist kissing him.

He returned her gaze for a long moment, and it seemed to her he felt the same thing she was feeling. His lips parted as if to kiss her, but after a moment he spoke instead. His words were soft and gentle, but not so fulfilling as a kiss.

"I…I find myself strangely drawn to you, Karlyn. You intrigue me greatly. I would…call you friend."

"Friend?" she said softly. "Oh, of course. Yes, I would like that."

"Do you wish to walk some more?"

"Yes, of course. Let's walk."

But they did not move. Instead he took her other hand and pulled her closer to him. They were only inches apart from one another and she could feel his breath on her forehead.

"I like the way you smell," he whispered.

She put her head on his chest and he began stroking her soft blond hair. She closed her eyes and let him embrace her in his strong arms.

"I like the way your body feels against mine."

As they stood there under the moonlight time lost all meaning. She listened intently to the quickening beat of his heart. Her own blood was racing, filling her with fire, and when he lifted her face to his she surrendered utterly to her desire.

Their kiss was long and full of passion and Karlyn was filled with life and light as the moment swept her away. Her eyes were closed lightly and she was focused on Martyn, on the kiss, with every fiber of her being. It lasted forever and was over in an instant. When they parted she opened her eyes and gazed with longing at his perfect face.

For a long time they did not move or speak, but then Martyn caressed her cheek and said, "You are a breath of fresh air to a man who has been suffocating. I am drawn to you in ways I cannot understand."

"I feel the same way. Martyn, I feel…"

She could not finish her sentence before surrendering to the urge to kiss him again. They kissed deeply, and no words were spoken again for a long while.

Slowly, as if in a dream, they eased to the ground, comfortable upon soft moss sprinkled with pine needles. She lay flat upon her back and he leaned over her and gazed longingly at her. His face was framed in silver moonlight and she was able to perceive the glow of magic around him…the magic of the Fair Folk, or perhaps only the enchantment of passion.

For Karlyn, the forest moved that night and the mountains quaked. The stars spun in the sky and the earth beneath her shifted. She died that night and found a home among the stars, soaring through the heavens, floating, flying, swimming in the clouds, growing, loving, lusting, becoming one with the world, one with a man, one with love, one, one, One, burning under the stars, the sky, living fully, expressing, actualizing, becoming, touching, going, dying, coming, starving, feasting. Changing.

There was a sudden rush and she soared to the peaks of the world, beyond them, beyond the stars, flashing like thunder, illuminating the sky, flashing like lightning, burning, burning, bursting...

And then she was floating back to the world gently, gently. Silently but for her and Martyn's gentle gasping sighs. Then there was only peace. Contentment.

Love.

She woke much later. The chill of the night swept over her bare flesh, but the heat of passion warmed her from inside. The first thing she noticed was that Martyn was no longer beside her. Rising up on one elbow, she looked to the edge of the clearing where she saw him, still unclad, staring silently into the dark forest. His slim, pale form seemed to glow in the moonlight, and his strong, lithe muscles were visible under his skin. She felt a pang in her breast. Already she desired him again.

"Anything interesting out there?" she asked softly.

He turned around. For a moment she thought he looked worried, almost fearful of something, but quickly his expression melted into a warm smile.

"I was only thinking, my love. By the One, you look glorious."

"Come to me, then," she said. "I want you again."

And he came to her, and again they embraced as lovers, and this time she soared even higher then before. But when it was over and they lay together looking at the stars, and she noticed a hint of worry once again creep into his face.

"Martyn, what's wrong? Is it me? Did I do something wrong? This is all new to me."

He looked at her and his expression became compassionate, yet at the same time sad. He touched her cheek and said, "You did nothing wrong, Karlyn. Nothing at all. In fact, everything you did was beyond right. You make me feel...whole. Fulfilled. And yet, what we have shared...it is against everything I have been taught all my life. It is against...against nature."

Suddenly all the warmth rushed away from Karlyn, leaving her with cold panic. "What are you talking about?" she cried. "It is against nature to know love? Certainly it's happened fast, faster than seems natural, but we cannot deny our feelings!"

Martyn shook his head sadly. "I said nothing of denying my feelings. I feel for you...perhaps I love you. I am drawn to you by a force I cannot explain. But there are things you do not know, Karlyn, ancient laws of the Fair Folk which forbid what we have just done. For a Fairy and a human to touch as we have touched, it is treason against Faerie itself. And treason is punishable by death."

The more she heard, the more she shook her head in disbelief. "Treason? Death? What kind of pointless law would separate two people in love, regardless of race?"

"The law is not pointless," answered Martyn. "It is based on old texts which contain the wisdom of the ancients. They were far more knowledgeable than we are today, and they spoke of terrible consequences should a Fairy and a human mate. It could mean the end of both our races. Oh, if only I would have listened to my head instead of my heart!"

Karlyn stared at him in silence. She didn't know what to feel. Everything was jumbled inside her and she couldn't think of anything to say. So instead of speaking, she got dressed and started walking back toward town. Adrift in conflicting emotion, it didn't occur to her to be afraid of the dark forest. Vaguely she was aware of Martyn following her, perhaps protecting her, but she did not turn to see him. He did not speak to her, and when she at last reached the outskirts of the village and looked back, he was nowhere to be found.

She wondered if she would ever see him again. Feeling numb, as if someone had just shown her the light of heaven only to snatch it away an instant later, she made her way to the farmhouse she shared with Brok. She wondered how she would explain where she'd been. She wondered, but didn't particularly care.

In the light of day she felt a little better. Her heart still ached for Martyn, but she busied herself with her chores and thought about him as little as possible. When Brok asked her where she had been, she told him she was out walking with her new friends, the strangers who had recently come to town. He warned her to be careful around strangers and asked her not to stay out so late, but after saying this he kissed her on the cheek and let it drop.

She was not in the mood to oversee any wedding plans, so she spent the day alone tending the flowers surrounding Brok's house. Keeping a garden had always helped her relax and forget her troubles, and today she truly needed to forget.

But of course she couldn't forget him. For better or for worse, she loved Martyn. Somehow she knew she always would.

Martyn and the four Fairies assigned to him marched purposefully through the village of Barton Hills. What a sight they must have looked to the quaint farmers and craftsmen who populated the little town! Four beautiful strangers striding down the streets and through the fields all day long was certainly cause for talk. But the strangers were always friendly and free with coin, so the villagers didn't mind their eccentric behavior. Not much, at least.

From time to time, Martyn consulted the gem at the end of his wand. He noticed it glowing very faintly a few hours into their search, and he excitedly led his men in the direction the wand indicated. The others smiled and congratulated him. Even if it was not the thing they sought which caused the gem to glow, it had to be a magical artifact of some power. *Something* was in or near the village, and they would soon find it.

Martyn had been glad when Correth assigned him to the village itself. Although he knew his feelings for Karlyn were wrong, he couldn't bare the thought of being far from her. As long as his quest kept him in the village, he could be near her without causing suspicion.

But surely she hated him now! He had taken her there in the forest after knowing her only a day, and then he told her their love could not be. But what else could he have done? If they were discovered, he would be put to death and she would be held captive until it was certain she was not with child. If she was, the child would be torn from her body and killed.

He prayed she wasn't carrying his child. And he knew he could not risk loving her again.

At the same time he knew, given the opportunity, he *would* risk it.

"Martyn," said Avryl, the smallish Fairy who strode beside him, "the wand glows more brightly. We must be getting closer to something."

Martyn shook himself out of his thoughts and glanced down at the gem. It was indeed brighter. "You are right," he said. "There is something of Fairy-make hidden in this village."

As they walked toward the eastern edge of town, the gem of the glow-wand shined brighter and brighter. Martyn's anticipation was so keen he was able to put Karlyn temporarily out of his mind. Perhaps he was within reach of the *Tynn's* goal!

He crested a low hill and saw a wooden building sitting alone among some trimmed shrubs and small trees. A new sign out front indicated they were approaching The Dragon's Den. Martyn smiled at the reference to the fierce mythological creature. Were there such a thing as dragons, this modest wooden building would be the last place he would expect to find one.

Martyn continued down the hill toward the building, his men following close behind. Although it was by no means a grand structure, it was the largest he had seen in Barton Hills, save only the Silver Shield. He reached the door and was about to knock when he noticed, hanging from a nail, a small sign which read "open." Still smiling to himself, he opened the door and went in.

He was pleasantly surprised and amused by what he saw inside. He had not expected a place like this to exist in a village as small and simple as Barton Hills. All around him were strange and exotic objects: ornaments, tools, objects of art, and toys of foreign lands and forgotten times. Some of the things he recognized as being crafted in Eglak before the civil war, or in Estron before Vorik Seth's shadow split it down the middle. Nothing, however, appeared to be of Fairy-make.

"What manner of place is this?" he asked, aloud but to himself.

"It's my shop," said a female voice off to his right, "the Dragon's Den, a place of curious wonders." A woman emerged from behind a shelf with a dust-cloth in her hand. She had her blond hair pulled back, and youthful green eyes looked out from an unlined face. She was attractive in a simple and pure way, similar to Karlyn yet different. She was slimmer of face and body, and on the surface prettier. But she did not stir Martyn's heart the way Karlyn did; that would have been impossible.

"Wonders indeed," said Martyn, reaching out to touch a silver statuette of a dove. "Who might you be, young lady, and where did you come by this marvelous merchandise?"

The woman smiled. "I'm Ara Mills. As for these goods, well, let's just say my grandfather was quite a collector. A well traveled collector. He had to buy this building just to store his things, none of which he could ever bare to part with. I, on the other hand, have no problem parting with these goods, if the price is right. But what brings you to my shop, strangers? Shopping for antiques?"

Martyn's smile widened. "Something like that." He paused and bowed deeply. "I am Martyn du Sharrel. My friends and I have been searching high and low for a special item…a family heirloom, if you will. We have it on good authority it is somewhere in this land. With so many marvels gathered here under one roof, I cannot help but wonder if you might have the thing we seek."

Ara chuckled. "I don't know, but feel free to look around. And if you find anything else that strikes your fancy, let me know. My prices are fair, and always negotiable."

Martyn bowed again and said, "Thank you, dear lady." He motioned for the others to follow him and began to scan the many shelves.

It wasn't long before he came to a closed door. When he pointed his wand at the door, the gem began to shine brilliantly. "Avryl," he whispered, "look!"

Avryl nodded and grinned. "There is something of worth through there. Perhaps the Father of Nom is as wise as they say."

Putting the wand away, Martyn turned to Ara and said, "What is through this door, good shopkeeper?"

She shrugged. "The basement. If you think there are a lot of things in the shop, you should see what I've got down there. Even if I keep this place open for twenty years I doubt I'll ever sell it all."

"Would it be possible to have a look downstairs?" asked Martyn.

"Oh, I don't think so," said Ara. "You wouldn't be able to find anything down there, anyway. It's not organized and it's packed so tightly you can barely walk."

Martyn hated to use magic to manipulate other people's minds, but he needed to check the basement. Although he himself was not skilled at the *Charin-ta*, he knew his companion was. "Avryl," he whispered.

The smaller Fairy nodded his understanding. With a tiny warping of reality which Martyn could sense with his spirit, Avryl Shaped Ara's perceptions.

"Fine lady," Avryl said, "I implore you, it is very important we search your entire shop. Allow us to go downstairs. I promise we will not be long."

"Well," said Ara with a sigh, "I suppose it could do no harm. Just be careful; things are stacked rather precariously down there."

"Thank you so much," said Martyn sincerely as Ara crossed the shop toward them.

She opened the door and ushered them down the stairs. When she left them to their own devices, Martyn took out his wand. It was glowing fiercely.

The others murmured excitedly, but Martyn kept his mind on his task. He pushed his way past heavy boxes and chests, moved between statues and shelves heaped with dusty relics. The wand was now bright enough to light the entire room. It almost hurt to look at it.

"Here!" he exclaimed, pointing to a small chest wedged in the corner between two large boxes. "In here must rest our goal, or at least some other Faerie artifact of great power. Avryl, open the chest."

"Of course, Martyn."

But when Avryl knelt down and put pulled at the chest's lid, it would not open. He tried to pry it with his knife, but the lid still would not budge. He looked up and shook his head.

"What is wrong?" questioned Martyn.

"Is it stuck?" asked one of the others.

Avryl shrugged. "It is closed tight, almost as if an enchantment were upon it. I cannot sense anything magical about the chest, though."

"Let me see," said Martyn. He knew he would have no more luck sensing magic than Avryl. The short Fairy had always been a stronger Shaper than Martyn.

Martyn bent over the chest and examined it. This close to a source of magic, he had to put the wand away for fear of being blinded. He grabbed the chest and yanked with all his might. The lid might as well have been a giant stone slab for all he could move it. But as he pulled in vain upon the lid, he noticed something resting in the corner *behind* the chest. Curious, he ceased his labor and reached into the small area between the corner and the chest. His hand fell upon a smooth sphere which he gripped and pulled free.

He held it up for all to see. It was a clear glass globe, about four inches in diameter. It was sturdy and heavy, and he could sense enchantment within it. So could the others, for they gazed at it with obvious wonder.

"What...what is it?" asked one of his companions.

"It is a memory glass," said Martyn. "A very rare and marvelous thing. I had one as a child, given to me by my grandfather, who had gotten it from *his* grandfather."

"Memory glass?" asked Avryl. "What is it for?"

Martyn smiled a small smile, remembering all the hours he spent gazing into his grandfather's glass. "It is a recording device. You place it upon your breast and meditate on your life, your experiences. Your memories. Your thoughts fill the glass, and there they remain for all time, waiting until someone comes along and unlocks them. This person then experiences your life, as if in a dream."

"Can anyone retrieve the memories?" asked another.

"No, not just *anyone*." answered Martyn. "Only your direct descendants can use the glass to obtain your memories, or someone very skilled in Shaping. An Elder might be able to do it, but not a lesser Brother."

"It must be a rare magic indeed," said Avryl.

"Rare it is, and strong as well. It must have been the memory glass which made the wand glow. The chest and its contents, it seems, must remain a mystery. They are unimportant anyway. That which we seek is not here."

Without consulting the wand again, Martyn climbed the stairs. Ara was waiting for them in the shop, and he brought the glass to her.

"What did you find down there?" she asked.

"Only this glass sphere," said Martyn. "It is not what we came for, but it caught my eye. How much for it, my lady?"

She turned it over in her hands and looked at it with a discerning eye. At length she handed it back to him and said, "Eight silver."

He laughed. "I fear I do not carry silver, good Ara. Would you accept this in its stead?"

He watched her eyes grow wide as he pulled a handful of gold from his purse. He counted out ten coins and placed them on the counter.

"That...that will be fine," she stammered.

Martyn laughed a friendly laugh and bowed even more deeply than he had before. "Thank you, Ara, and good day to you!" he exclaimed as he left the shop. The others bowed, bade Ara farewell, and followed him outside.

As they walked back toward the center of town, Avryl caught up to him and asked, "Are there anyone's memories inside the glass?"

"No, my friend. This glass is empty. I wonder how it happened to end up in this place."

"Who can say?" replied Avryl. "Perhaps it is part of a larger destiny."

Martyn couldn't suppress a chuckle. "Why not? Even here, in Barton Hills, the One touches everyone and everything. We are all part of a larger destiny."

"Yes," said Avryl. "Yes we are."

A few days passed and the strangers were seen less and less in Barton Hills, yet their visit remained the talk of the town. A few of them were still guests at the Silver Shield, including Martyn and his companions. The others stopped back occasionally, but their visits were shorter and less frequent as their search took them deeper into Tyridan.

Karlyn spent her days planning her wedding and trying to keep Martyn out of her mind. Despite her best efforts, her mind would often wander to the night in the forest she spent with the Fairy. When she thought of his body against hers, his soft breath on her neck, her heart would quicken and her blood would race. She had to remind herself Martyn had turned his back on her. And she was going to marry Brok.

But the beautiful Fairy was occupying her thoughts ever more frequently, and six days after the two of them had lain together in the forest she went to the tavern where she knew she would find him. She was just going to peek though the door, hoping to catch a glimpse of him as he sat at a table drinking or talking to his companions. But when she arrived, something drew her inside.

"Karlyn!" said Derik over his shoulder as he filled a mug from the keg behind the bar. "Preparations for the wedding feast are going well. How's the guest list looking?"

She walked right past him without answering. In the far corner, Martyn sat with two of his friends. They were talking quietly together, but when Martyn saw her coming, he looked away from the others and stood up to greet her. His look of surprise quickly melted into a casual smile.

"Well...the lady Karlyn! What a surprise! What brings you here, good lady?"

She stopped and stared. No words would come. After all, she hadn't been expecting a confrontation. She merely wanted to see Martyn, to look at his fair face one last time.

"What is wrong?" he asked. His companions looked at her questioningly. Martyn turned to them and quietly said, "She is still in awe of us, my friends. She is the only one in town who can see us for what we are."

"She had better put her eyes back in her head before any of the other towns-folk start to wonder why she is so impressed," said another Fairy.

Karlyn shook herself out of her shock and moved to an empty chair. "I am sorry," she managed to say. "I didn't mean to stare. I just...I just wanted to check in with you, to see how you are enjoying your visit. I feel...somewhat responsible for you, since I am the first person from the town to meet you."

Martyn and the others chuckled. "There is no need to feel responsible," he said. "We are quite well. But since you are here, why not join us for a drink?"

Karlyn hesitated, wondering if it would be better if she got up and left at once. But when she met Martyn's gaze, all she could do was say, "That would be lovely."

One drink became two, and two became three, and before she knew it the afternoon had melted to evening and the evening to night. She spoke at length about the history of the town, her tongue becoming freer with each drink she consumed. The Fairies told heroic tales of their history, apparently glad to have someone to talk to who knew what they were. Martyn's companions eventually excused themselves, suggesting Martyn come with them. They needed rest, they said, for in the morning they were to ride to Riverton to continue their quest.

"I will be along shortly," he said. "The lady may need someone to see her home."

Accepting his answer, the other Fairies went to their rooms.

For an awkward moment Karlyn and Martyn stared at one another without speaking. Then they both started saying something at the same time. Eyes locked, they began to laugh softy.

"You go first," she said.

Martyn sobered and said, "I meant what I said the other day. About the laws of Faerie, I mean. It is very forbidden for your race and mine to love one another as we have. Emotionally…and physically. Yet…I have thought of you often over these last few days. You consume me. I do not understand it, cannot comprehend it, but I love you. I want to be with you as long and as often as I can."

"Grok, Martyn, I want the same thing! What are we to do?"

He leaned over the table, meeting her half way. "Meet me at the stables in an hour. We will go to our special place in the Northwood. Perhaps we can make plans to meet there each night for as long as I remain in this area."

She nodded excitedly. She felt her blood heating and hoped it didn't show on her face. Breathlessly she said, "What of later? What will we do when you must return to Faerie?"

"I do not know. We must discuss that when the time comes. But for now, we must use our time together as best we can. One hour?"

She nodded. He stood, bowed, and went upstairs. She sat at the table for a few minutes longer, urgent need building beneath her breast. At last she raced out of the tavern, counting the minutes until she could see her love again.

For the next week, time swept by in a sweet rush of excitement and ecstasy. Her days were filled with anticipation and longing and her nights were blessed with tenderness and passion. They met in the woods, made love, and talked for hours. Sometimes their love was urgent and furious, other times it was slow and gentle. It was always wonderful. She never felt so safe and contented as she did in his arms, and she began to stay with him later and later. So strong was their bond she could hardly bare to leave his side.

Of course, when she returned home she had to answer to Brok. He was more concerned for her than angry with her, and he always believed her excuses for being out so late. She told him she spent her evenings with Ara or her other friends, making important plans for the wedding. She hated lying to him, but she didn't know what to do. He was one of her best friends, but Martyn was her life.

One night she confessed to Martyn her plans to marry Brok. "Of course, I can't go through with it now. You are the one I love. I'm so sorry I didn't tell you sooner."

Martyn only smiled. "I already know of the upcoming wedding, Karlyn." When she gaped at him in shock and open dismay, he chuckled and said, "How could I not have known? Everyone is talking about it."

She sighed and said, "I guess I thought you were too busy to listen to gossip. You and your friends have been spending almost all your time searching for…something."

"Yes, but there is more to life than our quest. Part of the mission of any *Tynn* is to gather information about the outside world. As such, we are always listening to gossip and rumor, however insignificant it may seem."

"You must think very poorly of me," she said.

"No, not at all." He touched her cheek with the backs of his fingers and stroked her gently. "I could never find any fault with you. I love you."

They kissed, and under the stars and the moonlight they moved the earth with their love.

Another week passed, and both of them knew their time together was growing short. They could not see each other as often, for Martyn's quest took him ever further from Barton Hills and he could not return every night. He told her his companions were growing suspicious of his frequent ventures into the woods, and he had to be careful to avoid their watchful eyes. She, too, felt suspicious eyes on her, both at home and in town. Brok was showing more concern for her nightly absences, and even Ara was starting to ask questions. Ara was a perceptive woman, and she knew there was something going on with Karlyn and the strange visitors. As a friend, however, she promised to keep her suspicions to herself.

"Just be careful," she said to Karlyn one day. "I don't know what you are doing, and I don't mean to pry, but I care about you and don't want to see you hurt."

"Don't worry about me," said Karlyn. "I am happier than I've ever been."

Ara gave her a worried glance. "I hope it lasts. These strangers won't be around forever."

But Karlyn didn't want to think about that. She *couldn't* think about it. She continued to plan a wedding she never intended to have, and she continued to see Martyn whenever she could.

Toward the end of the third week since the Fair Folk had come to town, close to the time the *Tynn* was to move on, Karlyn became violently ill. The illness was not caused by something she had eaten, nor was it the normal sickness of the stomach from which the townsfolk suffered from time to time. She had seen enough women with this particular illness to know what it meant.

Karlyn was with child. Somehow she was sure of it beyond all question.

That night she told Martyn she was carrying his baby. Shock and dismay twisted his face.

"By the One! Karlyn, you must be wrong. This cannot be…what have we done?"

"Martyn," she said, putting her hands on his chest, "this isn't bad news! We are going to have a baby! This ties us together forever; it completes our love!"

He made a visible effort to calm himself. "I am sorry. My people believe such a child will be an abomination. It is for this reason our races are not permitted to mate. Oh, I wish this had not happened. I do not know what to do!"

She hugged him. "It's already done. Listen to me, Martyn. Has there ever been a coupling of our two races? Has there ever been a child born of a human and a Fairy?"

He pulled away slightly and looked down into her eyes. "No…none of which I am aware."

"Then how do you know it's a bad thing? How can your people know?"

A quizzical look passed over him. "It is written in the ancient texts. It is spoken in the Law."

"So you accept it on blind faith? There is no proof?"

He shook his head. "No, there is no proof." They were both silent for a time, and soon his worried expression turned calm, almost glad. "The law is based on a passage in a book, a passage no one even claims to understand. By the One, Karlyn, you are right! There is absolutely no reason to believe our child will be a monster."

They embraced tightly and spoke of future plans. They would run away together, far to the South where neither of their peoples would find them. They would raise their child in peace and love, and they would live their days as husband and wife. They built a dream for themselves that night, a fantasy life they would make reality as soon as they could. Long they lay in each other's arms, and Karlyn was swept once again into a warm dream of love and happiness.

But the next night the fantasy came crashing down, and the dream became a nightmare.

It didn't happen right away. At first the dream was as good as ever. They made love under the night sky and spoke together of the future and their child. In the middle of their talk, Martyn reached toward his pile of clothes and took hold of a small leather purse.

"What are you doing?" asked Karlyn, lying naked on her side with her head propped on her hand.

"I want to show you something," he said. He took a small glass sphere out of his purse and held it out for her to see.

"It's lovely," she said. "What is it?"

"A memory glass. I found it in your friend's shop a few weeks ago and it caught my eye." He continued to explain what the glass was, what it could do. Then he said, "I think it might be a fine gift for our son or daughter. We can both place our memories into the glass so our child might know of our love and how he or she came to be."

"I've never seen anything magical before," she said in wonder. "How can such a small thing hold a lifetime of memories?"

"Here," he said, offering it to her. "You will see. Just lie down, place it upon your breast, and remember."

She did as he told her, and after a moment she began to drift into a dream. The magic of the glass pulled at her memories, and she remembered her life more vividly than she would have thought possible. A stream of thoughts passed from her into the glass, and she felt Fairy-magic moving through her body and soul. She tingled all over, feeling warm and content. After a few minutes, it ended. The tale of her life was recorded in the glass globe which rested on her breast.

"That was amazing," she said. "I just remembered my entire life! Is it all recorded in the glass?"

Martyn smiled. "Only the parts the glass thinks important. Like all artifacts of Faerie, it has a mind of its own. One can try to impress one's will upon it, but unless one is a master of magic, the glass will pick and choose what it wishes to record. Do not worry, though; whatever it has recorded will paint a vivid and accurate picture of your life for our child."

Then Martyn took the glass and lay upon the earth. She watched as he fell into a peaceful trance. The globe glowed white for a few minutes while he dreamed his life into it, and then it stopped. He took the globe into his hand, sat up, and smiled.

They talked for a while longer and then embraced once again on the soft ground, locking in a kiss of passion and love.

This kiss, both tender and urgent, was the last they would ever share. It was warm and deep and long, and it would live always in Karlyn's memory as both sweet and bitter, but it was over too soon in a burst of noise and light.

The trees around them shook noisily as the clomping of many hoofs sounded in the clearing. A bright glow illuminated the space around Karlyn and Martyn, and they looked up in panic. Above them, atop their horses, were six Fairies of Martyn's *Tynn*, including the one known as Avryl and the leader, Captain Correth. As they looked down upon the couple, their gazes were harsh and fiery.

"Treachery!" cried one of the Fairies. "You devil, your actions fly in the face of the One himself!"

"I told you this was happening," said another to the Captain. "You refused to believe me. Martyn was taken with this…this *human* from the very start."

Avryl shook his head sadly and said nothing.

The Captain shook with controlled rage. "For the sake of the One, put some clothes on. My disappointment knows no bounds, Martyn. You have damned yourself and this woman."

Karlyn was in a panic. She was too scared to flee, like a deer blinded by the light of a hunter's lantern. Martyn held her close, but he was shaking as well. Slowly he let go of her and reached for their clothes.

"Here," he whispered to her. "It is best to do as they say. Put them on."

She complied numbly. The dream was over. Somehow she knew there would be no reasoning with these Fairies. She and Martyn were doomed.

When they were clothed, Correth dismounted and drew his blade. "Martyn, we are leaving here tomorrow. We are returning to Fairhaven. There, you will be tried before the King and, in all likelihood, you will be hanged." He looked bitter and sad, betrayed and confused. His jaw shook and sweat formed on his brow. Suddenly he shouted, "Why! Why, damn you! You were my favorite! You showed such promise! Now, you bastard, you have thrown it all away."

"For love," muttered Martyn. "I love her. She is my life, Correth. My life."

"Seth take you!" cried the Captain. The others looked at him in dismay. His anger at Martyn had driven him to speak an oath which, apparently, was strong enough to horrify even the angry Fairies. "May the hordes of Mul Kytuer stampede over your corpse! Avryl, shackle the traitor."

Avryl dismounted with chains and shackles and locked them around Martyn's ankles and wrists. Martyn hung his head and did not try to resist.

"When I heard of your treachery I created these bonds by Shaping some vines from a tree," said Correth. "I prayed to the One I would not have to use them." He seemed calmer now, and he put his hand on Martyn's shoulder. "Come. We camp north of here."

"What of the woman?" asked Avryl.

"You must kill her," said another Fairy.

"Indeed! She may bear Martyn's child!"

As Correth turned his glare on Karlyn, Martyn screamed, "No! She is not with child! I swear it, swear by the One! Spare her. It is my fault. All my fault."

"You are not with child?" Correth asked Karlyn. "Is this true?"

Terrified, she found it within herself to speak a single word.

"Yes," she lied.

"She cannot be believed! Kill her."

"Kill them both!"

Correth raised his hand to silence the group. "You are right, of course. Martyn we will take with us, to be tried under our Law as it must be. This woman, however, is not protected by the law of Faerie. She must die here, tonight. But you, my friends, need not bear witness to such brutality. Go. Prepare the camp. Leave Martyn and the woman to me."

"But Captain..." began Avryl.

"Go!" he cried. "I order you. Do you really want to see this woman's blood spilled? She is innocent, a victim of fate. I take responsibility, for I am your Captain, but I will not have the rest of you hardened by what I must do tonight. I order you, ride!"

So ordered, the others rode away without another word.

"And now, girl, you must pay the price for Martyn's evil. I am sorry."

"No!" cried Martyn. "By the One, by the Crafter himself, I implore you..."

Light flashed from Correth's fingertips and sound like thunder tore the air. Deadly magic lit the sky. Karlyn screamed what she thought to be her death cry.

The light died and the sound faded. Karlyn stood, shaken but unharmed. They stood silently for a moment, gazing at one another, as darkness and silence fell once again around them.

"That was for the benefit of the others," said Correth. "You are dead now, woman. Our people believe it is so, and thus it is so. We will not return to Barton Hills in your lifetime, so you may go back there and resume your life. I trust you have not lied to me about the child. Forget Martyn. As you are dead in our minds, he will soon be dead in fact."

"No, leave him here," sobbed Karlyn. What good was her life if she could not spend it with him? "He is of no use to you now, especially not dead! Please…"

"Karlyn," whispered Martyn, reaching out to her. "It must be this way. Our law…I am sorry." He turned away from her toward his Captain. "Oh, Correth, praise the One. You will be blessed for your mercy this day."

"Or cursed. We shall see. I could not kill an innocent. Pray my mercy is not folly."

"It is not," said Martyn, weeping. "Mercy is never folly."

"We shall see," repeated Correth.

As he lifted the shackled Martyn onto the back of his horse, Karlyn ran at him and beat on him with her small fists. Correth easily shoved her away and fluidly mounted.

"Grok damn you!" she cried as she fell to the ground. Her face was twisted and her stomach sick and knotted. She shook impotently as oceans streamed down her face. "Damn you to Hell!"

Without another word, Correth spurred his horse into motion, carrying her beloved Martyn into the trees and out of her life forever.

The journey back to Fairhaven took three weeks of steady riding. During those weeks Martyn lived in a haze, barely eating or sleeping, mostly oblivious to the shackles binding him and the Fairies surrounding him. His heart and mind were still with Karlyn. The others rarely spoke to him, and when they did he seldom replied. They had taken him from his love, his reason for living, and no words could bring him peace. At times he felt his heart breaking, but for the most part he felt nothing.

One day of the journey was very much like the next, and it seemed in its monotony to drag on forever, but at last they passed into Faerie and entered the grand capitol city of Fairhaven. Correth had sent word ahead of Martyn's treachery, and crowds of Fair Folk thronged in the street to see this strange sight, this rare Fairy criminal. As far as any of them knew, no Fairy had broken the law of the realm for centuries, and Martyn was a curiosity.

Martyn looked into the faces of his many accusers; some were angry, some curious, some sad. A few shouted curses at him and others merely asked him why. Why would he lay with a human woman? What did she offer him that no Fairy maid could?

He had no answer for them. Surrounded by the members of his *Tynn*, he rode toward the palace where he would be tried that very day. He prayed the trial would be quick. He had no illusions how it would end, but he was loathe to face the King as a traitor. The best he could hope for was a quick trial and an immediate execution. He welcomed the grave. There was nothing else for him here.

Beneath the palace there was a small dungeon, and it was here they took Martyn to await his trial. Seldom were there any prisoners, for evil could not freely enter the forests of the Fair Folk. But as the cell door slammed shut and his escorts left, Martyn heard the sounds of footsteps in the cell beside him. The other prisoner didn't speak, and Martyn had no desire to initiate conversation. He was still too numb to be curious about his dungeon-mate.

He waited in the dark for more than an hour, and then the main door leading down to the dungeon opened. He saw a large figure outlined in the light, saw the figure make its way down the stairs. Martyn had seen that shape enough times to know exactly who it was: Father Sang, the leader of the Order of Nom.

Sang did not approach Martyn's cell, but rather stopped to speak to the other prisoner.

"My *Tynn* has returned. They have been unsuccessful in recovering my prize."

A deep, raspy voice said, "I knew they would fail. It is not for your hands any more than it is for your King's. My master will crush your people in time; it is foreordained."

"Urdrokk will crush us? Nay, his time is ended, Razzyn Kane. For nigh on eighty years he has cowered in some hiding-hole, waiting to whither and die. The Seth needs a stronger general, one who can conquer and command the Fair Folk."

The one called Razzyn Kane laughed. "Do you think you will be the one? Fool! You could never be the equal of the great sorcerer."

"No? You are a powerful sorcerer, Kane, and it took only a small part of my power to bind you and force you to tell me your secrets."

"And yet they availed you not. I told you your precious prize was in Tyridan, yet your *Tynn* failed to find it."

Martyn's shock and horror broke through his numbness. Sang plotted against the King! Sang had captured this sorcerer and used his knowledge to plan the downfall of Faerie!

The Father of Nom was a slave to Vorik Seth.

"NO!" cried Martyn. "By the One, Sang, have you gone mad?" Martyn leapt up and grabbed the bars of his cell. Father Sang slowly turned his head to face the imprisoned Fairy.

Slowly a smile curled his lips. "Ah, Martyn, there you are. I wondered where they stashed you to await your trial." He sauntered over to the cell, smiling serenely all the while. "So you have heard my plan. What ever will you do about it?"

Martyn was wild with fear. His heart thumped urgently. "I'll tell the King! I'll shout it out as loud as I can! 'Father Sang is the *real* traitor,' I'll say."

"You will say nothing of the kind!" exclaimed Sang. "You will admit your guilt before the King and beg for death." Sang waved his hands in the air and powerful magic encompassed Martyn. He fought it, but Sang was far too powerful. Martyn struggled to move his mouth but no words came out. He was entirely in Father Sang's power.

Sang leaned toward him and whispered, "Now you cannot speak unless I will it. You alone know of my crimes against Faerie. You alone know I plan to uncover the Talisman of Unity and use it to unite the Fair Folk under one will: mine. I will be King. We will be a strong people, able to survive in the new world that is coming. A world ravaged by darkness and terror." He grinned, his face twisting and becoming hideous. "The One is growing weak and tired. The Seth's day is coming. And only those who serve him will be allowed to live."

Martyn cried out, but he could form no words. Then he felt Sang loosen his magic, and Martyn shouted, "Seth take you! You are a horror! I must tell the King, the Talisman must be found, and you must…ugh!" Again his throat constricted and he could say no more.

"Thank you for shutting him up," said the deep voice from the adjacent cell. "His ranting is tiresome."

"Pray I do not begin to find *your* ranting tiresome, Kane," said Sang. "I may have use for you yet, which is the only reason you still live." He spared one last look at Martyn and hurried up the stairs. The vicious grin never left his face.

That evening Martyn stood before the King and Queen, the Councilors and Elders, and was unable to utter one word in his defense. Father Sang looked on from his seat near the King and spoke out fervently for the "traitor's" death. In the end Martyn spoke the words Sang's enchantment dictated, asking to be punished for his terrible crime. Begging for death. He wanted to shout, *Sang is the traitor, not me! He wants you dead; he wants the Talisman of Unity for his own! He sides with the Seth! THE SETH, damn you!"*

But he said none of these things. Sang's magic wouldn't let him. When it was finished, the King decreed Martyn would hang at dawn, and Martyn was dragged away, still in chains, to spend the night crying in the dungeon. And cry he did: for Sang's treason, for his King's ignorance, for his parents and his sister Kari *(Where was she? Did she know of the trial?)*. He cried for his people, wondering if they would indeed fall to Vorik Seth. But most of all he cried for Karlyn, his lost love, and for the life they might have had.

His last tears that night were for the child he would never know.

My child, he cried. *My child! I will love you always.*

Kari pushed her way through the throng massing around the hastily erected gallows standing in the town square. Panic and grief surged through her heart. Today, her brother was to die.

She had gotten the message the day before after returning from a successful hunt. Word of his affair with a human had spread through the towns surrounding Fairhaven like a firestorm. Her parents were stricken with grief, and they could not face the horror of their son's impending execution. For this reason, Kari was the only one of the family to make the journey to Fairhaven to witness the hanging.

She too was filled with heartache, but she could not let Martyn face his death alone. Someone had to be there for him, and she was strong enough to be the one. She struggled to bite back her pain as she reached the front of the crowd.

A wooden platform stood before her, and upon it was a thin, black pillar from which her brother would hang. It was freshly made, but to her it stank of death and horror. It was an instrument of justified murder, and looking upon it tore her heart in two.

Sickened, she looked away from the gallows and took in the crowd. The majority of the onlookers seemed uncomfortable, even embarrassed, being there. An execution was such a rare event that curiosity made it impossible not to attend. But the Fair Folk were not people who took delight at another's death, even if it was the death of a traitor. Still, there were those who looked eager, and those who seemed angry. Were they angry about Martyn's supposed treachery or at the execution itself? Kari wasn't sure.

Perhaps it is both.

The sounds of drums came suddenly from the palace above. A slow bass rhythm steadily pounded, low and ominous like a dying heart. Guards appeared from the palace gate, marching slowly toward the gallows to the beat of the drum.

Thoom! Thoom!

And then, dressed in simple brown clothes, head bowed, came Martyn himself. His eyes were shut and his face bore no readable expression. The crowd was silent as he passed, save a few who cried out in hatred or disgust. Kari's throat thickened and her stomach clenched. She closed her eyes to hold back the tears.

Thoom! Thoom!

She listened to the drums, listened to the murmurs of the crowd around her. Soon she heard the footsteps of the guards as they neared her. Sobbing now, she forced her eyes open so she could see her brother as he passed.

He was coming toward her, almost near enough to touch. If it weren't for the guards she would have run to him, hugged him close, and cried into his chest. Instead she screamed his name. She was no longer able to control the flood of tears which washed down her cheeks. He looked up, and his blank expression melted away into a passionate mix of conflicting emotion.

"Kari!" he cried. Desperately, he broke through the surprised guards and ran to her side. "Ah, Kari, praise the One you are here."

"Oh, Martyn," she cried, throwing her arms around him.

Before the guards could pull him away, he reached into a pocket in his pants and pulled out a spherical object. "Keep it safe," he whispered to her. "Keep it hidden. You will know who to give it to when the time comes."

She took it without thinking and slipped it into her purse as the guards roughly tore Martyn away from her.

"Tell our parents I love them," he cried.

She tried to answer, but the words would not come.

Thoom! Thoom!

She watched him climb the gallows, witnessed the solemn hangman slip the noose about his neck. She barely heard a soldier read the charges and ask if Martyn had any final words. Kari hardly realized what was happening as Martyn shook his head, declining the right to speak.

The guards backed away.

Thoom!

The executioner placed his hand on the wooden lever which would open the trap door beneath Martyn's feet.

Thoom!

Kari's heart stopped. The hangman pulled the lever.

Thoom!

Just before rope went taught, Martyn screamed one word.

"KARLYN!"

The drums ceased. Martyn jerked once. His neck snapped.

Kari screamed and screamed. Those around her tried to comfort her, but nothing in the world could assuage her sorrow.

Martyn, her brother, whom she loved above all others, was dead.

CHAPTER 23

Red Rain

"*NO!*" screamed Alec Mason, jerking upright. Thunder pounded in his chest and sweat swam down his brow. He didn't know where he was. Panic ravaged him as he gasped desperately for air. The last thing he remembered, he was standing in Fairhaven watching Martyn hang.

"Alec?" said a familiar voice. Alec glanced around wildly, his jaw dropped and his eyes wide, looking at people he almost recognized.

"Alec, it's me, Kraig," said a muscular man as he put his hand on Alec's shoulder. Alec flinched at his touch but did not pull away.

It was coming back to him now. He wasn't in Fairhaven at Martyn's execution. He hadn't even been born then. This was more than two decades into the future, and he was Alec Mason, son of Martyn the Fairy and Karlyn of Barton Hills. He was among friends. He looked from Kraig's worried face to the faces of the others, all of whom were standing over him like concerned, protective older brothers.

"Oh, wounds!" he cried, "Grok's wounds! It was terrible. They killed him. They killed my father!" He broke into tears, crying on Kraig's big shoulder.

At once, both Michael and Lorn bent down to try to console him. Lorn just put his hand out in an offer of silent support, but Michael patted his shoulder and spoke gently.

"It happened a long, long time ago, Alec. Your father has joined with the One now and is at peace."

"I...I know," sobbed Alec, "but you didn't see it. You don't know what it was like! And...and that *bastard!* Father Sang. Even back then he plotted against the King. Salin wasn't the first to plan to use the Talisman of Unity to bend the Fair Folk to evil. Sang had the idea twenty years ago! Martyn knew…he *knew*, damn it! But he couldn't…Sang put a spell…"

The tears continued to flow and Alec could say no more. The others gazed at him helplessly. Michael ran both hands through his hair and gazed hopelessly at the sky.

"By the One," he said. "The Fair Folk are supposed to be above corruption. I thought the recent revolt was unprecedented, but it appears I was wrong. If Sang's treason began more than twenty years ago, who knows how deeply the Seth's shadow has already spread into Faerie?"

Lorn turned to Michael sternly. "It must be an isolated event, Michael. I cannot and will not believe Vorik Seth has wide-spread control over the Fair Folk. If he did, he would have used them already. He wouldn't need Salin to steal the Talisman if he could already control them."

Michael nodded in agreement. "You are right, of course. Still, the corruption of Fairies, however rare it may be, causes me great heartache."

Alec slowly pulled himself together. "I'll be all right," he said. "We should get moving. Salin already has too much of a head start." He wiped the tears from his eyes and the sweat from his brow. Kraig offered him a hand to help him get up, which Alec gladly accepted.

"Do you want to talk about it?" asked the peacekeeper.

Alec shook his head. "Maybe later. I just want to ride now. It's…it's too much to think about just now. It's too big for my mind."

As they mounted the horses and resumed their journey, the others left Alec in peace. Alec appreciated their understanding. It gave him time to sort through what he had just learned, to come to terms with the past. He was the son of Martyn and Karlyn, not Brok and Karlyn. And that meant Kari, the woman who had given Alec the memory glass, was his aunt! Alec wondered what he would say to her if he should ever meet her again. Would it be awkward? Painful?

Alec also wondered about the parts of the story that weren't in the glass. What happened to Karlyn after Martyn was torn out of her life? Alec knew she eventually married Brok, but was she ever truly happy? Did he know about her affair with Martyn? Did he know Alec was not truly his son?

Perhaps Ara would be able to tell him more. After all, she and Karlyn had been close friends. He would be sure to question her if he ever made it back to Fairhaven.

As the afternoon wore on, Alec resolved to put the tragic tale of his parents out of his mind, at least for the present. Dwelling on it wouldn't accomplish anything, and he really had more important things to deal with. First and foremost, the others were depending on him to track the sorcerer. He concentrated on the pull of the Talisman, which still called to him strongly, pulling him ever westward.

His mind firmly on his task once again, he decided it was time to join the others. He had been riding quite a distance in front of them, not looking back, but now he waited for them to catch up. Michael was the first to reach him, and he greeted Alec with a smile.

"You are feeling better, I take it?"

Alec returned the smile. "A bit. I'm anxious to catch up to Salin and put this ordeal behind us."

"As am I," answered the Wizard. "Your experiences with Salin go back only weeks; I have had to deal with the black sorcerer for centuries."

Alec held Michael's gaze, trying to understand how a man could have lived so long. He simply couldn't believe his companion was hundreds of years old. "Michael, I've been thinking," said Alec. "I know you are the Second of the Three, and I know Salin is one of the strongest sorcerers in the world, but I still don't understand how you two can be so old. Does magic itself give you a long or indefinite life span? Is magic why the Fair Folk live so long?"

Michael shook his head and chuckled softly. "You would like to have a lesson now? Very dedicated of you." He paused for a minute and then said, "Well, it has to do with being close in spirit with the One. The Fair Folk, whose spirits are naturally tied to the One, drink from his endless spring of life, refreshing their bodies and their minds. Thus they age only slowly, and in the end return to unite with the One. The closer they are to the One, the longer they can live.

"It is the same with humans who learn to Shape. The more powerful human Shapers, those who become close in spirit with the One, are gifted with extended life spans, but seldom can they live as long as the Fair Folk. I, on the other hand, along with my two brothers, are so close to the One we hardly age at all. Even when my loss of faith kept me from using my power, I was still closely tied to the One and did not age.

"Sorcerers are a different breed. They have forsaken the One, and so the One has forsaken them. Yet, Vorik Seth grants those who serve him loyally some semblance of immortality. They age in appearance, quickly becoming old and gnarled on the outside, but still retain the vitality of youth within. Their long life spans are not linked to their strength in magic, but rather are a dark gift from their dark master. It is said the Seth often grants some form of immortality even to his servants who have little or no talent in magic. Groshem the Dark, his highest general prior to Salin, was said to have lived three hundred years before he fell out of favor with his master and was replaced."

"How is it Vorik Seth has the power to grant immortality?" asked Kraig, who was riding behind Alec and off to the left.

"As I have told Alec in his lessons, Vorik Seth has the combined power of all the Seths who came before him. In the power he holds, he is very nearly the equal of the One. In theory, he has the power to send his spirit forth into the world and tear it apart or control it as he wishes. The only thing holding him back is the will of the One, with whom he is constantly at war. You see, Vorik Seth, like every user of magic upon this world, depends on the One for the power to Shape, and the One is constantly trying to hold his power back from the Seth. Since the Seth is almost the equal of the One, he is able to steal a vast amount of the One's strength, but not enough to ravage the world as he wishes. Still, it is enough to provide his servants with powers they could not otherwise imagine."

"We pray constantly that the One may remain vigilant in his struggle with the Seth," said Lorn. "If he should falter, even for an instant, Vorik Seth's victory is assured."

"The One will never falter," said Michael. "It is utterly unthinkable. Still, Vorik Seth, through his servants and the power he does manage to steal, may yet be victorious. It is up to those who are faithful to the One to stand against evil. Therein lies the only hope for this world."

They rode on in silence for a while, and Alec thought about what Michael had said. The more Alec learned about the One and the way magic worked, the less he believed he would ever be able to Shape. There was just so much to know, and too much of it boggled his mind. Looking at Michael, it was still hard to accept that the man had lived for centuries.

"So how old are you, anyway?" asked Alec.

Michael did not answer for a long while. Finally, he said, "I do not know."

"What?"

"I remember the last seven hundred years or so, some of it quite vividly. Beyond that, there are only impressions, memories so vague they are hardly memories at all. I remember coming through a fire, and I remember being held prisoner in a steel fortress which flew in the sky. There were weapons that you cannot imagine: bows without strings which fired pure light, swords without blades which could cut a man in two easier than your Flame. Of my child-hood and youth I remember nothing. I do not even know what my name was."

"It wasn't Michael?"

"No. Michael is something I just started calling myself in the last hundred years. Before that, I was known as Nul, which means Wizard in the ancient tongue of Eglak. And of course, the Fair Folk and some of the people further west know me as Elsendarin, which also means Wizard."

"How could you have no memory of those years?" asked Kraig.

"It is possible the human mind simply does not have the capacity to retain the memories of a life as long as mine. Or perhaps, as I sometimes think, something happened to me which burned out my older memories. What ever it was, it happened to my brothers as well. The other two remember no more than I do of those ancient days. Besides the impressions which sometimes come to us, we know only what is preserved in the history books. Some of those books speak of the deeds of the Three, but we do not know if we really did those things. We do not even know if we were the original Three, or replacements for those who came before us. And perhaps worst of all, we do not know how or why we became the Three. We have accepted that our pur-pose is and has always been to fight darkness in the name of the One, but we cannot know for certain if this mission was appointed to us by the One him-self."

They continued their journey in silence, a silence broken only by occasional quiet singing from Horren. Despite the seriousness of their mission, the Addin had fallen into a pleasant mood and spent much time with his smiling gaze fixed on the forest around him. He was a woodsman, and the woods of Faerie were like no other. The others were focused completely on the task at hand, but Horren was just glad to be back among the glorious trees.

"The whole forest is like an Addingrove," he whispered. "It is in woods like these my people were meant to live."

Alec spared a smile for the Addin but didn't reply. His mind was filled with the pull of the Talisman, which seemed to be growing further away but was still strong. He wondered how far they would have to travel before they caught Salin. Would it be too late? He had no idea where Salin was taking the thing, and he didn't know how long it would take the sorcerer to master the Talis-man's magic. Once he did, the Fair Folk were his to command, and all hope would be lost.

Late in the afternoon, they passed just south a Fairy village, the name of which Lorn translated from a signpost. It was Greenbrook, he told them, a town larger than Lehnwood but not nearly so grand as Fairhaven. It was a town which thrived on trade, for it lay along the banks of the River Lye, which provided a route for trade ships to and from the towns further north. Furs and hides common in the north were traded for the crops which grew more freely in southern Faerie. Of course, the people of the north were the Dark Folk, so Michael suggested they stay clear of the town. Since dark Fairies were relatively common in Greenbrook, a group of them loyal to Salin could pass unnoticed. Alec was glad to oblige Michael's wishes, for he, too, wanted to avoid confrontation. Besides, the Talisman did not pass through the village and time was of the essence.

They rode on into the night until they became too weary to travel. They set camp in a little niche formed by a cluster of white rocks and some tall pine. Kraig and Lorn fed and groomed the horses while Michael and Alec prepared a simple meal. Horren went in search of some branches, roots, and nuts, saying he could not eat anything as disgusting as the dead flesh on which humans seemed to thrive. After their meal, they decided on an order for guard duty and turned in for the night.

The next day passed as quickly and as uneventfully as the previous. Alec led them to the southwest, always feeling the Talisman drawing him on. He knew Salin was still moving, still gaining ground on them, but he felt no danger of losing the trail. The further the Talisman drew away from him, the weaker he felt its pull, but from what he experienced so far, he thought he would always feel it a little no matter how far away it was. Somehow it had become a part of him, and even Salin's magic hadn't broken the bond completely.

Over the course of the day, both Lorn and Michael had expressed an interest in continuing Alec's training, even now, on the road. They came to the agreement they would take turns, each training Alec every other night. Alec ran a hand through his hair as he shook his head in wonder. Why did they think it so important he continue learning Shaping and swordplay? There just wasn't time!

But Alec didn't seem to have any say in the matter. They stopped an hour earlier than they had the previous evening to give Alec time for his lesson. Tonight he was with Lorn, who drilled him rigorously while the others talked quietly among themselves as they set up the camp and prepared dinner. Lorn had him run through all the forms he knew, first with Flame and then with a wooden practice sword Lorn had carried from Fairhaven. As before when Alec had used a practice sword, he had a hard time concentrating and fumbled his way clumsily through the forms.

"That was good," said Lorn when Alec had finished.

"Good?" panted the baker. "I nearly fell over my own feet! Half way through, I forgot three maneuvers. Grok, what's wrong with me?"

Lorn took a long moment to look Alec up and down. "Alec, I've been watching you and discussing your progress with Michael. I've decided you shouldn't use Flame when you practice anymore."

Alec's eyes went wide with shock, and for some reason, anger. He gripped defensively at his sword. "No! That's insane. I...I have to use it. It's mine!"

Lorn put his hands on Alec's shoulders and squeezed. "This is just the reaction I was expecting. Alec, Flame is a magic sword. It is a powerful weapon, and it has saved your life in the past, but it has dangers of its own."

"Dangers? I don't know what you are talking about." He tried to pull away, but Lorn held him too tightly.

"Yes you do. First of all, look at how you are acting. Why are you being so defensive? Why are you so possessive of the blade?"

"Well...because it's mine. The mummy gave it to me. It belongs to me; why shouldn't I use it?" Suddenly suspicion overcame Alec. "You want it, don't you? You don't want me to use it anymore because you want it for yourself! Well, Lorn, you can't have it! Flame is mine, I tell you! Mine!"

"Alec Mason, you get a hold of yourself!" Lorn gave him a good shake. "Think. You offered me the sword once and I did not take it. I do not want it. The fact that you are so suspicious of me should tell you something. You are irrational when it comes to the sword. You are not yourself. Have you ever felt so possessive of anything before?"

Alec frowned, his fading anger replaced by confusion. "Well, no. It...does seem kind of strange, doesn't it? I mean, I never act like this."

"No, you do not. Like I said, things of magic can be dangerous to those who use them lightly. Your sword, like the Talisman, has a will of its own. It is using its will to influence your feelings. You are becoming possessive of the sword because the sword has become possessive of *you*. And I would wager a stack of gold that when you hold the sword in battle, the feelings you experience are not entirely your own. Anger, perhaps, or a thirst for killing?"

Alec bowed his head and ran both hands through his hair. "Grok's wounds. Sometimes it's so strong I almost can't stop myself, even after the battle's over. I...I thought I was becoming some sort of monster. But it's not me at all."

"No, Alec. It is not you. It is the sword. Of course, the benefits of a magic weapon such as Flame cannot be denied. When you wield it, your confidence increases. It enhances your skill and improves your concentration, allowing you to do things you could never do without it. When you fight with Flame, you look like you have been training for years rather than a few weeks."

"Then all my skill, all the progress I thought I'd made, is just the sword. I should have known. Why should I have any talent in swordplay?"

Lorn smiled warmly. "But you do have talent, Alec. Why, that is the reason I made you run through the forms without the sword: to test your talent. The things you have learned and mastered, the things you have done even with a practice sword, are far beyond what you should be able to do at this stage. It takes years to master the blade. Some warriors, very respected warriors, never master it completely. But you, my friend, are well on your way. You have a natural talent, and in time, you will be able to develop it. Give yourself a few years, and you will be a true master."

Alec managed a smile. He knew Lorn well enough to know when he gave praise, it was well deserved. "So what should I do in the meantime? Like you said, Flame is too valuable for me to lay aside, especially when I know there's still danger ahead."

"You cannot lay it aside; this is certain. Just do not use it to train. If you are forced into a real battle again, you will need the advantage the sword gives you. Just remember who you are and do not give in to the sword's bloodlust. In time, when you learn more of magic, you will be the master of the sword, not the other way around. Until then, touch it only when you must."

Alec nodded in agreement and Lorn announced the lesson was at an end. They joined the others for a small meal and then settled into their blankets. Under the clear skies of Faerie, sleep was peaceful and undisturbed.

By noon on the next day, they had passed out of Faerie. Alec felt a perceptible change in the air, as if a glorious magic which had made him glad to be alive had just been taken away. Actually, Alec knew this was precisely what had happened. The webs of enchantment which made Faerie a safe and wondrous land had been left behind. The forest was just a forest now, the trees only trees. They did not glow with silvery light and they did not radiate life and health. Alec's spirits sank into his boots and it took the rest of the day for his mood to improve. He kept reminding himself he had lived his entire life in a place where magic was unknown and he did not need it to be happy. By evening, he had still not been able to convince himself entirely.

As twilight took hold of the sky above them, Kraig brought his horse side by side with Alec's.

"Do you still feel it? The Talisman, I mean."

"Of course. Salin's still moving, and he's gained at least a day on us. Don't worry, though, I'm in no danger of losing the trail. The pull is getting weaker, but I can still feel it tugging at me, even in my sleep. We'll find Salin, eventually. I'm just worried about what's going to happen when we do."

"I'm sure Michael's got that covered. Our job is just to get him there; he'll deal with the sorcerer."

"Right. At least we have the thing the King gave us, the *Lyll Una*, whatever it is. Michael and Lorn seem to think it's pretty important. Maybe it will help us defeat Salin."

"Maybe," said Kraig. "I wouldn't want to speculate. I don't know anything about magic, like you and Michael."

"Me?" Alec laughed. "Don't give me so much credit, Kraig. I haven't been able to light a candle with magic yet. I can't even figure out how I'm supposed to do it. There are these Seven Laws, right, but only six can be put into words, and I don't even understand those six! It's hopeless."

"You'll figure it out, Alec. After this journey's over and we've got the Talisman back, you'll have plenty of time to sort out this magic stuff."

"I hope I have the chance," said Alec.

The peacekeeper gave Alec a crooked smile and continued riding beside him. Alec was glad to have Kraig for a friend. They had not been very close back home, mostly because Kraig was a good six or seven years older than Alec, but since they left Barton Hills they had become fast friends. Traveling with the likes of Lorn and Michael could be intimidating and at times infuriating. Kraig's down-to-earth manner was a comfort to Alec.

The day passed quickly. When they stopped for the night it was time for Alec's lesson. He spent an hour listening to Michael lecture on the intricacies of the Seven Laws and another half-hour in meditation to try to "see" the spirit of the One. At the end of the lesson, as always, Michael asked him what he had seen. Alec replied he had seen nothing unusual, save at one point a tree he was looking at seemed to lose its solidity. He could not explain it any more clearly, but Michael looked pleased.

Later, Horren announced he was going for a walk through the woods, and Michael went to his blankets for the night. Alec, Kraig, and Lorn remained sitting around the small cook-fire, finishing the last of the brown stew Lorn had prepared. He had managed to catch some rabbits, and the meal was a welcome change from the dried meat and trail rations they had been eating. As Kraig threw down his empty bowl, he took a long look at Lorn and rubbed his beard in thought.

"What is it?" asked Lorn.

"That stew wasn't bad at all, Lorn," said Kraig with a grin. "Of course, for all we know, you could have been a cook before you settled down in Bordonhold. Only trouble is, cooks can't usually wield a sword like you can." His grin faded as he regarded the warrior more closely. "What's your story, Lorn? You know your way around these lands like you've been traveling them all your life, you fight like a master, and the Fairies treat you like some sort of visiting lord. Yet, when we found you in Bordonhold, you were throwing your life away to the bottle."

Lorn bowed his head. "My business is my own."

"Stop it," said Kraig. "You've come too far to start moping around again. And we've come too far together for secrets. Lorn, we've been traveling together for weeks, but we don't even know who you are!"

"Kraig's right," said Alec. "Even Michael has started to open up to us a little bit. We're all in this together; we have to help each other however we can. Maybe we could help you better if we know something about you."

For a long moment, Lorn was silent, and then he let out a long sigh. "I have been doing my best to forget my past, but each night my dreams remind me. You are right when you say I have come a long way. Without this journey to give me purpose, I would be back in Bordonhold drowning my sorrows with all the ale I could afford…or steal. Thanks to all of you, I have found myself again, and sometimes I can forget my heartache and do what must be done. But at night when I am alone I remember, and the pain comes."

He sat up straight and his eyes became hard. He was suddenly filled with a strength that reminded Alec of King Elyahdyn. He spoke, and his voice was low and steady and filled with authority. "I am David Lourne du Carren, the Prince of Eglak. My father is Breyden Mala du Carren, Lord of Eglak and High King of the Eglacian Union."

Alec tried to close his gaping mouth, but his jaw wouldn't work. Kraig was struck speechless as well, and for a time Lorn sat there, his powerful gaze holding them both. Then, finally, Alec said, "Prince? You're the Prince of Eglacia?"

He couldn't believe it. Eglacia! The Kingdom of Eglak was the keystone of the union of kingdoms which surrounded it: Tyridan, Madagon, Riglak Nord, Margon, Pren Dalah, Estron, and others Alec could not remember. Each land had its own King, but since ancient times each King bowed to the High King of Eglak. The Eglacian Union, or Eglacia as it was commonly called, covered practically all the known world. Over the last few centuries, however, the kingdoms had gained more and more autonomy until Eglacia was a union in name only. These days the High King had little power over the lands outside of Eglak, but he was still respected out of tradition. Everyone knew of the High King, even if many didn't even know his name. In farming villages like Barton Hills, few people even remembered the name of their local lord.

"Yes, I am a prince, for all it is worth. I am a prince in exile, for my older brother has accused me of crimes I did not commit, treasons I would never even consider. My father has grown tired in his old age and has become reliant on the advice of my brother Thorne. Thorne has poisoned him against me, saying I plotted father's death, and Thorne's as well, so I would be king. He brought evidence against me, damning evidence I could not refute. I was exiled and may not return under pain of death."

Alec was shaking his head in disbelief. "Why…why would your brother do this? Did he hate you so much?"

Lorn's lips pressed together as if to hold back a rush of emotion. Then, he breathed deeply and continued. "We were as close as brothers could be. When we were children, we practiced swordplay in the courtyard together while Father's Bladeknights watched. We hunted together in the royal forests and laughed together at the childish pranks we played on our tutors. Even as young adults we remained close, although he was groomed to be king and I was busy training to become First Bladeknight. Yet one day, quite suddenly, Thorne changed. He became angry, greedy, and began coveting our Father's power. He began to abuse women, taking serving women to his bed whenever he could, whether they were willing or not. Strangely enough, Father and his advisors could not, or would not, see the changes in Thorne. The servants were afraid to speak, and Thorne silenced the local nobility with gifts of gold and land. The worse he behaved, the more popular he appeared to become.

"One day, four years ago, I found him on Father's throne, a satisfied look in his eyes. I told him he was not King yet. He said, 'But I will be, dear brother, and sooner than you think. And then…think of the things I can do!' I said, 'From what I have seen lately, you are not fit to be king. Besides, Father has a great deal of life left in him, and you'll not see the throne for a good, long time.' He laughed and said, 'We shall see.'

"By the way he was acting, I knew what he was planning. He did not even try to hide it from me. Someday soon, I knew he would kill our father so he might be King. But somehow he managed to turn it around. Soon I found myself on trial for the crime Thorne was plotting, and my own father spoke the words which condemned me to exile."

"How did he do it?" asked Kraig. "How did he frame you?"

Lorn shook his head. "It doesn't matter. Suffice it to say he produced evidence and witnesses to back him up. I left in disgrace, and all the citizens of Varnia hissed and jeered at me as the guards dragged me from the city. My only small victory was, before I left, I was able to speak with a group of Bladeknights still loyal to me. I told them to keep a close eye on Thorne and to protect King Breyden at all costs. Since I have not yet heard word of my father's passing, I assume they have done their job well.

"Yet I still dread the day when my brother ascends the throne. We have already lost Northern Eglak, first to civil war and then to the forces of the Seth. When Thorne takes the throne in Varnia, I fear Southern Eglak will be lost as well."

"Surely there is something you can do," said Kraig. "You have friends, allies among the Fair Folk. Perhaps they could…"

"No. As long as Father is still alive there is hope he will see the truth. When he does, he will end my exile and cast down his first son. If I storm Varnia with a force of Fairy shapers, it will look like I really am trying to take the throne by force. Moreover, some might believe my motive to be pure jealousy, for Thorn has recently taken the Lady Hannah as his bride, and the Lady was once the love of my life. Besides, I could never ask the Fair Folk to join me in such an ordeal. They do more than they need to for humanity already. Without their vigilance, sorcerers like Salin Urdrokk would have long since overrun the world."

Alec was still trying to get the thought into his head: Lorn was a prince. His situation was even more tragic than Alec had imagined. No wonder he had fallen into such a depression! It wasn't just for his own exile, Alec was sure, but for his homeland as well. If this Thorne was truly as heartless as Lorn made him out to be, he could bring the whole land to ruin if he became king. Alec's heart went out to his companion.

"Lorn…or, Prince David…or, should I call you…?"

"Lorn is just fine," said Lorn.

"Lorn, then. If we'd have known…it must be so hard for you. I'm sorry."

Lorn shook his head. "Do not worry about me. The purpose I've found since I've left Bordonhold has made me stronger. Even if I never return home, I can have a satisfying life. You have given me this gift."

Alec smiled and Kraig wore a satisfied expression. At long last they had gotten Lorn to open up to them. Alec felt like he had gotten to know the warrior better in the last ten minutes than he had in all the weeks they'd been traveling together. They sat in silence together, and it was a comfortable silence, a quiet moment shared by friends. At last Kraig announced he was turning in, and Lorn stood to take the first shift guarding the camp. Soon Alec lay down to go to sleep, saddened by Lorn's tale, but satisfied there were no more secrets between them.

They pressed on for the next four days. Each day was much like the one before it, and most of their time was spent riding in tedious silence. On the eve of their sixth day out of Fairhaven, however, Alec made an announcement.

"Wait," he said, reining his horse in.

"What is it?" asked Kraig.

Alec gazed off into the distance, cocking his head as if listening. "The Talisman has stopped moving. It's calling to me more loudly now, more clearly. It's closer. Salin's either stopped for an extended rest or he has reached his destination."

"Excellent," said Michael. "Let us not tarry here, then." He motioned for Alec to lead them onward.

The Wizard looked pleased, and the way he purposefully peered down the path Alec chose betrayed how anxious he was to catch the sorcerer. They were all anxious now, and nervous energy hung in the air amongst them. Even Horren dropped his cheery demeanor and began mumbling something about "grinding black old Salin's bones."

The forest thinned out and became a region of hilly brown grassland, punctuated by dry bushes and an occasional oak or spruce. They were far to the west of the rich, green, grassy hills they had passed through on their way to Faerie. Lorn ventured they were somewhere between the forests of Faerie and Ogrynwood, in a region where the boundary between them was ambiguous. Far to the south, he said, was the kingdom of Madagon, Tyridan's western neighbor.

When they camped that night, Alec cleared his head and listened to Michael's lecture. The Wizard, for the first time during one of Alec's lessons, demonstrated some simple magic. He made balls of light dance in the air and juggled them as the others watched in delight. He told Alec to watch carefully, not with his eyes, but with his spirit. For a time Alec saw only what his eyes could see: colored balls of light leaping from one of Michael's hands to the other. But when he let himself go, when he stopped concentrating so hard, he saw something entirely different. There were particles in the air…no, the particles *were* the air. Michael was doing something with those particles, bending them somehow, changing their basic structure so they glowed. He was condensing the glowing particles, Shaping them into tight clusters, so it appeared he created balls of light from nothingness. But, Alec realized, Michael wasn't creating something new; he was simply using what was all around him. He was Shaping air into light. For a moment Alec saw even more, saw how the Wizard was using invisible fingers to mold reality as he wished, and for that moment Alec thought he could do it as well. It seemed like it would be the easiest thing in the world. But when the moment passed, the vision was gone, and magic was again a mystery to the young baker.

The next day they set out early, and the call of the Talisman sang strongly to Alec's heart. He knew they would reach their destination before the day was out, unless Salin starting moving again. Time and time again over the course of the morning, Alec had to fight the urge to turn his horse around, to flee from the confrontation so close at hand. So many people were depending on him to be strong, but he didn't know if he could.

This is crazy. We're hunting Salin and we've almost caught him. Grok's wounds, we must be mad!

But Michael was with him, and Lorn and Horren and Kraig, and so Alec pressed on, feeling somewhat heartened by the presence of his friends. But Salin cast fear into his heart. He had witnessed first hand the demon's vast power and was filled with horror at the certainty he would witness it again. And yet he struggled, and pressed onward, and ignored the growing terror gnawing at his heart.

Salin paced back and forth through the inner sanctum of the temple. The cold walls of black stone pressed in on him, making his sanctuary feel like a prison. He had been pouring over the Talisman for a day now and had managed to unlock some of the secrets which would allow him to control the Fair Folk, but he still had a long way to go. Salin could be a patient man when he had to be, but he feared time was no longer on his side.

Something was coming. He could feel it. And as it drew closer, he knew by the vast, pure energy it spewed forth it could be only one thing: the *Lyll Una*. The Word of the One.

The King of the Fairies must have been desperate to invoke the *Lyll Una*. It was the greatest sacrifice a Fairy-king could make. Of course, it only made sense he would invoke the Word in Faerie's darkest hour. It was the one thing he could do, the one bit of magic he could perform, which would have a chance against the sorcerer. Whoever was carrying it possessed a weapon even

Salin could not defend against. But Salin would not be defeated so easily. He was not above acting in desperation himself.

He knelt at the black altar, over which his Sorcerer's Chain was draped. He meditated for a moment, feeling dark powers swirling about him, and then laid both hands upon the thick, black links of the Chain. He stood, lifting the heavy Chain and clutching its length to his breast. The metal was unnaturally cold, and he relished the deathly chill as it settled into his bones.

The long Chain dragged on the floor behind him as he stepped away from the altar. He clutched it tighter, knowing how lucky he was to have been granted such a gift. To his knowledge, only three such Chains had ever been crafted, and as far as he knew, only the one he now held still existed. It was a direct conduit to the Seth's power. It was sorcery's answer to the *Lyll Una.*

As much as he loved to gaze upon it, to hold it lovingly in his arms, he was loathe to actually use its power. Each use destroyed several links of the Chain. The more power he drew through the Chain, the more links were destroyed. Salin's Chain was once much longer.

Using the Sorcerer's Chain was dangerous in other ways, as well. With each use, he gave more of himself over to Vorik Seth. When the Chain was gone, it was said, the sorcerer who used it could no longer even sneeze unless the Seth willed it. Salin knew he was forever tied to his master, but currently he had his free will, and could serve his master in his own way. When the Chain was gone, he would be nothing but a puppet on a string.

Desperate times demanded desperate acts. The Fairy-King knew it and Salin knew it as well. The sorcerer needed time, and if someone was bringing the *Lyll Una* to his temple, he would do what must be done.

He wrapped himself in the Sorcerer's Chain and began to chant. Purple energy began to crackle about him. Outside, the skies would soon begin to cloud over. The clouds would be red.

He didn't care how many links of the Chain he needed to use. Someone, probably the cursed Second of the Three, was carrying the Word of the One to his door step. The fool had to be stopped. Salin continued to chant, summoning forth the greatest of Vorik Seth's powers he could channel through the Chain.

With a scream that threatened to crack the very stone of the temple, Salin called forth the Blood Mist.

Late in the afternoon they came to a vast open area, the far boundary of which was formed by a thick curve of trees. Alec scanned the area between them and the trees, noting its short brown grass, its stubby bushes, and its lack of anything else. He wasn't surprised by the absence of small animals or birds; the clearing was dry and dead. Briefly he wondered what had happened here to make it this way.

"We're close," he said. "Very close. He's got to be somewhere just beyond those trees."

"At a full gallop, we could cross this clearing in half an hour," said Lorn.

"I do not like this," said Michael. "Salin is no fool; he must know we are coming after him. Besides, sorcerers and Shapers are sensitive to powerful magic. He might be able to sense my presence, even from this distance. He can certainly sense the *Lyll Una*, unless he is so wrapped up in his work he is oblivious to everything else. We must be extremely cautious."

"I'm all for caution," said Kraig. "but this is a waste of time. If Salin knows we're coming, it's folly to stand around and give him more time to prepare."

The Addin, who had grown uncharacteristically introspective of late, began to growl. "The boy's right. This is the time for action. Salin is ours."

Alec wondered why Horren was so passionately hateful of the sorcerer. Ever since he had first met the Addin, the mere mention of the Salin's name stirred him to anger. Granted, at times Horren buried the anger under his typical humor, but it was always there, like smoldering embers that would burst into flame if someone stoked the fire. Hatred for Salin was more than justified, but in Horren's case it seemed personal.

"I am only suggesting we proceed carefully," said Michael. "Otherwise, I agree with you. It is time to end this thing. Lead us onward, Alec."

Without another word, Alec bolstered his courage and tugged on the reigns. His horse started forward, and the others followed close behind. As they rode into the dead grassland, a quiet encircled them, a silence somehow complete despite the dull clomps of the horse's hooves on dry grass. A more lifeless place Alec could not imagine.

When they had progressed to the mid-point of the clearing, a roar of thunder rolled toward them from the west. The sky, already gray, became darker as clouds blew toward them from beyond the trees. In the darkening sky it was hard to tell, but Alec thought the clouds looked peculiar. They were low and vast, and the light that filtered through them was blood red.

Michael motioned for Alec to stop. He was looking into the sky, watching the clouds roll in as red lighting brightened the sky. When the first drops of bloody rain fell from the sky, his features clenched in panic.

"No. No, he cannot!"

Lorn rode to Michael's side, his eyes wide but his manner tightly calm. "Is this what I think it is? Michael, can you stop this?"

"Can I stop...?" Michael trailed off and began shaking his head. "This is the Blood Mist! Salin cannot be doing this on his own. No human could Shape this into being. The hand of the Seth is in this!"

As if to punctuate what Michael had just said, thick red mist came rolling in from every direction. It was as if they were at the hub of a vast wheel of mist, a hub getting smaller by the second. Soon the red fog would close around them completely.

"What is this Blood Mist?" asked Alec. "What can it do to us?"

Michael looked on the verge of calamity. "It can kill us. Horribly. The mist itself can only make you weary, draining your strength and filling you with fear. But out of the mist comes worse horrors, horrors like...ah, One! They come!"

Alec turned to look into the mist rolling quickly toward them over the grass. Vague, dark shapes formed within the red haze, shapes which grew in size as they drew more of the fog to themselves. Transparent and red, the human-shaped figures drifted toward the companions.

"Blood wraiths," muttered Lorn.

As more of the wraiths became visible in the mist, the companions dismounted and formed a tight circle, their backs facing inward. Michael forced down his panic and held his arms in the air. Globes of brilliance formed around each of his hands.

"Lorn, take my sword. It is magical and can destroy these things. Alec, your weapon should be potent against them as well. I will try to hold as many back as possible, but you might have to defend the others. I fear Kraig and Horren have no weapon capable of wounding creatures made of mist."

"Great!" cried Kraig. "What are we supposed to do?"

"Pray," said Lorn, drawing the rune-engraved sword from Michael's sheath.

The mist closed in, borne on winds of sorcery. The panicked horses bolted, disappearing into the mist. The wraiths came faster. One moment they were still far away; the next, they were upon the companions.

Orange fire leaped into Alec's sword and took hold of his heart. His sword arced outward as the first blood wraith came within reach. The blade passed through the misty creature, and with a shrill howl it came apart and faded into the air.

Out of the corner of his eye, Alec could see lights flashing from where Michael stood. The red darkness became bright and yellow, and shrill cries filled the air. Vaguely Alec was aware he could feel reality being manipulated around him. Michael was tearing the wraiths apart by turning the mist, their very substance, to light.

"Alec, look out!"

Alec ducked just as a red shadow passed overhead. If it weren't for Kraig's timely warning, the wraith would have touched his flesh. He wasn't sure what it would have done, but he had no desire to find out. Thrusting upward, he dissipated another misty form with his sword's orange fire.

To his left, Lorn fought madly. Blood wraiths were materializing from the mist all around him. He was swinging Michael's blade furiously to keep them away from Kraig and Horren. No matter how many he returned to mist by the magic of the sword, more kept coming forth to take their place. He moved with practiced finesse and dance-like grace, and his phenomenal skill kept the wraiths at bay. Yet the things kept coming, and Alec wondered how long the warrior could last.

Two came at Alec from the right, and he was saved from their touch by the speed and skill Flame magically imparted to him. Two strokes destroyed them, but another came immediately on their heels.

The red rain was falling more fiercely now, and its touch stung Alec's exposed flesh. The mist itself had trapped them in a tight ring, and in seconds it would close over them. A tendril of it encircled Alec's leg, and at once he felt the strength drain out of his body. His eyes fluttered with weariness and he lowered his sword.

And then a blood wraith touched him. His eyes shot wide open as his scream filled the air, and he felt a wound tearing open where the thing's hand lay. Blood was pouring from the wound, or rather, being *pulled* from the wound to become part of the attacking creature. The wraith's color deepened as Alec's blood mixed with its hazy body.

Orange fire pulsed in Alec's hand, the rage it induced eradicating all weariness. His sword came up, tearing through the wraith and sending it to oblivion. The blood that had infused into its being was flung outward, spattering the ground and Alec's clothes and face. Through his rage, he was vaguely sickened by the fact that the blood was his own.

The mist was touching them all now, and Alec heard someone flop to the ground, unable to resist the fatigue it induced. He turned around in time to see Michael swaying in the mist, his eyes barely open. But the Wizard stayed upright and forced his eyes wide, thrusting his arms into the mist while chanting furiously. Brilliance flashed from his open palms, and the mist recoiled, withdrawing at least twenty feet from the party. Dozens of wraiths were caught in the light as well, and their banshee cries filled the red darkness as they were burned from existence.

It was Kraig who had fallen, and now Lorn stood directly over him, his blade protecting the fallen peacekeeper from the oncoming wraiths. More than ten poured out of the mist and converged on Lorn. Alec cried out as they fell upon the warrior, their misty hands grabbing him everywhere. Thinking about what one wraith had been able to do to himself, Alec watched in horror at what he was certain was Lorn's demise.

But the rune-written blade sang loudly, carving through the wraiths like the mist they were. Lorn, unhurt, stood tall, furiously driving back his attackers. Alec breathed a sigh of relief and cursed himself for a fool. Of course the wraiths hadn't been able to harm Lorn; they were creatures of magic! Alec felt a little better knowing at least one of them would survive the assault, but he had no time to be thankful for it. The mist was closing in again, and another group of wraiths was coming right at him.

Michael's silver light flashed once again, and more of the wraiths burned to nothingness. The mist rolled back as well, but not as far this time. Was the Wizard growing weary, his magic becoming less effective? As Alec brought his sword up to defend against his attackers, he said a prayer that Michael would hold out a while longer.

The blood wraiths kept coming. Empowered by Flame, Alec sent a dozen more to their misty doom. But the attack was unrelenting, and Michael's flashes of power became weaker and less frequent. The Blood Mist encircled them and at last closed upon them, and Alec felt unbearable fatigue settle into his bones. His movements became sluggish, his swings and thrusts slow and dull. Once, when lethargy pulled his sword arm down and made him sway helplessly, an unaffected Lorn came to his rescue, hewing the wraiths apart. But even Lorn was slowing down, not from the magic, but from simple, natural exertion. Alec fell to the ground, the red mist he was breathing conquering him at last.

From where he lay he could see Michael, the Wizard gasping for air as he tried to Shape away the mist one last time. His hands glowed faintly, but his power was waning. Wraiths surrounded him, closing in slowly, while the Blood Mist swirled around him and red rain burned his flesh. As thunder roared through the air and bloody lightning filled the sky with fire, Michael fell to his knees. His power was spent, and the spell of the mist drew him down into lassitude.

Alec heard Horren cry out. For all the Addin's power, he was defenseless against these creatures of magic. Lorn was grunting with effort, probably trying to defend the woodsman. Alec groaned. No power in the world could have helped him stand, and his eyelids were becoming as heavy as bricks. He was hardly aware of the forms of the blood wraiths as they bent down over him.

Suddenly, miraculously, a dazzling white light blazed into existence. Alec's eyes, even being half closed, were seared by it, and he thought that he would surely go blind. But he did not go blind, and the light blazed on, burning away the Blood Mist in an instant of white fire. The horrible screams of dying blood wraiths rent the air. Alec lay on the ground gazing upward, unable, and unwilling, to close his eyes against the silver blaze around him.

The light expanded outward, filling the whole of the vast clearing. It shot up into the sky in a thick shaft, burning away the red clouds and purifying the falling rain. Sounds like thunder, but deeper and richer, filled the air, and for a moment Alec thought he was hearing the voice of a god. Perhaps he was.

The light slowly faded, except at its source, where it held on a moment longer. Michael stood bathing in the light, both hands wrapped around a slim, glowing rod which he had raised above his head. The globe of light shrank, becoming smaller and dimmer, until it settled around the rod. In another moment, it flickered out entirely. The rod itself had stopped glowing, and all that remained of it was a blackened husk. Soon, even this crumbled away, and the dust of the *Lyll Una* fell over Michael's hands and drifted to the ground.

The mist was entirely gone. The rain had stopped. The sky was not even overcast any longer, and the afternoon sun shown down brightly upon them. Alec slowly got up. His wound was throbbing painfully, but he was no longer the least bit tired. Kraig was fully awake as well, and was being helped to his feet by Lorn. Horren had a few raw wounds, but otherwise he was fine.

Alec walked over to Michael, who still had his hands above his head, clutching at nothing. The Wizard's gaze was locked skyward, and his face bore a look of wonder and, at the same time, loss.

"It is gone," he said, his tone soft and sad. "The Word has been Spoken, and its power is gone. I had no choice. It was the only thing that could have saved us."

Alec put his hand on Michael's shoulder. "You did the right thing. Thank Grok the King gave us the *Lyll Una*; without it, we'd all be dead."

Finally Michael lowered his arms and looked at Alec. "But it was for Salin. Don't you understand, Alec? The Word of the One was our best chance at defeating the sorcerer. But it has been used now, expended, and there will never be another until the next King of Faerie grants one. Even I cannot call forth the Word."

Lorn came over and offered the rune-graven sword to Michael, who dismissed it with a wave. The warrior shrugged and said, "There was nothing else you could do. It was just bad luck Salin had the Blood Mist waiting for us."

"It was not luck," said Michael. "He sent the Blood Mist for a reason." Revelation dawned on his face. "Of course! He could sense the Word, and he knew his own magic could not prevail against it. He called the Blood Mist not to kill us, but to force us to use the *Lyll Una*."

Kraig came over with Horren. They both were frowning. "More bad news," said Kraig. "The horses are dead. When they ran off into the mist, the wraiths tore them to pieces. You don't want to see what's left of them."

"Wounds," said Alec. "Losing the horses is a shame, but as far as reaching our destination, it doesn't matter. We're so close we can reach Salin by the end of the day, even on foot."

"I wonder how he called the Mist," said Lorn. "Only Vorik Seth himself has *that* kind of power."

Michael rubbed his chin, considering. "Have you ever heard of a Sorcerer's Chain?"

"Sorcerer's Chain?" Lorn's brows drew together in confusion. "I was always taught Sorcerer's Chains were only myth."

Michael shook his head. "Oh, they are real enough, although rare in the extreme. Salin has got to have one. It is the only way he could have called the Blood Mist."

"If he has a Chain, then we are doomed," said Lorn. "We cannot fight such power."

Michael allowed himself a hint of a smile. "We will not have to. Salin would only use it as a last resort. Each use consumes some of the Chain, and when it is gone, the Seth owns him, body and soul. Can you imagine how much of the Chain must have been consumed to do what he just did? No, he dare not touch it again. He serves Vorik Seth, but he fears him, too. Salin wants to keep his soul to himself for as long as he can."

Alec was hardly following the conversation. Now that they were out of danger, the pull of the Talisman was overwhelming him. They were so close! Fear of Salin told him to run far and fast, but the Talisman's call tugged at his heart. He didn't think he could turn back now if he had to.

"Come on," he said. "Let's get this over with."

The others voiced their agreement, and they plodded onward over the dead grass. The sun was falling in the west, dropping behind the row of trees still some distance away. The afternoon was slipping away, and before long twilight would take hold of the sky. Alec wondered if they would reach Salin before then. Regardless, he was not about to stop until he brought them to their goal. The sorcerer knew they were coming. They could delay no longer.

Alec's gaze was fixed straight ahead. He knew exactly where the Talisman was now: what direction, how close. It sang to his heart. The song was beautiful, but no longer pure. Salin had already tampered with it. He had already blackened it with the dark poison of his magic. Alec felt like weeping.

Toward the trees, toward destiny, the companions marched.

Salin leaned on the altar in exhaustion. He felt wrecked, but nevertheless he wore a fiendish grin. The *Lyll Una* was gone. The fools would still come, of course, but they no longer possessed a weapon potent against him. Even Michael's skill would not be sufficient. The Second was so much less than he had been and Salin was so much more.

The sorcerer looked down at his Chain and dropped it to the altar in disgust. Two links left. Useless!

Still, that didn't matter. He had the Talisman of Unity, and the power it would grant him would dwarf anything he would have been able to accomplish with the Chain. He picked it up from the pedestal beside the altar and turned it over and over in his hands. Already he had unlocked so many of its secrets, and soon, so very soon, he would discover the rest. He couldn't wait until the Fair Folk bent knee before him and called him lord. Such thoughts sent shivers of ecstasy down his old, gnarled frame.

Enemies were coming, but they could be dealt with. Tor was here, among others. Let them deal with the distractions. Salin had more important matters to ponder.

Satisfied, he turned all his thoughts toward the Talisman. With fingers of thought, he began peeling away its secrets like the layers of an onion. A green glow filled it and him, and each second brought him closer to becoming the new Lord of Faerie...the new King of the World.

CHAPTER 24

A Few Days in Fairhaven

Ara's room at the palace was warm and comfortable; nevertheless, she found little comfort in the thoughts consuming her as she stared out the window at the city below. Four days had passed since she and Landyn had gone before the King, four days since Landyn had spoken his warning. King Elyahdyn had listened intently to the minstrel and had taken seriously his claims that another attack was forthcoming. The King ordered additional guards posted around the palace and called for increased patrols throughout the city. The Order of Nom, now under the command of Elder Toros, walked among the people of Fairhaven, keeping a watchful eye for any hint of a threat. To appearances, Fairhaven was more than prepared for any raid.

Ara knew differently, however. The fact of the matter was that anyone—any soldier in the King's army, any guard or Brother of Nom—could be a traitor. It was not only the *dark* Fairies who had fought on Salin's side three days ago. It was impossible to tell who was with the King and who was against him.

Sarah had suggested the King have someone "read" his soldiers and guards to see who could be trusted. Elyahdyn had bowed his head sadly, saying there had been only two readers in the city besides Devra, both of whom had vanished in the fighting. Devra herself was in no condition to conduct so many readings, even if there had been time. They would simply have to have faith that most of Fairhaven's defenders were still loyal to the King.

As Ara gazed out the window, she pondered the other problems facing the city. First of all, no one had any idea when the attack might come. The way Landyn had talked, it seemed there would be another assault that same day, perhaps sooner than they could prepare a defense. But the attack did not come that day, nor did it come in the days since, and the defenders of the city grew more and more anxious. There was an expectant tension in Fairhaven, as if everyone was watching the sky for a storm they knew was coming. Ara couldn't figure out why the attackers would wait, why they wouldn't press the advantage they had already gained with the first assault. Perhaps they were biding their time until the soldiers let their guard down, or perhaps they were waiting for reinforcements. Maybe Landyn had simply been mistaken about a second attack. Whatever the case, as the days passed anxiety and suspicion grew in Fairhaven.

To make matters worse, a great change had come over the King. When Ara had first seen him in the Hall of the Council, he had been an imposing figure, strong and sure and full of majesty. Something about the way he stood and spoke made him seem so much larger than he actually was. Simply put, his presence inspired awe.

More recently, however, he appeared greatly diminished. He seemed tired all the time; his face was haggard and gray. His robes suddenly seemed too large for him, and he hunched within them as if he were trying to hide. His voice spoke commands as it had before, but now those commands lacked conviction. The several times Ara had seen him in the last few days, it appeared he had trouble staying awake, as if he were not the least bit interested in the things happening around him.

Once, one of the red-robed Brothers took her aside and explained to her what had happened. The King had invoked the greatest magic a mortal being could call forth, the *Lyll Una*, the Word of the One. Drawing such power to oneself was a terrible strain on the body, spirit, and mind, and it would, at best, leave one physically wrecked. Such an act of sacrifice could only be made by a person of the highest bloodline of Faerie, the royal bloodline. And such was its toll on the body and spirit each king could do it only once. In time, perhaps, the King would become more like his former self, but he would never again be the powerful Shaper he'd been, and his health would never be the same.

It was the Queen, now, who presided most often in the audience chamber. Mahv issued commands in the name of the King, and she met the people who came to the palace seeking guidance. She had taken an immediately liking to Ara and had invited her and Sarah to dine with her on the second evening since the attack.

"The King will be taking his nourishment in our rooms for a while," she said, "but I must, as Queen, sit at the formal table with our guests and advisors. I would be honored if the two of you would sit with me, for there are things I would discuss with both of you."

They had, of course, accepted gracefully. At dinner, after she and the advisors discussed the situation in Fairhaven, the Queen turned to Sarah and said, "I hear you have been doing well in learning the workings of your special ring."

Sarah smiled proudly. "Well, Lady Devra has been teaching me to create flame from air with the help of the ring. I can start small fires sometimes, but I haven't really come very far. Actually, I'm happy to take it slow. I've already had a…bad experience with the ring."

"I have heard," said the Queen. "You were lucky to have survived. In times of great emotion, one can invoke the power of a Rage Ring without even knowing how. However, in such situations, the wielder of the ring retains no control over the power. It can run amok, feeding on itself and everything around it, or it can fail utterly at the most inopportune of times. Knowledge and control are the only protection against such wild magic."

"You sound like Lady Devra," said Sarah with a grin. Almost at once, her smile vanished. "Grok, I hope she recovers. I went to see her this morning and she wasn't doing very well."

The Queen shook her head sadly, but a hint of a smile still touched her lips. "The best healers in Fairhaven attend her. She will be fine. But in the meantime, I feel it imperative your lessons with the ring continue. I, myself, have some experience with magical Fairy artifacts and would be glad to continue your training."

Sarah looked as stunned as Ara felt. "But…but you're the Queen. Surely you don't have the time train me personally!"

"Nonsense. As you say, I am the Queen and can do as I wish. Although I will be quite busy in the days to come, I am certain I can find an hour or two a day to show you the ways of *Nahl-Shyfir*. Your ability is rare among humans and is too valuable to leave undeveloped. We will begin tomorrow after the noontide meal."

"As you wish, Queen Mahv," said Sarah.

The Queen then chatted informally with Ara, asking her about her life, the land she came from, and her journey here. She was keenly interested in Kari and Jinn and she appeared amused at Ara's description of Landyn.

"We must have him perform at the palace," she said. "It would be interesting to see how a human minstrel compares with our own entertainers."

Later that evening, when Ara had left the company of the Queen to walk through one of Fairhaven's beautiful parks with Landyn, she told the minstrel of Mahv's interest in him. He smiled proudly, saying he would show these Fair Folk what a real musician could do.

"In fact," he stated as they walked down a paved path through a well-tended grove, "I am quite anxious to perform again. It has been far too long since I have played before an audience. I will have to spend some time growing accustomed to the feel of a lute in my hands. Perhaps you will join me for a song?"

Ara smiled but shook her head. "I'm not quick at learning new songs, and I doubt the songs I know appeal to someone of your sophisticated tastes. I appreciate the offer, though."

Landyn gave her a serious look. "It is an offer I don't make lightly. I am very particular about who I will and will not perform with. I have heard you sing, Ara, and your voice is beyond lovely. The whole reason I sought you out in the first place was to ask you to sing with me."

Ara chuckled. "You got a lot more than you bargained for. Oh, Landyn, I'm sorry for dragging you into this."

"My lady," he said with mock seriousness, bowing deeply before her, "I would not have missed it for the world."

He knelt before her, took her hand in both of his, and placed a soft, gentlemanly kiss upon it. Ara pulled her hand away with a sly smile and began to walk away.

"You rogue," she said over her shoulder.

He hopped to his feet and hurried after her, grinning. "You know me too well."

They walked back to the palace together, and Ara reluctantly took her leave of the minstrel. She had considered inviting him to spend some time with her in her room, but she was not quite ready for what she knew would happen. It had been a long time since she had been with a man, since Sarah's father died, in fact. As much as she liked Landyn, and as much as she missed the things she knew he could do for her, she knew the time was not right. There was too much else going on, and they had not known one another long enough, anyway. If only he wasn't so charming!

The following morning, she had broken fast with Landyn and Sarah before joining them for an extended tour of Fairhaven. Their guide for the tour was a Fairy named Vyrdan, a minor lord from Lehnwood whom Landyn had befriended. Sarah knew him as well, Ara soon discovered. He was the one leading the patrol which had discovered Alec, Sarah, and the rest when they had first come to Faerie. Now, he happily led them around the city, pointing out places of interest and talking at length about himself. From his own description, it seemed he could have fought off half of Salin's attack by himself. When Ara asked him if he was worried another assault might come, Vyrdan shrugged and said, "If it does, we will be ready."

After the midday meal, Sarah joined the Queen in the royal garden for her lesson. Ara watched from a bench not far away as the Queen borrowed Sarah's ring, slid it on her finger, and with a wave of her hand made beautiful shapes out of fire. At first she painted abstract designs in the air, but then the flames became discernible forms: large birds, swans, lions, and swirling schools of orange fish. At the end of her display, the Queen shot an impressive shaft of flame high into the air, which burst at its peak into hundreds of flashing stars. Sarah laughed with joy, amazed such wonderful things could be done with the ring.

From where she sat, Ara couldn't hear everything being said, but the Queen spoke for a long time. She demonstrated certain hand motions, explaining the significance of each one, and taught Sarah mystic words and phrases that would help bring out the potential of the ring. Sarah practiced with the ring, and by the end of the lesson she had formed a small ball of flame which hovered in the air before her. At the Queen's instruction, Sarah pointed at the ball and began moving her arm. Her brow furrowed in concentration as the sphere began to move where she pointed. In a few seconds, the ball of flames sputtered and was gone, but Queen Mahv beamed at her student, obviously pleased.

Sarah was pleased as well and spent the rest of the afternoon practicing on her own. Afterwards, she went to eat dinner with some of her friends, and Ara dined in a local tavern with Landyn.

Now as a gentle twilight streaked the sky, Ara watched from her window and enjoyed a moment of peace. The sky's beauty enabled her to put her concerns aside and relax, if only for a moment. Too soon, a knock on her door brought her back to the present.

"Come in," she said, turning away from the window.

The door opened and Sarah stepped in. She was wearing a long green gown that one of the Queen's maids had found for her, and her blond hair was brushed and feathered. For the first time, Ara looked at her daughter and saw a young woman rather than a girl. She was so proud of Sarah, of her ability to meet all the challenges the last several weeks had set before her.

"What are you smiling about, mother?" asked Sarah.

"Oh, nothing," said Ara. "You look wonderful."

"Thank you," she said, twirling to show off her gown. "I have three more of these back in a wardrobe in my room. You don't think the neckline is too low?"

Ara chuckled. "Maybe for the straight-laced farmers back in Barton Hills, but around here it's almost conservative. The lower neckline flatters you more so than it would me. You're developing certain…*assets* I haven't been blessed with."

It was true. Sarah's chest filled out the dress better than Ara's would have. Sarah took a quick look at her cleavage and sighed.

"I'm just glad it's summer. Otherwise I'd be freezing."

Ara crossed the room and gave her daughter a hug. "What brings you by? I thought you'd be spending the evening with your friends."

"I was going to, but I decided I'd rather spend some time with you. I mean, we were only reunited three days ago. Before that, I thought you might be dead! Now that I've got you back, I want to see you as much as possible before…before things get crazy again."

Sarah's face turned grim and Ara hugged her again. "Don't worry. Elder Toros is working with the Captain of the Guard to organize a defense against invaders. Between the Brothers and the King's army, we don't have anything to worry about. Those invaders had the element of surprise last time. This time, they won't catch Fairhaven off guard. Thanks to Landyn."

Sarah shrugged noncommittally. "Of course, none of it matters if Alec and the others don't get the Talisman back. Oh, mother, I miss Alec! If only he hadn't had to go. It's so dangerous! If Alec doesn't make it, I don't know if I can…oh, Grok!"

She threw her arms around Ara, and Ara squeezed her hard. Sarah was sobbing gently, trying her best to stay in control.

"It's hard, I know," she said softly into Sarah's ear. "That's what it means to love someone: to hurt when they're not around, to worry for them if they're away too long. I know how much he means to you. I've known longer than you have. Just have faith everything will work out all right. Do you think Kraig or the others would let anything happen to him? He's in good hands, Sarah. He'll be back before you know it."

Sarah slowly pulled away and wiped a tear from her cheek. She managed a brief smile and said, "I keep telling myself he'll be fine, but it's so hard. I just got back one person I love and just as suddenly I've lost another. That's why I needed to see you. I need to be around people I love."

Putting her arm around her daughter, Ara said, "Why don't we go for a walk? It's a beautiful evening and some fresh air will be sure to lift your spirits."

And so the two of them went out into the royal gardens, and they walked and talked for the next few hours. Sarah's mood seemed to improve as the evening wore on, and Ara found herself feeling happier as well. They were hundreds of miles from Barton Hills, but whenever she looked at her daughter Ara felt as if she were home.

Just past noon the next day, Sarah met Queen Mahv for her next lesson. From her place on the bench, Ara saw the incredible progress Sarah was making. By focusing her mind on the ring, she was now able to call forth fire at will. As before, she made a small sphere of flame and moved it by pointing, but this time it lasted longer and moved quickly where she commanded. She tried increasing the size, but the ball grew only a little bigger before the effort was too much for her and she let it flash out.

Mahv showed her how to make licks of flame dance in the air, and Sarah soon mastered the technique. One time, however, she lost control of the blaze and the Queen had to wave her hands furiously, magically dousing the fire. She cautioned Sarah against trying to do things beyond her abilities, but at the end of the lesson she was more than pleased with Sarah's progress.

"Your daughter is amazing," she said to Ara as the three of them walked back to the palace. "Most Fairies would be able to use her ring instinctively, of course, but very few humans could develop the talent which is coming so easily to her. You should be very proud of her."

Ara couldn't suppress a grin. "I'd be proud of her if she had no talent in magic whatsoever. She's a remarkable girl…a remarkable woman."

Sarah was blushing. "Please, stop!"

When they had left the company of the Queen, Ara asked Sarah to come to her room. "I have something I want to give you," she said.

"What is it?" Sarah asked curiously.

"Something to keep you safe while you practice with your ring."

When they reached her room, Ara opened her wardrobe and removed something she had placed far back on the top shelf, out of view. She ran her fingers in a ring around it, feeling the smooth gold which contained a precious magic. She held it out to Sarah, whose eyes widened in recognition.

"That's the gold circlet Alec found in the chest along with my ring and the Talisman." Ara nodded. "Why did you bring it from Barton Hills? How is it going to keep me safe?"

"It's a long story," Ara began, taking a seat on the edge of her bed, "but I'll make it as short as I can. On the night you and Alec vanished, the night Salin went on his rampage in Barton Hills, I was sitting in the shop examining this circlet, entranced by its beauty, its perfection of form. That's when Salin came in. I never saw him, but he spoke to me, telling me I had to die. Flame erupted all around me, and the shop came down around my ears. But the circlet began to glow, and its glow encompassed me before the fire could burn me. It protected me, Sarah, and I never even felt any heat! I was too stunned to think at that moment, but when I sorted it out later I realized the circlet was magical and its power had saved me from the fire.

"From then on, I kept it hidden. After all, it was my secret advantage. If Salin tried to kill me again, I could survive his attack as long as he struck with fire. And from what I'd seen in Barton Hills, fire seemed to be his weapon of choice.

"After I arrived here with Landyn and the others, I stashed it in the wardrobe to keep it safe. With everything going on since then, I'd practically forgotten about it. But seeing you out there throwing fire around, knowing you could get hurt if it gets out of control, reminded me I had something which could protect you. Wear this circlet whenever you use your ring. I don't want you to get burned again like you did in the tomb."

Hesitantly, Sarah reached out for the golden headpiece. "Are you sure? I mean, you need the protection as much as I do. If there is another attack, you'll need any advantage you can get."

"We all will," said Ara. "If there is an attack, I hope both of us will be safely stashed away in the palace. You need this more than I do; these days, you expose yourself to fire as a matter of course. Besides, I think perhaps these artifacts were designed to work together. A ring that makes fire and a headpiece that protects from it are a perfect match, especially when the ring is designed so emotion can bring forth an uncontrollable inferno. Take it and wear it."

Sarah finally took the circlet and placed it upon her head. It fit her perfectly. She smiled and said, "How do I look?"

"Beautiful," said Ara. "And safe. It does my heart good to know you won't be burning yourself to a crisp out there."

Sarah laughed, and the sound of her laughter lifted Ara's heart. "Thank you, Mother. I think I'll go out and practice a little. You never know when juggling balls of fire is going to come in handy."

Ara sighed. "Be careful! You should be protected by the circlet, but you never know what could go wrong."

"Spoken like a true mother," laughed Sarah as she headed out the door.

The following evening, Ara dined with Landyn, Kari, and Vyrdan at the Woodhelm Inn, a refined establishment which Vyrdan claimed served the best hot meals in all of Fairhaven. It was nearly a mile from the palace, so by the time they arrived at the Inn Ara's stomach was rumbling restlessly. The smells wafting out of the kitchen made her mouth water in anticipation.

The Inn was crafted of a fine, dark wood, both inside and out, and the dim lantern light set a quiet, relaxing atmosphere. A few Fairies playing quiet music in one corner completed the mood. A serving woman smiled at them and led them to a table toward the center of the room, taking their order when they had been seated. Ara looked around the place, impressed by its subtle decor and quiet patrons.

"I've never been in a place quite like this," she said. "No one's shouting or singing or dancing on the tables. No one is trying to pinch the tavern girls."

Vyrdan laughed quietly. "Woodhelm Inn is a different eating establishment than most, my lady. The owners demand good behavior of their guests. This is a place where fine food and drink can be enjoyed in peace. There are a few other places like it in Faerie, but none serve food so delectable."

As they sat waiting for their meals to arrive, Landyn said, "I've asked Kari to join us tonight for a few reasons. First of all, since we arrived here we've barely seen each other. I must admit, good Fairy, I had grown rather used to your company on the road." He flashed Kari a perfect smile, to which she only raised an eyebrow. "Secondly, I know you've been doing some investigating into the possibility of a second attack. People are beginning to think my warning of a second attack was mistaken. But I know what I saw. I need to know if you have uncovered any new information."

Vyrdan sighed. "Must we discuss this tonight? I was under the impression we were to have a pleasant evening together to forget our troubles. Besides, I do not believe I have been properly introduced to this fine lady." He indicated Kari with a smile and a nod. "I am Vyrdan, lord of house Manrell, chief defender of Lehnwood. I serve directly under the Lady Devra."

Kari, only slightly less like iron than usual, said, "It is a pleasure. I am Kari du Sharrel. I am originally from Greenhold, but I have been away from Faerie for many years."

"Indeed," said Landyn. "She was living in a little village called Markway when I met her. I never even suspected she was of the Fair Folk. I was always under the impression that Fairies were...well, quite a bit *different* than human beings. It turns out you are a little taller and thinner than us, perhaps your noses and ears are a little sharper, your eyes a little brighter…but otherwise, we are the same."

"The same?" laughed Vyrdan. "I would not say so. There are many differences deeper than the flesh, differences you cannot see. And of course, the forms we show to you are not necessarily forms we were born with."

"What do you mean?" asked Ara.

"It is part of our magic to change our appearance to please ourselves. It is not a conscious effort, but rather a development that takes place over time, as we find flaws in ourselves and correct them. Without magic many of us would look rather mundane, I'm sorry to say. Not everyone can be blessed with natural beauty. Of course, in a way it is natural. We are, after all, creatures of magic."

"So…what would you look like if you hadn't used magic to change yourself?"

Vyrdan shrugged. "Who knows? Perhaps I would be ugly as a toad. Perhaps I would be nearly as beautiful as I am now. It is too late to go back, but of course I never would want to."

Ara should have learned to believe anything about the Fair Folk by now, but she was still struck by the strangeness of every new bit of magic she discovered. Briefly she wondered if the true appearance of the Fair Folk was human-like at all. Could it be that in their natural forms they were so strange as to be unrecognizable? She had heard the Dark Folk were monstrous in their natural forms, and they changed to resemble dark-skinned versions of the Fair Folk when they left their homes. Could it be the original forms of the Fairies were just as strange?

Probably not. She was just speculating without any real information. How could a people as noble and as lovely as the Fairies be anything less than perfect?

"This is all very interesting," said Landyn, "but if we could go back to the matter at hand? What have you discovered, Kari?"

Both as hard and as beautiful as a diamond, Kari folded her arms. "Nothing. Or at least next to nothing."

"What do you mean?"

"I located some tracks on the outskirts of the city. There were enough different feet passing into the city to belong to a small army. They passed through the forest maze by a quick, secret way. Once inside the city, the tracks become lost among the jumbled footsteps of the highly traveled roads."

Landyn frowned in confusion. "What does this mean? Does the enemy walk among us even now?"

"I do not know. All I know is that someone, quite a lot of someones, passed into the city through a secret way. It was not us; we knew only the normal paths. It was not Salin and his first group of raiders; the tracks are too fresh. A large number of people entered the city only a few days ago."

Vyrdan shook his head. "How can this be? The guards saw nothing. And if they have already penetrated our defenses, why haven't they attacked yet?"

"Like I said, my knowledge is next to nothing. There are tracks, but I do not know who they belong to or what they can mean."

"Well, it has got to mean something," said Landyn. "At least it confirms there is *something* going on. It gives my warning some credibility. Have you told the King or the Queen what you've discovered?"

"Not yet," said Kari. "I wanted to have more to go on before I went to see them." Her eyes betrayed reluctance when she mentioned the rulers of Faerie. Vyrdan must have caught the look in her eyes, for he regarded her carefully.

"Is there perhaps another reason why you hesitate to go to them, my lady?" he said. "Perhaps you would rather they were not warned for some reason?"

Ara gave him a scolding frown. "Don't imply anything about Kari's loyalty. She agreed to help me when I was desperate to find my daughter. And since we've arrived, she's taken it upon herself to investigate the possibility of a second assault. She didn't have to do that. She's obviously on our side. She has nothing against the King."

Kari's cold exterior faltered for an almost imperceptible moment. "That is...not entirely true."

Everyone's gaze locked on the Fairy.

"I am loyal to the land of Faerie. I love it with all my heart. And yet, I had to leave it years ago because the memories it held for me were too painful. When the King condemned my brother to death, I knew he was only serving justice, but the knowledge did not save my heart from breaking. I had to leave before it broke completely."

"To death?" questioned Vyrdan, astonished. "But no Fairy has been condemned to death in centuries. Except for the one who sired young Alec Mason...Martyn...ah, by the One."

"Martyn du Sharell. My brother. My closest friend."

Ara was reeling. Vaguely she remembered that when Kari burst into the Hall of the Council, she mentioned she had a brother named Martyn. Ara hadn't had enough information to put the pieces together at the time, but now...

"We grew up together in Greenhold," continued Kari, "raised by wonderful parents. He was only about seventeen years older than me, yet he quickly became my idol. He was intelligent, strong, and ambitious, and he would often tell me of his plans to travel to Fairhaven and study with the Order of Nom. For a time he planned to become a Keeper of the Tomb, but much to our parent's relief the Keepers were disbanded when the Tomb was deemed too dangerous. This was about sixty years ago, when I was only a child of fifty. Martyn had just reached adulthood and was ready to seek his destiny. He took me for a long walk, telling me he had to go, but would return soon with stories of the world, and would tell me what the grand city of Fairhaven was like. I told him to say hello to the King for me. He laughed and hugged me, and the next morning he was on his way.

"Years passed before I saw him again. Missives he sent to me and my parents told us he had not been deemed strong enough to join the Order of Nom, but he was perfectly happy serving as a soldier in the King's army. Of course, war was nearly unheard of, but the soldiers trained hard and patrolled the land vigilantly. His skills and ambitions served him well, for he rose to the rank of captain quickly. We were so proud of him. I wanted to follow in his footsteps, but of course women were not encouraged to become soldiers. My talent in tracking was discovered early, and I was to serve Faerie as a guide and hunter. Later, it was discovered I had the talents in Shaping my brother lacked, so an instructor from the Order of Nom took me under his wing and helped me develop my skills.

"Meanwhile, Martyn was selected to serve in a *Tynn*. I was thrilled for him, for at last he would be able to realize his dream of seeing lands outside of our own. His *Tynn* was to travel to Eglak by way of Naar to re-establish communication between our King and the High King of Eglacia. He was gone for many years, and when he at last returned he came to see me, and he told me tales of the land of humans which thrilled and mystified me. I was a strong Shaper and respected tracker by this time, but I still idolized my brother, and envied him a little. He had gone where most of the Fair Folk only dream: the realms of humans.

"He stayed with us for nearly two years before returning to his duties in Fairhaven. Afterwards, he kept in touch through letters. Soon he wrote us that he had been chosen as a palace guard, the highest honor for a soldier in the King's Army. He served at the palace for a several years, until such time as the next *Tynn* was being sent out into the world. This time, their mission was to explore Tyridan. He was not permitted to divulge the true nature of their mission, but it seemed to be something of great importance. At any rate, he went to Tyridan and I never saw him again.

"You see, he broke one of the highest laws of Faerie, a law considered almost sacred. In Tyridan, he fell in love with a human woman and he lay with her. For this love, he was brought back to Fairhaven in chains. For this love, he was executed. When we received word, my parents fell into a deep grief and I grew bitter and angry. I left home then, unable to deal with my parents' grief, unable to come to terms with my love for Faerie and my hatred for the law which condemned my brother to death. The King did what law required, but this answer failed to satisfy me.

"I traveled within Faerie for some time, lost and alone until I came to Brahnah, the strange homeland of the Sprites. There I met Jinn, who desired to leave Faerie for reasons of his own. Thus, together, we decided to venture into the world beyond the forests we knew. We wandered Naar and Eglacia for years before settling at Markway.

"I never wanted to return to Faerie. But Ara's plight moved me, and I agreed to bring her here to find her daughter. Now that I am back I will do everything in my power to serve this land, to protect it from the horrors threatening it. You need not worry about my loyalties, Vyrdan. I have little love for the King personally, but I believe in what he stands for. I would never betray him or the Queen. Certainly not to the likes of Salin Urdrokk and these dark Fairy traitors."

Vyrdan looked across the table, regarding Kari with an unreadable frown. He drew a deep breath and said, "Perhaps I have misjudged you. It is not like me to leap to conclusions in haste, but these are trying times. It is hard to know who to trust. I am sorry for your brother, but law is law. Yet, perhaps the laws will someday be changed. Alec Mason does not seem to be the evil offspring we feared would come of such a union. As we have come to know, he just may be the savior of us all."

That was an exaggeration, thought Ara, but Alec certainly was important. He was the only one who could track down the Talisman now that Salin had it. The Talisman itself had chosen Alec, both to find it and to wield it.

"Be that as it may," said Landyn, leaning forward across the table, "we might not be here for him to save if we aren't ready for this second assault. Now it may not be my place to worry so much about it, but since I am the one who first learned of it, I feel responsible. What can we do to prepare?"

Vyrdan said, "The guards at the palace are doing double duty, and the patrols around the city have been increased. I've already stationed my men...the ones I can still trust...at various points throughout Fairhaven. They will report to me should anything happen. Aside from that, I do not think there is anything we can do."

Kari nodded her agreement. "I have already done what I can. I have determined they are here. Until they act, we can only wait."

"What about Jinn?" asked Landyn. "I imagine he would be good at hiding in the shadows, uncovering secrets. What has he been doing?"

Kari snorted. "Jinn has been a faithful companion over the years. He has many fine traits, but courage is not one of them. When he learned Fairhaven might be the target of another attack, he was quick to develop a case of homesickness. He set out for Brahnah yesterday."

They were interrupted as serving women came carrying plates of steaming food: thick slabs of smoking ham, bowls of buttery corn and beans, warm brown bread, a big wedge of yellow cheese, and plenty of fresh fruit. Another woman brought a full jug of dark wine and sat it in the center of the table. She bowed and smiled and left them to their meal.

For a while they were too busy eating to talk. The food was marvelous, and Ara found she was even hungrier than she thought. Food at the palace was exceptional in its way, but this meal was a feast which reminded her of holidays at home. The ham reminded her of a Groksday roast pig, and she found herself reminiscing about the last time she had spent the spring holiday with her daughter and her friends.

The food improved their spirits considerably, and soon their conversation moved on to happier topics. Landyn spoke of the ballad he was busy composing, the one which would make him famous. Vyrdan told a few anecdotes of his time serving as Captain of the Guard in Lehnwood. Kari even broke a smile once or twice during the course of the evening. As for herself, Ara was glad for a little light conversation for a change.

But when the meal was long over and the wine was gone, when the hour grew late and they said their goodnights, Vyrdan bade them be careful. "It is a fairly long walk back to the palace, and we do not know what is out there."

Landyn sighed as he stroked his perfectly trimmed beard. "We will be wary. I just wish there was something more we could do. If only there was some way we could draw them out, make them declare themselves before they are ready..."

Out of the blue, a burst of inspiration struck Ara. She thought perhaps she should keep it to herself. After all, who was she to offer suggestions in this crisis? But it was too important. What if her plan could work?

"Wait a moment," she said. "maybe there is a way."
Curious eyes locked on Ara as she mapped out her plan.

Gwendolyn wasn't exactly pleased with her current situation. The cellar of the merchant's home in which she and her sister were forced to hide wasn't exactly uncomfortable, but it was a far cry from their palace in Varnia. As the daughter of a wealthy noble, she was accustomed to luxury.

To relieve her boredom, she began Shaping delicate ice sculptures out of thin air. First, she formed a long-necked swan, carving the minute details of its features with the chisel of her mind. When it was complete, she began creating a likeness of herself. Perhaps it betrayed her vanity, but she herself was her favorite subject to render in ice. She was beautiful in a cold, wintry way, like ice itself. Since she was a girl, she had always loved the colder months the best. When ice and snow covered the land, she was in her glory. And when, as a teenager, she discovered the ways of sorcery, she was quick to master the cold art of Shaping frozen water. She could make things of icy beauty, like her sculptures. She could call snow down from the sky even in summer, just for the joy of it. And she could kill with a glance by freezing a man's blood as it coursed through his body. This was her favorite thing to do.

Of course, there were easier ways to kill, more efficient and faster. With a wave of her hand, she could fling countless spears of ice in every direction. She could make storms of hail strong enough to pummel even an armored man to death. Freezing the blood was harder, took more concentration, but it was more rewarding. Ah, the look in a man's eye when the cold starts to creep through his veins, when his movements start to slow, when he knows frigid death is claiming him from within…

She concentrated on her sculpture. She had allowed her mind to wander, and the eyes weren't quite right. She melted away a bulge under the right eye and corrected the size of the eyebrows. Then she proceeded to make her waist a little slimmer, her fingers a little longer. Why do a thing if you weren't going to do it right?

"You know, if you are vain enough to want to immortalize yourself with a statue, you should choose a medium that will not melt in an hour or two; marble or bronze perhaps?"

As always, Stiletta greeted her with a sarcastic grin. She was attractive too, in her way, but her beauty smoldered like red coals. Hot passions she could not hide always boiled just under the surface. The only things she and Gwendolyn shared were their loyalty to Salin and their disdain for almost everything else. The rivalry between them was as sharp and precise as one of Stiletta's knives.

"Seth's grin, sister, your very presence is a bane to me. Leave me to finish my work in peace."

"I would gladly do so, but the dark whore Salin left in charge has summoned us. There has been a change of plans. The attack can wait no longer."

"What? But this is foolish! Our numbers are too small to take on all of Fairhaven. Surely Salin has not been able to master the Talisman yet?"

Stiletta laughed soundlessly. "No, even he cannot work so quickly. I do not doubt before long the weaker minds of Faerie will fall under his command, but we no longer have the luxury to wait until this happens. Granted, the attack would be easier if our numbers were swelled with the sorcerer's new mind slaves, but we have to act now."

"Why?" questioned Gwendolyn. "We've waited this long. Surely a few more days cannot hurt."

"The King and Queen are fleeing Fairhaven. Some of their advisors and many of Elders and Brothers of Nom are going with them. Salin's orders were specific. They are all to die. We cannot let them escape."

The sorceress was not convinced. "But how important can they really be? Once Salin has mastered the Talisman, even the most powerful Brothers will kneel before him."

"Yes, given time. But the Brothers, especially the Elders, are incredibly strong of will. It may take them a long while to fall, especially if their King is still alive to lead them. Who knows what they may be able to accomplish if they can fend off Salin's influence long enough. They may even find a way to fight him. No, Salin is right. The most powerful minds of Faerie must be put down. The rest will fall under his influence as easily as trained dogs."

Gwendolyn cursed silently. Stiletta was right. She hated to admit it, especially when Gwendolyn herself should have seen it first. She was the sorceress, not Stiletta. She was supposed to know how these things worked.

"Very well," she said, putting the finishing touches on her sculpture. "Let us go see what Gothra's plan is. It had better be a good one."

"I am certain it is," Stiletta said through a grin. "At any rate, I'm tired of waiting. We've been hiding down here for days like rats in a hole. My knives grow thirsty for Fairy blood."

Gwendolyn took a last look at the sculpture before her. Her mind had been preoccupied; it was not her best work. Sighing, she followed her sister without another word.

Before leaving the merchant's house, they put on light cloaks and pulled hoods up over their heads to hide their features. As humans, they would immediately have been recognized as strangers in Fairhaven. They were only going across the street, and it was a little-traveled street on the outskirts of town, but they couldn't take any chances. Too much depended on secrecy.

It was amazing how good the Dark Folk were at secrecy. Two nights ago, when their small army had entered Fairhaven, the dark sorcerers had worked some sort of magic she had never encountered. They cast a cloak of darkness around the army, a cloak as black as the night, which rendered them effectively invisible. Unseen, they advanced with unnatural stealth through the forest maze and entered the city. They passed so near to sentries and patrols of soldiers that Gwendolyn thought they would surely be discovered, but the sorcery kept them hidden. Once inside, they secreted themselves in the homes of Fairies who were sympathetic to their cause. There, they waited for the call. Gothra l'Uarach, the dark Fairy in charge of the invasion, had several sorcerers roaming the city, looking for evidence that the first of the Fair Folk were falling under Salin's influence. They were to take command of those weak-minded fools and give the sign the attack was to begin.

It would have been so easy. More and more of the Fair Folk would have turned to Salin's side as the attack progressed, creating confusion and distrust among Fairhaven's defenders. Soon, only the King and his strongest allies would have been left to fight against Gothra's forces. Alone, they would easily fall.

But if the King and his Shapers escaped now, who knows what damage they could do before they were finally caught and slain! Perhaps none, but this was a risk Gothra, apparently, wasn't willing to take. The attack would take place now, prematurely, to prevent the land's monarch from living to oppose Salin.

They came to the small farmer's hovel where Gothra and her sorcerers were hiding. It was an unlikely place for one of Salin's highest captains to hide, but that was why she had chosen it. Besides, the "farmer" in question was himself a slave to Salin, and under his tiny home was a cellar large enough to serve as Gothra's base of operations.

Stiletta pushed open the farmer's door and went inside without a glance at her sister. Gwendolyn followed behind her and, taking no time to acknowledge the farmer or his wife as they tried to greet the sisters, progressed down the stone staircase which led to the cellar.

It was a dim, gray stone room, several times larger than the house resting above it. There was some sparse furniture, including a few small beds, but nothing which provided the least bit of luxury or comfort. Gwendolyn couldn't help but wrinkle her nose in disgust. How could anyone live like this, even for a few days?

A dozen or so dark Fairies stood in clusters around the room, Gothra's chief sorcerers and warriors, the lieutenants of the invasion force. A handsome light-skinned Fairy stood at the front with Gothra. Gwendolyn recognized him as Rhyan, a warrior who had joined their cause only recently. He had been useful, for up until the first attack he had been placed highly as a trusted captain in Faerie's army.

Gothra saw the sisters arrive and spared them an insincere grin. There was a certain enmity between Salin's servants. Gothra was jealous of Stiletta and Gwendolyn's position as personal agents of Salin, and the sisters resented Gothra being granted leadership of this mission. Still, they were forced to work together for the good of the cause.

Gothra called for the group's attention, and when she had it, she began to speak. "Seth's greetings to you all. As you have heard, the time for the assault has come sooner than we had planned. It would have been easier if we had been able to wait, but the problem is not as difficult as it may seem. We are strong enough to crush the King and the Brothers of Nom, for they are weak and disorganized, and they do not know who among them can be trusted. Indeed, many highly placed brothers, even elders, are loyal not to their King, but to their new master, Salin Urdrokk. The day of Salin's victory is close at hand!"

A rousing speech, but Gwendolyn was not impressed. She did not join the others in cheering and applauding Gothra's words. She needed more than empty words. She needed Gothra to prove she had a plan which could lead them to victory.

Over the course of the next few minutes, Gothra proved it.

In the crowded streets in front of the palace, Ara watched as the King and Queen descended the grand spiral staircase. They were both dressed in their royal finery, but now, more than ever, the King appeared to be swallowed by his clothes. His face was sunken and weak, and he needed to be helped down the stairs. She had not imagined that one single act of magic could take such a toll on someone, especially someone as mighty as the King of Faerie. She prayed his sacrifice would enable Alec and the others to defeat Salin Urdrokk. It had to! From what she had learned, the King had tapped directly into the power of a god. How could the sorcerer stand up to that?

They royal carriage waited for Elyahdyn and Mahv at the foot of the great palace stairs. Upon a row of sleek horses sat the advisors and Brothers who had been chosen to accompany them on their journey. It had been announced earlier in the day that the King and Queen had chosen to retreat to a village further east, further from Salin's influence and the Dark Folk homeland. The Council, it was said, had determined that the King and Queen were too valuable to perish here should Fairhaven be attacked again. They had advised the royal couple to leave the city and the King had agreed.

Of course, it was all a lie. The King and Queen weren't really planning on going anywhere. It was all a ploy, a scheme to draw out the enemy before they were ready to attack. As the trap grew closer to being sprung, Ara's mouth grew dry and her knees became weak. She was nervous, and with good reason. This entire, dangerous plan had been her idea.

Sarah stood to her right, Landyn to her left. The three of them were positioned in such a way that it would be easy for them to retreat into the palace if and when the attack began. Vyrdan was nearby with a small number of his men to help usher Ara and the others to safety. Ara would have rather stayed safely in the palace while her plan was carried out, but she knew it might look suspicious if the rather well known human guests of the King and Queen were not present to see them off. They had to do everything they could to conceal the fact that this was a trap.

It was a good trap, she thought. Vyrdan had organized the details. Brothers of Nom, dressed in simple farmer's clothes, were mixed in with the crowd. The best warriors in the city, the ones most likely to be loyal, were stationed in doorways, on rooftops, in alleyways, anywhere it would not seem likely. They, too, where in disguise. Of course, there were other Brothers and soldiers placed in plain sight, but they were only for show. Sadly, they were likely to be the first casualties if an attack was forthcoming.

There was much more to the counterattack than that, but Ara didn't know the details. She had come up with the plan, but she hardly understood military strategy. Vyrdan, however, proved to be an expert in the field. Salin's allies would be hard pressed to get through the defenses he had set up.

The King and Queen stopped at the foot of the palace stairs. Despite his obvious weakness, the King managed a wave and a smile. He could do no more, however, and the Queen took his arm and led him down to the carriage. First Advisor Syndar, who had been following close behind them, made the obligatory farewell speech in his King's stead, keeping it short and to the point. Then he followed the royal couple toward the carriage.

This is it. If anything is going to happen, it will happen now.

Most of the observers in the crowd knew nothing of what was truly going on, yet Ara felt the tension in the air thicken as the King and Queen walked down middle of the road, making themselves vulnerable to attack. Time seemed to stand still, and for a long moment it seemed nothing would happen.

And then the air turned rank with black smoke. Seemingly out of nowhere, and to everyone's surprise, thick, sooty clouds billowed across the road, choking and blinding the onlookers. The attack was so fast, the magic so unexpected, most of the would-be defenders dropped to their knees, coughing and gagging helplessly. Ara herself went into a fit of hoarse coughs as the black soot filled her lungs, and her eyes watered and stung as she tried to gaze into the cloud.

Through the swirling darkness, she saw chaos erupt. The crowd surged as people tried to move away from the noxious cloud, stumbling over one another as they gasped for air. As they bolted in all directions away from the King's carriage, others, somehow unaffected by the cloud, ran forward purposefully. The sound of metal scraping leather filled the air as swords were unsheathed. Ara saw the dark forms, swords aloft, converge on the unprotected carriage.

Assassins! she meant to cry out loud, but smoke got in her throat and she hacked uncontrollably instead. In a panic, she realized her plan had backfired completely. The King and Queen of Faerie were about to be cut down and it was all her fault.

And then there was a mighty gust of wind, and the smoke nearest the carriage was swept away. Queen Mahv stood at the center of the cloud, her arms spread wide as if she could push away the smoke with her hands. Her brow was creased in concentration. She closed her fists and the wind whipped harder, pushing the deadly cloud back further. The area around her became clear as the wind dispersed the fog, and five dark Fairy swordsmen stood plainly revealed. They did not slow their charge, however, and their deadly blades remained poised to strike the King and Queen.

From somewhere above, bows twanged. No longer protected by the cloud's shadowy cloak, the assassins had become easy targets for hidden bowmen. Seven arrows flew from windows, towers, and staircases surrounding the street, and four struck home in dark Fairy hearts or necks. The remaining three thunked into the ground harmlessly, leaving one attacker racing for the Queen. Braving the flailing wind, he launched himself toward her vulnerable form.

Lightning blazed. In an instant, a brittle, black form fell to the ground at the Queen's feet, its sword clattering on the pavement before her. She breathed in relief as her eyes flashed gratefully toward her rescuer. Ara followed the Queen's gaze and saw Elder Toros, still sitting atop his beige horse, smiling grimly as wisps of lightning flashed from his smoking hand.

"Come on," said Landyn, grabbing her hand. "I don't know where Vyrdan's gotten to, but I've got to get you to safety."

The smoke had cleared enough that she could breathe and speak normally. "All right, I'm coming. Grok, this is worse than I thought it would be. Sarah, let's go."

But before she could turn to her daughter, the attack began again with renewed vigor. Dark Folk flooded the street, swords were pulled from sheaths, and steel clanged against steel as the Fair Folk leapt forth to defend their King. To make matters worse, blasts of flame and lighting fell amidst the defenders, sending them screaming to their deaths. And then rocks of ice began to fall from the sky.

Ice? In summer?

Ara heard a feminine laugh nearby. She spun to face a woman whose beauty resembled ice itself, a blond, blue-eyed, light skinned woman waving her hands madly in the air. As she waved, a wind whipped up around her, hurling the ice storm in the direction she indicated. She kept her ice away from the main thrust of the attack, forcing back defenders without harming too many of her allies.

"Grok!" Ara called out to anyone who could hear, "someone stop that woman! She's bringing a storm!"

Landyn was pulling her away. She groped behind her, reaching for her daughter. But her hands caught only air.

"Sarah?"

As she turned, she saw Sarah step toward the ice woman, her fire ring blazing to life. Ara cried out her daughter's name, begging Sarah to follow her and Landyn to safety. Sarah didn't turn around, but her voice carried clearly over the din.

"I'll stop her, mother. There's no one else who can."

It was true. Things were so chaotic no one else had heard Ara's warning, and the soldiers and Shapers of Faerie were already fighting for their lives. But Ara's heart screamed out for Sarah, and her hands reached out desperately to grab her daughter, to pull her away from danger. But she was far too late. Landyn was dragging Ara toward the palace now, and a wave of shouting combatants swept between her and Sarah. All she could see were grim warriors facing off in a deadly contest and all she could hear was the clamor of steel. Sarah was lost to her.

As she reached the palace the hail stones fell harder.

CHAPTER 25

Of Fire and Ice

Alec stepped out of the curved grove of trees and gazed at the unkempt garden spreading before him. Weeds and ugly vines pushed themselves out of the dirt in a chaotic tangle, twisting into shapes as random as they were unsightly. Michael stepped out of the woods and stood beside him, casting magical light into the hideous garden. The Wizard shook his head and sighed.

"I think we have found him. For some reason Salin has always been fond of strange gardens such as this. I think it pleases him to grow horrible weeds as some enjoy growing flowers and herbs. He mocks life any way he can."

As the others stepped into the garden, Michael threw his light forward. Hunching in the dim illumination, perhaps a hundred yards away, stood a large building of black brick. Wide stairs led up to the wooden double doors, which were framed by tall, engraved pillars of black stone. The pillars supported a stone awning which arched upward at the center, and into the stone was carved a black hand twisted into a claw.

"One," muttered Michael. "That symbol. No wonder Salin came here."

"What is it?" asked Alec.

"The symbol of Vorik Seth. This is a temple erected in his name."

"A temple to the Seth?" questioned Lorn. "I thought they were all destroyed."

"Apparently not," said Michael, starting across the twisted garden.

"Wait," said Alec, hurrying after his teacher. "A temple? Temples are built for gods, not...not demons."

"To some, the Seth is a god. There was a time when there were as many temples dedicated to Vorik Seth as there were to Lars. Part of the work of the Three was to seek out these temples and destroy them. Centuries ago there were many people who worshipped the Seth, for he was a god who actually walked within the world, more immediate, more real, than any other god. Most of these people were not evil like Salin, simply misguided. Many of those misguided fools lost their lives defending these temples."

"Why was it so important they be destroyed?" asked Kraig.

"They were...*are*...focal points of Vorik Seth's power. Evil is stronger in such places and the influence of the One is less. The land on which these temples were built has been touched by the Seth's power; he has invested it with his evil. It seems we are at more of a disadvantage than I thought."

Horren, who had been lagging behind, caught up to the others and said, "You need to learn to think more positively, Elsendarin. Salin's master abides far, far west of here. The shadow he casts is long, but not as long as this, I think. Salin himself is our only concern, and together we can surely crush him."

"Do you really think so?" questioned Michael as he stepped over a twist of gnarled roots. "You are prone to overconfidence. Remember how easily he defeated you in Fairhaven. He defeated us all, claimed his prize, and escaped with ease. And now, as if he were not already powerful enough, we must attack him here, at his place of power. We do not even have the advantage of surprise. He sent the Blood Mist, so he already knows we are on our way."

"Unless," said Lorn, "he believes we died in the Blood Mist."

"He knows we survived," said Michael. "He knew the *Lyll Una* would be enough to disperse the mist. By forcing us to expend its power before we reached his hiding place, he deprived us of the only weapon which would have given us a reasonable chance at victory. He knows what he is doing."

"What are our chances now?" asked Alec.

Michael shrugged. "Pray for a miracle, Alec Mason."

As the dark temple grew nearer, Alec realized it was far larger than it had first appeared. It was only twenty or thirty feet high, but the dark brick structure sprawled out across the weed-choked ground for forty yards or more. The clawed fist on the black awning became more distinct, and as Alec gazed upon it he was filled with dread.

"I do not like this," said Lorn. "There is no one in sight. Surely Salin would not leave his stronghold unguarded."

"No," answered Michael. "We must be wary."

"We should have some sort of plan," said Kraig. "Are we just going to go knock on the door and say, 'Hey, here we are?'"

"There is no other way in," said the Wizard, "but rest assured, I am not going to knock."

"As for a plan," said Lorn, "just get me close to him. His sorcery cannot harm me and his flesh is as susceptible to my steel as any other's."

"Of course," said Michael, "if you can get to his flesh through the cloak of invulnerability he will obviously cast upon himself. I fear only I will be effective against him, at least until I can wear him down enough so a sword might slip through his weakened defenses. Still, even without magic, he is a fierce opponent. He was once First Bladeknight to an ancient King of Eglak, and his prowess with the sword has never been lessened by the years."

"Then you must wear him out," said Horren, "drain his magic so we can crush him."

Alec shook his head. Both Lorn and Horren actually seemed anxious for this conflict. Michael discussed it calmly and matter-of-factly. Besides Alec himself, only Kraig had the sense to look nervous.

They had nearly reached the stairs now and the dark shape of the temple filled Alec's vision. The blackness of the already dark night seemed to deepen, and shadows cast in the gray moonlight hunched ominously around them. Suddenly Alec heard a sound like something crunching its way toward them through the dense vegetation.

"What is that?" he cried.

Before anyone had a chance to respond, a thick brown vine wrapped itself around Kraig and lifted him into the air. He cried out, struggling futilely to free his arms so he could grab his axe. Alec stared in disbelief as the horrible weeds and vines rustled and writhed to life, twisting around the legs and ankles of his companions.

"Grok's wounds!" cried Alec as the ground burst open beneath him, bent roots reaching up to bind him.

"One!" grunted Michael, gritting his teeth in frustration. He was already half bound by writhing weeds.

The plants were growing out of control, snapping and twisting to bind and consume the companions. The roots were like steel bars, the vines like chains. Brute strength would not be enough to break these bonds, and Alec could not reach his weapon to cut himself free. No one could. The assault was too quick, too complete.

The vines which had lifted Kraig brought him crashing back to the ground, where weeds rushed over him like a wave, burying his thrashing form in seconds. Alec screamed his friend's name as he struggled against his own bonds.

Horren was covered to his chest in thick green vines which struggled to pull him downward. He fought as hard as he could to stay erect, but even his huge muscles were failing him. His face knotted with effort, and with rage.

"He cannot do this!" cried the woodsman. "Twisting nature in this way!" His eyes were wild, red, his mouth clenched in a grimace of hate. "Plants are my domain, Urdrokk," he shouted. "Not yours!" He lifted his one free hand above his head, shaking his fist madly. *"Mine!"*

He turned his raging eyes upon the vines gripping him like a vice. "Let go!" he screamed. Alec thought he had lost his mind.

But the vines obeyed.

Slowly, as if with great reluctance, the vines disentangled from Horren's torso, then his legs. His eyes held them, and it was as if the plants recoiled from his anger. When he was free, he threw his arms open, and the weeds and vines bent away from him, forming a circle with him at the center.

"In this, at least, I am your better, sorcerer," he rumbled. "Even so far from my Addingrove I hold some power over things which grow in the earth. Even here, in your perverse garden."

He started walking forward, toward where Kraig lay buried under crushing weeds. Everywhere he stepped, the plants bent away from him. If Alec didn't know better, he would have thought the vegetation capable of fear.

"Release him!" cried Horren.

Rustling loudly, hurrying to obey, the growth withdrew from the peace-keeper's still form. Horren roared his anger, and the vines and weeds and roots dropped from Alec, Lorn and Michael. Alec took a deep breath and shook some clinging leaves and dirt from his clothes and hair. Michael brushed himself off calmly while Lorn gave a salute to the Addin.

"Well done," said the warrior. "I thought your power over plants was tied to your Addingrove."

Horren grinned wildly. "It is, for the most part. My influence here is weak, but not so weak I cannot break this simple enchantment. Salin has not studied nature as I have. He should not trifle with things he does not understand."

"Wisdom that should be heeded by all," said Michael, locking his gaze on Horren. "You bear great anger toward the sorcerer, but you cannot fight him. He has vast powers which you, old friend, cannot comprehend."

"Bah! You just distract him with your magic, Elsendarin, and I will grind him to paste."

Kraig had just risen, taken a few deep breaths, and brushed himself off. Blood dripped from a few small scratches on his face and arms, but he appeared to be fine otherwise. "We should move on," he said. "Who knows what other surprises the sorcerer has for us."

"Are you all right?" asked Alec.

"I'm fine." He hefted his axe, gripping if firmly in his powerful fist. "And I'm anxious for a chance to use this."

"You may get it sooner than you think," said Lorn.

The warrior stepped over the stilled piles of roots and weeds, and the others followed close behind. Soon they were free of the deadly garden and within twenty yards of the temple's front stairs. Fear thumped in Alec's chest, rattled in his bones. His mind insisted he turn around, his heart begged him to run from the evil shrine before him. Yet his legs would not obey. The Talisman called him so strongly, filled his being so completely, he could do nothing but walk on. The Talisman *needed* Alec, needed him and called to him, begging to be set free. The irresistible force pulling Alec toward the temple was a poor substitute for courage, but it was all he had.

And then, roaring madly, the ogres came charging from each side of the temple, massive spiked clubs raised overhead. At once, Alec heard Lorn draw his blade, saw Kraig ready his axe. Michael remained standing calmly while Horren charged the ogres, his mad grin still intact.

The first wave of ogres cut them off from the stairs while the second charged in at them from each side. Still more poured around the sides of the temple, and the air rang with their cries of hate. Somewhere past his panic, Alec wondered where all the ogres had been hiding. There were twenty...then thirty...then forty...*and they kept coming!*

Like an avalanche the gray-skinned monsters fell upon Horren, Lorn, and Kraig, threatening to sweep them away like so much jetsam. But Horren smashed outward with arms like tree trunks, fists like battering rams, bursting gray heads like ripe melons. At the same time Lorn, using the enchanted blade Michael had appropriated from Tor, slashed with such skill the first three ogres who charged him were efficiently eviscerated. Kraig's great strength and heavy axe took its toll on the beasts as well, spraying blood onto the temple stairs.

Alec's hand drifted toward Flame, but his heart was not in it. His fear raged uncontrollably, and the sword refused to ignite in the orange glow which would have instilled bloodlust in Alec's heart and skill in his body. Conflicting with the fear was the Talisman's song, begging, demanding, that Alec ignore what was going on around him and continue toward the stairs.

"Do not move," said Michael calmly, standing inches away to Alec's right. The ogres were only feet away from them now, a dozen or more of them bearing down directly on Alec. How could he not *move?*

With a wave of his arm, the Wizard tore the ground asunder. Alec felt something in the air shift, some sort of energy reaching out from Michael, gripping the earth, tearing it apart. The result was devastating. Ogres were flung back, blinded by the blast, pummeled by chunks of earth as forceful as catapult rocks. They tripped on each other and fell, some buried under waves of earth, some crushed by chunks of bedrock torn free by Michael's fury. A score of ogres screamed their death cries, another score fled before the Wizard's wrath.

But further away, creatures not affected by the quake were undaunted. A full thirty of them stood before the stairs to the temple, advancing on the already struggling Lorn, Horren, and Kraig. Despite a strong start, the odds were proving too much for the fighters. The Addin was still crushing anything that came close to him; his stamina and fury seemed to spring from a bottomless well. Lorn was faring less well, however. No matter how skillful he was, he was only a man, and the ogres were more than willing to sacrifice themselves to tire him. Kraig was already half buried in huge corpses, making it impossible to defend against living ogres.

A few of the creatures broke away from the conflict and rushed at Alec and Michael. The Wizard sent a stream of flame at their attackers, but somehow one skirted the fire and came at Alec from the side. The ogre came so fast, so unexpectedly, there was no way Michael could get between it and the baker.

Orange fire or no, Alec lifted his sword to meet the oncoming beast. Fear raged within him, but one thought spurred him to action. One thought broke through his terror, and it wasn't the call of the Talisman.

It was Sarah.

He had recently found love and was in no hurry to lose it. He wanted to live so he might return to her, so their love might grow and flourish.

He swung his blade with passion and fury, taking his fear and using it, channeling it to give him strength. As Flame bit into the charging ogre, taking its arm in a spray of blood and splintered bone, Alec cried one word.

"*Sarah!*"

The ogre dropped back, stunned. Alec pressed his advantage, charging forth and slicing open its stomach with a powerful sweep of his blade. The sword did not glow; it did not lend him skill or speed. As the ogre fell and Alec pierced its neck with his bloody blade, Alec realized what he had done. Unaided by his companions or the magic of his sword, he had survived deadly combat. More than survived: he had *won*.

And in doing so, he had mastered his fear. It was still there, deep in his heart, but it was quiet and dull and no longer paralyzed him. He raised his blade in triumph as the Talisman's song rang in his mind and fed his passion. Let Salin send his ogres. Alec was ready.

But ready though he was, he could never fight the bellowing, clattering, fighting press of ogres surrounding Lorn, Horren, and Kraig. The three men would certainly fall if Michael did not soon intervene. Alec looked to the Wizard, who was surveying the battle as if to determine where to best spend his energies.

Alec ran over to him. "This is madness!" he exclaimed.

Quietly and matter-of-factly, Michael turned to him and replied, "This is war."

Too calmly to seem sane, Michael walked into the crush of monsters. He lifted his hands, palms outwards, and lightning blazed loudly into the raging throng. Death sizzled from his hands, blasting ogre after ogre as he waded toward his companions. Smoking gray bodies fell everywhere. The path where Michael passed remained open; no ogre dared to walk in his wake.

Alec took the opportunity to heed the Talisman's call. He ran into the path Michael had opened, racing to catch up to the Wizard before the ogres regained their courage and crushed in upon him. Soon he found himself directly behind Michael, who continued blasting his way toward their companions.

Soon all five of them stood side by side. The ogres retreated to a safe distance, fearfully respecting Michael's magic, Horren's strength, Lorn's skill, and Alec's newfound courage. Yet it seemed they had reached a stale-mate. The temple stairs were blocked by twenty or more ogres, and still more waited in the darkness, surrounding the companions. Lorn's heavy breathing suggested he wouldn't last through another battle, and Kraig swayed on his feet, severely wounded. Horren was hunched and ready, snarling like an animal, but Alec saw blood running down the huge man's chest and legs and pouring from a wound on his scalp. Even Michael had broken a sweat.

Through a growl, Horren said, "I will hold them here. Go find Salin. Kill the bastard."

"But you are wounded," said Lorn. "These ogres will kill you."

"I am the only one with the strength to keep them at bay. Elsendarin's magic would suffice, but only he can slay Salin. He has to go. I have to stay."

"But how can we get through them?" asked Kraig. "They're guarding the stairs."

"Watch and learn, boy," growled the Addin.

Propelled by his powerful legs, Horren bounded toward the stairs. His roar was terrifying, and the ogres scrambled to get out of his way. He continued up the stairs until he stood before the tall wooden doors, and with a yell he smashed them with his fists. They buckled inward, the large iron hinges cracking. He smashed them again, and the wood splintered, the hinges snapped, and the doors crashed inward.

By now the ogres had rallied. They were racing toward the stairs, toward the Addin, perceiving him to be the most dangerous threat to them and their master. He hurled himself down the stairs, landing amidst the massing creatures. His fists battered at them, crushing them, and again they parted in fear.

"Now!" he called. "Before they find their courage!"

"You heard him," muttered Lorn, already rushing toward the doorless entry. "This is our chance!"

Michael and Kraig followed him, racing up the stairs, and the call of the Talisman pulled Alec along behind them. Now that the way was clear, he could not resist.

He rushed past Horren just as the ogres regrouped and began carefully circling their prey. Alec ran up the wide staircase and passed under the threshold. Before he knew it, he was inside Salin Urdrokk's stronghold.

He was in the temple of Vorik Seth.

Lorn and Kraig were waiting for him just inside the doorway. Michael stood further inside, casting light down a dank hallway.

"Hurry," said the Wizard. "Horren will not be able to hold them back forever."

Alec spared a look back before starting down the hall, and his heart cried out for the Addin. The ogres, a score of them at the least, charged Horren as one. He struck hard, struck furiously, but sheer numbers threatened to overwhelm him. Just before Kraig reached out to drag Alec away from the gaping entryway, a flood of gray creatures buried the woodsman and forced him to the ground.

Horren! Ah, Grok, Horren!

He meant to cry out loud, but his throat was too dry for speech. As he was pulled along, both by Kraig's grasp and the Talisman's plea, he felt his heart beginning to break. He longed to run back out, cleave at the ogres with Flame, take as many of them apart as he could before they smashed him to bloody pieces. Horren needed help! But suicide was pointless. Even so, Alec did not see how they could possibly win. Salin had too many defenses, too many slaves. This was his place of power.

And they had already lost Horren.

Gwendolyn carefully picked her way through the fighting, deftly avoiding the skirmishes springing up all over the streets of Fairhaven. She had already done her part in the battle, and she had no intention of risking herself further. Let Stiletta join the dark Fairies in their raid, adding her knives and daggers to their swords and sorcery. Stiletta reveled in danger, thrived at being in the midst of battle. She liked to be spattered with the hot blood of fallen foes.

Gwendolyn, on the other hand, favored a cold kill: impersonal, dispassionate, and preferably from a safe distance. Her power complimented her style. She saw no need to stay close to the conflict when she could kill men from afar, keeping herself out of harm's way.

When she reached a flowery garden at the top of a high hill, far from the center of town and away from the noisy chaos of war, she paused to catch her breath. Fighting had broken out near the garden, of course, as it had over the rest of the city, but compared to the conflict near the palace it seemed a peaceful place. As she stood and gazed at the struggle below, armed Fairies rushed past her, focused on the calamity beyond. They were farmers, merchants, and townsfolk of every profession and rank, taking up arms to defend their home. They were oblivious to the lone woman standing quietly in their midst, just as they were oblivious to the traitors who ran among them, Fairies dedicated to Salin who would strike them down before they could lift a finger to help their King.

She let them pass. She could have killed them, or at least a great number of them, if she had desired. But they were irrelevant and she did not wish to spare the power. Her attentions were focused elsewhere. The ice storm she had created had kept the defenders away from the King and Queen, and now, as she concentrated, it rolled eastward past the palace, continuing to rain icy death on the soldiers who raced to battle. The pattern in which she moved her storm was predetermined, a pattern known to Gothra's forces, but not to the soldiers of Fairhaven. Thus, the dark Fairies and their allies were always a step ahead of the storm, drawing the King's soldiers directly into its deadly path. Heavy stones of ice pounded down upon Fairhaven's defenders, forcing them away from the main thrust of the attack, assuring Gothra's victory.

Gwendolyn stared at the sky above the palace, and with a push from her mind, she moved the storm eastward. From her vantage upon the garden hill, she could see the King's men preparing a charge, massing their forces to break through the raider's defenses. She nudged her raging storm clouds until the King's defenders stood under their shadow, and then she broke the clouds open, tearing ice from them and sending it down upon the soldiers. Fists of ice roared from the sky as if they had been hurled from a giant sling, cracking helmets and shattering bones, felling soldiers by the score. Many of Gwendolyn's victims were able to back out of the storm's way, but they were wounded and disoriented, and the charge had been foiled.

The sorceress smiled. Because of her talent, the defenders didn't have a chance. Salin's victory was assured, and he would be well pleased with Gwendolyn for the part she played. Perhaps he would at last grant her the knowledge she coveted, the secrets of power he had promised her when she first pledged herself to him. The secrets he would teach his greatest servant would set her apart from the others, set her above even Tor, and, more importantly, her sister. If she was lucky, however, she wouldn't have to worry about Stiletta any longer. Perhaps Stiletta would be killed in the battle below. Thinking such thoughts made Gwendolyn's smile widen.

A second group of townsfolk came running through the garden. This time, Gwendolyn had power to spare for them. As they ran past she flung out her arms, and long daggers of ice sprang from her fingers. Launched like bolts from a crossbow, the daggers impaled the running Fairies through the centers of their backs. Cries of death rang out as a dozen bodies fell as one to the cold earth.

Ice. Like a killer's logic, like Gwendolyn's heart, it was cold and deadly. The deaths she had just caused pleased her, but they did not warm her. Only Salin's promises of forbidden knowledge had the power to do that.

Consumed with thoughts of ice, she was ill prepared for the blast of fire which flared suddenly past her. If she had not instinctively flung herself to the side, she would have been scorched badly, perhaps killed. Gaping in amazement, she turned to face the source of the blaze.

Before her, a lone child stood. She was a pretty young thing with blond hair, blue eyes, and a gaze trying hard to portray confidence but failing. Although she was just a child, she was wreathed in a power many an experienced sorcerer would envy. An amber glow surrounded her and fire bled from her outstretched hands. Still, she was only a girl, and she was afraid. Gwendolyn's smile returned.

"That's enough killing," said the girl.

The sorceress chuckled. "Do you think? I was just getting started."

Thrusting her hand outward, she sent a cold spear toward the girl's heart. The girl reacted immediately, burning the spear to steam before it had traveled half the distance toward her.

"Very good, child," said Gwendolyn, mildly impressed. "You have been taught well. You have been practicing magic for, what, a month? Two?" Clenching her fists, she caused two great pillars of ice to burst from the ground on either side of the child. "I've been a sorceress for twenty *years*, girl!" The child lost her footing as the earth erupted around her, and Gwendolyn willed a spike to rise up just under her. The sorceress would have preferred to play with the girl a while, but she had to return her concentration to the storm before it dissipated.

Fire erased the spike from existence before it was fully formed. The girl then set her power to the pillars, turning the ice itself into raw flame. Before Gwendolyn could react, she was on her feet, eyes hardening as she faced her attacker.

She's better than I imagined. I cannot afford to play games with this girl.

Fast as a thought, a wave of flame burned toward her. Gwendolyn's thoughts were just as fast, however, and she met the flame with a gush of icy water, dousing it completely. She pressed her advantage at once, freezing the air directly around the girl. The child must have felt the chill surrounding her, for she sent forth a circle of fire to compensate. This time, however, Gwendolyn was prepared.

The sorceress continued bending the air, changing it to water, freezing it with her will. She stepped toward the struggling girl, reaching out with her hands and mind to erect a shield of ice. Steam rose from the clashing powers of fire and ice, and the air sizzled with energy. The girl desperately wreathed herself in flame, fighting with her whole heart and mind to fend off the sorceress's icy embrace. But she was too slow, too inexperienced, and the fires of her will slowly froze at Gwendolyn's touch.

As the last of the girl's fire flickered and went out, the sorceress said, "I am Gwendolyn of Varnia, girl, ice sorceress and favored of Salin. Think on my name as you die, and know Fairhaven itself will shortly fall!"

With that, she bent over the cowering child, drawing her icy shield closed. The wind whipped fiercely, and summer was lost to the cold blue of winter.

Gwendolyn allowed herself a chilling laugh as she reached out to touch her handiwork.

Still laughing, she turned and walked away from the garden. She left the pretty girl to die alone, encased in a massive block of solid ice.

"Let go of me, Landyn, or I swear I'll kick you where you'll feel it most!"

The minstrel gave her a look of frustration mixed with concern and continued to hold her arm tightly.

"Ara, you can't go out there. Fairhaven is a battlefield and the ice storm hasn't let up. You'll be killed!"

"I can't stay here, not with Sarah in danger. She went after the sorceress, alone! I have to help her."

"There is nothing you can do, Ara. You'll never even find her out in that madness. Just pray for her. Pray for us all."

Finally Ara sagged in his arms. She felt drained, as if her helplessness had sapped the last of her strength. Landyn was right, of course. There was nothing she could do.

They stood in her room at the palace, near the window looking out over the town square where the battle had begun. Ara pulled away from Landyn's embrace and walked to the window, wringing her hands nervously. She put her face to the glass and looked out on the conflict below.

"Are you sure this is a good idea?" said Landyn. "A pane of glass will not protect you should a stray arrow or bolt of sorcery find its way to your window."

Ara didn't look back as she replied, "I have to look. I have to know what's happening out there."

Although the storm obscured her view, she was able to see a mass of people in the square, running and shouting and clashing swords. In the chaos she could make out fallen warriors, spilling their life onto the paved streets and the trampled grass. The attackers seemed to have gained an advantage, and the dark Fairies and those who stood with them were pushing the defenders back. They were using the storm to their advantage, moving with it was if they knew the path it would take. Fairhaven's soldiers, on the other hand, kept getting drawn into the storm. They had to retreat quickly to avoid injury and death, leaving their foes time to regroup and renew their attack.

A bold group of defenders, however, braved the storm to clear a path for the King and Queen, holding shields above their heads to fend off the falling rocks of ice. The shields cracked under the crushing hail and many of the Fairies fell, but many more survived to defend the royal couple from the invaders who pressed toward them. To Ara's surprise, Vyrdan himself was leading the group, waving his sword and shouting orders to the others. He had darted out of the storm to engage a group of Dark Folk who had nearly reached the King's carriage, cutting down two of them with quick, masterful strokes. He held his cracked shield in front of him to deflect flashing blades, simultaneously skewering an attacker who rushed him from the side. He shouted something to the Fairies who had just joined him, and at his command they split into two groups to surround the invaders.

His tactic proved a success. The raiders turned outward to defend themselves from Vyrdan's soldiers, and a path was opened from the carriage to the palace. Vyrdan and one of his companions rushed to the Queen, who was standing fearlessly outside the carriage. While Vyrdan grasped his Queen's hand, his companion rushed in to get the King. Within moments they were running down the cleared path toward the palace.

Almost at once the raiders realized their mistake, and some attempted to peel away from the melee to chase their prey. Most of those who turned away from Vyrdan's warriors were pursued and cut down with ease, but a few outran the soldiers and gained on the King and his escort. Vyrdan bade the Queen to run ahead, ordering his companion to take the King and do the same. Then he turned to face the raiders, his legs spread and his sword at the ready.

Three dark Fairies ran at him, swinging their swords toward his neck. His own blade was like lightning, flashing to impale one attacker while his shield battered the second aside. The third attacker slashed fiercely as he ran past, opening a raw cut across Vyrdan's right shoulder. Vyrdan cried out in pain and nearly dropped his blade. While the third dark Fairy raced onward after the King, the one Vyrdan had struck with his shield recovered his wits and charged the wounded warrior. Vyrdan's face was tight with pain as he tried to ignore his slashed shoulder and lift his sword. His wounded arm refused to move, however, and only his shield saved him from the dark Fairy's solid strike. But the already damaged shield cracked in half under the powerful blow, and the pieces fell away uselessly, leaving Vyrdan defenseless.

Ara's heart raced as the dark warrior drew his weapon back and swung it at Vyrdan's exposed neck. At the last instant Vyrdan dropped to his knees, and the blade whisked over his head. Faster than her eye could follow, Vyrdan's sword was in his left hand and its blade skewered his foe through the stomach.

Meanwhile, the last attacker thrust his blade toward the fleeing King. Vyrdan's companion turned just in time to deflect the attack, but trying to run backwards and fight at the same time threw him off balance. With a casual shove, his assailant easily thrust him to the side. The King, now unguarded, was within easy reach of the assassin's blade.

Suddenly lightning flared from the Queen's fingers. The blast caught the assassin full in the chest, knocking him back. He hit the ground writhing and convulsing, spitting up blood as his blackened skin sizzled and smoked.

By this time, Vyrdan and his companion had reached the King and were helping him to the stairs. While the dark attackers struggled to get past Vyrdan's warriors, the King and Queen reached the relative safety of the palace.

"Thank Grok," said Ara. "Now if the Brothers of Nom stationed in the palace can keep these raiders out, the King and Queen should be safe."

"And so will we," added Landyn. As he continued to survey the battle, he said, "Vyrdan certainly was impressive out there. If all the Fair Folk were as skilled as him and his men, we wouldn't have anything to worry about."

"But they're not. Most of them aren't warriors at all. And..." she stammered, her voice catching on a lump of emotion, "and Sarah's out there somewhere, chasing after the sorceress."

"Sarah has become rather skilled with her ring, Ara. How do you know she hasn't won already?"

"Because," she replied, gazing anxiously at the cold gray sky, "the hail is still falling."

Sarah had never been so cold in her life. For some reason, she couldn't move, couldn't even breathe. Darkness surrounded her, and it was getting hard to stay awake. The cold was drawing her down toward oblivion, slowing her thoughts and dulling her mind. She couldn't remember where she was or how she had gotten there. The cold and the darkness had driven away her memories, and only one thought remained clear to her.

I'm going to die.

She could feel her life slipping away into the cold, and she wanted to let it go. All she wanted to do was sleep. Only sleep would end the chilling pain seeping through her flesh to freeze her bones. She knew sleep, if it came, would be a deep slumber from which she would never awaken. She let it come, knowing she could not fight it even if she wanted to, and the chill began to fade as numbness settled into her mind and body.

And yet with numbness came a new clarity. Images flashed into her mind, images of people she knew and cared for. She saw her mother, who had bravely traveled into the unknown out of concern for her. She saw brave Kraig, who had protected Sarah well during her own journey. And she saw Alec, whom she loved above all. Her heart was filled with need for him as she remembered how bravely he faced the dangers which stood before him. She remembered how he had agreed to lead the others in their pursuit of the dangerous sorcerer, Salin Urdrokk. Only he could track the Talisman and save the Fair Folk.

It all came back to her in a rush. Alec was fighting his battle and she had to fight hers. She was in Fairhaven, where noble warriors engaged a deadly foe, but as hard as they struggled, they were doomed to fail. It was the storm keeping them from victory. The storm caused by a sorceress, a woman called…

Gwendolyn! Grok, I've got to stop her!

Sarah finally realized where she was. Gwendolyn had frozen her in a block of ice. Gwendolyn, who was helping Salin destroy Fairhaven!

Sarah knew what she had to do.

She let rage fill her, rage at what had been done to Fairhaven, rage at what had been done to her. That murderess had frozen her solid and left her to die! Then she had laughed about it; she had even bragged!

I'm going to kill her.

The fires of her rage flared. At once the cold was driven from her bones and the numbness fled her mind. Enveloped in fiery passion, she let her will explode, driving flame into the ice binding her. The sudden heat caused the ice to crack. Flexing her mind, she tore the ice asunder. She was suddenly free, and she lifted her arms and gasped for precious air. Chunks of ice were hurled violently into the air and burned into steam before they could fall back to the earth.

Consumed with power she had no idea how to control, Sarah stepped forward. The fire raged around her, whirling and roaring wildly, trying to burn her to ash. Sarah stepped through it unhurt. She was completely protected by the circlet her mother had given her. The air was still gray and icy, but no chill could touch her now. Her power burned too hotly.

She scanned the area around the garden, and found a path leading down from the burning hilltop. Far down the path, the object of her rage was escaping.

"Gwendolyn!" she cried. The name was bitter on her tongue.

As the sorceress turned with a look of disbelief on her face, Sarah charged. She couldn't control her fire, couldn't stop it or guide it, so she decided to take it directly to her foe. At first the sorceress looked down the path, considering flight, but then she chose to stand her ground. Her chilling smile returned, and she laughed aloud as she caused a cold wind to rise around her.

"Impressive," she called, barely audible over the wind and the crackling of Sarah's flame. "Your power is strong, but you lack control." She raised both hands above her head. "Observe what power can do when it is coupled with control!"

A white cone of frozen air burst from her hands. Sarah ran toward it, unable to stop her charge now that the Rage Ring drove her. Frigid wind met raging flame, hissing and causing billowing smoke to fill the air. Sarah felt a stinging breeze, but her fires protected her from the brunt of the blast. The flames wreathing her flickered in the wind and were diminished, but they were not doused completely. She felt her ring drawing power from her surroundings, from Sarah herself, pouring more and more energy into the fire. The ring had a will of its own, and its only priority was to sustain and increase the flame it had created.

Gwendolyn, seeing her tactic had been only partially successful, sprayed water onto the ground between her and Sarah. It froze immediately, and Sarah lost her footing and began sliding down the hill, out of control. She screamed as her body rammed into a huge tree and she felt something in her hip crack. Agony shot through her, piercing pain like thousands of needles shooting down her leg.

"The strength of your power is not the only thing," lectured Gwendolyn, smiling at Sarah's pain, "knowing how to use it creatively is the key. You need to observe your surroundings and use them to your advantage."

"Shut the hell up!" cried Sarah, grasping her fractured hip. The tree she had slid into was on fire now, burning with a flame she had no power to stop.

"Oh, I am sorry, little one; I did not mean to criticize. But look at you. Even now that you have lost, you still let your power run out of control. It cannot touch me, of course, but you are likely to do quite a bit of damage to the city you sought to save. You really should have waited until you were fully trained before attempting to combat your betters."

Sarah winced as she tried to stand. "'Betters?' You may be more powerful than I am, more experienced, but no slave of Salin Urdrokk is my 'better.' He's just going to use you until he doesn't need you any more, and then you're finished. You're nothing but a cheap whore to him."

Gwendolyn's eyes flared angrily. Her cool demeanor was cracking. "Enough, you little witch! I've toyed with you long enough."

The sorceress waved her hands and began to chant, and a shadow fell upon Sarah. She looked up and saw a massive rock of ice forming in the sky directly above her. It grew and grew, somehow suspended in the air, turning as if it were hanging from a chain. When it was at least as large as a house, the roaring wind snapped the invisible chain and the rock began to fall.

Gwendolyn was laughing. The shadow over Sarah grew as the rock plummeted toward her. She struggled to crawl out of the way, but the stabbing pain in her hip crippled her. She screamed a curse, enraged she had come this far only to die at the hands of a sorcerer's slave.

The ring took hold of her rage and turned it into an inferno. A firestorm swept upward from her, carried on her screams of pain and futility. The block of ice smoked and sizzled, caught in a blaze as hot as the sun. Pieces of it were torn away, melted, reduced to steam. At last it struck the ground, so reduced it missed Sarah completely.

"By the Seth, would you just die?" cried Gwendolyn.

Sarah felt as if she might. The ring was drawing too much of her strength, and she felt her heart struggling to keep beating. Her body was too weak to keep Shaping this fire, but the ring would not let her stop. It was drawing the very life from her in order to sustain its fire!

She knew of one way to stop the flame, but she dared not stop it yet. If she did, she would be easy prey for Gwendolyn. Somehow she had to end this now, before the sorceress killed her or the ring did. Using every last ounce of strength and willpower left to her, she forced herself up on her good leg. She could barely see through her pain, could barely hear through the roar of the fire feeding on her life. Gritting her teeth to keep from screaming, she launched herself down the hill straight at Gwendolyn.

The very ice the sorceress had laid on the ground to stop Sarah provided the girl with an easy way down the hill. She slid down gracelessly, but the ice path took her right where she needed to go.

As she had intended from the first, she took her fire to the ice queen.

"No!" cried the woman. "No fire!"

Gwendolyn waved her hands wildly, churning the air, but she could not Shape ice quickly enough to hinder Sarah's wild slide. The firestorm which was focused on Sarah since she'd broken free of her ice prison whipped around Gwendolyn, and the sorceress was forced to use all her power to defend herself. She chilled the air, threw snow and cold water into the fire, did everything she could to beat back the flame.

Her efforts were enough to preserve her, but she had no power left to focus on Sarah. Crying out, the girl slammed into the sorceress, knocking her from her feet. The two of them, enveloped in a furious blaze of fire and ice, clawed at one another as they tumbled down the hill.

"Witch!" cried Gwendolyn, "You will ruin everything!"

When they stopped rolling, Sarah ended up on top of the sorceress. They were at the foot of the hill, near a flower bed bordered with fist-sized rocks of various colors. Without giving herself a chance to think about what she was doing, Sarah picked up a rock in both hands and lifted it above her head. Gwendolyn screamed.

And then Sarah crushed the woman's face with the rock.

She lifted the bloody rock and brought it down again, tears streaming down her cheeks. She struck again and again, and it wasn't until she had broken the sorceress's skull open and was spattered with gore that she realized what she had done.

Physically drained and emotionally wrecked, Sarah collapsed on Gwendolyn's corpse. As she rolled off, she used the last of her strength to pull the Rage Ring from her finger. At once the fire around her was gone, save where it had caught on trees and plants. She lay on her back, breathing heavily and feeling sick.

It was strangely quiet. Besides the crackle of the little fires remaining, nothing stirred in the scorched and frozen garden. Even the sounds of battle were distant and unimportant. Pain and weariness blurred Sarah's perception, and consciousness was slipping away quickly. She hoped she would be found soon and carried to safety, for she knew she could not move again on her own. Still, weariness gave her an odd sort of peace: she didn't know if she was going to live or die, but she found it hard to care. She had killed Gwendolyn and ended the sorceress's storm. The dark Fairies' strategy was foiled. As she faded to oblivion, Sarah smiled.

She had given Fairhaven a fighting chance.

CHAPTER 26

The Seventh Law

For the third time since they had entered the dark temple, Alec heard muffled footsteps echoing down the corridor in front of them. Immediately he held his breath and pushed himself flat against the wall as Michael, Lorn, and Kraig did the same. He glanced over at Michael, who had his finger to his lips to signal for silence. For a moment the footsteps came closer, but whoever they belonged to chose a different corridor and after a moment they faded to silence.

"Lucky again," whispered Kraig. "Who do you imagine it could be?"

Michael risked brightening his light a little so he could see Kraig's face. Since they had entered the dank corridors of the temple, he had dimmed his magical light to decrease the chances of being spotted.

"Who knows? Probably not Salin himself; I am certain he is too busy with the Talisman to patrol the halls. I would guess he has many guardians here to insure he will not be disturbed while locked in his studies."

"Studies," muttered Lorn. "This is not the word I would choose for what Salin is up to in here."

"I think it's safe now," whispered Kraig. "We had better get on with it."

Alec more than agreed with the peacekeeper. He liked Kraig's practical philosophy. While others sometimes discussed things to death, he was always ready to act. Some, perhaps, would call this quality of Kraig's impatience, but Alec saw it as decisiveness.

They continued down the corridor with Alec leading the way. Although he knew the general direction and distance to the Talisman, he was not always sure which path would take him closer or through which door it might lay. The entry corridor of the temple had led them to a disused meeting room, where worshipers of Vorik Seth had once met to offer him their dark prayers. Three doorways in the back of the room had led to three slim hallways, each leading off into darkness toward the deeper areas of the temple. Alec had chosen the middle doorway since it seemed to him he could feel the Talisman's call more strongly from there.

Since then, they had come across several doors on either side of the straight hall, and two places where other hallways crossed. Alec had not risked opening any of the doors since it didn't feel like the Talisman was pulling him toward them. But as time went on, he became less and less sure of what he was doing. Maybe Salin was behind one of the doors they had already passed, and maybe he had already mastered the Talisman's secrets. Perhaps he was watching them somehow, laughing at the stupid baker leading his group around blindly.

Perhaps Salin had already won. The thought made Alec's repressed fear writhe in his gut, and it was all he could do to keep moving forward.

"Grok," he whispered. "This is impossible! We can't win!"

Kraig grabbed his shoulder. "Get yourself together, Alec! We're nearly there."

"Give him some space, Kraig," said Michael. "He will take us where we need to go. I do not think he could turn back now if he wanted to. The Talisman has too strong a hold on him."

Alec knew Michael was right. Although he had resolved to see this thing through to the end, although he moved forward with a determination of will he never knew he possessed, it was the Talisman's call which insured he would not falter or turn back. The closer he got to the Talisman, the harder it was to resist its song.

They were coming to another intersection when the footsteps came again. This time there were many soft footfalls upon the stone floor, as if a large group of people wearing soft-soled leather boots was about to round the corner.

"This way," said Michael, opening a door on the left wall. "We cannot risk a confrontation."

They rushed into the small room and Michael pulled the door shut behind them. Empty, decaying shelves indicated they were in some sort of long-abandoned storage closet. A vaguely moldy smell hung in the air.

Outside the tight room, the footsteps grew louder. Before long the owners of the footsteps were walking right past the door, their boots making soft sounds on the stone floor. Alec was holding his breath, fearful of making any noise lest he give himself away. He tried to count the guards as they went past, and although he could not accurately guess their number, he knew there were many of them. He wondered what manner of man or creature Salin had chosen to guard his stronghold.

After the footfalls echoed into the distance, Michael said, "They are gone. There must have been a score of them, what ever they were."

No one answered as the Wizard opened the door a crack and peeked into the hall. When he was satisfied the way was clear, he led them outside and let Alec take the lead. Alec walked ahead carefully and at the intersection took a right.

"I think it's this way," he whispered. "It's so close I feel like I can reach out and…"

Suddenly Kraig screamed and fell to his knees. When Alec whirled to look at his big companion, he saw Kraig's face clenched in a grimace of pain. The bloodied point of an arrow was sticking out of his left shoulder, inches from his heart.

A second arrow appeared from the darkness aimed perfectly at Lorn's chest. The warrior jerked aside at the last moment with incredible speed and grace, and the arrow only nicked his shoulder. Knocked off course, it broke in half against the stone wall.

"Get down!" cried Lorn, grabbing his shoulder as he ran toward the hidden bowman.

"Lorn, you'll be killed!" called Alec, reaching out after his companion.

Another arrow shot out of the shadows, but it missed Lorn by an arm's length. Alec almost breathed a sigh of relief before he realized the arrow wasn't aimed at Lorn, but at Alec himself! Stunned, he had no chance to avoid the shaft as it headed straight for the center of his face.

As if it had struck something solid, the arrow bounced back just before it could skewer Alec's head. He breathed a sigh of relief and turned to Michael, who was standing expressionless beside him.

"Did you do that?" breathed Alec.

"Thank me later," Michael answered. "See to Kraig. I have to make sure Lorn does not get himself killed."

Lorn had already disappeared into the shadows beyond the place where the hallways crossed. Just as Michael started after him the familiar sound of footsteps returned, this time louder and faster. Before Michael could reach the intersection, gray figures closed in from each side of the intersecting hallway to block his way. He slowed, unsure of this new threat he was facing.

Alec's attention was torn between these newcomers and the wounded peacekeeper. Kraig was still on his knees, sagging under the pain of his pierced shoulder. Meanwhile, slender gray men were advancing toward Michael. They were not armed, and they were dressed only in gray rags and dusty shoes of soft leather. Their faces were haggard and blank, and their eyes glowed a sickly yellow.

"What are they?" whispered Alec.

As if he had heard the baker, Michael called, "I have never seen such creatures!" As they advanced toward him, the Wizard waved his hands in an arc, and flames spread out in front of him. Fire filled the corridor and enveloped the creatures, but their strange gray skin repelled the flame and they walked through it unharmed. Michael backed up a step and threw a lightning bolt at the nearest creature. The bolt reflected off its flesh and struck the ceiling.

"One! This is impossible!" He reached for his sword, but it was not there. He had given it to Lorn.

The gaunt men advanced, and Michael continued backing out of the way. One creature unexpectedly lunged for him and managed to lay a hand on his arm before Michael could react. The Wizard jerked back, but his arm began to smolder where the thing had touched him. He cried out in pain or surprise and began to run back toward Alec and Kraig.

"Run! Give me some room to figure out how to fight these things!"

Alec helped Kraig to his feet. The peacekeeper gritted his teeth and grunted, bearing the pain of the arrow still stuck in his shoulder. The two of them hurried down the corridor, giving Michael the time and space he required. Alec hurried onward for Kraig's sake, but in his heart he wished there was a way to reach Lorn. These gray creatures had effectively cut them off from the warrior.

"Oh, wounds, Lorn!" exclaimed Alec.

Through gritted teeth, Kraig grunted, "Lorn can handle himself. We have to worry about those...those things!"

As they reached the end of the corridor, the gaunt creatures close behind, the call of the Talisman was nearly screaming out to Alec. It was shattering his thoughts, filling him with a driving need. He was vaguely aware of Kraig's heavy breathing as the burly man lumbered along next to him. He heard a rumble and a crash behind him which should have meant something, but his attention was keenly focused on the large black door at the end of the corridor. The Talisman was *there*, most assuredly in the hands of Salin Urdrokk.

With utter certainty, Alec knew they had arrived.

A loud boom shook Alec out of his single-minded trance, and he turned just in time to see a large section of the ceiling collapsing. Michael had done something, had brought the ceiling down on top of the gaunt men. Alec heard the things screaming hoarsely, saw them flailing desperately as large stones tumbled down to crush their bones. They were impervious to fire and lightning, but simple falling rock destroyed them.

Two of the creatures won free of the falling rock, however, and threw themselves at Michael. He dodged the first, but the second lay its hand on his chest, burning straight through his shirt and searing his skin. As he screamed and fell to the side, both of the rag-clad men launched themselves directly at Alec.

Suddenly Flame was in his hand, still cold and dark, but sharp and deadly just the same. Moving with practiced precision, his body remembering its training, he sliced outward with the blade and took off the nearest creature's head. Fear boiled within him, but for the sake of his companions, for the sake of the girl who never left his mind, he buried it deeply and stood tall.

But for all his conviction, he simply wasn't fast enough to defend against the second thing's attack. It came at him more quickly than he expected, its smoldering hands reaching out to burn him.

And then Kraig was there, axe in hand, pushing Alec out of the way to stand directly in the creature's path. Gritting his teeth and ignoring his pain, he cut the thing a gaping wound across the chest. But the gaunt creature did not fall; instead, it reached out and embraced the peacekeeper with both arms.

As Kraig's flesh began to smolder under the gray man's touch, Alec leapt forward and tore the creature off him. His hands smoked where he touched it, but he continued holding it while Kraig hefted his axe. Ignoring his own steaming skin, the peacekeeper brought the axe down on the gaunt man's head and split it in half.

Alec dropped the dead thing, and both he and Kraig leaned against the wall, gasping in pain. Alec had some burns from the gray creatures' strange touch, but Kraig's condition was much worse. In addition to having an arrow through his shoulder, his skin was black and blistered where the gaunt thing had embraced him. He was sweating profusely and for some reason he was starting to shiver.

"What…what is happening to me?"

Michael, slowly rising to his feet, took a gasping breath as he recovered from the gray man's touch. "Acid. Those things…they secrete acid through their flesh. You have been burned badly and you are going into shock."

"You have to help him!" exclaimed Alec.

"Of course. I should be able to reverse these burns, given time."

Kraig shook his head. "No. There is no time. We're too close. That's right, isn't it Alec? This door...this is where he is."

Alec nodded. "Yes, but..."

"No, listen. We've made a lot of noise out here. He's been warned. Get in there and stop him while there's still time. Don't give him any more time to prepare."

While Alec stood there gaping at Kraig indecisively, the fallen rocks began to move. The soft patter of many leather shoes echoed from the far side of the rocks.

"More of them have arrived," said Kraig, standing up. "They're digging their way through." He stood tall, sweating dripping off his big, hard muscles. "I'll hold them here. You deal with Salin."

"No!" cried Alec. "Horren's already made that sacrifice. We've lost Lorn. We can't lose you, too."

"It's the only way," said Kraig. The rocks were shifting, falling away. "Go, or it has all been for nothing."

Alec looked at Michael. The Wizard smiled grimly at Kraig. "Good luck, friend. No Bladeknight could ever claim more courage than you." Michael turned to Alec. "We must go."

"What? You mean you're not going to...Grok! I give up!"

Alec turned away from both of them. All this self-sacrifice was tearing him apart. It was time to make his own sacrifice. He closed his eyes and, putting Kraig and Horren and Lorn out of his mind, surrendered to the call of the Talisman.

It took him to the end of the corridor, to the black door. He turned the latch and, slightly surprised at finding the door unlocked, pushed it open.

The room beyond was large and dark, decorated completely in black. The curled claw of Vorik Seth hung on the wall at the far end of the room, and beneath it was a long black altar. Upon the altar sat the Talisman of Unity, burning with a sickly green glow. Alec's stomach churned at seeing the Talisman so corrupted. He longed to rush into the room and reclaim it, purify it somehow.

Consumed with thoughts of the Talisman, he almost failed to notice the old man hunched over the altar, gazing with single-minded intent at his prize. Dressed in black robes, rubbing his gnarled, spotted hands over the Talisman, Salin Urdrokk began to laugh.

Without so much as looking up, he said, "It is about time you arrived, Alec Mason. I thought you would miss my victory entirely." He rubbed his hands together and smiled. "Tell your friend Michael he is too late to stop me. The Fair Folk are *mine*."

Sarah was startled awake by the touch of a hand on her shoulder. She didn't recall losing consciousness, but with what she had been through it didn't surprise her. Her first impulse on waking was to squirm away from the person touching her, but when she looked up and realized who it was, she relaxed.

"Gryn!" she said, recognizing the boyish face of Alec's friend. "What are you doing here?"

"We have been trying to help the wounded," he said, his face drawn in an uncharacteristic grimace. "A group of us have been going around the city, taking people to the Houses of Rest. The healers are working nonstop." His eyes, which had been locked on Sarah, flickered to Gwendolyn's bloodied corpse. "Who was she? Not a friend of yours, I hope."

Sarah ignored the question. "Gryn, you're no fighter. It's far too dangerous out here!"

"You should listen to your own advice," he said, noting her wounds. "Besides, I am not entirely unprotected."

For the first time Sarah noticed a burly Fairy standing behind Gryn, wielding a battle-axe as large and deadly as the one Kraig carried. She recognized him as Gorah, the old Fairy who had tutored the peacekeeper in the way of the axe. He gave Sarah a quick bow before turning away to scan the area around the garden.

Gryn extended his hand in an offer of help. "Can you stand? We have to get to shelter as quickly as possible. The Dark Folk have been on the defense since the storm ended, but they're not beaten yet. If it were not for the Order of Nom, they might have conquered us already."

"How bad is it, Gryn? How are things at the palace?"

Gorah turned toward them, his fist tight around his axe. "We are running out of time. I just spotted a group of raiders heading this way from the western quarter. A few farmers with swords bar their path, but I fear they will not hold them long."

"All right," said Sarah, grabbing Gryn's hand. "I guess we'd better get moving."

But when she tried to stand, daggers of pain shot up her leg into her cracked hip. A brief cry escaped her lips before she could stifle it.

"Grok, that hurts!" she gritted. "Can...can one of you carry me? I'm not going to be able to make it on foot."

Gorah shrugged and shook his head. "Women. Always more trouble than they are worth." Sliding his axe into his belt, he leaned over to pick her up.

Without warning a cry fell on them from above. Sarah looked to the top of the hill and saw a squad of raiders running toward her. Among them were several slate-skinned warriors, but the rest were Fairies native to Fairhaven. They were screaming curses, mouths wide with hate, and they waved bloodied weapons in their tight fists. Sarah was shocked to see so many of the Fair Folk standing with their dark brethren, until she saw their eyes. Their eyes glowed brightly with a sick green intensity, the same glow which had surrounded the Talisman of Unity when Salin had first taken it.

"Wounds!" she cried. "They're under a spell! Salin has them!"

As if to confirm her suspicion, cries of hate began to arise from the west, where several of the defending farmers gleefully joined their former assailants in slaughtering their kinfolk. When only green-eyed farmers were left standing, the raiders and their new allies turned toward Sarah and the others.

"One!" spat Gorah. "They have us surrounded. Damned traitors."

"No, not traitors," Sarah explained urgently. "Look at their eyes! Salin has mastered the Talisman, and the weakest of you are falling under his will!"

Gorah and Gryn fell speechless. Their jaws dropped as they realized what was happening. "I do not believe it," muttered Gorah. "This cannot be happening."

As the attackers closed in from both east and west, Sarah once again tried to stand. The screams of hatred grew louder and closer. She grappled urgently with her pain, but in the end she could only sag back to the ground, defeated.

"I'll have to make a stand," said Gorah.

"You cannot do it!" cried Gryn. "There are scores of them!"

"We have no choice!" cried the old Fairy. He was right. There was nowhere to go, and the enemy was upon them.

Sarah turned her worried gaze upon Gryn, who was staring at her with panic in his eyes. And then without transition, there was something else in his eyes: a sickly green light which told her his will was no longer his own.

His face tightened and his eyes clamped shut. "I will not...kill her!" he grunted. His hands went to his face, and he collapsed to the ground, writhing.

Sarah knew he would not be able to fight the influence of the Talisman for long. None of the others had been able to resist, from what she could see. As the attackers swarmed down around them, taking her attention away from the young Fairy, she tried to embrace the fires of the Rage Ring. And yet, despite her churning emotions, her previous confrontation had left her too wrecked to summon even a tiny flame. She was defenseless against the oncoming horde.

Gorah's axe sang and his skill made Kraig look like a clumsy ox. Sarah had never imagined someone could wield an axe with such finesse, but Gorah almost looked like Lorn as he danced among the attackers, bringing them down one after another in a rain of blood and limbs. And yet he was only one man, and they were many, and soon he was lost in a wave of screaming foes and slashing blades.

For a moment the raiders were still, and then they turned their attention to Sarah and Gryn. Unable to summon her power, Sarah knew there was nothing she could do to defend herself, so she strove to crush her panic and face her death bravely. She knew Alec would have done the same. Two green-eyed Fairies charged her, goaded on by laughing Dark Folk. Swords were raised to impale her. She closed her eyes…

…and opened them again as inspiration struck her. As fast as she could, she shoved her hand into the purse she always wore attached to her belt. She fumbled around frantically, knowing she only had a few seconds to find what she was seeking. And then her hand fell upon it: the almost forgotten glass vial which had been Horren's gift to her.

She tore it free of the purse, scattering her other belongings on the ground in front of her. As a green-eyed Fairy swung his blade toward her neck, she yanked the stopper from the seemingly empty vial and prayed something would happen.

Something did. At once an invisible force threw back her attacker. Then, as the rest of the mind-controlled Fairies swarmed around her, the unseen force took on shape and color and grew until it towered over Sarah's assailants. Horren had said some sort of tree spirit resided in the magical vial, a dying spirit who wished to do one last good deed before it perished. Once released from the container it would not live long, but perhaps it would cling to life long enough to fulfill its last desire.

It grew in a swirl of browns and reds and greens, the color of mud and roots and leaves and life. Large, translucent hands reached out and thrust her assailants away, battering them about as if they were rag dolls. The spirit was especially harsh with the dark Fairies, snapping them like twigs in a hurricane. It swirled loudly, breaking bones and hurling bodies into the air, killing or incapacitating every last one of the raiders in sight.

It ended as quickly as it began. When the threat was over, the swirling colors began to slow. But before they could stop, Gryn leapt to his feet with a hateful look in his eyes. He cried out in anger and charged Sarah, and a fist of swirling light reached out to crush him.

"No! Don't kill him!" cried Sarah.

Responding to her wishes, the fist merely grabbed the young Fairy, lifted him into the air, and set him down gently. When he tried to charge Sarah again, the swirling colors focused into a smaller fist and struck him across the jaw, just hard enough to render him unconscious.

The swirls slowed again, and this time they stopped moving entirely. Sarah could make out a vague, faded form, somewhat man-shaped but larger even than Horren. It seemed to fray at the edges. Its features were indistinct, but Sarah had the impression it was smiling.

Thank you.

The voice rang in her head, and at first she thought she was imagining things. But then she looked at the radiant being in front of her, and she was sure it was speaking to her.

"I…I should be thanking *you*," she said.

No. The great Addin gave me a chance to strike one last blow against evil, and by freeing me you allowed my last wish to be fulfilled.

"But…but what are you? How did you fit in that vial?"

The spirit seemed to chuckle. *Once, a very long time ago, there were many woodland spirits like me. The Addins were our masters, and under their guidance we protected the forests from those who would bring them harm. But the growing powers of darkness have poisoned the wood, and my kind are all but extinct. I am one of the last. As for how I could fit into such a little vial…well, that is just magic, I suppose.*

"Will you stay and help us? I'm afraid this war is not over yet, and we're going to need all the help we can find."

I am sorry, young one, but death is calling and I cannot remain in this realm any longer. I depart gladly, for my last wish has been granted. Good-bye, child. Remain vigilant.

The colors swirled one last time, and then the spirit was gone.

For a moment Sarah lay still, unable to pull her eyes away from the place where the spirit had stood. But then her eyes and mind drifted to the devastation around her, and the bleak reality of her peril brought her back to the present. Most of the green-eyed Fairies were unconscious rather than dead; somehow the spirit had known they were not acting of their own will and had spared them. The dark raiders, however, the spirit had slain without mercy. Sarah closed her eyes against the terrible sight and prayed it would soon be over, prayed she would be rescued before more raiders or their new, unwilling allies appeared. She had no strength left to do anything more.

Kari charged through the ranks of farmers and merchants who were flailing uselessly against the dark warriors attacking them. As she had done many times throughout the day, she Shaped a funnel of wind powerful enough to force the raiders back, giving her allies time to regroup. Then she caught as many raiders as she could in crushing ropes of air, squeezing the life out of them before they had a chance to react. Her stomach churned at having to use her magic this way, but she had no choice. She had to do whatever it took to protect her homeland and her people, even if it meant killing other Fairies.

As the defenders rallied around her, she cursed Jinn for abandoning her, for running from the fight he knew was coming. She knew she shouldn't be so hard on him; sprites were hardly known for their bravery. Still, with his mastery of shape-changing, he would have been more than capable of holding his own in the battle. He had his own priorities, however, and had left for his home in Brahnah soon after they had arrived in Fairhaven.

Suddenly Kari felt something slash the back of her leg. She cried out in surprise, shocked that one of the attackers had been able to get behind her. She spun to face him and realized she had been attacked by one of her own allies! He was grinning wildly, holding his sword above his head, and his eyes were glowing with a repulsive green light. Kari wasn't sure what was going on, but she knew if she took the time to ask questions she wouldn't live to find the answer.

Already weary, she tried to focus her magic on her new attacker. But things were happening too quickly, and she could only save herself from his next strike by throwing herself out of the way. Instantly she realized several more of her companions had turned on her, their eyes glowing brightly green.

She called for help, and those of her allies who were still themselves sprung to her aid. Most of them were not warriors, but they were brave and loved their home, and they would do anything to defend it. They didn't understand why their friends and neighbors had turned on them, but they adapted quickly to the situation. Kari couldn't help but admire their valor as they leapt to her rescue.

But the defenders were hesitant to attack people they had known and trusted for years, and this gave the green-eyes an edge. By now the dark raiders who survived Kari's attack had rejoined the fight, and the defenders were falling to their blades and losing ground. They were surrounded, outnumbered, and exhausted. Kari aided them with magic as best she could, but she knew, short of a miracle, their struggles would be in vain.

All over the field of battle, things were the same. The core of the conflict was taking place in a large park, just north of the palace. Kari's group was on a high ridge at the eastern end of the park, and from there she could see everything that was happening. Still striking out with bursts of air, she glanced to the conflict which continued to rage below.

The soldiers and Shapers of Fairhaven were fighting a losing battle, falling under waves of Salin's servants, both dark and fair. After the ice storm had quite suddenly ended, the soldiers rallied and it seemed they would be victorious, but several Brothers of Nom revealed themselves as traitors and turned the tide back to Salin's favor. Now, more and more Fair Folk were turning on their companions, the green glow in their eyes visible even from a distance. Fairy blood washed the grass and the gardens, and final defeat seemed inevitable.

As Kari turned away from the cries of agony and death to repel her own attackers with a forceful blast of air, a new sound grabbed her attention. She turned to the west and looked upon a sight she almost couldn't believe. There, where the raiders had nearly crushed all resistance, a wild battle-cry echoed from a wooded grove. Then, from out of the trees burst scores upon scores of screaming sprites, those in the front riding ponies and small horses, those in the rear running and leaping after them. All of them had assumed their hideous battle-shapes, sporting elongated, clawed hands and extended jaws with tusk-like, razor-sharp teeth. And riding on a sleek white pony at the lead was Jinn himself, holding a clawed fist above his head in a fierce salute.

Like demons they fell upon the enemy, tearing flesh with razor claws and deadly teeth. The mounted sprites leapt from their saddles, hurling themselves through the air and into the midst of their foes. They were fast and furious, spinning and running and leaping among the dark folk, dealing out sharp death at every turn. Jinn was the quickest and most ferocious of them all, slashing the life from raider after raider as he gleefully waded through the fray.

Kari was filled with hope and also with pride. She should have known her dearest friend would not truly abandon her. With renewed vigor, Kari threw out a wind which blew her opponents off the ridge, and she followed them down to join Jinn and his people in the battle below. Perhaps the tide was turning again. Perhaps Fairhaven would stand after all.

Lorn ran blindly down the corridor, heading toward a light shining dimly through the shadows. Out of the light shot another arrow, but Lorn was expecting it and was able to duck under it. If he sprinted, he thought, he might be able to reach the hidden archer before he had a chance to nock another shaft.

Lorn picked up his pace. He ran as fast as his legs would carry him, knowing at close range he wouldn't be fast enough to dodge arrows. Alec and the others might think Lorn had lost his mind to go running into the darkness toward the bowman, but to Lorn it was the only sane thing to do. The bowman, whoever he was, was too good to be ignored. His shafts were too accurate. He would be able to fell the companions one by one from the safety of the shadows. As long as he remained hidden and unchallenged, he might single-handedly bring them to ruin.

Lorn refused to take this chance. He had no qualms about risking his own life to stop the archer. Despite his immunity to the direct effects of magic, he knew he would stand little chance against Salin himself. The sorcerer was too intelligent; he would find a way around Lorn's immunity. Stopping the archer was a task Lorn could accomplish. It was Michael's job to deal with Salin; Lorn's responsibility was to make sure he lived to do it.

The warrior stepped into a pool of light cast by a small torch mounted on the wall. He had reached a dead end, and the only thing he saw there was a sturdy longbow and a single arrow lying discarded on the floor. The archer had seemingly fled, and yet there were no doors, no side passages. Where had he gone?

A flicker of movement caused Lorn to jerk to the side. He brought his sword around defensively, but he was too slow to stop a blade which flashed out of nowhere to cut a deep gash across the knuckles of his sword hand. He cried out in pain and surprise, and his weapon clattered uselessly to the floor.

Defenseless, he threw his back to the wall. Into the light stepped a man in black leather, not quite as tall as Lorn but somewhat broader. He had long back hair slicked back in a pony tail, and his features were square and hard. In a way, Lorn felt he was looking into some sort of twisted mirror. Apart from the physical similarities, there was a seriousness of purpose about the man which reminded Lorn of himself. If Lorn had had other experiences, made other choices, he could have been in this man's place.

Never taking his eyes away from Lorn, the man leaned over and snatched up the warrior's sword. "This is mine," he said. "I thank you for returning it to me."

"You must be Tor," said Lorn. "We have not met face to face, but the others have told me a little about you. Former Watcher to the high lords of Valaria. Very impressive. The Watchers of Tyridan are held in nearly as high a regard as Eglak's Bladeknights."

"Fah!" spat Tor, holding his re-acquired sword in front of him. "The skills of your so-called Bladeknights are feeble compared to the talent and dedication of the Watchers. And I have developed talents of my own far beyond those any other Watcher."

"A lofty claim," answered Lorn. "Then why is it you have sold yourself to one such as Salin?"

Tor laughed. "For power, obviously. For the promise of immortality. You must have realized I already command some sorcery, or did you think anyone could blend perfectly into the shadows so as to seem invisible?"

"So that is how you were able to take me by surprise. Very clever. What do you plan to do now, Tor? Kill me in cold blood before going after my companions?"

The Watcher sneered. "The thought had crossed my mind, but I am not entirely without honor. Here."

With his left hand, he tossed into the air the broad sword he had just used to slash Lorn's knuckles. Lorn instinctively reached out with his sword arm to catch the weapon, but his wounded right hand could not grip it properly and the blade clattered to the floor. Tor chucked and closed in on the warrior.

"You can't claim I didn't give you a chance," he said, swinging his rune-graven blade at Lorn.

Instantly Lorn dived to the floor, rolling under Tor's swing and snatching up the broad sword in his left hand. His roll took him right to Tor's legs, and the Watcher had to leap over him to avoid being thrown from his feet. Lorn stabbed upward as Tor leapt, but the Watcher was too quick and the warrior's unpracticed left arm too slow. Lorn was barely able to climb to his feet before his foe was upon him again.

He clumsily brought his blade up just in time to block a solid swing. The force of the blow knocked him back and he fell against the wall. Only by rolling to the left did he avoid Tor's next downward blow.

The magical longsword tossed sparks as it cleft a gash into the stone wall. Tor turned toward Lorn with almost supernatural speed and renewed his assault. Lorn stumbled back to avoid Tor's thrust, and suddenly his back was against the dead-end wall. He had nowhere else to go. Tor gracefully spun in the air, bringing his blade around to his opponent's throat.

By sheer desperation, Lorn managed to place his blade vertically between his neck and the Watcher's steel. The force of the strike sent stinging pain through Lorn's arm, but his neck was spared. Fiercely, he kicked outward as hard as he could, slamming the heel of his right foot into his enemy's stomach. Tor stumbled back, bent over and groaning.

Lorn launched himself forward. His left arm swung out wildly, and his blade missed Tor by a large margin. Still bent over, the Watcher managed to shuffle to the side and watched Lorn fumble uncontrollably past. He then struck out with practiced ease, his blade scoring a slash across the warrior's back. His groans changed to laughter as Lorn flopped to the ground on his belly.

Rolling to his back, Lorn struggled to remember his training. He had studied long and hard with his father, the King of Eglak, learning all there was to know about every manner of blade. He practiced swordplay with both his right and left hand, repeating the forms until he could perform them with great facility no matter which hand held his blade. By the end of his training, he was besting his father's Bladeknights.

But that was long ago, and since then he had forgotten half of what he had known about fighting. He hadn't held a sword in his left hand since his training had ended, all those years ago. He had since been a vagrant, then a drunk, and even though he had recently put this behind him to pick up the sword again, he was not ready to fight someone as skilled as Tor. Not with his left hand, at any rate.

And yet he could not give up. He owed it to Alec and Michael, to Kraig and Sarah and Horren, to struggle on as best he could. Without them, he would still be sitting in a tavern in Bordonhold, drinking until the peacekeeper realized he couldn't pay and threw him out. And if he gave up now, it was very possible Tor would kill his companions before they even had a chance at Salin himself.

Tor was standing over him, the point of his blade falling toward Lorn's chest. At the last instant the warrior rolled to the side, and blue sparks flew as Tor's blade pierced cold stone. Lorn scrambled out from between his foe's legs, springing to his feet with the grace of a cat. He breathed deeply and felt the calm of his training wash over him. By the time Tor freed his blade from the floor and turned to face him, Lorn had found his center of gravity and had remembered who he was. For the first time since the battle had begun, he felt stable and sure.

"Impressive," said Tor. "You do well under pressure. And you do know the proper stance and how to hold a sword. I was beginning to wonder."

Lorn didn't waste time responding. He danced forward, flicking his blade toward Tor to test his reflexes. The Watcher was fast, knocking his attack away with a casual tap. He was grinning, obviously not impressed at his opponent's attack. He retaliated with a downward cut which Lorn was hard pressed to parry.

They circled around and around one another, thrusting and parrying, swinging and blocking, dancing smoothly to the steady rhythm of clanging steel. Tor seemed to be having the time of his life, completely at ease as he effortlessly glided around his foe. Lorn, on the other hand, was hurting and tired, sweat dripping from his furrowed brow as he jerked his sword from right to left, using everything he had just to stay alive. He was at a disadvantage for several reasons, not the least of which was that Tor was wielding an enchanted weapon. Yet he was remembering his training, forcing enough dexterity from his left hand to keep Tor's steel from his flesh.

Little by little, though, the Watcher was wearing him down. His heart was racing and he was gasping for breath, and his arm trembled under the weight of his sword. Tor continued to smile as if he were immune to fatigue. He didn't even break a sweat. Still, Lorn's training was with him, and part of his training entailed studying a foe, uncovering his weaknesses. Tor's style seemed flawless at first, his thrusts perfect and his parries impeccable.

But always to the right. No matter what I do, he always parries left to right.

Embraced in the calm of his training, Lorn knew exactly how to use this knowledge. He waited until he had an opening and then he struck.

Tor parried casually, with the effortless grace Lorn had come to expect. But the warrior's attack had been a feint, and he thrust a second time before the Watcher could react. Because of Tor's predictable parry, Lorn knew exactly where to strike.

He lashed out, slashing a long cut along his foe's left side. Tor grunted loudly, his eyes flaring with shock. Immediately he reciprocated with a strike of his own, but Lorn parried easily, knowing exactly where the thrust was coming from. He had found an edge, and now he knew he was fighting his opponent on even ground.

As their blades clashed anew, fiercely but precisely meeting again and again with a ringing clamor, Tor began to concentrate more wholly on the battle at hand. No longer was his every motion performed with practiced nonchalance. Soon he was fighting as frantically and passionately as Lorn was. Now more than ever they looked like dancers performing to some wild, rapid song, their movements choreographed by a madman. Beautiful and deadly, they continued their dance, clashing blades faster than the eye could follow.

The opening Lorn needed was *there*, but he was too slow to take advantage of it. In a moment it was *there* again, but Tor recovered and beat his sword aside.

There.

Sweat poured from his brow. Left handed, he kept missing his opportunity. *There*, and *there* again.

Lars! I cannot do it!

Tor cut him across the chest. Lorn nearly lost his rhythm, but pure concentration saved him. He could not keep this up much longer.

There.

The pattern of their dance was repeating itself over and over. Lorn was almost certain Tor hadn't seen it yet. If he had, he might have already corrected his mistake, or taken advantage of a mistake Lorn was making.

There.

Must concentrate…anticipate…there…and…

"There."

Tor's eyes stared at him in utter disbelief. They locked gazes for a long moment as time seemed to stand still. Then, as if in slow motion, the watcher began to slide back. His sword clattered to the ground, and he gripped Lorn's blade with both hands, tried to hold himself up. He looked at Lorn's outstretched arm, at the sword in his hand. His gaze followed the blade to where it entered his chest, and he groaned as he realized the weapon had run him all the way through. Blood gushed out of his chest and over his hands, making it impossible for him to hold on any longer.

"Seth's grin," he muttered. "Who…who *are* you?"

He slid off the blade and fell flat on his back. Blood sprayed from his wound and bubbled from his mouth. His body jerked several times as he choked on the frothing red fluid. After a moment he went still, but his dead eyes continued to gaze their bewilderment at Lorn.

"I am Lorn," answered the warrior, although Tor was beyond hearing him. "Prince of Eglak. Seth take you."

Stopping only to pick up Tor's enchanted blade, Lorn hurried as best he could back down the corridor. He prayed he could find the others before they got themselves into any more trouble.

Followed closely by Landyn, Ara hurried out of her room when she heard the commotion in the hall. Servants were running in a panic deeper into the palace, and guards were racing toward the stairs with swords unsheathed. From her window, Ara had witnessed fighting near the palace stairs, but nothing she had seen indicated the gates had been breached.

"Ara, what are you doing?" cried Landyn, grabbing her arm. "Get back in your room!"

"I want to see what's going on," she answered as she pulled away from him.

"You are infuriating!" he exclaimed, chasing after her.

She knew he was right, but she just couldn't hide under her bed while so much was happening around her. She was restless and upset, sick with worry for her daughter, and she desperately needed to do something. She pushed her way past some fleeing servants to get a closer look at what the guards were doing.

At the far end of the hall, near where the gates led out to the spiral staircase which descended from the palace, the guards were engaged in a fierce conflict against a group of dark Fairy warriors. For a moment Ara did not understand how they had gotten inside the palace, but then her gaze fell upon the vast opening where the massive gates should have been. They had not been battered open or burned down; they were simply gone.

"Grok's wounds," she whispered. "How could this happen?"

"Sorcery," said a voice behind her. "Powerful sorcery."

She turned to see Elder Toros, his red robes torn and stained with blood.

"Elder Toros," she said. "Where have you been? The last I saw, you were out in the middle of the fighting."

"I found my way back to the palace through the secret ways. But if you'll excuse me, there is a small matter of a missing gate to which I must attend. And there is a traitor I must find. Those gates were protected by carefully Shaped enchantments; only someone who knew them well could unmake them."

As he ran toward the struggling guards, Ara shook her head and turned to Landyn. "There are too many traitors," she said. "It seems half the Order of Nom is on Salin's side, as well as a good number of Fairhaven's soldiers and citizens. I thought Fairies were supposed to be incorruptible."

"That's what the old tales say," said Landyn. "But we are entering a new age, ushered in by Salin Urdrokk. He's changing all the rules."

Ara watched as Elder Toros forced his way through the combatants, clearing his way with shoves of solid air. She could not see much past the gaping gateway, but from the flood of dark Fairies entering the hall she guessed there were many more waiting on the stairs beyond. The guards would be overrun in minutes unless Toros could somehow remake the gate.

He called for guards to protect him as he stood near the gateway. He began chanting and performing arcane gestures. Dark Folk swarmed around him, and only the vigilance of the palace guards kept their lethal blades from the Elder. After a moment, something started to happen. The raiders just outside the gateway found themselves pressing up against an invisible barrier. Toros's magic was sealing the breach!

But no sooner did the barrier begin to form than something caused the Elder to cry out, grasp his head in both hands, and fold over in pain. The raiders pushing at the invisible wall fell forward, the way before them once again clear. Gritting his teeth in determination, Toros began Shaping again.

"Brother Grond!" he shouted. "Traitor! I feel your hand in this. Where ever you are, know you have done nothing to the gate I cannot easily undo. Do not attempt to attack me again or I will shatter your mind as you have tried to shatter mine."

And yet Toros *was* attacked again, and although he was able to fend off this attack as easily as the last, more raiders were able to press through the breach. More guards had arrived on the scene, as well as a few Brothers apparently loyal to the King, but the odds were still no better than even. At least, thought Ara, none of the attackers had been able to break through the guards to gain entry deeper into the palace.

But just as the thought occurred to her, four guards fell as one, perfectly placed knives jutting from each of their necks. Through the opening created by their deaths darted a woman, as lithe and graceful as a cat. Already she had more knives in her hands, and as she ran she was scanning the hall for targets. She had not seen Ara and Landyn yet, but she certainly would in a moment.

"Come on!" cried the minstrel, pulling forcefully on Ara's arm. He wasn't giving her any choice this time. He yanked her back until they reached her room, and then he pulled her in and slammed the door shut. In a moment they heard the woman's light footfalls as she ran unmolested down the corridor.

"We have to stop her," said Ara. "She's going to try to assassinate Elyahdyn and Mahv!"

"I know," said Landyn. "Stay here."

He opened the door and darted out, his short sword jumping into his hand. Ara, in no mood to be left behind, hurried after him. They rounded the corner and headed toward the King and Queen's rooms, but there was no sign of the woman they were pursuing. She was incredibly fast and had gotten too far ahead of them.

"I thought I told you to stay in your room," said Landyn when he noticed her behind him.

"You did. I ignored you."

"Infuriating!" he huffed as he burst into the throne room.

Sprawled on the floor were two dead guards and a Brother of Nom, all three with their throats neatly cut. Near them stood Vyrdan, pinned to the wall by a long knife driven through his shoulder, just to the left of his heart. He was breathing in gasps and sweat poured down his face, but his eyes focused as his head turned toward Landyn and Ara.

"It was her," he gritted. "The witch I fought in the first attack. Stiletta, she called herself. Never…never seen someone so fast."

"We'll be back for you, Vyrdan," said the minstrel. "Hang on." He started toward the King and Queen's private rooms.

"No, not that way!" said the pinned Fairy. "I…knew it wasn't safe here. Sent them…with two guards…toward the Hall of the Council…toward the secret passages. Stiletta's on her way there now. Go!"

And they went, running as fast as they could toward the Grand Hall. The hallways were cleared of people, for the servants had hidden themselves away in every room or closet that seemed safe, and all the guards had gone to defend the breached gate. In the chaos they had overlooked the beautiful assassin who had slipped into their midst.

Ara had never seen Landyn move so quickly. He pulled ahead of her, his fine cape flowing behind him, and crashed through the double doors leading into the Grand Hall. She followed as fast as she could, but it was several long seconds before she passed through the entry to join the minstrel.

The two guards Vyrdan had sent with the King and Queen lay dead on a table, one with a dagger through his eye and the second gutted. At the far end of the room, near the front table where the King presided at Council meetings, Stiletta stood with her back to Ara, holding the King and Queen at her mercy. She had a short sword poised at the King's neck and a dagger held at the Queen's heart. Ara knew given half a chance, the Queen would be able to defend herself with magic, but she doubted any defense would be quick enough to stop the assassin's blade. From the ease with which Stiletta had torn through so many well-trained guards, Ara guessed the woman was one of the most dangerous people in the world.

Landyn was half way across the room, flying straight down the center isle to where the assassin stood. She casually turned her head, smiling at him as if she had all the time in the world. Then she took her dagger away from the Queen, and with a graceful flick of her wrist, hurled it at Landyn.

At once the Queen moved, but faster than a thought Stiletta kicked her in the stomach. Mahv fell to the ground wincing in agony. At the same time, Landyn dived to the side, desperately trying to avoid the dagger which raced for his heart. The dagger bit into his arm and he cried out, but he did not slow his charge.

Then he was upon Stiletta, and she was forced to pull her sword away from the King's throat to defend herself. But as soon as she had met Landyn's first strike with an easy parry, she spun to deliver a round-house kick to the King's jaw. He crumpled to the ground before he could offer any sort of resistance. Even taking the time to fell the King, the assassin had plenty of time to meet Landyn's next attack. She answered him at once with a lightning slash across his waist.

Landyn was good with his blade, but he was severely outmatched. He was immediately on the defense and had to fall back to avoid being skewered. He parried madly, meeting her advances with all the skill he possessed. Ara knew she needed to help him, but she had no weapon and she didn't know what she could possibly do against such an enemy.

When Landyn had retreated to the center of the room, the grinning assassin slipped her sword past his defenses and pierced his stomach. He fell over, gripping his gut in an attempt to keep his life from spilling over the floor. He dropped to his side and curled up in a ball, grimacing fiercely against his agony. Stiletta, still smiling, stepped over him.

"I do not believe we've met," she said to Ara. "I am Stiletta. And you are a fool who is in over her head."

"I only do what needs to be done," replied Ara. "It's the only way I know how to live my life."

The assassin laughed. "Very noble. But you need not worry about 'living your life' any longer. I will relieve you of this petty concern right now."

Ara realized she had waited too long to act. Seemingly from nowhere, a shining knife appeared in Stiletta's hand, and faster than a thought, she drew it back to throw it. Ara's muscles tensed, preparing to dive out of the way, but things were happening too fast. She couldn't possibly move in time.

But as the knife left Stiletta's hand, the assassin looked down in surprise, distracted by something grabbing her ankle. Landyn, still clenched with pain, was trying to pull her down. She cursed him and easily kicked his hand away, but his efforts had succeeded in one respect. At the last instant Stiletta's concentration had been shaken and her throw was not true. The knife thunked loudly into the wall, a mere inch from Ara's ear.

Angrily, Stiletta turned her attention to Landyn, raising her sword to finish him once and for all. Ara's heart pounded in her chest, bursting with the emotions raging within her. Adrenaline thundered through her veins, and quickly, without a thought, she tore the assassin's knife from the wall.

"Bitch!" she cried, hurling the knife toward its owner.

Stiletta looked up just in time to watch the dagger impale her through her right eye. As the hilt slammed against her face, throwing her back, her face widened in an expression of disbelief. To all appearances, she felt no pain or horror at the moment of her death. As she slammed to the floor, landing hard on her back, her dying expression was one of surprise.

Ara took only a second to catch her breath and recover from what had just happened. She didn't think about the fact that she had come within an inch of her life or that she had just taken someone else's. Instead she raced to Landyn's side, taking his head in her hands.

"Leave me," he muttered. "I am done for. See to the King and Queen."

"Nonsense," she said. "You…you'll be fine." She fumbled over her words, choking back tears. "There are healers…I'll get you to a House of Rest. Damn you, Landyn, you have an epic to write!"

"I hope it…has a happy ending," he said.

With that, he closed his eyes.

"What…what do you mean, the Fair Folk are yours?" stammered Alec, his eyes wide as he regarded the grinning sorcerer.

"I think it is self-explanatory, boy," snarled Salin, grabbing the glowing Talisman in a knobby fist and presenting it to Alec. "This thing, this sacred Talisman, has finally succumbed to my will. Already I feel the minds of the Fair Folk, and minds I feel I can control. Say goodbye to your friends in Fairhaven, Alec; I fear they are about to meet their doom at the hands of my Fairy puppets!"

Alec stood in the doorway, renewed horror rooting him to the spot. Why had he bothered to come here? He had witnessed Salin's mighty sorcery, and he had nothing which could stand against such power. The Talisman screamed in his head, pleading with him to do something, but even if there was something he could have done, he could not force himself to move through his terror. Salin's eyes spoke naked threats for which he had no answer.

Alec stumbled as someone shouldered him aside and hurried into the room. It was Michael, and a halo of power surrounded him as he advanced on the sorcerer.

"Stay back, Alec. Leave Urdrokk to me."

The Wizard unleashed a fiery bolt of death in Salin's direction, but the sorcerer laughed as it broke harmlessly on an invisible wall before him. "How very uncreative, Nul," he mocked. "How very predictable. You have been without your powers too long."

Michael did not waste time on words. With a wave of his hand, he caused the altar to leap into the air and hurl itself at his enemy. Instead of grinding the sorcerer to paste against the wall as it should have, it spit in two and flew harmlessly to either side of him. As it shattered against the wall its deadly splinters sprayed the room, but not one touched Salin. Cloaked in shadows, he roared in confident laughter.

"You see? Predictable. There is nothing you can do which I cannot counter."

This time Michael was moved to speech. "You are a fool, Urdrokk! I have defeated you in the past and I shall defeat you again!"

The sorcerer bared his decaying teeth in a sardonic grin. "You remember the past differently than I do. In your prime you did little more than battle me to a stalemate. Call it victory, if your ego demands it. Make no mistake; this time there will be no stalemate."

"On that point, at least, we are in agreement."

Michael flung himself forward, surrounding himself with webs of power Alec's training allowed him to recognize. With vast energies he formed a wedge of solid light, and he drove it toward Salin's invisible shield, seeking any tiny crack in which it might find purchase. Salin, obviously not prepared for such a direct assault, stopped smiling.

The wedge found purchase, and with a wrenching sound and a burst of light, the shield came down. Michael, never slowing for an instant, charged Salin with globes of fire in his fists. Grimacing, Salin spun, and his dark cloaks spread out in the air around him. The shadows they cast spun outward, destroying all light where their inky blackness fell. In the face of such darkness,

Michael's flame was doused and the power surrounding him quenched. Surprised, he stumbled into the shadow and fell to his knees before Salin.

Chains, apparently of steel, broke free of the stone floor around the Wizard and bound him tightly where he knelt. Salin's shadow hung over him, and with the eyes of his training Alec understood what the shadow was: the complete absence of the One. Wrapped in such a void, Shaping would be impossible.

"A worthy effort," said Salin. "The Nul I knew never would have attempted a physical assault, unless he was in the mood to do battle with steel rather than magic. Speaking of which, I am disappointed you did not see fit to bring a blade. I have not met a swordsman to test my metal since I destroyed the Lord of Estron, decades ago."

As Michael struggled futilely against his bonds, Salin turned back to Alec. "Perhaps I will let Nul live," he said. "Lord Vorik has captured and mastered his brother by learning his Secret Name. Perhaps Nul will become my plaything as Siv has become my master's. I'm sure I can discover the Second's Secret Name, as I discovered the Third's.

Through his struggles, Michael looked up in horror. "Siv? You...lie! The Three...cannot be mastered! The Names of Power...through which we touch the One...are in our minds alone. You cannot have learned his Name...as you claim."

Salin could not restrain a chuckle. "You are mistaken. His Name was discovered by someone, I know not who, and recorded in a text of ancient sorcery. I unearthed the text and therein read his Name. I sold my knowledge to the Seth for access to the Talisman of Unity. Thereby I have secured my place as the highest of Vorik Seth's captains!"

"You've secured...only your...damnation."

"Oh, do shut up! You are defeated, you whimpering dog. This is my place of power, and here my shadow is an extension of the Seth himself. Where you kneel, helplessly wrapped in chains, you are sealed off from your precious One. Your newly found power is useless, now!"

Alec knew it was true. To Shape, Michael's spirit had to be touching the spirit of the One. Surrounded by Salin's shadow of sorcery, Michael was helpless. And the chains binding him insured he could not move free of the shadow.

"You...truly *are* a fool, Salin," said Michael. He was gasping for breath now, unable to fill his lungs as the chains pulled tighter.

"I? I am the fool? Look at yourself, at how I have brought you low, and reconsider who is the fool."

Suddenly Michael roared, and miraculously the chains broke before his power. He stood, taking the chains into the fists of his magic and hurling them at the Sorcerer. Salin had to leap back out of the way, and the mystic shadow he was casting vanished.

"How...?" he began.

Michael wrapped Salin in his own chains, pulling them tight enough to choke him. "You forget the first of the Seven Laws, the one you and your kind choose to ignore. All things are a part of the One! All things, including the chain you used to bind me! You attempted with your shadow to block me from the One, but through the chains you allowed within the shadow I was able to touch his spirit. I was able to touch it...and do *this!*"

With a thrust of his arm, Michael pulled the chains even tighter around the sorcerer. Salin began thrashing, making constricted sounds in his throat. Alec's heart leapt with hope; it seemed Michael had at last found a way to defeat his nemesis.

But his hope was doused in an instant as the chains suddenly vanished in a flash of light. Salin stood erect, gasping for breath, and his face assumed a vengeful, hate-filled grimace. He turned toward Michael, and the two old foes stood still as they appraised each other.

"Nice try," said the sorcerer, "but you can do better."

"No question about it," answered the Wizard, his eyes narrowing.

Alec's body tightened in anticipation. The room was thick with tension, and great power gathered near the combatants. Something was going to happen, something loud and bright and lethal. Alec turned away from the building conflagration, instinctively bringing his arm up to shield his eyes. For a long moment he stood there, bent away from the combatants with his eyes squeezed shut. Dangerous power hung in the air, power enough to rend the temple stone from stone. He could feel it hovering, compressing, energizing the air itself.

But nothing happened. Eventually he looked up and saw that neither Michael or Salin had moved. To all appearances, they had become unblinking statues, gazes locked and faces clenched in concentration. Only beads of sweat rolling down both their foreheads showed they were still living, breathing human beings.

Suddenly Alec understood what was happening. The duel in which Michael and Salin were locked was taking place on a purely spiritual level. They were concentrating their power totally upon one another, each of them focusing all his energy on trying to break the other's mind and spirit. Magic was heavy in the air, but to one not sensitive to its presence it would seem nothing was happening at all. Only because Michael had opened Alec's eyes to the One could he perceive the vast forces which clashed before him.

This had been Michael's plan all along, Alec suddenly realized. This type of spiritual combat would exhaust a Shaper or sorcerer completely, leaving him, for a time, unable to achieve the perfect union of body, spirit, and mind necessary to Shape. Eventually, one of the combatants would succumb to weariness. Alec could only pray it would be Salin.

But perhaps, he thought, there was something he could do to help. Mustering his courage, he drew Flame from its ivory sheath and advanced toward Salin. The sorcerer was so intent on his nemesis that maybe he would not notice Alec until it was too late. Alec wished the sword would glow orange and invest him with its lust for blood, but because of his fear it remained dead and cold in his hand.

Unfortunately, he never reached Salin. After he took three steps, an invisible fist burst from the sorcerer's mind, knocking Alec back against the wall and pinning him there. Apparently Salin's power was sufficient to continue his battle with Michael and keep Alec at bay simultaneously. Alec struggled against the fist, but with no magic of his own he was helpless.

To Alec's eyes, the air burned red with power. The weight of it pressed on him, threatened to crush him. He didn't know how Michael and Salin could stand it. A loud buzzing filled the room, a sizzling sound like cooking meat. It grew in Alec's ears until it was drowned by the sound of screams. Power blazed white, blinding Alec to everything else around him. Pain assaulted all his senses and his voice joined the other's in screaming. Blind, unhearing, Alec slumped to the ground, vaguely aware Salin's fist no longer held him. Through his agony he grasped at the hope Salin had been defeated.

And then at once the power around him was gone, releasing him from the pain which had been crushing him. He had crumpled to the floor and was gasping for breath, but he was able to push himself to his knees as the bright points of pressure dancing in front of his eyes began to clear. His hearing returned slowly, and in the absence of blinding energy the world around him became visible.

But returning sight brought with it renewed horror. The first thing he saw was Michael sprawled lifeless on the ground, his eyes open but glazed and his limbs twisted unnaturally. Then his gaze fell upon Salin, bent and gasping but still very much alive. The sorcerer looked up and locked eyes with Alec, and his wrecked expression slowly became one of sinister victory.

"Fool," he breathed, "you should have known this could end no other way. You could have lived at least a little while longer, Alec Mason, if you had not followed this pathetic worm to my place of power. You should have run far and fast." Slowly, as if to savor the moment, Salin unsheathed his rune-graven long-sword. "This is Hellsedge, a blade forged in the smithies of Vorik Seth himself. It has not tasted innocent blood for quite some time, and it hungers. Since the worm forced me to exhaust my sorcery to burn out his mind, I am afraid you must die by the blade."

Burn out his mind? Oh, Michael, what has he done to you!

Salin advanced slowly, and Alec fumbled with Flame, trying to assume the fighting stance he had been taught. But his mind was on the Wizard, on what had just happened to him. Salin had won, although he'd temporarily expended his magic in the process. Or…or had this been Michael's plan all along? Did he engage Salin in a contest of spirit, knowing the only way he could suppress the sorcerer's power was to sacrifice himself? The thought enraged and horrified Alec at the same time. Horren, Lorn, Kraig, and now Michael, all sacrificed themselves to bring Alec to this moment. To leave him alone at the mercy of Salin Urdrokk.

Those bastards! How dare they do this to me! Michael, you idiot! Did you think I could fight him?

Rage and horror filled him. The song of the Talisman exploded anew in his mind. Salin walked toward him, grinning like a skull. It was too much. Something in him snapped.

With a burst of light, his sword flamed orange. At once he felt hate consume him, and he turned his red gaze on the sorcerer. He charged, feeling at once wild and confident, crazed yet sure. His training coupled with the skill imparted to him by his sword made his movements precise, his attack perfect. Sure-footed, he engaged Salin in a dance of death.

Flame met Hellsedge and sparks rained down upon the combatants. Salin's toothy grin widened as he realized his kill would not be so easy after all. Apparently he relished a challenge.

Meeting Alec thrust for thrust, Salin exclaimed, "Ah, this is rich! The baker from Barton Hills turns out to be quite the swordsman! You surprise me, Alec Mason."

Through his red hatred, Alec was surprised as well. Salin had been bent over and wheezing following his battle with Michael, but now the ancient, gnarled sorcerer was fighting like a master, wielding his blade as skillfully as Lorn. He gave no sign he was tired in the least. Alec tried to get a strike past the sorcerer's defenses, but a masterful parry knocked his blade aside as if it were a mere annoyance. Alec embraced the vengeful passions Flame offered him, but deep down he knew bloodlust could only take him so far.

Around and around they went, Salin grinning like a fiend all the while. It seemed so easy for him, thrusting and swinging, parrying and ducking, clashing Hellsedge against Flame again and again in furious succession. Alec let the sword guide him, giving himself over completely to its desires. Even so, he could barely move quickly enough to keep up with Salin's fury. In the beginning they appeared to be on equal footing, but it quickly became obvious Alec was on the defensive. Soon, his every movement was a parry or block. Salin was so fast, his strikes so true, Alec's every action was dedicated to keeping Hellsedge away from his flesh.

As he stumbled back to avoid a blow he could not block, Alec realized he would never win this way. He was no match for someone who had once been First Bladeknight of Eglak. He wondered if even Lorn would triumph over Salin in a test of steel. For Alec, at least, there could be no victory, not with the sword. If he was to survive, he would have to turn to his other training.

Magic? He had never in all his lessons been able to perform even the simplest of Shapings. He had never come to an understanding of the Seventh Law, the Law on which all the others hinged. But he could see magic, could feel it, and if he could do those things, why could he not use it? Most of his mind was consumed with Flame's passion and with his struggle for survival, but with a small part of himself he sought to touch the spirit of the One.

All things, living and not, and all energy, are a part of the One. The One is pure and good, and thus nothing done with his power shall be done for the sake of Evil.

Alec ducked to avoid Salin's whistling steel as he quoted the First Law. Everything was part of the One. Alec had no trouble perceiving this. The spirit of the One was pervasive; it existed in everything around him. The One was everything in the world: the One *was* the world.

Reality is fluid, not set in stone as most believe. The particles of reality are always moving, flowing, and those who understand how can control the flow.

Even now, as Alec held flame aloft to stop Hellsedge from splitting his skull, he could see reality, not as it appeared, but as it *was*. Things he had always accepted to be solid were not; flowing particles swam up and down the walls, through the air, among the sparks which flew as his blade rang against Salin's. If only he could reach out to them as Michael could, grab them with his spirit and turn them against the sorcerer!

Energy is simply material in another form. Energy, too, whether it be lighting, fire, light, or heat, is under the dominion of the Shaper.

It was true. Desperately leaping back to avoid the sorcerer's vicious advance, Alec witnessed the light which filled the room dancing in front of him, millions of tiny particles flowing and spinning through the air. Anyone should have been able to see them, to reach out and grab them and Shape them. How could he have been so blind all his life as to think light was just light?

The power of Shaping derives from the world around you; it is not a part of your being. The forces of nature are bound together as One, and everything touches everything else.

Salin was driving him back now, and Flame danced madly, barely able to fend off the sorcerer's skillful advance. Alec struggled to keep a part of his mind on the Seven Laws, knowing it was his only hope. In the meantime he tried a simple thrust, but the effort almost got him killed. He brought his sword around just in time to knock Salin's blade away from his heart.

All living things have spirit. By perceiving our own spirits, we may perceive the spirit of the One. When we perceive the One, we perceive all things, for all things are the One.

In some small way, Alec had been able to perceive his own spirit almost from the first day he had begun his training. This was how he had become aware of the true fluid nature of the world. But he had never been able to use his spirit to his advantage. Frustration plagued his every attempt at reaching out with his spirit to touch the world. Now, diving to the floor headfirst to avoid being decapitated, he tried in vain to reach out with his spirit.

Control of the fluid reality is done by a perfect union of the spirit, body, and mind. Without perfect union, Shaping is not possible.

Alec rolled across the floor, moving as fast as he could to stay away from Salin. He didn't even have time to rise to his feet, let alone try to unify his spirit, body, and mind. His heart was hammering in his chest, and sweat was covering him head to toe. Never in his life had he been pushed so far. When he looked up, he saw Salin had not lost his grin. The sorcerer seemed to be having the time of his life.

There was one more Law, but Michael had not given Alec words to describe it. According to the Wizard, there were no words. Understanding of the last Law was to come when a person had mastered the first six. Gulping air, Alec struggled with the six Laws he knew, praying for some sort of revelation. Salin was nearly upon him.

For some reason, the sorcerer slowed, and Alec took the moment to force himself to his feet. Salin, apparently, was enjoying the contest too much to end it so soon. He sauntered toward Alec slowly, holding his sword loosely and chuckling to himself. Only when Alec was on his feet and had assumed a solid stance did Salin press forward once more.

They clashed again, but this time Salin was driving Alec back relentlessly. There seemed to be no end to the old man's stamina. Alec's head was swimming, and even the blazing orange rage of Flame was losing its power to sustain him. He was tripping and fumbling; his feet were becoming lead weights. The only reason he wasn't dead yet was because Salin was playing with him. Desperate for any chance at all, he cast his mind back on his lessons, trying to recall every word Michael had ever said to him.

"I have told you before Shapers follow the Seven Laws. Now listen to me closely, Alec, for this is of the utmost importance."

Of course it was of the utmost importance. But only if he could actually make it work! Salin swept his sword around, and this time Alec was too slow and tired to block it. Salin's blade scored a deep gash across Alec's left shoulder, and Alec shrieked in pain.

"By following the Seven Laws, by accepting them totally, a Shaper can do marvelous things."

He struggled to accept the Laws, but it was impossible for him to accept that which he could not understand. Salin was laughing in glee now, and he battered Alec's blade out of the way and planted a solid kick in the youth's stomach. His apparent frailness belied a wiry strength of body, and Alec felt as if he had been kicked by a horse. He flew backwards, landing hard with his back to the wall. Pain swam before his eyes, rang in his mind.

"By accepting the fluid nature of everything around you, you can do almost anything your mind conceives, bend reality to suit your needs. You can change common rocks into gold."

Through the ache penetrating and surrounding his whole body, Alec saw Salin standing over him, raising his blade. With everything he had, Alec lifted Flame to stop Salin's downward cut. The two blades met and sizzling sparks burned the air. Alec saw the sparks as bright particles flowing through a sea of darker ones. The world was nothing more than bright and dark particles, tiny dots flowing forever across all creation. And penetrating all these particles, binding them together, was a vast and glorious spirit: the spirit of the One. For the first time, Alec saw the whole picture.

"You can make air glow and bring light to the darkness."

And Alec knew he that *could* do it, that he had the power to bring light to the darkness. But he still wasn't sure how, and he didn't have much time to learn. Salin bashed at Alec's blade, battering it down, striking it again and again until Alec's strength was gone. Then, with a flick of his wrist, he cut the baker across the wrist of his sword arm, and Flame clattered to the ground.

"You need never be concerned about hunger again, for you can turn dirt into rice or a shoe into a loaf of bread."

Laughing, Salin looked down at where Alec lay limply against the wall. "The game is finished, young Alec. With your death, your bond with the Talisman will be shattered completely, and I will be able to easily gain full mastery over the Fair Folk. You have come far since I found you in Barton Hills, but it would take quite a bit more than a baker with a magic sword to defeat Salin Urdrokk."

"You can turn air into fire."

As Salin drew back his sword, a strange calm fell over Alec. It was as if the certainty of impending death had taken away all his earthy concerns, made all his fear and pain and frustration irrelevant. The certainty that it was at last truly over gave his mind clarity, gave his body contentment, and gave his spirit freedom. He instantly perceived how the three parts of his being were inter-related, how they worked together to form a whole. He saw, at long last, how they could be perfectly unified. He knew, with little effort, he could make it so.

With a thought, he made it so.

"You can turn air into fire. Mud into iron."

Salin thrust his sword toward Alec's heart. To Alec's eyes, it was as if the blade were moving infinitely slowly, as if it would take all of eternity to reach its mark. But Alec's motions, too, were infinitely slow, even more so, and there was no way he could ever avoid or block the falling blade. But his mind was churning, his body thriving, his spirit reaching out. All six Laws blazed through his mind at once, and he saw for the first time they had a meaning beyond their mere words. Taken together, by one whose mind, body, and soul were perfectly unified, they meant something vast. And suddenly Alec knew what the meaning was.

With utter clarity, Alec understood the Seventh Law.

"You can turn air into fire. Mud into iron. A sword into water."

Energy flared. The world moved.

"A sword into water."

Alec Mason Shaped.

Cold water splashed him in the face. For a moment he just sat there, feeling it run down his forehead and cheeks, trickle off the tip of his nose, drip from his chin. When he finally looked up, what he saw was a completely astounded Salin Urdrokk.

Salin was standing over him, still posed in the lunge which was to be his killing stroke. In his outstretched hand he held a useless hilt of a sword. He gaped at it in disbelief, unable to fathom how the sword's blade had become harmless water in mid-stroke. His jaw hung slackly, and his head moved back and forth slowly, as if he was struggling to deny what his eyes were telling him. He began working his mouth, and at last words came.

"Impossib…"

Alec's hand fell upon the hilt of his sword. He snatched it up, and with a fluid motion he thrust forward toward the sorcerer's chest. Flame slid easily through Salin's ribs, and the old man gasped as the fiery blade lanced his heart. He turned his dumbfounded gaze toward Alec, and his eyes filled with horror at the sudden discovery of his own mortality. The sorcerer convulsed once, blood oozing from his mouth. Slowly, his eyes rolled up into his head. Then he fell face first to the cold stone floor, his weight driving Flame the rest of the way through his chest. His body tensed and a final breath hissed out from between his teeth.

Salin Urdrokk was dead.

A long while passed before Alec realized what had happened. From where he sat against the wall, he turned his head to look at Salin's body as it spilled its lifeblood across the floor. The red stain grew outward from the corpse until Alec was sitting in it, but even so he couldn't bring himself to move. He sat there for a long while, clutching his wounded arm, too exhausted to feel any sort of emotion. He knew he had won, but he felt anything but victorious. He felt numb. He closed his eyes, wanting nothing so much as to drift into a deep, oblivious sleep.

"That was…well done…Alec."

His eyes darted open at the sound of the familiar voice. Hope tore through his numbness as his turned toward the source of the voice, toward Michael. The Wizard was sitting against the wall opposite Alec, his body so limp and frail he looked like he would never move again. But he *had* moved; he was no longer sprawled on the floor like some broken and discarded doll. Still, his face was pale and his breathing ragged, and Alec's hope at finding his companion alive was tempered with concern.

"Salin…Salin told me he…burned out your mind," stammered Alec.

Michael chuckled and began to cough. When he was able to suppress the cough, he said, "Salin was prone to exaggeration. He hurt me…badly…but it is nothing from which I cannot recover. I will be restored, although it will take me some time."

"Can you get up? Will you be able to walk?"

Michael grunted as he pushed himself to his knees. "I think I can manage." When he at last was on his feet, he swayed back and forth and had to lean on the wall for support. "But perhaps…I could use some help," he sighed.

Alec struggled to his feet. He was tired and wounded as well, but he found he was in better condition than Michael. He took a few deep breaths and went to help Michael.

"Let's get out of here, if we can," he said. "Salin's slaves may still be around."

"Then don't forget your sword," said Michael.

Alec looked disgustedly at Salin's gory corpse, loathing to go near it. But he needed his sword, so he turned the body on its side with his foot and gripped the hilt. With a solid pull, he yanked the blade from Salin's chest. Standing straight, he took one last look at his fallen foe. He couldn't resist giving the corpse a solid kick.

"Bastard!" he shouted.

Michael gave him a stern look. "He is already dead, Alec. There is no need for that. Besides, we have to take the Talisman and be gone from here."

"Grok! I nearly forgot about the Talisman!"

Alec walked toward the Talisman, which had fallen to the floor during the battle. With Salin's death its call to Alec had been silenced and the perverse green light which had filled it was doused. When Alec lifted it from the stone floor, it began to glow dazzlingly white, and the shadows filling the temple were banished in its hallowed light. Alec's heart sang, for with the Talisman of Unity restored to him he felt whole.

"The Talisman has chosen you wisely, Alec," said Michael, smiling.

Alec returned the smile, relishing the feeling of the Talisman's light and warmth flowing over and through him. Then he went to Michael and allowed the Wizard to slip an arm over his shoulder for support. Together, sheltered by the Talisman's light, they gratefully took their leave of Salin Urdrokk's inner sanctum.

Once out in the hall, Alec was greatly relieved to see Kraig leaning against the wall, wounded and breathing heavily, but still alive. There had been a massive battle, but Kraig had been victorious. Gray bodies were strewn up and down the hall, many of them hacked to pieces.

"Thank Grok you're alive," said Alec, rushing to his friend's side. "How did you do this? How did you fight so many of them?"

Kraig smiled through his short beard. "I didn't. Not alone, anyway. Lorn was here."

"Lorn?" asked Alec. "Where is he now?"

Kraig shrugged. "He tried to get in to help you two, but the door was somehow sealed. Nothing he did could break it open."

Michael nodded. "The sealed door was Salin's doing. I felt him use sorcery to bolt the door. I suppose he did not want any surprises once he had Alec and me at his mercy. Lorn's immunity to magic wouldn't have been able to get him through; it was not magic blocking his way, but the door itself."

Kraig nodded. "Anyway, when he couldn't get in to help you, he rushed off to find Horren. He was going crazy not being of any use here, so he went to see if he could help the Addin."

"I hope they are both all right," said Michael. "We left Horren with an army of ogres."

But when they emerged from the temple, what they found was a completely destroyed army of ogres. Horren and Lorn were both bloody and raw, and the Addin's right arm was hanging uselessly at his side, nearly severed. But they were alive, and to Alec nothing else mattered. No one had had to sacrifice himself after all.

Lorn was so glad to see Alec he threw his arms around the young man and grinned from ear to ear. He and Horren were both amazed when Alec explained what had happened with Salin, but Kraig only smiled. "I knew you had it in you, Alec," was all he said. After they finished congratulating Alec on his incredible victory, they at last turned their backs on the dark temple and headed homeward. On foot it would be a long journey, but even wounded and tired Alec knew they were up to it. Compared to what they had just faced, a walk through the wilderness would be a simple thing.

And so they stumbled onward into the night, their spirits high as the Talisman's radiant blaze lit their way. They had defeated Salin and freed the Fair Folk from his tyranny, and in doing so they had restored hope to the world. Even Michael couldn't stop smiling. The night passed quickly as they walked, and so euphoric were they not a one of them felt the need to stop for sleep.

And when the dawn came, Alec imagined it was the most marvelous dawn to grace the sky since the world began.

CHAPTER 27

The Feast of Nom

Ara rushed into the House of Rest, her heart pounding in anticipation. When Brother Morgan had come to her in her room at the palace and had given her the news, she could scarcely believe it. It had been so long she had nearly given up hope.

"Rayannah," she said, spying the old healer across the room. "Where is he? Can I see him?"

The old Fairy looked at her sternly. "He needs his rest, Ara. I let you come in here enough times while he slept, thinking it could do no harm, but now that he is waking you may be tempted to stay too long."

Ara exhaled slowly to calm herself. "Rayannah, I'll only be a moment. Please?"

The old woman rolled her eyes. "All right, child, go on in. I swear you people make it impossible to do my job!"

Ara smiled in thanks and hurried to one of the private rooms in back. The room was similar to the one which Sarah had shared with Lady Devra, only a little smaller. Ara thought of the many times over the last two weeks she had visited her daughter here, as Sarah recuperated from her broken hip and her cuts and bruises. The healers were skilled, and with their magics they mended her hip many times faster than it could have healed on its own. Sarah was released from the House days ago. She had taken to spending time with Gryn and her other friends and helping however she could in the process of rebuilding Fairhaven. The rest of her time she spent pining for Alec.

As she stepped into the room, her eyes immediately fell upon the bed and the figure who lay there, head propped up on pillows as he perused an old book. His eyes flicked up toward his visitor and his lips curled in a smile.

"Ara!" he exclaimed. "Yours is the prettiest face I have seen in days."

"Landyn," she said, smiling. "Besides Rayannah, I'd guess mine is the *only* face you've seen in days. Or weeks, rather. You've been unconscious since the attack, and that was nearly two weeks ago."

"So I've been told. I took quite a wound from the assassin, Stiletta, and as I hear it I was nearly dead by the time you and the palace guards got me to the House of Rest. The way Rayannah tells it, saving my life was an intolerable burden on her and her staff. I told her I'd repay her with a song, but she just grunted and left the room."

"Don't let her worry you," Ara said with a smile. "She's like that with everyone. Oh, Landyn. I'm just glad to see you're all right."

She reached out her hand to him and he gripped it solidly. They smiled at one another for a long moment, and then he said, "How is Sarah? I heard she was in Rayannah's care for quite some time."

"She had broken her hip, but she's better now."

"How did she stop the ice sorceress? That must have been worthy of a song."

Ara sighed. "She hasn't been very forthcoming about that. Whenever I ask her, she gets quiet and turns away. All I know is when the soldiers found her, the sorceress's corpse was nearby, her head all smashed in. I suppose Sarah doesn't want to remember she was capable of killing someone so brutally."

"She saved Fairhaven, Ara. If Gwendolyn kept sending her ice storms, the defenders wouldn't have held out as long as they did."

"I know, and I told her so. She just needs some time. She'll be all right when Alec gets back, of that I'm certain."

Landyn's smile faded. "I hope he and the others get back safely. I wish there was a way we could know they're alive and well."

"We know they defeated Salin," she answered. "There's that much, at least. After you went down, the battle turned seriously against us. Without Stiletta and the ice sorceress, the dark Fairies should have been outnumbered and easily defeated, but more and more of the Fair Folk started turning to their side. Before we knew it, nearly half of the people of Fairhaven were attacking their own. Their eyes were glowing green and their screams were hateful and terrifying. Salin had them, Landyn. That was when we knew we were going to lose.

"But then, in an instant, everything changed. Suddenly the green light was gone from their eyes. Some of them fell over and wept for what they had done, and others just stood there disoriented. But soon they all rose up, filled with anger at how they had been used. They fought harder and braver than ever, and soon the raiders were on the run. The archers took out a number of the Dark Folk as they fled, and some Shapers brought many more of them down. The Sprites Jinn brought tore through most of those who broke through to the forest. Only a handful escaped.

"You see, Landyn? Something broke Salin's hold over the Fair Folk. The Talisman was taken from him…or he was killed."

"Alec and the others succeeded in their mission," said Landyn.

"Yes. This doesn't mean they survived and will make it back to Fairhaven. But it does give me hope. I've been praying to Grok, Lars, even the One the Fairies are always going on about, for their safe return. Sarah needs Alec, all of Fairhaven needs Michael, and I certainly wouldn't want anything to happen to the others."

Landyn's smile returned. He rubbed her hand for a while and finally said, "You were amazing in the Grand Hall. Put a dagger right through Stiletta's eye, just like you did to that ogre in Ogrynwood. I had to practice for years to gain that kind of accuracy, especially under pressure."

Ara grinned. "Never underestimate a desperate woman." She bent down and gave him a quick kiss on the cheek. "I promised Rayannah I wouldn't be long. I'll see you tomorrow?"

"I certainly hope so. I will be out of here in a few days, Ara, and then we'll have to catch up on lost time. I'm looking forward to those long walks through the parks and gardens we used to take. I'm looking forward to getting to know you better in times of peace. Things have been a little crazy since we met, you know."

"So they have. I'm looking forward to a little peace and quiet as well. Until tomorrow, Landyn."

"Until tomorrow."

She took her leave of the House, her face flush with emotion. She was looking forward to more than peace and quiet. She was anxious to spend more time with Landyn, and not just walking through parks, either. She hoped he felt the same way about her. But there were other things to do, and she made an effort to put Landyn out of her mind as she went about her tasks.

Two more days passed. Ara had joined Sarah in planting seeds in the new gardens of Fairhaven, to grow grass and flowers over the hundreds of bodies the soldiers had buried. The bodies of the enemies were gathered and burned, not deserving the dignity of being returned to the earth in the Fairy tradition. But the soldiers and Shapers and guards and citizens who had fought in Fairhaven's defense all had a place in the Garden of Honor, and all their names were to be carved on grand monuments being built there.

That afternoon, there was a great commotion in the square in front of the palace. Ara and Sarah hurried to the square to see what was happening, and they joined a cheering throng of Fairies gathered along both sides of the street. When Ara saw what they were cheering about, she cried out in delight, and her daughter screamed and embraced her in a fierce hug.

For coming down the street, mounted on grand steeds, were the five who had set out more than three weeks ago in pursuit of Salin Urdrokk. Michael rode a shining white horse, sitting proud and straight on its bare back. Lorn rode at his side, bold and strong in his shiny black leather and a flowing cloak fit for a king. Kraig came slightly behind, all smiles through his thick beard, and beside him walked Horren, who looked joyous despite having one arm in a sling. They waved at the people around them, greeting the grateful onlookers with joy and sincerity.

And in the front, sitting tall and strong, was a radiant Alec Mason. His blond hair fell about his shoulders and curled down toward the center of his back, longer and more lovely than Ara had ever remembered it being. In his arms and legs were strength, and in his face was confidence. His tight shirt of brown leather showed a firm, flat stomach. Not a trace of his boyish fat remained. Around his neck he wore the Talisman of Unity, and it shown white and pure with a radiant light. Here rode a man she had known and loved since he was a small boy. Here rode a man she had never seen in her life.

"Praise Grok!" cried Sarah. "Praise the One! Alec! Alec, I love you!"

She ran to him, and he smiled from ear to ear as he reached down with a strong arm and swooped her up onto his white horse's back. She wrapped her arm around him and began kissing his neck, and he turned to plant a long, hard kiss on her lips. Every Fairy in the street cheered as they kissed, waving triumphant fists in the air. A loud and glorious chant rose up and filled all of Fairhaven.

"Hail Alec Mason, rescuer of the Talisman! Hail Elsendarin and Lorn *Narn-sahn*, who stand against the darkness! Hail Horren Addin, master of the forest, and mighty Kraig, keeper of the peace! All hail the saviors of Faerie! All hail the saviors of the world!"

The chant continued and grew until every voice in Fairhaven had joined in, including the King and Queen who were watching from a balcony high in the palace. Alec and the others dismounted, and with Sarah, Ara, and an escort of guards, they mounted the stairs and entered the palace.

"All hail the Saviors of Faerie! All hail the saviors of the world!"

After a long and detailed conference with the King, the Queen, the advisors and several Elders, they retreated to a quiet sitting room deep within the palace to relax and spend a quiet moment among friends. Ara sat on a plush chair at one end of the room. Michael and Kraig sat to either side of her, and across from her was Lorn and, sitting cross-legged on the floor, the massive Horren. Sarah and Alec sat on a couch together, all smiles as their arms encircled one another and their hands clasped lovingly. Vyrdan had joined them, the knife wound in his shoulder fully healed. Kari stood beside him, and at her feet sat Jinn. Only Landyn was missing, but he was still recovering in the House of Rest.

For a moment, Ara caught Alec and Kari looking at one another, as if both wanted to say something but did not know how. Alec looked nervous, perhaps wondering how to broach the subject of his blood-tie to the Fairy. After an awkward moment, Kari smiled a sad but warm smile and her typically cold expression melted away completely.

"I…I can see some of Martyn in you, young Alec. He was a great man, and I would guess you resemble him in more than just looks."

Alec smiled and said, "Thank you, Kari. I wish I had known him."

Ara shifted in her seat then, grimacing. "I *did* know him," she said.

"What?" exclaimed Kari, shifting her gaze from Alec to Ara. "You knew my brother?"

"Only briefly," answered Ara, "when he and his companions visited Barton Hills more than twenty years ago. At the time I had no idea he was a Fairy." She turned her sympathetic eyes toward Alec. "But I guess…I guess I always suspected he might be your father, Alec. Karlyn…your mother…was one of my dearest friends. I knew she loved him."

Alec looked at her, his eyes full of questions. "But…but she loved Brok, too, didn't she? She was happy with him?"

Ara smiled. "Yes, she loved Brok. It wasn't the same, of course: she never felt the passion for him she felt with Martyn, but Karlyn and Brok shared a deep and meaningful friendship. He helped her get over the pain of losing Martyn, although she never told him the whole truth about it. I don't know if he ever knew or suspected you weren't his natural son. But he loved you dearly; that is certain. The poor man…he was so heart-broken over Karlyn's death he left town after she died, leaving you in the care of the Kulnips. We never heard from him again."

For a moment silence filled the room, and Alec's melancholy eyes held Ara's gaze. But then Lorn ended the silence with a deep sigh, fixing his own sad eyes on the former baker.

"In a way you are the lucky one, Alec. You had two fathers, both of whom loved you very much. My own father thinks I betrayed him. My brother turned against me and cast me from my home. Someday, I hope I can return and set the matter aright. But not just yet. I have found a home here, a new family, a purpose. A man can ask for nothing more."

The mood in the room was heavy, but after a grim moment Vyrdan broke the tension, blurting out, "By the One, people, this is meant to be a celebration! Let us lighten our moods with tales of our great victory!" He began the storytelling with a greatly exaggerated tale of his own bravery, and after a few minutes they were laughing at his enthusiastic speech. They continued talking for quite some time, telling each other the tales of their triumphs. Ara was stunned at Alec's description of his battle with Salin, how he had changed the sorcerer's sword to water and then stabbed him through the heart. Sarah was so proud. She couldn't stop kissing him all over his face and neck. He was proud of her, too, when he heard how she had saved Fairhaven by defeating Gwendolyn.

"It's finally over," he said, a smile in his eyes. "I've said it before, but this time I know it's true. Salin's dead, the Talisman is back in our hands, and Fairhaven is at peace."

"We have struck a great blow against the shadow," said Lorn. "When we stopped to rest in Greenbrook, where we acquired our new horses, we heard many tales from the citizens there. They'd had a battle of their own, as Fairies' eyes became green and they went on murdering sprees. Some of the green-eyes fled the city at once, heading westward, probably toward Salin's temple. Many of the Dark Folk were there as well, as it is a trading city. Most of those were innocent, not at all involved in Salin's plan, but they, too, were susceptible to his control when he ruled the Talisman. I imagine this sort of chaos broke out all over Faerie. If not for Alec and Michael, Salin would rule all the Fairies now, both dark and fair."

"Lorn brings up a point we must all remember," said Michael. "Not all the Dark Folk are evil. Really, only a small number of them had allied themselves with Salin. When next we encounter them, we must not let our prejudices color our view against them. For the most part, they were as much innocent victims in his scheme as the rest of us."

"But they are more corruptible by their very nature," said Kari. "We must treat them with caution."

"Caution, yes," said Michael, "but not unwarranted suspicion."

The talked turned lighter then, and soon they were laughing and discussing what they would do now that it was over.

"Well, as much as I wish I could go home, I've got to stay here and continue my training," said Alec. "The Talisman has chosen me, and until the King is strong again, only I can use it for the cause of good. I still don't know how to use it, but with Michael, Lorn, and the Brothers teaching me I'm sure I will figure it out eventually. And...as much as I don't like to think about it, there is something else I have to do. When I am ready, I must return to *Faryn-Gehna*, the ancient Tomb of the Fairies, and try to break the tomb's curse. I gave my word to the Lord of the Dead."

Michael nodded seriously. "I agree it must be done; for such an oath as you gave must not be taken lightly. When it is time, I will accompany you to the tomb. Together we will find the means to end this terrible curse."

"I don't want you to go, Alec, but I know you have to fulfill your oath," said Sarah, kissing him again. "And I'm sure you'll be ready soon. You can use magic now."

Alec shrugged. "Not as well as you might think. Actually, not really at all. I haven't been able to light a candle with magic since I turned Salin's sword into water. I can still perceive the spirit of the One, and I can see how things fit together, flowing forever into each other, but I haven't been able to reach out with my spirit as I did then. It was like I had a revelation, but then shadows took it away. The Seventh Law is as much a mystery to me now as it was before."

Michael waved away Alec's concern. "Not to worry. Learning to Shape is often like that. The Seventh Law is elusive, and often one may understand it one day and forget it the next. Whatever it takes, Alec, I will help you master it. I will not give up on you."

"I won't either," giggled Sarah, nibbling at his ear.

"That tickles!" cried Alec, laughing out loud.

Ara smiled, feeling warm and glad. She had traveled far, and had come through so much, but at last all her wishes were being fulfilled. She was with her daughter again in a time of peace, and Sarah was happier than she had ever been. Ara relaxed in her chair, listening contentedly as the others laughed and chattered around her.

And so the day passed, and it was a day of joy and celebration across all of Fairhaven.

But the official celebration did not start until the next day, which by coincidence was the most sacred of the Fairy holidays, the Feast of Nom. The day was dedicated to Nom, the Name, a mysterious entity the Fair Folk believed was the Maker of All, the Crafter of the Universe. It was He, or She, who first Spoke, giving life and power to the One, who in turn granted life to everything else. The Order of Nom was obviously named after this entity, although they did not pray to Him or speak of Him except on the day of His Feast. Such was the custom of the Fair Folk, who on other days held the One above all other gods.

This day the celebration of the Feast was grander than it had ever been, for in addition to honoring the Crafter they were celebrating the return of the heroes and the victory they represented. All over the city, and indeed, all over Faerie, the names of Alec Mason, rescuer of the Talisman; Elsendarin the Wizard, Second of the Three; Lorn the *Narnsahn*, Son of the King; Kraig the Mighty, the Keeper of Peace; and Horren Addin, Master of the Forests, were spoken and honored with great praise. Sarah and Ara Mills were also granted the status of heroes, as were Landyn, Minstrel of Freehold and Vyrdan, lord of house Manrell. They were all gathered together in the great ball room of the King and Queen, where the royal couple presided in all their glory and majesty. The King had recovered much of his former strength and poise, and he looked grand cloaked in royal purple and gold, his long, silver hair flowing down his back. All his councilors and sages were gathered around him, and his people spread out before him, as he spoke praise to the saviors of Faerie.

Alec Mason, dressed in rich golden robes and wearing the Talisman of Unity shining white upon his breast, was called to kneel before the King. He knelt, and King Elyahdyn del Kennthal proclaimed him Alec *Faryn-Lahdyne* and *Narnfahn*, that is, Fairy-friend and Ward of the King. Alec accepted his new titles gladly, promising to honor them as best he could.

And the day went on, and there was dancing and singing, and Landyn of Freehold performed the greatest ballads of the land, joined in song by the beautiful Ara Mills. They feasted all day long, drinking and reveling late into the night, praising Nom and the One and the Heroes of Faerie, and saying prayers for their honored dead. At the stroke of midnight, the Queen, aided by Sarah's ring, put on a display of fireworks so grand all stopped their celebrations to watch. Alec watched from the balcony of his room at the palace, his arm around Sarah's waist. They shared a long kiss and then went down to be with the others for the rest of the celebration.

In the square they met with Ara and Landyn, who had watched the fireworks hand in hand, and Michael, who was laughing and talking with a fully-recovered Lady Devra. Lorn and Kraig were also there, and Vyrdan and Kari and Jinn, and Syndar and Toros, and Gryn and all Alec's friends. They hugged, and laughed, and talked about everything and nothing, and continued celebrating with the rest of the city all the night through.

And when dawn at last came, and Fairhaven slept, Alec kissed Sarah long and deep at the door of her bedchamber before retiring to his own room. There he lay down, knowing at last he would never be the baker of Barton Hills. He had a new destiny, one he knew he would have to embrace with the whole of his heart.

He thought of Sarah, and of his friends here in Fairhaven, and of the Talisman glowing warmly against his chest. He decided that his new life wouldn't be so bad after all.

"No," he said quietly as he pulled the covers up around him, "it won't be bad at all."

Warm and content, Alec Mason slept.

Epilogue: Shadows Waiting

"Why are you grinning like that? Doesn't Salin's failure disturb you at all?"

From his place on his crumbling throne, Vorik Seth chuckled at the man trapped in the globe of green light. With skeletal hands he pushed himself up and crossed slowly toward his captive.

"Failure? For all your vaunted wisdom you do not to understand. The fool Salin may have died, but he did not fail in the task I set before him."

The gray, muscular man in the globe grimaced in confusion. "He lost the Talisman, Vorik. You lost any hope you ever had of gaining control of the Fair Folk. You can keep me here and use me as you please, but it will bring you no closer to victory. The One…"

"The One is a fool to put his trust in the likes of you! Ah, dear Siv, how easy it was for me to call you here and bind you with the information Salin brought to me. With but a word I can send you against your brother Nul, or command you to wreak destruction upon the world of man."

The man's face was drawn in anger, and with massive fists he pounded against the shield of light. "Then why don't you do it! Why don't you strip me of my will and make me dance like a puppet on a string!"

The Seth leaned toward his captive, placing his face, little more than a black skull with a hint of rotted flesh stretched over it, right against the solid light. "Because it would be merciful to do so, and I am without mercy. It gives me great pleasure to see you watch in horror as your world comes crumbling down. I will use you eventually, of this you must have no doubt, but until such time as I have need of you, you will bear witness to my unfolding victory."

Vorik could see his prisoner's impatience building. Siv gripped his long, gray hair in his big fists and began tugging at it with impotent rage.

Banes of Lars, I've not had so much fun in millennia! thought Vorik.

"What *victory?* Salin is dead, damn you, his revolution ended! You made me watch everything: the attack on Fairhaven, Nul and the others battling their way through Salin's temple, everything!" He was practically foaming at the mouth. "And yet you say Salin didn't fail!"

Vorik circled the emerald cage slowly, his tattered black robes dragging on the ground behind him. "It depends on your point of view, Third of the Three. From Salin's point of view, rotting on the floor of his stronghold, he certainly failed. But the task which he failed was uniting the Fair Folk under one will: his own. This was not a task I gave him, but one he took on himself. In failing this task, however, he succeeded in something greater."

"Greater?"

Vorik circled faster now, enjoying the confused look on the Enchanter's face. "He drew out Alec Mason, made him aware of his legacy, his potential for power."

Siv looked at the floor, rubbing his high forehead with one meaty hand. "How in Hell does that help *you?*"

"You don't know what Mason really is, and neither does he. No one does, save the gods and, of course, me."

"Of course I know what he is. A hybrid of Fairy and human. All the Fair Folk know…"

"They know nothing! Yes, his father was a Fairy. His mother was human. The Fair Folk were suspicious of Mason's heritage at first, as their laws advised, but now they embrace him as one of their own. The fools! They should have paid closer attention to the wisdom of their ancestors. Alec Mason, it is said, possesses the magic of death, but neither the Fairies nor Mason himself knows what this really means. What he is, or will become, is not a new thing at all, as they in their narrow thinking believe."

"What…what is he?" questioned the Third of the Three.

Vorik was silent for a long moment. "All you need to know is, whatever else he may be, Mason is *mine.*" He paused for a moment, his eyes smoldering with vicious delight. Then he said, "Do you know what your brother is doing?"

"What?" said the captive, looking up suddenly. "Of course; he's in Fairhaven helping to…"

"No, not him. The other. The one you call Vor."

"The First? I have no idea where…"

"He is doing my work," said Vorik through a rotted grin. "Unknowingly, but willingly. Do you wish to speak of corruption? Salin's was nothing compared to your brother's. Power? Vor could have crushed Urdrokk. In his mind he serves only his own selfish desires, but his deeds aid my cause."

"Damn you, what have you done with him?"

"I?" The Seth laughed as heartily as his ruined lungs allowed. "I merely stood by and watched his mind sink into greed and a bloated sense of self-worth. He is quite mad, you know. He wants to rule the world."

"You bastard! You lie!"

"Oh, I lie, do I? Look into my mirror, O Mighty Enchanter, and despair!"

With a twitch of his mind, Vorik opened a scrying vortex in the air before Siv's glowing prison. The Third looked into the vortex and his eyes grew wide with horror at what he saw. There was murder and betrayal, corruption and horror. Blood washed the streets of a grand city and decay hung in the air like a fog. In the center of it all stood Vor, the Magus, First of the Three.

"NO!" cried Siv, falling to his knees. "How could the One allow this?" Tears poured from his eyes, tears of grief and madness. "NO!"

Vorik Seth laughed long and loud, and with a thought he rose into the air. He began floating toward the room's exit.

"Wait!" cried Siv, looking up. "Where are you going?" His red face was streaked with tears. "You never leave the throne room."

The Seth stopped for a moment, hovering gently in mid-air. "Salin may have done me a great service, but he *is* dead. It is time to find a new agent to do my work in the land of mortals. And I know just the woman."

As he floated from the dark throne room, he heard the prisoner cry, "At least close the scrying vortex!"

Without looking back, Vorik Seth said, "No."

As the door slammed shut, dark laughter rang throughout the tower, laughter which would have been heard all across the land of Mul Kytuer were there any living beings to hear it. Siv listened to the laughter and gazed into the vortex, unable to close his eyes or look away.

It was hours before he could stop screaming.

0-595-32320-0

Printed in the United States
80014LV00001B/1-18